TOM CRINGLE'S LOG

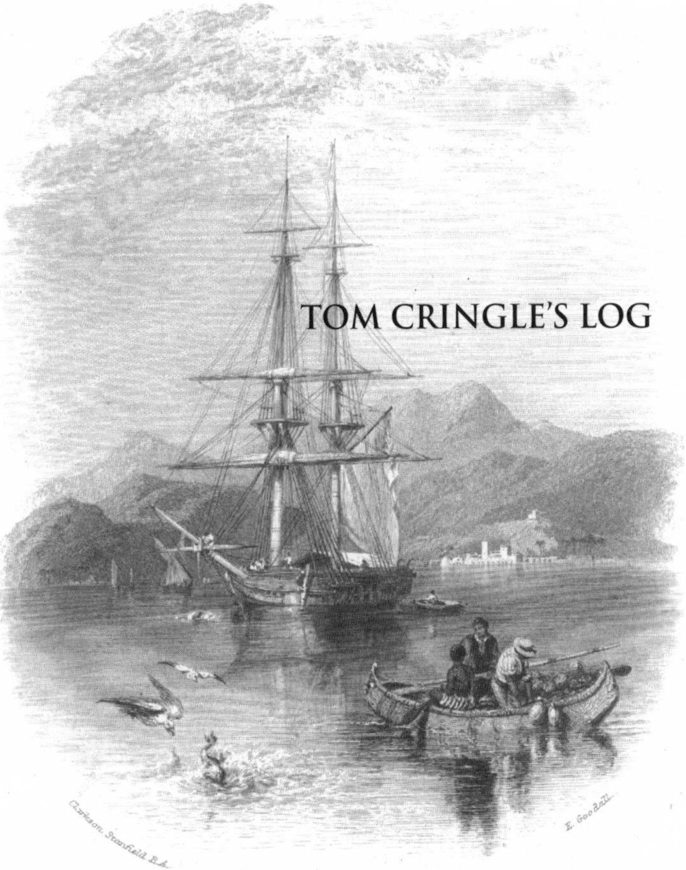

"The Torch was lying at Anchor in Bluefields Bay."

Tom Cringle's Log, Page 82.

OTHER NAUTICAL FICTION PUBLISHED BY MCBOOKS PRESS

By Alexander Kent
Midshipman Bolitho
Stand into Danger
In Gallant Company
Sloop of War
To Glory We Steer
Command a King's Ship

By Captain Frederick Marryat
Frank Mildmay OR The Naval Officer
Mr Midshipman Easy
Newton Forster OR The Merchant Service

By W. Clark Russell
Wreck of the Grosvenor

By Rafael Sabatini
Captain Blood

TOM CRINGLE'S LOG

by
Michael Scott

"I am as a weed,
Flung from the rock on ocean's foam to sail,
Where'er the surge may sweep, the tempest's
breath prevail."

CHILDE HAROLD.

CLASSICS OF NAUTICAL FICTION SERIES

McBOOKS PRESS
ITHACA, NEW YORK

Book and cover design by Paperwork.
Cover painting is *The Prisoners of Cabrera* by Francois Musin, 1820–1888, courtesy of Fine Art Photographic Library Ltd.

Library of Congress Cataloging-in-Publication Data

Scott, Michael, 1789-1835.
  Tom Cringle's log / by Michael Scott.
    p. cm. — (Classics of nautical fiction series)
  ISBN 0-935526-51-X (pbk.)
    I. Title. II. Series.
PR5299.S6T66 1998
                    98-38971
                     CIP

Tom Cringle's Log was first published serially in *Blackwood's Magazine,* beginning in 1829. This text is based on the 1869 edition published by William Blackwood and Sons in Edinburgh and London. A few corrections were made for consistency and clarity, but most of the original spelling and punctuation remain intact.

Distributed to the book trade by:
Login Trade, 1436 West Randolph, Chicago, IL 60607, 800-626-4330.

Additional copies of this book may be ordered from any bookstore or directly from McBooks Press, 120 West State Street, Ithaca, NY 14850. Please include $3.00 postage and handling with mail orders. New York State residents must add 8% sales tax. All McBooks Press publications can also be ordered by calling toll-free 1-888-BOOKS11 (1-888-266-5711).

Visit the McBooks Press website at http://www.McBooks.com.

Printed in the United States of America

9 8 7 6 5 4 3 2 1

PREFACE

PLUMBING the sea of literature that has washed over our libraries to bring back an authentic record of time, place, and manner of life is likely to teach us more than we set out to find. In the case of *Tom Cringle's Log,* we approach the 19th century world of the West Indies through the eyes of Michael Scott, a British colonial and traveller.

With that, we take in the encounters of native Brits, accustomed to a cool, often cloudy climate, with the astonishing weather, terrain, and vegetation of the tropics. We share in the ongoing struggle—by turns, challenging, vicious, tedious, even ludicrous—to establish an outpost of one society's culture, mores and habits on the altogether alien soil which is home to another. And perhaps most significantly, we confront the complicated interactions of white Europeans with the Other—especially the black Other, but to a lesser degree, with Jews, Indians, and Spaniards.

Scott, whose *Log* first appeared anonymously in *Blackwood's Magazine,* was gifted with impressive powers of description. Through them, we find sweeping pictures of ocean-going ships and untouched island paradises, as well as minor details of period architecture, of table settings and—in great precision—of clothing. But true to his time, his training, and his station in life, when Scott turns his description on the blacks in his story, by and large, they suffer in any comparison with the dominant whites. Almost no level is too low for him to assume in making a black character appear inferior: "his blubber-lips," "his hair, if hair it could be called," his "tarnished" clothing, his "dingy paws." To Scott, these characters are almost all buffoons. His delineations of their dialogue is right out of the vaudeville hall, and his assessments of motivation and character are stereotypical, and hence suspect, in the extreme. Even when he paints a person of color in complimentary terms,

Scott's praise is couched in an understanding between the author and an audience of his contemporaries of the subject's fundamental inferiority.

Yet blacks are not the only characters Scott tars with his vivid brush, though the black players in his story are portrayed with a disdain which is axiomatic. Similar prejudices are brought to bear on his depictions of women. Drawing upon the favored conventions of his time, Scott portrays his female characters as "delicate" and "infantile." They weep; they are tender; they are weak; and "they don't improve by age." Scott describes the features of a beautiful woman in the terms of a statue or a fine painting, emphasizing material qualities and marginalizing the immaterial. Bound within sexist, racist and imperialist Christian frameworks, the Other of Scott's log emerges as cliché and caricature rather than with any actual human characteristics.

Tom Cringle's Log has been hailed as "one of the most accurate pictures of West Indian life, both afloat and on shore, during the early part of the 19th century." Certainly, if we have learned anything in the intervening two centuries, it is that accuracy is closely connected to the eye and mind of the beholder. But our access to real accuracy is in learning more—always more—about the way things were.

S.K. LIST AND SARAH C. PATTEN

PREFATORY NOTICE
FROM THE 1869 EDITION

THE FEW particulars which we know with regard to the Author of *Tom Cringle's Log* may be compressed almost into a sentence. The name of the writer of that series of papers (which first appeared in *Blackwood's Magazine*) was Michael Scott. He was born in Glasgow, on the 30th October 1789, and attended the High School and University there. In October 1806 he sailed for Jamaica, where he remained in the management of various estates till 1810, when he joined a mercantile house in Kingston, Jamaica. It was in the course of his employment in this establishment, and of the numerous visits which he had occasion to pay to the neighbouring islands and to the Spanish Main, that he acquired that familiarity with the character of West Indian society, with the wild and adventurous nature of a nautical life, and with the scenes and aspects of a tropical climate, which afterwards imparted so much of truth and vivacity to his sketches. Arriving in this country in 1817, he married in 1818; but again returned to Jamaica, and did not finally settle in Scotland till 1822. In 1829 he addressed to the late Mr Blackwood some fragments, under the pseudonym of Tom Cringle, in which—brief and slenderly connected as they were—that publisher at once discerned the traces of original talent, and of great powers of description. He urged him to proceed, and to weave his materials into a connected form, uniting them by some common link, which, without subjecting the writer to the strict rules of narrative composition, would keep up a personal and continuous interest in the movement of the story. The anticipations of Mr Blackwood as to the popularity of these remarkable sketches were completely fulfilled. Their truth of local painting, placing the reader at once amidst the wonders and the terrors of a torrid clime—their strong contrasts, and ever-shifting rapidity of narration—the broad and often extravagant flood of humour which was shed over all these particulars of the reckless life, of the sea and the plantations, instantly attracted public attention and favour. No series of papers which has appeared in *Blackwood's Magazine* ever enjoyed more general or continued popularity: they were characterised by the *Quarterly Review** as the most brilliant series of magazine papers of the time; and by Coleridge, in his *Table Talk* as "most excellent." When reprinted in two volumes, an unusually large edition was almost immediately disposed of; on the Continent they have been generally read and admired; and in Germany more than once translated.

During the publication of these sketches, Mr Scott preserved his *incognito* even towards his publisher. Mr Blackwood died without knowing, except by report from other sources, the real name of their author. Mr Scott himself died at Glasgow, on the 7th November 1835.

---

* No. C., p. 377

CHAPTER I.

THE LAUNCHING OF THE LOG.

"While rapidly the marksman's shot prevailed,
And aye as if for death some lonely trumpet wailed."
Gertrude of Wyoming.

DAZZLED BY the glories of Trafalgar, I, Thomas Cringle, one fine morning in the merry month of May, in the year one thousand eight hundred and so and so, magnanimously determined in my own mind that the United Kingdom of Great Britain and Ireland should no longer languish under the want of a successor to the immortal Nelson, and being then of the great perpendicular altitude of four feet four inches, and of the mature age of thirteen years, I thereupon betook myself to the praiseworthy task of tormenting, to the full extent of my small ability, every man and woman who had the misfortune of being in any way connected with me, until they had agreed to exert all their interest, direct or indirect, and concentrate the same in one focus upon the head and heart of Sir Barnaby Blueblazes, vice-admiral of the red squadron, a Lord of the Admiralty, and one of the old plain K.B.'s (for he flourished before the time when a gallant action or two tagged half of the letters of the alphabet to a man's name, like the tail of a paper kite), in order that he might be graciously pleased to have me placed on the quarterdeck of one of his Majesty's ships of war without delay.

The stone I had set thus recklessly a-rolling had not been in motion above a fortnight, when it fell with unanticipated violence, and crushed the heart of my poor mother, while it terribly braised that of me, Thomas; for as I sat at breakfast with the dear old woman one fine Sunday morning, admiring my new blue jacket and snow-white trousers, and shining well-soaped face, and nicely brushed hair, in the pier glass over the chimney-piece, I therein saw the door behind me open, and Nicodemus, the waiting-man, enter, and deliver a letter to the old lady, with a formidable-looking seal.

I perceived that she first ogled the superscription, and then the seal, very ominously, and twice made as if she would have broken the missive open, but her heart seemed as often to fail her. At length she laid it down—heaved a long deep sigh—took off her spectacles, which appeared dim, dim—wiped them, put them on again, and, making a sudden effort, tore open the letter, read it hastily over, but not so rapidly as to prevent her hot tears falling with a small tiny tap tap on the crackling paper.

Presently she pinched my arm, pushed the blistered manuscript under my nose, and, utterly unable to speak to me, rose, covered her face with her hands, and left the room weeping bitterly. I could hear her praying in a low, solemn, yet sobbing and almost inarticulate voice, as she crossed the passage to her own dressing room. "Even as thou wilt, O Lord—not mine, but thy holy will be done; yet, oh! it is a bitter bitter thing for a widowed mother to part with her only boy."

Now came my turn, as I read the following epistle three times over, with a most fierce countenance, before thoroughly understanding whether I was dreaming or awake—in truth, poor little fellow as I was, I was fairly stunned.

"Admiralty, *such a date.*

DEAR MADAM,—It gives me very great pleasure to say that your son is appointed to the Breeze frigate, now fitting at Portsmouth for foreign service. Captain Wigemwell is a most excellent officer, and a good man, and the schoolmaster on board is an exceedingly decent person, I am informed; so I congratulate you on his good fortune in beginning his career, in which I wish him all success, under such favourable auspices. As the boy is, I presume, all ready, you had better send him down on Thursday next, at latest, as the frigate will go to sea, wind and weather permitting, positively on Sunday morning.

"I remain, my dear Madam,
"Yours very faithfully,
"BARNABY BLUEBLAZES, K.B."

However much I had been moved by my mother's grief, my false pride came to my assistance, and my first impulse was to chant a verse of some old tune, in a most doleful manner. "All right—all right," I then exclaimed, as I thrust half a doubled-up muffin into my gob; but it was all chew chew, and no swallow— not a morsel could I force down my parched throat, which tightened like to throttle me.

Old Nicodemus had by this time again entered the room, unseen and unheard, and startled me confoundedly, as he screwed his words in his sharp cracked voice into my larboard ear. "Jane tells me your mamma is in a sad taking, Master Tom. You ben't going to leave us, all on a heap like, be you? Surely you'll stay until your sister comes from your uncle Job's? You know there are only two on ye—You won't leave the old lady all alone, Master Thomas, will ye?" The worthy old fellow's voice quavered here, and the tears hopped over his old cheeks through the flour and tallow like peas, as he slowly drew a line down the forehead of his well-powdered pate with his forefinger.

"No—no—why, yes," exclaimed I, fairly overcome; "that is—oh Nic, Nic,—you old fool, I wish I could cry, man—I wish I could cry!" and straightway I hied me to my chamber, and wept until I thought my very heart would have burst.

In my innocence and ignorance, child as I was, I had looked forward to several months' preparation; to buying and fitting of uniforms, and dirks, and cocked hat, and swaggering therein, to my own great glory, and the envy of all my young relations; and especially I desired to parade my fire-new honours before the large dark eyes of my darling little creole cousin, Mary Palma; whereas I was now to be bundled on board at a few days' warning, out of a ready-made furnishing shop, with lots of ill-made, glossy, hard-mangled duck trousers, the creases as sharp as the backs of knives, and—"Oh, it never rains but it pours," exclaimed I; "surely all this promptitude is a little *de plus* in Sir Barnaby."

However, away I was trundled at the time appointed, with an aching heart, to Portsmouth, after having endured the misery of a first parting from a fond mother and a host of kind friends; but, miserable as I was, according to my preconceived determination, I began my journal the very day I arrived, that nothing connected with so great a man should be lost, and most weighty did the matters therein related appear to me at the time; but, seen through the long vista of, I won't say how many years, I really must confess that the Log, for long long after I first went to sea in the Breeze, and subsequently when removed to the old Kraaken line-of-battle ship, both of which were constantly part of blockading squadrons, could be compared to nothing more fitly than a dish of trifle, anciently called syllabub, with a stray plum here and there scattered at the bottom. But when, after several weary years, I got away in the dear old Torch, on a separate cruise, incidents came fast enough with a vengeance— stern, unyielding, iron events, as I found to my heavy cost, which spoke out trumpet-tongued and fiercely for themselves, and whose tremendous simplicity required no adventitious aid in the narration to thrill through the hearts of others. So, to avoid yarn-spinning, I shall evaporate my early Logs, and blow off as much of the froth as I can, in order to present the residuum free of flummery to the reader—just to give him a taste here and there, as it were, of the sort of animal I was at that time. Thus:

Thomas Cringle, his Log-book.—

Arrived in Portsmouth, by the Defiance, at ten a.m., on such a day. Waited on the Commissioner, to whom I had letters, and said I was appointed to the Breeze. Same day, went on board and took up my berth; stifling hot; mouldy biscuit; and so on. My mother's list makes it fifteen shirts, whereas I only have twelve.

Admiral made the signal to weigh, wind at S.W., fresh and squally. Stockings should be one dozen worsted, three of cotton, two of silk; find only half a dozen worsted, two of cotton, and one of silk. Fired a gun and weighed.

Sailed for the fleet off Vigo, deucedly sea-sick; was told that fat pork was the best specific, if bolted half raw; did not find it much of a tonic;—passed a terrible night, and for four hours of it obliged to keep watch, more dead than alive. The very second evening we were at sea, it came on to blow, and the night fell very dark, with heavy rain. Towards eight bells in the middle watch, I was standing on a gun, well forward on the starboard side, listening to the groaning of the maintack, as the swelling sail, the foot of which stretched transversely right athwart the ship's deck in a black arch, struggled to tear it up, like some dark impalpable spirit of the air striving to burst the chains that held him and escape high up into the murky clouds, or a giant labouring to uproot an oak, and wondering in my innocence how hempen cord could brook such strain— when just as the long-waited-for strokes of the bell sounded gladly in mine ear, and the shrill clear note of the whistle of the boatswain's mate had been followed by his gruff voice, grumbling hoarsely through the gale, "Larboard watch, ahoy!" the look-out at the weather gangway, who had been relieved, and beside whom I had been standing a moment before, stepped past me, and scrambled up on the booms. "Hillo, Howard, where away, my man?" said I.

"Only to fetch my—"

Crack!—the maintack parted, and up flew the sail with a thundering flap, loud as the report of a cannon-shot, through which, however, I could distinctly hear a heavy *smash,* as the large and ponderous blocks at the clew of the sail struck the doomed sailor under the ear, and whirled him off the booms into the sea, where he perished, as heaving-to was impossible, and useless if practicable, as his head must have been smashed to atoms.

This is one of the stray plums of the trifle; what follows is a whisk of the froth, written when we looked into Corunna, about a week after the embarkation of the army:—

MONODY ON THE DEATH OF SIR JOHN MOORE.

Farewell, thou pillar of the war,
Warm-hearted soldier, Moore, farewell,
In honor's firmament a star,
As bright as e'er in glory fell.

Deceived by weak or wicked men,
How gallantly thou stoodst at bay,
Like lion hunted to his den,
Let France tell, on that bloody day.

No boastful splendour round thy bier,
No blazoned trophies o'er thy grave;
But thou hadst more, the soldier's tear,
The heart-warm offering of the brave.

On Lusitania's rock-girt coast,
All coffinless thy relics lie,
Where all but honour bright was lost,
Yet thy example shall not die.

Albeit no funeral knell was rung,
Nor o'er thy tomb in mournful wreath
The laurel twined with cypress hung,
Still shall it live while Britons breathe.

What though, when thou wert lowly laid,
Instead of all the pomp of woe,
The volley o'er thy bloody bed
Was thundered by an envious foe?—

Inspired by it in after time,
A race of heroes will appear,
The glory of Britannia's clime,
To emulate thy bright career.

And there will be, of martial fire,
Those who all danger will endure;
Their first, best aim, but to aspire
To die thy death—*the death of Moore.*

To return. On the evening of the second day, we were off Falmouth, and then got a slant of wind that enabled us to lie our course.

Next morning, at daybreak, saw a frigate in the north-east quarter, making signals;—soon after we bore up. Bay of Biscay—tremendous swell—Cape Finisterre—blockading squadron off Cadiz—in-shore squadron—and so on, all trifle and no plums.

At length the Kraaken, in which I had now served for some time, was ordered home; and, sick of knocking about in a fleet, I got appointed to a fine eighteen-gun sloop, the Torch, in which we sailed, on such a day, for the North Sea—wind foul—weather thick and squally; but towards evening on the third day, being then off Harwich, it moderated, when we made more sail, and stood on, and next morning, in the cold, miserable, drenching haze of an October daybreak, we passed through a fleet of fishing-boats at anchor. "At anchor," thought I, "and in the middle of the sea,"—but so it was—all with their tiny cabooses, smoking cheerily, and a solitary figure, as broad as it was long, stiffly walking to and fro on the confined decks of the little vessels. It was now that I knew the value of the saying, "A fisherman's walk, two steps and overboard." With regard to these same fishermen, I cannot convey a better notion of them, than by describing *one* of the two North Sea pilots whom we had on board. This pilot was a tall, raw-boned subject, about six feet or so, with a blue face—I could not call it red—and a hawk's bill nose of the colour of bronze. His head was defended from the weather by what is technically called a south-west— pronounced sow-west—cap, which is in shape like the *thatch* of a dustman, composed of canvass, well tarred, with no snout, but having a long flap hanging down the back to carry the rain over the cape of the jacket. His chin was imbedded in a red comforter that rose to his ears. His trunk was first of all eased in a shirt of worsted stocking-net; over this he had a coarse linen shirt, then a thick cloth waistcoat; a shag jacket was the next layer, and over that was rigged the large cumbrous pea-jacket, reaching to his knees. As for his lower spars, the rig was still more peculiar;—first of all, he had on a pair of most comfortable woollen stockings, what we call fleecy hosiery—and the *beauties* are peculiar- ly nice in this respect—then a pair of strong fear-naught trowsers; over these again are drawn up another pair of stockings, thick, coarse, rig-and-furrow as we call them in Scotland, and above all this were drawn a pair of long, well- greased, and *liquored* boots, reaching half-way up the thigh, and altogether impervious to wet. However comfortable this *costume* may be in bad weather *in*-board, it is clear enough that any culprit so swathed would stand a poor chance of being saved were he to fall *over*board. The wind now veered round and round, and baffled, and checked us off, so that it was the sixth night after we had taken our departure from Harwich before we saw Heligoland light. We then bore away for Cuxhaven, and I now knew for the first time that we had a government emissary of some kind or another on board, although he had hitherto confined himself strictly to the captain's cabin.

All at once it came on to blow from the north-east, and we were again driven back among the English fishing-boats. The weather was thick as buttermilk, so we had to keep the bell constantly ringing, as we could not see the jib-boom end from the forecastle. Every now and then we heard a small, hard, clanking tinkle, from the fishing-boats, as if an old pot had been struck instead of a bell, and a faint hollo, "Fishing-smack," as we shot past them in the fog, while we could scarcely see the vessels at all. The morning after this particular time to which I allude, was darker than any which had gone before it; absolutely you could not see the breadth of the ship from you; and as we had not taken the sun for five days, we had to grope our way almost entirely by the lead. I had the forenoon watch, during the whole of which we were amongst a little fleet of fishing-boats, although we could scarcely see them; but being unwilling to lose ground by lying to, we fired a gun every half hour, to give the small craft notice of our vicinity, that they might keep their bells agoing. Every three or four minutes the marine drum-boy, or some amateur performer—for most sailors would give a glass of grog any day to be allowed to beat a drum for five minutes on end—beat a short roll, and often as we drove along, under a reefed foresail, and close-reefed topsails, we could hear the answering tinkle before we saw the craft from which it proceeded; and when we did perceive her as we flew across her stern, we could only see it, and her mast, and one or two well-swathed, hardy fishermen, the whole of the little vessel forward being hid in a cloud.

I had been invited this day to dine with the captain,—Mr Splinter, the first-lieutenant, being also of the party; the cloth had been withdrawn, and we had all had a glass or two of wine a-piece, when the fog settled down so thickly, although it was not more than five o'clock in the afternoon, that the captain desired that the lamp might be lit. It was done, and I was remarking the contrast between the dull, dusky, brown light, or rather the palpable London fog, that came through the skylight, and the bright yellow sparkle of the lamp, when the master came down the ladder. "We have shoaled our water to five fathoms, sir—shells and stones. Here, Wilson, bring in the lead."

The leadsman, in his pea-jacket and shag trowsers, with the rain-drop hanging to his nose, and a large knot in his cheek from a junk of tobacco therein stowed, with pale, wet visage, and whiskers sparkling with moisture, while his long black hair hung damp and lank over his fine forehead and the stand-up cape of his coat, immediately presented himself at the door, with the lead in his claws, an octagonal-shaped cone, like the weight of a window-sash, about eighteen inches long, and two inches diameter at the bottom, tapering away nearly to a point at top, where it was flattened, and a hole pierced for the line to be fastened to. At the lower end—the butt-end, as I would say—there was a hollow scooped out, and filled with grease, so that when the lead was cast, the quality of the soil, sand, shells, or mud, that came up adhering to this lard, indicated, along with the depth of water, our situation in the North Sea; and by this, indeed, we guided our course, in the absence of all opportunity of ascertaining our position by observations of the sun.

The captain consulted the chart—"Sand and shells; why, you should have deeper water, master. Any of the fishing-boats near you?"

"Not at present, sir; but we cannot be far off some of them."

"Well, let me know when you come near any of them."

A little after this, as became my situation, I rose and made my bow, and went on deck. By this time the night had fallen, and it was thicker than ever, so that, standing beside the man at the wheel, you could not see farther forward than the booms: yet it was not dark either—that is, it was moonlight, so that the haze, thick as it was, had that silver gauze-like appearance, as if it had been luminous in itself, that cannot be described to any who has not seen it. The gun had been fired just as I came on deck, but no responding tinkle gave notice of any vessel being in the neighbourhood. Ten minutes, it may have been a quarter of an hour, when a short roll of the drum was beaten from the forecastle, where I was standing. At the moment I thought I heard a holla, but I could not be sure. Presently I saw a small light, with a misty halo surrounding it, just under the bowsprit,

"Port your helm," sang out the boatswain,—"hard-a-port, or we shall be over a fishing-boat!"

A cry arose from beneath—a black object was for an instant distinguishable—and the next moment a crash was heard. The spritsail-yard rattled, and broke off sharp at the point where it crossed the bowsprit; and a heavy smashing thump against our bows told, in fearful language, that we had run her down. Three of the men and a boy hung on by the rigging of the bowsprit, and were brought safely on board; but two poor fellows perished with their boat. It appeared that they had broken their bell; and although they saw us coming, they had no better means than shouting, and showing a light, to advertise us of their vicinity.

Next morning the wind once more chopped round, and the weather cleared, and in four-and- twenty hours thereafter we were off the mouth of the Elbe, with three miles of white foaming shoals between us and the land at Cuxhaven, roaring and hissing, as if ready to swallow us up. It was low water, and, as our object was to land the emissary at Cuxhaven, we had to wait, having no pilot for the port, although we had the signal flying for one all morning, until noon, when we ran in close to the green mound which constituted the rampart of the fort at the entrance. To our great surprise, when we hoisted our colours and pennant, and fired a gun to leeward, there was no flag hoisted in answer at the flag-staff, nor was there any indication of a single living soul on shore to welcome us. Mr Splinter and the captain were standing together at the gangway —"Why, sir," said the former, "this silence somewhat surprises me: what say You, Cheragoux?" to the government emissary or messenger already mentioned, who was peering through the glass close by.

"Why, mi lieutenant, I don't certain dat all ish right on sore dere."

"No?" said Captain Deadeye; "why, what *do* you see?"

"It ish not so mosh vat I shee, as vat I no shee, sir, dat trembles me. It cannot surely be possib dat de Prussian and Hanoverian troop have left de place, and dat dese dem Franceman ave advance so far as de Elbe *autrefois*, dat ish, once more?"

"French!" said Deadeye: "poo, nonsense; no French here-abouts; none nearer than those cooped-up in Hamburgh with Davoust, take my word for it,"

"I sall take your vord for anyting else in de large vorld, mi captain; but I see someting glance behind dat rampart, parapet you call, dat look dem like de shako of de *infanterie légère* of dat villain de Emperor Napoleon. Ah! I see de red-worsted epaulet of de grenadier also; *sacre!* vat is dat pof of vite smoke?"

What it was we soon ascertained to our heavy cost, for the shot that had been fired at us from a long 32-pound gun, took effect right abaft the foremast, killing three men outright, and wounding two. Several other shots followed, but with less sure aim. Returning the fire was of no use, as our carronades could not have pitched their metal much more than half way; or, even if they had been long guns, they would merely have plumped the balls into the turf rampart, without hurting any one. So we wisely hauled off, and ran up the river with the young flood for about an hour, until we anchored close to the Hanoverian bank, near a gap in the dike, where we waited till the evening.

As soon as the night fell, a boat with muffled oars was manned, to carry the messenger on shore, I was in it; Mr Treenail, the second-lieutenant, steering. We pulled in right for a breach in the dike, lately cut by the French, in order to inundate the neighbourhood; and as the Elbe at high water is hereabouts much higher than the surrounding country, we were soon sucked into the current, and had only to keep our oars in the water, pulling a stroke now and then to give the boat steerage way. As we shot through the gap into the smooth water beyond, we once more gave way, the boat's head being kept in the direction of lights that we saw twinkling in the distance, apparently in some village beyond the inner embankment, when all at once we dashed in amongst thousands of wild geese, which rose with a clang, and a concert of quacking, screaming, and hissing, that was startling enough. We skimmed steadily on in the same direction—"Oars, men!" We were by this time close to a small cluster of houses, perched on the forced ground or embankment, and the messenger hailed in German.

"Qui vive?" sang out a gruff voice; and we heard the clank of a musket, as if some one had cast it from his shoulder, and caught it in his hands, as he brought it down to the charge. Our passenger seemed a little taken aback; but he hailed again, still in German. *"Parole,"* replied the man. A pause. "The watchword, or I fire." We had none to give.

"Pull round, men," said the lieutenant, with great quickness; pull the starboard oars; we are in the wrong box; back water the larboard. That's it! give way, men."

A flash—crack went the sentry's piece, and ping sang the ball over our heads. Another pause. Then a volley from a whole platoon. Again all was dark and silent. Presently a field-piece was fired, and several rockets were let off in our direction, by whose light we could see a whole company of French soldiers standing to their arms, with several cannon, but we were speedily out of the reach of their musketry. Several round shots were now fired, that hissed, ricochetting along the water close by us. Not a word was spoken in the boat all this time; we continued to pull for the opening in the dike, although, the current being strong against us, we made but little way; while the chance of being cut off by the *Johnny Crapeaus* getting round the top of the embankment, so as to command the gap before we could reach it, became every moment more alarming.

The messenger was in great tribulation, and made several barefaced attempts to stow himself away under the stern sheets.

The gallant fellows who composed the crew strained at their oars until everything cracked again; but as the flood made, the current against us increased, and we barely held our own. "Steer her out of the current, man," said the lieutenant to the coxswain; the man put the tiller to port as he was ordered.

"Vat you do soch a ting for, Mr Capitain Lieutenant?" said the emissary. "Oh! you not pershave you are rone in onder de igh bank! How you sall satisfy me no France *infanterie légère* dere, too, more as in de fort, eh? How you sall satisfy me, Mister Capitain Lieutenant, *eh?*"

"Hold your blasted tongue, will you," said Treenail, "and the infantry légère be damned simply. Mind your eye, my fine fellow, or I shall be much inclined to see whether you will be légère in the Elbe, or no. Hark!"

We all pricked up our ears, and strained our eyes, while a bright, spitting, sparkling fire of musketry opened at the gap, but there was no *ping pinging* of the shot overhead.

"They cannot be firing at us, sir," said the coxswain; "none of them bullets are telling hereaway."

Presently a smart fire was returned in three distinct clusters from the water, and whereas the firing at first had only lit up the dark figures of the French soldiery, and the black outline of the bank on which they were posted, the flashes that answered them showed us three armed boats attempting to force the passage. In a minute the firing ceased; the measured splash of oars was heard, as boats approached us.

"Who goes there?" sung out the lieutenant.

"Torches," was the answer.

"All's well, Torches," rejoined Mr Treenail; and presently the jolly-boat, and launch, and cutter of the Torch, with twenty marines, and six-and-thirty seamen, all armed, were alongside.

"What cheer, Treenail, my boy?" quoth Mr Splinter.

"Why, not much; the French, who we were told had left the Elbe entirely, are still here, as well as at Cuxhaven, not in force certainly, but sufficiently strong to pepper us very decently in the outgoing."

"What, are any of the people hurt?"

"No," said the garrulous emissary. "No, not hurt, but some of us frightened leetle piece—ah, very mosh, *je vous assure.*"

"Speak for yourself, Master Plenippo," said Treenail. "But Splinter, my man, now since the enemy have occupied the dike in front, how the deuce shall we get back into the river?—tell me that."

"Why," said the senior-lieutenant, "we must go as we came."

And here the groans from two poor fellows who had been hit were heard from the bottom of the launch. The cutter was by this time close to us, on the larboard side, commanded by Mr Julius Caesar Tip, the senior midshipman, vulgarly called in the ship *Bathos,* from his rather unromantic name. Here also a low moaning evinced the precision of the Frenchmen's fire.

"Lord, Mr Treenail, a sharp brush that was."

"Hush!" quoth Treenail. At this moment three rockets hissed up from the dark sky, and for an instant the hull and rigging of the sloop of war at anchor in the river glanced in the blue-white glare, and vanished again, like a spectre, leaving us in more thick darkness than before.

"Gemini! what is that, now?" quoth Tip again, as we distinctly heard the commixed rumbling and rattling sound of artillery, scampering along the dike.

"The ship has sent up these rockets to warn us of our danger," said Treenail. "What is to be done? Ah, Splinter, we are in a scrape—there they have brought up field-pieces, don't you hear?"

Splinter had heard it as well as his junior officer. "True enough, Treenail; so the sooner we make a dash through the opening the better."

"Agreed."

By some impulse peculiar to British sailors, the men were just about cheering, when their commanding officer's voice controlled them. "Hark, my brave fellows, silence, as you value your lives."

So away we pulled, the tide being now nearly on the turn, and presently we were so near the opening that we could see the signal-lights in the rigging of the sloop of war. All was quiet on the dike.

"Thank God, they have retreated, after all," said Mr Treenail.

"Whoo—o, whoo—o," shouted a gruff voice from the shore.

"There they are still," said Splinter. "Marines, stand by; don't throw away a shot. Men, pull like fury. So—give way, my lads; a minute of that strain will shoot us alongside of the old brig—that's it—hurrah!"

"Hurrah!" shouted the men in answer; but his and their exclamations were cut short by a volley of musketry. The fierce mustaches, pale faces, glazed shakoes, blue uniforms, and red epaulets, of the French infantry, glanced for a moment, and then all was dark again.

"Fire!" The marines in the three boats returned the salute, and by the flashes we saw three pieces of field-artillery in the very act of being unlimbered. We could distinctly hear the clash of the mounted artillerymen's sabres against their horses' flanks as they rode to the rear, their burnished accoutrements glancing at every sparkle of the musketry. We pulled like fiends, and, being the fastest boat, soon headed the launch and cutter, who were returning the enemy's fire brilliantly, when crack—a six-pound shot drove our boat into staves, and all hands were the next moment squattering in the water. I sank a good bit, I suppose, for I rose to the surface half drowned, and giddy and confused, and striking out at random, the first thing I recollected was a hard hand being wrung into my neckerchief, while a gruff voice shouted in my ear—

"*Rendez vous, mon cher?*"

Resistance was useless. I was forcibly dragged up the bank, where both musketry and cannon were still playing on the boats, which had, however, by this time got a good offing. I soon knew they were safe, by the Torch opening a fire of round and grape on the head of the dike, a certain proof that the boats had been accounted for. The French party now ceased firing, and retreated by the edge of the inundation, keeping the dike between them and the brig, all except the artillery, who had to scamper off, running the gauntlet on the crest of the embankment, until they got beyond the range of the carronades. I was conveyed between two grenadiers along the water's edge so long as the ship was firing; but when that ceased, I was clapped on one of the limbers of the field-guns, and strapped down to it between two of the artillerymen.

We rattled along until we came up to the French bivouac, where, round a large fire, kindled in what seemed to have been a farmyard, were assembled about fifty or sixty French soldiers. Their arms were piled under the low projecting roof of an outhouse, while the fire flickered upon their dark figures, and glanced on their bright accoutrements, and lit up the wall of the house that composed one side of the square. I was immediately marched between a file of men into a small room, where the commanding officer of the detachment was seated at a table, a blazing wood fire roaring in the chimney. He was a genteel, slender, dark man, with very large black mustaches, and fine sparkling black eyes, and had apparently just dismounted, for the mud was fresh on his boots and trousers. The latter were blue, with a broad gold lace down the seam, and fastened by a strap under his boot, from which projected a long fixed spur, which to me was remarkable as an unusual dress for a *militaire,* the British army being, at the time I write of, still in the age of breeches and gaiters or tall boots, long cues, and pipeclay—that is, those troops which I had seen at home, although I believe the great Duke had already relaxed a number of these absurdities in Spain.

His single-breasted coat was buttoned up to his throat, and without an inch of lace except on his crimson collar, which fitted close round his neck, and was richly embroidered with gold acorns and oak leaves, as were the crimson cuffs to his sleeves. He wore two immense and very handsome gold epaulets.

"My good boy," said he, after the officer who had captured me had told his story, "so your Government thinks the Emperor is retreating from the Elbe?"

I was a tolerable French scholar as times went, and answered him as well as I could.

"I have said nothing about that, sir; but from your question, I presume you command the rear-guard, colonel?"

"How strong is your squadron on the river?" said he, parrying the question.

"There is only one sloop of war, sir;"—and I spoke the truth.

He looked at me, and smiled incredulously; and then continued—

"I don't command the rear-guard, sir. But I waste time—are the boats ready?"

He was answered in the affirmative.

"Then set fire to the houses, and let off the rockets; they will see them at Cuxhaven—men, fall in-march"—and off we all trundled towards the river again.

When we arrived there we found ten Blankenese boats, two of them very large, and fitted with sliding platforms. The four field-pieces were run on board, two into each; one hundred and fifty men embarked in them and the other craft, which I found partly loaded with sacks of corn. I was in one of the smallest boats with the colonel. When we were all ready to shove off, "Lafont," said he, "are the men ready with their *couteaux?*"

"They are, sir," replied the sergeant.

"Then cut the horses' throats—but no firing." A few bubbling groans, and some heavy falls, and a struggling splash or two in the water, showed that the poor artillery horses had been destroyed.

The wind was fair up the river, and away we bowled before it. It was clear to me that the colonel commanding the post had overrated our strength, and, under the belief that we had cut him off from Cuxhaven, he had determined on falling back on Hamburgh.

When the morning broke we were close to the beautiful bank below Altona. The trees were beginning to assume the russet hue of autumn, and the sun shone gaily on the pretty villas and *bloomin Gartens* on the hill-side, while here and there a Chinese pagoda, or other fanciful pleasure-house, with its gilded trellised works, and little bells depending from the eaves of its many roofs, glancing like small golden balls, rose from out the fast thinning recesses of the woods. But there was no life in the scene—'twas "Greece, but living Greece no more"—not a fishing-boat was near, scarcely a solitary figure crawled along the beach.

"What is that?" after we had passed Blankenese, said the colonel, quickly. "Who are those?" as a group of three or four men presented themselves at a sharp turning of the road, that wound along the foot of the hill close to the shore.

"The uniform of the Prussians," said one.

"Of the Russians," said another.

"Poo," said a third, "it is a picket of the prince's;" and so it was, but the very fact of his having advanced his outposts so far, showed how he trembled for his position. After answering their hail, we pushed on, and as the clocks were striking twelve we were abreast of the strong beams that were clamped together with iron, and constituted the boom or chief water defence of Hamburgh. We passed through, and found an entire regiment under arms close by the Custom-house. Somehow or other I had drunk deep of that John Bull prejudice which delights to disparage the physical conformation of our Gallic neighbours, and hugs itself with the absurd notion "that on one pair of English legs doth march three Frenchmen." But when I saw the weather-beaten soldier-like veterans who formed this compact battalion, part of the *élite* of the first *corps,* more commanding in its aspect from severe service having worn all the gilding and lace away—"there was not a piece of feather in the host"—I felt the reality before me fast overcoming my preconceived opinion. I had seldom or ever seen so fine a body of men—tall, square, and muscular, the spread of their shoulders set off by their large red worsted epaulets, and the solidity of the mass increased by their wide trousers, which in my mind contrasted advantageously with the long gaiters and tight integuments of our own brave fellows.

We approached a group of three mounted officers, and in a few words the officer whose prisoner I was explained the affair to the *chef de bataillon,* whereupon I was immediately placed under the care of a sergeant and six rank and file, and marched along the chief canal for a mile, where I could not help remarking the numberless large rafts—you could not call them boats—of unpainted pine timber, which had arrived from the upper Elbe, loaded with grain; with gardens, absolute gardens, and cowhouses, and piggeries on board; while their crews of *Fierlanders,* men, women, and children, cut a most extraordinary appearance,—the men in their jackets, with buttons like pot-lids, and trousers fit to carry a month's provender and a couple of children in; and the women with bearings about the quarters as if they had cut holes in large cheeses, three feet in diameter at least, and stuck themselves through them— such sterns—and as to their costumes, all very fine in a Flemish painting, but the devils appeared to be awfully nasty in real life.

We carried on until we came to a large open space fronting a beautiful piece of water, which I was told was the Alster. As I walked through the narrow streets, I was struck with the peculiarity of the gables of the tall houses being all turned towards the thoroughfare, and with the stupendous size of the churches. We halted for a moment in the porch of one of the latter, and my notions of decency were not a little outraged, by seeing it filled with a squadron of dragoons, the men being in the very act of cleaning their horses. At length we came to the open space on the Alster, a large parade, faced by a street of splendid houses on the left hand, with a row of trees between them, and the water on the right. There were two regiments of foot bivouacking here, with their arms piled under the trees, while the men were variously employed, some on duty before the houses, others cleaning their accoutrements, and others again playing at all kinds of games. Presently we came to a crowd of soldiers clustered round a particular spot, some laughing, others cracking coarse jests, but none at all in the least serious. We could not get near enough to see distinctly what was going on; but we afterwards saw, when the crowd had dispersed, three men in the dress of respectable burghers, hanging from a low gibbet,—so low in fact, that although their heads wore not six inches from the beam, their feet were scarcely three from the ground. I was here placed in a guard-house, and kept there until the evening, when I was again marched off under my former escort, and we soon arrived at the door of a large mansion, fronting this parade, where two sentries were walking backwards and forwards before the door, while five dragoon horses, linked together, stood in the middle of the street, with one soldier attending them, but there was no other particular bustle to mark the headquarters of the general commanding. We advanced to the entrance—the sentries carrying arms—and were immediately ushered into a large saloon, the massive stair winding up along the walls, with the usual heavy wooden balustrade. We ascended to the first floor, where we were encountered by three aides-de-camp, in full dress, leaning with their backs against the hardwood railing, laughing and joking with each other, while two right opposite cast a bright flashing light on their splendid uniforms all *décoré* with one order or another. We approached.

"Whence, and whom have we here?" said one of them, a handsome young man, apparently not above twenty-two, as I judged, with small tiny black, jet-black, mustaches, and a noble countenance; fine dark eyes, and curls dark and clustering.

The officer of my escort answered, "A young Englishman—*enseigne de vaisseau.*"

I was no such thing, as a poor middy has no commission, but only his rating, which even his captain, without a court-martial, can take away at any time, and turn him before the mast.

At this moment I heard the clang of a sabre and the jingle of spurs on the stairs, and the group was joined by my captor, Colonel ✳✳✳.

"Ah, colonel!" exclaimed the aides in a volley, "where the devil have you come from? We thought you were in Bruxelles at the nearest."

The colonel put his hand on his lips and smiled, and then slapped the young officer who spoke first with his glove. "Never mind, boys, I have come to help you *here*—you will need help before long;—but how is ————!" Here he made a comical contortion of his face, and drew his ungloved hand across his throat. The young officers laughed, and pointed to the door. He moved towards it, preceded by the youngest of them, who led the way into a very lofty and handsome room, elegantly furnished, with some fine pictures on the walls, a handsome sideboard of plate, a rich Turkey carpet—an unusual thing in Germany—on the floor, and a richly gilt pillar at the end of the room farthest from us, the base of which contained a stove, which, through the joints of the door of it, appeared to be burning cheerily.

There were some very handsome sofas and ottomans scattered through the room, and a grand piano in one corner, the furniture being covered with yellow or amber-coloured velvet, with broad heavy draperies of gold fringe, like the bullion of an epaulet. There was a small round table near the stove, on which stood a silver candlestick, with four branches filled with wax tapers; and bottles of wine, and glasses. At this table sat an officer, apparently about forty-five years of age. There was nothing very peculiar in his appearance; he was a middle-sized man, well made apparently. He sat on one chair, with his legs supported on another.

His *white*-topped boots had been taken off, and replaced by a pair of slipshod slippers; his splashed white kerseymere pantaloons, seamed with gold, resting on the unfrayed velvet cushion; his blue coat, covered with rich embroidery at the bosom and collar, was open, and the lappels thrown back, displaying a crimson velvet facing, also richly embroidered, and an embroidered scarlet waistcoat; a large solitary star glittered on his breast, and the grand cross of the Legion of Honour sparkled at his buttonhole; his black neckerchief had been taken off; and his cocked hat lay beside him on a sofa, massively laced, the edges richly ornamented with ostrich down; his head was covered with a red velvet cap, with a thick gold cord twisted two or three turns round it, and ending in two large tassels of heavy bullion; he wore very large epaulets; and his sword had been inadvertently, as I conjectured, placed on the table, so that the steel hilt rested on the ornamental part of the metal stove.

His face was good, his hair dark, forehead without a wrinkle, high and massive, eyes bright and sparkling, nose neither fine nor dumpy—a fair enough proboscis as noses go. There was an expression, however, about the upper lip and mouth that I did not like—a constant nervous sort of lifting of the lip, as it were; and as the mustache appeared to have been recently shaven off, there was a white blueness on the upper lip, that contrasted unpleasantly with the dark tinge which he had gallantly wrought for on the glowing sands of Egypt, and the bronzing of his general features from fierce suns and parching winds. His bare neck and hands were delicately fair, the former firm and muscular, the latter slender and tapering, like a woman's. He was reading a gazette, or some printed paper, when we entered; and although there was a tolerable clatter of muskets, sabres, and spurs, he never once lifted his eye in the direction where we stood. Opposite this personage, on a low chair, with his legs crossed, and eyes fixed on the ashes that were dropping from the stove, with his brown cloak hanging from his shoulders, sat a short stout personage, a man about thirty years of age, with fair flaxen hair, a florid complexion, a very fair skin, and massive German features. The expression of his face, so far as such a countenance could be said to have any characteristic expression, was that of fixed sorrow. But before I could make any other observation, the aide-de-camp approached with a good spice of fear and trembling, as I could see.

"Colonel ∗ ∗ ∗ to wait on your highness."

"Ah!" said the officer to whom he spoke,—"ah, colonel, what do you here? Has the emperor advanced again?"

"No," said the officer, "he has not advanced; but the rearguard were cut off by the Prussians, and the ——— light, with the ——— grenadiers, are now in Cuxhaven."

"Well," replied the general, "but how come *you* here?"

"Why, marshal, we were detached to seize a depot of provisions in a neighbouring village, and had made preparations to carry them off, when we were attacked through a gap in the dike by some armed boats from an English squadron, and hearing a distant firing at the very moment, which I concluded to be the Prussian advance, I conceived all chance of rejoining the main army at an end, and therefore I shoved off in the grain-boats, and *here* I am."

"Glad to see you, however," said the general, "but sorry for the cause why you have returned.—Whom have we got here—what boy is that?"

"Why," responded the colonel, "that lad is one of the British officers of the force that attacked us."

"Ha," said the general again—"how did you capture him?"

"The boat (one of four) in which he was, was blown to pieces by a six-pound shot. He was the only one of the enemy who swam ashore. The rest, I am inclined to think, were picked up by the other boats."

"So," grumbled the general,—"British ships in the Elbe!"

The colonel continued. "I hope, marshal, you will allow him his parole?—he is, as you see, quite a child."

"Parole!" replied the marshal,—"parole! such a mere lad cannot know the value of his promise."

A sudden fit of rashness came over me.

"He is a mere boy," reiterated the marshal. "No, no—send him to prison;" and he resumed the study of the printed paper he had been reading.

I struck in, impelled by despair, for, young as I was, I knew the character of the man before whom I stood, and I remembered that even a tiger might be checked by a bold front—"I *am* an Englishman, sir, and incapable of breaking my plighted word."

He laid down the paper he was reading, and slowly lifted his eyes, and fastened them on me,—"Ha," said he, "ha—so young—so reckless!"

"Never mind him, marshal," said the colonel. "If you will grant him his parole, I—"

"Take it, colonel—take it—take his parole, not to go beyond the ditch."

"But I decline to give any such promise," said I, with a hardihood which at the time surprised me, and has always done so.

"Why, my good youth," said the marshal in great surprise, "why will you not take advantage of the offer—a kinder one, let me tell you, than I am in the habit of making to an enemy?"

"Simply, sir, because I will endeavour to escape on the very first opportunity."

"Ha!" said the marshal once more, "this to my face? Lafontaine,"—to the aide-de-camp—"a file of soldiers." The handsome young officer hesitated—hung in the wind, as we say, for a moment—moved, as I imagined, by my extreme youth. This irritated the marshal—he rose, and stamped on the floor. The colonel essayed to interfere. "Sentry—sentry—a file of grenadiers—take him forth, and—" here he energetically clutched the steel hilt of his sword, and instantly dashed it from him—"*Sacre!* the devil—what is that?" and straightway he began to *pirouette* on one leg round the room, shaking his right hand and blowing his fingers.

The officers in waiting could not stand it any longer, and burst into a fit of laughter, in which their commanding officer, after an unavailing attempt to look serious—I should rather write fierce—joined; and there he was, the bloody Davoust—Duke of Auerstad—Prince of Eckmuhl—the Hamburgh Robespierre—the terrible Davoust—dancing all around the room, in a regular *guffaw*, like to split his sides. The heated stove had made his sword, which rested on it, nearly red-hot.

All this while the quiet, plain-looking little man sat still. He now rose; but I noticed that he had been fixing his eyes intently on me. I thought I could perceive a tear glistening in them as he spoke,

"Marshal, will you intrust that boy to me?"

"Poo," said the prince, still laughing, "take him—do what you will with him;"—then, as if suddenly recollecting himself, "But, Mr ∗ ∗ ∗, *you* must be answerable for him—he must be at hand if I want him."

The gentleman who had so unexpectedly patronised me rose and said, "Marshal, I promise."

"Very well," said Davoust. "Lafontaine, desire supper to be sent up."

It was brought *in,* and my new ally and I were shown *out.*

As we went down stairs, we looked into a room on the ground floor, at the door of which were four soldiers with fixed bayonets. We there saw, for it was well lit up, about twenty or five-and-twenty respectable-looking men, very English in appearance, all to their long cloaks, an unusual sort of garment to my eye at that time. The night was very wet, and the aforesaid garments were hung on pegs in the wall all around the room, which being strongly heated by a stove, the moisture rose up in a thick mist, and made the faces of the burghers indistinct.

They were busily engaged talking to each other, some to his neighbour, the others across the table, but all with an expression of the most intense anxiety.

"Who are these?" said I to my guide.

"Ask no questions *here,*" said he, and we passed on.

I afterwards learned that they were the hostages seized on for the contribution of fifty millions of francs, which had been imposed on the doomed city, and that this very night they had been torn from their families, and cooped up in the way I had seen, where, they were advertised, they must remain until the money should be forthcoming.

As we walked along the streets, and crossed the numerous bridges over the canals and branches of the river, we found all the houses lit up, by order, as I learned, of the French marshal. The rain descended in torrents, sparkling past the lights, while the city was a desert, with one dreadful exception; for we were waylaid at almost every turn by groups of starving lunatics, their half-naked figures and pale visages glimmering in the glancing lights, under the dripping rain and, had it not been for the numerous sentries scattered along the thoroughfares, I believe we should have been torn to pieces by bands of *moping* idiots, now rendered ferocious from their sufferings, in consequence of the madhouses having been cleared of their miserable, helpless inmates, in order to be converted into barracks for the troops. At all of these bridges sentries were posted, past which my conductor and myself were franked by the sergeant who accompanied us giving the countersign. At length, civilly touching his cap, although he did not refuse the piece of money tendered by my friend, he left us, wishing us good-night, and saying the coast was clear.

We proceeded, without further challenge, until we came to a very magnificent house, with some fine trees before it. We approached the door, and rang the door-bell. It was immediately opened, and we entered a large desolate-looking vestibule, about thirty feet square, filled in the centre with a number of bales of goods and a variety of merchandise, while a heavy wooden stair, with clumsy oak balustrades, wound round the sides of it. We ascended, and, turning to the right, entered a large well-furnished room, with a table laid out for supper, with lights, and a comfortable stove at one end. Three young officers of cuirassiers, in their superb uniforms, whose breast and back pieces were glittering on a neighbouring sofa, and a colonel of artillery, were standing round the stove. The colonel, the moment we entered, addressed my conductor:—

"Ah, * * *, we are devilish hungry—*Ich bin dem Verhungern, nahe*—and were just on the point of ordering in the provender, had you not appeared."

"A little more than that," thought I; for the food was already smoking on the table.

Mine host acknowledged the speech with a slight smile.

"But whom have we here?" said one of the young dragoons. He waited a moment—*"Etes vous Français?"* I gave him no answer. He then addressed me in German—*"Sprechen sie gelaüfig Deutsch?"*

"Why," chimed in my conductor, "he does speak a little French indifferently enough; but still—"

Here I was introduced to the young officers, and we all sat down at table; the colonel, civility itself, pressing my host to drink *his own* wine, and eat *his own* food, and even rating the servants for not being sufficiently alert in their attendance on *their own* master.

"Well, my dear * * * how have you sped with the prince?"

"Why, colonel," said my protector, in his cool, calm way, "as well as I expected. I was of some service to him when he was here before, at the time he was taken so very ill, and he has not forgotten it; so I am not included amongst the unfortunate *détenus* for the payment of the fine. But that is not all; for I am allowed to go to-morrow to my father's, and here is my passport."

"Wonders will never cease," said the colonel; "but who is that boy?"

"He is one of the crew of the English boats which tried to cut off Colonel * * * the other evening, near Cuxhaven. His life was saved by a very laughable circumstance certainly; merely by the marshal's sword, from resting on the stove, having become almost red-hot." And here he detailed the whole transaction as it took place, which set the party a-laughing most heartily.

I will always bear witness to the extreme amenity with which I was now treated by the French officers. The evening passed over quickly. About eleven we retired to rest, my friend furnishing me with clothes, and warning me that next morning he would call me at daylight, to proceed to his father's country-seat, where he intimated that I must remain in the mean time.

Next morning I was roused accordingly, and a long, low, open carriage rattled up to the door, just before day-dawn. Presently the *réveille* was beaten, and answered by the different posts in the city and on the ramparts.

We drove on, merely showing our passport to the sentries at the different bridges, until we reached the gate, where we had to pull up until the officer on duty appeared, and had scrupulously compared our personal appearance with the written description. All was found correct, and we drove on.

It surprised me very much, after having repeatedly heard of the great strength of Hamburgh, to look out on the large mound of green turf that constituted its chief defence. It is all true that there was a deep ditch and glacis beyond; but there was no covered way, and both the scarp and counterscarp were simple earthen embankments; so that, had the ditch been filled with fascines, there was no wall to face the attacking force after crossing it,—nothing but a green mound, precipitous enough, certainly, and crowned with a low parapet of masonry, and bristling with batteries about half-way down, so that the muzzles of the guns were flush with the neighbouring country beyond the ditch. Still there was wanting, to my imagination, the strength of the high perpendicular wall, with its gaping embrasures and frowning cannon. All this time it never occurred to me that to breach such a defence as that we looked upon was impossible. You might have plumped your shot into it until you had converted it into an iron mine, but no chasm could have been forced in it by all the artillery in Europe; so that battering in breach was entirely out of the question; and this, in truth, constituted the great strength of the place.

We arrived, after an hour's drive, at the villa belonging to my protector's family, and walked into a large room, with a comfortable stove, and extensive preparations made for a comfortable breakfast.

Presently three young ladies appeared. They were his sisters; blue-eyed, fair-haired, white-skinned, round-sterned, plump little partridges.

"*Haben sie gefrühstücht?*" said the eldest.

"*Pas encore,*" said he in French, with a smile. "But, sisters, I have brought a stranger here, a young English officer, who was recently captured in the river."

"An English officer!" exclaimed the three ladies, looking at me, a poor, little, dirty midshipman, in my soiled linen, unbrushed shoes, dirty trousers and jacket, with my little square of white cloth on the collar; and I began to find the eloquent blood mantling in my cheeks and tingling in my ears; but their kindly feelings got the better of a gentle propensity to laugh, and the youngest said—

"*Sie sind gerade zu rechter zeit gekommen:*" when, finding that her German was Hebrew to me, she tried the other tack—"*Vous arrivez à propos, le déjeûné est prêt.*"

However, I soon found that the moment they were assured that I was in reality an Englishman, they all spoke English, and exceedingly well too. Our meal was finished, and I was standing at the window looking out on a small lawn, where evergreens of the most beautiful kinds were checkered with little round clumps of most luxuriant hollyhocks, and the fruit-trees in the neighbourhood were absolutely bending to the earth under their loads of apples and pears. Presently my friend came up to me; my curiosity could no longer be restrained.

"Pray, my good sir, what peculiar cause, may I ask, have you for showing me, an entire stranger to you, all this unexpected kindness? I am fully aware that I have no claim on you."

"My good boy, you say true; but I have spent the greatest part of my life in London, although a Hamburgher born, and I consider you, therefore, in the light of a countryman. Besides, I will not conceal that your gallant bearing before Davoust riveted my attention, and engaged my good wishes."

"But how come you to have so much influence with the mon—— general, I mean?"

"For several reasons," he replied. "For those, amongst others, you heard the colonel—who has taken the small liberty of turning me out of my own house in Hamburgh—mention last night at supper. But a man like Davoust cannot be judged of by common rules. He has, in short, taken a fancy to me, for which you may thank your stars—although your life has been actually saved by the prince having burned his fingers.—But here comes my father."

A venerable old man entered the room, leaning on his stick. I was introduced in due form.

"He had breakfasted in his own room," he said, "having been ailing; but he could not rest quietly, after he had heard there was an Englishman in the house, until he had himself welcomed him."

I shall never forget the kindness I experienced from these worthy people. For three days I was fed and clothed by them as if I had been a member of the family.

Like a boy as I was, I had risen on the fourth morning at grey dawn, to be aiding in dragging the fish-pond, so that it might be cleaned out. This was an annual amusement, in which the young men and women in the family, under happier circumstances, had been in the invariable custom of joining; and, changed as these were, they still preserved the fashion. The seine was cast in at one end, loaded at the bottom with heavy sinks, and buoyant at the top with cork floats. We hauled it along the whole length of the pond, thereby driving the fish into an enclosure, about twenty feet square, with a sluice towards the pond, and another fronting the dull ditch that flowed past beyond it. Whenever we had hunted the whole of the finny tribes (barring those slippery youths the eels, who, with all their cleverness, were left to dry in the mud) into the toils, we filled all the tubs, and pots, and pans, and vessels of all kinds and descriptions, with the fat, honest-looking Dutchmen, the carp and tench, who really submitted to their captivity with all the resignation of most ancient and quiet fish, scarcely indicating any sense of its irksomeness, except by a lumbering sluggish flap of their broad heavy tails.

A transaction of this kind could not take place amongst a group of young folk without shouts of laughter, and it was not until we had caught the whole of the fish in the pond, and placed them in safety, that I had leisure to look about me. The city lay nearly four miles distant from us. The whole country round Hamburgh is level, except the right bank below it of the noble river on which it stands, the Elbe. The house where I was domiciled stood on nearly the highest point of this bank, which gradually sloped down into a swampy hollow, nearly level with the river. It then rose again gently until the swell was crowned with the beautiful town of Altona, and immediately beyond appeared the ramparts and tall spires of the noble city itself.

The morning had been thick and foggy, but as the sun rose, the white mist that had floated over the whole country gradually concentrated and settled down into the hollow between us and Hamburgh, covering it with an impervious veil, which even extended into the city itself, filling the lower part of it with a dense white bank of fog, which rose so high that the spires alone, with one or two of the most lofty buildings, appeared above the rolling sea of white fleece-like vapour, as if it had been a model of the stronghold, in place of the reality, packed in white wool, so distinct did it appear, diminished as it was in the distance. On the tallest spire of the place, which was now sparkling in the early sunbeams, the French flag, the pestilent *tricolor*, that upastree, waved sluggishly in the faint morning breeze.

It attracted my attention, and I pointed it out to my patron. Presently it was hauled down, and a series of signals was made at the yard-arm of a spar that had been slung across it. Who can they be telegraphing to? thought I, while I could notice my host assume a most anxious and startled look, while he peered down into the hollow; but he could see nothing, as the fog bank still filled the whole of the space between the city and the acclivity where we stood.

"What is that?" said I; for I heard, or thought I heard, a low, rumbling, rushing noise in the ravine. Mr * * * heard it as well as I, apparently, for he put his finger to his lips—as much as to say, "Hold your tongue, my good boy—*nous verrons*."

It increased—the clattering of horses' hoofs, and the clang of scabbards were heard, and, in a twinkling, the hussar caps of a squadron of light dragoons emerged from out the fog bank, as, charging up the road, they passed the small gate of green basketwork at a hand-gallop. I ought to have mentioned before, that my friend's house was situated about half-way up the ascent, so that the rising ground behind it in the opposite direction from the city shut out all view towards the country. After the dragoons passed, there was an interval of two minutes, when a troop of flying artillery, with three six-pound field-pieces, rattled after the leading squadron, the horses all in a lather, at full speed, with the guns bounding and jumping behind them as if they had been playthings, followed by their *caissons.* Presently we could see the leading squadron file to the right—clear the low hedge—and then disappear over the crest of the hill. Twenty or thirty pioneers, who had been carried forward behind as many of the cavalry, were now seen busily employed in filling up the ditch, and cutting down the short scrubby hedge; and presently, the artillery coming up also, filed off sharply to the right, and formed on the very summit of the hill, distinctly visible between us and the grey cold streaks of morning. By the time we had noticed this, the clatter in our immediate neighbourhood was renewed, and a group of mounted officers dashed past us, up the path, like a whirlwind, followed, at a distance of twenty yards, by a single cavalier, apparently a general officer. These did not stop, as they rode at speed past the spot where the artillery were in position, but, dipping over the summit, disappeared down the road, from which they did not appear to diverge, until they were lost to our view beyond the crest of the hill. The hum and buzz, and, anon, the "measured tread of marching men," in the valley between us and Hamburgh, still continued. The leading files of a light infantry regiment now appeared, swinging along at a round trot, with their muskets poised in their right hands—no knapsacks on their backs. They appeared to follow the route of the group of mounted officers, until we could see a puff of white smoke, then another and a third from the field-pieces, followed by thudding reports, there being no high ground nor precipitous bank nor water in the neighbourhood to reflect the sound, and make it emulate Jove's thunder. At this they struck across the fields, and, forming behind the guns, lay down flat on their faces, where they were soon hid from our view by the wreaths of white smoke, as the sluggish morning breeze rolled it down the hill-side toward us.

"What the deuce can all this mean—is it a review?" said I, in my innocence.

"A *reconnoissance* in force," groaned my friend. "The Allied troops must be at hand—now, God help us!"

The women, like frightened hares, paused to look up in their brother's face, as he kept his eye steadily turned towards the ridge of the hill, and, when he involuntarily wrung his hands, they gave a loud scream, and ran off into the house.

The breeze at this moment "aside the shroud of battle cast," and we heard a faint bugle-call, like an echo, wail in the distance, from beyond the hill. It was instantly answered by the loud, startling *blare* of a dozen of the light infantry bugles above us on the hill-side, and we could see them suddenly start from their lair, and form; while between us and the clearing morning sky, the cavalry, magnified into giants in the strong relief on the outline of the hill, were driven in straggling patrols, like chaff, over the summit—their sabres sparkling in the level sunbeams, and the reports of the red flashes of their pistols crackling down upon us.

"They are driven in on the infantry," said Mr ✳ ✳ ✳. He was right—but the light battalion immediately charged over the hill, with a loud hurrah, after admitting the beaten horse through their intervals, who, however, to give the devils their due, formed again in an instant, under the shelter of the high ground. The artillery again opened their fire—the cavalry once more advanced, and presently we could see nothing but the field-pieces, with their three separate groups of soldiers standing quietly by them—a sure proof that the enemy's pickets were now out of cannon-shot, and had been driven back on the main body, and that the *reconnoissance* was still advancing.

What will not a habitual exposure to danger do, even with tender women?

"The French have advanced, so let us have our breakfast, Julia, my dear," said Mr ✳ ✳ ✳, as we entered the house. "The Allied forces would have been welcome, however; and surely, if they do come, they will respect our sufferings and helplessness."

The eldest sister, to whom be spake, shook her head mournfully; but, nevertheless, betook herself to her task of making coffee.

"What rumbling and rattling is that?" said ✳ ✳ ✳ to an old servant who had just entered the room.

"Two waggons with wounded men, sir, have passed onwards towards the town."

"Ah!" said mine host, in great bitterness of spirit.

But *allons*, we proceeded to make the best use of our time—ham, good—fish, excellent—eggs, fresh—coffee, superb—when we again heard the field-pieces above us open their fire, and in the intervals we could distinguish the distant rattle of musketry. Presently this rolling fire slackened, and, after a few scattering shots here and there, ceased altogether; but the cannon on the hill still continued to play. We were by this time all standing in a cluster in the porch of the villa, before which stood the tubs with the finny spoil of the fish-pond, on a small paddock of velvet grass, about forty yards square, separated from the high-road by a low ornamental fence of green basket-work, as already mentioned. The firing from the great guns increased, and every now and then I thought I heard a distant sound, as if the reports of the guns above us had been reflected from some precipitous bank.

"I did not know that there was any echo here," said the youngest girl.

"Alas, Janette!" said her brother, "I fear that is no echo;" and he put up his hand to his ear, and listened in breathless suspense. The sound was repeated.

"The Russian cannon replying to those on the hill!" said Mr * * *, with startling energy. "God help us! it can no longer be an affair of posts; the heads of the Allied columns must be in sight, for the French skirmishers are unquestionably driven in."

A French officer at this moment rattled past us down the road at speed, and vanished in the hollow, taking the direction of the town. His hat fell off, as his horse swerved a little at the open gate as he passed. He never stopped to pick it up. Presently a round shot, with a loud ringing and hissing sound, pitched over the hill, and knocked one of the fish-tubs close to us to pieces, scattering the poor fish all about the lawn. With the recklessness of a mere boy I dashed out, and was busy picking them up, when Mr * * * called to me to come back.

"Let us go in and await what may befall; I dread what the ty——" here he prudently checked himself, remembering, no doubt, "that a bird of the air might carry the matter,"—"I dread what *he* may do, if they are really investing the place. At any rate, here, in the very arena where the struggle will doubtless be fiercest, we cannot abide. So go, my dearest sisters, and pack up whatever you may have most valuable or most necessary. Nay, no tears; and I will attend to our poor old father, and get the carriage ready, if, God help me, I dare use it."

"But where, in the name of all that is fearful, shall we go?" said his second sister. "Not back to Hamburgh—not to endure another season of such deep degradation—not to be exposed to the—. O brother, you saw we all submitted to our fate without a murmur, and laboured cheerfully on the fortifications, when compelled to do so by that inhuman monster Davoust, amidst the ribaldry of a licentious soldiery, merely because poor Janette had helped to embroider a standard for the brave Hanseatic Legion—you know how we bore this"—here the sweet girl held out her delicate hands, galled by actual and unwonted labour—"and many other indignities, until that awful night, when—No, brother, *we* shall await the arrival of the Russians, even should we see our once happy home converted into a field of battle; but into the city *we* shall *not* go."

"Be it so then, my dearest sister.—Wilhelm, put up the *stuhl wagen.*"

He had scarcely returned into the breakfast-room, when the door opened, and the very handsome young officer, the aide-de-camp of the prince, whom I had seen the night I was carried before Davoust, entered, splashed up to the eyes, and much heated and excited. I noticed blood on the hilt of his sword. His orderly sat on his foaming steed, right opposite where I stood, wiping his bloody sabre on his horse's mane. The women grew pale; but still they had presence of mind enough to do the honours with self-possession. The stranger wished us a good morning; and on being asked to sit down to breakfast, he unbuckled his sword, threw it from him with a clash on the floor, and then, with all the grace in the world, addressed himself to discuss the *comestibles*. He tried a slight approach to jesting now and then; but seeing the heaviness of heart which prevailed amongst the women, he, with the good-breeding of a man of the world, forbore to press his attentions.

Breakfast being finished, and the ladies having retired, he rose, buckled on his sword again, drew on his gloves, and taking his hat in his hand, he advanced to the window, and desired his men to "fall in."

"Men!—what men? " said poor Mr ✳ ✳.

"Why, the marshal has had a company of *sapeurs* for these three days back in the adjoining village—they are now here."

"Here!" exclaimed ✳ ✳ ✳; "what do the sappers *here?*" Two of the soldiers carried slow matches in their hands, while their muskets were slung at their backs. "There is no mine to be sprung here?"

The young officer heard him with great politeness, but declined giving any answer. The next moment he turned towards the ladies, and was making himself as agreeable as time and circumstances would admit, when a shot came crashing through the roof, broke down the ceiling, and, knocking the flue of the stove to pieces, rebounded from the wall, and rolled harmlessly beneath the table. He was the only person who did not start, or evince any dread. He kicked the bullet out of the way, and merely cast his eyes upward and smiled. He then turned to poor * * *, who stood quite collected, but very pale, near where the stove had stood, and held out his hand to him.

"On my honour," said the young soldier, "it grieves me to the very heart; but I must obey my orders. It is no longer an affair of posts; the enemy is pressing on us in force. The Allied columns are in sight; their cannon-shot have but now penetrated your roof; we have but driven in their pickets; very soon they will be here; and in the event of their advance, my orders are to burn down this house and the neighbouring village."

A sudden flush rushed into Mr * * *'s face. "Indeed! does the prince really —"

The young officer bowed, and with something more of sternness in his manner than he had yet used, he said, "Mr * * *, I duly appreciate your situation, and respect your feelings; but the Prince of Eckmuhl is my superior officer; and under other circumstances"—Here he slightly touched the hilt of his sword.

"For myself I don't care," said * * *, "but what is to become of my sisters!"

"They must proceed to Hamburgh."

"Very well—let me order the *stuhl wagen,* and give us, at all events, half an hour to move our valuables."

Here Mr * * * exchanged looks with his sisters.

"Certainly," said the young officer, "and I will myself see you safe into the city."

Who says that eels cannot be made used to skinning? The poor girls continued their little preparations with an alacrity and presence of mind that truly surprised me. There was neither screaming nor fainting, and by the time the carriage was at the door, they, with two female domestics, were ready to mount. I cannot better describe their vehicle, than by comparing it to a canoe mounted on four wheels, connected by a long perch with a coach-box at the bow, and three gig bodies hung athwart ships, or slung inside of the canoe, by leather thongs, At the moment we were starting, Mr * * * came close to me and whispered, "Do you think your ship will still be in the river?"

I answered that I made no doubt she was.

"But even if she be not," said he, "the Holstein bank is open to us. Anywhere but Hamburgh *now*." And the scalding tears ran down his cheeks.

At this moment there was a bustle on the hill top, and presently the artillery began once more to play, while the musketry breezed up again in the distance. A mounted bugler rode halfway down the hill, and sounded the *recall*. The young officer hesitated. The man waved his hand, and blew the *advance*.

"It must be for us—answer it." His bugle did so. "Bring the pitch, men—the flax—so now—break the windows, and let the air in—set the house on fire; and, Sergeant Guido, remain to prevent it being extinguished—I shall fire the village as we pass through."

He gave the word to face about; and, desiring the men to follow at the same swinging run with which the whole of the infantry had originally advanced, he spurred his horse against the hill, and soon disappeared.

My host's resolution seemed now taken. Turning to the sergeant—"My good fellow, the *reconnoissance* will soon be returning; I shall precede it into the town."

The man, a fine *vieux moustache,* hesitated.

My friend saw it, and hit him in a Frenchman's most assailable quarter.

"The ladies, my good man—the ladies!—You would not have them drive in *pell-mell* with the troops, exposed most likely to the fire of the Prussian advanced-guard, would you?"

The man grounded his musket, and touched his cap—"Pass on."

Away we trundled, until, coming to a cross-road, we turned down towards the river; and at the angle we could see thick wreaths of smoke curling up into the air, showing that the barbarous order had been but too effectually fulfilled.

"What is that?" said ✳ ✳ ✳.

A horse, with his rider entangled and dragged by the stirrup, passed us at full speed, leaving a long track of blood on the road.

"Who is that?"

The coachman drove on, and gave no answer; until, at a sharp turn, we came upon the bruised and now breathless body of the young officer, who had so recently obeyed the savage behests of his brutal commander. There was a musket-shot right in the middle of his fine forehead, like a small blue point, with one or two heavy black drops of blood oozing from it. His pale features wore a mild and placid expression, evincing that the numberless lacerations and bruises, which were evident through his torn uniform, had been inflicted on a breathless corpse.

The *stuhl wagen* had carried on for a mile farther or so, but the firing seemed to approximate, whereupon our host sang out, *"Fahrt zu, Schwager— Wir kommen nicht weiter."*

The driver of the *stuhl wagen* sculled along until we arrived at the beautiful, at a mile off, but the beastly, when close to, village of Blankenese.

When the *voiture* stopped in the village, there seemed to be a *nonplusation,* to coin a word for the *nonce,* between my friend and his sisters. They said something very sharply, and with a degree of determination that startled me. He gave no answer. Presently the Amazonian attack was renewed.

"We *shall* go on board," said they.

"Very well," said he; "but have patience, have patience!"

"No, no. *Wann wird man sich einschiffen müssen?*"

By this time we were in the heart of the village, and surrounded with a whole lot, forty at the least, of Blankenese boatmen. We were not long in selecting one of the fleetest-looking of those very fleet boats, when we all trundled on board; and I now witnessed what struck me as being an awful sign of the times. The very coachman of the *stuhl wagen,* after conversing a moment with his master, returned to his team, tied the legs of the poor creatures as they stood, and then with a sharp knife cut their jugular veins through and through on the right side, having previously reined them up sharp to the left, so that, before starting, we could see three of the team, which consisted of four superb bays, level with the soil, and dead; the near wheeler only holding out on his fore-legs.

We shoved off at eleven o'clock in the forenoon; and after having twice been driven into creeks on the Holstein shore by bad weather, we arrived about two next morning safely all board the Torch, which immediately got under weigh for England. After my story had been told to the captain, I left my preserver, his father, and his sisters in his hands, and I need scarcely say that they had as hearty a welcome as the worthy old soul could give them, and dived into the midshipmen's berth for a morsel of comfort, where, in a twinkling, I was far into the secrets of a pork-pie.

CHAPTER II.

THE CRUISE OF THE TORCH.

> "Sleep, gentle sleep—
> Wilt thou, upon the high and giddy mast,
> Seal up the ship-boy's eyes, and rock his brains
> In cradle of the rude imperious surge;
> And in the visitation of the winds,
> Who take the ruffian billows by the top,
> Curling their monstrous heads, and hanging them

With deaf'ning clamours in the slippery clouds
That, with the hurly, death itself awakes.
Canst thou, O partial sleep! give thy repose
To the wet sea-boy in an hour so rude?"

King Henry IV., Part II.

HELIGOLAND LIGHT—north and by west—so many leagues—wind baffling—weather hazy—Lady Passengers on deck for the first time.

Arrived in the Downs—ordered by signal from the guardship to proceed to Portsmouth. Arrived at Spithead—ordered to fit to receive a general officer, and six pieces of field artillery, and a Spanish Ecclesiastic, the Canon of ————. Plenty of great guns, at any rate—a regular park of artillery.

Received General ✳ ✳ ✳ and his wife, and aide-de-camp, and two poodle-dogs, one white man-servant, one black ditto, and the Canon of ————, and the six nine-pound field-pieces, and sailed for the Cave of Cork.

It was blowing hard as we stood in for the Old Head of Kinsale—pilot boat breasting the foaming surge like a sea gull—"Carrol Cove" in her tiny mainsail—pilot jumped into the main channel—bottle of rum swung by the lead line into the boat—all very clever.

Ran in, and anchored under Spike Island. A line-of-battle ship, three frigates, and a number of merchantmen at anchor—men-of-war lovely craft—bands playing—a good deal of the pomp and circumstance of war. Next forenoon, Mr Treenail, the second-lieutenant, sent for me.

"Mr Cringle," said he, "you have an uncle in Cork, I believe?"

I said I had.

"I am going there on duty to-night; I daresay, if you asked the captain to let you accompany me, he would do so." This was too good an offer not to be taken advantage of. I plucked up courage, made my bow, asked leave, and got it; and the evening found my friend the lieutenant, and myself, after a ride of three hours, during which I, for one, had my bottom sheathing grievously rubbed, and a considerable botheration at crossing the Ferry at Passage, safe in our inn at Cork. I soon found out that the object of my superior officer was to gain information amongst the crimp shops, where ten men who had run from one of the West Indiamen, waiting at Cove for convoy, were stowed away, but I was not let farther into the secret; so I set out to pay my visit, and after passing a pleasant evening with my friends, Mr and Mrs Job Cringle, the lieutenant dropped in upon us about nine o'clock. He was heartily welcomed; and under the plea of our being obliged to return to the ship early next morning, we soon took leave, and returned to the inn. As I was turning into the public room, the door was open, and I could see it full of blowsy-faced monsters, glimmering and jabbering, through the mist of hot brandy grog and gin twist; with poodle Benjamins, and greatcoats, and cloaks of all sorts and sizes, steaming on their pegs, with Barcelonas and comforters, and damp travelling caps of seal-skin, and blue cloth, and tartan, arranged above the same. Nevertheless, such a society in my juvenile estimation, during my short *escapade* from the middy's berth, had its charms, and I was rolling in with a tolerable swagger, when Mr Treenail pinched my arm.

"Mr Cringle, come here into my room."

From the way in which he spoke, I imagined, in my innocence, that his room was at my elbow; but no such thing—we had to ascend a long, and not over-clean staircase, to the fourth floor, before we were shown into a miserable little double-bedded room. So soon as we had entered, the lieutenant shut the door.

"Tom," said he, "I have taken a fancy to you, and therefore I applied for leave to bring you with me; but I must expose you to some danger, and, I will allow, not altogether in a very creditable way either. You must enact the spy for a short space."

I did not like the notion, certainly, but I had little time for consideration.

"Here," he continued—"here is a bundle." He threw it on the floor. "You must rig in the clothes it contains, and make your way into the celebrated crimp-shop, in the neighbourhood, and pick up all the information you can regarding the haunts of the pressable men at Cove, especially with regard to the ten seamen who have run from the West Indiaman we left below. You know the Admiral has forbidden pressing at Cork, so you must contrive to frighten the blue jackets down to Cove, by representing yourself as an apprentice of one of the merchant vessels, who had run from his indentures, and that you had narrowly escaped from a press-gang this very night *here*."

I made no scruples, but forthwith arrayed myself in the slops contained in the bundle; in a pair of shag trousers, red flannel shirt, coarse blue cloth jacket, and no waistcoat.

"Now," said Mr Treenail, "stick a quid of tobacco in your cheek, and take the cockade out of your hat; or stop, leave it, and ship this striped woollen nightcap—so—and come along with me."

We left the house, and walked half a mile down the *Quay.*

Presently we arrived before a kind of low grog-shop—a bright lamp was flaring in the breeze at the door, one of the panes of the glass of it being broken.

"Before I entered, Mr Treenail took me to one side—"Tom, Tom Cringle, you must go into this crimp-shop; pass yourself off for an apprentice of the Guava, bound for Trinidad, the ship that arrived just as we started, and pick up all the knowledge you can regarding the whereabouts of the men, for we are, as you know, cruelly ill manned, and must replenish as we best may." I entered the house, after having agreed to rejoin my superior officer so soon as I considered I had obtained my object. I rapped at the inner door, in which there was a small unglazed aperture cut, about four inches square; and I now, for the first time, perceived that a strong glare of light was cast into the lobby, where I stood, by a large argand with a brilliant reflector, that, like a magazine lantern, had been mortised into the bulkhead, at a height of about two feet above the door in which the spy-hole was cut. My first signal was not attended to; I rapped again, and, looking round, I noticed Mr Treenail flitting backwards and forwards across the doorway, in the rain, his pale face and his sharp nose, with the sparkling drop at the end on't, glancing in the light of the lamp. I heard a step within, and a very pretty face now appeared at the wicket.

"Who are you saking here, an' please ye?"

"No one in particular, my dear; but if you don't let me in, I shall be lodged in jail before five minutes be over."

"I can't help that, young man," said she; "but where are ye from, darling?"

"Hush—I am run from the Guava, now lying at the Cove."

"Oh," said my beauty, "come in;" and she opened the door, but still kept it on the chain in such a way, that although, by bobbing, I creeped and slid in beneath it, yet a common-sized man could not possibly have squeezed himself through. The instant I entered, the door was once more banged to, and the next moment I was ushered into the kitchen, a room about fourteen feet square, with a well-sanded floor, a huge dresser on one side, and over against it a respectable show of pewter dishes in racks against the wall. There was a long stripe of a deal table in the middle of the room—but no tablecloth—at the bottom of which sat a large, bloated, brandy, or rather whisky faced savage, dressed in a shabby greatcoat of the hodden grey worn by the Irish peasantry, dirty swandown vest, and greasy corduroy breeches, worsted stockings, and well-patched shoes; he was smoking a long pipe. Around the table sat about a dozen seamen, from whose wet jackets and trousers the heat of the blazing fire, that roared up the chimney, sent up a smoky steam that cast a halo round a lamp which depended from the roof, and hung down within two feet of the table, stinking abominably of coarse whale oil. They were, generally speaking, hardy, weather-beaten men, and the greater proportion half, or more than half, drunk. When I entered, I walked up to the landlord.

"Yo ho, my young un! Whence and whither bound, my hearty?"

"The first don't signify much to you," said I, "seeing I have wherewithal in my locker to pay my shot; and as to the second, of that hereafter; so, old boy, let's have some grog, and then say if you can ship me with one of them colliers that are lying alongside the quay?"

"My eye, what a lot of brass that small chap has!" grumbled mine host. "Why, my lad, we shall see to-morrow morning; but you gammons so about the rhino, that we must prove you a bit; so, Kate, my dear,"—to the pretty girl who had let me in—"score a pint of rum against—Why, what is your name?"

"What's that to you?" rejoined I, "let's have the drink, and don't doubt but the shiners shall be forthcoming."

"Hurrah!" shouted the party, most of them now very tipsy. So the rum was produced forthwith, and as I lighted a pipe and filled a glass of swizzle, I struck in, "Messmates, I hope you have all shipped?"

"No, we han't," said some of them.

"Nor shall we be in any hurry, boy," said others.

"Do as you please, but I shall, as soon as I can, I know; and I recommend all of you making yourselves scarce to-night, and keeping a bright look-out."

"Why, boy, why?"

"Simply because I have just escaped a press-gang, by bracing sharp up at the corner of the street, and shoving into this dark alley here."

This called forth another volley of oaths and unsavoury exclamations, and all was bustle and confusion, and packing up of bundles, and settling of reckonings.

"Where," said one of the seamen,—"where do you go to, my lad?"

"Why, if I can't get shipped to-night, I shall trundle down to Cove immediately, so as to cross at Passage before daylight, and take my chance of shipping with some of the outward-bound that are to sail, if the wind holds, the day after to-morrow. There is to be no pressing when the blue Peter flies at the fore— and that was hoisted this afternoon, I know, and the foretopsail will be loose to-morrow.

"D——n my wig, but the small chap is right," roared one.

"I've a bloody great mind to go down with him," stuttered another, after several unavailing attempts to weigh from the bench, where he had brought himself to anchor.

"Hurrah!" yelled a third, as he hugged me, and nearly suffocated me with his maudlin caresses, "I trundles wid you too, my darling, by the piper!"

"Have with you, boy—have with you," shouted half-a-dozen other voices, while each stuck his oaken twig through the handkerchief that held his bundle, and shouldered it, clapping his straw or tarpaulin hat, with a slap on the crown, on one side of his head, and staggering and swaying about under the influence of the poteen, and slapping his thigh, as he bent double, laughing like to split himself, till the water ran over his cheeks from his drunken half-shut eyes, while jets of tobacco-juice were squirting in all directions.

I paid the reckoning, urging the party to proceed all the while, and indicating Pat Doolan's at the Cove as a good rendezvous; and, promising to overtake them before they reached Passage, I parted company at the corner of the street, and rejoined the lieutenant.

Next morning we spent in looking about the town—Cork is a fine town—contains seventy thousand inhabitants *more* or *less*—safe in that—and three hundred thousand pigs, driven by herdsmen, with coarse grey greatcoats. The pigs are not so handsome as those in England, where the legs are short, and tails curly; here the legs are long, the flanks sharp and thin, and tails long and straight.

All classes speak with a deuced brogue, and worship graven images; arrived at Cove to a late dinner—and here follows a great deal of nonsense of the same kind.

By the time it was half-past ten o'clock, I was preparing to turn in, when the master at arms called down to me,—

"Mr Cringle, you are wanted in the gunroom."

I put on my jacket again, and immediately proceeded thither, and on my way I noticed a group of seamen, standing on the starboard gangway, dressed in pea-jackets, under which, by the light of a lantern, carried by one of them, I could see they were all armed with pistol and cutlass. They appeared in great glee, and as they made way for me, I could hear one fellow whisper, "There goes the little beagle." When I entered the gunroom, the first-lieutenant, master, and purser, were sitting smoking and enjoying themselves over a glass of cold grog—the gunner taking the watch on deck—the doctor was piping anything but mellifluously on the double flageolet, while the Spanish priest, and aide-de-camp to the general, were playing at chess, and wrangling in bad French. I could hear Mr Treenail rumbling and stumbling in his stateroom, as he accoutred himself in a jacket similar to those of the armed boat's crew whom I had passed, and presently he stepped into the gunroom, armed also with cutlass and pistol.

"Mr Cringle, get ready to go in the boat with me, and bring your arms with you."

I now knew whereabouts I was, and that my Cork friends were the quarry at which we aimed. I did as I was ordered, and we immediately pulled on shore, where, leaving two strong fellows in charge of the boat, with instructions to fire their pistols and shove off a couple of boat-lengths should any suspicious circumstance indicating an attack take place, we separated, like a pulk of Cossacks coming to the charge, but without the *hourah,* with orders to meet before Pat Doolan's door, as speedily as our legs could carry us. We had landed about a cable's length to the right of the high precipitous bank—up which we stole in straggling parties—on which that abominable congregation of the most filthy huts ever pig grunted in is situated, called the Holy Ground. Pat Doolan's domicile was in a little dirty lane, about the middle of the village. Presently ten strapping fellows, including the lieutenant, were before the door, each man with his stretcher in his hand. It was a very tempestuous, although moonlight, night, occasionally clear, with the moonbeams at one moment sparkling brightly in the small ripples on the filthy puddles before the door, and on the gem-like water-drops that hung from the eaves of the thatched roof, and lighting up the dark statue-like figures of the men, and casting their long shadows strongly against the mud wall of the house; at another, a black cloud, as it flew across her disk, cast everything into deep shade; while the only noise we heard was the hoarse dashing of the distant surf, rising and falling on the fitful gusts of the breeze. We tried the door. It was fast.

"Surround the house, men," said the lieutenant in a whisper. He rapped loudly. "Pat Doolan, my man, open the door, will ye?" No answer. "If you don't, we shall make free to break it open, Patrick, dear."

All this while the light of a fire, or of candles, streamed through the joints of the door. The threat at length appeared to have the desired effect. A poor decrepit old man undid the bolt and let us in. *"Ohon a ree! Ohon a ree!* What make you all this boder for—come you to help us to wake poor ould Kate there, and bring you the whisky wid you?"

"Old man, where is Pat Doolan?" said the lieutenant.

"Gone to borrow whisky, to wake ould Kate, there;—the howling will begin whenever Mother Doncannon and Misthress Conolly come over from Middleton, and I look for dem every minute."

There was no vestige of any living thing in the miserable hovel, except the old fellow. On two low trestles, in the middle of the floor, lay a coffin with the lid on, on the top of which was stretched the dead body of an old emaciated woman in her grave-clothes, the quality of which was much finer than one could have expected to have seen in the midst of the surrounding squalidness. The face of the corpse was uncovered, the hands were crossed on the breast, and there was a plate of salt on the stomach.

An iron cresset, charged with coarse rancid oil, hung from the roof, the dull smoky red light flickering on the dead corpse, as the breeze streamed in through the door and numberless chinks in the walls, making the cold, rigid, sharp features appear to move, and glimmer, and gibber as it were, from the changing shades. Close to the head there was a small door opening into an apartment of some kind, but the coffin was placed so near it that one could not pass between the body and the door.

"My good man," said Treenail to the solitary mourner, "I must beg leave to remove the body a bit, and have the goodness to open that door."

"Door, yere honour! It's no door o' mine and it's not opening that same that old Phil Carrol shall busy himself wid."

"Carline," said Mr Treenail, quick and sharp, "remove the body." It was done.

"Cruel heavy the old dame is, sir, for all her wasted appearance," said one of the men.

The lieutenant now ranged the press-gang against the wall fronting the door, and, stepping into the middle of the room, drew his pistol and cocked it. "Messmates," he sang out, as if addressing the skulkers in the other room, "I know you are here; the house is surrounded—and unless you open that door now, by the powers, but I'll fire slap into you!" There was a bustle, and a rumbling tumbling noise within. "My lads, we are now sure of our game," sang out Treenail, with great animation; "sling that clumsy bench there." He pointed to an oaken form about eight feet long and nearly three inches thick. To produce a two-inch rope, and junk it into three lengths, and rig the battering-ram, was the work of an instant. "One, two, three,"—and bang the door flew open, and there were our men stowed away, each sitting on the top of his bag, as snug as could be, although looking very much like condemned thieves. We bound eight of them, thrusting a stretcher across their backs, under their arms, and, lashing the fins to the same by good stout lanyards, we were proceeding to stump our prisoners off to the boat, when, with the innate devilry that I have inherited, I know not how, but the original sin of which has more than once nearly cost me my life, I said, without addressing my superior officer, or any one else directly, "I should like now to scale my pistol through that coffin. If I miss, I can't hurt the old woman; and an eyelet hole in that coffin itself will only be an act of civility to the worms."

I looked towards my superior officer, who answered me with a knowing shake of the head. I advanced, while all was silent as death—the sharp click of the pistol lock now struck acutely on my own ear. I presented, when—crash— the lid of the coffin, old woman and all, was dashed off in an instant, the corpse flying up in the air, and then falling heavily on the floor, rolling over and over, while a tall handsome fellow, in his striped flannel shirt and blue trousers, with the sweat pouring down over his face in streams, sat up in the shell.

"All right," said Mr Treenail; "help him out of his berth."

He was pinioned like the rest, and forthwith we walked them all off to the beach. By this time there was an unusual bustle in the Holy Ground, and we could hear many an anathema curses—not loud but deep—ejaculated from many a half-opened door as we passed along. We reached the boat, and time it was we did so, for a number of stout fellows, who had followed us in a gradually increasing crowd until they amounted to forty at the fewest, now nearly surrounded us, and kept closing in. As the last of us jumped into the boat, they made a rush, so that if we had not shoved off with the speed of light, I think it very likely that we should have been overpowered. However, we reached the ship in safety, and the day following we weighed, and stood out to sea with our convoy.

It was a very large fleet, nearly three hundred sail of merchant vessels— and a noble sight truly.

A line-of-battle ship led, and two frigates and three sloops of our class were stationed on the outskirts of the fleet, whipping them in, as it were. We made Madeira in fourteen days, looked in, but did not anchor; superb island—magnificent mountains—white town,—and all very fine, but nothing particular happened for three weeks. One fine evening (we had by this time progressed into the trades, and were within three hundred miles of Barbadoes) the sun had set bright and clear, after a most beautiful day, and we were bowling along right before it, rolling like the very devil; but there was no moon, and although the stars sparkled brilliantly, yet it was dark, and as we were the sternmost of the men-of-war, we had the task of whipping in the sluggards. It was my watch on deck. A gun from the commodore, who showed a number of lights. "What is that, Mr Kennedy?" said the captain to the old gunner. "The commodore has made the night-signal for the sternmost ships to make more sail and close, sir." We repeated the signal and stood on, hailing the dullest of the merchantmen in our neighbourhood to make more sail, and firing a musket-shot now and then over the more distant of them. By-and-by we saw a large West Indiaman suddenly haul her wind and stand across our bows.

"Forward there!" sung out Mr Splinter; "stand by to fire a shot at that fellow from the boat gun if he does not bear up. What can he be after? Sergeant Armstrong"—to a marine, who was standing close by him in the waist—"get a musket, and fire over him."

It was done, and the ship immediately bore up on her course again; we now ranged alongside of him on his larboard quarter.

"Ho, the ship, ahoy!"—"Hillo!" was the reply. "Make more sail, sir, and run into the body of the fleet, or I shall fire into you: why don't you, sir, keep in the wake of the commodore?" No answer. "What meant you by hauling your wind just now, sir?"

"Yesh, yesh," at length responded a voice from the merchantman.

"Something wrong here," said Mr Splinter. "Back your maintopsail, sir, and hoist a light at the peak; I shall send a boat on board of you. Boatswain's mate, pipe away the crew of the jolly-boat." We also hove to, and were in the act of lowering down the boat, when the officer rattled out—"Keep all fast with the boat; I can't comprehend that chap's manœuvres for the soul of me. He has not hove to." Once more we were within pistol-shot of him. "Why don't you heave to, sir? " All silent.

Presently we could perceive a confusion and noise of struggling on board, and angry voices, as if people were trying to force their way up the hatches from below; and a heavy thumping on the deck, and a creaking of the blocks, and rattling of the cordage, while the mainyard was first braced one way, and then another, as if two parties were striving for the mastery. At length a voice hailed distinctly—"we are captured by a ———." A sudden sharp cry, and a splash overboard, told of some fearful deed.

"We are taken by a privateer or pirate," sung out another voice. This was followed by a heavy crunching blow, as when the spike of a butcher's axe is driven through a bullock's forehead deep into the brain.

By this time all hands had been called, and the word had been passed to clear away two of the foremost carronades on the starboard side, and to load them with grape.

"On board there—get below, all you of the English crew, as I shall fire with grape," sung out the captain.

The hint was now taken. The ship at length came to the wind—we rounded to, under her lee—and an armed boat, with Mr Treenail, and myself, and sixteen men, with cutlasses, were sent on board.

We jumped on deck, and at the gangway Mr Treenail stumbled and fell over the dead body of a man, no doubt the one who had hailed, last, with his skull cloven to the eyes, and a broken cutlass-blade sticking in the gash. We were immediately accosted by the mate, who was lashed down to a ring-bolt close by the bits, with his hands tied at the wrists by sharp cords, so tightly that the blood was spouting from beneath his nails.

"We have been surprised by a privateer schooner, sir; the lieutenant of her, and several men, are now in the cabin."

"Where are the rest of the crew?"

"All secured in the forecastle, except the second-mate and boatswain, the men who hailed you just now; the last was knocked on the head, and the former was stabbed and thrown overboard."

We immediately released the men, eighteen in number, and armed them with boarding-pikes. "What vessel is that astern of us? " said Treenail to the mate. Before he could answer, a shot from the brig fired at the privateer showed she was broad awake. Next moment Captain Deadeye hailed. "Have you mastered the prize crew, Mr Treenail?" "Ay, ay, sir." "Then bear up on your course, and keep two lights hoisted at your mizen-peak during the night, and blue Peter at the maintopsail yardarm when the day breaks; I shall haul my wind after the suspicious sail in your wake."

Another shot, and another, from the brig—the time between each flash and the report increasing with the distance. By this the lieutenant had descended to the cabin, followed by his people, while the merchant crew once more took charge of the ship, crowding sail into the body of the fleet.

I followed him close, pistol and cutlass in hand, and I shall never forget the scene that presented itself when I entered. The cabin was that of a vessel of five hundred tons, elegantly fitted up; the panels filled with crimson cloth, edged with gold mouldings, with superb damask hangings before the stern windows and the side berths, and brilliantly lighted up by two large swinging lamps hung from the deck above, which were reflected from, and multiplied in, several plate-glass mirrors in the panels. In the recess, which in cold weather had been occupied by the stove, now stood a splendid grand piano, the silk in the open work above the keys corresponding with the crimson cloth of the panels; it was open, a Leghorn bonnet with a green veil, a parasol, and two long white gloves, as if recently pulled off, lay on it, with the very mould of the hands in them.

The rudder case was particularly beautiful; it was a richly carved and gilded palm-tree, the stem painted white and interlaced with golden fretwork, like the lozenges of a pine-apple, while the leaves spread up and abroad on the roof.

The table was laid for supper, with cold meat, and wine, and a profusion of silver things, all sparkling brightly: but it was in great disorder, wine spilt, and glasses broken, and dishes with meat upset, and knives, and forks, and spoons, scattered all about. She was evidently one of those London West Indiamen on board of which I knew there was much splendour and great comfort. But, alas! the hand of lawless violence had been there. The captain lay across the table, with his head hanging over the side of it next to us, and unable to help himself, with his hands tied behind his back, and a gag in his mouth; his face purple from the blood running to his head, and the white of his eyes turned up, while his loud stertorous breathing but too clearly indicated the rupture of a vessel on the brain.

He was a stout portly man, and although we released him on the instant, and had him bled, and threw water on his face, and did all we could for him, he never spoke afterwards, and died in half an hour.

Four gentlemanly-looking men were sitting at table, lashed to their chairs, pale and trembling, while six of the most ruffian-looking scoundrels I ever beheld stood on the opposite side of the table in a row fronting us, with the light from the lamps shining full on them. Three of them were small but very square mulattoes; one was a South American Indian, with the square high-boiled visage and long, lank, black glossy hair of his caste. These four had no clothing besides their trousers, and stood with their arms folded, in all the calmness of desperate men caught in the very fact of some horrible atrocity, which they knew shut out every hope of mercy. The two others were white Frenchmen, tall, bushy-whiskered, sallow desperadoes, but still, wonderful to relate, with, if I may so speak, the manners of gentlemen. One of them squinted, and had a hare-lip, which gave him a horrible expression. They were dressed in white trousers and shirts, yellow silk sashes round their waists, and a sort of blue uniform jackets, blue Gascon caps, with the peaks, from each of which depended a large bullion tassel, hanging down on one side of their heads. The whole party had apparently made up their minds that resistance was vain, for their pistols and cutlasses, some of them bloody, had all been laid on the table, with the butts and handles towards us, contrasting horribly with the glittering equipage of steel, and crystal, and silver things, on the snow-white damask table-cloth. They were immediately seized and ironed, to which they submitted in silence. We next released the passengers, and were overpowered with thanks, one dancing, one crying, one laughing, and another praying. But, merciful Heaven! what an object met our eyes! Drawing aside the curtain that concealed a sofa fitted into a recess, there lay, more dead than alive, a tall and most beautiful girl, her head resting on her left arm, her clothes disordered and torn, blood on her bosom, and foam on her mouth, with her long dark hair loose and dishevelled, and covering the upper part of her deadly pale face, through which her wild sparkling black eyes, protruding from their sockets, glanced and glared with the fire of a maniac's, while her blue lips kept gibbering an incoherent prayer one moment, and the next imploring mercy, as if she had still been in the hands of those who knew not the name; and anon, a low hysterical laugh made our very blood freeze in our bosoms, which soon ended in a long dismal yell, as she rolled off the couch upon the hard deck, and lay in a dead faint.

Alas the day!—a maniac she was from that hour. She was the only daughter of the murdered master of the ship, and never awoke, in her unclouded reason, to the fearful consciousness of her own dishonour and her parent's death.

The Torch captured the schooner, and we left the privateer's men at Barbadoes to meet their reward, and several of the merchant sailors were turned over to the guardship, to prove the facts in the first instance, and to serve his Majesty as impressed men in the second,—but scrimp measure of justice to the poor ship's crew.

Anchored at Carlisle Bay, Barbadoes. Town seemed built of cards—black faces—showy dresses of the negroes—dined at Mr C——'s—capital dinner—little breeze-mill at the end of the room, that pumped a solution of saltpetre and water into a trough of tin, perforated with small holes, below which, and exposed to the breeze, were ranged the wine and liqueurs, all in cotton bags; the water then flowed into a well, where the pump was stepped, and thus was again pumped up and kept circulating.

Landed the artillery, the soldiers, officers, and the Spanish Canon—discharged the whole battery.

Next morning, weighed at day—dawn, with the trade for Jamaica, and soon lost sight of the bright blue waters of Carlisle Bay and the smiling fields and tall cocoa-nut trees of the beautiful island. In a week after we arrived off the east end of Jamaica; and that same evening, in obedience to the orders of the admiral on the Windward Island station, we hove to in Bull Bay, in order to land despatches, and secure our tithe of the crews of the merchant-vessels bound for Kingston, and the ports to leeward, as they passed us. We had fallen in with a pilot canoe of Morant Bay with four negroes on board, who requested us to hoist in their boat, and take them all on board, as the pilot schooner to which they belonged had that morning bore up for Kingston, and left instructions to them to follow her in the first vessel appearing afterwards. We did so, and now, as it was getting dark, the captain came up to Mr Treenail.

"Why, Mr Treenail, I think we had better heave to for the night, and in this case I shall want you to go in the cutter to Port Royal to deliver the despatches on board the flag-ship."

"I don't think the admiral will be at Port Royal, sir," responded the lieutenant; "and, if I might suggest, those black chaps have offered to take me ashore here on the *Palisadoes,* a narrow spit of land, not above one hundred yards across, that divides the harbour from the ocean, and to haul the canoe across, and take me to the agent's house in Kingston, who will doubtless frank me up to the pen where the admiral resides, and I shall thus deliver the letters, and be back again by day-dawn."

"Not a bad plan," said old Deadeye; "put it in execution, and I will go below and get the despatches immediately."

The canoe was once more hoisted out; the three black fellows, the pilot of the ship continuing on board, jumped into her alongside.

"Had you not better take a couple of hands with you, Mr Treenail?" said the skipper.

"Why, no, sir, I don't think I shall want them; but if you will spare me Mr Cringle I will be obliged, in case I want any help."

We shoved off, and as the glowing sun dipped under Portland Point, as the tongue of land that runs out about four miles to the southward, on the western side of Port Royal harbour, is called, we arrived within a hundred yards of the *Palisadoes*. The surf, at the particular spot we steered for, did not break on the shore in a rolling curling wave, as it usually does, but smoothed away under the lee of a small sandy promontory that ran out into the sea, about half a cable's length to windward, and then slid up the smooth white sand without breaking, in a deep clear green swell, for the space of twenty yards, gradually shoaling, the colour becoming lighter and lighter until it frothed away in a shallow white fringe, that buzzed as it receded back into the deep green sea, until it was again propelled forward by the succeeding billow.

"I say, friend Bungo, how shall we manage? You don't mean to swamp us in a shove through that surf, do you?" said Mr Treenail.

"No fear, massa, if you and toder leetle man-of-war buccra only keep dem seat when we rise on de crest of de swell dere."

We sat quiet enough. Treenail was coolness itself, and I aped him as well as I could. The loud murmur, increasing to a roar, of the sea, was trying enough as we approached, buoyed on the last long undulation.

"Now sit still, massa, bote."

We sank down into the trough, and presently were hove forwards with a smooth sliding motion up on the beach—until grit, grit, we stranded on the cream-coloured sand, high and dry.

"Now, jomp, massa, jomp."

We leapt with all our strength, and thereby toppled down on our noses; the sea receded, and before the next billow approached we had run the canoe twenty yards beyond high-water mark.

It was the work of a very few minutes to haul the canoe across the sand-bank, and to launch it once more in the placid waters of the harbour of Kingston. We pulled across towards the town, until we landed at the bottom of Hanover Street; the lights from the cabin windows of the merchantmen glimmering as we passed, and the town only discernible from a solitary sparkle here and there. But the contrast when we landed was very striking. We had come through the darkness of the night in comparative quietness; and in two hours from the time we had left the old Torch, we were transferred from her orderly deck to the bustle of a crowded town.

One of our crew undertook to be the guide to the agent's house. We arrived before it. It was a large mansion, and we could see lights glimmering in the ground-floor; but it was gaily lit up aloft. The house itself stood back about twenty feet from the street, from which it was separated by an iron railing.

We knocked at the outer gate, but no one answered. At length our black guide found out a bell-pull, and presently the clang of a bell resounded throughout the mansion. Still no one answered. I pushed against the door, and found it was open, and Mr Treenail and myself immediately ascended a flight of six marble steps, and stood in the lower piazza, with the hall, or vestibule, before us. We entered. A very well-dressed brown woman, who was sitting at her work at a small table, along with two young girls of the same complexion, instantly rose to receive us.

"Beg pardon," said Mr Treenail, "pray, is this Mr ———'s house?"

"Yes, sir, it is."

"Will you have the goodness to say if he be at home?"

"Oh yes, sir, he is dere upon dinner wid company," said the lady.

"Well," continued the lieutenant, "say to him, that an officer of his Majesty's sloop Torch is below, with despatches for the admiral."

"Surely, sir,—surely," the dark lady continued; "Follow me, sir; and dat small gentleman [Thomas Cringle, Esquire, no less!]—him will better follow me too."

We left the room, and turning to the right, landed in the lower piazza of the house, fronting the north. A large clumsy stair occupied the easternmost end, with a massive mahogany balustrade, but the whole affair below was very ill lighted. The brown lady preceded us; and, planting herself at the bottom of the staircase, began to shout to some one above—

"Toby!—Toby!—buccra gentlemen arrive, Toby." But no Toby responded to the call.

"My dear madam," said Treenail, "I have little time for ceremony. Pray usher us up into Mr ———'s presence."

"Den follow me, gentlemen, please."

Forthwith we all ascended the dark staircase until we reached the first landing-place, when we heard a noise as of two negroes wrangling on the steps above us.

"You rascal!" sang out one, "take dat; larn you for teal my wittal!"—then a sharp crack, as if he had smote the culprit across the pate; whereupon, like a shot, a black fellow, in a handsome livery, trundled down, pursued by another servant with a large silver ladle in his hand, with which he was belabouring the fugitive over his flint-hard skull, right against our hostess with the drumstick of a turkey in his hand, or rather in his mouth.

"'Top, you tief!—top, you tief!—for me piece dat," shouted the pursuer.

"You dam rascal!" quoth the dame. But she had no time to utter another word, before the fugitive pitched, with all his weight, against her; and at the very moment another servant came trundling down with a large tray full of all kinds of meats—and I especially remember that two large crystal stands of jellies composed part of his load—so there we were regularly capsized, and caught all of a heap in the dark landing-place, halfway up the stair; and down the other flight tumbled our guide, with Mr Treenail and myself, and the two blackies on the top of her, rolling in our descent over, or rather into, another large mahogany tray which had just been carried out, with a tureen of turtle soup in it, and a dish of roast-beef, and platefuls of land-crabs, and the Lord knows what all besides.

The crash reached the ear of the landlord, who was seated at the head of his table in the upper piazza, a long gallery about fifty feet long by fourteen wide, and he immediately rose and ordered his butler to take a light. When he came down to ascertain the cause of the uproar, I shall never forget the scene.

There was, first of all, mine host, a remarkably neat personage, standing on the polished mahogany stair, three steps above his big servant, who was a very well-dressed respectable elderly negro, with a candle in each hand; and beneath him, on the landing-place, lay two trays of viands, broken tureens of soup, fragments of dishes, and fractured glasses, and a chaos of eatables and drinkables, and table gear scattered all about, amidst which lay scrambling my lieutenant and myself, the brown housekeeper, and the two negro servants, all more or less covered with gravy and wine dregs. However, after a good laugh, we gathered ourselves up, and at length we were ushered on the scene. Mine host, after stifling big laughter the best way he could, again sat down at the head of his table, sparkling with crystal and wax-lights, while a superb lamp hung overhead. The company was composed chiefly of naval and military men, but there was also a sprinkling of civilians, or *muftees,* to use a West India expression. Most of them rose as we entered, and after they had taken a glass of wine, and had their laugh at our mishap, our landlord retired to one side with Mr Treenail, while I, poor little middy as I was, remained standing at the end of the room, close to the head of the stairs. The gentleman who sat at the foot of the table had his back towards me, and was not at first aware of my presence. But the guest at his right hand, a happy-looking, red-faced, well-dressed man, soon drew his attention towards me. The party to whom I was thus indebted seemed a very jovial-looking personage, and appeared to be well known to all hands, and indeed the life of the party, for, like Falstaff, he was not only witty in himself, but the cause of wit in others.

The gentleman to whom he had pointed me out immediately rose, made his bow, ordered a chair, and made room for me beside himself, where, the moment it was known that we were direct from home, such a volley of questions was fired off at me that I did not know which to answer first. At length, after Treenail had taken a glass or two of wine, the agent started him off to the admiral's pen in his own gig, and I was desired to stay where I was until he returned.

The whole party seemed very happy, my boon ally was fun itself, and I was much entertained with the mess he made when any of the foreigners at table addressed him in French or Spanish. I was particularly struck with a small, thin, dark Spaniard, who told very feelingly how the night before, on returning home from a party to his own lodgings, on passing through the piazza, he stumbled against something heavy that lay in his grass-hammock, which usually hung there. He called for a light, when, to his horror, he found the body of his old and faithful valet lying in it, *dead* and cold, with a knife sticking under his fifth rib—no doubt intended for his master. The speaker was Bolivar. About midnight, Mr Treenail returned, we shook hands with Mr ———, and once more shoved off; and, guided by the lights shown on board the Torch we were safe *home* again by three in the morning, when we immediately made sail, and nothing particular happened until we arrived within a day's sail of New Providence. It seemed that, about a week before, a large American brig, bound from Havanna to Boston, had been captured in this very channel by one of our men-of-war schooners, and carried into Nassau; out of which port, for their own security, the authorities had fitted a small schooner, carrying six guns and twenty-four men. She was commanded by a very gallant fellow—there is no disputing that—and he must needs emulate the conduct of the officer who had made the capture; for in a fine clear night, when all the officers were below rummaging in their kits for the killing things they should array themselves in on the morrow, so as to smite the Fair of New Providence to the heart at a blow—*Whiss*—a shot flew over our mast-head.

"A small schooner lying to right ahead, sir," sang out the boatswain from the forecastle.

Before we could beat to quarters, another sang between our masts. We kept steadily on our course, and as we approached our pigmy antagonist, he bore up. Presently we were alongside of him.

"Heave to," hailed the strange sail; "heave to, or I'll sink you."

The devil you will, you midge, thought I.

The captain took the trumpet—"Schooner, ahoy"—no answer—"D——n your blood, sir, if you don't let everything go by the run this instant, I'll fire a broadside. Strike, sir, to his Britannic Majesty's sloop Torch."

The poor fellow commanding the schooner had by this time found out his mistake, and immediately came on board, where, instead of being lauded for his gallantry, I am sorry to say he was roundly rated for his want of discernment in mistaking his Majesty's cruiser for a Yankee merchantman. Next forenoon we arrived at Nassau.

In a week after we again sailed for Bermuda, having taken on board ten American skippers, and several other Yankees, as prisoners of war.

For the first three days after we cleared the Passages, we had fine weather —wind at east-south-east; but after that it came on to blow from the north-west, and so continued without intermission during the whole of the passage to Bermuda. On the fourth morning after we left Nassau, we descried a sail in the southeast quarter, and immediately made sail in chase. We overhauled her about noon; she hove to, after being fired at repeatedly; and, on boarding her, we found she was a Swede from Charleston, bound to Havre-de-Grace. All the letters we could find on board were very unceremoniously broken open, and nothing having transpired that could identify the cargo as enemy's property, we were bundling over the side, when a nautical-looking subject, who had attracted my attention from the first, put in his oar.

"Lieutenant," said he, "will you allow me to put this barrel of New York apples into the boat as a present to Captain Deadeye, from Captain ✳✳✳ of the United States navy?"

Mr Treenail bowed, and said he would; and we shoved off and got on board again, and now there was the devil to pay, from the perplexity old Deadeye was thrown into, as to whether, here in the heat of the American war, he was bound to take this American captain prisoner or not. I was no party to the councils of my superiors, of course, but the foreign ship was finally allowed to continue her course.

The next day I had the forenoon watch; the weather had lulled unexpectedly, nor was there much sea, and the deck was all alive, to take advantage of the fine *blink*, when the man at the mast-head sang out—"Breakers right ahead, sir."

"Breakers!" said Mr Splinter, in great astonishment. "Breakers!—why, the man must be mad! I say, Jenkins ———"

"Breakers close under the bows," sang out the boatswain from forward.

"The devil!" quoth Splinter, and he ran along the gangway, and ascended the forecastle, while I kept close to his heels. We looked out ahead, and there we certainly did see a splashing, and boiling, and white foaming of the ocean, that unquestionably looked very like breakers. Gradually, this splashing and foaming appearance took a circular whisking shape, as if the clear green sea, for a space of a hundred yards in diameter, had been stirred about by a gigantic invisible *spurtle*, until everything hissed again; and the curious part of it was, that the agitation of the water seemed to keep ahead of us, as if the breeze which impelled us had also floated it onwards. At length the whirling circle of white foam ascended higher and higher, and then gradually contracted itself into a spinning black tube, which wavered about for all the world like a gigantic *loch-leech* held by the tail between the finger and thumb, while it was poking its vast snout about in the clouds in search of a spot to fasten on.

"Is the boat-gun on the forecastle loaded?" said Captain Deadeye.

"It is, sir."

"Then luff a bit—that will do—fire."

The gun was discharged, and down rushed the black wavering pillar in a watery *avalanche,* and in a minute after the dark heaving billows rolled over the spot whereout it arose, as if no such thing had ever been.

This said troubling of the waters was neither more nor less than a waterspout, which again is neither more nor less than a whirlwind at sea, which gradually whisks the water round and round, and up and up, as you see straws so raised, until it reaches a certain height, when it invariably breaks. Before this I had thought that a waterspout was created by some next to supernatural exertion of the power of the Deity, in order to suck up water into the clouds, that they, like the wine-skins in Spain, might be filled with rain.

The morning after, the weather was clear and beautiful, although the wind blew half a gale. Nothing particular happened until about seven o'clock in the evening. I had been invited to dine with the gunroom officers this day, and every thing was going on smooth and comfortable, when Mr Splinter spoke. "Say, master, don't you smell gunpowder?"

"Yes, I do," said the little master, "or something deuced like it."

To explain the particular comfort of our position, it may be right to mention that the magazine of a brig sloop is exactly under the gunroom. Three of the American skippers had been quartered on the gunroom mess, and they were all at table. Snuff, snuff, smelled one, and another sniffled,—"Gunpowder, I guess, and in a state of ignition."

"Will you not send for the gunner, sir?" said the third. Splinter did not like it, I saw, and this quailed me.

The captain's bell rang. "What smell of brimstone is that, steward?"

"I really can't tell," said the man, trembling from head to foot; "Mr Splinter has sent for the gunner, sir."

"The devil!" said Deadeye, as he hurried on deck. We all followed. A search was made.

"Some matches have caught in the magazine," said one.

"We shall be up and away like sky-rockets," said another.

Several of the American masters ran out on the jib-boom, coveting the temporary security of being so far removed from the seat of the expected explosion, and all was alarm and confusion, until it was ascertained that two of the boys, little skylarking vagabonds, had stolen some pistol cartridges, and had been making lightning, as it is called, by holding a lighted candle between the fingers, and putting some loose powder into the palm of the hand, and then chucking it up into the flame. They got a sound flogging on a very unpoetical part of their corpuses, and once more the ship subsided into her usual orderly discipline. The northwester still continued, with a clear blue sky, without a cloud overhead by day, and a bright cold moon by night. It blew so hard for the three succeeding days, that we could not carry more than close-reefed topsails to it, and a reefed foresail. Indeed, towards six bells in the forenoon watch of the third day, it came thundering down with such violence, and the sea increased so much, that we had to hand the foretopsail.

This was by no means an easy job. "Ease her a bit," said the first-lieutenant,—"there—shake the wind out of her sails for a moment, until the men get the canvass in"—whirl, a poor fellow pitched off the lee foreyardarm into the sea. "Up with the helm—heave him the bight of a rope." We kept away, but all was confusion, until an American midshipman, one of the prisoners on board, hove the bight of a rope at him. The man got it under his arms, and after hauling him along for a hundred yards at the least—and one may judge of the velocity with which he was dragged through the water, by the fact that it took the united strain of ten powerful men to get him in—he was brought safely on board, pale and blue, when we found that the running of the rope had crushed in his broad chest, below his arms, as if it had been a girl's waist, indenting the very muscles of it and of his back half an inch deep. He had to be bled before he could breathe, and it was an hour before the circulation could be restored, by the joint exertions of the surgeon and gunroom steward, chafing him with spirits and camphor, after he had been stripped and stowed away between the blankets in his hammock.

The same afternoon we fell in with a small prize to the squadron in the Chesapeake, a dismantled schooner, manned by a prize crew of a midshipman and six men. She had a signal of distress, an American ensign, with the union down, hoisted on the jury-mast, across which there was rigged a solitary lug-sail. It was blowing so hard that we had some difficulty in boarding her, when we found she was a Baltimore pilot-boat-built schooner, of about 70 tons burden, laden with flour, and bound for Bermuda. But three days before, in a sudden squall, they had carried away both masts short by the board, and the only spar which they had been able to rig, was a spare topmast which they had jammed into one of the pumps—fortunately she was as tight as a bottle—and stayed it the best way they could. The captain offered to take the little fellow who had charge of her, and his crew and cargo, on board, and then scuttle her; but no—all he wanted was a cask of water and some biscuit; and having had a glass of grog, he trundled over the side again, and returned to his desolate command. However, he afterwards brought his prize safe into Bermuda.

The weather still continued very rough, but we saw nothing until the second evening after this. The forenoon had been even more boisterous than any of the preceding, and we were all fagged enough with "make sail," and "shorten sail," and "all hands," the whole day through; and as the night fell, I found myself, for the fourth time, in the maintop. The men had just lain in from the maintopsail yard, when we heard the watch called on deck,—"Starboard watch, ahoy!"—which was a cheery sound to us of the larboard, who were thus released from duty on deck, and allowed to go below.

The men were scrambling down the weather shrouds, and I was preparing to follow them, when I jammed my left foot in the grating of the top, and capsized on my nose. I had been up nearly the whole of the previous night, and on deck the whole of the day, and actively employed too, as during the greater part of it it blew a gale. I stooped down in some pain, to see what had bolted me to the grating; but I had no sooner extricated my foot, than, over-worked and over-fatigued as I was, I fell over in the soundest sleep that ever I have enjoyed before or since, the back of my neck resting on a coil of rope, so that my head hung down within it.

The rain all this time was beating on me, and I was drenched to the skin. I must have slept for four hours or so, when I was awakened by a rough thump on the side from the stumbling foot of the captain of the top, the word having been passed to shake a reef out of the topsails, the wind having rather suddenly gone down. It was done; and now broad awake, I determined not to be caught napping again, so I descended, and swung myself in on deck out of the main rigging, just as Mr Treenail was mustering the crew at eight bells. When I landed on the quarterdeck, there he stood abaft the binnacle, with the light shining on his face, his glazed hat glancing, and the rain-drop sparkling at the brim of it. He had noticed me the moment I descended.

"Heyday, Master Cringle, you are surely out of your watch. Why, what are you doing here, eh?"

I stepped up to him, and told him the truth, that, being over-fatigued, I had fallen asleep in the top.

"Well, well, boy," said he, "never mind, go below, and turn in; if you don't take your rest, you never will be a sailor."

"But what do you see aloft?" glancing his eye upwards, and all the crew on deck, as I passed them, looked anxiously up also amongst the rigging, as if wondering what I saw there, for I had been so chilled in my snoose, that my neck, from resting in the cold on the coil of rope, had become stiffened and rigid to an intolerable degree; and although, when I first came on deck, I had, by a strong exertion, brought my *caput* to its proper bearings, yet the moment I was dismissed by my superior officer, I for my own comfort was glad to conform to the contraction of the muscle, whereby I once more staved along the deck, *glowering* up into the heavens, as if I had seen some wonderful sight there.

"What do you see aloft?" repeated Mr Treenail, while the crew, greatly puzzled, continued to follow my eyes, as they thought, and to stare up into the rigging.

"Why, sir, I have thereby got a stiff neck—that's all, sir."

"Go and turn in at once, my good boy—make haste, now; tell our steward to give you a glass of hot grog, and mind your hand that you don't get sick."

I did as I was desired, swallowed the grog, and turned in; but I could not have been in bed above an hour, when the drum beat to quarters, and I had once more to bundle out on the cold wet deck, where I found all excitement. At the time I speak of, we had been beaten by the Americans in several actions of single ships, and our discipline improved in proportion as we came to learn, by sad experience, that the enemy was not to be undervalued. I found that there was a ship in sight, right ahead of us—apparently carrying all sail. A group of officers were on the forecastle with night-glasses, the whole crew being stationed in dark clusters round the guns at quarters. Several of the American skippers were forward amongst us, and they were of opinion that the chase was a man-of-war, although our own people seemed to doubt this. One of the skippers insisted that she was the Hornet, from the unusual shortness of her lower masts, and the immense squareness of her yards. But the puzzle was, if it were the Hornet, why she did not shorten sail. Still this might be accounted for, by her either wishing to make out what we were before she engaged us, or she might be clearing for action. At this moment a whole cloud of studdingsails were blown from the yards as if the booms had been carrots; and to prove that the chase was keeping a bright look-out, she immediately kept away, and finally bore up dead before the wind, under the impression, no doubt, that she would draw ahead of us, from her gear being entire, before we could rig out our light sails again.

And so she did for a time, but at length we got within gunshot. The American masters were now ordered below, the hatches were clapped on, and the word passed to see all clear. Our shot was by this time flying over and over her, and it was evident she was not a man-of-war. We peppered away—she could not even be a privateer; we were close under her lee quarter, and yet she had never fired a shot; and her large swaggering Yankee ensign was now run up to the peak, only to be hauled down the next moment. Hurrah! a large cotton-ship from Charlestown to Bordeaux—prize to H.M.S. Torch!

She was taken possession of, and proved to be the Natches, of four hundred tons burden, fully loaded with cotton.

By the time we got the crew on board, and the second-lieutenant, with a prize crew of fifteen men, had taken charge, the weather began to lour again, nevertheless we took the prize in tow, and continued on our voyage for the next three days, without anything particular happening. It was the middle watch, and I was sound asleep, when I was startled by a violent jerking of my hammock, and a cry "that the brig was amongst the breakers." I ran on deck in my shirt, where I found all hands, and a scene of confusion such as I never had witnessed before. The gale had increased, yet the prize had not been cast off, and the consequence was, that by some mismanagement or carelessness, the swag of the large ship had suddenly hove the brig in the wind, and taken the sails aback. We accordingly fetched stern way, and ran foul of the prize, and there we were, in a heavy sea, with our stern grinding against the cotton-ship's high quarter.

The mainboom, by the first rasp that took place after I came on deck, was broken short off, and nearly twelve feet of it hove right in over the taffrail; the vessels then closed, and the next rub ground off the ship's mizen channel as clean as if it had been sawed away. Officers shouting, men swearing, rigging cracking, the vessels crashing and thumping together, I thought we were gone, when the first-lieutenant seized his trumpet—"Silence, men; hold your tongues, you cowards, and mind the word of command!"

The effect was magical.—"Brace round the foreyard-round with it; set the jib—that's it—fore-topmast staysail—haul—never mind if the gale takes it out of the bolt-rope"—a thundering flap, and away it flew in truth down to leeward, like a puff of white smoke.—"Never mind, men, the jib stands. Belay all that—down with the helm, now—don't you see she has stern way yet? Zounds! we shall be smashed to atoms if you don't mind your hands, you lubbers—main-topsail sheets let fly—there she pays off, and has headway once more—that's it: right your helm, now—never mind his spanker-boom, the forestay will stand it: there—up with helm, sir—we have cleared him—hurrah!" And a near thing it was too, but we soon had everything snug; and although the gale continued without any intermission for ten days, at length we ran in and anchored with our prize in Five-Fathom Hole, off the entrance to St George's Harbour.

It was lucky for us that we got to anchor at the time we did, for that same afternoon one of the most tremendous gales of wind from the westward came on that I ever saw. Fortunately it was steady and did not veer about, and having good ground-tackle down, we rode it out well enough. The effect was very uncommon; the wind was howling over our mast-heads, and amongst the cedar bushes on the cliffs above, while on deck it was nearly calm, and there was very little swell, being a weather shore; but half a mile out at sea all was white foam, and the tumbling waves seemed to meet from north and south, leaving a space of smooth water under the lee of the island, shaped like the tail of a comet, tapering away, and gradually roughening and becoming more stormy, until the roaring billows once more owned allegiance to the genius of the storm.

There we rode, with three anchors ahead, in safety through the night; and next day, availing of a temporary lull, we ran up and anchored off the Tanks. Three days after this, the American frigate President was brought in by the Endymion and the rest of the squadron.

I went on board, in common with every officer in the fleet, and certainly I never saw a more superb vessel; her scantling was that of a seventy-four, and she appeared to have been fitted with great care. I got a week's leave at this time, and, as I had letters to several families, I contrived to spend my time pleasantly enough.

Bermuda, as all the world knows, is a cluster of islands in the middle of the

Atlantic. There are Lord knows how many of them, but the beauty of the little straits and creeks which divide them no man can describe who has not seen them. The town of St George's, for instance, looks as if the houses were cut out of chalk; and one evening the family where I was on a visit proceeded to the main island, Hamilton, to attend a ball there. We had to cross three ferries, although the distance was not above nine miles, if so far. The 'Mudian women are unquestionably beautiful—so thought Thomas Moore, a tolerable judge, before me. By the by, touching this 'Mudian ball, it was a very gay affair—the women pleasant and beautiful; but all the men, when they speak, or are spoken to, shut one eye and spit;—a lucid and succinct description of a community.

The second day of my sojourn was fine—the first fine day since our arrival—and with several young ladies of the family, I was prowling through the cedar wood above St George's, when a dark good-looking man passed us; he was dressed in tight worsted net pantaloons and Hessian boots, and wore a blue frock-coat and two large epaulets, with rich French bullion, and a round hat. On passing, he touched his hat with much grace, and in the evening I met him in society. It was Commodore Decatur. He was very much a Frenchman in manner, or, I should rather say, in look, for although very well bred, he, for one ingredient, by no means possessed a Frenchman's volubility; still, he was an exceedingly agreeable and very handsome man.

The following day we spent in a pleasure cruise amongst the three hundred and sixty-five islands, many of them not above an acre in extent—fancy an island of an acre in extent!—with a solitary house, a small garden, a red-skinned family, a piggery, and all around clear deep pellucid water. None of the islands, or islets, rise to any great height, but they all shoot precipitously out of the water, as if the whole group had originally been one huge platform of rock, with numberless grooves subsequently chiselled out in it by art.

We had to wind our way amongst these many small channels for two hours, before we reached the gentleman's house where we had been invited to dine; at length, on turning a corner, with both lateen sails drawing beautifully, we ran bump on a shoal; there was no danger, and knowing that the 'Mudians were capital sailors, I sat still. Not so Captain K——, a round plump little *homo*,— "Shove her off, my boys, shove her off." She would not move, and thereupon he, in a fever of gallantry, jumped overboard up to the waist in full fig; and one of the men following his example, we were soon afloat. The ladies applauded, and the captain sat in his wet *breeks* for the rest of the voyage, in all the consciousness of being considered a hero. Ducks and onions are the grand staple of

Bermuda, but there was a fearful dearth of both at the time I speak of—a knot of young West India merchants, who, with heavy purses and large credits on England, had at this time domiciled themselves in St George's, to batten on the spoils of poor Jonathan, having monopolised all the good things of the place. I happened to be acquainted with one of them, and thereby had less reason to complain; but many a poor fellow, sent ashore on duty, had to put up with but Lenten fare at the taverns. At length, having refitted, we sailed in company with the Rayo frigate, with a convoy of three transports, freighted with a regiment for New Orleans, and several merchantmen bound for the West Indies.

"The still vexed Bermoothes"—I arrived at them in a gale of wind, and I sailed from them in a gale of wind. What the climate may be in the summer I don't know; but during the time I was there it was one storm after another.

We sailed in the evening with the moon at full, and the wind at west-northwest. So soon as we got from under the lee of the land the breeze struck us, and it came on to blow like thunder so that we were all soon reduced to our storm staysails; and there we were, transports, merchantmen, and men-of-war, rising on the mountainous billows one moment, and the next losing sight of everything but the water and sky in the deep trough of the sea, while the seething foam was blown over us in showers from the curling manes of the roaring waves. But overhead, all this while, it was as clear as a lovely winter moon could make it, and the stars shone brightly in the deep blue sky; there was not even a thin fleecy shred of cloud racking across the moon's disc. Oh, the glories of a northwester!

But the devil seize such glory! Glory, indeed! with a fleet of transports, and a regiment of soldiers on board! Glory! why, I daresay five hundred rank and file, at the fewest, were all cascading at one and the same moment—a thousand poor fellows turned outside in, like so many pairs of old stockings. Any glory in that? But to proceed.

Next morning the gale still continued, and when the day broke there was the frigate standing across our bows, rolling and pitching, as she tore her way through the boiling sea, under a close-reefed main-topsail and reefed foresail, with topgallant-yards and royal masts, and everything that could be struck with safety in war-time, down on deck. There she lay, with her clear black bends, and bright white streak, and long tier of cannon on the maindeck, and the carronades on the quarterdeck and forecastle grinning through the ports in the black bulwarks, while the white hammocks, carefully covered by the hammock-cloths, crowned the defences of the gallant frigate fore and aft, as she delved through the green surge—one minute rolling and rising on the curling white crest of a mountainous sea, amidst a hissing snow-storm of spray, with her bright copper glancing from stem to stern, and her scanty white canvass swelling aloft, and twenty feet of her keel forward occasionally hove into the air clean out of the water, as if she had been a sea-bird rushing to take wing—and the next, sinking entirely out of sight-hull, masts, and rigging—behind an intervening sea, that rose in hoarse thunder between us, threatening to overwhelm both us and her. As for the transports, the largest of the three had lost her fore-topmast, and had bore up under her foresail; another was also scudding under a close-reefed fore-topsail; but the third or head-quarter ship was still lying-to to windward, under her storm staysails. None of the merchant vessels were to be seen, having been compelled to bear up in the night, and to run before it under bare poles.

At length, as the sun rose, we got before the wind, and it soon moderated so far that we could carry reefed topsails and foresail; and away we all bowled, with a clear, deep, cold, blue sky, and a bright sun overhead, and a stormy leaden-coloured ocean with whitish green-crested billows, below. The sea continued to go down, and the wind to slacken, until the afternoon, when the commodore made the signal for the Torch to send a boat's crew, the instant it could be done with safety, on board the dismasted ship to assist in repairing damages and in getting up a jury-foretopmast.

The damaged ship was at this time on our weather-quarter; we accordingly handed the fore-topsail, and presently she was alongside. We hailed her, that we intended to send a boat on board, and desired her to heave-to, as we did, and presently she rounded to under our lee. One of the quarter-boats was manned, with three of the carpenter's crew, and six good men over and above her complement; but it was no easy matter to get on board of her, let me tell you, after she had been lowered, carefully watching the rolls, with four hands in. The moment she touched the water, the tackles were cleverly unhooked, and the rest of us tumbled on board, shin leather growing scarce, when we shoved off. With great difficulty, and not without wet jackets, we, the supernumeraries, got on board, and the boat returned to the Torch. The evening when we landed in the lobster-box, as Jack loves to designate a transport, was too far advanced for us to do anything towards refitting that night; and the confusion and uproar and numberless abominations of the crowded craft, were irksome to a greater degree than I expected, after having been accustomed to the strict and orderly discipline of a man-of-war. The following forenoon the Torch was ordered by signal to chase in the south-east quarter, and, hauling out from the fleet, she was soon out of sight.

"There goes my house and home," said I, and a feeling of desolateness came over me, that I would have been ashamed at the time to have acknowledged. We stood on, and worked hard all day in repairing the damage sustained during the gale.

At length dinner was announced, and I was invited, as the officer in charge of the seamen, to go down. The party in the cabin consisted of an old *gizzened* major, with a brown wig, and a voice melodious as the sharpening of a saw—I fancied sometimes that the vibration created by it set the very glasses in the steward's pantry a-ringing—three captains and six subalterns, every man of whom, as the devil would have it, played on the flute, and drew bad sketches, and kept journals. Most of them were very white and blue in the gills when we sat down, and others of a dingy sort of whitey-brown, while they ogled the viands in a most suspicious manner. Evidently most of them had but small confidence in their *moniplies;* and one or two, as the ship gave a heavier roll than usual, looked wistfully towards the door, and half rose from their chairs, as if in act to bolt. However, hot brandy grog being the order of the day, we all, landsmen and sailors, got on astonishingly, and numberless long yarns were spun of what "what's-his-name of this, and so-and-so of t'other, did or did not do."

About half-past five in the evening the captain of the transport, or rather the agent, an old lieutenant in the navy, and our host, rang his bell for the steward.

"Whereabouts are we in the fleet, steward?" said the ancient.

"The sternmost ship of all, sir," said the man.

"Where is the commodore?"

"About three miles ahead, sir."

"And the Torch, has she rejoined us?"

"No, sir; she has been out of sight these two hours; when last seen she was in chase of something in the south-east quarter, and carrying all the sail she could stagger under."

"Very well, very well."

A song from Master Waistbelt, one of the young officers. Before he had concluded the mate came down. By this time it was near sundown.

"Shall we shake a reef out of the main and mizen topsails, sir, and set the mainsail and spanker? The wind has lulled, sir, and there is a strange sail in the north-west that seems to be dodging us—but she may be one of the merchantmen, after all, sir."

"Never mind, Mr Leechline," said our gallant captain. "Mr Bandalier—a song if you please."

Now, the young soldiers on board happened to be men of the world, and Bandalier, who did not sing, turned off the request with a good-humoured laugh, alleging his inability with much suavity; but the old rough Turk of a tar-bucket chose to fire at this, and sang out—"Oh, if you don't choose to sing when you are asked, and to sport your damned fine airs—"

"Mr Crowfoot—"

"Captain," said the agent, piqued at having his title by courtesy withheld.

"By no means," said Major Sawrasp, who had spoken—"I believe I am speaking to *Lieutenant* Crowfoot, agent for transport No. ———, wherein it so happens I am commanding officer—so—"

Old Crowfoot saw he was in the wrong box, and therefore hove about, and backed out in good time—making the *amende* as smoothly as his gruff nature admitted, and trying to look pleased.

Presently the same bothersome mate came down again—

"The strange sail is creeping up on our quarter, sir."

"Ay?" said Crowfoot, "how does she lay?"

"She is hauled by the wind on the starboard tack, sir," continued the mate.

We now went on deck, and found that our suspicious friend had shortened sail, as if he had made us out, and was afraid to approach, or was lying by until nightfall.

Sawrasp had before this, with the tact and ease of a soldier and a gentleman, soldered his feud with Crowfoot, and, with the rest of the lobsters, was full of fight. The sun at length set, and the night closed in, when the old major again addressed Crowfoot.

"My dear fellow, can't you wait a bit, and let us have a rattle at that chap?" And old Crowfoot, who never bore a grudge long, seemed much inclined to fall in with the soldier's views; and, in fine, although the weather was now moderate, he did not make sail. Presently the commodore fired a gun, and showed lights. It was the signal to close. "Oh, time enough," said old Crowfoot—"what is the old man afraid of?" Another gun—and a fresh constellation on board the frigate. It was "an enemy in the north-west quarter."

"Hah, hah," sang out the agent, "is it so? Major, what say you to a brush—let her close, eh?—should like to pepper her wouldn't you—three hundred men, eh?"

By this time we were all on deck—the schooner came bowling along under a reefed mainsail and jib, now rising, and presently disappearing behind the stormy heavings of the roaring sea, the rising moon shining brightly on her canvass pinions, as if she had been an albatross skimming along the surface of the foaming water, while her broad white streak glanced like a silver ribbon along her clear black side. She was a very large craft of her class, long and low in the water, and evidently very fast; and it was now clear, from our having been unable as yet to sway up our fore-topmast, that she took us for a disabled merchantman, which might be cut off from the convoy.

As she approached we could perceive by the bright moonlight that she had six guns of a side, and two long ones on pivots—the one forward on the forecastle, and the other choke up to the mainmast.

Her deck was crowded with dark figures, pike and cutlass in hand: we were by this time so near that we could see a trumpet in the hand of a man who stood in the fore rigging, with his feet on the hammock netting, and his back against the shrouds. We had cleared away our six eighteen-pound carronades, which composed our starboard broadside, and loaded them, each with a round shot and a bag of two hundred musket-balls, while three hundred soldiers in their foraging jackets, and with their loaded muskets in their hands, were lying on the deck, concealed by the quarters, while the blue-jackets were sprawling in groups round the carronades.

I was lying down beside the gallant old major, who had a bugler close to him, while Crowfoot was standing on the gun nearest us; but getting tired of this recumbent position, I crept aft, until I could see through a spare port.

"Why don't the rascals fire?" quoth Sawrasp.

"Oh, that would alarm the commodore. They intend to walk quietly on board of us; but they will find themselves mistaken a little," whispered Crowfoot.

"Mind, men, no firing till the bugle sounds," said the major.

The word was passed along.

The schooner was by this time ploughing through it within half pistol-shot, with the white water dashing away from her bows, and buzzing past her sides—her crew as thick as peas on her deck. Once or twice she hauled her wind a little, and then again kept away from us, as if irresolute what to do. At length, without hailing, and all silent as the grave, she put her helm a-starboard, and ranged alongside.

"Now, my boys, give it him," shouted Crowfoot—"Fire!"

"Ready, men," shouted the major—"Present,—fire!"

The bugles sounded, the cannon roared, the musketry rattled, and the men cheered, and all was hurra, and fire, and fury. The breeze was strong enough to carry the smoke forward, and I saw the deck of the schooner, where the moment before all was still and motionless, and filled with dark figures till there scarcely appeared standing room, at once converted into a shambles. The blasting fiery tempest had laid low nearly the whole mass, like a maize-plat before a hurricane; and such a cry arose, as if

> "Men fought on earth,
> And fiends in upper air."

Scarcely a man was on his legs, the whole crew seemed to have been levelled with the deck, many dead, no doubt, and most wounded, while we could see numbers endeavouring to creep towards the hatches, while the black blood, in horrible streams, gushed through her scuppers across the bright white streak that glanced in the moonlight.

Some one on board of the privateer now hailed, "We have surrendered; cease firing, sir." But devil a bit—we continued blazing away—a lantern was run up to his main gaff, and then lowered again.

"We have struck, sir," shouted another voice; "don't murder us—don't fire, sir, for Godsake."

Put fire we still did; no sailor has the least compunction at even *running down* a privateer. Mercy to privateersmen is unknown. "Give them the stem," is the word, the curs being regarded by Jack at the best as highwaymen; so when he found we still peppered away, sailing two feet for our one, he hauled his wind, and speedily got beyond range of our carronades, having all this time never fired a shot. Shortly after this we ran under the Rayo's stern—she was lying to.

"Mr Crowfoot, what have you been after? I have a mind to report you, sir."

"We could not help it, sir," sang out Crowfoot, in a most dolorous tone, in answer to the captain of the frigate; "we have been nearly taken, sir, by a privateer, sir—an immense vessel, sir, that sails like a witch, sir."

"Keep close in my wake then, sir," rejoined the captain, in a gruff tone, and immediately the Rayo bore up.

Next morning we were all carrying as much sail as we could crowd. By this time we had gotten our jury-foretopmast up, and the Rayo, having kept astern in the night, was now under topsails and top-gallantsails, with the wet canvass at the head of the sails, showing that the reefs had been freshly shaken out— rolling, wedge-like on the swell, and rapidly shooting ahead, to resume her

station. As she passed us, and let fall her foresail, she made the signal to make
more sail, her object being to get through the Caicos Passage, into which we
were now entering before nightfall. It was eleven o'clock in the forenoon. A fine
clear breezy day, fresh and pleasant, sometimes cloudy overhead, but always
breaking away again, with a bit of a sneezer and a small shower. As the sun rose
there were indications of squalls in the north-eastern quarter, and about noon
one of them was whitening to windward. So "hands by the topgallant clew-
lines" was the word, and we were all standing by to shorten sail when the
commodore came to the wind as sharp and suddenly as if he had anchored; but
on a second look I saw his sheets were let fly, haulyards let go, and apparently
all was confusion on board of her. I ran to the side and looked over. The long
heaving dark-blue swell had changed into a light-green hissing ripple.

"Zounds, Captain Crowfoot, shoal water—why it breaks—we shall be
ashore!"

"Down with the helm-brace round the yards," shouted Crowfoot; "that's it—
steady—luff, my man;" and the danger was so imminent that even the
studding-sail haulyards were not let go, and the consequence was that the
booms snapped off like carrots as we came to the wind.

"Lord help us! we shall never weather that foaming reef there: set the
spanker—haul out—haul down the foretopmast-staysail—so, mind your luff,
my man."

The frigate now began to fire right and left, and the hissing of the shot overhead was a fearful augury of what was to take place; so sudden was the accident
that they had not had time to draw the round shot. The other transports were
equally fortunate with ourselves in weathering the shoal, and presently we
were all close hauled to windward of the reef, until we weathered the easternmost prong, when we bore up. But poor Rayo! she had struck on a coral reef,
where the Admiralty charts laid down fifteen fathoms water; and although
there was some talk at the time of an error in judgment, in not having the lead
going in the chains, still do I believe there was no fault lying at the door of her
gallant captain. By the time we had weathered the reef the frigate had swung
off from the pinnacle of rock on which she had been in a manner impaled, and
was making all the sail she could, with a fothered sail under her bows, and
chain-pumps clanging, and whole cataracts of water gushing from them, clear
white jets spouting from all the scuppers, fore and aft. She made the signal to
close. The next, alas! was the British ensign, seized, union down in the main
rigging, the sign of the uttermost distress. Still we all bowled along together,

but her yards were not squared, nor her sails set with her customary precision, and her lurches became more and more sickening, until at length she rolled so heavily, that she dipped both yardarms alternately in the water, and reeled to and fro like a drunken man.

"What is that splash?"

It was the larboard-bow gun, a long eighteen-pounder, hove overboard, and, watching the roll, the whole broadside, one after another, was cast into the sea. The clang of the chain-pumps increased, the water rushed in at one side of the main-deck and out at the other, in absolute cascades from the ports. At this moment the whole fleet of boats were alongside, keeping way with the ship, in the light, breeze. Her main-topsail was hove aback, while the captain's voice resounded through the ship.

"Now, men—all hands—bags and hammocks—starboard watch, the starboard side—larboard watch, the larboard side—no rushing now—she will swim this hour to come."

The bags, and hammocks, and officers' kits, were handed into the boats; the men were told off over the side as quietly by watches as if at muster, the officers last. At length the first-lieutenant came down. By this time she was settling perceptibly in the water; but the old captain still stood on the gangway, holding by the iron stanchion, where, taking off his hat, he remained uncovered for a moment, with the tears standing in his eyes. He then replaced it, descended, and took his place in the ship's launch—the last man to leave the ship; and there was little time to spare, for we had scarcely shoved off a few yards, to clear the spars of the wreck, when she sended forward, heavily and sickly, on the long swell. She never rose to the opposite heave of the sea again, but gradually sank by the head. The hull disappeared slowly and dignifiedly, the ensign fluttered and vanished beneath the dark ocean—I could have fancied reluctantly—as if it had been drawn down through a trap-door. The topsails next disappeared, the foretopsail sinking fastest; and last of all, the white pennant at the main-topgallantmast head, after flickering and struggling in the wind, flew up in the setting sun as if imbued with life, like a stream of white fire, or as if it had been the spirit leaving the body, and was then drawn down into the abyss, and the last vestige of the Rayo vanished for ever. The crew, as if moved by one common impulse, gave three cheers.

The captain now stood up in his boat—"Men, the Rayo is no more, but it is my duty to tell you, that although you are now to be distributed amongst the transports, you are still amenable to martial law: I am aware, men, this hint may not be necessary, still it is right you should know it."

When the old hooker clipped out of sight, there was not a dry eye in the whole fleet. "There she goes, the dear old beauty," said one of her crew. "There goes the blessed old black b——h," quoth another. "Ah, many a merry night have we had in the clever little craft," quoth a third; and there was really a tolerable shedding of tears and squirting of tobacco-juice. But the blue ripple had scarcely blown over the glass-like surface of the sea where she had sunk, when the buoyancy of young hearts, with the prospect of a good furlough amongst the lobster-boxes, for a time, seemed to be uppermost among the men. The officers, I saw and knew, felt very differently.

"My eye!" sang out an old quartermaster in our boat, perched well forward, with his back against the ring in the stem, and his arms crossed, after having been busily employed rummaging in his bag—"my eye, what a pity—oh, what a pity!—"

Come, there is some feeling, *genuine,* at all events, thought I.

"Why," said Bill Chestree, the captain of the foretop, "what *is* can't be helped, old Fizgig; old Rayo has gone down, and—"

"Old Rayo be d——d, Master Bill," said the man, "but may I be flogged, if I han't forgotten half-a-pound of negrohead baccy in Dick Catgut's bag."

"Launch ahoy!" hailed a half-drunken voice from one of the boats astern of us. "Hillo," responded the coxswain. The poor skipper even pricked up his ears. "Have you got Dick Catgut's fiddle among ye?" This said Dick Catgut was the corporal of marines, and the prime instigator of all the fun amongst the men. "No, no," said several voices, "no fiddle here." The hail passed round among the other boats, "No fiddle." "I would rather lose three days' grog than have his fiddle mislaid," quoth the man who pulled the bow oar.

"Why don't you ask Dick himself?" said our coxswain.

"Ay, true enough—Dick, Dick Catgut!" but no one answered. Alas! poor Dick was nowhere to be found; he had been mislaid as well as his fiddle. He had broken into the spirit-room, as it turned out, and, having got drunk, did not come to time when the frigate sank.

Our ship, immediately after the frigate's crew had been bestowed and the boats got in, hoisted the commodore's light, and the following morning we fell in with the Torch, off the east end of Jamaica, which, after seeing the transports safe into Kingston, and taking out me and my people, bore up through the Gulf, and resumed her cruising-ground on the edge of the Gulf Stream, between 25° and 30° north latitude.

CHAPTER III.

THE QUENCHING OF THE TORCH.

"Then rose from sea to sky the wild farewell."

—Don Juan.

THE EVENING was closing in dark and rainy, with every appearance of a gale from the westward, and the weather had become so thick and boisterous that the lieutenant of the watch had ordered the look-out at the mast-head down on deck. The man, on his way down, had gone into the maintop to bring away some things he had placed there in going aloft, and was in the act of leaving it, when he sang out—"A sail on the weather bow."

"What does she look like?"

"Can't rightly say, sir; she is in the middle of the thick weather to windward."

"Stay where you are a little.—Jenkins, jump forward, and see what you can make of her from the foreyard."

Whilst the topman was obeying his instruction, the look-out again hailed— "She is a ship, sir, close-hauled on the same tack—the weather clears, and I can see her now."

The wind, ever since noon, had been blowing in heavy squalls, with appalling lulls between them. One of these gusts had been so violent as to bury in the sea the lee-guns in the waist, although the brig had nothing set but her close-reefed main-topsail and reefed foresail. It was now spending its fury, and she was beginning to roll heavily, when, with a suddenness almost incredible to one unacquainted with these latitudes, the veil of mist that had hung to windward the whole day was rent and drawn aside, and the red and level rays of the setting sun flashed at once, through a long arch of glowing clouds, on the black hull and tall spars of his Britannic Majesty's sloop Torch. And, true enough, we were not the only spectators of this gloomy splendour; for, right in the wake of the moon-like sun, now half sunk in the sea, at the distance of a mile or more lay a long warlike-looking craft, apparently a frigate or heavy corvette, rolling heavily and silently in the trough of the sea, with her masts, yards, and the scanty sail she had set, in strong relief against the glorious horizon.

Jenkins now hailed from the foreyard—"The strange sail is bearing up, sir."

As he spoke a flash was seen, followed, after what seemed a long interval, by the deadened report of the gun, as if it had been an echo, and the sharp, half-ringing half-hissing sound of the shot. It fell short, but close to us, and was evidently thrown from a heavy cannon, from the length of the range.

Mr Splinter, the first-lieutenant, jumped from the gun he stood on— "Quartermaster, keep her away a bit," and dived into the cabin to make his report.

Captain Deadeye was a staid, stiff-rumped, wall-eyed, old first-lieutenant-ish-looking veteran, with his coat of a regular Rodney cut, broad skirts, long waist, and stand-up collar, over which dangled either a queue or a marlinspike with a tuft of oakum at the end of it,—it would have puzzled Old Nick to say which. His lower spars were eased in tight unmentionables of what had once been white kerseymere, and long boots, the coal-scuttle tops of which served as scuppers to carry off the drainings from his coat-flaps in bad weather: he was, in fact, the "last of the sea-monsters," but, like all his tribe, as brave as steel, and, when put to it, as alert as a cat.

He no sooner heard Splinter's report than he sprang up the ladder, brushing the tumbler of swizzle he had just brewed clean out of the fiddle into the lap of Mr Saveall, the purser, who had dined with him, and nearly extinguishing the said purser by his arm striking the bowl of the pipe he was smoking, thereby forcing the shank half-way down his throat.

"My glass, Wilson," to his steward.

"She is close to, sir; you can see her plainly without it," said Mr Treenail, the second-lieutenant, from the weather nettings, where he was reconnoitring.

After a long look through his starboard blinker (his other skylight had been shut up ever since Aboukir), Captain Deadeye gave orders to "clear away the weather-bow gun;" and as it was now getting too dark for flags to be seen distinctly, he desired that three lanterns might be got ready for hoisting vertically in the main-rigging.

"All ready forward there?"

"All ready, sir."

"Then hoist away the lights, and throw a shot across her forefoot—Fire!" Bang went our carronade, but our friend to windward paid no regard to the private signal; he had shaken a reef out of his topsails, and was coming down fast upon us.

It was clear that old Blowhard had at first taken him for one of our own cruisers, and meant to *signalise* him, "all regular and shipshape," to use his own expression. Most of us, however, thought it would have been wiser to have made sail and widened our distance a little, in place of bothering with old-fashioned manœuvres, which might end in our catching a tartar; but the skipper had been all his life in line-of-battle ships or heavy frigates; and it was a tough job, under any circumstances, to persuade him of the propriety of "up-stick-and-away," as we soon felt to our cost.

The enemy, for such he evidently was, now all at once yawed, and indulged us with a sight of his teeth; and there he was, fifteen ports of a side on his maindeck, with the due quantum of carronades on his quarterdeck and forecastle; whilst his short lower-masts, white canvass, and the tremendous hoist in his topsails, showed him to be a heavy American frigate; and it was equally certain that he had cleverly hooked us under his lee, within comfortable range of his long twenty-fours. To convince the most unbelieving, three jets of flame, amidst wreaths of white smoke, now glanced from his maindeck; but in this instance the sound of the cannon was followed by a sharp crackle and a shower of splinters from the foreyard.

It was clear we had got an ugly customer—poor Jenkins now called to Treenail, who was standing forward near the gun which had been fired—"Och, sir, and it's badly wounded we are here."

The officer was a Patlander, as well as the seaman. "Which of you, my boy?"—the glowing seriousness of the affair in no way checking his propensity to fun,—"Which of you—you, or the yard?"

"Both of us, your honour; but the yard badliest."

"The devil!—Come down, then, or get into the top, and I will have you looked after presently."

The poor fellow crawled off the yard into the foretop, as he was ordered, where he was found after the brush, badly wounded by a splinter in the breast.

Jonathan, no doubt, "calculated," as well he might, that this taste of his quality would be quite sufficient for a little eighteen-gun sloop close under his lee; but the fight was not to be so easily taken out of Deadeye, although even to his optic it was now high time to be off.

"All hands make sail, Mr Splinter; that chap is too heavy for us.—Mr Kelson," to the carpenter, "jump up and see what the foreyard will carry. Keep her away, my man," to the seaman at the helm.—"Crack on, Mr Splinter, set the fore-topsail,—shake all the reefs out, and loose topgallant-sails;—stand by to sheet home; and see all clear to rig the booms out, if the breeze lulls."

In less than a minute we were bowling along before it; but the wind was breezing up again, and no one could say how long the wounded foreyard would carry the weight and drag of the sails. To mend the matter, Jonathan was coming up hand over hand with the freshening breeze, under a press of canvass; it was clear that escape was next to impossible.

"Clear away the larboard guns!" I absolutely jumped off the deck with astonishment—who could have spoken it? It appeared such downright madness to show fight under the very muzzles of the guns of an enemy, half of whose broadside was sufficient to sink us. It was the captain, however, and there was nothing for it but to obey.

In an instant the creaking and screaming of the carronade slides, the rattling of the carriage of the long twelve-pounder amidships, the thumping and punching of handspikes and the dancing and jumping of Jack himself, were heard through the whistling of the breeze, as the guns were being shotted and run out. In a few seconds all was still again, but the rushing sound of the vessel going through the water, and of the rising gale amongst the rigging.

The men stood clustered at their quarters, their cutlasses buckled round their waists, all without jackets and waistcoats, and many with nothing but their trousers on.

"Now, men, mind your aim; our only chance is to wing him. I will yaw the ship, and as your guns come to bear, slap it right into his bows. Starboard your helm, my man, and bring her to the wind." As she came round, blaze went our carronades and long gun in succession, with good will and good aim, and down came his foretop-sail on the cap, with all the superincumbent spars and gear; the head of the topmast had been shot away. The men instinctively cheered. "That will do; now knock off, my boys, and let us run for it. Keep her away again; make all sail."

Jonathan was for an instant paralysed by our impudence; but just as we were getting before the wind, he yawed, and let drive his whole broadside; and fearfully did it transmogrify us.

Half an hour before we were as gay a little sloop as ever floated, with a crew of a hundred and twenty as fine fellows as ever manned a British man-of-war. The iron shower sped—ten of the hundred and twenty never saw the sun rise again; seventeen more were wounded, three mortally; we had eight shot between wind and water, our maintop-mast shot away as clean as a carrot, and our hull and rigging otherwise regularly cut to pieces. Another broadside succeeded; but by this time we had bore up—thanks to the loss of our after-sail, we could do nothing else; and what was better luck still, whilst the loss of our maintop-mast paid the brig off on the one hand, the loss of headsail in the frigate brought her as quickly to the wind on the other; thus most of her shot fell astern of us; and before she could bear up again in chase, the squall struck her, and carried her maintop-mast overboard.

This gave us a start, crippled and bedevilled though we were; and as the night fell, we contrived to lose sight of our large friend. With breathless anxiety did we carry on through that night, expecting every lurch to send our remaining topmast by the board; but the weather moderated, and next morning the sun shone on our blood-stained decks at anchor off the entrance to St George's harbour.

I was the mate of the watch, and as the day dawned I had amused myself with other younkers over the side, examining the shot-holes and other injuries sustained from the fire of the frigate, and contrasting the clean, sharp, well-defined apertures made by the 24-pound shot from the long guns—with the bruised and splintered ones from the 32-pound carronades; but the men had begun to wash down the decks, and the first gush of clotted blood and water from the scuppers fairly turned me sick. I turned away, when Mr Kennedy our gunner, a good steady old Scotchman, with whom I was a bit of a favourite, came up to me—"Mr Cringle, the captain has sent for you; poor Mr Johnstone is fast going, he wants to see you."

I knew my young messmate had been wounded, for I had seen him carried below after the frigate's second broadside; but the excitement of a boy, who had seldom smelt powder fired in anger before, had kept me on deck the whole night, and it never once occurred to me to ask for him, until the old gunner spoke.

I hastened down to our small confined berth, where I saw a sight that quickly brought me to myself. Poor Johnstone was indeed going; a grape-shot had struck him, and torn his belly open. There he lay in his bloody hammock on the deck, pale and motionless as if he had already departed, except a slight twitching at the corners of his mouth, and a convulsive contraction and distension of his nostrils. His brown ringlets still clustered over his marble forehead, but they were drenched in the cold sweat of death. The surgeon could do nothing for him, and had left him; but our old captain—bless him for it—I little expected from his usual crusty bearing to find him so employed—had knelt by his side, and, whilst he read from the Prayer-book one of those beautiful petitions in our Church service to Almighty God for mercy to the passing soul of one so young, and so early cut off, the tears trickled down the old man's cheeks, and filled the furrows worn in them by the washing up of many a salt spray. On the other side of his narrow bed, fomenting the rigid muscles of his neck and chest, sat Misthress Connolly, one of three women on board—a rough enough creature, heaven knows! in common weather: but her stifled sobs showed that the mournful sight had stirred up all the woman within her. She had opened the bosom of the poor boy's shirt, and untying the ribbon that fastened a small gold crucifix round his neck she placed it in his cold hand. The young midshipman was of a respectable family in Limerick, her native place, and a Catholic— another strand of the cord that bound her to him. When the captain finished reading, he bent over the departing youth, and kissed his cheek. "Your young messmate just now desired to see you, Mr Cringle, but it is too late; he is insensible and dying." Whilst he spoke, a strong shiver passed through the boy's frame, his face became slightly convulsed, and all was over!

The captain rose, and Connolly, with a delicacy of feeling which many might not have looked for in her situation, spread one of our clean mess table-cloths over the body. "And is it really gone you are, my poor dear boy!" forgetting all difference of rank in the fulness of her heart. "Who will tell this to your mother, and nobody here to wake you but ould Kate Connolly, and no time will they be giving me, nor whisky—Ochon! ochon!"

But enough and to spare of this piping work. The boatswain's whistle now called me to the gangway, to superintend the handing up, from a shore-boat alongside, a supply of the grand staples of the island—ducks and onions. The three 'Mudians in her were characteristic samples of the inhabitants. Their faces and skins, where exposed, were not tanned, but absolutely burnt into a fiery-red colour by the sun. They guessed and drawled like any buckskin from Virginia, superadding to their accomplishments their insular peculiarity of always shutting one eye when they spoke to you. They are all Yankees at bottom; and if they could get their 365 *islands*—so they call the large stones on which they live—under weigh, they would not be long in towing them into the Chesapeake.

The word had been passed to get six of the larboard guns and all the shot over to the other side, to give the brig a list of a streak or two a-starboard, so that the stage on which the carpenter and his crew were at work over the side, stopping the shot-holes about the water-line, might swing clear of the wash of the sea. I had jumped from the nettings, where I was perched, to assist in unbolting one of the carronade slides, when I slipped and capsized against a peg sticking out of one of the scuppers. I took it for something else, and d——d the ring-bolt incontinently. Caboose, the cook, was passing with his mate, a Jamaica negro of the name of John Crow, at the time. "Don't d——n the remains of your fellow-mortals, Master Cringle; that is my leg." The cook of a man-of-war is no small beer; he is his Majesty's warrant-officer, a much bigger wig than a poor little mid, with whom it is condescension on his part to jest.

It seems to be a sort of rule that no old sailor who has not lost a limb, or an eye at least, shall be eligible to the office; but as the kind of maiming is so far circumscribed that all cooks must have two arms, a laughable proportion of them have but one leg. Besides the honour, the perquisites are good; accordingly, all old quartermasters, captains of tops, &c., look forward to the cookdom, as the cardinals look to the popedom; and really there is some analogy between them, for neither are preferred from any especial fitness for the office. A cardinal is made pope because he is old, infirm, and imbecile—our friend Caboose was made cook because he had been Lord Nelson's coxswain, was a drunken rascal, and had a wooden leg; for as to his gastronomical qualifications, he knew no more of the science than just sufficient to watch the copper where the salt junk and potatoes were boiling. Having been a little in the wind overnight, he had quartered himself, in the superabundance of his heroism, at a gun where he had no business to be, and in running it out he had jammed his toe in a scupper hole, so fast that there was no extricating him; and notwithstanding his piteous entreaty, "to be eased out handsomely, as the leg was made out of a plank of the Victory, and the ring at the end out of one of her bolts," the captain of the gun, finding, after a stout pull, that the man was like to come "home in his hand *without* the leg," was forced "to break him short off," as he phrased it, to get him out of the way, and let the carriage traverse. In the morning when he sobered, he had quite forgotten where the leg was, and how he broke it; he therefore got Kelson to splice the stump with the butt-end of a mop; but in the hurry it had been left three inches too long so he had to jerk himself up to the top of his peg at every step. The doctor, glad to breathe the fresh air after the horrible work he had gone through, was leaning over the side speaking to Kelson. When I fell, he turned round and drew Cookee's fire on himself. "Doctor, you have not prescribed for me yet."

"No, Caboose, I have not; what is wrong?"

"Wrong, sir? why, I have lost my leg, and the captain's clerk says I am not in the return!—Look here, sir, had Doctor Kelson not coopered me, where should I have been?—Why, doctor, had I been looked after, amputation might have been unnecessary; a *fish* might have done, whereas I have had to be *spliced*."

He was here cut short by the voice of his mate, who had gone forward to slay a pig for the gunroom mess. "Oh, Lad, oh! Massa Caboose!—dem dam Yankee! —De Purser killed, massa!—Dem shoot him troo de head!—Oh, Lad!"

Captain Deadeye had come on deck. "You John Crow, what is wrong, with you?"

"Why, de Purser killed, captain, dat all."

"Purser killed?—Doctor, is Saveall hurt?"

Treenail could stand it no longer. "No, sir, no; it is one of the gunroom pigs that we shipped at Halifax three cruises ago; I am sure I don't know how he survived one, but the seamen took a fancy to him, and nicknamed him the Purser. You know, sir, they make pets of anything and everything at a pinch!"

Here John Crow drew the carcass from the hog-pen, and sure enough a shot had cut the poor Purser's head nearly off. Blackee looked at him with a most whimsical expression; they say no one can fathom a negro's affection for a pig. "Poor Purser! de people call him Purser, sir, because him knowing chap; him cabbage all de grub, slush, and stuff in him own corner, and give only de small bit, and de bad piece, to de oder pig; so, captain—"

Splinter saw the poor fellow was like to get into a scrape.

"That will do, John Crow—forward with you now, and lend a hand to cat the anchor.—All hands up anchor!" The boatswain's hoarse voice repeated the command, and he in turn was re-echoed by his mates; the capstan was manned, and the crew stamped round to a point of war most villanously performed by a bad drummer and a worse fifer, in as high glee as if those who were killed had been snug and well in their hammocks on the berth deck, in place of at the bottom of the sea, with each a shot at his feet. We weighed, and began to work up, tack and tack, towards the island of Ireland, where the arsenal is, amongst a perfect labyrinth of shoals, through which the 'Mudian pilot *cunned* the ship with great skill, taking his stand, to our no small wonderment, not at the gangway or poop, as usual, but on the bowsprit end, so that he might see the rocks under foot, and shun them accordingly, for they are so steep and numerous (they look like large fish in the clear water), and the channel is so intricate, that you have to go quite close to them. At noon we arrived at the anchorage, and hauled our moorings on board.

We had refitted, and been four days at sea, on our voyage to Jamaica, when the gunroom officers gave our mess a blow-out.

The increased motion and rushing of the vessel through the water, the groaning of the masts, the howling of the rising gale, and the frequent trampling of the watch on deck, were prophetic of wet jackets to some of us; still, midshipman-like, we were as happy as a good dinner and some wine could make us, until the old gunner shoved his weather-beaten phiz and bald pate in at the door. "Beg pardon, Mr Splinter, but if you will spare Mr Cringle on the forecastle for an hour until the moon rises."

("Spare, quotha, is his Majesty's officer a joint stool?")

"Why, Mr Kennedy, why? here, man, take a glass of grog."

"I thank you, sir. It is coming on a roughish night, sir; the running ships should be crossing us hereabouts; indeed more than once I thought there was a strange sail close aboard of us, the scud is flying so low, and in such white flakes; and none of us have an eye like Mr Cringle, unless it be John Crow, and he is all but frozen."

"Well, Tom, I suppose you *will* go"—*Anglice,* from a first-lieutenant to a mid—"Brush instanter."

Having changed my uniform for shag-trousers, pea-jacket, and south-west cap, I went forward, and took my station, in no pleasant humour, on the stowed foretopmast-staysail, with my arm round the stay. I had been half an hour there, the weather was getting worse, the rain was beating in my face, and the spray from the stem was flashing over me, as it roared through the waste of sparkling and hissing waters. I turned my back to the weather for a moment, to press my hand on my strained eyes. When I opened them again, I saw the gunner's gaunt high-featured visage thrust anxiously forward; his profile looked as if rubbed over with phosphorus, and his whole person as if we had been playing at snap-dragon. "What has come over you, Mr Kennedy?—who is burning the blue-light now?"

"A wiser man than I am must tell you that; look forward, Mr Cringle—look there; what do your books say to that?"

I looked forth, and saw, at the extreme end of the jib-boom, what I had read of, certainly, but never expected to see, a pale, greenish, glow-worm-coloured flame, of the size and shape of the frosted glass shade over the swinging lamp in the gun-room. It drew out and flattened as the vessel pitched and rose again; and as she sheered about, it wavered round the point that seemed to attract it, like a soap-sud bubble blown from a tobacco-pipe before it is shaken into the air; at the core it was comparatively bright, but gradually faded into a halo. It shed a baleful and ominous light on the surrounding objects; the group of sailors on the forecastle looked like spectres, and they shrunk together, and whispered when it began to roll slowly along the spar towards where the boatswain was sitting at my feet. At this instant something slid down the stay, and a cold clammy hand passed round my neck. I was within an ace of losing my hold, and tumbling overboard. "Heaven have mercy on me, what's that?"

"It's that skylarking son of a gun, Jem Sparkle's monkey, sir. You, Jem, you'll never rest till that brute is made shark bait of."

But Jackoo vanished up the stay again, chuckling and grinning in the ghostly radiance, as if he had been the "Spirit of the Lamp." The light was still there, but a cloud of mist, like a burst of vapour from a steam boiler, came down upon the gale, and flew past, when it disappeared. I followed the white mass as it sailed down the wind; it did not, as it appeared to me, vanish in the darkness, but seemed to remain in sight to leeward, as if checked by a sudden flaw; yet none of our sails were taken aback. A thought flashed on me. I peered still more intensely into the night. I was now certain. "A sail, broad on the lee bow."

The ship was in a buzz in a moment. The captain answered from the quarterdeck—"Thank you, Mr Cringle. How shall we steer?"

"Keep her away a couple of points, sir—steady."

"Steady," sang the man at the helm; and the slow melancholy cadence, although a familiar sound to me, now moaned through the rushing of the wind, and smote upon my heart as if it had been the wailing of a spirit.

I turned to the boatswain, who was standing beside me—"Is that you, or *Davy* steering, Mr Nipper? If you had not been here bodily at my elbow, I could have sworn that was your *voice.*"

When the gunner made the same remark, it startled the poor fellow; he tried to take it as a joke, but could not. "There may be a laced hammock, with a shot in it, for some of us ere morning."

At this moment, to my dismay, the object we were chasing shortened—gradually fell abeam of us, and finally disappeared.

"The Flying Dutchman."

"I can't see her at all now."

"She will be a fore-and-aft-rigged vessel that has tacked, sir," said the gunner. And sure enough, after a few seconds, I saw the white object lengthen, and draw out again abaft our beam.

"The chase has tacked, sir," I sang out; "put the helm down, or she will go to windward of us."

We tacked also, and time it was we did so, for the rising moon now showed us a large schooner under a crowd of sail. We edged down on her, when, finding her manœuvre detected, she brailed up her flat sails, and bore up before the wind. This was our best point of sailing, and we cracked on, the captain rubbing his hands—"It's my turn to be the *big un* this time." Although blowing a strong north-wester, it was now clear moonlight, and we hammered away from our bow guns; but whenever a shot told amongst the rigging, the injury was repaired as if by magic. It was evident we had repeatedly hulled her, from the glimmering white streaks along her counter and across her stern, occasioned by the splintering of the timber, but it seemed to produce no effect.

At length we drew well up on her quarter. She continued all black hull and white sail, not a soul to be seen on deck, except a dark object which we took for the man at the helm. "What schooner's that?" No answer. "Heave-to, or I'll sink you." Still all silent. "Sergeant Armstrong, do you think you could pick off that chap at the wheel?" The marine jumped on the forecastle, and levelled his piece, when a musket-shot from the schooner crashed through his skull, and he fell dead. The old skipper's blood was up. "Forecastle, there! Mr Nipper, clap a canister of grape over the round shot into the boat-gun, and give it to him."

"Ay, ay, sir!" gleefully rejoined the boatswain, forgetting the augury and everything else in the excitement of the moment. In a twinkling the square foresail, topsail, top-gallant, royal, and studdingsail haulyards were let go by the run on board of the schooner, as if they had been shot away, and he put his helm hard a-port, as if to round to.

"Rake him, sir, or give him the stem. He has *not* surrendered. I know their game. Give him your broadside, sir, or he is off to windward of you like a shot.—No, no! we have him now; heave-to, Mr Splinter, heave-to!" We did so, and that so suddenly, that the studdingsail booms snapped like pipe-shanks, short off by the irons. Notwithstanding, we had shot two hundred yards to leeward before we could lay our maintopsail to the mast. I ran to windward. The schooner's yards and rigging were now black with men, clustered like bees swarming, her square-sails were being close furled, her fore-and-aft sails set, and away she was, close-hauled and dead to windward of us.

"So much for undervaluing our American friends," grumbled Mr Splinter.

We made all sail in chase, blazing away to little purpose; we had no chance on a bowline, and when our *amigo* had satisfied himself of his superiority by one or two short tacks, he deliberately hauled down his flying jib and gaff-topsail, took a reef in his mainsail, triced up the bunt of his foresail, and fired his long thirty-two at us. The shot came in at the third aftermost port on the starboard side, and dismounted the carronade, smashing the slide, and wounding three men. The second shot missed, and as it was madness to remain to be peppered, probably winged, whilst every one of ours fell short, we reluctantly kept away on our course, having the gratification of hearing a clear well-blown bugle on board the schooner play up "Yankee Doodle."

As the brig fell off, our long gun was run out to have a parting crack at her, when the third and last shot from the schooner struck the sill of the mid-ship port, and made the white splinters fly from the solid oak like bright silver sparks in the moonlight. A sharp piercing cry rose into the air—my soul identified that death-shriek with the voice that I had heard, and I saw the man who was standing with the lanyard of the lock in his hand drop heavily across the breech, and discharge the gun in his fall. Thereupon a blood-red glare shot up into the cold blue sky, as if a volcano had burst forth from beneath the mighty deep, followed by a roar, and a shattering crash, and a mingling of unearthly cries and groans, and a concussion of the air and of the water, as if our whole broadside had been fired at once. Then a solitary splash here, and a dip there, and short sharp yells, and low choking bubbling moans, as the hissing fragments of the noble vessel we had seen fell into the sea, and the last of her gallant crew vanished for ever beneath that pale broad moon. *We were alone,* and once more all was dark, and wild, and stormy. Fearfully had that ball sped, fired by a dead man's hand. But what is it that clings, black and doubled, across that fatal cannon, dripping and heavy, and choking the scuppers with clotting gore, and swaying to and fro with the motion of the vessel, like a bloody fleece?

"Who is it that was hit at the gun there?"

"Mr Nipper the boatswain, sir. The last shot has cut him in two."

After this most melancholy incident we continued on our voyage to Jamaica, nothing particular occurring until we anchored at Port Royal, where we had a regular overhaul of the old bark; and after this was completed, we were ordered down to the leeward part of the island to afford protection to the coasting trade. One fine morning, about a fortnight after we had left Port Royal, the Torch was lying at anchor in Bluefields Bay. It was between eight and nine; the land-wind had died away, and the sea-breeze had not set in—there was not a breath stirring. The pennant from the masthead fell sluggishly down, and clung amongst the rigging like a dead snake, whilst the folds of the St George's ensign that hung from the mizen-peak were as motionless as if they had been carved in marble.

The anchorage was one unbroken mirror, except where its glasslike surface was shivered into sparkling ripples by the gambols of a skipjack, or the flashing stoop of his enemy the pelican; and the reflection of the vessel was so clear and steady, that at the distance of a cable's length you could not distinguish the waterline, nor tell where the substance ended and shadow began, until the casual dashing of a bucket overboard for a few moments broke up the phantom ship; but the wavering fragments soon reunited, and she again floated double, like the swan of the poet. The heat was so intense that the iron stanchions of the awning could not be grasped with the hand, and where the decks were not screened by it, the pitch boiled out from the seams. The swell rolled in from the offing in long shining undulations, like a sea of quicksilver, whilst every now and then a flying-fish would spark out from the unruffled bosom of the heaving water, and shoot away like a silver arrow, until it dropped with a flash into the sea again. There was not a cloud in the heavens, but a quivering blue haze hung over the land, through which the white sugar-works and overseers' houses on the distant estates appeared to twinkle like objects seen through a thin smoke, whilst each of the tall stems of the cocoa-nut trees on the beach, when looked at steadfastly, seemed to be turning round with a small spiral motion, like so many endless screws. There was a dreamy indistinctness about the outlines of the hills, even in the immediate vicinity, which increased as they receded, until the Blue Mountains in the horizon melted into sky. The crew were listlessly spinning oakum, and mending sails, under the shade of the awning; the only exceptions to the general languor were John Crow the black, and Jackoo the monkey. The former (who was an *improvisatore* of a rough stamp) sat out on the bowsprit, through choice, beyond the shade of the canvass, without hat or shirt, like a bronze bust, busy with his task, whatever that might be, singing at the top of his pipe, and between whiles confabulating with his hairy ally, as if he had been a messmate. The monkey was hanging by the tail from the dolphin-striker, admiring what John Crow called "his own dam ogly face in the water."

"Tail like yours would be good ting for a sailor, Jackoo, it would leave his two hands free aloft—more use, more hornament, too, I'm sure, den de piece of greasy junk dat hangs from de captain's tafferel.—Now I shall sing to you how dat Corromantee rascal, my fader, was sell me on de Gold Coast—

> "Two red nightcap, one long knife,
>   All him get for Quackoo,
>   For gun next day him sell him wife—
>   You tink dat good song, Jackoo?"

"Chockoo, chockoo," chattered the monkey, as if in answer.

"Ah, you tink so—sensible honimal!—What is dat? shark?—Jackoo, come up, sir: don't you see dat big shovel-nosed fis looking at you? Pull your hand out of de water—Gara-mighty!"

The negro threw himself on the gammoning of the bowsprit to take hold of the poor ape, who, mistaking his kind intention, and ignorant of his danger, shrunk from him, lost his hold, and fell into the sea. The shark instantly sank to have a run, then dashed at his prey, raising his snout over him, and shooting his head and shoulders three or four feet out of the water, with poor Jackoo shrieking in his jaws, whilst his small bones crackled and crunched under the monster's triple row of teeth.

Whilst this small tragedy was acting—and painful enough it was to the kind-hearted negro—I was looking out towards the eastern horizon, watching the first dark-blue ripple of the sea-breeze, when a rushing noise passed over my head. I looked up and saw a gallinaso, the large carrion-crow of the tropic, sailing, contrary to the habits of its kind, seaward over the brig. I followed it with my eye, until it vanished in the distance, when my attention was attracted by a dark speck far out in the offing, with a little tiny white sail. With my glass I made it out to be a ship's boat, but I saw no one on board, and the sail was idly flapping about the mast.

On making my report, I was desired to pull towards it in the gig; and as we approached, one of the crew said he thought he saw some one peering over the bow. We drew nearer, and I saw him distinctly.

"Why don't you haul the sheet aft and come down to us, sir?"

He neither moved nor answered; but as the boat rose and fell on the short sea raised by the first of the breeze, the face kept mopping and mowing at us over the gunwale.

"I will soon teach you manners, my fine fellow! give way, men"—and I fired my musket, when the crow that I had seen rose from the boat into the air, but immediately alighted again, to our astonishment, vulture-like with outstretched wings, *upon the head*.

Under the shadow of this horrible plume, the face seemed on the instant to alter like the hideous changes in a dream. It appeared to become of a death-like paleness, and anon streaked with blood. Another stroke of the oar—the chin had fallen down, and the tongue was hanging out. Another pull—the eyes were gone, and from their sockets brains and blood were fermenting and flowing down the cheeks. It was the face of a putrefying corpse. In this floating coffin we found the body of another sailor, doubled across one of the thwarts, with a long Spanish knife sticking between his ribs, as if he had died in some mortal struggle, or, what was equally probable, had put an end to himself in his frenzy; whilst alone, the bottom of the boat, arranged with some show of care, and covered by a piece of canvass stretched across an oar above it, lay the remains of a beautiful boy, about fourteen years of age, apparently but a few hours dead. Some biscuit, a roll of jerked beef, and an earthen water-jar, lay beside him, showing that hunger at least could have had no share in his destruction—*but the pipkin was dry, and the small water-cask in the bow was staved and empty.*

We had no sooner cast our grappling over the bow, and begun to tow the boat to the ship, than the abominable bird that we had scared settled down into it again, notwithstanding our proximity, and began to peck at the face of the dead boy. At this moment we heard a gibbering noise, and saw something like a bundle of old rags roll out from beneath the stern-sheets, and, whatever it was, apparently make a fruitless attempt to drive the gallinaso from its prey. Heaven and earth, what an object met our eyes! It was a full-grown man, but so wasted that one of the boys lifted him by his belt with one hand. His knees were drawn up to his chin, his hands were like the talons of a bird, while the falling-in of his chocolate-coloured and withered features gave an unearthly relief to his forehead, over which the horny and transparent skin was braced so tightly that it seemed ready to crack. But in the midst of this desolation his deep-set coal-black eyes sparkled like two diamonds with the fever of his sufferings; there was a fearful fascination in their flashing brightness, contrasted with the death-like aspect of the face and rigidity of the frame. When sensible of our presence he tried to speak, but could only utter a low moaning sound. At length—*"Agua, agua"*—we had not a drop of water in the boat. *"El muchacho esta muriendo de sed—Agua."*

We got on board, and the surgeon gave the poor fellow some weak tepid grog. It acted like magic. He gradually uncoiled himself; his voice, from being weak and husky, became comparatively strong and clear. *"El Hijo—Agua para mi Pedrillo—No le hace para mi—Oh la noche pasado, la noche pasado!"* he was told to compose himself, and that his boy would be taken care of. *"Dexa me verlo entonces, oh Dios, dexa me verlo"*—and he crawled, grovelling on his chest, like a crushed worm, across the deck, until he got his head over the portsill, and looked down into the boat. He there beheld the pale face of his dead son; it was the last object he ever saw—*"Ay de mi!"* he groaned heavily, and dropped his face against the ship's side. He was dead.

After spending several months in the service already alluded to, we were ordered on a cruise off the coast of Terra Firma.

Morillo was at this time besieging Carthagena by land, while a Spanish squadron, under Admiral Enrile, blockaded the place by sea; and it pleased the officer who commanded the inshore division to conceive, while the old Torch was quietly beating up along the coast, that we had an intention of forcing the blockade.

The night before had been gusty and tempestuous—all hands had been called three times, so that at last, thinking there was no use in going below, I lay down on the stern-sheets of the boat over the stern—an awkward berth certainly, but a spare tarpauling had that morning been stretched over the afterpart of the boat to dry, and I therefore ensconced myself beneath it. Just before daylight, however, the brig, by a sudden shift of wind, was taken aback, and fetching stern-way, a sea struck her. How I escaped I never could tell, but I was pitched right in on deck over the poop, and much bruised, where I found a sad scene of confusion, with the captain and several of the officers in their shirts, and the men tumbling up from below as fast as they could—while, amongst other incidents, one of our passengers who occupied a small cabin under the poop, having gone to sleep with the stern port open, the sea had surged in through it with such violence as to wash him out on deck in his shirt, where he lay sprawling among the feet of the men. However, we soon got all right, and in five minutes the sloop was once more tearing through it on a wind; but the boat where I had been sleeping was smashed into staves, all that remained of her being the stem and stern-post dangling from the tackles at the ends of the davits.

At this time it was grey dawn, and we were working up inshore, without dreaming of breaking the blockade, when it fell stark calm. Presently the Spanish squadron, anchored under Punto Canoa, perceived us, when a corvette, two schooners, a cutter, and eight gunboats, got under weigh, the latter of which soon swept close to us, ranging themselves on our bows and quarters; and although we showed our colours, and made the private international signal, they continued firing at us for about an hour, without however doing any damage, as they had chosen a wary distance. At length some of the shot falling near us, the skipper cleared for action, and with his own hand fired a 32-pounder at the nearest gunboat, the crew of which bobbed as if they had seen the shot coming. This opened the eyes of the Dons, who thereupon ceased firing; and as a light breeze had now set down, they immediately made sail in pursuit of a schooner that had watched the opportunity of their being employed with us to run in under the walls, and was at this moment chased by a ship and a gunboat, who had got within gun-shot, and kept up a brisk fire on her. So soon as the others came up, all hands opened on the gallant little hooker who was forcing the blockade, and peppered away; and there she was like a hare, with a whole pack of harriers after her, sailing and sweeping in under their fire towards the doomed city. As the wind was very light, the blockading squadron now manned their boats, and some of them were coming fast up, when a rattle of musketry from the small craft sent them to the right about, and presently the chase was safely at anchor under the battery of Santa Catalina.

But the fun was to come—for by this time some of the vessels that had held her in chase had got becalmed under the batteries, which immediately opened on them cheerily; and down came a topgallant-mast here, and a topsail-yard there, and a studdingsail t'other place—and such a squealing and creaking of blocks, and rattling of the gear—while yards braced hither and thither, and toppinglifts let go, and sheets let fly, showed that the Dons were in a sad quandary; and no wonder, for we could see the shot from the long 32-pounders on the walls, falling very thick all around several of them. However, at four P.M. we had worked up alongside of the Commodore, when the old skipper gave our friend such a rating, that I don't think he will ever forget it.

On the day following our being fired at, I was sent, being a good Spaniard, along with the second-lieutenant—poor Treenail—to Morillo's headquarters. We got an order to the officer commanding the nearest post on shore, to provide us with horses; but before reaching it we had to walk, under a roasting sun, about two miles through miry roads, until we arrived at the barrier, where we found a detachment of artillery, but the commanding officer could only give us one poor broken-winded horse, and a jackass, on which we were to proceed to headquarters on the morrow; and here, under a thatched hut of the most primitive construction, consisting simply of cross sticks and palm branches, we had to spend the night, the poor fellows being as kind as their own misery would let them.

Next morning we proceeded, accompanied by a hussar through dreadful roads, where the poor creatures we bestrode sank to the belly at every flounder, until about four P.M., when we met two negroes, and found to our great distress that the soldier who was our guide and escort had led us out of our way, and that we were in very truth then travelling towards the town. We therefore hove about and returned to Palanquillo, a village that we had passed through that very morning, leaving the hussar and his horse sticking fast in a slough. We arrived about nightfall, and, as the village was almost entirely deserted, we were driven to take up our quarters in an old house that seemed formerly to have been used as a distillery. Here we found a Spanish lieutenant and several soldiers quartered, all of them suffering more or less from dysentery; and, after passing a very comfortless night on hard benches, we rose at grey dawn with our hands and faces blistered from mosquito-bites, and our hair full of wood ticks or *garapatos*. We again started on our journey to headquarters, and finally arrived at Torrecilla at two o'clock in the afternoon. Both the commander-in-chief, Morillo and Admiral Enrile, had that morning proceeded to the works at Boca Chica, so we only found El Señor Montalvo, the captain-general of the province, a little kiln-dried diminutive Spaniard. Morillo used to call him *"uno moñeco Creollo,"* but withal he was a gentleman-like man in his manners.

He received us very civilly; we delivered our despatches; and the same evening we made our bow, and, having obtained fresh horses, set out on our return, and arrived at the village of Santa Rosa at nine at night, where we slept; and next morning continuing on our journey, we got once more safely on board of the old brig at twelve o'clock at noon, in a miserable plight, not having had our clothes off for three days. As for me, I was used to roughing it, and in my humble equipment any disarrangement was not particularly discernible; but in poor Treenail, one of the nattiest fellows in the service, it was a very different matter. He had issued forth on the enterprise eased in tight blue pantaloons that fitted him like his skin, over which were drawn long well-polished Hessian boots, each with a formidable tassel at top, and his coat was buttoned close up to the chin, with a blazing swab on the right shoulder, while a laced cocked hat and dress sword completed his equipment. But alas! when we were accounted for on board of the old Torch there was a fearful dilapidation of his external man. First of all, his inexpressibles were absolutely torn into shreds by the briers and prickly bushes through which we had been travelling, and fluttered from his waistband like the stripes we see depending from an ancient Roman or Grecian coat of armour; his coat had only one skirt, and the bullion of the epaulet was reduced to a strand or two, while the tag that held the brim or flaps of the cocked hat up had given way, so that although he looked fierce enough, stem on, still, when you had a stern view, the after part hung down his back like the tail of the hat of one of Landseer's flying dustmen.

After this we experienced, with little intermission, most dreadful weather for two weeks, until at length we were nearly torn in pieces, and the captain was about abandoning his ground, and returning to Port Royal, when it came on to blow with redoubled violence. We struggled against it for twelve hours, but were finally obliged to heave-to, the sea all the while running tremendously high.

About noon on the day I speak of the weather had begun to look a little better, but the sea had if anything increased. I had just come on deck when Mr Splinter sang out—"Look out for that sea, quartermaster!—Mind your starboard helm!—Ease her, man—ease her!"

On it came, rolling as high as the foreyard, and tumbled in over the bows, green, clear, and unbroken. It filled the deep waist of the Torch in an instant, and as I rose, half smothered in the midst of a jumble of men, pigs, hencoops, and spare spars, I had nearly lost an eye by a floating boarding-pike that was lanced at me by the *jaugle* of the water. As for the boats on the booms, they had all gone to sea separately, and were bobbing at us in a squadron to leeward, the launch acting as commodore, with a crew of a dozen sheep, whose bleating as she rose on the crest of a wave came back upon us, faintly blending with the hoarse roaring of the storm, and seeming to cry, "No more mutton for you, my boys!"

At length the lee ports were forced out—the pumps promptly rigged and manned—buckets slung and at work down the hatchways; and although we had narrowly escaped being swamped, and it continued to blow hard, with a heavy sea, the men, confident in the qualities of the ship, worked with glee, shaking their feathers and quizzing each other. But anon a sudden and appalling change came over the sea and the sky, that made the stoutest amongst us quail and draw his breath thick. The firmament darkened—the horizon seemed to contract—the sea became black as ink—the wind fell to a dead calm—the teeming clouds descended and filled the murky arch of heaven with their whirling masses, until they appeared to touch our mast-heads, but there was neither lightning nor rain, not one glancing flash, not one refreshing drop—the windows of the sky had been sealed by Him, who had said to the storm, "Peace, be still."

During this death-like pause, infinitely more awful than the heaviest gale, every sound on board, the voices of the men, even the creaking of the bulkheads, was heard with startling distinctness; and the water-logged brig, having no wind to steady her, laboured so heavily in the trough of the sea that we expected her masts to go overboard every moment.

"Do you see and hear that, sir?" said Lieutenant Treenail to the captain.

We all looked eagerly forth in the direction indicated. There was a white line, in fearful contrast with the clouds and the rest of the ocean, gleaming on the extreme verge of the horizon—it grew broader—a low increasing growl was heard—a thick blinding mist came driving up astern of us, whose small drops pierced into the skin like sharp hail.

"Is it rain?"

"No, no—salt, salt."

And now the fierce Spirit of the Hurricane himself, the sea Azrael, in storm and in darkness, came thundering on with stunning violence, tearing off the snowy scalps of the tortured billows, and with tremendous and sheer force crushing down beneath his chariot-wheels their mountainous and howling ridges into one level plain of foaming water. Our chain-plates, strong fastenings, and clenched bolts drew like pliant wires, shrouds and stays were torn away like the summer gossamer, and our masts and spars, crackling before his fury like dry reeds in autumn, were blown clean out of the ship, over her bows, into the sea.

Had we shown a shred of the strongest sail in the vessel, it would have been blown out of the bolt-rope in an instant; we had, therefore, to get her before the wind, by crossing a spar on the stump of the foremast, with four men at the wheel, one watch at the pumps, and the other clearing the wreck. But our spirits were soon dashed, when the old carpenter, one of the coolest and bravest men in the ship, rose through the forehatch, pale as a ghost, with his white hairs streaming straight out in the wind. He did not speak to any of us, but clambered aft towards the capstan, to which the captain had lashed himself.

"The water is rushing in forward like a mill-stream, sir; we have either started a *butt,* or the wreck of the foremast has gone through her bows, for she is fast settling down by the head."

"Get the boatswain to *fother* a sail then, man, and try it over the leak; but don't alarm the people, Mr Kelson."

The brig was, indeed, rapidly losing her buoyancy, and, when the next heavy sea rose ahead of us, she gave a drunken sickening lurch, and pitched right into it, groaning and trembling in every plank, like a guilty and condemned thing, in the prospect of impending punishment.

"Stand by, to heave the guns overboard."

Too late, too late—Oh God, that cry!—I was stunned and drowning, a chaos of wreck was beneath me and around me and above me, and blue agonised gasping faces, and struggling arms, and colourless clutching hands, and despairing yells for help, where help was impossible; when I felt a sharp bite on the neck, and breathed again. My Newfoundland dog, Sneezer, had snatched at me, and dragged me out of the eddy of the sinking vessel.

For life, for dear life, nearly suffocated amidst the hissing spray, we reached the cutter, the dog and his helpless master.

∽∾∾

For three miserable days I had been exposed, half-naked and bareheaded, in an open boat, without water, or food, or shade. The third fierce cloudless West Indian noon was long passed, and once more the dry burning sun sank in the west, like a red-hot shield of iron. In my horrible extremity, I imprecated the wrath of Heaven on my defenceless head, and, shaking my clenched hands against the brazen sky, I called aloud on the Almighty, "Oh, let me never see him rise again!" I glared on the noble dog, as he lay dying at the bottom of the boat; madness seized me, I tore his throat with my teeth, not for food, but that I might *drink* his hot blood—it flowed, and, vampire-like, I would have gorged myself; but as he turned his dull, grey, glazing eye on me, the pulses of my heart stopped, and I fell senseless.

When my recollection returned, I was stretched on some fresh plantain-leaves, in a low smoky hut, with my faithful dog lying beside me, whining and licking my hands and face. On the rude joists that bound the rafters of the roof together, rested a light canoe with its paddles, and over against me, on the wall, hung some Indian fishing implements and a long-barrelled Spanish gun. Underneath lay a corpse, wrapped in a boat-sail, on which was clumsily written, with charcoal—"The body of John Deadeye, Esq., late Commander of his Britannic Majesty's Sloop, Torch."

There was a fire on the floor, at which Lieutenant Splinter, in his shirt and trousers, drenched, unshorn, and death-like, was roasting a joint of meat, whilst a dwarfish Indian, stark naked, sat opposite to him, squatting on his hams, more like a large bullfrog than a man, and fanning the flame with a palm leaf. In the dark corner of the hut half-a-dozen miserable sheep shrank huddled together. Through the open door I saw the stars in the deep blue heaven, and the cold beams of the newly-risen moon were dancing in a long flickering *wake* of silver light on the ever-heaving bosom of the ocean, whilst the melancholy murmur of the surf breaking on the shore came booming on the gentle night-wind. I was instantly persuaded that I had been nourished during my delirium; for the fierceness of my sufferings was assuaged, and I was comparatively strong. I anxiously inquired of the lieutenant the fate of our shipmates.

"All gone down in the old Torch; and had it not been for the launch and our four-footed friends there, I should not have been here to have told it; but raw mutton, with the wool on, is not a mess to thrive on, Tom. All that the sharks have left of the captain and five seamen came ashore last night. I have buried the poor fellows on the beach where they lay as well as I could, with an oar-blade for a shovel, and the *bronze ornament* there," pointing to the Indian, "for an assistant."

Here he looked towards the body; and the honest fellow's voice shook as he continued.

"But seeing you were alive, I thought, if you did recover, it would be gratifying to both of us, after having weathered it so long with him through gale and sunshine, to lay the kind-hearted old man's head on its everlasting pillow as decently as our forlorn condition permitted."

As the lieutenant spoke, Sneezer seemed to think his watch was up, and drew off towards the fire. Clung and famished, the poor brute could no longer resist the temptation, but, making a desperate snatch at the joint, bolted through the door with it, hotly pursued by the bullfrog.

"Drop the leg of mutton, Sneezer," roared the lieutenant,

"Drop the mutton—drop it, sir, drop it, drop it." And away raced his Majesty's officer in pursuit of the canine pirate.

After a little, he and the Indian returned, the former with the joint in his hand; and presently the dog stole into the hut after them, and patiently lay down in a corner, until the lieutenant good-humouredly threw the bone to him after our comfortless meal had been finished.

I was so weak that my shipmate considerately refrained from pressing his society on me, and we therefore all betook ourselves to rest for the night.

CHAPTER IV.

SCENES ON THE COSTA FIRME.

"Here lies a sheer hulk, poor Tom Bowline."

I WAS awakened by the low growling and short bark of the dog. The night was far spent; the tiny sparks of the fireflies that were glancing in the doorway began to grow pale; the chirping of the crickets and lizards, and the *snore* of the tree-toad, waxed fainter, and the wild cry of the tiger-cat was no longer heard. The *terral* or land-wind, which is usually strongest towards morning, moaned loudly on the hillside, and came rushing past with a melancholy *sough* through the brushwood that surrounded the hut, shaking off the heavy dew from the palm and cocoa-nut trees, like large drops of rain.

The hollow tap of the woodpecker; the clear flute-note of the *pavo del monte;* the discordant shriek of the macaw; the shrill *chirr* of the wild guinea-fowl; and the chattering of the paroquets, began to be heard from the wood. The ill-omened gallinaso was sailing and circling round the hut, and the tall flamingo was stalking on the shallows of the lagoon, the haunt of the disgusting alligator, that lay beneath, divided from the sea by a narrow mud-bank, where a group of pelicans, perched on the wreck of one of our boats, were pluming themselves before taking wing. In the east, the deep blue of the firmament, from which the lesser stars were fast fading, all but the "Eye of Morn," was warming into magnificent purple, and the amber rays of the yet unrisen sun were shooting up, streamer-like, with intervals between, through the parting clouds, as they broke away with a passing shower, that fell like a veil of silver gauze between us and the first primrose-coloured streaks of a tropical dawn.

"That's a musket-shot," said the lieutenant. The Indian crept on his belly to the door, dropped his chin on the ground, and placed his open palms behind his ears. The distant wail of a bugle was heard, then three or four dropping shots again, in rapid succession. Mr Splinter stooped to go forth, but the Indian caught him by the leg, uttering the single word "Españoles."

On the instant, a young Indian woman with a shrieking infant in her arms, rushed to the door. There was a blue gunshot wound in her neck, from which two or three large black clotting gouts of blood were trickling. Her long black hair was streaming in coarse braids, and her features were pinched and sharpened, as if in the agony of death. She glanced wildly behind, and gasped out, *"Escapa, Oreeque, escapa, para mi soi muerto ya."* Another shot, and the miserable creature convulsively clasped her child, whose small shrill cry I often fancy I hear to this hour blending with its mother's death-shriek, and, falling backwards, rolled over the brow of the hill out of sight. The ball had pierced the heart of the parent through the body of her offspring. By this time a party of Spanish soldiers had surrounded the hut, one of whom, kneeling before the low door, pointed his musket into it. The Indian, who had seen his wife and child thus cruelly shot down before his face, now fired his rifle, and the man fell dead. *"Siga mi Querida Bondia—maldito."* Then springing to his feet, and stretching himself to his full height, with his arms extended towards heaven, while a strong shiver shook him like an ague fit, he yelled forth the last words he ever uttered, *"Venga la suerte, ya soi listo,"* and resumed his squatting position on the ground.

Half-a-dozen musket-balls were now fired at random through the wattles of the hut, while the lieutenant, who spoke Spanish well, sang out lustily that we were English officers who had been shipwrecked.

"Mentira," growled the officer of the party, *"Piratas son ustedes."* "Pirates leagued with Indian bravoes; fire the hut, soldiers, and burn the scoundrels!"

There was no time to be lost; Mr Splinter made a vigorous attempt to get out, in which I seconded him with all the strength that remained to me but they beat us back again with the butts of their muskets.

"Where are your commissions, your uniforms, if you be British officers?"— We had neither, and our fate appeared inevitable.

The doorway was filled with brushwood, fire was set to the hut, and we heard the crackling of the palm thatch, while thick stifling wreaths of white smoke burst in upon us through the roof.

"Lend a hand, Tom, now or never, and kick up the dark man there;" but he sat still as a statue. We laid our shoulders to the end wall, and heaved at it with all our might; when we were nearly at the last gasp it gave way, and we rushed headlong into the middle of the party, followed by Sneezer with his shaggy coat, that was full of clots of tar, blazing like a torch. He unceremoniously seized *"par le queue,"* the soldier who had throttled me, setting fire to the skirts of his coat, and blowing up his cartouche-box. I believe, under Providence, that the ludicrousness of this attack saved us from being bayoneted on the spot. It gave time for Mr Splinter to recover his breath, when, being a powerful man, he shook off the two soldiers who had seized him, and dashed into the burning hut again. I thought he was mad, especially when I saw him return with his clothes and hair on fire, dragging out the body of the captain. He unfolded the sail it was wrapped in, and pointing to the remains of the naval uniform in which the mutilated and putrifying corpse was dressed, he said sternly to the officer, "We are in your power, and you may murder us if you will; but that was my captain four days ago, and you see at least *he* was a British officer—satisfy yourself." The person he addressed, a handsome young Spaniard, with a clear olive complexion, oval face, small brown mustaches, and large black eyes, shuddered at the horrible spectacle, but did as he was requested.

When he saw the crown and anchor, and his Majesty's cipher on the appointments of the dead officer, he became convinced of our quality, and changed his tone *"Es verdad, son de la marina Englesa.* But, gentlemen, were there not three persons—in the hut?"

There were indeed—the flames had consumed the dry roof and walls with incredible rapidity, which by this time had fallen in, but Oreeque was nowhere to be seen. I thought I saw something move in the midst of the fire, but it might have been fancy. Again the white ashes heaved, and a half-consumed hand and arm were thrust through the smouldering mass, then a human head, with the scalp burnt from the skull, and the flesh from the scalp and cheekbones; the trunk next appeared, the bleeding ribs laid bare, and the miserable Indian, with his limbs like scorched rafters, stood upright before us, like a demon in the midst of the fire. He made no attempt to escape, but, reeling to and fro like a drunken man, fell headlong, raising clouds of smoke and a shower of sparks in his fall. Alas! poor Oreeque, the newly-risen sun was now shining on your ashes, and on the dead bodies of the ill-starred Bondia and her child, whose bones, ere his setting, the birds of the air and beasts of the forest will leave as white and fleshless as your own.

The officer, who belonged to the army investing Carthagena, now treated us with great civility; he heard our story, and desired his men to assist us in burying the remains of our late commander.

We remained all day on the same part of the coast, but towards evening the party fell back on the outpost to which they belonged. After travelling an hour or so we emerged from a dry river-course, in which the night had overtaken us, and came suddenly on a small plateau, where the post was established on the promontory of *"Punto Canoa."* There may be braver soldiers at a charge— although that I doubt, if they be properly led—but none more picturesque in a *bivouac* than the Spanish. A gigantic wild cotton-tree, to which our largest English oaks would have been but as dwarfs, rose on one side, and overshadowed the whole level space. The bright beams of the full moon glanced among the topmost leaves, and tipped the higher branches with silver, contrasting strangely with the scene below, where a large watchfire cast a strong red glare on the surrounding objects, throwing up dense volumes of smoke, which eddied in dun wreaths—amongst the foliage, and hung in the still night-air like a canopy, about ten feet from the ground, leaving the space beneath comparatively clear.

A temporary guard-house, with a rude verandah of bamboos and palm-leaves, had been built between two of the immense spurs of the mighty tree, that shot out many yards from the parent stem like wooden buttresses, whilst overhead there was a sort of stage, made of planks laid across the lower boughs, supporting a quantity of provisions covered with tarpaulins. The sentries in the background, with their glancing arms, were seen pacing on their watch; some of the guard were asleep on wooden benches, and on the platform amongst the branches, where a little baboon-looking old man, in the dress of a drummer, had perched himself, and sat playing a Biscayan air on a sort of bagpipe; others were gathered round the fire cooking their food or cleaning their arms. It shone brightly on the long line of Spanish transports that were moored below, *stem on* to the beach, and on the white sails of the armed craft that were still hovering under weigh in the offing, which, as the night wore on, stole in, one after another, like phantoms of the ocean, and, letting go their anchors with a splash, and a hollow rattle of the cable, remained still and silent like the rest. Farther off, it fell in a crimson stream on the surface of the sheltered bay, struggling with the light of the gentle moon, and tinging with blood the small waves that twinkled in her silver wake, across which a guard boat would now and then glide, like a fairy thing, the arms of the men flashing back the red light.

Beyond the influence of the hot smoky glare, the glorious planet reassumed her sway in the midst of her attendant stars, and the relieved eye wandered forth into the lovely night, where the noiseless sheet-lightning was glancing, and ever and anon lighting up for an instant some fantastic shape in the fleecy clouds, like prodigies forerunning the destruction of the stronghold over which they impended; while beneath, the lofty ridge of the convent-crowned Popa, the citadel of San Felipé bristling with cannon, the white batteries and many towers of the fated city of Carthagena, and the Spanish blockading squadron at anchor before it, slept in the moonlight.

We were civilly received by the captain, who apologised for the discomfort under which we must pass the night. He gave us the best he had, and that was bad enough, both of food and wine, before showing us into the hut, where we found a rough deal coffin lying on the very bench that was to be our bed. This he ordered away with all the coolness in the world. "It was *only* one of his people who had died that morning of *vomito,* or yellow fever."

"Comfortable country this," quoth Splinter, "and a pleasant morning we have had of it, Tom!"

Next morning we proceeded towards the Spanish headquarters, provided with horses through the kindness of the captain of the outpost, and preceded by a guide on an ass. He was a *moreno,* or man of colour, who, in place of bestriding his beast, gathered his limbs under him, and sat cross-legged on it like a tailor; so that when you saw the two "end on," the effect was laughable enough, the flank and tail of the ass appearing to constitute the lower part of the man, as if he had been a sort of composite animal like the ancient satyr. The road traversed a low swampy country, from which the rank moisture arose in a hot palpable mist, and crossed several shallow lagoons, from two to six feet deep, of tepid, muddy, brackish water, some of them half a mile broad, and swarming with wild waterfowl. On these occasions, our friend the Satyr was signalled to make sail ahead on his donkey to pilot us; and as the water deepened, he would betake himself to swimming in its wake, holding on by the tail and shouting, *"Cuidado Burrico, Cuidado que no te ahogas."*

While passing through the largest of these we noticed several calabashes about pistol-shot on our right; and as we fancied one of them bobbed now and then, it struck me they might be Indian fishing-floats. To satisfy my curiosity I hauled my wind, and, leaving the track we were on, swam my horse towards the group. The two first that I lifted had nothing attached to them, but proved to be mere empty gourds floating before the wind; but when I tried to seize the largest it eluded my grasp in a most incomprehensible manner, and slid away astern of me with a curious hollow gabbling sort of noise, whereupon my palfrey snorted and reared, and nearly capsized me over 'his bows. What a noble fish, thought I, as I tacked in chase, but my Bucephalus refused to face it. I therefore bore up to join my companions again; but in requital of the disappointment, smashed the gourd in passing with the stick I held in my hand, when, to my unutterable surprise, and amidst shouts of laughter from our *moreno,* the head and shoulders of an Indian, with a quantity of sedges tied round his neck, and buoyed up by half-a-dozen dead teal fastened by the legs to his girdle, started up before me. *"Ave Maria, purisima!* you have broken my head, señor." But as the vegetable helmet had saved his skull, of itself possibly none of the softest, a small piece of money spliced the feud between us; and as he fitted his pate with another calabash, preparatory to resuming his cruise, he joined in our merriment, although from a different cause. "What *can* these English simpletons see so very comical in a poor Indian catching wild-ducks?"

Shortly after, we entered a forest of magnificent trees, whose sombre shade, on first passing from the intolerable glare of the sun, seemed absolute darkness. The branches were alive with innumerable tropical birds and insects, and were laced together by a thick tracery of withes along which a guana would occasionally dart, coming nearest of all the reptiles I had seen to the shape of the fabled dragon.

But how different from the clean stems and beautiful green sward of our English woods! Here, you were confined to a quagmire by impervious underwood of prickly pear, penguin, and speargrass; and when we rode under the drooping branches of the trees, that the leaves might brush away the halo of musquitoes, flying ants, and other winged plagues that buzzed about our temples, we found, to our dismay, that we had made bad worse by the introduction of a whole colony of *garapatos,* or wood-ticks, into our eyebrows and hair. At length, for the second time, so far as I was concerned, we reached the headquarters at Torrecilla, and were well received by the Spanish commander-in-chief, a tall, good-looking, soldierlike man, whose personal qualities had an excellent foil in the captain-general of the province, an old friend of mine, as already mentioned, and who certainly looked full as like a dancing-master, or, at the best, *perruquier en general* to the staff, as a viceroy.

General Morillo, however, had a great share of Sancho Panza shrewdness, and I will add kindness, about him. We were drenched and miserable when we arrived, yet he might have turned us over, naturally enough, to the care of his staff. No such thing; the first thing he did was to walk both of us behind a canvass screen that shut off one end of the large barn-like room, where a long table was laid for dinner. This was his sleeping apartment; and drawing out of a leather bag two suits of uniform, he rigged us almost with his own hands. Presently a point of war was sounded by half-a-dozen trumpeters, and Splinter and I made our appearance, each in the dress of a Spanish general. The party consisted of Morillo's personal staff, the captain-general, the *enquisidor-general,* and several colonels and majors of different regiments. In all, twenty people sat down to dinner; among whom were several young Spanish noblemen, some of whom I had met on my former visit, who, having served in the Peninsular war under the great Duke, made their advances with great cordiality. Strange enough—Splinter and I were the only parties present in uniform; all the others, priests and soldiers, were clothed in gingham coats and white trousers.

The besieging force at this time was composed of about five thousand Spaniards, as fine troops as I ever saw, and three thousand Creoles, under the command of that desperate fellow Morales. I was not long in recognising an old friend of mine in the person of Captain Bayer, an aide-de-camp of Morillo, amongst the company. He was very kind and attentive, and rather startled me by speaking very tolerable English *now,* from a kindly motive I make no question, whereas, when I had known him before in Kingston, he professed to speak nothing but Spanish or French. He was a German by birth, and lived to rise to the rank of colonel in the Spanish army, where he subsequently greatly distinguished himself, but he at length fell in some obscure skirmish in New Granada; and my old ally Morillo, Count of Carthagena, is now living in penury, an exile in Paris.

After being, as related, furnished with food and raiment, we retired to our *quatres*, a most primitive sort of couch, being a simple wooden frame, with a piece of canvass stretched over it. However, if we had no mattresses, we had none of the disagreeables often incidental to them, and fatigue proved a good opiate, for we slept soundly until the drums and trumpets of the troops, getting under arms, awoke us at daylight. The army was under weigh to occupy Carthagena, which had fallen through famine and we had no choice but to accompany it.

I knew nothing of the misery of a siege but by description; the reality even to me, case-hardened as I was by my own recent sufferings, was dreadful. We entered by the gate of the *raval*, or suburb. There was not a living thing to be seen in the street; the houses had been pulled down, that the fire of the place might not be obstructed in the event of a lodgment in the outwork. We passed on, the military music echoing mournfully amongst the ruined walls, to the main gate, or *Puerto de Tiera,* which was also open, and the drawbridge lowered. Under the archway we saw a delicate female, worn to the bone, and weak as an infant, gathering garbage of the most loathsome description, the possession of which had been successfully disputed by a carrion crow. A little farther on, the bodies of an old man and two small children were putrefying in the sun; while beside them lay a miserable, wasted, dying negro, vainly endeavouring to keel) at a distance with a palm branch a number of the same obscene birds that were already devouring the carcass of one of the infants; before two hours the faithful servant and those he attempted to defend were equally the prey of the disgusting gallinaso. The houses, as we proceeded, appeared entirely deserted, except where a solitary spectre-like inhabitant appeared at a balcony, and feebly exclaimed, "Viva los Españoles! Viva Fernando Septimo!" We saw no domestic animal whatsoever, not even a cat or a dog; but I will not dwell on these horrible details any longer.

One morning, shortly after our arrival, as we strolled beyond the land gate, we came to a place where four *banquillos* (a sort of short bench or stool, with an upright post at one end firmly fixed into the ground) were placed opposite a dead wall. They were painted black, and we were not left long in suspense as to their use; for solemn music, and the roll of muffled drums in the distance, were fearful indications of what we were to witness.

First came an entire regiment of Spanish infantry, which, filing off, formed three sides of a square—the wall near which the *banquillos* were placed forming the fourth; then eight priests, and as many choristers, chanting the service for the dying; next came several mounted officers of the staff, and four firing-parties of twelve men each. Three Spanish-American prisoners followed, dressed in white, with crucifixes in their hands, each supported, more dead than alive, by two priests; but when the fourth victim appeared, we could neither look at nor think of anything else.

On inquiry we found he was an Englishman, of the name of S——; English, that is, in all except the place of his birth, for his whole education had been English, as were his parents and all his family; but it came out, accidentally I believe, on his trial, that he had been *born* at Buenos Ayres, and having joined the patriots, this brought treason home to him, which he was now led forth to expiate. Whilst his fellow-sufferers appeared crushed down to the very earth, under their intense agony, so that they had to be supported as they tottered towards the place of execution, he stepped firmly and manfully out, and seemed impatient, when at any time, from the crowding in front, the procession was obliged to halt. At length they reached the fatal spot, and his three companions in misery being placed astride on the *banquillos,* their arms were twisted round the upright posts, and fastened to them with cords, *their backs being towards the soldiers.* Mr S—— walked firmly up to the vacant bench, knelt down, and covering his face with his hands, rested his head on the edge of it. For a brief space he seemed to be engaged in prayer, during which he sobbed audibly, but soon recovering himself, he rose, and folding his arms across his breast, sat down slowly and deliberately on the *banquillo,* facing the firing-party with an unshrinking eye.

He was now told that he must turn his back and submit to be tied like the others. He resisted this, but on force being attempted to be used, he sprung to his feet, and stretching out his hand, while a dark red flush passed transiently across his pale face, be exclaimed in a loud voice, "Thus, thus, and not otherwise, you *may* butcher me, but I am an Englishman and no traitor, nor will I die the death of one." Moved by his gallantry, the soldiers withdrew, and left him standing. At this time the sun was intensely hot—it was high noon—and the monk who attended Mr S—— held an umbrella over his head; but the preparations being completed, he kissed him on both cheeks, while the hot tears trickled down his own, and was stepping back, when the unhappy man said to him, with the most perfect composure, *"Todavia padre, todavia, mucho me gusta la sombra."* But the time had arrived, the kind-hearted monk was obliged to retire. The signal was given, the musketry rattled, and they were as clods of the valley. "Truly," quoth old Splinter, *"a man does sometimes become a horse by being born in a stable."*

Some time after this we were allowed to go to the village of Turbaco, a few miles distant from the city, for change of air. On the third morning after our arrival, about the dawning, I was suddenly awakened by a shower of dust on my face, and a violent shaking of the bed, accompanied by a low grumbling unearthly noise, which seemed to pass immediately under where I lay. Were I to liken it to anything I had ever experienced before, it would be to the lumbering and tremor of a large waggon in a tempestuous night, heard and felt through the thin walls of a London house. Like—yet how fearfully different!

In a few seconds the motion ceased, and the noise gradually died away in hollow echoes in the distance—whereupon ensued such a crowing of cocks, cackling of geese, barking of dogs, lowing of kine, neighing of horses, and shouting of men, women, and children amongst the negro and coloured domestics, as baffles all description; whilst the various white inmates of the house (the rooms, for air and coolness, being without ceiling, and simply divided by partitions run up about ten feet high) were, one and all, calling to their servants and each other, in accents which did not by any means evince great composure. In a moment this hubbub again sank into the deepest silence—man, and the beasts of the field and the fowls of the air, became mute with breathless awe at the impending tremendous manifestation of the power of that Almighty Being in whose hands the hills are as a very little thing—for the appalling voice of the earthquake was once more heard growling afar off, like distant thunder mingling with the rushing of a mighty wind, waxing louder and louder as it approached, and upheaving the sure and firm-set earth into long undulations, as if its surface had been the rolling swell of the fathomless ocean. The house rocked, pictures of saints fell from the walls, tables and chairs were overturned, the window-frames were forced out of their embrasures and broken in pieces; beams and rafters groaned and screamed, crushing the tiles of the roof into ten thousand fragments. In several places the ground split open into chasms a fathom wide, with an explosion like a cannon-shot; the very foundation of the house seemed to be sinking under us; and whilst men and women rushed like maniacs naked into the fields, with a yell as if the Day of Judgment had arrived, and the whole brute creation, in an agony of fear, made the most desperate attempts to break forth from their enclosures into the open air, the end wall of my apartment was shaken down, and, falling outwards with a deafening crash, disclosed, in the dull, grey, mysterious twilight of morning, the huge gnarled trees that overshadowed the building, bending and groaning amidst clouds of dust, as if they had been tormented by a tempest, although the air was calm and motionless as death.

CHAPTER V.

THE PICCAROON.

"Ours the wild life in tumult still to range."—The Corsair.

SOME TIME after this we once more returned to Carthagena, to be at hand should any opportunity occur for Jamaica, and were lounging about one forenoon on the fortifications, looking with sickening hearts out to seaward, when a voice struck up the following negro ditty close to us:—

> "Fader was a Corramantee,
>> Moder was a Mingo,
> Black picaniny buccra wantee,
>> So dem sell a me, Peter, by jingo.
>> Jiggery, jiggery, jiggery."

"Well sung, Massa Bungo!" exclaimed Mr Splinter; "where do you hail from, my hearty?"

"Hillo! Bungo, indeed! free and easy dat, anyhow. Who you yousef, eh?"

"Why, Peter," continued the lieutenant, "don't you know me?"

"Cannot say dat I do," rejoined the negro, very gravely, without lifting his head, as he sat mending his jacket in one of the embrasures near the water-gate of the arsenal—"Have not de honour of your acquaintance, sir."

He then resumed his scream, for song it could not be called:—

> "Mammy Sally's daughter
>> Lose him shoe in an old canoe

> Dat lay half full of water,
> And den she knew not what to do.
> Jiggery, jig—"

"Confound your jiggery, jiggery, sir! But I know you well enough, my man; and you can scarcely have forgotten Lieutenant Splinter of the Torch, one would think?"

However, it was clear that the poor fellow really had not known us; for the name so startled him, that, in his hurry to unlace his legs from under him, as he sat tailor-fashion, he fairly capsized out of his perch, and toppled down on his nose—a feature, fortunately, so flattened by the hand of nature, that I question if it could have been rendered more obtuse had he fallen out of the maintop on a timber-head, or a marine officer's.

"Eh!—no—yes, him sure enough; and who is de picaniny hofficer—Oh! I see, Massa Tom Cringle? Garamighty, gentlemen, where have you drop from? Where is de old Torch? Many a time hab I, Peter Mangrove, pilot to Him Britannic Magesty squadron, taken de old brig in and through amongst de keys at Port Royal!"

"Ay, and how often did you scour her copper against the coral reefs, Peter?"

His Majesty's pilot gave a knowing look, and laid his hand on his breast— "No more of dat if you love me, massa."

"Well, well, it don't signify now, my boy; she will never give you that trouble again—foundered—all hands lost, Peter, but the two you see before you."

"Werry sorry, Massa Plinter, werry sorry—What! de black cook's-mate and all?—But misfortune can't be help. Stop till I put up my needle, and I will take a turn wid you." Here he drew himself up with a great deal of absurd gravity. "Proper dat British hofficer in distress should assist one anoder—we shall consult togeder.—How can I serve you?"

"Why, Peter, if you could help us to a passage to Port Royal, it would be serving us most essentially. When we used to be lying there a week seldom passed without one of the squadron arriving from this; but here have we been for more than a month without a single pennant belonging to the station having looked in: our money is running short, and if we are to hold on in Carthagena for another six weeks, we shall not have a shot left in the locker—not a copper to tinkle on a tombstone."

The negro looked steadfastly at us, then carefully around. There was no one near.

"You see, Massa Plinter, I am desirable to serve you, for one little reason of my own; but, beside dat, it is good for me at present to make some friend wid de hofficer of de squadron, being as how dat I am absent widout leave."

"Oh, I perceive—a large R against your name in the master-attendant's books, eh?"

"You have hit it, sir, werry close; besides, I long mosh to return to my poor wife, Nancy Cator, dat I leave, wagabone dat I is, just about to be confine."

I could not resist putting in my oar.

"I saw Nancy just before we sailed, Peter—fine child that; not quite so black as you, though."

"Oh, massa," said Snowball, grinning, and showing his white teeth, "you know I am soch a terrible black fellow—But you are a leetle out at present, massa—I meant, about to be confine in de workhouse for stealing de admiral's Muscovy ducks;" and he laughed loud and long.—"However, if you will promise dat you will stand my friends, I will put you in de way of getting a shove across to de east end of Jamaica; and I will go wid you too, for company."

"Thank you," rejoined Mr Splinter; "but how do you mean to manage this? There is no Kingston trader here at present, and you don't mean to make a start of it in an open boat, do you?"

"No, sir, I don't; but in de first place—as you are a gentleman, will you try and get me off when we get to Jamaica? Secondly, will you promise dat you will not seek to know more of de vessel you may go in, nor of her crew, than dey are willing to tell you, provided you are landed safe?"

"Why, Peter, I scarcely think you would deceive us, for you know I saved your bacon in that awkward affair, when through drunkenness you plumped the Torch ashore, so—"

"Forget dat, sir—forget dat! Never shall poor black pilot forget how you saved him from being seized up, when de gratings, boatswain's mates, and all, were ready at de gangway—never shall poor black rascal forget dat."

"Indeed, I do not think you would wittingly betray us into trouble, Peter; and as I guess you mean one of the forced traders, we will venture in her, rather than kick about here any longer, and pay a moderate sum for our passage."

"Den wait here five minute"—and so saying, he slipped down through the embrasure into a canoe that lay beneath, and in a trice we saw him jump on board of a long low nondescript kind of craft that lay moored within pistol-shot of the walls.

She was a large shallow vessel, coppered to the bends, of great breadth of beam, with bright sides, like an American, so painted as to give her a clumsy mercantile sheer externally, but there were many things that belied this to a nautical eye: her copper, for instance, was bright as burnished gold on her very sharp bows and beautiful run; and we could see, from the bastion where we stood, that her decks were flush and level. She had no cannon mounted that were visible; but we distinguished grooves on her well-scrubbed decks, as from the recent traversing of carronade slides, while the bolts and rings in her high and solid bulwarks shone clear and bright in the ardent noontide. There was a tarpauling stretched over a quantity of rubbish, old sails, old junk, and hen-coops, rather ostentatiously piled up forward, which we conjectured might conceal a long gun.

She was a very taught-rigged hermaphrodite, or brig forward and schooner aft. Her foremast and bowsprit were immensely strong and heavy, and her mainmast was so long and tapering, that the wonder was how the few shrouds and stays about it could support it; it was the handsomest stick we had ever seen. Her upper spars were on the same scale, tapering away through topmast, topgallant-mast, royal and skysail-masts, until they fined away into slender wands. The sails, that were loose to dry, were old, and patched, and evidently displayed to cloak the character of the vessel by an ostentatious show of their unserviceable condition; but her rigging was beautifully fitted, every rope lying in the chafe of another being carefully served with hide. There were several large bushy-whiskered fellows lounging about the deck, with their hair gath-ered into dirty net-bags, like the fishermen of Barcelona; many had red silk sashes round their waists, through which were stuck their long knives, in shark-skin sheaths. Their numbers were not so great as to excite suspicion; but a certain daring, reckless manner, would at once have distinguished them, independently of anything else, from the quiet hard-worked, red-shirted, merchant seaman.

"That chap is not much to be trusted," said the lieutenant; "his bunting would make a few jackets for Joseph, I take it." But we had little time to be crit-ical, before our friend Peter came paddling back with another blackamoor in the stern, of as ungainly an exterior as could well be imagined. He was a very large man, whose weight every now and then, as they breasted the short sea, cocked up the snout of the canoe with Peter Mangrove in it, as if he had been a cork, leaving him to flourish his paddle in the air, like the weather-wheel of a steam-boat in a sea-way. The new-comer was strong and broad-shouldered, with long muscular arms, and a chest like Hercules; but his legs and thighs were, for his bulk, remarkably puny and misshapen. A thick fell of black wool, in close tufts, as if his face had been stuck full of cloves, covered his chin and upper-lip; and his hair, if hair it could be called, was twisted into a hundred short plaits, that bristled out, and gave his head, when he took his hat off, the appearance of a porcupine. There was a large sabre-cut across his nose and down his cheek, and he wore two immense gold earrings. His dress consisted of short cotton drawers, that did not reach within two inches of his knee, leaving his thin cucumber shanks (on which the small bullet-like calf appeared to have been stuck before, through mistake, in place of abaft) naked to the shoe; a check shirt, and an enormously large Panama hat, made of a sort of cane, split small, and worn shovel-fashion. Notwithstanding, he made his bow by no means ungracefully, and offered his services in choice Spanish, but spoke English as soon as he heard who we were.

"Pray, sir, are you the master of that vessel?" said the lieutenant.

"No, sir, I am the mate, and I learn you are desirous of a passage to Jamaica." This was spoken with a broad Scotch accent.

"Yes, we are," said I, in very great astonishment, "but we will not sail with the devil; and who ever saw a negro Scotchman before, the spirit of Nicol Jarvie conjured into a blackamoor's skin!"

The fellow laughed. "I am black, as you see; so were my father and mother before me." And he looked at me, as much as to say, I have read the book you quote from. "But I was born in the good town of Port-Glasgow notwithstanding, and many a voyage I have made as cabin-boy and cook in the good ship the Peggy Bogle, with worthy old Jock Hunter; but that matters not. I was told you wanted to go to Jamaica; I daresay our captain will take you for a moderate passage-money. But here he comes to speak for himself.—Captain Vanderbosh, here are two shipwrecked British officers, who wish to be put on shore on the east end of Jamaica; will you take them, and what will you charge for their passage?"

The man he spoke to was nearly as tall as himself; he was a sunburnt, angular, raw-boned, iron-visaged veteran, with a nose in shape and colour like the bowl of his own pipe, but not at all, according to the received idea, like a Dutchman. His dress was quizzical enough—white-trousers, a long-flapped embroidered waistcoat that might have belonged to a Spanish grandee,—with an old-fashioned French-cut coat, showing the frayed marks where the lace had been stripped off, voluminous in the skirts, but very tight in the sleeves, which were so short as to leave his large bony paws, and six inches of his arm above the wrist, exposed; altogether, it fitted him like a purser's shirt on a handspike.

"Vy, for von hondred thaler I will land dem safe in Mancheoneal Bay; but how shall ve manage, Villiamson? De cabin vas point yesterday."

The Scotch negro nodded. "Never mind; I daresay the smell of the paint won't signify to the gentlemen."

The bargain was ratified; we agreed to pay the stipulated sum, and that same evening, having dropped down with the last of the sea-breeze, we set sail from Bocca Chica, and began working up under the lee of the headland of Punto Canoa. When off the San Domingo Gate, we burned a blue-light, which was immediately answered by another in-shore of us. In the glare we could perceive two boats, full of men. Any one who has ever played at snapdragon, can imagine the unearthly appearance of objects when seen by this species of fire-work. In the present instance it was held aloft on a boat-hook, and cast a strong spectral light on the band of lawless ruffians, who were so crowded together that they entirely filled the boats, no part of which could be seen. It seemed as if two clusters of fiends, suddenly vomited forth from hell, were floating on the surface of the midnight sea, in the midst of brimstone flames. In a few moments our crew was strengthened by about forty as ugly Christians as I ever set eyes on. They were of all ages, countries, complexions, and tongues, and looked as if they had been kidnapped by a pressgang as they had knocked off from the Tower of Babel. From the moment they came on board, Captain Vanderbosh was shorn of all his glory, and sank into the petty officer while, to our amazement, the Scottish negro took the command, evincing great coolness, energy, and skill. He ordered the schooner to be wore as soon as we had shipped the men, and laid her head off the land, then set all hands to shift the old suit of sails, and to bend new ones.

"Why did you not shift your canvass before we started?" said I to the Dutch captain, or mate, or whatever he might be.

"Vy vont you be content to take a quiet passage and hax no question?" was the uncivil rejoinder, which I felt inclined to resent, until I remembered that we were in the hands of the Philistines, where a quarrel would have been worse than useless. I was gulping down the insult as well as I could, when the black captain came aft, and, with the air of an equal, invited us into the cabin to take a glass of grog. We had scarcely sat down before we heard a noise like the swaying up of guns, or some other heavy articles, from the hold.

I caught Mr Splinter's eye—he nodded, but said nothing. In half an hour afterwards, when we went on deck, we saw by the light of the moon twelve eighteen-pound carronades mounted, six of a side, with their accompaniments of rammers and sponges, water-buckets, boxes of round, grape, and canister, and tubs of wadding, while the coamings of the hatchways were thickly studded with round-shot. The tarpauling and lumber forward had disappeared, and there lay long Tom, ready levelled, grinning on his pivot.

The ropes were all coiled away, and laid down in regular man-of-war fashion; while an ugly gruff beast of a Spanish mulatto, apparently the officer of the watch, walked the weatherside of the quarterdeck in the true pendulum style. Look-outs were placed aft, and at the gangways and bows, who every now and then passed the word to keep a bright look-out, while the rest of the watch were stretched silent, but evidently broad awake, under the lee of the boat. We noticed that each man had his cutlass buckled round his waist—that the boarding-pikes had been cut loose from the main boom, round which they had been stopped, and that about thirty muskets were ranged along a fixed rack that ran athwart ships near the main hatchway.

By the time we had reconnoitred thus far the night became overcast, and a thick bank of clouds began to rise to windward; some heavy drops of rain fell, and the thunder grumbled at a distance. The black veil crept gradually on, until it shrouded the whole firmament, and left us in as dark a night as ever poor devils were out in. By-and-by a narrow streak of bright moonlight appeared under the lower edge of the bank, defining the dark outlines of the tumbling multitudinous billows on the horizon as distinctly as if they had been pasteboard waves in a theatre.

"Is that a sail to windward in the clear, think you?" said Mr Splinter to me in a whisper. At this moment it lightened vividly. "I am sure it is," continued he— "I could see her white canvass glance just now."

I looked steadily, and at last caught the small dark speck against the bright background, rising and falling on the swell of the sea like a feather.

As we stood on, she was seen more distinctly, but, to all appearance, nobody was aware of her proximity. We were mistaken in this, however, for the captain suddenly jumped on a gun, and gave his orders with a fiery energy that startled us.

"Leroux!" A small French boy was at his side in a moment. Forward, and call all hands to shorten sail; but, *doucement,* you land-crab!—Man the fore clew-garnets.—Hands by the topgallant clew-lines—jib down-haul—rise tacks and sheets—peak and throat haulyards—let go—clew up—settle away the main-gaff there!"

In almost as short a space as I have taken to write it, every inch of canvass was close furled—every light, except the one in the binnacle, and that was cautiously masked, carefully extinguished—a hundred and twenty men at quarters, and the ship under bare poles. The head-yards were then squared, and we bore up before the wind. The stratagem proved successful; the strange sail could be seen through the night-glasses cracking on close to the wind, evidently under the impression that we had tacked.

"Dere she goes, chasing de Gobel," said the Dutchman.

She now burned a blue-light, by which we saw she was a heavy cutter—without doubt our old fellow-cruiser the Spark. The Dutchman had come to the same conclusion.

"My eye, captain, no use to dodge from her; it is only dat footy little King's cutter on de Jamaica station."

"It is her, true enough," answered Williamson; "and she is from Santa Martha with a freight of specie, I know. I will try a brush with her, by—"

Splinter struck in before he could finish his irreverent exclamation. "If your conjecture be true, I know the craft—a heavy vessel of her class, and you may depend on hard knocks, and small profit if you do take her; while if she takes you—"

"I'll be hanged if she does"—and he grinned at the conceit—then setting his teeth hard, "or rather, I will blow the schooner up with my own hand before I strike; better that than have one's bones bleached in chains on a key at Port Royal. But you see you cannot control us, gentlemen; so get down into the cable-tier, and take Peter Mangrove with you. I would not willingly see those come to harm who have trusted me."

However, there was no shot flying as yet, we therefore stayed on deck. All sail was once more made; the carronades were cast loose on both sides, and double-shotted, the long-gun slewed round, the tack of the fore-and-aft foresail hauled up, and we kept by the wind, and stood after the cutter, whose white canvass we could still see through the gloom like a snow-wreath.

As soon as she saw us, she tacked and stood towards us, and came bowling along gallantly, with the water roaring and flashing at her bows. As the vessels neared each other they both shortened sail, and finding that we could not weather her, we steered close under her lee.

As we crossed on opposite tacks, her commander hailed, "Ho, the brigantine, ahoy!"

"Hillo!" sung out Blackie, as he backed his maintop-sail.

"What schooner is that?"

"The Spanish schooner Caridad."

"Whence, and whither bound!"

"Carthagena to Porto Rico."

"Heave-to, and send your boat on board."

"We have none that will swim, sir."

"Very well, bring-to, and I will send mine."

"Call away the boarders," said our captain, in a low stern tone; "let them crouch out of sight behind the boat."

The cutter wore, and hove-to under our lee quarter, within pistol-shot; we heard the rattle of the ropes running through the davit-blocks, and the splash of the jolly-boat touching the water, then the measured stroke of the oars, as they glanced like silver in the sparkling sea, and a voice calling out," Give way, my lads."

The character of the vessel we were on board of was now evident; and the bitter reflection that we were chained to the stake on board of a pirate, on the eve of a fierce contest with one of our own cruisers, was aggravated by the consideration, that the cutter had fallen into a snare by which a whole boat's crew would be sacrificed before a shot was fired.

I watched my opportunity as she pulled up alongside, and called out, leaning well over the nettings, "Get back to your ship!—treachery! get back to your ship!"

The little French serpent was at my side with the speed of thought, his long clear knife glancing in one hand, while the fingers of the other were laid on his lips. He could not have said more plainly, "Hold your tongue, or I'll cut your throat;" but Sneezer now startled him by rushing between us, and giving a short angry growl.

The officer in the boat had heard me imperfectly; he rose up—"I won't go back, my good man, until I see what you are made of;" and as he spoke he sprang on board, but the instant he got over the bulwarks, he was caught by two strong hands, gagged, and thrown bodily down the main-hatchway.

"Heave," cried a voice, "and with a will!" and four cold 32-pound shot were hove at once into the boat alongside, which, crashing through her bottom, swamped her in a moment, precipitating the miserable crew into the boiling sea. Their shrieks still ring in my ears as they clung to the oars and some loose planks of the boat.

"Bring up the officer, and take out the gag," said Williamson.

Poor Walcolm, who had been an old messmate of mine, was now dragged to the gangway half-naked, his face bleeding, and heavily ironed, when the black-amoor, clapping a pistol to his head, bid him, as he feared instant death, hail "that the boat had swamped under the counter, and to send another." The poor fellow, who appeared stunned and confused, did so, but without seeming to know what he said.

"Good God," said Mr Splinter, "don't you mean to pick up the boat's crew!"

The blood curdled to my heart, as the black savage answered in a voice of thunder, "Let them drown and be d——d! Fill, and stand on!

But the clouds by this time broke away, and the mild moon shone clear and bright once more upon this scene of most atrocious villany. By her light the cutter's people could see that there was no one struggling in the water now, and that the people must either have been saved, or were past all earthly aid; but the infamous deception was not entirely at an end.

The captain of the cutter, seeing we were making sail, did the same, and after having shot ahead of us, hailed once more.

"Mr Walcolm, why don't you run to leeward, and heave-to, sir?"

"Answer him instantly, and hail again for another boat," said the sable fiend, and cocked his pistol.

The click went to my heart. The young midshipman turned his pale mild countenance, laced with his blood, upwards towards the moon and stars, as one who had looked his last look on earth; the large tears were flowing down his cheeks, and mingling with the crimson streaks, and a flood of silver light fell on the fine features of the poor boy, as he said firmly, "Never." The miscreant fired, and he fell dead.

"Up with the helm, and wear across her stern." The order was obeyed. "Fire!" The whole broadside was poured in, and we could hear the shot rattle and tear along the cutter's deck, and the shrieks and groans of the wounded, while the white splinters glanced away in all directions.

We now ranged alongside, and close action commenced, and never do I expect to see such an infernal scene again. Up to this moment there had been neither confusion nor noise on board the pirate—all had been coolness and order; but when the yards locked the crew broke loose from all control—they ceased to be men—they were demons, for they threw their own dead and wounded, as they were mown down like grass by the cutter's grape, indiscriminately down the hatchways to get clear of them. They had stripped themselves almost naked; and although they fought with the most desperate courage, yelling and cursing, each in his own tongue, most hideously, yet their very numbers, pent up in a small vessel, were against them. At length, amidst the fire and smoke and hellish uproar, we could see that the deck had become a very shambles; and unless they soon carried the cutter by boarding, it was clear that the coolness and discipline of my own glorious service must prevail, even against such fearful odds, the superior size of the vessel, greater number of guns, and heavier metal. The pirates seemed aware of this themselves, for they now made a desperate attempt forward to carry their antagonist by boarding, led on by the black captain. Just at this moment the cutter's main-boom fell across the schooner's deck, close to where we were sheltering ourselves from the shot the best way we could; and while the rush forward was being made, by a sudden impulse Splinter and I, followed by Peter and the dog (who with wonderful sagacity, seeing the uselessness of resistance, had cowered quietly by my side during the whole row), scrambled along it as the cutter's people were repelling the attack on her bow, and all four of us, in our haste, jumped down on the poor Irishman at the wheel.

"Murder, fire, rape, and robbery!—it is capsized, stove in, sunk, burned, and destroyed I am! Captain, captain, we are carried aft here—Och, hubbaboo for Patrick Donnally!"

There was no time to be lost; if any of the crew came aft we were dead men, so we tumbled down through the cabin skylight, men and beast, the hatch having been knocked off by a shot, and stowed ourselves away in the side berths. The noise on deck soon ceased—the cannon were again plied—gradually the fire slackened, and we could hear that the pirate had scraped clear and escaped. Some time after this the lieutenant commanding the cutter came down. Poor Mr Douglas! both Splinter and I knew him well. He sat down and covered face with his hands, while the blood oozed down between fingers. He had received a cutlass wound on the head in the attack. His right arm was bound up with his neckcloth, and he was very pale.

"Steward, bring me a light.—Ask the doctor how many are killed and wounded; and—do you hear?—tell him to come to me when he is done forward, but not a moment sooner. To have been so mauled and duped by a buccanneer; and my poor boat's crew—"

Splinter groaned. He started—but at this moment the man returned again. "Thirteen killed, your honour, and fifteen wounded; scarcely one of us untouched." The poor fellow's own skull was bound round with a bloody cloth.

"God help me! God help me! but they have died the death of men. Who knows what death the poor fellows in the boat have died!"—Here he was cut short by a tremendous scuffle on the ladder, down which an old quartermaster was trundled neck and crop into the cabin. "How now, Jones?"

"Please your honour," said the man, as soon as he had gathered himself up, and had time to turn his quid and smooth down his hair; but again the uproar was renewed, and Donnally was lugged in, scrambling and struggling between two seamen—"this here Irish chap, your honour, has lost his wits, if so be he ever had any, your honour. He has gone mad through fright."

"Fright be d——d!" roared Donnally; "no man ever frightened me; but as his honour was skewering them bloody thieves forward, I was boarded and carried aft by the devil, your honour—pooped by Beelzebub, by ———," and he rapped his fist on the table until everything on it danced again. "There were four of them, yeer honour—a black one and two blue ones—and a piebald one, with four legs and a bushy tail—each with two horns on his head, for all the world like those on Father M'Cleary's red cow—no, she was humbled—it is Father Clannachan's, I mane—no, not his neither, for his was the parish bull; fait, I don't know what I mane, except that they had all horns on their heads, and vomited fire, and had each of them a tail at his stern, twisting and twining like a conger eel, with a blue light at the end on't."

"And dat's a lie, if ever dere was one," exclaimed Peter Mangrove, jumping from the 'berth. "Look at me, you Irish tief, and tell me if I have a blue light or a conger eel at my stern!"

This was too much for poor Donnally. He yelled out, "You'll believe your own eyes now, yeer honour, when you see one o' dem bodily before you! Let me go— let me go!" and, rushing up the ladder, he would, in all probability, have ended his earthly career in the salt sea, had his bullet-head not encountered the broadest part of the purser, who was in the act of descending, with such violence, that he shot him out of the companion several feet above the deck, as if he had been discharged from a culverin; but the recoil sent poor Donnally, stunned and senseless, to the bottom of the ladder. There was no standing all this; we laughed outright, and made ourselves known to Mr Douglas, who received us cordially, and in a week we were landed at Port Royal.

CHAPTER VI.

THE CRUISE OF THE SPARK.

"Ours are the tears, though few, sincerely shed."

—The Corsair.

THE ONLY other midshipman on board the cutter beside young Walcolm, whose miserable death we had witnessed, was a slight delicate little fellow, about fourteen years old, of the name of Duncan; he was the smallest boy of his age I ever saw, and had been badly hurt in repelling the attack of the pirate. His wound was a lacerated puncture in the left shoulder from a boarding-pike, but it appeared to be healing, kindly, and for some days we thought he was doing well. However, about five o'clock in the afternoon on which we made Jamaica, the surgeon accosted Mr Douglas as we were walking the deck together.

"I fear little Duncan is going to slip through my fingers after all, sir."

"No!—I thought he had been better."

"So he was till about noon, when a twitching of the muscles came on, which I fear betokens lockjaw; he wavers, too, now and then—a bad sign of itself where there is a fretting wound."

We went below, where, notwithstanding the wind-sail that was let down close to where his hammock was slung, the heat of the small vessel was suffocating. The large coarse tallow candle in the purser's lantern, that hung beside his shoulder, around which the loathsome cockroaches fluttered like moths in a summer evening, filled the between-decks with a rancid oily smell, and with smoke as from a torch, while it ran down and melted like fat before a fire. It cast a dull sickly gleam on the pale face of the brown-haired girlish-looking lad, as he lay in his narrow hammock. When we entered, an old quartermaster was rubbing his legs, which were jerking about like the limbs of a galvanised frog, while two of the boys held his arms, also violently convulsed. The poor little fellow was crying and sobbing most piteously, but made a strong effort to compose himself and "be a man" when he saw us.

"This is so good of you, Mr Cringle!—you will take charge of my letter to my sister, I know you will? I say, Anson," to the quartermaster, "do lift me up a little 'till I try and finish it.—It will be a sore heart to poor Sarah; she has no mother now, nor father, and aunt is not over kind;" and again he wept bitterly.

"Confound this jumping hand, it won't keep steady, all I can do.—I say, doctor, I shan't die this time, shall I?"

"I hope not, my fine little fellow."

"I don't think I shall; I shall live to be a man yet, in spite of that bloody buccaneer's pike—I know I shall." God help me, the death-rattle was already in his throat, and the flame was flickering in the socket; even as he spoke the muscles of his neck stiffened to such a degree that I thought he was choked, but the violence of the convulsion quickly subsided. "I am done for, doctor!"—he could no longer open his mouth, but spoke through his clenched teeth—"I feel it now!—God Almighty receive my soul, and protect my poor sister!" The archenemy was indeed advancing to the final struggle, for he now gave a sudden and sharp cry, and stretched out his legs and arms, which instantly became as rigid as marble, and in his agony he turned his face to the side I stood on, but he was no longer sensible. "Sister," he said with difficulty—"don't let them throw me overboard; there are sharks here."

"Land on the lee-bow!" sang out the man at the mast-head. The common life sound would not have moved any of us in the routine of duty, but, bursting in under such circumstances, it made us all start as if it had been something unusual; the dying midshipman heard it, and said, calmly, "Land!—I will never see it.—But how blue all your lips look.—It is cold, piercing cold, and dark, dark." Something seemed to rise in his throat, his features sharpened still more, and he tried to gasp, but his clenched teeth prevented him—he was gone.

I went on deck with a heavy heart, and, on looking in the direction indicated, I beheld the towering Blue Mountain peak rising high above the horizon, even at the distance of fifty miles, with its outline clear and distinct against the splendid western sky, now gloriously illumined by the light of the set sun. We stood on under easy sail for the night, and next morning, when the day broke, we were off the east end of the magnificent island of Jamaica. The stupendous peak now appeared to rise close aboard of us, with a large solitary star sparkling on his forehead, and reared his forest-crowned summit high into the cold blue sky, impending over us in frowning magnificence, while the long dark range of the Blue Mountains, with their outlines hard and clear in the grey light, sloped away on each side of him as if they had been the Giant's shoulders. Great masses of white mist hung on their sides about half-way down, but all the valleys and coasts as yet slept in the darkness. We could see that the land-wind was blowing strong inshore, from the darker colour of the water, and the speed with which the coasters, only distinguishable by their white sails, slid along; while astern of us, out at sea, yet within a cable's length, for we had scarcely shot beyond its influence, the prevailing trade-wind blew a smart breeze coming up strong to a defined line, beyond which and between it and the influence of the land-wind, there was a belt of dull lead-coloured sea, about half a mile broad, with a long heavy ground-swell rolling, but smooth as glass, and without even a ripple on the surface, in the midst of which we presently lay dead becalmed.

The heavy dew was shaken in large drops out of the wet flapping sails, against which the reef-points pattered like hail as the vessel rolled. The decks were wet and slippery, and our jackets saturated with moisture; but we enjoyed the luxury of cold to a degree that made the sea-water when dashed about the decks, as they were being holystoned, appear absolutely warm. Presently all nature awoke in its freshness so suddenly that it looked like a change of scene in a theatre. The sun, as yet set to us, rose to the huge peak, and glanced like lightning on his summit, making it gleam like a ruby; presently the clouds on his shaggy ribs rolled upwards, enveloping his head and shoulders, and were replaced by the thin blue mists which ascended from the valleys, forming a fleecy canopy, beneath which appeared hill and dale, woods and cultivated lands, where all had been undistinguishable a minute before, and gushing streams burst from the mountain sides like gouts of froth, marking their course in the level grounds by the vapours they sent up. Then breeze-mill towers burst into light, and cattle-mills, with their cone-shaped roofs, and overseers' houses, and water-mills, with the white spray falling from the wheels, and sugar-works, with long pennants of white smoke streaming from the boiling-house chimneys seaward in the morning wind. Immediately after, gangs of negroes were seen at work; loaded waggons, with enormous teams of fourteen to twenty oxen dragging them, rolled along the roads; long strings of mules, loaded with canes, were threading the fields; drogging vessels were seen to shove out from every cove; the morning song of the black fisherman was heard, while their tiny canoes, like black specks, started up suddenly on all sides of us, as if they had floated from the bottom of the sea; and the smiling scene burst at once, and as if by magic, on us, in all its coolness and beauty, under the cheering influence of the rapidly rising, sun. We fired a gun, and made the signal for a pilot; upon which a canoe, with three negroes in it, shoved off from a small schooner lying-to about a mile to leeward. They were soon alongside, when one of the three jumped on board. This was the pilot, a slave, as I knew; and I remember the time when, in my innocence, I would have expected to see something very squalid and miserable; but there was nothing of the kind, for I never in my life saw a more spruce salt-water dandy, in a small way. He was well dressed, according to a seaman's notion—clean white trousers, check shirt with white lapels, neatly fastened at the throat with a black ribbon, smart straw hat; and altogether he carried an appearance of comfort—I was going to write independence—about him, that I was by no means prepared for. He moved about with a swaggering roll, grinning and laughing with the seamen.

"I say, blackie," said Mr Douglas.

"John Lodge, massa, if you please, massa; blackie is not politeful, sir;" whereupon he showed his white teeth again.

"Well, well, John Lodge, you are running us in too closely;" and the remark seemed seasonable enough to a stranger, for the rocks on the bold shore were now within half pistol-shot,

"Mind your eye," shouted old Anson. "You will have us ashore, you black rascal!"

"You, sir, what water have you here?" sang out Mr Splinter.

"Salt water, massa," rapped out Lodge, fairly dumfounded by such a volley of questions. "You hab six fadom good here, massa;" but suspecting he had gone too far—"I take de Tonnant, big ship as him is, close to dat reef, sir, you might have jump ashore, so you need not frighten for your leetle dish of a hooker; beside, massa, my character is at 'take, you know," then another grin and bow.

There was no use in being angry with the poor fellow, so he was allowed to have his own way until we anchored in the evening at Port Royal.

The morning after we arrived, I went ashore with a boat's crew to perform the magnanimous operation of cutting brooms; we pulled for Green Bay, under the guns of the Twelve Apostles—a heavy battery of twelve cannon, where there is a tombstone with an inscription, setting forth that the party over whom it was erected had been actually swallowed up in the great earthquake that destroyed the opposite town, but subsequently disgorged again—being, perchance, an unseemly morsel.

We approached the beach—"Oars"—the men laid them in.

"What sort of nuts be them, Peter Coamings?" said the coxswain to a new hand who had been lately impressed, and was now standing at the bow ready to fend off.

Peter broke off one of the branches from the bush nearest him.

"Smite my timbers, do the trees here bear shell-fish?"

The tide in the Gulf of Mexico does not ebb and flow above two feet, except at the springs, and the ends of the drooping branches of the mangrove-trees, that here cover the shore, are clustered, within the wash of the water, with a small well-flavoured oyster. The first thing the seamen did, when they got ashore, was to fasten an oakum tail to the rump of one of the most lubberly of the cutter's crew; they then gave him ten yards' law, when they started in chase, shouting amongst the bushes, and switching each other like the veriest schoolboys. I had walked some distance along the beach, pelting the amphibious little creatures, half crab, half lobster, called soldiers, which kept shouldering their large claws, and running out and in their little burrows, as the small ripple twinkled on the sand in the rising sun, when two men-of-war's boats, each with three officers in the stern, suddenly pulled round a little promontory that intercepted my view ahead. Being somewhat out of the line of my duty, so far from my boat, I squatted amongst the brushwood, thinking they would pass by; but, as the devil would have it, they pulled directly for the place where I was ensconced, beached their boats, and jumped on shore. "Here's a mess," thought I.

I soon made out that one of the officers was Captain Pinkem of the Flash, and that the parties saluted each other with that stern courtesy which augured no good.

"So, so, my masters, not enough of fighting on the coast of America, but you must have a little private defacing of God's image amongst yourselves?"

Pinkem spoke first. "Mr Clinch" (I now knew he addressed the first-lieutenant of the flag-ship),—"Mr Clinch, it is not too late to prevent unpleasant consequences; I ask you again, at the eleventh hour, will you make an apology?"

He seemed hurried and fidgety in his manner; which rather surprised me, as I knew he was a seasoned hand in these matters, and it contrasted unfavourably with the calm bearing of his antagonist, who by this time had thrown his hat on the ground, and stood with one foot on the handkerchief that marked his position, the distance, twelve paces, having already been measured. By the by, his position was deucedly near in a line with the grey stone behind which I lay perdu; nevertheless, the risk I ran did not prevent me noticing that he was very pale, and had much the air of a brave man come to die in a bad cause. He looked upwards for a second or two, and then answered, slowly and distinctly, "Captain Pinkem, I now repeat what I said before; this rencontre is none of my seeking. You accuse me of having spoken slightingly of you seven years ago, when I was a mere boy. You have the evidence of a gallant officer that

I did so; therefore I may not gainsay it; but of uttering the words imputed to me, I declare, upon my honour, I have no recollection." He paused.

"That won't do, my fine fellow," said Pinkem.

"You are unreasonable," rejoined Clinch, in the same measured tone, "to expect further *amende* for uttering words which I have no conviction of having spoken; yet to any other officer in the service I would not hesitate to make a more direct apology, but you know your credit as a pistol-shot renders this impossible."

"Sorry for it, Mr Clinch—sorry for it."

Here the pistols were handed to the principals by their respective seconds. In their attitudes, the proficient and the novice were strikingly contrasted (by this time I had crept round so as to have a view of both parties, or rather, if the truth must be told, to be out of the line of fire). Pinkem stood with his side accurately turned towards his antagonist, so as to present the smallest possible surface; his head was, as it struck me, painfully slewed round, with his eye looking steadily at Clinch, over his right shoulder, whilst his arm was brought down close to his thigh, with the cock of the pistol turned outwards, so that his weapon must have covered his opponent by the simple raising of his arm below the elbow. Clinch, on the other hand, stood fronting him, with the whole breadth of his chest; holding his weapon awkwardly across his body, with both hands. Pinkem appeared unwilling to take him at such advantage, for, although violent and headstrong, and but too frequently the slave of his passions, he had some noble traits in his character.

"Turn your feather-edge to me, Mr Clinch; take a fair chance, man."

The lieutenant bowed, and I thought would have spoken, but he was checked by "the *fear* of being thought to fear;" however, he took the advice, and in an instant the word was given—"Are you both ready?"

"Yes."

"Then fire!"

Clinch fired without deliberation. I saw him, for my eyes were fixed on him, expecting to see him fall. He stood firm, however, which was more than I did, as at the instant a piece of the bullion of an epaulet, at first taken for a pellet of baser metal, struck me sharply on the nose, and shook my equanimity confoundedly; at length I turned to look at Pinkem, and there he stood with his arm raised, and pistol levelled, but he had not fired. He stood thus whilst I might have counted ten, like a finger-post, then, dropping his hand, his weapon went off, but without aim, the bullet striking the sand near his feet, and down he came headlong to the ground. He fell with his face turned towards me, and I never shall forget the horrible expression of it. His healthy complexion had given place to a deadly blue, the eyes were wide open and straining in their sockets, the upper lip was drawn up, showing his teeth in a most frightful grin, the blood gushed from his mouth as if impelled by the strokes of a force-pump, while his hands griped and dug into the sand.

Before the sun set he was a dead man.

"A neat morning's work, gentlemen," thought I.

The two surgeons came up, opened his dress, felt his pulse, and shook their heads; the boats' crews grouped around them—he was lifted into his gig, the word was given to shove off, and—I returned to my broom-cutters.

When we got on board, the gunner, who had the watch, was taking his fisherman's walk on the starboard side of the quarterdeck, and kept looking steadily at the land, as if to avoid seeing poor little Duncan's coffin, that lay on a grating near the gangway. The crew, assisted by thirty men from the flag-ship, were employed in twenty different ways, repairing damages, and were bustling about, laughing, joking, and singing, with small regard to the melancholy object before their eyes, when Mr Douglas put his head up the ladder—"Now, Jackson, if you please."

The old fellow's countenance fell as if his heart was wrung by the order he had to give.

"Aloft there! lie out, you Perkins, and reeve a whip on the starboard yardarm to lower Mr—" The rest stuck in his throat, but, as if ashamed of his soft-heartedness, he throw as much gruffness as he could into his voice as he sang out, "Beat to quarters there!—knock off, men!"

The roll of the drum stayed the confusion and noise of the people at work in an instant, who immediately ranged themselves, in their clean frocks and trousers, on each side of the quarterdeck. At a given signal, the white deal coffin, wrapped in its befitting pall—the meteor flag of England—swung high above the hammock nettings, between us and the bright blue sky, to the long clear note of the boatswain's whistle, which soon ending in a short cherup, told that it now rested on the thwarts of the boat alongside. We pulled ashore, and it was a sight perchance to move a woman, to see the poor little fellow's hat and bit of a dirk lying on his coffin, whilst the body was carried by four ship boys, the eldest scarcely fourteen. I noticed the tears stand in Anson's eyes as the coffin was lowered into the grave—the boy had been wounded close to him,—

and when we heard the hollow rattle of the earth on the coffin—an unusual sound to a sailor—he shuddered.

"Yes, Master Cringle," he said, in a whisper, "he was as kind-hearted and as brave a lad as ever trode on shoe leather. None of the larkings of the men in the clear moonlight nights ever reached the cabin through him; nor was he the boy to rouse the watch from under the lee of the boats in bad weather, to curry with the lieutenant, while he knew the look-outs were as bright as beagles; and where was the man in our watch that wanted 'baccy while Mr Duncan had a shiner left?" The poor fellow drew the back of his horny hand across his eyes, and grumbled out as he turned away, "And here am I, Bill Anson, such a swab as to be ashamed of being sorry for him."

We were now turned over into the receiving-ship, the old Shark, and fortunately there were captains enough in port to try us for the loss of the Torch, so we got over our court-martial speedily, and the very day I got back my dirk the packet brought me out a lieutenant's commission. Being now my own master for a season, I determined to visit some relations I had in the island, to whom I had never yet been introduced; so I shook hands with old Splinter, packed my kit, and went to the wharf to charter a wherry to carry me up to Kingston. The moment my object was perceived by the black boatmen, I was surrounded by a mob of them, pulling and hauling each other, and shouting forth the various qualifications of their boats, with such vehemence, that I was nearly deafened.

"Massa, no see Pam be Civil, sail like a witch, tack like a dolphin?"

"Don't believe him, massa; Ballahoo is de boat dat can beat him."

"Big lie dat, as I am a gentleman!" roared a ragged black vagabond.

"Come in de Monkey, massa; no flying fis can beat she."

"Don't boder de gentleman," yelled a fourth—"massa love de Stamp-and-go—no so, massa?" as he saw me make a step in the direction of his boat. "Oh yes, so get out of de way, you black rascals"—the fellow was black as a sloe himself—"make room for man-of-war buccra; him leetle just now, but will be admiral one day."

So saying, the fellow who had thus appropriated me, without more ado, levelled his head like a battering-ram and began to batter in breach all who stood in his way. He first ran a tilt against Pam be Civil, and shot him like a rocket into the sea; the Monkey fared no better; the Ballahoo had to swim for it; and having thus opened a way by main force, I at length got safely moored in the stern-sheets; but just as we were shoving off, Mr Callaloo, the clergyman of Port

Royal, a tall yellow personage, begged for a passage, and was accordingly taken on board. As it was high-water, my boatman chose the five-foot channel, as the boat channel near to Gallows Point is called, by which a long stretch would be saved, and we were cracking on cheerily, my mind full of my recent promotion, when scur, scur, scur, we stuck fast on the bank. Our black boatmen, being little encumbered with clothes, jumped overboard in a covey like so many wild-ducks, shouting as they dropped into the water, "We must all get out—we must all get out;" whereupon Mr Callaloo, a sort of Dominie Sampson in his way, promptly leaped overboard up to his waist in the water. The negroes were thunderstruck.

"Massa Parson Callaloo, you mad surely, you mad!"

"Children, I am not mad, but obedient; you said we must all get out!"

"To be sure, massa, and you see we all *did* get out."

"And did you not see that I got out too?" rejoined the parson, still in the water, and somewhat nettled.

"Oh, lud, massa! we no mean you—we meant poor nigger, not white man parson."

"You said *all*, children, and thereupon I leaped," pronouncing, the last word in two syllables—"be more correct in your grammar next time."

The worthy but eccentric old chap then scrambled on board again, amidst the suppressed laughter of the boatmen, and kept his seat, wet clothes and all, until we reached Kingston.

CHAPTER VII.

SCENES IN JAMAICA.

"Excellent—why this is the best fooling when all is done."

Twelfth Night

I CONFESS that I did not promise myself much pleasure from my cruise ashore. Somehow or other I had made up my mind to believe that in Jamaica, putting aside the magnificence and natural beauty of the face of the country, there was little to interest me, I had pictured to myself the slaves—a miserable squalid, half-fed, ill-clothed, over-worked race—and their masters, and the white inhabitants generally, as an unwholesome-looking crew of saffron-faced tyrants, who wore straw hats with umbrella brims, wide trousers, and calico jackets, living on pepper pot and land crabs, and drinking sangaree and smoking cigars the whole day—in a word, that all that Bryan Edwards and others had written regarding the civilisation of the West Indies was a fable. But I was agreeably undeceived; for although I did meet with some extraordinary characters, and witnessed not a few rum scenes, yet, on the whole, I gratefully bear witness to the great hospitality of the inhabitants, both in the towns and in the country. In Kingston the society was extremely good, as good, I can freely affirm, as I ever met with in any provincial town anywhere; and there prevailed a warmth of heart, and a kindliness, both in the males and females of those families to which I had the good fortune to be introduced, that I never experienced *out* of Jamaica.

At the period I am describing, the island was in the hey-day of its prosperity, and the harbour of Kingston was full of shipping. I had never before seen so superb a mercantile haven; it is completely land-locked, and the whole navy of England might ride in it commodiously.

On the sea-face it is almost impregnable, for it would be little short of a miracle for an invading squadron to wind its way through the labyrinth of shoals and reefs lying off the mouth of it, amongst which the channels are so narrow and intricate that at three or four points the sinking of a sand barge would effectually block up all ingress; but, independently of this, the entrance at Port Royal is defended by very strong works—the guns ranging the whole way across—while, a little farther on, the attacking ships would be exposed to a cross fire from the heavy metal of the Apostles' Battery; and, even assuming all these obstacles to be overcome, and the passage into the harbour forced, before they could pass the narrows, to get up to the anchorage at Kingston, they would be blown out of the water by a raking fire from sixty pieces of large cannon on Fort Augusta, which is so situated that they would have to turn to windward for at least half-an-hour, in a strait which, at the widest, would not allow them to reach beyond musket-shot of the walls. Fortunately, as yet Mr Canning had not called his New World into existence, and the whole of the trade of Terra Firma, from Porto Cavello down to Chagres, the greater part of the trade of the islands of Cuba and San Domingo, and even that of Lima and San Blas, and the other ports of the Pacific, carried on across the Isthmus of Darien, centred in Kingston, the usual supplies through Cadiz being stopped by the advance of the French in the Peninsula. The result of this princely traffic, more magnificent than that of Tyre, was a stream of gold and silver flowing into the Bank of England to the extent of three millions of pounds sterling annually, in return for British manufactures; thus supplying the sinews of war to the government at home, and, besides the advantage of so large a mart, employing an immense amount of British tonnage, and many thousand seamen; and in numberless ways opening up new outlets to British enterprise and capital. Alas! alas! where is all this now? The echo of the empty stores might answer "where!"

On arriving at Kingston, my first object was to seek out Mr * * *, the admiral's agent, and one of the most extensive merchants in the place, in order to deliver some letters to him, and get his advice as to my future proceedings. Mr Callaloo undertook to be my pilot, striding along abeam of me, and leaving in his wake two serpentine dottings on the pavement from the droppings of water from his voluminous coat-skirts, which had been thoroughly soaked by his recent ducking.

Everything appeared to be thriving, and we passed along, the hot sandy streets were crowded with drays conveying goods from the wharfs to the stores, and from the stores to the Spanish Posadas. The merchants of the place, active sharp-looking men, were soon grouped under the piazzas in earnest conversation with their Spanish customers, or perched on top of the bales and boxes just landed, waiting to hook the gingham-coated, Moorish-looking Dons, as they came along with cigars in their mouths, and a train of negro servants following them with fire-buckets on their heads, filled with *pesos fuertes.* The appearance of the town itself was novel and pleasing; the houses, chiefly of two storeys, looked as if they had been built of cards, most of them being surrounded with piazzas from ten to fourteen feet wide, gaily painted green and white, and formed by the roofs projecting beyond the brick walls or shells of the houses. On the ground-floor these piazzas are open, and in the lower part of the town, where the houses are built contiguous to each other, they form a covered way, affording a most grateful shelter from the sun, on each side of the streets, which last are unpaved, and more like dry river-courses than thoroughfares in a Christian town. On the floor above, the balconies are shut in with a sort of movable blinds, called "jealousies," like large-bladed Venetian blinds, fixed in frames, with here and there a glazed sash to admit light in bad weather when the blinds are closed. In the upper part of the town the effect is very beautiful, every house standing detached from its neighbour, in its little garden filled with vines, fruit-trees, stately palms, and cocoa-nut-trees, with a court of negro houses and offices behind, and a patriarchal-looking draw-well in the centre, generally overshadowed by a magnificent wild tamarind. When I arrived at the great merchant's place of business, I was shown to a lofty cool room, with a range of desks along the walls where a dozen clerks were quill-driving. In the centre sat my man, a small, sallow, yet perfectly gentleman-like personage.

"Dat is massa," quoth my black usher.

I accordingly walked up to him, and presented my letter. He never lifted his head from his paper, which I had half a mind to resent; but at the moment there was a bustle in the piazza, and a group of naval officers, amongst whom was the admiral, came in. My silent friend was now alert enough, and profuse of his bows and smiles.

"Who have we here? Who is that boy, L——?" said the admiral to his secretary.

"Young Cringle, sir; the only one except Mr Splinter saved from the Torch; he was first on the Admiralty list t' other day."

"What, the lad Willoughby spoke so well of? "

"The same, sir; he got his promotion by last packet."

"I know, I know. I say, Mr Cringle, you are appointed to the Firebrand, do you know that?" I did not know it, and began to fear my cruise on shore was all up. "But I don't look for her from Havanna for a month; so leave your address with L——, that you may get the order to join when she does come."

It appeared that I had seen the worst of the agent, for he gave me a very kind invitation to stay some days with him, and drove me home in his ketureen—a sort of sedan chair, with the front and sides knocked out, and mounted on a gig body.

Before dinner we were lounging about the piazza, and looking down into the street, when a negro funeral came past, preceded by a squad of drunken black vagabonds, singing and playing on gumbies, or African drums, made out of pieces of hollow trees, about six feet long, with skins braced over them, each carried by one man, while another beats it with his open hands. The coffin was borne along on the heads of two negroes—a negro carries everything on his head, from a bale of goods to a wineglass or tea-cup. It is a practice for the bearers, when they come near the house of any one against whom the deceased was supposed to have had a grudge, to pretend that the coffin will not pass by, and in the present case, when they came opposite to where we stood, they began to wheel round and round, and to stagger under their load, while the choristers shouted at the top of their lungs.

"We beg you, shipmate, for come along—do, broder, come away;" then another reel. "What, you no wantee go in a hole, eh? You hab grudge 'gainst somebody lif here, eh?"—another devil of a lurch—"Massa * * *'s housekeeper, eh? Ah, it must be!"—A tremendous stagger—"Oh, Massa * * *, dollar for drink; something to hold play" negro wake, "in Spring-path," the negro burying-ground; "Bediacko say him won't pass 'less you give it." And here they began to spin round more violently than before; but at the instant a drove of bullocks coming along, they got entangled amongst them, and down went body and bearers and all, the coffin bursting in the fall, and the dead corpse, with its white grave-clothes and black face, rolling over and over in the sand amongst the feet of the cattle. It was immediately caught up, however, bundled into the coffin again, and away they staggered, drumming and singing as loudly as before.

The party at dinner was a large one; everything in good style, wines superb, turtle, &c., magnificent, and the company exceedingly companionable. A Mr Francis Fyall (a great planting attorney—that is, an agent for a number of proprietors of estates who preferred living in England, and paying a commission to him for managing in Jamaica, to facing the climate themselves), to whom I had an introduction, rather posed me, by asking me during dinner, if I would take anything in the *long way* with him, which he explained by saying he would be glad to take a glass of small beer with me. This, after a deluge of Madeira, Champagne, and all manner of light wines, was rather trying; but I kept my countenance as well as I could. One thing, I remember, struck me as remarkable; just as we were rising to go to the drawing-room a cloud of winged ants burst in upon us through the open windows, and, had it not been for the glass-shades, would have extinguished the candles; but when they had once settled on the table they deliberately wriggled themselves free of their wings, as one would cast off a greatcoat, and crept away in their simple and more humble capacity of creeping things.

Next day I went to wait on my relation, Mrs Palma. I had had a confoundedly hot walk through the burning sandy streets, and was nearly blinded by the reflection from them, as I ascended the front stairs. There are no carpets in the houses in Jamaica; but the floors, which are often of mahogany, are beautifully polished, and shine like a well-kept dinner table. They are, of course, very slippery, and require wary walking till one gets accustomed to them. The rooms are made exceedingly dark during the heat of the day, according to the prevailing practice in all ardent climates. A black footman, very handsomely dressed, all to his bare legs (I thought at first he had black silk stockings on), preceded me, and when he reached the drawing-room door, asked my name. I told him, "Mr Cringle,"—whereupon he sang out, to my dismay—"Massa Captain Ringtail to wait pan Misses."

This put me out a *leetle*—especially as I heard some one say—"Captain who?—what a very odd name!"

But I had no time for reflection, as I had not blundered three steps out of the glare of the piazza, into the palpable obscure of the darkened drawing-room, black as night from the contrast, when I capsized headlong over an ottoman in the middle of the apartment, and floundered right into the centre of a group of young ladies, and one or two lapdogs, by whom it was conjointly occupied. Trying to recover myself, I slipped on the glass-like floor, and came down stern foremost; and being now regularly at the slack end, for I could not well get lower, I sat still, scratching my caput in the midst of a gay company of morning visitors, enjoying the gratifying consciousness that I was distinctly visible to them, although my dazzled optics could as yet distinguish nothing. To add to my pleasurable sensations, I now perceived, from the coldness of the floor, that in my downfall the catastrophe of my unmentionables had been grievously rent, but I had nothing for it but sitting patiently still amidst the suppressed laughter of the company, until I became accustomed to the twilight, and they, like bright stars, began to dawn on my bewildered senses in all their loveliness, and prodigiously handsome women some of them were, for the Creoles, so far as figure is concerned, are generally perfect, while beautiful features are not wanting, and my travel had reconciled me to the absence of the rose from their cheeks. My eldest cousin Mary (where is there a name like Mary?) now approached; she and I were old friends, and many a junketing we used to have in my father's house during the holidays, when she was a boarding-school girl in England. My hardihood and self-possession returned, under the double gratification of seeing her, and the certainty that my blushes (for my cheeks were glowing like hot iron) could not have been observed in the subdued green light that pervaded the room.

"Well, Tom, since you are no longer dazzled, and see us all now, you had better get up, hadn't you—you see mamma is waiting there to embrace you?"

"Why, I think myself I had better; but when I broached-to so suddenly, I split my lower canvass, Mary, and I cannot budge until your mother lends me a petticoat."

"A what? you are crazy, Tom—"

"Not a whit, not a whit, why I have split my—ahem. This is speaking plain, an't it?"

Away tripped the sylph-like girl, and in a twinkling re-appeared with the desired garment, which in a convulsion of laughter she slipped over my head as

I sat on the floor; and having fastened it properly round my waist, I rose and paid my respects to my warm-hearted relations. But that petticoat—it could not have been the old woman's, there could have been no such virtue in an old woman's petticoat; no, no, it must either have been a charmed garment, or—or—Mary's own; for from that hour I was a lost man, and the devoted slave of her large black eyes, and high pale forehead. "Oh, murder—you speak of the sun dazzling; what is it to the lustre of that same eye of yours, Mary!"

In the evening I escorted the ladies to a ball (by the way, a West India ball-room being a perfect lantern, open to the four winds of heaven, is cooler, notwithstanding the climate, than a ball-room anywhere else), and a very gay affair it turned out to be, although I had more trouble in getting admittance than I bargained for, and was witness to as comical a row (considering the very frivolous origin of it, and the quality of the parties engaged in it) as ever took place even in that peppery country, where, I verily believe, the temper of the people, generous though it be in the main, is hotter than the climate, and that, God knows! is sudoriferous enough. I was walking through the entrance saloon with my fair cousin on my arm, stepping out like a hero to the opening crash of a fine military band, towards the entrance of the splendid ball-room filled with elegant company, brilliantly lighted up and ornamented with the most rare and beautiful shrubs and flowers, which no European conservatory could have furnished forth, and arched overhead with palm branches and a profusion of evergreens, while the polished floor, like one vast mirror, reflected the fine forms of the pale but lovely black-eyed and black-haired West Indian dames, glancing amidst the more sombre dresses of their partners, while the whole group was relieved by being here and there spangled with a rich naval or military uniform. As we approached, a constable put his staff across the doorway.

"Beg pardon, sir, but you are not in full dress."

Now this was the first night whereon I had sported my lieutenant's uniform, and with my gold swab on my shoulder, the sparkling bullion glancing in the corner of my eye at the very moment, my dress-sword by my side, gold buckles in my shoes, and spotless white trousers, I had, in my innocence, considered myself a deuced killing fellow, and felt proportionably mortified at this address.

"No one can be admitted in trousers, sir," said the man.

"Shiver my timbers!" I could not help the exclamation, the transactions of the morning crowding on my recollection, "shiver my timbers! is my fate in this strange country to be for ever irrevocably bound up in a pair of breeches?"

My cousin pinched my arm. "Hush, Tom; go home and get mamma's petticoat."

The man was peremptory; and as there was no use in getting into a squabble about such a trifle, I handed my partner over to the care of a gentleman of the party, who was fortunately accoutred according to rule, and, stepping to my quarters, I equipped myself in a pair of tight nether integuments, and returned to the ball-room. By this time there was the devil to pay; the entrance saloon was crowded with military and naval men, high in oath, and headed by no less a person than a general officer, and a one-armed man, one of the chief civil officers in the place, and who had been a sailor in his youth. I was just in time to see the advance of the combined column to the door of the ballroom, through which they drove the picket of constables like chaff, and then halted. The one-armed functionary, a most powerful and very handsome man, now detached himself from the phalanx, and strode up to the advanced-guard of stewards clustered in front of the ladies, who had shrunk together into a corner of the room like so many frightened hares.

The place being now patent to me, I walked up to comfort my party, and could see all that passed. The champion of the Excluded had taken the precaution to roll up the legs of his trousers, and to tie them tightly at the knee with his garters, which gave him the appearance of a Dutch skipper; and in all the consciousness of being now properly arrayed, he walked up to one of the men in authority—a small pot-bellied gentleman, and set himself to intercede for the attacking column, the head of which was still lowering at the door. But the little steward speedily interrupted him.

"Why, Mr Singlefist, rules must be maintained, and let me see," here he peered through his glass at the substantial supporters of our friend, "as I live, you yourself are inadmissible."

The giant laughed.

"Damn the body, he must have been a tailor! Charge, my fine fellows, and throw the constables out of the window, and the stewards after them. Every man his bird; and here goes for my Cock Robin." With that he made a grab at his Lilliputian antagonist, but missed him, as he slid away amongst the women like an eel, while his pursuer, brandishing his wooden arm on high, to which I now perceived for the first time that there was a large steel hook appended, exclaimed, in a broad Scotch accent, "Ah, if I had but caught the *creature*, I would have clapt this in his mouth, and played him like a salmon."

At this signal in poured the mass of soldiers and sailors; the constables vanished in an instant, the stewards were driven back upon the ladies; and such fainting and screaming, and swearing and threatening, and shying of cards, and fixing of time and place for a cool turn in the morning, it had never been my good fortune to witness before or since. "My wig!" thought I, "a precious country, where a man's life may be periled by the fashion of the covering to his nakedness!"

Next day Mr Fyall—who, I afterwards learned, was a most estimable man in substantials, although somewhat eccentric in small matters—called and invited me to accompany him on a cruise amongst some of the estates under his management. This was the very thing I desired; and three days afterwards I left my kind friends in Kingston, and set forth on my visit to Mr Fyall, who lived about seven miles from town.

The morning was fine as usual, although about noon the clouds, thin and fleecy and transparent at first, but gradually settling down more dense and heavy, began to congregate on the summit of the Liguanea Mountains, which rise about four miles distant to a height of near 5000 feet, in rear of the town. It thundered, too, a little now and then in the same direction, but this was an everyday occurrence in Jamaica at this season; and as I had only seven miles to go, off I started in a gig of mine host's, with my portmanteau well secured under a tarpauling, in defiance of all threatening appearances, crowding sail, and urging the noble roan that had me in tow close upon thirteen knots. I had not gone above three miles, however, when the sky in a moment changed from the intense glare of a tropical noontide to the deepest gloom, as if a bad angel had suddenly overshadowed us, and interposed his dark wings between us and the blessed sun; indeed, so instantaneous was the effect, that it reminded me of the withdrawing of the foot-lights in a theatre. The road now wound round the base of a precipitous spur from the Liguanea Mountains, which, instead of melting into the level country by gradual decreasing undulations, shot boldly out nearly a mile from the main range, and so abruptly, that it seemed mortised into the plain, like a rugged promontory running into a frozen lake. On looking up along the ridge of this prong, I saw the lowering mass of black clouds gradually spread out, and detach themselves from the summits of the loftier mountains, to which they had clung the whole morning, and begin to roll slowly down the hill, seeming to touch the tree tops, while along their lower edges hung a fringe of dark vapour, or rather shreds of cloud in rapid motion, that shifted about, and shot out and shortened like streamers.

As yet there was no lightning nor rain, and in the expectation of escaping the shower, as the wind was with me, I made more sail, pushing the horse into a gallop, to the great discomposure of the negro who sat beside me.

"Massa, you can't escape it, you are galloping into it; don't massa hear de sound of de rain coming along against de wind, and smell de earthy smell of him like one new-made grave?"

"The sound of the rain." In another clime, long, long ago, I had often read at my old mother's knee, "And Elijah said unto Ahab, there is a *sound* of abundance of rain, prepare thy chariot, and get thee down, that the rain stop thee not; and it came to pass, in the meanwhile, that the heaven was dark with clouds and wind, and there was a great rain."

I looked, and so it was; for in an instant a white sheet of the heaviest rain I had ever seen (if rain it might be called, for it was more like a waterspout) fell from the lower edge of the black cloud, with a strong rushing noise, that increased as it approached to a loud roar like that of a waterfall. As it came along, it seemed to devour the rocks and trees, for they disappeared behind the watery screen the instant it reached them. We saw it ahead of us for more than a mile coming along the road, preceded by a black line from the moistening of the white dust, right in the wind's eye, and with such an even front, that I verily believe it was descending in bucketsful on my horse's head, while as yet not one drop had reached me. At this moment the adjutant-general of the forces, Colonel F——, of the Coldstream Guards, in his tandem, drawn by two sprightly blood bays, with his servant, a light boy, mounted Creole fashion on the leader, was coming up in my wake at a spot where the road sank into a hollow, and was traversed by a watercourse already running knee-deep, although dry as a bone but the minute before.

I was now drenched to the skin, the water pouring out in cascades from both sides of the vehicle, when, just as I reached the top of the opposite bank, there was a flash of lightning so vivid, accompanied by an explosion so loud and tremendous, that my horse, trembling from stem to stern, stood dead still; the dusky youth by my side jumped out, and buried his snout in the mud, like a porker in Spain nuzzling for acorns, and I felt more queerish than I would willingly have confessed to. I could have knelt and prayed. The noise of the thunder was a sharp ear-piercing crash, as if the whole vault of heaven had been made of glass, and had been shivered at a blow by the hand of the Almighty.

It was, I am sure, twenty seconds before the usual roar and rumbling reverberation of the report from the hills, and among the clouds, was heard.

I drove on, and arrived just in time to dress for dinner; but I did not learn till next day, that the flash which paralyzed me, had struck dead the colonel's servant and leading horse, as he ascended the bank of the ravine, by this time so much swollen, that the body of the lad was washed off the road into the neighbouring gully, where it was found, when the waters subsided, entirely covered with sand.

I found the party congregated in the piazza round Mr Fyall, who was passing his jokes, without much regard to the feelings of his guests, and exhibiting as great a disregard of the common civilities and courtesies of life as can well be imagined. One of the party was a little red-faced gentleman, Peregrine Whiffle, Esquire, by name, who, in Jamaica parlance, was designated an *extraordinary* master in Chancery; the overseer of the pen, or breeding farm, in the great house, as it is called, or mansion-house, in which Mr Fyall resided, and a merry, laughing, intelligent, round, red-faced man; he was either Fyall's head clerk, or a sort of first-lieutenant; these personages and myself composed the party. The dinner itself was excellent, although rather of the rough and round order; the wines and food intrinsically good; but my appetite was not increased by the exhibition of a deformed, bloated, negro child, about ten years old, which Mr Fyall planted at his elbow, and, by way of practical joke, stuffed to repletion with all kinds of food and strong drink, until the little dingy brute was carried out drunk.

The wine circulated freely, and by-and-by Fyall indulged in some remarkable stories of his youth—for he was the only speaker—which I found some difficulty in swallowing, until at length, on one thumper being tabled, involving an impossibility, and utterly indigestible, I involuntarily exclaimed, "By Jupiter!"

"You want any ting, massa?" promptly chimed in the black servant at my elbow, a diminutive, kiln-dried old negro.

"No," said I, rather caught

"Oh, me tink you call for Jupiter."

I looked in the baboon's face—"Why, if I did, what then?"

"Only me Jupiter, at massa sarvice, dat all."

"You are; no great shakes of a Thunderer, eh? and who is that tall square man standing behind your master's chair?"

"Daddy Cupid, massa."

"And the old woman who is carrying away the dishes in the piazza?"

"Mammy Weenus."

"Daddy Cupid and Mammy Weenus—*Shade* of Homer!"

Jupiter, to my surprise, shrunk from my side, as if he had received a blow, and the next moment I could hear him communing with Venus in the piazza.

"For true, dat leetle man-of-war buccra must be Obeah man; how de debil him come to sabé dat it was stable-boy Homer who broke de candle *shade* on massa right hand, dat one wid de piece broken out of de edge?" and here he pointed towards it with his *chin*—a negro always points with his chin.

I had never slept on shore out of Kingston before; the night season in the country in dear old England, we all know, is usually one of the deepest stillness—here it was anything but still;—as the evening closed in, there arose a loud humming noise, a compound of the buzzing, and chirping, and whistling, and croaking of numberless reptiles and insects, on the earth, in the air, and in the water. I was awakened out of my first sleep by it, not that the sound was disagreeable, but it was unusual; and every now and then a beetle, the size of your thumb, would bang in through the open window, cruise round the room with a noise like a humming-top, and then dance a quadrille with half-a-dozen bats; while the fire-flies glanced like sparks, spangling the folds of the muslin curtains of the bed. The croak of the tree-toad, too, a genteel reptile, with all the usual lovable properties of his species, about the size of the crown of your hat, sounded from the neighbouring swamp like some one snoring in the piazza, blending harmoniously with the nasal concert got up by Jupiter, and some other heathen deities, who were sleeping there almost naked, excepting the head, which every negro swathes during the night with as much flannel and as many handkerchiefs as he can command. By the way, they all slept on their faces—I wonder if this will account for their flat noses.

Next morning we started at daylight, cracking along at the rate of twelve knots an hour in a sort of gig, with one horse in the shafts, and another hooked on abreast of him to a sort of studdingsail-boom, or outrigger, and followed by three mounted servants, each with a led horse and two sumpter mules.

In the evening we arrived at an estate under Mr Fyall's management, having passed a party of maroons immediately before. I never saw finer men—tall, strapping fellows, dressed exactly as they should be and the climate requires; wide duck trousers, over these a loose shirt, of duck also, gathered at the waist by a broad leathern belt, through which, on one side, their short cutlass is stuck, while on the other hangs a leathern pouch for ball; and a loose thong across one shoulder, supports on the opposite hip a large powder-horn and haversack. This, with a straw hat, and a short gun in their hand, with a sling to be used on a march, completes their equipment—in better keeping with the climate than the padded coats, heavy caps, tight cross-belts, and ponderous muskets of our regulars. As we drove up to the door, the overseer began to bawl, "Boys, boys!" and kept blowing a dog-call. All servants in the country in the West Indies, be they as old as Methuselah, are called boys. In the present instance, half-a-dozen black fellows forthwith appeared to take our luggage, and attend on "massa" in other respects. The great man was as austere to the poor overseer as if he had been guilty of some misdemeanour, and after a few short crabbed words, desired him to get supper, "do you hear?"

The meat consisted of plantation fare—salted fish, plantains, and yams, and a piece of goat mutton. Another "observe,"—a South-Down mutton, after sojourning a year or two here, does not become a goat exactly, but he changes his heavy warm fleece, and wears long hair; and his progeny after him, if bred on the hot plains, never assume the wool again. Mr Fyall and I sat down, and then in walked four mutes, stout young fellows, not over well dressed, and with faces burnt to the colour of brick-dust. They were the bookkeepers, so called because they *never* see a book, their province being to attend the negroes in the field, and to superintend the manufacture of sugar and rum in the boiling and distilling houses.

One of them, the head bookkeeper, as he was called, appeared literally roasted by the intensity of the sun's rays.

"How is Baldy Steer?" said the overseer to this person.

"Better to-day, sir,—I drenched him with train-oil and sulphur."

"The devil you did," thought I. "Alas! for Baldy."

"And Mary, and Caroline, and the rest of that lot?"

"Are sent to Perkins's Red Rover, sir; but I believe some of them are in calf already by Bullfinch—and I have cut Peter for the lampas."

The knife and fork dropped from my hands. "What can all this mean? is this their boasted kindness to their slaves? One of a family drenched with train-oil and brimstone, another cut for some horrible complaint never heard of before, called lampas, and the females sent to the Red Rover, some being in calf already!" But I soon perceived that the baked man was the cow-boy or shepherd of the estate, making his report of the casualties amongst his bullocks, mules, and heifers.

"Juliet Ridge will not yield, sir," quoth another.

"Who is this, next? a stubborn concern *she* must be."

"The liquor is very poor." Here he helped himself to rum and water, the rum coming up about an inch in the glass, regular half-and-half, fit to float a marlinspike.

"It is more than yours is," thought I; and I again stared in wonderment, until I perceived he spoke of the juice of a cane patch.

At this time a tall, lathy gentleman came in, wearing a most original cut coatee. He was a most extraordinary built man; he had absolutely no body, his bottom being placed between his shoulders; but what was wanted in corpus was made up in legs; indeed he looked like a pair of compasses, buttoned together at the shoulders, and supporting a yellow phiz half a yard long, thatched with a fell of sandy hair, falling down lank and greasy on each side of his face. Fyall called him Buckskin, which, with some other circumstances, made me guess that he was neither more nor less than an American smuggler.

After supper, a glass of punch was filled for each person; the overseer gave a rap on the table with his knuckles, and off started the bookkeepers like shots out of shovels, leaving the Yankee, Mr Fyall, the overseer, and myself, at table.

I was very tired, and reckoned on going to bed now—but no such thing. Fyall ordered Jupiter to bring a case from his gigbox, containing some capital brandy. A new brewage of punch took place, and I found about the small hours that we were all verging fast towards drunkenness, or something very like that same. The Yankee was specially plied by Fyall, evidently with an object, and he soon succeeded in making him helplessly drunk.

The fun now "grew fast and furious,"—a large wash-tub was ordered in, placed under a beam at the corner of the room, and filled with water; a sack and a three-inch rope were then called for, and promptly produced by the blackies, who, apparently accustomed to Fyall's pranks, grinned with delight. Buckskin was thrust into the sack, feet foremost; the mouth of it was then gathered round his throat with a string and I was set to splice a bight in the rope, so as to fit under his arms without running, which might have choked him. All things being prepared, the slack end was thrown over the beam. He was soused in the tub, the word was given to hoist away, and we ran him up to the roof, and then belayed the rope round the body of the overseer, who was able to sit on his chair, and that was all. The cold bath, and the being hung up to dry, speedily sobered the American, but his arms being within the sack, he could do nothing for his own emancipation: he kept swearing, however, and entreating, and dancing with rage, every jerk drawing the cord tighter round the waist of the overseer who, unaware of his situation, thought himself bewitched as he was drawn with violence by starts along the floor, with the chair as it were glued to him. At length the patient extricated one of his arms, and laying hold of the beam above him, drew himself up, and then letting go his hold suddenly, fairly lifted the drunken overseer, chair and all, several feet from the ground, so as to bring them on a level with himself, and then, in mid air, began to pummel his counterpoise with right goodwill. At length, fearful of the consequences from the fury into which the man had worked himself, Fyall and I dashed out the candles and fled to our rooms, where, after barricading the doors, we shouted to the servants to let the gentlemen down.

The next morning had been fixed for duck-shooting, and the overseer and I were creeping along amongst the mangrove bushes on the shore to get a shot at some teal, when we saw our friend, the pair of compasses, crossing the small bay in his boat, towards his little pilot-boat-built schooner, which was moored in a small creek opposite, the brushwood concealing everything but her masts. My companion, as wild an Irishman as I ever knew, hailed him.

"Hillo, Obediah—Buckskin—you Yankee rascal, heave to. Come ashore here—come ashore."

Obed, smoking his pipe, deliberately uncoiled himself—I thought as he rose there was to be no end of him—and stood upright in the boat like an ill-rigged jurymast.

"I say, Master Tummas, you ben't no friend of mine, I guess, a'ter last night's work; you hears how I coughs?" and he began to wheezle and crow in a most remarkable fashion.

"Never mind," rejoined the overseer;" if you go round that point, and put up the ducks—by the piper, but I'll fire at you!"

Obed neighed like a horse expecting his oats, which was meant as a laugh of derision. "Do you think your birding-piece can touch me here away, Master Tummas?" and again he *nichered* more loudly than before.

"Don't provoke me to try, you yellow snake you!"

"Try, and be d——d, and there's a mark for thee," unveiling a certain part of his body.

The overseer, or *busha*, to give him his Jamaica name, looked at me and smiled, then coolly lifted his long Spanish barrel and fired. Down dropped the smuggler, and ashore came the boat.

"I am mortally wounded, Master Tummas," quoth Obed; and I was confoundedly frightened at first, from the unusual proximity of the injured part to his head; but the overseer, as soon as he could get off the ground, where he had thrown himself in an uncontrollable fit of laughter, had the man stripped and laid across a log, where he set his servant to pick out the pellets with a penknife.

Next night I was awakened out of my first sleep by a peculiar sort of tap, tap, on the floor, as if a cat with walnut shells had been moving about the room. The feline race, in all its varieties, is my detestation, so I slipped out of bed to expel the intruder; but the instant my toe touched the ground, it was seized as if by a smith's forceps. I drew it into bed, but the annoyance followed it; and in an agony of alarm and pain I thrust my hand down, when my thumb was instantly manacled to the other suffering member. I now lost my wits altogether, and roared murder, which brought a servant in with a light, and there I was, thumb and toe, in the clinch of a land-crab.

I had been exceedingly struck with the beauty of the negro villages on the old-settled estates, which are usually situated in the most picturesque spots, and I determined to visit the one which lay on a sunny bank full in view from my window, divided on two sides from the cane pieces by a precipitous ravine, and on the other two by a high logwood hedge, so like hawthorn that I could scarcely tell the difference, even when close to it.

At a distance it had the appearance of one entire orchard of fruit-trees, where were mingled together the pyramidal orange, in fruit and in flower, the former in all its stages, from green to dropping ripe,—the citron, lemon, and lime-trees, the stately, glossy-leaved star-apple, the golden shaddock and grape-fruit, with their slender branches bending under their ponderous yellow fruit,—the cashew, with its apple like that of the cities of the plain, fair to look at, but acrid to the taste, to which the far-famed nut is appended like a bud,— the avocada, with its Brobdignag pear as large as a purser's lantern,—the bread-fruit, with a leaf, one of which would have covered Adam like a bishop's apron, and a fruit, for all the world, in size and shape, like a blackamoor's head; while for underwood you had the green, fresh, dew-spangled plantain, round which, in the hottest day, there is always a halo of coolness,—the coco root, the yam, and granadillo, with their long vines twining up the neighbouring trees and shrubs like hop-tendrils,—and pease and beans, in all their endless variety of blossom and of odour, from the Lima bean, with a stalk as thick as my arm, to the mouse pea, three inches high—the pine-apple, literally growing in, and constituting, with its prickly leaves, part of the hedgerows,—the custard-apple, like russet-bags of cold pudding,—the cocoa and coffee bushes, and the devil knows what all that is delightful in nature besides; while aloft, the tall graceful cocoa-nut, the majestic palm, and the gigantic wild cotton-tree, shot up here and there like minarets far above the rest, high into the blue heavens.

I entered one of the narrow winding footpaths, where an immense variety of convolvuli crept along the penguin fences, disclosing their delicate flowers in the morning freshness (all that class here shut shop at noon), and passion flowers of all sizes, from a soup-plate to a thumb-ring.

The huts were substantially thatched with palm-leaves, and the walls woven with a basket-work of twigs, plastered over with clay, and whitewashed—the floors were of baked clay, dry and comfortable. They all consisted of a hall and a sleeping-room off each side of it: in many of the former I noticed mahogany sideboards and chairs, and glass decanters, while a whole lot of African drums and flutes, and sometimes a good gun, hung from the rafters; and it would have gladdened an Irishman's heart to have seen the adjoining piggeries. Before one of the houses an old woman was taking care of a dozen black infants, little, naked, glossy, black guinea-pigs, with party-coloured beads tied round their loins, each squatted like a little Indian pagod in the middle of a large wooden bowl, to keep it off the damp ground.

While I was pursuing my ramble, a large conch-shell was blown at the overseer's house, and the different gangs turned in to dinner; they came along dancing and shouting, and playing tricks on each other in the little paths, in all the happy anticipation of a good dinner, and an hour and a-half to eat it in, the men well clad in Osnaburg frocks and trousers, and the women in baize petticoats and Osnaburg shifts, with a neat printed calico short-gown over all.

"And these are slaves," thought I, "*and this is West Indian bondage!* Oh that some of my well-meaning anti-slavery friends were here, to judge from the evidence of their own senses!"

The following night there was to be a grand play or wake in the negro houses over the head cooper, who had died in the morning, and I determined to be present at it, although the overseer tried to dissuade me, saying that no white person ever broke in on these orgies; that the negroes were very averse to their doing so; and that neither he, nor any of the white people on the estate, had ever been present on such an occasion. This very interdict excited my curiosity still more; so I rose about midnight, and let myself gently down through the window, and shaped my course in the direction of the negro houses, guided by a loud drumming, which, as I came nearer, every now and then sank into a low murmuring roll, when a strong bass voice would burst forth into a wild recitative; to which succeeded a loud piercing chorus of female voices, during which the drums were beaten with great vehemence; this was succeeded by another solo, and so on. There was no moon, and I had to thread my way along one of the winding footpaths by star-light. When I arrived within a stone-cast of the hut before which the play was being held, I left the beaten track, and crept onwards until I gained the shelter of the stem of a wild cotton-tree, behind which I skulked unseen.

The scene was wild enough. Before the door a circle was formed by about twenty women, all in their best clothes, sitting on the ground, and swaying their bodies to and fro, while they sang in chorus the wild dirge already mentioned, the words of which I could not make out; in the centre of the circle sat four men playing on *gumbies,* or the long drum formerly described, while a fifth stood behind them with a conch-shell, which he kept sounding at intervals. Other three negroes kept circling round the outer verge of the circle of women, naked all to their waist-cloths spinning about and about with their hands above their heads, like so many dancing dervishes. It was one of these three that from time to time took up the recitative, the female chorus breaking in after each line. Close to the drummers lay the body in an open coffin, supported on two low stools or trestles; a piece of flaming resinous wood was stuck in the ground at the head, and another at the feet; and a lump of kneaded clay, in which another torch-like splinter was fixed, rested on the breast. An old man, naked like the solo singer, was digging a grave close to where the body lay. The following was the chant:—

"I say, broder, you can't go yet."
THEN THE CHORUS OF FEMALE VOICES.
"When do morning star rise, den we put you in a hole."
CHORUS AGAIN.
"Den you go in a Africa, you see Fetish dere."
CHORUS.
"You shall nyam goat dere, wid all your family."
CHORUS
"Buccra can't come dere; say, dam rascal, why you no work?"
CHORUS.
"Buccra can't catch Duppy.* no, no."
CHORUS

Three calabashes, or gourds, with pork, yams, and rum, were placed on a small bench that stood close to the head of the bier, and at right angles to it.

Duppy, ghost.

In a little while, the women, singing-men, and drummers, suddenly gave a loud shout, or rather yell, clapped their hands three times, and then rushed into the surrounding cottages, leaving the old grave-digger alone with the body.

He had completed the grave, and had squatted himself on his hams beside the coffin, swinging his body as the women had done, and uttering a low moaning sound, frequently ending in a loud *pech*, like that of a pavior when he brings down his rammer.

I noticed he kept looking towards the east, watching, as I conjectured, the first appearance of the morning star, but it was as yet too early.

He lifted the gourd with the pork, and took a large mouthful.

"How is dis! I can't put dis meat in Quacco's coffin, dere is salt in de pork; Duppy can't bear salt," another large mouthful—"Duppy hate salt too much," —here he ate it all up, and placed the empty gourd in the coffin. He then took up the one with boiled yam in it, and tasted it also.

"Salt here too—who de debil do such a ting?—must not let Duppy taste dat." He discussed this also, placing the empty vessel in the coffin, as he had done with the other. He then came to the calabash with the rum. There is no salt here, thought I.

"Rum! ah, Duppy love rum—if it be well strong, let me see—Massa Niger, who put water in dis rum, eh? Duppy will never touch dat"—a long pull—"no, no, never touch dat." Here he finished the whole, and placed the empty vessel beside the others; then gradually sank back on his hams with his mouth open, and his eyes starting from the sockets, as he peered up into the tree, apparently at some terrible object. I looked up also, and saw a large yellow snake, nearly ten feet long, let itself gradually down directly over the coffin, between me and the bright glare (the outline of its glossy mottled skin glancing in the strong light, which gave its dark opaque body the appearance of being edged with flame, and its glittering tongue, that of a red-hot wire), with its tail round a limb of the cotton-tree, until its head reached within an inch of the dead man's face, which it licked with its long forked tongue, uttering a loud hissing noise.

I was fascinated with terror, and could not move a muscle; at length the creature slowly swung itself up again, and disappeared amongst the branches.

Quashie gained courage, as the rum began to operate, and the snake to disappear. "Come to catch Quacco's Duppy, before him get to Africa, sure as can be. De metody parson say de debil old sarpant—dat must be old sarpant, for I never see so big one, so it must be de debil."

He caught a glimpse of my face at this moment; it seemed that I had no powers of fascination like the snake, for he roared out, "Murder, murder, de debil, de debil, first like a sarpant, den like himself; see him white face behind de tree; see him white face behind de tree;" and then, in the extremity of his fear, he popped, head foremost, into the grave, leaving his quivering legs and feet sticking upwards, as if he had been planted by the head, like a forked parsnip reversed.

At this uproar, a number of negroes ran out of the nearest houses, and, to my surprise, four white seamen appeared suddenly amongst them, who, the moment they got sight of my uniform, as I ran away, gave chase, and having overtaken me, as I stumbled in the dark path, immediately pinioned me. They were all armed, and I had no doubt were part of the crew of the smuggling schooner, and that they had a depot amongst the negro houses.

"Yo ho, my hearty, heave-to, or here goes with a brace of bullets."

I told them who I was, and that curiosity alone brought me there.

"Gammon, tell that to the marines; you're a spy, messmate, and on board you go with us, so sure as I be Paul Brandywine."

Here was a change with a vengeance. An hour before I was surrounded by friends, and resting comfortably in my warm bed, and now I was a prisoner to a set of brigands, who were smugglers at the best, and what might they not be at the worst? I had no chance of escape by any sudden effort of strength or activity, for a piece of a handspike had been thrust across my back, passing under both of my arms, which were tightly lashed to it, as if I had been trussed for roasting, so that I could no more run, with a chance of escape, than a goose without her pinions. After we left the negro houses, I perceived, with some surprise, that my captors kept the beaten track, leading directly to, and passed the overseer's dwelling. "Come, here is a chance, at all events," argued I to myself. "If I got within hail, I will alarm the lieges, if a deuced good pipe don't fail me."

This determination had scarcely been formed in my mind, when, as if my very thoughts had been audible, the smuggler next me on the right hand drew a pistol, and held it close to my starboard ear.

"Friend, if you tries to raise the house, or speaks to any Niger or other person we meets, I'll walk through your skull with two ounces of lead."

"You are particularly obliging," said I; "but what do you promise yourselves by carrying me off? Were you to murder me, you would be none the richer; for I have no valuables about me, as you may easily ascertain by searching me."

"And do you think that freeborn Americans like we have kidnapped you for your dirty rings, and watch, and mayhap a few dollars, which I takes you to mean by your, 'waluboles,' as you calls them?"

"Why, then, *what* in the devil's name have you kidnapped me for?" And I began to feel my choler overpowering my discretion, when Mr Paul Brandywine, who I now suspected to be the mate of the smuggler, took the small liberty of jerking the landyard that had been made fast to the middle of the handspike, so violently, that I thought both my shoulders were dislocated; for I was fairly checked down on my back, just as you may have seen a pig-merchant on the Fermoy road bring an uproarious boar to his marrow-bones; while the man who had previously threatened to blow my brains out, knelt beside me, and civilly insinuated, that "if I was tired of my life, he calculated I had better speak as loud again."

There was no jest in all this; so I had nothing for it but to walk silently along with my escort, after having gathered myself up as well as I could. We crept so close under the windows of the overseer's house, where we picked up a lot of empty ankers, slung on a long pole, that I fancied I heard, or really did hear, some one snore—oh how I envied the sleeper! At length we reached the beach, where we found two men lying on their oars, in what, so far as I could distinguish, appeared to be a sharp swift-looking whale-boat—which they kept close to, with her head seaward, however, to be ready for a start, should anything suspicious appear near to them. The boat-keeper hailed promptly, "Who goes there?" as they feathered their oars.

"The tidy little Wave," was the answer.

No more words passed; and the men, who had, in the first instance, pulled a stroke or two to give the boat way, now backed water, and tailed her on to the beach, when we all stepped on board.

Two of my captors now took each an oar; we shoved off, and glanced away through the darkness, along the smooth surface of the sparkling sea, until we reached the schooner, by this time hauled out into the fairway at the mouth of the cove, where she lay hove short, with her mainsail hoisted up, riding to the land-wind, and apparently all ready to cant and be off the moment the boat returned.

As we came alongside, the captain of her, my friend Obediah, as I had no difficulty in guessing, from his very out-of-the-way configuration, dark as it was, called out, "I says, Paul, who have you got into the starn-sheets there?"

"A bloody spy, captain; he who was with the overseer when he peppered your sheathing t'other morning."

"Oho, bring him on board—bring him on board. I knows there be a man-of-war schooner close aboard of the island somewheres hereabouts. I sees through it all, smash my eyes!—I sees through it. But what kept you, Paul? Don't you see the morning star has risen?"

By this time I stood on the deck of the little vessel, which was not above two feet out of the water; and Obediah, as he spoke, pointed to the small dark pit of a companion, for there was no light below, nor indeed anywhere on board, except in the binnacle, and that carefully masked, indicating, by his threatening manner, that I was to get below as speedily as possible.

"Don't you see the morning star, sir? Why, the sun will be up in an hour, I calculate, and then the sea-breeze will be down on us before we get anything of an offing."

The mention of the morning star recalled vividly to my recollection the scene I had so recently witnessed at the negro wake; it seemed there was another person beside poor Quacco, likely to be crammed into a hole before the day broke, and to be carried to Africa too, for what I knew; but one must needs go when the devil drives, so I slipped down into the cabin, and the schooner having weighed, made sail to the northward.

CHAPTER VIII.

THE CHASE OF THE SMUGGLER.

"Would I were in an alehouse in London, I would give all my fame
    for a pot of ale, and safety."

King Henry V.

THE CRIB in which I was confined was as dark as pitch, and, as I soon found, as hot as the Black-hole in Calcutta. I don't pretend to be braver than my neighbours, but I would pluck any man by the beard who called me coward. In my small way I had in my time faced death in various shapes; but it had always been above board, with the open heaven overhead, and generally I had a goodly fellowship in danger, and the eyes of others were upon me. No wonder, then,

that the sinking of the heart within me, which I now experienced for the first
time, was bitter exceedingly, and grievous to be borne. Cooped up in a small
suffocating cabin, scarcely eight feet square, and not above five feet high, with
the certainty of being murdered, as I conceived, were I to try to force my way on
deck; and the knowledge that all my earthly prospects, all my dreams of promotion, were likely to be blasted and for ever ruined by my sudden spiriting
away, not to take into the heavy tale the misery which my poor mother and my
friends must suffer, when they came to know it—and "who will tell this to thee,
Mary?" rose to my throat, but could get no further for a cursed bump that was
like to throttle me. Why should I blush to own it—when the gypsy, after all,
jinked an old rich goutified coffee-planter at the eleventh hour, and married
me, and is now the mother of half-a-dozen little Cringles or so? However, I
made a strong effort to bear my misfortunes like a man, and, folding my arms, I
sat down on a chest to abide my fate, whatever that might be, with as much
composure as I could command, when half-a-dozen cockroaches flew flicker
flicker against my face.

     For the information of those who have never seen this delicious insect, I
take leave to mention here, that, when full grown, it is a large dingy brown-
coloured beetle, about two inches long, with six legs, and two feelers as long as
its body. It has a strong anti-hysterical flavour, something between rotten
cheese and asafœtida, and seldom stirs abroad when the sun is up, but lies concealed in the most obscure and obscene crevices it can creep into; so that,
when it is seen, its wings and body are thickly covered with dust and dirt of various shades, which any culprit who chances to fall asleep with his mouth open
is sure to reap the benefit of, as it has a great propensity to walk into it, partly
for the sake of the crumbs adhering to the masticators, and also, apparently,
with a scientific desire to inspect, by accurate admeasurement with the aforesaid antennae, the state and condition of the whole potato-trap.

     At the same time I felt something gnawing the toe of my boot, which I
inferred to be a rat—another agreeable customer for which I had a special
abhorrence; but as for beetles of all kinds, from my boyhood up, they had been
an abomination unto me, and a cockroach is the most abominable of all beetles; so between the two I was speedily roused from my state of supine, or
rather dogged endurance; and, forgetting the geography of my position, I
sprang to my feet, whereby I nearly fractured my skull against the low deck
above—I first tried the skylight—it was battened down; then the companion
hatch—it was locked; but the ladder leading up to it being cooler than the noi-

some vapour bath I had left, I remained standing in it, trying to catch a mouthful of fresh air through the joints of the door. All this while we had been slipping along shore, with the land-wind on our beam, at the rate of five or six knots, but so gently and silently that I could distinctly hear the roar of the surf, as the long smooth swell broke on the beach, which, from the loudness of the noise, could not be above a mile to windward of us. I perceived, at the same time, that the schooner, although going free, did not keep away, nor take all the advantage of the land-wind to make his easting, before the sea-breeze set down, that he might have done, so that it was evident he did not intend to beat up, so as to fetch the Crooked Island Passage, which would have been his course, had he been bound for the States; but was standing over to the Cuba shore, at that time swarming with pirates.

It was now good daylight, and the *terral* gradually died away, and left us rolling gunwale under, as we rose and fell on the long seas, with our sails flapping, bulkheads creaking and screaming, and mainboom jig-jigging, as if it would have torn everything to pieces. I could hear my friend Obed walking the deck, and whistling manfully for the sea-breeze, exclaiming from time to time in his barbarous lingo, "Souffle, souffle, San Antonio." But the saint had no bowels, and there we lay roasting until near ten o'clock in the forenoon. During all this period, Obed, who was shortsighted, kept desiring his right arm, Paul Brandywine, to keep a bright look-out for the sea-breeze to windward, or rather to the eastward, for there was no wind—because he knowed it oftentimes tumbled down right sudden and dangerous at this season about the corner of the island hereabouts; and the pride of the morning often brought a shower with it, fit to level a maize-plat smooth as his hand."

"No black clouds to windward yet, Paul?"

Paul could see nothing, and the question was repeated three or four times.

"There is a small black cloud about the size of my hand to windward, sir, right in the wake of the sun, just now, but it won't come to anything; I sees no signs of any wind."

"And Elijah said to his servant, Go up now, and look towards the sea; and he went up, and looked, and said, There is nothing. And he said, Go again seven times; and it came to pass the seventh time, that he said, Behold, there ariseth a little cloud out of the sea, like a man's hand."

I knew what this foreboded, which, as I thought, was more than friend Obed did; for he shortened no sail, and kept all his kites abroad, for no use as it struck me, unless he wished to wear them out by flapping against the masts. He was indeed a strange mixture of skill and carelessness; but, when fairly stirred up, one of the most daring and expert and self-possessed seamen I had ever seen, as I very soon had an ugly opportunity of ascertaining.

The cloud on the horizon continued to rise rapidly, spreading over the whole eastern sky, and the morning began to lower very ominously; but there was no sudden squall, the first of the breeze coming down as usual in cats' paws, and freshening gradually; nor did I expect there would be, although I was certain it would soon blow a merry capful of wind, which might take in some of the schooner's small sails, and pretty considerably bother us, unless we could better our offing speedily, for it blew right on shore, which, by the setting-in of the sea-breeze, was now close under our lee.

At length the sniffler reached us, and the sharp little vessel began to *speak*, as the rushing sound through the water is called; while the wind sang like an Æolian harp through the taught weather-rigging. Presently I heard the word given to take in the two gaff-topsails and flying jib, which was scarcely done when the moaning sound roughened into a roar, and the little vessel began to yerk at the head seas as if she would have cut through them, in place of rising to them, and to lie over as if Davy Jones himself had clapperclawed the mast-heads, and was in the act of using them as levers to capsize her; while the sails were tugging at her, as if they would have torn the spars out of her so that I expected every moment, either that she would turn over, keel up, or that the masts would snap short off by the deck.

All this, which I would without the smallest feeling of dread, on the contrary with exhilaration, have faced cheerily on deck in the course of duty, proved at the time, under my circumstances, most alarming and painful to me; a fair-strae death out of the maintop, or off the weather yard-arm, would to my imagination have been an easy exit comparatively; but to be choked in this abominable hole, and drowned darkling like a blind puppy—the very thought made me frantic, and I shouted and tumbled about, until I missed my footing and fell backwards down the ladder, from the bottom of which I scuttled away to the lee-side of the cabin, quiet, through absolute despair and exhaustion from the heat and closeness.

I had remarked that from the time the breeze freshened the everlasting Yankee drawling of the crew, and the endless confabulation of the captain and his mate, had entirely ceased, and nothing was now heard on deck but the angry voice of the raging cry elements, and at intervals a shrill piercing word or two from Obed, in the altered tone of which I had some difficulty in recognising his pipe, which rose clear and distinct above the roar of the sea and wind, and was always answered by a prompt, sharp, "Ay, ay, sir," from the men. There was no circumlocution, nor calculating, nor guessing now, but all hands seemed to be doing their duty energetically and well. "Come, the vagabonds are sailors after all, we shan't be swamped this turn;" and I resumed my place on the companion ladder with more ease of mind, and a vast deal more composure, than when I was pitched from it when the squall came on. In a moment after I could hear the captain sing out, loud even above the howling of the wind and rushing of the water, "There it comes at last—put your helm hard a-port—down with it, Paul, down with it, man—luff, and shake the wind out of her sails, or over she goes, clean and for ever." Everything was jammed, nothing could be let go, nor was there an axe at hand to make short work with the sheets and haulyards; and for a second or two I thought it was all over, the water rushing half-way up her decks, and bubbling into the companion through the crevices; but at length the lively little craft came gaily to the wind, shaking her plumage like a wild-duck; the sails were got in, all to the foresail, which was set with the bonnet off, and then she lay-to, like a sea-gull, without shipping a drop of water. In the comparative stillness I could now distinctly hear every word that was said on deck.

"Pretty near it; rather close shaving that same, captain," quoth Paul, with a congratulatory chuckle; "but I say, sir, what is that wreath of smoke rising from Annotta Bay over the headland?"

"Why, how should I know, Paul? Negroes burning brush, I guess."

"The smoke from brushwood never rose and flew over the bluff with that swirl, I calculate; it is a gun, or I mistake."

And he stepped to the companion, for the purpose, as I conceived, of taking out the spy-glass, which usually hangs there in brackets fitted to hold it: he undid the hatch and pushed it back, when I popped my head out, to the no small dismay of the mate; but Obed was up to me, and while with one hand he seized the glass, he ran the sliding top sharp up against my neck, till he pinned me into a kind of pillory, to my great annoyance; so I had to beg to be released, and once more slunk back into my hole. There was a long pause; at length Paul, to whom the skipper had handed the spy-glass, spoke.

"A schooner, sir, is rounding the point!"

As I afterwards learned, the negroes who had witnessed my capture, especially the old man who had taken me for his infernal majesty, had raised the alarm, so soon as they could venture down to the overseer's house, which was on the smuggling boat shoving off, and Mr Fyall immediately despatched an express to the Lieutenant commanding the Gleam, then lying in Annotta Bay, about ten miles distant, when she instantly slipped and shoved out.

"Well, I can't help it if there be," rejoined the captain.

Another pause.

"Why, I don't like her, sir; she looks like a man-of-war—and that must have been the smoke of the gun she fired on weighing."

"Eh?" sharply answered Obed, "if it be, it will be a hanging matter if we are caught with this young splice on board; he may belong to her, for what I know. Look again, Paul."

A long, long look.

"A man-of-war schooner, sure enough, sir; I can see her ensign and pennant, now that she is clear of the land."

"O Lord, O Lord!" cried Obed, in great perplexity, "what shall we do?"

"Why, pull foot, captain," promptly replied Paul; "the breeze has lulled, and in light winds she will have no chance with the tidy little Wave."

I could now perceive that the smugglers made all sail, and I heard the frequent swish-swish of the water, as they threw bucketsful on the sails to thicken them and make them hold more wind, while we edged away, keeping as close to the wind, however, as we could without stopping her way.

"Starboard," quoth Obed—"rap full, Jem—let her walk through it, my boy—there, main and foresail, flat as boards; why, she will stand the main-gaff-topsail yet—set it, Paul, set it;" and his heart warmed as he gained confidence in the qualifications of his vessel. "Come, weather me now, see how she trips it along—pooh! I was an ass to quail, wan't I, Paul?"

"No chance now," thought I, as I descended once more; "I may as well go and be suffocated at once." I knocked my foot against something in stepping off the ladder, which, on putting down my hand, I found to be a tinder-box, with steel and flint. I had formerly ascertained there was a candle in the cabin, on the small table, stuck into a bottle; so I immediately struck a light, and as I knew that meekness and solicitation, having been tried in vain, would not serve me, I determined to go on the other tack, and to see how far an assumption of coolness and self-possession, or, it might be, a dash of bravado, whether true or feigned, might not at least insure me some consideration and better treatment from the lawless gang into whose hands I had fallen.

So I set to and ransacked the lockers, where, amongst a vast variety of miscellaneous matters, I was not long in finding a bottle of very tolerable rum, some salt junk, some biscuit, and a *goglet*, or porous earthen jar, of water, with some capital cigars. By this time I was like to faint with the heat and smell; so I filled a tumbler with good half-and-half, and swigged it off. The effect was speedy; I thought I could eat a bit, so I attacked the salt junk and made a hearty meal, after which I replenished my tumbler, lighted a cigar, pulled off my coat and waistcoat, and with a sort of desperate glee struck up, at the top of my pipe, "Ye Mariners of England." My jovialty was soon noticed on deck.

"Eh, what be that?" quoth Obed,—"that be none of our ditties, I guess—who is singing below there?"

"We be all on deck, sir," responded Paul.

"It can't be the spy, eh?—sure enough it must be he, and no one else; the heat and choke must have made him mad."

"We shall soon see," said Paul, as he removed the skylight, and looked down into the cabin.

Obed looked over his shoulder, peering at me with his little short-sighted pigs' eyes, into which, in my pot valiancy, I immediately chucked half a tumbler of very strong grog, and under cover of it attempted to bolt through the skuttle, and thereby gain the deck; but Paul, with his shoulder-of-mutton fist, gave me a very unceremonious rebuff, and down I dropped again.

"You makes yourself at home, I sees, and be hanged to you," said Obed, laying the emphasis on the last word, pronouncing it "yoo-oo" in two syllables.

"I do, indeed, and be d——d to yoo-oo," I replied; "and why should I not? the visit was not volunteered, you know; so come down, you long-legged Yankee smuggling scoundrel, or I'll blow your bloody buccaneering craft out of the water like the peel of an onion. You see I have got the magazine scuttle up, and *there* are the barrels of powder, and here is the candle, so—"

Obed laughed like the beginning of the bray of the jackass before he swings off into his "heehaw, heehaw." "Smash my eyes, man, but them barrels be full of pimento, all but that one with the red mark, and that be crackers fresh and sharp from the Brandywine mills."

"Well, well, gunpowder or pimento, I'll set fire to it if you don't be civil."

"Why, I *will* be civil; you are a curious chap, a brave slip, to carry it so, with no friend near; so, civil I will be."

He unlocked the companion hatch, and came down to the cabin, doubling his long limbs up like foot-rules, to suit the low roof.

"Free and easy, my man," continued the captain, as he entered. "Well, I forgive you—we are quits now—and if we were not beyond the island craft, I would put you ashore, but I can't stand back now."

"Why, may I ask?"

"Simply, because one of your men-of-war schooners an't more than hull down astern of me at this moment; she is working up in shore, and has not chased me as yet; indeed she may save herself the trouble, for ne'er a schooner in your blasted service has any chance with the tidy little Wave."

I was by no means sure of this.

"Well, Master Obediah, it may turn up as you say—and in a light wind I know you will either sail or sweep away from any one of them; but, to be on the square with you, if it comes on to blow, that same hooker, which I take to be his Britannic Majesty's schooner Gleam, will, from his greater beam and superior length, outcarry and forereach on you—ay, and weather on you too, hand over hand; so this is my compact—if he nails you, you will require a friend at court, and I will stand that friend; if you escape—and I will not interfere either by advice or otherwise, either to get you taken or to get you clear—will you promise to put me on board of the first English merchant vessel we fall in with, or, at the longest, to land me at St Jago de Cuba, and I will promise you, on my honour, notwithstanding all that has been said or done, that I will never hereafter inform against you, or in any way get you into trouble if I can help it. Is it done? Will you give me your hand upon it?"

Obed did not hesitate a moment; he clenched my hand, and squeezed it till the blood nearly spouted from my finger-ends. One might conceive of Norwegian bears greeting each other after this fashion, but I trust no Christian will ever, in time coming, subject my digits to a similar species of torture.

"Agreed, my boy; I *have* promised, and you may depend on me. Smuggler though I be, and somewhat worse on occasion mayhap, I never breaks my word."

There was an earnestness about the poor fellow in which I thought there could be no deception, and from that moment we were on what I may call a very friendly footing for a prisoner and his jailer.

"Well, now, I believe you, so let us have a glass of grog, and—"

Here the mate sang out, "Captain, come on deck, if you please; quickly, sir, quickly."

By this time it had begun to breeze up again, and as the wind rose, I could see the spirits of the crew *fell*, as if conscious they had no chance if it freshened. When we went on deck, Paul was still peering through the telescope.

"The schooner has tacked, sir." A dead silence; then giving the glass a swing, and driving the joints into each other with such vehemence as if he would have broken them in pieces, he exclaimed, "She is after us, so sure as I ben't a niger."

"No! Is she though?" eagerly inquired the captain, as he tried at length seized the spy-glass, twisting and turning it about and about, as he tried to hit his own very peculiar focus. At length he took a long, breathless look, while the eyes of the whole crew, some fifteen hands or so, were riveted upon him with the most intense anxiety.

"What a gaff-topsail she has got—my eye!—and a ringtail with more cloths in it than our squaresail—and the breeze comes down stronger and stronger!"

All this while I looked out equally excited, but with a very different interest. "Come, this will do," thought I; "she *is* after us; and if old Dick Gasket brings that fiery sea-breeze he has now along with him, we shall puzzle the smuggler, for all his long start."

"There's a gun, sir," cried Paul, trembling from head to foot. "Sure enough," said the skipper; "and it must be a signal. And there go three flags at the fore. She must, I'll bet a hundred dollars, have taken our tidy little Wave for the admiral's tender that was lying in Morant Bay."

"Blarney," thought I; "tidy as your little Wave is, she won't deceive old Dick—he is not the man to take a herring for a horse; she *must* be making signals to some man-of-war in sight."

"A strange sail right ahead," sang out three men from forward all at once.

"Didn't I say so?"—I had only *thought* so. "Come, Master Obediah, it thickens now; you're in for it," said I.

But he was not in the least shaken; as the matter grew serious, he seemed to brace up to meet it. He had been flurried at the first, but he was collected and cool as a cucumber *now*, when he saw everything depending on his seamanship and judgment. Not so Paul, who seemed to have made up his mind that they must be taken.

"Jezebel Brandywine, you are but a widowed old lady, I calculate. I shall never see the broad, smooth Chesapeake again—no more peach brandy for Paul;" and, folding his arms, he set himself doggedly down on the low taffrail.

Little did I think at the time how fearfully the poor fellow's foreboding was so soon to be fulfilled.

"There again," said I, "a second puff to windward." This was another signal-gun, I knew; and I went forward to where the captain was reconnoitring the sail ahead through the glass. "Let me see," said I, "and I will be honest with you, and tell you if I know her."

He handed me the glass at once, and the instant I saw the top of her courses above the water, I was sure, from the red cross in her foresail, that she was the Firebrand, the very corvette to which I was appointed. She was so well to windward, that I considered it next to impossible that we should weather her; but Obediah seemed determined to try it. After seeing his little vessel snug under mainsail, foresail, and jib, which was as much as she could stagger under, and everything right and tight, and all clear to make more sail should the breeze lull, he ordered the men below, and took the helm himself. What queer animals sailors are! We were rising the corvette fast; and on going aft again from the bows, where I had been looking at her, I cast my eye down the hatchway into the men's berth, and there were the whole crew at breakfast, laughing and joking, and enjoying themselves as heartily, apparently—nay, I verily believe in reality—as if they had been in a yacht on a cruise of pleasure, in place of having one enemy nearly within gunshot astern, and another trying to cut them off ahead.

At this moment the schooner in chase luffed up in the wind, and I noticed the foot of the foresail lift. "You'll have it now, friend Obed; there's at you in earnest." While I spoke, a column of thick white smoke spouted over the bows of the Gleam, about twenty yards dead to windward, and then blew back again amongst the sails and rigging as if a gauze veil had for an instant been thrown over the little vessel, rolling off down the wind in whirling eddies, growing thinner and thinner, until it disappeared altogether. I heard the report this time, and the shot fell close alongside of us.

"A good mark with that apple," coolly observed the captain; "the Long Tom must be a tearer, to pitch its mouthful of iron this length."

Another succeeded; and if I had been still pinned up in the companion, there would have been no log now, for it went crash through into the hold.

"Go it, my boys," shouted I; "a few more as well aimed, and heigh for the Firebrand's gun-room!"

At the mention of the Firebrand I thought Obed started, but he soon recovered himself, and looking at me with all the apparent composure in the world, he smiled as he said, "Not so fast, lieutenant; you and I have not drank our last glass of swizzle yet, I guess. If I can but weather that chap ahead, I don't fear the schooner."

The corvette had by this time answered the signal from the Gleam, and had hauled his wind also, so that I did not conceive it possible that the Wave could scrape clear, without coming tinder his broadside.

"You won't try it, Obed, surely?"

"Answer me this, and I'll tell you," rejoined he. "Does that corvette *now* carry long 18's or 32-pound carronades?"

"She carries 32-pound carronades."

"Then you'll not sling your cot in her gunroom this cruise."

All this time the little Wave was carrying to it gallantly, her jib-boom bending like whalebone, and her long slender topmasts whipping about like a couple of fishing-rods, as she thrashed at it, sending the spray flashing over her mastheads at every pitch; but notwithstanding her weatherly qualities, the heavy cross sea, as she drove into it, headed her off bodily, and she could not prevent the Gleam from creeping up on her weather-quarter where she peppered away from her long 24-pounder, throwing the shot over and over us.

To tack, therefore, would have been to run into the lion's mouth, and to bear up was equally hopeless, as the corvette, going free, would have chased her under water; the only chance remaining was to stand on, and trust to the breeze taking off, and try to weather the ship, now about three miles distant on our lee bow, braced sharp up on the opposite tack, and evidently quite aware of our game.

As the corvette and the Wave neared each other, he threw a shot at us from the boat gun on his topgallant forecastle, as if to ascertain beyond all doubt the extent of our insanity, and whether we were serious in our attempt to weather him and escape.

Obed held right on his course, like grim Death. Another bullet whistled over our mastheads, and, with the aid of the glass, I could see, by the twinkling of feet, and here and there a busy peering face through the ports, that the crew were at quarters fore and aft, while fourteen marines or so were all ready rigged on the poop, and the nettings were bristling through the whole length of the ship, with fifty or sixty small-arm men.

All this I took care to communicate to Obediah. "I say, my good friend, I see little to laugh at in all this. If you do go to windward of him at all, which I greatly doubt, you will have to cross his fore-foot within pistol-shot at the farthest, and then you will have to rasp along his whole broadside of great and small, and they are right well prepared and ready for you, that I can tell you; the skipper of that ship has had some hedication, I guess, in the war on your coast, for he seems up to your tricks, and I don't doubt but he will tip you the stem, if need be, with as little compunction as I would kill a cockroach, devil confound the whole breed! There—I see his marines and small-arm men handling their fire-locks, as thick as sparrows under the lee of a hedge in a snowstorm, and the people are training the bull-dogs fore and aft. Why, this is downright stark star-ing lunacy, Obed; we shall be smashed like an egg-shell, and all hands of us whipped off to Davy, from your cursed foolhardiness."

I had made several pauses in my address, expecting an answer, but Obed was mute as a stone. At length I took the glass from my eye, and turned round to look at him, startled by his silence.

I might have heard of such things, but I had never before seen the working of the spirit so forcibly and fearfully demonstrated by the aspect of the outward man. With the exception of myself, he was the only man on deck, as before men-tioned, and by this time he was squatted down on it, with his long legs and thighs thrust down into the cabin, through the open skylight. The little vessel happened to carry a weather helm, so that his long sinewy arms, with their large veins and leaders strained to cracking, covered but a small way below the elbow by his jacket, were stretched as far as they could clutch the tiller to windward, and his enormous head, supported on his very short trunk, that seemed to be countersunk into the deck, gave him a most extraordinary appearance. But this was not all; his complexion, usually sallow and sunburnt, was now ghastly and blue, like that of the corpse of a drowned man; the mus-cles of the neck, and the flesh of the cheeks and chin were rigid and fixed, and shrunk into one-half of their usual compass; the lips were so compressed that they had almost entirely disappeared, and all that marked his mouth was a black line; the nostrils were distended, and thin and transparent, while the forehead was shrivelled into the most minute and immovable wrinkles, as if done with a crimping instrument; while over his eyes, or rather his eye, for he kept one closed as if it had been hermetically sealed, he had lashed with half-a-dozen turns of spun-yarn a wooden socket, like the butt-end of an opera glass, fitted with some sort of magnifier, through which he peered out ahead most intensely, stooping down, and stretching his long bare neck to its utmost reach, that he might see under the foot of the foresail.

I had scarcely time to observe all this, when a round shot came through the head of the mainsail, grazing the mast, and the very next instant a bushel of grape, from one of the bow guns, a 32-pound carronade, was crashed in on us amidships. I flung down the glass, and dived through the companion into the cabin—I am not ashamed to own it; and any man who would undervalue my courage in consequence, can never, taking into consideration the peculiarities of my situation, have known the appalling sound, or infernal effect of a discharge of grape. Round shot in broadsides is a joke to it; musketry is a joke to it; but only conjure up in your imagination, a shower of iron bullets, of the size of well-grown plums, to the number of from sixty to one hundred and twenty, taking effect within a circle, not above ten feet in diameter, and that all this time there was neither honour nor glory in the case, for I was a miserable captive, and I fancy I may save myself the trouble of farther enlargement.

I found that the crew had by this time started and taken up the planks of the cabin floor, and had stowed themselves well down into the run, so as to be as much out of harm's way as they could manage; but there was neither fear nor flinching amongst them; and although totally devoid of all gasconade—on the contrary, they had taken all the precautions men could do in their situation, to keep out of harm's way, or at least to lessen the danger—there they sat, silent, and cool, and determined. "I shall never undervalue an American as an enemy again," thought I. I lay down on the side of the little vessel, now nearly level as she lay over, alongside of Paul Brandywine, in a position that commanded a view of Obed's face through the small scuttle. Ten minutes might have elapsed —a tearing crash—and a rattle on the deck overhead, as if a shower of stones had been thrown from aloft on it.

"That's through the mainmast, I expect," quoth Paul.

I looked from him to the captain; a black thick stream of blood was trickling down behind his ear. Paul had noticed it also.

"You are hurt by one of them splinters, I see; give me the helm now, Captain;" and, crushed down as the poor fellow appeared to be under some fearful and mysterious consciousness of impending danger, he nevertheless addressed himself to take his captain's place.

"Hold your blasted tongue"—was the polite rejoinder.

"I say, captain," shouted your humble servant, "you may as well eat peas with a pitchfork, as try to weather him. You are hooked, man, flounder as you will. Old Nick can't shake you clear—so I won't stand this any longer;" and, making a spring; I jammed myself through the skylight, until I sat on the deck, looking aft and confronting him, and there we were, stuck up like the two kings of Brentford, or a couple of *smiling cherries* on one stalk, I have often laughed at the figure we must have cut, but at the time there was that going on that would have made Comus himself look grave. I had at length fairly aroused the sleeping devil within him.

"Look out, *there,* lieutenant—look out there,"—and he pointed with his sinister claw down to leeward. I did so—whew!—what a sight for poor Master Thomas Cringle! "You are booked for an outside place,—Master Tommy," thought I to myself—for *there* was the corvette in very truth—she had just tacked, and was close aboard of us on our lee quarter, within musket-shot at the farthest, bowling along upon a wind, with the green, hissing, multitudinous sea surging along her sides, and washing up in foam, like snow-flakes, through the midship ports, far aft on the quarterdeck, to the glorification of Jack, who never minds a wet jacket so long as he witnesses the discomfiture of his ally Peter Pipeclay. The press of canvass she was carrying laid her over, until her copper sheathing, clear as glass, and glancing like gold, was seen high above the water throughout her whole length, above which rose her glossy jet black bends, surmounted by a milk-white streak, broken at regular intervals into eleven goodly ports, from which the British cannon, ugly customers at the best, were grinning, tompion out, open-mouthed at us; and above all, the clean, well-stowed white hammocks filled the nettings, from taffrail to cat-head—oh! that I had been in one of them, snug on the berth deck! Aloft, a cloud of white sail swelled to the breeze, till the cloth seemed inclined to say good-by to the bolt ropes, bending the masts like willow-wands (as if the devil, determined to beat Paganini himself, was preparing fiddlesticks to play a spring with, on the cracking and straining weather shrouds and backstays), and tearing her sharp wedge-like bows out of the bowels of the long swell, until the cutwater, and ten yards of the keel next to it, were hove clean out of the sea, into which she would descend again with a roaring plunge, burying everything up to the hause-holes, and driving the brine into mist, over the fore-top, like vapour from a waterfall, through which, as she rose again, the bright red copper on her bows flashed back the sunbeams in momentary rainbows. We were so near, that I could with the naked eye distinctly see the faces of the men. There were at least 150 determined fellows at quarters, and clustered with muskets in their hands, wherever they could be posted to most advantage.

There they were in groups about the ports (I could even see the captains of the guns examining the locks), in their clean white frocks and trousers, the officers of the ship, and the marines, clearly distinguishable by their blue or red jackets.—*I could discern the very sparkle of the epaulets.*

High overhead the red cross, that for a thousand years "has braved the battle and the breeze," blew out strong from the peak, like a sheet of flickering white flame, or a thing instinct with life, struggling to tear away the ensign haulyards, and to escape high into the clouds; while from the main-royal mast-head the long white pennant streamed upwards into the azure heavens, like a ray of silver light. Oh! it was a sight "most beautiful to see," as the old song hath it,—but I confess I would have preferred that pleasure from t'other side of the hedge.

There was no hailing nor trumpeting, although, as we crossed on opposite tacks when we first weathered her, just before she hove in stays I had heard a shrill voice sing out, "Take good aim, men—fire!" But *now* each cannon in thunder shot forth its glance of flame, without a word being uttered, as she kept away to bring them to bear in succession, while the long feathery cloud of whirling white smoke that shrouded her sides from stem to stern, was sparkling brilliantly throughout with crackling musketry, for all the world like fireflies in a bank of night fog from the hills, until the breeze blew it back again through the rigging, and once more unveiled the lovely craft in all her pride and glory.

"You see all that," said Obed.

"To be sure I do, and I feel something too;" for a sharp rasping jar was repeated in rapid succession three or four times, as so many shot struck our hull, and made the splinters glance about merrily; and the musket-balls were mottling our top sides and spars, plumping into the timber, *whit, whit!* as thick as ever you saw schoolboys plastering a church-door with clay pellets. There was a heavy groan, and a stir amongst the seamen in the run.

"And, pray, do you see and hear all that yourself, Master Obed? The iron has clenched some of your chaps down there. Stay a bit, you shall have a better dose presently, you obstinate old ———."

He waved his hand, and interrupted me with great energy—"I *dare* not give in, I cannot give in; all I have in the world swims in the little hooker, and strike I will not so long as two planks stick together."

"Then," quoth I, "you are simply a damned, cold-blooded, calculating scoundrel—brave I will never call you." I saw he was now stung to the quick.

"Lieutenant, smuggler as I am, don't goad me to what worse I may have been; there are some deeds done in my time which, at a moment like this, I don't much like to think upon. I am a desperate man, Master Cringle; don't, for your own sake as well as mine, try me too far."

"Well, but—" persisted I. He would hear nothing.

"Enough said, sir, enough said; there was not an honester trader, nor a hap-pier man in all the Union, until your infernal pillaging and burning squadron in the Chesapeake captured and ruined me; but I paid it off on the prize-master, although we were driven on the rocks after all. I paid it off, and, God help me, I have never thriven since, enemy although he was. I see the poor fellow's face yet, as I—" He checked himself suddenly, as if aware that he might say more than could be conveniently retracted. "But I *dare not* be taken; let that satisfy you, Master Cringle, so go below—below with you, sir"—I saw he had succeeded in lashing himself into a fury—"or, by the Almighty God, who hears me, I shall be tempted to do another remembrance of which will haunt me till my dying day!"

All this passed in no time, as we say, much quicker than one can read it; and I now saw that the corvette had braced up sharp to the wind again on the same tack that we were on; so I slipped down like an eel, and once more stretched myself beside Paul, on the lee side of the cabin. We soon found that she was indeed after us in earnest, by the renewal of the cannonade and the breezing up of the small arms again. Two round-shot now tore right through the deck, just beneath the larboard coamings of the main hatchway; the little vessel's deck, as she lay over, being altogether exposed to the enemy's fire, they made her whole frame tremble again, smashing everything in their way to shivers, and going right out through her bottom on the opposite side, within a dozen streaks of her keel, while the rattling of the clustered grapeshot every now and then made us start, the musketry all the while peppering away like a hail shower. Still the skipper, who I expected every moment to see puffed away from the tiller like smoke, held upon deck as if he had been bullet-proof, and seemed to escape the hellish tornado of missiles of all sorts and sizes by a miracle.

"He is in league with the old one, Paul," said I "howsoever, you must be nabbed, for you see the ship is fore-reaching on you, and you can't go on t'other tack, surely, with these pretty eyelet holes between wind and water on the weather side there? Your captain is mad—why *will you*, then, and all these poor fellows, go down because *he dare* not surrender, for some good deed of his own, eh?"

The roar of the cannon and noise of the musketry made it necessary for me to raise my voice here, which the small scuttle, like Dionysius's ear, conveyed unexpectedly to my friend the captain on deck.

"Hand me up my pistols, Paul."

It had struck me before, and I was now certain, that from the time he had become so intensely excited as he was now, he spoke with a pure English accent, without the smallest dash of Yankeeism.

"So so; I see—no wonder you won't strike, you renegade," cried I.

"You have tampered with my crew, sir, and abused me," he announced, in a stern, slow tone, much more alarming than his former fierceness, "so take that to quiet you;" and deuce take me if he did not, the moment he received the pistols from his mate, fire slap at me, the ball piercing the large muscle of my neck on the right side, missing the artery by the merest accident. Thinking I was done for, I covered my face with my hands, and commended myself to God, with all the resignation that could be expected from a poor young fellow in my grievous circumstances, expecting to be cut off in the *prima vera* of his days, and to part for ever from ————. Poo! that there line is not my forte. However, finding the hæmorrhage by no means great, and that the wound was in fact slight, I took the captain's rather strong hint to be still, and lay quiet until a 32-pound shot struck us bang on the quarter. The subdued force with which it came, showed that we were widening our distance, for it did not drive through and through with a crash, but lodged in a timber; nevertheless it started one of the planks across which Paul and I lay, and pitched us both with extreme violence bodily into the run amongst the men, three of them lying amongst the ballast, which was covered with blood, two badly wounded and one dead. I came off with some slight bruises, however; not so the poor mate. He had been nearest the end or *butt* that was started, which thereby struck him so forcibly that it fractured his spine, and dashed him amongst his shipmates, shrieking piercingly in his great agony, and clutching whatever he could grasp with his hands, and tearing whatever he could reach with his teeth, while his limbs below his waist were dead and paralysed.

"Water, water!" he cried, "water, for the love of God, water!" The crew did all they could; but his torments increased—the blood began to flow from his mouth—his hands became clay-cold and pulseless—his features sharp, blue, and death-like—his respiration difficult; the choking death-rattle succeeded, and in ten minutes he was dead.

This was the last shot that told—every report became more and more faint, and the musketry soon ceased altogether.

The breeze had taken off, and the Wave, resuming her superiority in light winds, *had escaped.*

CHAPTER IX.

CUBA FISHERMEN.

"El Pescador de Puerto Escondido
Pesca mas que Pescado
Quando la Luna redonda
Reflexado en la mar profunda.
Pero cuidado,
El pobre sera el nino perdido
Si esta per *Anglisman* cojido.
Ay de mi."

IT WAS now five in the afternoon, and the breeze continued to fall, and the sea to go down, until sunset, by which time we had run the corvette hull down, and the schooner nearly out of sight. Right ahead of us rose the high land of Cuba, to the westward of Cape Maize, clear and well defined against the northern sky; and as we neither hauled our wind to weather the east end of the island, nor edged away for St Jago, it was evident, beyond all doubt, that we were running right in for some one of the piratical haunts on the Cuba coast.

The crew now set to work, and removed the remains of their late messmate, and the two wounded men, from where they lay upon the ballast in the run, to their own berth forward in the bows of the little vessel; they then replaced the planks which they had started, and arranged the dead body of the mate along the cabin floor, close to where I lay, faint and bleeding, and more heavily bruised than I had at first thought.

The captain was still at the helm; he had never spoken a word either to me or any of the crew since he had taken the trifling liberty of shooting me through the neck, and no thanks to him that the wound was not mortal; but he now resumed his American accent, and began to drawl out the necessary orders for repairing damages.

When I went on deck shortly afterwards, I was surprised beyond measure to perceive the injury the little vessel had sustained, and the uncommon speed, handiness, and skill with which it had been repaired. However lazily the command might appear to have been given, the execution of it was quick as lightning. The crew, now reduced to ten working hands, had, with an almost miraculous promptitude, knotted and spliced the rigging, mended and shifted sails, fished the sprung and wounded spars, and plugged and nailed lead over the shot-holes, and all within half an hour.

I don't like Americans; I never did, and never shall like them; I have seldom met with an American gentleman, in the large and complete sense of the term. I have no wish to eat with them, drink with them, deal with, or consort with them in any way; but let me tell the whole truth, *nor fight* with them, were it not for the laurels to be acquired, by overcoming an enemy so brave, determined, and alert, and every way so worthy of one's steel, as they have always proved. One used to fight with a Frenchman as a matter of course, and for the fun of the thing as it were, never dreaming of the possibility of Johnny Crapeau beating us, where there was anything approaching to an equality of force; but, say as much as we please about larger ships and more men, and a variety of excuses which proud John Bull, with some truth very often, I will admit, has pertinaciously thrust forward to palliate his losses during the short war, a regard for truth and fair dealing, which I hope are no scarce qualities amongst British seamen, compels me to admit that, although I would of course peril my life and credit more readily with an English crew, yet I believe a feather would turn the scale between the two countries, so far as courage and seamanship go; and let it not be forgotten, although we have now regained our superiority in this respect, yet, in gunnery and small-arm practice, we were as thoroughly weathered on by the Americans during the war, as we over-topped them in the bull-dog courage with which our boarders handled those genuine English weapons, the cutlass and pike.

After the captain had given his orders, and seen the men fairly at work, he came down to the cabin, still ghastly and pale, but with none of that ferocity stamped on his grim features, from the outpouring of which I had suffered so severely. He never once looked my way, no more than if I had been a bundle of old junk; but, folding his hands on his knee, he sat down on a small locker, against which the feet of the dead mate rested, and gazed earnestly on his face, which was immediately under the open skylight, through which, by this time, the clear cold rays of the moon streamed full on it, the short twilight having already fled, chained as it is in these climates to the chariot-wheels of the burning sun. My eye naturally followed his, but I speedily withdrew it. I had often bent over comrades who had been killed by gunshot wounds, and always remarked, what is well known, that the features wore a benign expression, bland and gentle, and contented as the face of a sleeping infant, while their limbs were composed decently, often gracefully, like one resting after great fatigue, as if nature, like an affectionate nurse, had arranged the deathbed of her departing child with more than usual care, preparatory to his last long sleep; whereas those who had died from the thrust of a pike, the blow of a cutlass, or any violent fracture, however mild the living expression of their countenance might have been, were always fearfully contorted both in body and face.

In the present instance, the eyes were wide open, white, prominent, and glazed like those of a dead fish; the hair, which was remarkably fine, and had been worn in long ringlets, amongst which a large gold earring glittered, the poor fellow having been a nautical dandy of the first water, was drenched and clotted into heavy masses with the death-sweat, and had fallen back on the deck from his forehead, which was well formed, high, broad, and massive. His nose was transparent, thin, and sharp, the tense skin on the bridge of it glancing in the silver light as if it had been glass. His mouth was puckered on one side into angular wrinkles, like a curtain drawn up awry, while a clotted stream of black gore crept from it sluggishly down his right cheek, and coagulated in a heap on the deck. His lower jaw had fallen, and there he lay agape with his mouth full of blood.

His legs—indeed his whole body below his loins, where the fracture of the spine had taken place—rested precisely as they had been arranged after he died; but the excessive swelling and puffing out of his broad chest contrasted shockingly with the shrinking of the body at the pit of the stomach, by which the arch of the ribs was left as well defined as if the skin had been drawn over a skeleton, and the distortion of the muscles of the cheeks and throat evinced the fearful strength of the convulsions which had preceded his dissolution. It was evident, indeed, that throughout his whole person above the waist, the nervous system had been utterly shattered; the arms, especially, appeared to have been awfully distorted, for when crossed on his breast, they had to be forcibly fastened down at the wrists by a band of spun yarn to the buttons of his jacket. His right hand was shut, with the exception of the fore-finger, which was extended, pointing upwards; but the whole arm, from the shoulder down, had the horrible appearance of straggling to get free from the cord which confined it.

Obed, by the time I had noticed all this, had knelt beside the shoulder of the corpse, and I could see by the moonlight that flickered across his face as the vessel rolled in the declining breeze, that he had pushed off his eye the uncouth spyglass which he had fastened over it during the chase, so that it now stood out from the middle of his forehead like a stunted horn; but, in truth, "it was not exalted," for he appeared crushed down to the very earth by the sadness of the scene before him, and I noticed the frequent sparkle of a heavy tear as it fell from his iron visage on the face of the dead man. At length he untied the string that fastened the eye-glass round his head, and taking a coarse towel from a locker, he sponged poor Paul's face and neck with rum, and then fastened up his lower jaw with the lanyard. Having performed this melancholy office, the poor fellow's feelings could no longer be restrained by my presence.

"God help me I have not now one friend in the wide world. When I had neither home, nor food, nor clothing, he sheltered me, and fed me, and clothed me, when a single word would have gained him five hundred dollars, and run me up to the foreyardarm in a wreath of white smoke; but he was true as steel; and oh that he was now doing for me what I have done for him! who would have moaned over me—me, who am now without wife or child, and have disgraced all my kin! alack-a-day, alack-a-day!" And he sobbed and wept aloud, as if his very heart would have burst in twain. "But I will soon follow you, Paul; I have had my warning already; I know it, and I believe it." At this instant the dead hand of the mate burst the ligature that kept it down across his body, and slowly rose up and remained in a beckoning attitude. I was seized with a cold shivering from head to foot, and would have shrieked aloud, had it not been for very shame, but Obed was unmoved. "I know it, Paul. I know it. I am ready, and I shall not be long behind you."

He fastened the arm down once more, and having called a couple of hands to assist him, they lashed up the remains of their shipmate in his hammock, with a piece of iron ballast at his feet, and then, without more ado, handed the body up through the skylight; and I heard the heavy splash as they cast it into the sea. When this was done, the captain returned to the cabin, bringing a light with him, filled and drank off a glass of strong grog. Yet he did not even now deign to notice me, which was by no means soothing; and I found that, since *he* wouldn't speak, *I* must, at all hazards.

"I say, Obed, do you ever read your Bible?" He looked steadily at me with his lacklustre eyes. "Because, if you do, you may perhaps have fallen in with some such passages as the following:—'Behold I am in your hand; but know ye for certain, that if you put me to death, ye shall surely bring innocent blood upon yourselves.'"

"It is true, Mr Cringle, I feel the truth of it here," and he laid his large bony hand on his heart. "Yet I do not ask you to forgive me; I don't expect that you can or will; but unless the devil gets possession of me again—which, so sure as ever there was a demoniac in this world, he had this afternoon when you so tempted me—I hope soon to place you in safety, either in a friendly port, or on board of a British vessel; and then what becomes of me is of little consequence, now since the only living soul who cared a dollar for me is at rest amongst the coral branches at the bottom of the deep green sea."

"Why, man," rejoined I, "leave off this stuff; something has turned your brain, surely; people must die in their beds, you know, if they be not shot, or put out of the way somehow or other; and as for my small affair, why, I forgive you, man—from my heart I forgive you; were it only for the oddity of your scantling, mental and corporeal, I would do so; and you see I am not much hurt—so lend me a hand, like a good fellow, to wash the wound with a little spirits—it will stop the bleeding, and the stiffness will soon go off—so—"

"Lieutenant Cringle, I need not tell what I know you have found out, that I am *not* the vulgar Yankee smuggler, fit only to be made a butt of by you and your friends, that you no doubt at first took me for; but who or what I am, or what I may have been, you shall never know—but I will tell you this much—"

"Devil confound the fellow!—why, this is too much upon the brogue, Obed. Will you help me to dress my wound, man, and leave off your cursed sentimental speeches, which you must have gleaned from some old novel or another? I'll hear it all by-and-by."

At this period I was a reckless young chap, with strong nerves, and my own share of that animal courage which generally oozes out at one's finger ends when one gets married and turned of thirty; nevertheless I did watch with some anxiety the effect which my unceremonious interruption was to have upon him. I was agreeably surprised to find that he took it all in good part, and set himself, with great alacrity, and kindness even, to put me to rights, and so successfully that, when I was washed and cleansed, and fairly coopered up, I found myself quite able to take my place at the table; and having no fear of the College of Surgeons before my eyes, I helped myself to a little of the needful, and in the plenitude of my heart I asked Obed's pardon for my ill-bred interruption.

"It was not quite the thing to cut you short in the middle of your Newgate Calendar, Obed—beg pardon, your story I mean; no offence now, none in the world—eh? But where the deuce, man, got you this fine linen of Egypt?"— looking at the sleeves of the shirt Obed had obliged me with, as I sat without my coat. "I had not dreamt you had anything so luxurious in your kit."

I saw his brow begin to lower again, so the devil prompted me to advert, by way of changing the subject, to a file of newspapers, which, as it turned out, might have proved to be by far the most dangerous topic I could have hit upon. He had laid them aside, having taken them out of the locker when he was rummaging for the linen. "What have we here?—Kingston Chronicle, Montego Bay Gazette, Falmouth Advertiser. A great newsmonger you must be. What arrivals?—let me see;—you know I am a week from headquarters.—Let me see."

At first he made a motion, as if he would have snatched them out of my hands, but speedily appeared to give up the idea, merely murmuring, "What can it signify *now?*"

I continued to read—"Chanticleer from a cruise—Tonnant from Barbadoes—Pique from Port-au-Prince. Oh, the next interests me—the Firebrand is daily expected from Havanna; she is to come through the Gulf, round Care Antonio, and beat up the haunts of the pirates all along the Cuba shore." I was certain *now* that at the mention of this corvette mine host winced in earnest. This made me anxious to probe him further. "Why, what means this pencil mark—'Firebrand's number off the Chesapeake was 1022?' How the deuce, my fine fellow, do *you* know that?"

He shook his head, but said nothing, and I went on reading the pencil memoranda—"'But this is most probably changed; she now carries a red cross in the head of her foresail, and has very short lower masts, like the Hornet.'" Still he made me no answer. I proceeded—"Stop, let me see what merchant ships are about sailing. 'Loading for Liverpool, the John Gladstone, Peter Pondeorus, master;'" and after it again in pencil—"'*Only* sugar: goes through the Gulf.'— Only sugar," said I, still fishing; "too bulky, I suppose.—'Ariel, Jenkins, Whitehaven;'" remark—"'Sugar, coffee, and logwood.' 'Nuestra Señora de los Dolores, to sail for Chagres on 7th proximo;'" remark—"'Rich cargo of bale goods, but no chance of overtaking her.'—'El Rayo to sail for St Jago de Cuba on the 10th proximo;'" remark—"'Sails fast; armed with a long gun and musketry; thirty hands; about ten Spanish passengers; valuable cargo of dry goods; mainmast rakes well aft;—new cloth in the foresail about half-way up; will be off the Moro about the 13th.'—And what is this written in ink under the above?—'The San Pedro from Chagres, and Marianita from Santa Martha, although rich, have both got convoy.'—Ah, too strong for your friends, Obed— I see, I see.—'Francis Baring, Loan French, master'—an odd name, rather, for a skipper:" remark—"'Forty seroons of cochineal and some specie; is to sail from Morant Bay on 5th proximo, to go through the windward passage; may be expected off Cape St Nicolas on the 12th, or thereby.'" I laid down the paper and looked him full in the face. "Nicolas is an ominous name. I fear the good ship Francis Baring will find it so. Some of the worthy saint's clerks to be fallen in with off the Mole, eh? Don't you think as I do, Obed?" Still silent. "Why, you seem to take great delight in noting the intended departures and expected arrivals, my friend—merely to satisfy your curiosity, of course; but, to come to close quarters with you, captain, I now know pretty well the object of your visiting Jamaica now and then; you are indeed no vulgar *smuggler*."

"It is well for you and good for myself, Mr Cringle, that something weighs heavy at my heart at this moment, and that there is that about you which, notwithstanding your ill-timed jesting, commands my respect and engages my good-will—had it not been so, you would have been alongside of poor Paul at this moment." He leant his arms upon the table, and gazed intensely on my face, as he continued in a solemn tremulous tone—"Do you believe in auguries, Mr Cringle? Do you believe that 'coming events cast their shadows before?'"— Oh, that little Wiggy Campbell had been beside me, to have seen the figure and face of the man who now quoted him!

"Yes, I do; it is part of the creed of every sailor to do so; I do believe that people have had forewarnings of peril to themselves or their friends."

"Then what do you think of the mate beckoning me with his dead hand to follow him?"

"Why, you are raving, Obed; you saw that he had been much convulsed, and that the limb, from the contraction of the sinews, much was forcibly kept down in the position it broke loose from—the spunyarn gave way, and of course it started up—nothing wonderful in all this, although it did at the time somewhat startle me. I confess."

"It may be so, it may be so; I don't know," rejoined he, "but taken along with what I saw before—" Here his voice sank into so hollow and sepulchral a tone as to be almost unintelligible. "But there is no use in arguing on the subject. Answer me this, Lieutenant Cringle, and truly, so help you God at your utmost need. *Did the mate leave the cabin at any moment after I was wounded by the splinter?* And he seized one of my hands convulsively with his iron paw, while he pointed up through the open scuttle towards heaven with the other, which trembled like a reed. The moon shone strong on the upper part of his countenance, while the yellow smoky glare of the candle over which he bent, blending harshly and unharmoniously with the pale silver light, fell full on his uncouth figure, and on his long scraggy bare neck and chin and cheeks, giving altogether a most unearthly expression to his savage features, from the conflicting tints and changing shadows cast by the flickering moonbeams streaming fitfully through the skylight on the one hand, as the vessel rolled to and fro, and by the large torch-like candle on the other, as it wavered in the night wind. The Prince of the Powers of the Air might have sat for his picture by proxy. It was just such a face as one has dreamed of after a hot supper and cold ale, when the whisky had been forgotten—horrible, changing, vague, glimmering, and undefined; and as if something was still wanting to complete the utter frightfulness of his aspect, the splinter wound in his head burst afresh from his violent agitation, and streamed down in heavy drops from his forehead, falling warm on my hand. I was much shaken at being adjured in this tremendous way, *with the hot blood glueing our hands together,* but I returned his grasp as steadily as I could, while I replied, with all the composure he had left me, and that would not have quite filled a Winchester bushel—

"He never left my side from the time he offered to take your place after you had been wounded."

He fell back against the locker as if he had been shot through the heart; his grasp relaxed, he drew his breath very hard, and I thought he had fainted.

"Then it was *not* him that stood by me; I thought it *might* have been him, but I was a fool, it was impossible."

He made a desperate effort to recover his composure, and succeeded.

"And, pray, Master Obediah," quoth I, *"what did* you see?"

He answered me sharply—"Never mind, never mind—here, Potomac, lend us a hand to sling a cot for this gentleman; there now, see the lanyard is sound, and the lacing all tight and snug; now, put that mattress into it, and there is linen in the chest."

In a trice my couch was rigged, all comfortable, snow-white linen, nice pillow, soft mattress, &c., and Obed, filling me another tumbler, helped himself also; he then drank to my health, wished me a sound sleep, promised to call me at daylight, and, as he left the cabin, he said, "Mr Cringle, had it been my object to have injured you, I would not have waited until now. You are quite safe, so far as depends on me, so take your rest—good night, once more."

I tumbled into bed, and never once opened my eyes until Obed called me at daylight, that is, at five in the morning, according to his promise.

By this time we were well in with the Cuba shore; the land might be two miles from us, as we could see the white surf. Out at sea, although all around was clear as crystal, there was nothing to be seen of the Gleam or Firebrand, but there were ten or twelve fishing canoes, each manned with from four to six hands, close aboard of us; we seemed to have got becalmed in the middle of a small fleet of them. The nearest to us hailed in Spanish, in a very friendly way.

"Como estamos capitan, que hay de nuevo; hay algo de bueno, para los pobres *Pescadores?*" and the fellow who had spoken laughed loudly.

The captain desired him to come on board, and then drew him aside, conversing earnestly with him. The Spanish fisherman was a very powerful man; he was equipped in a blue cotton shirt, Osnaburg trousers, sandals of untanned bullock's hide, a straw hat, and wore the eternal greasy red sash and long knife. He was a bold, daring-looking fellow, and frequently looked frowningly on me, and shook his head impatiently, while the captain, as it seemed, was explaining to him who I was. Just in this nick of time my friend Potomac handed up my uniform coat (I had previously been performing my ablutions on deck in my shirt and trousers), which I put on, swab and all, thinking no harm. But there must have been mighty great offence, nevertheless, for the fisherman, in a twinkling, casting a fierce look at me, jumped overboard like a feather, clearing the rail like a flying-fish, and swam to his canoe, that had shoved off a few paces.

When he got on board he stood up and shook his clenched fist at Obed, shouting, "Picaro, traidor, Ingleses hay abordo, quieres engañarnos!" He then held up the blade of his paddle, a signal which all the canoes answered in a moment in the same manner, and then pulled towards the land, from whence a felucca, invisible until that moment, now swept out, as if she had floated up to the surface by magic, for I could neither see creek nor indentation on the shore, nor the smallest symptom of any entrance to a port or cove. For a few minutes the canoes clustered round this necromantic craft, and I could notice that two or three hands from each of them jumped on board; they then paddled off in a string, and vanished one by one amongst the mangrove bushes as suddenly as the felucca had appeared. All this puzzled me exceedingly—I looked at Obed—he was evidently sorely perplexed.

"I had thought to have put you on board a British vessel before this, or, failing that, to have run down and landed you at St Jago, Mr Cringle, as I promised; but you see I am prevented by these *honest* men there. Get below, and as you value your life, and I may say mine, keep your temper, and be civil."

I did as he suggested, but peeped out of the cabin skylight to see what was going on, notwithstanding. The felucca was armed with a heavy carronade on a pivot, and as full of men as she could hold—fierce, half-naked, savage-looking fellows; she swept rapidly up to us, and closing on our larboard quarter, threw about five-and-twenty of her genteel young people on board, who immediately secured the crew, and seized Obed. However, they, that is the common sailors, seemed to have no great stomach for the job, and had it not been for the fellow I had frightened overboard, I don't think one of them would have touched him. Obed bore all this with great equanimity.

"Why, Francisco," he said to this personage, in good Spanish, "why, what madness is this? your suspicions are groundless; it is as I tell you, he is my prisoner, and whatever he may have been to me, he can be no spy on you."

"Cuchillo entonces," was the savage reply.

"No, no," persisted Obediah, "get cool, man, get cool; I am pledged that no harm shall come to him; and further, I have promised to put him ashore at St Jago, and I *will* be as good as my word."

"You can't if you would," rejoined Francisco; "the Snake is at anchor under the Moro."

"Then he must go with us."

"We shall see as to that," said the other; then raising his voice, he shouted to his ragamuffins, "Comrades, we are betrayed; there is an English officer on board, who can be nothing but a spy; follow me!"

And he dashed down the companion ladder, knife in hand, while I sprang through the small scuttle, like a rat out of one hole when a ferret is put in at the other, and crept as close to Obed as I could. Francisco, when he missed me, came on deck again. The captain had now seized a cutlass in one hand, and held a cocked pistol in the other. It appeared he had greater control, the nature of which I now began to comprehend, over the felucca's people than Francisco bargained for, for at the moment the latter went below, they released him, and went forward in a body. My persecutor again advanced close up to me, seized me by the collar with one hand, and tried to drag me forward, brandishing his naked knife aloft in the other.

Obed stuck his pistol in his belt, and promptly caught his sword-arm; "Francisco," he exclaimed, still in Spanish, "fool, madman, let go your hold! let go, or by the heaven above us, and the hell we are both hastening to, I will strike you dead!"

The man paused, and looked round to his own people, and seeing one or two encouraging glances and gestures amongst them, he again attempted to drag me away from my hold on the taffrail. Something flashed in the sun and the man fell! His left arm, the hand of which still clutched my throat, while mine grasped its wrist, had been shred from his body by Obed's cutlass, like a twig; and, O God, my blood curdles to my heart even now when I think of it! the dead fingers kept the grasp sufficiently long to allow the arm to fall heavily against my side, where it hung for a second, until the muscles relaxed, and it dropped on the deck. The instant that Obed struck the blow, he caught hold of my hand, threw away his cutlass, and advanced towards the group of the felucca's men, pistol in hand.

"Am I not your captain, ye cowards—have I ever deceived you yet—have I ever flinched from heading you where the danger was greatest—have you not all that I am worth in your hands, and will you murder me now?"

"Viva, el noble capitan, viva!"

And the tide turned as rapidly in our favour as it had lately ebbed against us.

"As for that scoundrel, he has got no more than he deserves," said he turning to where Francisco lay, bleeding like a carcass in the shambles; "but tie up his arm, some of ye, I would be sorry he bled to death."

It was unavailing—the large arteries had emptied his whole life-blood—he had already gone to his account.

This most miserable transaction, with all its concomitant horrors, to my astonishment, did not seem to make much impression on Obed, who now, turning to me, said, with perfect composure—

"You have there another melancholy voucher for my sincerity," pointing to the body; "but time presses, and you must now submit to be blindfolded, and that without further explanation at present."

I did so with the best grace I could, and was led below, where two beauties, with loaded pistols and a drawn knife each, obliged me with their society, one seated on each side of me on the small locker, like two deputy butchers ready to operate on an unfortunate veal. It had now fallen dead calm, and from what I heard, I conjectured that the felucca was sweeping in towards the land with us in tow, for the sound of the surf grew louder and louder. By-and-by we seemed to slide beyond the long smooth swell into broken water, for the little vessel pitched sharp and suddenly, and again all was still, and we seemed to have sailed into some land-locked cove. From the loud echo of the voices on deck, I judged that we were in a narrow canal, the banks of which were reflecting the sound; presently this ceased, and although we skimmed along as motionless as before, I no longer heard the splash of the felucca's sweeps, the roar of the sea gradually died away, until it sounded like distant thunder, and I thought we touched the ground now and then, although slightly. All at once the Spanish part of the crew—for we still had a number of the felucca's people with us—sang out "Palanka," and we began to pole along a narrow marshy lagoon, coming so near the shore occasionally, that our sides were brushed by the branches of the mangrove bushes. Again the channel seemed to widen, and I could hear the felucca once more ply her sweeps. In about ten minutes after this the anchor was let go, and for a quarter of an hour nothing was heard on deck but the bustle of the people furling sails, coiling down the ropes, and getting everything in order, as is usual in coming into port. It was evident that several boats had boarded us soon after we anchored, as I could make out part of the greetings between the strangers and Obed, in which my own name recurred more than once. In a little while all was still again, and Obed called down the companion to my guards, that I might come on deck—a boon I was not long in availing myself of.

We were anchored nearly in the centre of a shallow swampy lagoon, about a mile across, as near as I could judge; two very large schooners, heavily armed, were moored ahead of us—one on each bow—and another, rather smaller, lay close under our stern; they all had sails bent, and everything apparently in high order, and were full of men. The shore, to the distance of a bow-shot from the water all around us, was low, marshy, and covered with an impervious jungle of thick strong reeds and wild canes, with here and there a thicket of mangroves; a little farther off, the land swelled into lofty hills, covered to the very summit with heavy timber, but everything had a moist, green, steamy appearance, as if it had been the region of perpetual rain. "Lots of yellow fever here," thought I, as the heavy rank smell of decayed vegetable matter came off, on the faint sickly breeze, and the sluggish fog-banks crept along the dull clay-coloured motionless surface of the tepid water. The sea view was quite shut out; I looked all round and could discern no vestige of the entrance. Right ahead there was about a furlong of land cleared at the only spot which one could call a beach, that is, a hard shore of sand and pebbles. Had you tried to get ashore at any other point your fate would have been that of the Master of Ravenswood—as fatal, that is, without the gentility; for you would have been suffocated in black mud in place of clean sea-sand. There was a long shed in the centre of this cleared spot, covered in with boards, and thatched with palm leaves; it was open below, a sort of capstan-house, where a vast quantity of sails, anchors, cordage, and most kinds of sea-stores, were stowed, carefully covered over with tarpauling. Overhead there was a flooring laid along the couples of the roof, the whole length of the shed, forming a loft of nearly sixty feet long, divided by bulkheads into a variety of apartments, lit by small rude windows in the thatch, where the crews of the vessels, I concluded, were occasionally lodged during the time they might be under repair. The boat was manned, and Obed took me ashore with him.

We landed near the shed I have described, beneath which we encountered about forty of the most uncouth and ferocious-looking rascals that my eyes had ever been blessed withal; they were of every shade, from the woolly negro and long-haired Indian, to the sallow American and fair Biscayan; and as they intermitted their various occupations of mending sails, fitting and stretching rigging, splicing ropes, making spun-yarn, coopering gun-carriages, grinding pikes and cutlasses, and filling cartridges, to look at me, they grinned and nodded to each other, and made sundry signs and gestures which made me regret many a past peccadillo that in more prosperous times I little thought on or repented of, and I internally prayed that I might be prepared to die as became a man, for my fate appeared to be sealed. The only ray of hope that shot into my mind, through all this gloom, came from the respect the thieves, one and all, paid the captain; and, as I had reaped the benefit of assuming an outward recklessness and daring, which I really did not at heart possess, I screwed myself up to maintain the same port still, and swaggered along, jabbering in my broken Spanish, right and left, and jesting even with the most infamous-looking scoundrels of the whole lot, while, God he knows, my heart was palpitating like a girl's when she is asked to be married. Obed led the way up a ladder into the loft, where we found several messes at dinner; and, passing through various rooms, in which a number of hammocks were slung, we at length arrived at the eastern end, which was boarded off into an apartment eighteen or twenty feet square, lighted by a small port-hole in the end, about ten feet from the ground. I could see several huts from this window, built just on the edge of the high wood, where some of the country people seemed to be moving about, and round which a large flock of pigs and from twenty to thirty bullocks were grazing. All beyond, as far as the eye could reach, was one continuous forest, without any vestige of a living thing; not even a thin wreath of blue smoke evinced the presence of a fellow-creature; I seemed to be hopelessly cut off from all succour, and my heart again died within me.

"I am sorry to say you must consider yourself a prisoner here for a few days," said Obed.

I could only groan.

"But the moment the coast is clear, I will be as good as my word, and land you at St Jago."

I groaned again. The man was moved.

"I would I could do so sooner," he continued; "but you see by how precarious a tenure I hold my control over these people; therefore I must be cautious, for your sake as well as my own, or they would make little of murdering both of us, especially as the fellow who would have cut your throat this morning has many friends amongst them; above all, I dare not leave them for any purpose for some days. I must recover my seat, in which, by the necessary severity you witnessed, I have been somewhat shaken. So good-by; there is cold meat in that locker, and some claret to wash it down with. Don't, I again warn you, venture out during the afternoon or night. I will be with you betimes in the morning. So good-by so long. Your cot, you see, is ready slung."

He turned to depart, when, as if recollecting himself, he stooped down, and taking hold of a ring, he lifted up a trap-door, from which there was a ladder leading down to the capstan-house.

"I had forgotten this entrance; it will be more convenient for me in my visits."

In my heart I believe he intended this as a hint that I should escape through the hole at some quiet opportunity; and he was descending the ladder, when he stopped and looked round, greatly mortified, as it struck me.

"I forgot to mention that a sentry has been placed, I don't know by whose orders, at the foot of the ladder, to whom I must give orders to fire at you, if you venture to descend. You see how the land lies: I can't help it."

This was spoken in a low tone, then aloud—"There are books on that shelf behind the canvass screen; if you can settle to them, they may amuse you."

He left me, and I sat down disconsolate enough. I found some Spanish books, and a volume of Lord Byron's poetry, containing the first canto of Childe Harold, two numbers of Blackwood, and several other English books and magazines, *the names of the owners on all of them being carefully erased.*

But there was nothing else that indicated the marauding life of friend Obediah, whose apartment I conjectured was now my prison, if I except a pretty extensive assortment of arms, pistols, and cutlasses, and a range of massive cases,—with iron clamps, which were ranged along one side of the room. I paid my respects to the provender and claret; the hashed chicken was particularly good; bones rather large or so, but flesh white and delicate. Had I known that I was dining upon a guana, or large wood lizard, I scarcely think I would have made so hearty a meal. Long cork, No. 2, followed ditto, No. 1; and as the shades of evening, as poets say, began to fall by the time I had finished it, I toppled quietly into my cot, said my prayers, such as they were, and fell asleep.

It must have been towards morning, from the damp freshness of the air that came through the open window, when I was roused by the howling of a dog, a sound which always moves me. I shook myself, but before I was thoroughly awake, it ceased; it appeared to have been close under my window.

I was turning to go to sleep again, when a female, in a small suppressed voice, sung the following snatch of a vulgar Port Royal ditty, which I scarcely forgive myself for introducing here to polite society:

> *"Young hofficer come home at night,*
> *Him gave me ring and kisses;*
> *Nine months, one picaniny white,*
> *Him white almost like missis.*
> *But missis fum* my back wid switch,*
> *Him say de shild for massa;*
> *But massa say him—"*

The singer broke off suddenly, as if disturbed by the approach of some one.

"Hush, hush, you old foolish ———" said a man's voice, in the same low whispering tone; "you will waken de dronken sentry dere, when we shall all be put in iron. Hush, he will know my voice more better."

It was now clear that some one wished to attract my attention besides, I had a dreamy recollection of having heard both the male and female voices before. I listened, therefore, all alive. The man began to sing in the same low tone

> *"Newfoundland dog love him master de morest*
> *Of all de dog ever I see;*
> *Let him starve him, and kick him, and cuff him de sorest,*
> *Difference none never makee to he."*

There was a pause for a minute or two.

"It no use," the same voice continued; "him either no dere, or he won't hear us."

"Stop," said the female, "stop; woman head good for someting. I know who be shall hear.—Here, good dog, sing psalm; good dog, sing psalm," and thereupon a long loud melancholy howl rose wailing through the night air.

---

*Fum—Flog

"If that be not my dear old dog Sneezer, it is a deuced good imitation of him," thought I.

The woman again spoke—"Youl leetle piece more, good dog," and the howl was repeated.

I was now certain. By this time I had risen and stood at the open window; but it was too dark to see anything distinctly below. I could barely distinguish two dark figures, and what I concluded was the dog sitting on end between them.

"Who are you? what do you want with me?"

"Speak softly, massa, speak softly, or de sentry may hear us, for all de rum I give him."

Here the dog recognised me, and nearly spoiled sport altogether; indeed it might have cost us our lives, for he began to bark and frisk about, and to leap violently against the end of the capstan-house, in vain endeavours to reach the window.

"Down, Sneezer, down, sir; you used to be a dog of some sense; down."

But Sneezer's joy had capsized his discretion, and the sound of my voice pronouncing his name drove him mad altogether, and he bounded against the end of the shed, like a battering-ram.

"Stop, man, stop," and I held down the bight of my neckcloth, with an end in each hand. He retired, took a noble run, and in a trice hooked his forepaws in the handkerchief, and I hauled him in at the window. "Now, Sneezer, down with you, sir, down with you, or your rampaging will get all our throats cut." He cowered at my feet, and was still as a lamb from that moment. I stepped to the window. "Now, who are you, and what do you want?" said I.

"Ah, massa, you no know me?"

"How the devil should I? Don't you see it is as dark as pitch?"

"Well, massa, I will tell you; it is *me*, massa."

"I make no great doubt of that; but who may *you* be?"

"Lord, you are de foolis person now; make *me* talk to him," said the female. "Massa, never mind he, dat stupid fellow is my husband, and surely massa know *me?*"

"Now, my very worthy friends, I think you want to make yourselves known to me; and if so, pray have the goodness to tell me your names, that is, if I can in any way serve you."

"To be sure you can, massa; for dat purpose I come here."

The woman hooked the word out of his mouth. "Yes, massa, you must know me as Nancy, and dat old stupid is my husband, Peter Mangrove, him who—"

Here Peter chimed in—"Yes, massa, Peter Mangrove is de person you have de honour to address, and—" here he lowered his voice still more, although the whole dialogue from the commencement had been conducted in no higher tone than a loud whisper—"we have secured one big large canoe, near de mout of dis dam hole, which, wid your help, I tink we shall be able to launch troo de surf; and once in smoot water, den no fear but we shall run down de coast safely before de wind till we reach St Jago."

My heart jumped against my ribs. Here's an unexpected chance, thought I. "But, Peter, how, in the name of mumbo jumbo, came you *here?*"

"Why, massa, you do forget a leetle, dat I am a Creole negro, and not a naked tatooed African, whose exploits, dat is de wonderful ting him *never* do in him's own country, him get embroidered and pinked in gunpowder on him breech; beside, I am a Christian gentleman like youshef; so d——n mumbo jumbo, Massa Cringle."

I saw where I had erred. "So say I, Peter, d——n mumbo jumbo particularly; but how came you here, man? tell me that."

"Why, massa, I was out in de pilot-boat schooner, wid my wife here, and five more hands, waiting for de outward bound, tinking no harm, when dem piratical rascal catch we, and carry us off. Yankee privateer bad enough; but who ever hear of pilot being carry off?—blasphemy dat—carry off pilot! Who ever dream of such a ting? every shivilized peoples respect pilot!—oh Lord"—and he groaned in spirit for several seconds.

"And the dog?" inquired I.

"Oh, massa, I could not leave him at home; and since you was good enough to board him wid us, he has messed wid us, ay and slept wid us; and when we started last, although he showed some dislike at going on board, I had only to say, Sneezer, we go look for you massa; and he make such a bound dat he capsize my old woman dere, heel over head; oh dear, what display, Nancy, you was exhibit!"

"Hold your tongue, Peter; you hab no decency, you old willain."

"Well, but, Peter, speak out; when are we to make the attempt? where are the rest of your crew?"

"Oh dear! oh dear! dat is de worstest; oh dear!" and he began to cry and sob like the veriest child. "Oh, massa"—after he had somewhat recovered himself;—"Oh massa, dese people debils. Why, de make all de oder on board walk de plank, wid two ten-pound shot, one at each foot, Oh, if you had seen de clear shining blue skin, as de became leetle and leetle, and more leetler, down far in de clear green sea! Oh dear! oh dear! Only to tink dat each wavering black spot was fellow-creature like one-shef, wid de heart's blood warm in his bosom at de very instant of time we lost sight of him for ever!"

"God bless me," said I; "and how did you escape, and the black dog, and the black—ahem—beg pardon—your wife I mean; how were you spared?"

"Ah, massa! I can't say; but bad as de were, de seemed to have a liking for brute beasts, so dem save Sneezer, and my wife, and myshef; we were de only quadrupeds saved out of de whole crew—Oh dear! oh dear!"

"Well, well; I know enough now. I will spare you the pain of any further recital, Peter; so tell me what I am to do."

"Stop, massa, till I see if de sentry be still sound. I know de fellow, he was one on dem; let me see"—and I heard him through the loose flooring boards walk to the foot of the trap ladder leading up to my berth. The soliloquy that followed was very curious of its kind. The negro had excited himself by a recapitulation of the cruelties exercised on his unfortunate shipmates, and the unwarrantable caption of himself and rib—a deed that in the nautical calendar would rank in atrocity with the murder of a herald or the bearer of a flag of truce. He kept murmuring to himself, as he groped about in the dark for the sentry—"Catch pilot! who ever hear of such a ting? I suppose dem would have pull down lighthouse, if dere had been any for pull.—Where is dis sentry rascal?—him surely no sober yet?"

The sentry had fallen asleep as he leant back on the ladder, and had gradually slid down into a sitting position, with his head leaning against one of the steps, as he reclined with his back towards it, thus exposing his throat and neck to the groping paw of the black pilot.

"Ah—here him is, snoring heavy as my Nancy—well, dronk still; no fear of him overhearing we—nice position him lie in—quite convenient—could cut his troat now—slice him like a pumpkin—de debil is surely busy wid me, Peter. I find de wery clasp-knife in my starboard pocket beginning to open of himshef."

I tapped on the floor with my foot.

"Ah, tank you, Massa Tom—de debil nearly get we all in a scrape just now. However, I see him is quite sound—de sentry dat is, for de oder never sleep, you know." He had again come under the window. "Now, lieutenant, in two word, to-morrow night at two bells, in de middle watch, I will be here, and we shall make a start of it; will you venture, sir?"

"Will I?—to be sure I will; but why not now, Peter? why not now?"

"Ah, massa, you no smell de daylight; near daybreak already, sir. Can't make try dis night, but to-morrow night I shall be here punctual."

"Very well, but the dog, man? If he be found in my quarters, we shall be blown, and I scarcely think he will leave me."

"Garamighty! true enough, massa! what is to be done? De people know de dog was catch wid *me*, and if he be found wid *you*, den de will sospect we communication togidder. What is to be done?"

I was myself not a little perplexed, when Nancy whispered, "De dog have more sense den many Christian person. Tell him he must go wid us dis *one* night, no tell him *dis* night, else him won't; say *dis one* night, and dat if him don't, we shall all be deaded; try him, massa."

I had benefited by more extraordinary hints before now, although, well as I knew the sagacity of the poor brute, I could not venture to hope it would come up to the expectations of Mrs Mangrove. But I'll try.—"Here, Sneezer, here, my boy; you must go home with Peter to-night, or we shall all get into a deuced mess; so here, my boy, here is the bight of the handkerchief again, and through the window you must go; come, Sneezer, come."

To my great joy and surprise, the poor dumb beast rose from where he had coiled himself at my feet, and after having actually embraced me, by putting his fore paws on my shoulders, as he stood on his hind legs, and licked my face from ear to ear, uttering a low, fondling, nuzzling sort of whine like a nurse caressing a child, he at once leapt on the window sill, put his fore paws through the handkerchief, and was dropped to the ground again. I could immediately perceive the two dark figures of the pilot and his wife, followed by the dog, glide away as noiselessly as if they had been spirits of the night, until they were lost under the shade of the thick jungle.

I turned in, and—what will not youth and fatigue do?—I fell once more fast asleep, and never opened my eyes until Obed shook me in my cot about eight o'clock in the morning.

"Good morning, lieutenant. I have sent up your breakfast, but you don't seem inclined to eat it."

"Don't you believe it, my dear Obed. I have been sound asleep till this moment; only stop till I have slipped on my—those shoes, if you please—thank you—waistcoat—that will do. Now—coffee, fish, yams, and plantains, and biscuit, white as snow, and short as—and eggs—and—zounds! claret to finish with?—Why, Obed, you surely don't desire that I should enjoy all these delicacies in solitary blessedness?"

"Why, I intend to breakfast with you, if my society be not disagreeable."

"Disagreeable! Not in the least, quite the contrary. That black grouper looks remarkably beautiful. Another piece of yam, if you please.—Shall I fill you a cup of coffee, Obed? For my own part, I always stow the ground tier of my cargo dry, and then take a top-dressing. Write this down as an approved axiom with all thorough breakfast-eaters. Why, man, you are off your feed; what are you turning up your ear for, in that incomprehensible fashion, like a duck in thunder? A little of the claret—thank you. The very best butter I have ever eaten out of Ireland—now, some of that avocado pear—and as for biscuit, Leman never came up to it. I say, man,—hillo, where are you?—rouse ye out of your brown study, man."

"Did you hear that, Mr Cringle?"

"Hear what?—I heard nothing," rejoined I; "but hand me over that land-crab.—Thank you, and you may send the spawl of that creeping thing along with it; that guana. I had a dislike to eating a lizard at first, but I have got over it somehow;—and a thin slice of ham, a small taste of the unclean beast, Obed—peach-fed, I'll warrant."

There was a pause. The report of a great gun came booming along, reverberated from side to side of the lagoon, the echoes growing shorter and shorter, and weaker and weaker, until they growled themselves asleep in a hollow rumble like distant thunder.

"Ha, ha! Dick Gasket for a thousand! Old Blowhard has stuck in your skirts, Master Obed—but, Lord help me, man! let us finish our breakfast; he won't be *here* this half hour."

I expected to see mine host's forehead lowering like a thunder cloud from my ill-timed funning; but to my surprise, his countenance exhibited more amenity than I thought had been in the nature of the beast, as he replied,—

"Why, lieutenant, the felucca put to sea last night, to keep a bright look-out at the mouth of our cove here. I suppose that is him overhauling some vessel."

"It may be so;—hush! there's another gun—*Two!*"

Obed changed countenance at the double report.

"I say, Obed, the felucca did not carry more than *one* gun when I saw her, and she has had no time to load and fire again."

He did not answer a word, but continued, with a piece of guana on the end of his fork in one hand, and a cup of coffee in the other, as if he had been touched by the wand of a magician. Presently we heard one or two dropping shots, quickly thickening into a rattle of musketry. He threw down his food, picked up his hat, and trundled down-stairs, as if the devil had kicked him. "Pedro que hay?" I could hear him say to some one below, who appeared to have arrived in great haste, for he gasped for breath

"Aqui viene la felucha," answered Pedro; "perseguido por dos lanchas cañoneras llenas de gente."

"Abordo entonces, abordo todo el mundo; arma, arma, aqui vienen los Engleses; arma, arma!"

And all from that instant was a regular hillabaloo. The drums on board the schooners beat to quarters, a great bell, formerly the ornament of some goodly ship, no doubt, which had been slung in the fork of a tree, clanged away at a furious rate, the crews were hurrying to and fro, shouting to each other in Creole Spanish and Yankee English, while every cannon-shot from the felucca or the boat-guns came louder and louder, and the small-arms peppered away sharper and sharper. The shouts of the men engaged, both friends and foes, were now heard, and I could hear Obed's voice on board the largest schooner, which lay full in view from my window, giving orders, not only to his own crew, but to those of the others. I heard him distinctly sing out, after ordering them to haul upon the spring on his cable, "Now, men, I need not tell you to fight bravely, for if you are taken every devil of you will be hanged, so hoist away the signal," and a small black ball flew up through the rigging, until it reached the maintopgallant-masthead of the schooner, where it hung a moment, and in the next blew out in a large *black* swallow-tailed flag, like a commodore's broad pennant.

"Now," shrieked he, "let me see who dares give in with *this* voucher for his honestly flying aloft!"

I twisted and craned myself out of the window, to get a view of what was going on elsewhere; however, I could see nothing but Obed's large schooner from it, all the other craft were out of the range of my eye, being hid by the projecting roof of the shed. The noise continued—the shouting rose higher than ever—the other schooners opened their fire, both cannon and musketry; and from the increasing vehemence of the Spanish exclamations, and the cheering on board Obed's vessels, I concluded the attacking party were having the worst of it. My dog Sneezer now came jumping and scrambling up the trap-stair, his paws slipping between the bars at every step, his mouth wide open, and his tongue hanging out, while he barked, and yelled, and gasped to get at me, as if his life depended on it. After him I could see the round woolly pate of Peter Mangrove, Esquire, as excited apparently as the dog, and as anxious to get up; but they got jammed together in a small hatch, and stuck there, man and beast. At length Peter spoke—

"Now, sir, now! Nancy has run on before to de beach wid two paddles; now for it, now for it."

Down trundled master and dog and pilot. By this time there was no one in the lower part of the shed, which was full of smoke, while the infernal tumult on the water still raged as furiously as ever—the shot of all sorts and sizes hissing and splashing and *ricochetting* along the smooth surface of the harbour, as if there had been a sleet of musket and cannon balls and grape. Peter struck out at the top of his speed, Sneezer and I followed. We soon reached the jungle, dashed through a path that had been recently cleared with a cutlass or billhook, for the twigs were freshly shred, and in about ten minutes reached the high wood. However, no rest for the wicked, although the row seemed lessening now.

"Some one has got the worst of it," said I.

"Never mind, massa," quoth Peter, "or we shan't get de betterest ourshef."

And away we galloped again, until I had scarcely a rag an inch square on my back, or *anywhere* else, and my skin was torn in pieces by the prickly bushes and spear-grass. The sound of firing now ceased entirely, although there was still loud shouting now and then.

"Push on, massa—dem will soon miss we."

"True enough, Peter—but what is that?" as we came to a bundle of clouts walloping about in the morass.

"De debil it must be, I tink," said the pilot "No my Nancy it is, sticking in the mud up to her waist; what shall us do? you tink, massa, we hab time for can stop to pick she out?"

"Heaven have mercy, Peter—yes, unquestionably."

"Well, massa, you know best."

So we tugged at the sable heroine, and first one leg came home out of the tenacious clay, with a plop, then the other was drawn out of the quagmire. We then relieved her of the paddles, and each taking hold of one of the poor half-dead creature's hands, we succeeded in getting down to the beach, about half a mile to leeward of the entrance to the cove. We found the canoe there, plumped Nancy stern foremost into the bottom of it for ballast, gathered all our remaining energies for a grand shove, and ran her like lightning into the surf, till the water flashed over and over us, reaching to our necks. Next moment we were both swimming, and the canoe, although full of water, beyond the surf, rising and falling on the swell. We scrambled on board, set Nancy to bale with Peter's hat, seized our paddles, and sculled away like fury for ten minutes right out to sea, without looking once about us, until a musket-shot whistled over our heads, then another, and a third; and I had just time to hold up a white hand-kerchief, to prevent a whole platoon being let drive at us from the deck of his Britannic Majesty's schooner Gleam, lying-to about a cable's length to wind-ward of us, with the Firebrand a mile astern of her out at sea. In five minutes we got on board of the former.

"Mercy on me, Tom Cringle, and is this the way we are to meet again?" said old Dick Gasket, as he held out his large, bony, sunburnt hand to me. "You have led me a nice dance, in a vain attempt to redeem you from bondage, Tom; but I am delighted to see you, although I have not had the credit of being your deliverer—very glad to see you, Tom; but come along, man, come down with me, and let me rig you, not quite a Stultze's fit, you know, but a jury rig you shall have, as good as Dick Gasket's kit can furnish forth, for really you are in a miserable plight, man."

"Bad enough indeed, Mr Gasket—many thanks though—bad enough, as you say; but I would that your boats' crew were in so good a plight."

Mr Gasket looked earnestly at me—"Why, I have my own misgivings Cringle; this morning at daybreak, the Firebrand in company, we fell in with an armed felucca. It was dead calm, and she was out of gun-shot, close in with the land. The Firebrand immediately sent the cutter on board, fully armed, with instructions to me to man the launch, and arm her with the boat-gun, and then to send both boats to overhaul the felucca. I did so, standing in as quickly as the light air would take me, to support them, the felucca all this while sweeping inshore as fast as she could pull. But the boats were too nimble for her, and our launch had already saluted her twice from the six-pounder in the bow, when the sea-breeze came thundering down in a white squall, that reefed our gaff-topsail in a trice, and blew away a whole lot of light sails, like so many paper-kites. When it cleared away, the devil a felucca, boat, or anything else, was to be seen. Capsized they could not have been, for all three were not likely to have gone that way; and as to any creek they could have run into, why we could see none. That they had pulled inshore, however, was our conclusion;

but here have we been, the whole morning, firing signal-guns every five minutes without success."

"Did you hear no firing after the squall?" said I.

"Why, some of my people thought they did, but it was that hollow, tremulous, reverberating kind of sound, that it might have been thunder; and the breeze blew too strong to have allowed us to hear musketry a mile and a half to windward. I did think I saw some smoke rise, and blow off now and then, but—"

"But me no buts, Master Richard Gasket; Peter Mangrove here, as well as myself, saw your people pursue the felucca into the lion's den, and I fear they have been crushed in his jaws." I briefly related what we had seen. Gasket was in great distress.

"They must have been taken, Cringle. The fools! to allow themselves to be trepanned in this way. We must stand out and speak the corvette. All hands make sail!"

I could not help smiling at the grandeur of Dick's emphasis on the *all,* when twenty hands, one-third of them boys and the rest landsmen, scrambled up from below, and began to pull and haul in no very seaman-like fashion. He noticed it.

"Ah, Tom, I know what you are grinning at, but I fear it has been no laughing matter to my poor boat's crew—all my best hands gone, God help me!"

Presently being under the Firebrand's lee quarter, we lowered down the boat and went on board, where, for the first time, the extreme ludicrousness of my appearance and following flashed on me. There we were, all in a bunch —the dog, Mr and Mrs Mangrove, and Thomas Cringle, gent.—such in appearance as I shall shortly describe them.

Old Richard Gasket, Esq., first clambered up the side, and made his bow to the Hon. Captain Transom, who was standing near the gangway, on the snow-white deck, amidst a group of officers, where everything was in the most apple-pie order, himself, both in mind and apparel, the most polished concern in the ship; while the whole crew, with the exception of the unfortunate absentees in the cutter, were scrambling to get a good view of us.

I have already said that my uniform was torn to pieces; trousers ditto; my shoes had parted company in the quagmire; and as for hat, it was left in my cot. I had a dirty bandage tied round my neck, performing the twofold office of a cravat and a dressing to my wound; while the blood from the scratches had dried in black streaks adown and across my face and paws, and

I was altogether so begrimed with mud that my mother would not have known me. Dick made his salaam, and then took up a position beside the sallyport, with an important face, like a showman exhibiting wild beastesses, a regular "stir-him-up-with-a-long-pole" sort of look. I followed him—"This is Lieutenant Cringle, Captain Transom."

"The devil it is!" said Transom, trying in vain to keep his gravity. "Why, I see it is—How do you do, Mr Cringle? glad to see you."

"This is Peter Mangrove, branch-pilot," continued Gasket, as Peter, bowing, tried to slide past out of sight.

Till this instant I had not time to look at him—he was even a much queerer-looking figure than myself. He had been encumbered with no garment besides his trousers when we started, and these had been reduced, in the scramble through the brake, to a waistband and two knee-bands, from which a few shreds fluttered in the breeze—the rest of his canvass having been entirely torn out of the bolt-ropes. For an upper dress he had borrowed a waistcoat without sleeves from the purser of the schooner, which hung loose and unbuttoned before; while behind, being somewhat of the shortest, some very prominent parts of his stern-frame were disclosed, as even an apology for a shirt he had none. Being a *decent* man, however, he had tied his large straw hat round his waist, by strings fastened to the broad brims, which nearly met behind, so that the crown covered his loins before like a petard, while the sameness of his black naked body was relieved by being laced with blood from numberless lacerations.

Next came the female—"This is the pilot's wife, Captain Transom;" again sang out old Dick; but decency won't let me venture on a description of poor Nancy's equipment, beyond mentioning that one of the Gleam's crew had given her a pair of old trousers, which, as a sailor has no bottom, and Nancy was not a sailor, were most ludicrously scanty at top, and devil another rag of any kind had the poor creature on, but a handkerchief across her bosom. There was no standing all this; the crew forward and in the waist were all on the broad grin, while the officers, after struggling to maintain their gravity until they were nearly suffocated, fairly gave in, and the whole ship echoed with the most uproarious laughter; a young villain, whether a mid or no I could not tell, yelling out in the throng, "Hurra for Tom Cringle's Tail!"

I was fairly beginning to lose countenance, when up jumped Sneezer to my relief out of the boat, with an old cocked-hat lashed on his head, a marine's jacket buttoned round his body, and his coal-black muzzle bedaubed with pipeclay, regularly monkeyfied—the momentary handiwork of some wicked little reefers—while a small pipe sang out quietly, as if not intended to reach the quarterdeck, although it did do so, "And here comes the *last joint* of Mr Cringle's Tail." The dog began floundering and jumping about, and walloping amongst the people, most of whom knew him, and immediately drew their attention from me and my party to himself; for away they all bundled forward, dog and men, tumbling and scrambling about like so many children, leaving the coast clear to me and my attendants. The absurdity of the whole exhibition had, for an instant, even under the very nose of a proverbially taught hand, led to freedoms which I believed impossible in a man-of-war. However, there was too much serious matter in hand, independently of any other consideration, to allow the merriment created by our appearance to last long.

Captain Transom, immediately on being informed how matters stood, with seaman-like promptitude, determined to lighten the Gleam, and send her in with the boats, for the purpose of destroying the haunt of the pirates, and recovering the men, if they were still alive; but before anything could be done it came on to blow, and for a week we had great difficulty in maintaining our position off the coast against the strength of the gale and lee current.

It was on the Sunday morning after I had escaped, that it moderated sufficiently for our purpose, when both vessels stood close in, and Peter and I were sent to reconnoitre the entrance of the port in the gig. Having sounded and taken the bearings of the land, we returned on board, when the Gleam's provisions were taken out and her water started. The ballast was then shifted, so as to bring her by the head, that she might thus draw less water by being on an even keel, all sharp vessels of her class requiring much deeper water aft than forward; the corvette's launch, with a 12-pound carronade fitted, was then manned and armed with thirty seamen and marines, under the command of the second-lieutenant; the jolly-boat and the two quarter-boats, each with twelve men, followed in a string, under the third-lieutenant, the master, and the senior midshipman; thirty picked hands were added to the schooner's crew; and I was desired to take the gig with six smart hands and Peter Mangrove, and to accompany the whole as pilot, but to pull out of danger so soon as the action commenced, so as to be ready to help any disabled boat, or to carry orders from the commanding officer.

At nine in the morning we gave three cheers, and, leaving the corvette with barely forty hands on board, the Gleam made sail towards the harbour's mouth, with the boats in tow; but when we got within musket-shot of the entrance, the breeze failed us, when the order of sailing was reversed, the boats now taking the schooner in tow, preceded by your humble servant in the gig. We dashed safely through the small canal of blue water, which divided the surf at the harbour's mouth, having hit it to a nicety; but when about a pistol-shot from the entrance, the channel narrowed to a muddy creek, not more than twenty yards wide, with high trees and thick underwood close to the water's edge. All was silent; the sun shone down upon us like the concentrated rays of a burning-glass, and there was no breeze to dissipate the heavy dank mist that hovered over the surface of the unwholesome canal, nor was there any appearance of a living thing, save and except a few startled waterfowl, and some guanas on the trees, and now and then an alligator, like a black log of charred wood, would roll off a slimy bank of brown mud, with a splash, into the water.

We rowed on, the schooner every now and then taking the ground, but she was always quickly warped off again by a kedge; at length, after we had in all proceeded, it might be, about a mile from the beach, we came to a boom of strong timber clamped with iron, stretching across the creek. We were not unprepared for this; one of two old 32-pound carronades, which, in anticipation of some obstruction of the sort, had been got on deck from amongst the Gleam's ballast, and properly slung, was now made fast to the middle timber of the boom, and let go, when the weight of it sank it to the bottom, and we passed on. We pulled on for about half a mile farther, when we noticed, high up on a sunny cliff that shot boldly out into the clear blue heavens, a small red flag suddenly run up to the top of a tall, scathed, branchless palm-tree, where it flared for a moment in the breeze like the flame of a torch, and then as suddenly disappeared. "Come, they are on the look-out for us, I see."

The hills continued to close on us as we advanced, and that so precipitously that we might have been crushed to pieces had half-a-dozen active fellows, without any risk to themselves—for the trees would have screened them—simply loosened some of the fragments of rock that impended over us so threateningly; it seemed as if a little finger could have sent them bounding and thundering down the mountain-side; but this either was not the game of the people we were in search of, or Obed's spirit and energy had been crushed out of him by the heart-depressing belief that his hours were numbered, for no active obstruction was offered.

We now suddenly rounded an abrupt corner of the creek, and there we were, full in front of the schooners, who, with the felucca in advance, were lying in line of battle, with springs on their cables. The horrible black pennant was, in the present instance, nowhere to be seen; indeed, why such an impolitic step as ever to have shown it at all was taken in the first attack I never could understand; for the force was too small to have created any serious fear of being captured (unless indeed it had been taken for an advanced-guard, supported by a stronger), while it must have appeared probable to Obediah that the loss of the two boats would, in all likelihood, lead to a more powerful attempt, when, if it were successful, the damning fact of having fought under such an infernal emblem must have insured a pirate's death on the gibbet to every soul who was taken, unless he had intended to have murdered all the witnesses of it. But since proof in my person and the pilot's existed, now, if ever, was the time for mortal resistance, and to have hoisted it, for they knew that they all fought with halters about their necks. They had all the Spanish flag, flying except the Wave, which showed American colours, and the felucca, which had a white flag hoisted, from which last, whenever our gig appeared, a canoe shoved off, and pulled towards us. The officer, if such he might be called, also carried a white flag in his hand. He was a daring-looking fellow, and dashed up alongside of me. The incomprehensible folly of trying, at this time of day, to cloak the real character of the vessels, puzzled me, and does so to this hour. I have never got a clue to it, unless it was that Obed's strong mind had given way before his superstitious fears, and others had now assumed the right of both judging and acting for him in this his closing scene. The pirate officer at once recognised me, but seemed neither surprised nor disconcerted at the strength of the force which accompanied me. He asked me, in Spanish, if I commanded it. I told him I did not, that the captain of the schooner was the senior officer.

"Then, will you be good enough to go on board with me, to interpret for me?"

"Certainly."

In half a minute we were both on the Gleam's deck, the crews of the boats that had her in tow lying on their oars.

"You are the commander of this force?" said the Spaniard.

"I am," said old Gasket, who had figged himself out in full puff, after the manner of the ancients, as if he had been going to church, instead of to fight; "and who the hell are you?"

"I command one of these Spanish schooners, sir, which your boats so unwarrantably attacked a week ago, although you are at peace with Spain. But even had they been enemies, they were in a friendly port, which should have protected them."

"All very good oysters," quoth old Dick; "and pray was it an honest trick of you to cabbage my young friend, Lieutenant Cringle there, as if you had been slavers kidnapping the Bungoes in the Bight of Biafra, and then to fire on and murder my people when sent in to claim him?"

"As to carrying off that young gentleman, it was no affair of ours; he was brought away by the master of that American schooner; but so far as regards firing on your boats, I believe they fired first. But the crews are not murdered; on the contrary, they have been well used, and are now on board that felucca. I am come to surrender the whole fifteen to you."

"The *whole fifteen!* and what have you made of the other *twelve?*"

"Gastados," said the fellow, with all the *sang froid* in the world,—"gastados [spent or expended] by their own folly."

"Oh, they are *expended*, are they? then give us the *fifteen*."

"Certainly, but you will in this case withdraw your force, of course?"

"We shall see about that—go and send us the men."

He jumped down into the canoe, and shoved off. Whenever he reached the felucca he struck the white flag, and hoisted the Spanish in its stead, and by hauling on a spring, he brought her to cover the largest schooner so effectually that we could not fire a shot at her without going through the felucca. We could see all the men leave this latter vessel in two canoes, and go on board one of the other craft. There was now no time to be lost, so I dashed at the felucca in the gig, and broke open the hatches, where we found the captured seamen and their gallant leader, Lieutenant * * *, in a sorry plight, expecting nothing but to be blown up, or instant death by shot or the knife. We released them, and, sending to the Gleam for ammunition and small-arms, led the way in the felucca, by Mr Gasket's orders, to the attack, the corvette's launch supporting us; while the schooner, with the other craft, were scraping up as fast as they could. We made straight for the largest schooner, which, with her consorts, now opened a heavy fire of grape and musketry, which we returned with interest. I can tell little of what took place till I found myself on the pirate's quarterdeck after a desperate tussle, and having driven the crew overboard, with dead and wounded men thickly strewn about, and our fellows busy firing at their surviving antagonists as they were trying to gain the shore by swimming.

Although the schooner we carried was the Commodore, and commanded by Obediah in person, yet the pirates—that is, the Spanish part of them—by no means showed the fight I expected. While we were approaching no fire could be hotter, and their yells and cheers were tremendous; but the instant we laid her alongside with the felucca, and swept her decks with a discharge of grape from the carronade, under cover of which we boarded on the quarter, while the launch's people scrambled up at the bows, their hearts failed, a regular panic overtook them, and they jumped overboard, without waiting for a taste either of cutlass or boarding-pike. The captain himself, however, with about ten Americans, stood at bay round the long gun, which, notwithstanding their great inferiority in point of numbers to our party, they manfully fired three several times at us, after we had carried her aft; but we were so close that the grape came past us like a round shot, and only killed one hand at each discharge; whereas, at thirty yards farther off, by having had room to spread, it might have made a pretty *tableau* of the whole party. I hailed Obed twice to surrender, while our people, staggered by the extreme hardihood of the small group, hung back for an instant; but he either did not hear me, or would not, for the only reply he seemed inclined to make was by slewing round the gun so as to bring me on with it, and the next moment a general rush was made, when the whole party was cut down, with three exceptions, one of whom was Obed himself, who, getting on the gun, made a desperate bound over the men's heads, and jumped overboard. He struck out gallantly, the shot pattering round him like the first of a thunder shower, but he dived, apparently unhurt, and I lost sight of him.

The other vessels having also been carried, the firing was all on our side by this time, and I, along with the other officers, was exerting myself to stop the butchery.

"Cease firing men; for shame, you see they no longer resist." And my voice was obeyed by all except the fifteen we had released, who were absolutely mad with fury—perfect fiends; such uncontrollable fierceness I had never witnessed—indeed, I had nearly cut one of them down before I could make them knock off firing.

"Don't fire, sir," cried I to one.

"Ay, ay, sir; but that scoundrel *made me wash his shirts,*" and he let drive at a poor devil, who was squattering and swimming away towards the shore, and shot him through the head.

"By heavens! I will run you through if you fire at that man!" shouted I to another—a marine—who was taking aim at no less a personage than friend Obed, who had risen to breathe, and was swimming after the others, *but the very last man of all.*

"No, by G——! *he made me wash his trousers, sir.*"

He fired; the pirate stretched out his arms turned slowly on his back, with his face towards me. I thought he gave me a sort of "Et tu, Brute" look, but I daresay it was fancy—his feet began to sink, and he gradually disappeared—a few bubbles of froth and blood marking the spot where he went down. He had been shot dead. I will not attempt to describe my feelings at this moment— they burned themselves in on my heart at the time, and the impression is indelible. Whether I had or had not acted, in one sense, unjustly, by thrusting myself so conspicuously forward in the attempt to capture him after what had passed between us, forced itself upon my judgment. I had certainly promised that I would, in no way that I could help, be instrumental in his destruction or seizure, provided he landed me at St Jago, or put me on board a friendly vessel. He did neither, so his part of the compact might be considered broken; but then it was out of his power to have fulfilled it; besides, he not only threatened my life subsequently, but actually wounded me; still, however, on great provoca- tion. But what "is writ, is writ." He has gone to his account, pirate as he was, murderer if you will; yet I had, and still have, a tear for his memory, and many a time have I prayed on my bare knees that his blue agonised dying look might be erased from my brain—but this can never be. What he had been I never learned; but it is my deliberate opinion that, with a clear stage and opportuni- ty, he would have forced himself out from the surface of society for good or for evil. The unfortunates who survived him, but to expiate their crimes on the gib- bet at Port Royal, said he had joined them from a New York privateer, but they knew nothing further of him beyond the fact that, by his skill and desperate courage, within a month he had, by common acclaim, been elected captain of the whole band. There was a story current on board the corvette, of a small trading craft, with a person answering his description, having been captured in the Chesapeake by one of the squadron, and sent to Halifax for adjudication (the master, as in most cases of the kind, being left on board), which from that hour had never been heard of, neither vessel, nor prize crew, nor captain, until two Americans were taken out of a slaver, off the Cape de Verds, by the Firebrand, about a year afterwards, after a most brave and determined attempt to escape, both of whom were, however, allowed to enter, but subsequently deserted off Sandy Hook by swimming ashore, in consequence of a pressed hand hinting that one of them, surmised to be Obed, had been the master of the vessel above mentioned.

All resistance having ceased, the few of the pirates who escaped having scampered into the woods, where it would have been vain to follow them, we secured our prisoners, and at the close of a bloody day—for fatal had it been to friend and foe—the prizes were got under weigh, and before nightfall we were all at sea, sailing in a fleet, under convoy of the corvette and Gleam.

CHAPTER X.

VOMITO PRIETO.

"This disease is beyond my practice."

—The Doctor in Macbeth.

THE SECOND- and acting-third-lieutenants were on board the prizes—the purser was busy in his vocation—the doctor ditto. Indeed, he and his mates had more on their hands than they could well manage. The first-lieutenant was engaged on deck, and the master was in his cot, suffering from a severe contusion; so when I got on board the corvette, and dived into the gunroom in search of some crumbs of comfort, the deuce a living soul was there to welcome me, except the gunroom steward, who speedily produced some cold meat, and asked me if I would take a glass of swizzle.

The food I had no great fancy to, although I had not tasted a morsel since six o'clock in the morning, and it was now eight in the evening; but the offer of the grog sounded gratefully in mine ear, and I was about tackling to a stout rummer of the same, when a smart dandified shaver, with gay mother-of-pearl buttons on his jacket, as thick set as peas, presented his tallow chops at the door.

"Captain Transom desires me to say that he will be glad of your company in the cabin, Mr Cringle."

"My compliments—I will wait on him so soon as I have had a snack. We have had no dinner in the gun-room to-day yet, you know, Mafame."

"Why, it was in the knowledge of that the captain sent me, sir. He has not had any dinner either; but it is now on the table, and he waits for you."

I was but little in spirits, and, to say sooth, was fitter for my bed than society; but the captain's advances had been made with so much kindliness, that I got up and made a strong endeavour to rouse myself; and, having made my toilet as well as my slender means admitted, I followed the captain's steward into the cabin.

I started—why, I could not well tell—as the sentry at the door stood to his arms when I passed in; and, as if I had been actually possessed by some wandering spirit, who had taken the small liberty of using my faculties and tongue without my concurrence, I hastily asked the man if he was an American? He stared in great astonishment for a short space, turned his quid, and then rapped out—as angrily as respect for a commissioned officer would let him—"No, by ———, sir!"

This startled me as much as the question I had almost unconsciously—and, I may say, involuntarily—put to the marine had surprised him, and I made a full stop, and leant back against the door-post. The captain, who was walking up and down the cabin, had heard me speak, but without comprehending the nature of my question, and now recalled me in some measure to myself by inquiring if I wanted anything. I replied, hurriedly, that I did not.

"Well, Mr Cringle, dinner is ready—so take that chair at the foot of the table, will you?"

I sat down, mechanically, as it appeared to me—for a strange swimming dizzy sort of sensation had suddenly overtaken me, accompanied by a whoreson tingling, as Shakespeare hath it, in my ears. I was unable to eat a morsel, but I could have drunk the ocean, had it been claret or vin-de-grave—to both of which I helped myself as largely as good manners would allow, or a little beyond, mayhap. All this while the captain was stowing his cargo with great zeal, and tifting away at the fluids as became an honest sailor, after so long a fast, interlarding his operations with a civil word to me now and then, without any especial regard as to the answer I made him, or, indeed, caring greatly whether I answered him or not.

"Sharp work you must have had, Mr Cringle; should have liked to have been with you myself. Help yourself before passing that bottle—zounds, man, never take a bottle by the bilge—grasp the neck, man, at least in this fervent climate—thank you. Pity you had not caught the captain, though. What you told me of that man very much interested me, coupled with the prevailing reports regarding him in the ship—daring dog he must have been—can't forget how gallantly he weathered us when we chased him."

I broke silence for the first time. Indeed, I could scarcely have done so sooner, even had I chosen it, for the gallant officer was rather continuous in his yarn-spinning. However, he had nearly dined, and was leaning back, allowing the champagne to trickle leisurely from a glass half a yard long, which he had applied to his lips, when I said—

"Well, the imagination does sometimes play one strange tricks; I verily believe in second sight now, captain, for at this very instant I am regularly the fool of my senses—but, pray, don't laugh at me;" and I lay back on my chair, and pressed my hands over my shut eyes and hot burning temples, which were now throbbing as if the arteries would have burst.

The captain, who was evidently much surprised at my abruptness, said something hurriedly and rather sharply in answer, but I could not for the life of me mark what it was. I opened my eyes again, and looked towards the object that had before riveted my attention. It was neither more nor less than the captain's cloak—a plain, unpretending, substantial blue garment, lined with white, which, on coming below, he had cast carelessly down on the locker that ran across the after-part of the cabin behind him. It was about eighteen feet from me, and as there was no light nearer it than the swinging lamp over the table at which we were seated, the whole of the cabin thereabouts was thrown considerably into shade. The cape of the cloak was turned over, showing the white lining, and was rather bundled, as it were, into a round heap, about the size of a man's head. When first I looked at it, there was a dreamy, glimmering indistinctness about it that I could not well understand, and I would have said, had it been possible, that the wrinkles and folds in it were beginning to be instinct with motion, to creep and crawl, as it were; at all events, the false impression was so strong as to jar my nerves, and make me shudder with horror. I knew there was no such thing, as well as Macbeth, but nevertheless it was with an indescribable feeling of curiosity, dashed with awe, that I stared intently at it, as if fascinated, while almost unwittingly I made the remark already mentioned.

I had expected that the unaccountable appearance which had excited my attention so strongly would have vanished with the closing of my eyes; but it did not, for when I looked at it again, the working and shifting of the folds of the cloth still continued, and even more distinctly than before.

"Very extraordinary all this," I murmured to myself.

"Pray, Mr Cringle, be sociable man," said the captain; "what the deuce do you see, that you stare over my shoulder in that way? Were I a woman, now, I should tremble to look behind me, while you were glaring aft in that wild, moonstruck sort of fashion."

"By all that is astonishing," I exclaimed, in great agitation, "if the folds of the cape have not arranged themselves into the very likeness of his dying face!—Why it *is* his face, and no fanciful grouping of my heated brain. Look there, sir—look there—I know it can't be—*but there he lies*—the very features and upper part of the body, lith and limb, as when he disappeared beneath the water when he was shot dead."

I felt the boiling blood, that had been rushing through my system like streams of molten lead, suddenly freeze and coagulate about my heart, impeding my respiration to such a degree that I thought I should have been suffocated. I had the feeling as if my soul was going to take wing. It was not fear, nor could I say I was in pain, but it was so utterly unlike anything I had ever experienced before, and so indescribable that I thought to myself—"this may be death."

"Why, what a changeable rose you are, Master Cringle," said Captain Transom, good-naturedly; "your face was like the north-west moon in a fog but a minute ago, and now it is as pale as a lily—blue-white, I declare. Why, my man, you must be ill, and seriously too."

His voice dissipated the hideous chimera—the folds fell, and relapsed into their own shape, and the cloak was once more a cloak, and nothing more. I drew a long breath. "Ah, it is gone at last, thank God!"—and then, aware of the strange effect my unaccountable incoherence must have had on the skipper, I thought to brazen it out by trying the free-and-easy line, which was neither more nor less than arrant impertinence in our relative positions. "Why, I have been heated a little, and amusing myself with sundry vain imaginings, but allow me to take wine with you, captain," filling a tumbler with vin-de-grave to the brim as I spoke. "Success to you, sir—here's to your speedy promotion—may you soon get a crack frigate; as for me, I intend to be Archbishop of Canterbury, or maid of honour to the Queen of Sheba, or something in the heathen mythology."

I drank off the wine, although I had the greatest difficulty in steadying my trembling hand, and carrying it to my lips; but notwithstanding my increasing giddiness, and the buzzing in my ears, and swimming of mine eyes, I noticed the captain's face of amazement as he exclaimed—

"The boy is either mad or drunk, by Jupiter!"

I could not stand his searching and angry look, and in turning my eye, it again fell on the cloak, which now seemed to be stretched out at greater length, and to be altogether more voluminous than it was before. I was forcibly struck with this, for I was certain no one had touched it.

"By heavens! it heaves," I exclaimed, much moved—"how is this? I never thought to have believed such things—it stirs again—it takes the figure of a man—as if it were a pall covering his body. Pray, Captain Transom, what trick is this?—Is there anything below that cloak there?"

"What cloak do you mean?"

"Why, that blue one lying on the locker there. Is there any cat or dog in the cabin?" and I started on my legs. "Captain Transom," I continued, with great vehemence, "for the love of God tell me what is there below that cloak."

He looked surprised beyond all measure.

"Why, Mr Cringle, I cannot for the soul of me comprehend you; indeed I cannot; but, Mafame, indulge him. See if *there be anything* below my cloak."

The servant walked to the locker, and lifted up the cape of it, and was in the act of taking it from the locker, when I impetuously desired the man to leave it alone.

"I can't look on him again," said I; while the faintishness increased, so that I could hardly speak. "Don't move the covering from his face, for God's sake—don't remove it," and I lay back in my chair, screening my eyes from the lamp with my hands, and shuddering with an icy chill from head to foot.

The captain, who had hitherto maintained the well-bred, patronising, although somewhat distant, air of a superior officer to an inferior who was his guest, addressed me now in an altered tone, and with a brotherly kindness.

"Mr Cringle, I have some knowledge of you, and I know many of your friends; so I must take the liberty of an old acquaintance with you. This day's work has been a severe one and your share in it, especially after your past fatigues, has been very trying, and as I will report it, I hope it may clap a good spoke in your wheel; but you are overheated, and have been over-excited; fatigue has broken you down, and I must really request you will take something warm, and turn in.—Here, Mafame, get the carpenter's mate to secure that cleat on the weather side there, and sling my spare cot for Mr Cringle.—You will be cooler here than in the gunroom."

I heard his words without comprehending their meaning. I sat and stared at him, quite conscious, all the time, of the extreme impropriety, not to say indecency, of my conduct; but there was a spell on me; I tried to speak, but could not; and, believing that I was either possessed by some dumb devil, or struck with palsy, I rose up, bowed to Captain Transom, and straightway hied me on deck.

I could hear him say to his servant, as I was going up the ladder, "Look after that young gentleman, Mafame, and send Isaac to the doctor, and bid him come here now;" and then in a commiserating tone—"Poor young fellow, what a pity!"

When I got on deck all was quiet. The cool fresh air had an instantaneous effect on my shattered nerves, the violent throbbing in my head ceased, and I began to hug myself with the notion that my distemper, whatever it might have been, had beaten a retreat.

Suddenly I felt so collected and comfortable, as to be quite alive to the loveliness of the scene. It was a beautiful moonlight night; such a night as is nowhere to be seen *without* the tropics, and not often *within* them. There was just breeze enough to set the sails to sleep, although not so strong as to prevent their giving a low murmuring flap now and then, when the corvette rolled a little heavier than usual on the long swell. There was not a cloud to be seen in the sky, not even a stray shred of thin fleecy gauze-like vapour, to mark the direction of the upper current of the air, by its course across the moon's disk, which was now at the full, and about half-way up her track in the liquid heavens.

The small twinkling lights from millions of lesser stars, in that part of the firmament where she hung, round as a silver pot-lid—shield, I mean—were swamped in the flood of greenish-white radiance shed by her, and it was only a few of the first magnitude, with a planet here and there, that were visible to the naked eye, in the neighbourhood of her crystal bright globe; but the clear depth, and dark translucent purity of the profound, when the eye tried to pierce into it at the zenith, where the stars once more shone and sparkled thick and brightly, beyond the merging influence of the pale cold orb, no man can describe *now*—one could, *once*—but, rest his soul, he is dead—and then to look forth far into the night, across the dark ridge of many a heaving swell of living water—but "Thomas Cringle, ahoy—where the devil are you cruising to?" So, to come back to my story. I went aft, and mounted the small poop, and looked towards the aforesaid moon—a glorious, resplendent, tropical moon, and not the paper lantern affair hanging in an atmosphere of fog and smoke, about which your blear-eyed poets *haver* so much. By the by, these gentry are fond of singing of the *blessed* sun—were they sailors they would *bless* the moon also, and be ——— to them, in place of writing much wearisome poetry regarding her *blighting* propensities. But I have lost the end of my yarn once more, in the strands of these parentheses.—Lord, what a word to pronounce in the plural!—I can no more get out now than a girl's silk-worm from the innermost of a nest of pill-boxes, where, to ride the simile to death at once, I have warped the thread of my story so round and round me, that I can't for the life of me unravel it. Very odd all this. Since I have recovered of this fever, everything is slack about me; I can't set up the shrouds and backstays of my mind, not to speak of bobstays, if I should die for it. The running rigging is all right enough, and the canvass is there; but I either can't set it, or when I do, I find I have too little ballast, or I get involved amongst shoals, and white water, and breakers,—don't you hear them roar?—which I cannot weather, and crooked channels, under some lee-shore, through which I cannot scrape clear. So down must go the anchor, as at present, and there—there goes the chain-cable rushing and rumbling through the hawse-hole. But I suppose it will be all right by-and-by, as I get stronger.

"But rouse thee, Thomas! Where *is* the end of this *yarn*, that you are blarneying about?"

"Avast heaving, you swab you—avast; if you had as much calomel in your corpus as I have at this present speaking—why, you would be a lad of more mettle than I take you for, that is all. You would have about as much quicksilver in your stomach, as I have in my purse, and all my silver has been *quick*, ever since I remember, like the jests of the gravedigger in Hamlet. But, as you say, where the devil *is* the end of this yarn?"

All here it is! so off we go again—And looked forward towards the rising moon, whose shining wake of glow-worm coloured light, sparkling in the small waves, that danced in the gentle wind on the heaving bosom of the dark-blue sea, was right ahead of us, like a river of quicksilver with its course diminished in the distance to a point, flowing towards us, from the extreme verge of the horizon, through a rolling sea of ink, with the waters of which, for a time, it disdained to blend. Concentrated, and shining like polished silver afar off— intense and sparkling as it streamed down nearer, but becoming less and less brilliant as it widened in its approach to us, until, like the stream of the great estuary of the Magdalena, losing itself in the salt waste of waters, it gradually melted beneath us and around us into the darkness.

I looked aloft—every object appeared sharply cut out against the dark firmament, and the swaying of the mastheads to and fro, as the vessel rolled, was so steady and slow, that *they* seemed stationary, while it was the moon and stars which appeared to vibrate and swing from side to side, high over head, like the vacillation of the clouds in a theatre, when the scene is first let down.

The masts and yards, and standing and running rigging, looked like black pillars, and bars, and wires of iron, reared against the sky, by some mighty spirit of the night; and the sails, as the moon shone dimly through them, were as dark as if they had been tarpaulings. But when I walked forward and looked aft, what a beauteous change! Now each mast, with its gently swelling canvass, the higher sails decreasing in size, until they tapered away nearly to a point, through topsail, topgallant-sail, royal and skysails, showed like towers of snow, and the cordage like silver threads, while each dark spar seemed to be of ebony, *fished* with ivory, as a flood of cold, pale, mild light streamed from the beauteous planet over the whole stupendous machine, lighting up the sand-white decks, on which the shadows of the men, and of every object that intercepted the moonbeams, were cast as strongly as if the planks had been inlaid with jet.

There was nothing moving about the decks. The look-outs aft, and at the gangways, sat or stood like statues half bronze, half alabaster. The old quarter-master, who was cunning the ship, and had perched himself on a carronade, with his arm leaning on the weather nettings, was equally motionless. The, watch had all disappeared forward, or were stowed out of sight under the lee of the boats; the first-lieutenant, as if captivated by the serenity of the scene, was leaning with folded arms on the weather-gangway, looking abroad upon the ocean, and whistling now and then, either for a wind or for want of thought. The only being who showed sign of life was the man at the wheel, and he scarcely moved, except now and then to give her a spoke or two, when the cheep of the tiller-rope, running through the well-greased leading-blocks, would grate on the ear as a sound of some importance; while in daylight, in the ordinary bustle of the ship, no one could say he ever heard it.

Three bells!—"Keep a bright look-out there," sang out the lieutenant.

"Ay, ay, sir," from the four look-out men, in a volley.

Then from the weather-gangway, " All's well," rose shrill into the night air.

The watchword was echoed by the man on the forecastle, re-echoed by the lee-gangway look-out, and ending with the response of the man on the poop. My dream was dissipated—and so was the first-lieutenant's, who had but little poetry in his composition, honest man.

"Fine night, Mr Cringle. Look aloft, how beautifully set the sails are; that mizen-topsail is well cut, eh? Sits well, don't it? But—Confound the lubbers! Boatswain's mate, call the watch."

Whi-whew, whi-whew, chirrup, chip, chip—the deck was alive in an instant, "as bees bizz out wi' angry fyke."

"Where is the captain of the mizen-top?" growled the man in authority.

"Here, sir."

"Here, sir!—look at the weather-clew of the mizen-topsail, sir—look at that sail, sir—how many *turns* can you count in that clew, sir? Spring it, you no-sailor you—spring, it, and set the sail again."

How weary, stale, flat, and unprofitable all this appeared to me at the time, I well remember; but the obnoxious *turns* were shaken out, and the sail set again so as to please even the fastidious eye of the lieutenant, who, seeing nothing more to find fault with, addressed me once more.

"Have had no grub since morning, Mr Cringle; all the others are away in the prizes; you are as good as one of us now, only want the order to join, you know—so, will you oblige me and take charge of the deck until I go below and change my clothes and gobble a bit?"

"Unquestionably—with much pleasure."

He forthwith dived, and I walked aft a few steps towards where the old quartermaster was standing on the gun.

"How is her head, quartermaster?"

"South-east and by south, sir. If the wind holds we shall weather Morant Point, I think, sir."

"Very like, very like.—What is that glancing backwards and forwards across the port-hole there, quartermaster?"

"I told you so, Mafame," said the man; "what are you skylarking about the mizen-chains for, man?—Come in, will you, come in."

The captain's caution to his servant flashed on me.

"Come in, my man, and give my respects to the captain, and tell him that I am quite well now; the fresh air has perfectly restored me."

"I will, sir," said Mafame, half ashamed at being detected in his office of inspector-general of my actions; but the doctor, to whom he had been sent, having now got a leisure moment from his labour in the shambles, came up and made inquiries as to how I felt.

"Why, doctor, I thought I was in for a fever half an hour ago, but it is quite gone off, or nearly so—there, feel my pulse."—It was regular, and there was no particular heat of skin.

"Why, I don't think there is much the matter with you. Mafame, tell the captain so; but turn in and take some rest as soon as you can, and I will see you in the morning—and here," feeling in his waistcoat pocket, "here are a couple of capers for you; take them now, will you"—(And he handed me two blue pills, which I the next moment chucked overboard, to cure some bilious dolphin of the liver complaint.) I promised to do so whenever the lieutenant relieved the deck, which would, I made no question, be within half an hour.

"Very well, that will do—good night. I am regularly done up myself," quoth the *medico*, as he descended to the gunroom.

At this time of night the prizes were all in a cluster under our lee quarter, like small icebergs covered with snow, and carrying every rag they could set. The Gleam was a good way astern, as if to whip them in, and to take care that no stray piccaroon should make a dash at any of them. They slid noiselessly along like phantoms of the deep, everything in the air and in the water was so still. I crossed to the lee side of the deck to look at them. The Wave, seeing some one on the hammock-nettings, sheered close to, under the Firebrand's lee quarter, and some one asked," Do you want to speak us?" The man's voice, reflected from the concave surface of the schooner's mainsail, had a hollow, echoing sound, that startled me.

"I should know that voice," said I to myself, "and the figure steering the schooner." The throbbing in my head and the dizzy feel which had capsized my judgment in the cabin, again returned with increased violence—"It was no deception after all," thought I, "no cheat of the senses—I now believe such things are."

The same voice now called out, "Come away, Tom; come away," no doubt to some other seaman on board the little vessel, but my heated fancy did not so construe it. The cold breathless fit again overtook me, and I ejaculated, "God have mercy upon me a sinner!"

"Why don't you come, Tom?" said the voice once more.

It was Obed's. At this very instant of time, the Wave forged ahead into the Firebrand's shadow, so that her sails, but a moment before white as wool in the bright moonbeams, suffered a sudden eclipse, and became black as ink.

"His dark spirit is there," said I audibly, "and calls me—go I will, whatever may befall."

I hailed the schooner, or rather I had only to speak, and that in a low tone, for she was now close under the counter—"Send your boat, for since *you* call I know I *must* come."

A small canoe slid off her deck; two shipboys got into it, and pulled under the starboard mizen-chains, which entirely concealed them, as they held on for a moment with a boat-hook in the dark shadow of the ship. This was done so silently that neither the look-out on the poop, who was rather on the weather side at the moment, nor the man at the lee gangway, who happened to be looking out forward, heard them or saw me, as I slipped down unperceived.

"Pull back again, my lads; quick now, quick."

In a moment I was alongside, the next I was on deck, and in this short space a change had come over the spirit of my dream, for I now was again conscious that I was on board the Wave with a prize crew. My imagination had taken another direction.

"Now, Mr—, I beg pardon, I forget your name,"—I had never heard it—"make more sail, and haul out from the fleet for Mancheoneal Bay; I have despatches for the admiral—So, crack on."

The midshipman who was in charge of her never for an instant doubted but that all was right; sail was made, and as the light breeze was the very thing for the little Wave, she began to *snore* through it like smoke. When she had shot a cable's length ahead of the Firebrand, we kept away a point or two, so as to stand more in for the land, and, like most maniacs, I was inwardly exulting at the success of my manœuvre, when we heard the corvette's bell struck rapidly. Her main-topsail was suddenly laid to the mast, whilst a loud voice echoed amongst the sails—"Any one see him in the waist—anybody see him forward there?"

"No, sir, no."

"Afterguard, fire, and let go the life-buoy—lower away the quarter-boats—jolly-boat also."

We saw the flash, and presently the small blue light of the buoy, blazing and disappearing, as it rose and fell on the waves, in the corvette's wake, sailed away astern, sparkling fitfully, like an *ignis fatuus*. The cordage rattled through the davit-blocks, as the boats dashed into the water—the splash of the oars was heard, and presently the twinkle of the life-buoy was lost in the lurid glare of the blue-lights, held aloft in each boat, where the crews were standing up, looking like spectres by the ghastly blaze, and anxiously peering about for some sign of the drowning man.

"A man overboard," was repeated from one to another of the prize crew.

"Sure enough," said I.

"Shall we stand back, sir?" said the midshipman.

"To what purpose?—there are enough there without us—no, no; crack on; we can do no good—carry on, carry on!"

We did so, and I now found severe shooting pains, more racking than the sharpest rheumatism I had ever suffered, pervading my whole body. They increased until I suffered the most excruciating agony, as if my bones had been converted into red-hot tubes of iron, and the marrow in them had been dried up with fervent beat, and I was obliged to beg that a hammock might be spread on deck, on which I lay down, pleading great fatigue and want of sleep as my excuse.

My thirst was unquenchable; the more I drank, the hotter it became. My tongue, and mouth, and throat were burning, as if molten lead had been poured down into my stomach, while the most violent retching came on every ten minutes. The prize crew, poor fellows, did all they could—once or twice they seemed about standing back to the ship, but "make sail, make sail," was my only cry. They did so, and there I lay without anything between me and the wet planks but a thin sailor's blanket and the canvass of the hammock, through the livelong night, and with no covering but a damp boat-cloak, raving at times during the hot fits, at others having my power of utterance frozen up during the cold ones. The men, once or twice, offered to carry me below, but the idea was horrible to me.

"No, no—not there—for heaven's sake not there! If you do take me down, I am sure I shall see him, and the dead mate—no—overboard rather, throw me overboard rather."

Oh, what would I not have given for the luxury of a flood of tears! But the fountains of mine eyes were dried up, and seared as with red-hot iron—my skin was parched, and hot, hot, as if every pore had been hermetically sealed; there was a hell within me and about me, as if the deck on which I lay had been steel at a white heat, and the gushing blood, as under the action of a force-pump, throbbed through my head, like as it would have burst on my brain—and such a racking, splitting headache—no language can describe it, and yet ever and anon in the midst of this raging fire, this furnace at my heart, seven times heated, a sudden icy shivering chill would shake me, and pierce through and through me, even when the roasting fever was at the hottest.

At length the day broke on the long, long, moist steamy light, and once more the sun rose to bless everything but me. As the morning wore on, my torments increased with the heat, and I lay sweltering on deck, in a furious delirium, held down forcibly by two men, who were relieved by others every now and then I while I raved about Obed, and Paul, and the scenes I had witnessed on board during the chase and in the attack. None of my rough but kind nurses expected I could have held on till nightfall; but shortly after sunset I became more collected, and, as I was afterwards told, whenever any little office was performed for me, whenever some drink was held to my lips, I would say to the gruff, sun-burnt, black-whiskered, square-shouldered top-man, who might be my Ganymede for the occasion, "Thank you, Mary; Heaven bless your pale face, Mary; bless you, bless you!"

It seemed my fancy had shaken itself clear of the fearful objects that had so pertinaciously haunted me before, and, occupying itself with pleasing recollections, had produced a corresponding calm in the animal; but the poor fellow to whom I had expressed myself so endearingly, was, I learned, most awfully put out and dismayed. He twisted and turned his iron features into all manner of ludicrous combinations under the laughter of his mates. "Now, Peter, may I be ———— but I would rather be shot at than hear the poor young gentleman so quiz me in his madness."

Then again, as I praised his lovely taper fingers—they were more like bunches of frosted carrots, dipped in a tar-bucket, with the tails snapt short off, where about all inch thick, *only*—

"My taper fingers—oh, Lord! Now, Peter, I can't stomach this any longer— I'll give you my grog for the next two days, if you will take my spell here—My taper fingers—murder!"

As the evening closed in we saw the high land of Jamaica, but it was the following afternoon before we were off the entrance of Mancheoneal Bay. All this period, although it must have been of great physical suffering, has ever, to my ethereal part, remained a dead blank. The first thing I remember afterwards was being carried ashore in the dark, in a hammock slung on two oars, so as to form a sort of rude palanquin, and laid down at a short distance from the overseer's house, where my troubles had originally commenced. I soon became perfectly sensible and collected, but I was so weak I could not speak: after resting a little, the men again lifted me and proceeded. The door of the dining-hall, which was the back entrance into the overseer's house, opened flush into the little garden through which we had come in—there were lights, and sounds of music, singing, and joviality within. The farther end of the room, at the door of which I now rested, opened into the piazza, or open verandah, which crossed it at right angles, and constituted the front of the house, forming, with this apartment, a figure somewhat like the letter T. I stood at the foot of the letter, as it wore, and as I looked towards the piazza, which was gaily lit up, I could see it was crowded with male and female negroes in their holiday apparel, with their wholesome, clear, brown-black skins—not *blue*-black as they appear in our cold country—and beautiful white teeth and sparkling black eyes, amongst whom were several gumbie-men and flute-players, and John Canoes, as the negro Jack Pudding is called; the latter distinguishable by wearing white false-faces, and enormous shocks of horsehair, fastened on to their woolly pates. Their character hovers somewhere between that of a harlequin and a clown, as they dance about, and thread through the negro groups, quizzing the women and slapping the men; and at Christmas time, the grand negro carnival, they don't confine their practical jokes to their own colour, but take all manner of comical liberties with the whites equally with their fellow-bondsmen.

The blackamoor visitors had suddenly, to all appearance, broken off their dancing, and were now clustered behind a rather remarkable group, who were seated at supper in the dining-room, near to where I stood, forming, as it were, the foreground in the scene. Mr Fyall himself was there, and a rosy-gilled, happy-looking man, who I thought I had seen before; this much I could discern, for the light fell strong on them, especially on the face of the latter, which shone like a star of the first magnitude, or a lighthouse in the red gleam. The usual family of the overseer—the book-keepers that is, and the worthy who had been the proximate cause of all my sufferings, the overseer himself—were there too, as if they had been sitting still at table where I saw them now, ever since I left them three weeks before—at least my fancy did me the favour to annihilate, for the nonce, all intermediate time between the point of my departure on the night of the cooper's funeral, and the moment when I now revisited them.

I was lifted out of the hammock, and supported to the door between two seamen. The fresh, nice-looking man before mentioned, Aaron Bang, Esquire, by name, an incipient planting attorney in the neighbourhood, of great promise, was in the act of singing a song, for it was during some holiday-time, which had broken down the stiff observances of a Jamaica planter's life. There he sat, lolling back on his chair, with his feet upon the table, and a cigar, half-consumed, in his hand. He had twisted up his mouth and mirth-provoking face, and, slewing his head on one side, he was warbling, *ore rotundo,* some melodious ditty, with infinite complacency, and, to all appearance, to the great delight of his auditory, when his eyes lighted on me: he was petrified in a moment—I seemed to have blasted him; his warbling ceased instantaneously—the colour faded from his cheeks—but there he sat, with open mouth, and in the same attitude, as if he still sung, and I had suddenly become deaf, or as if he and his immediate compotators, and the group of blackies beyond, had all been on the instant turned to stone by a slap from one of their own John

Canoes. I must have been in truth a terrible spectacle; my skin was yellow, not as saffron, but as the skin of a ripe lime; the *white* of my eyes, to use an Irishism, ditto; my mouth and lips had festered and *broke out* as we say in Scotland; my head was bound round with a napkin—none of the cleanest, you may swear; my dress was a pair of dirty duck trousers, and my shirt, with the boat-cloak that had been my only counterpane on board of the little vessel, hanging from my shoulders.

Lazarus himself could scarcely have been a more appalling object, when the voice of Him who spoke as never man spake, said, "Lazarus, come forth."

I made an unavailing attempt to cross the threshold, but could not. I was spellbound, or there was an invisible barrier erected against me which I could not overleap. The buzzing in my ears, the pain and throbbing in my head, and racking aches, once more bent me to the earth—ill and reduced as I was, a relapse, thought I; and I felt my judgment once more giving way before the sweltering fiend, who had retreated but for a moment to renew his attacks with still greater fierceness. The moment he once more entered into me—the instant that I was possessed—I cannot call it by any other name—an unnatural strength pervaded my shrunken muscles and emaciated frame, and I stepped boldly into the hall. While I had stood at the door, listless and feeble as a child, hanging on the arms of the two topmen, after they had raised me from the hammock, the whole party had sat silently gazing at me, with their faculties paralysed with terror. But now, when I stumped into the room like the marble statue in Don Juan, and glared on them, my eyes sparkling with unearthly brilliancy under the fierce distemper which had anew thrust its red-hot fingers into my maw, and was at the moment seething my brain in its hellish cauldron, the negroes in the piazza, one and all, men, women, and children, evanished into the night, and the whole party in the foreground started to their legs, as if they had been suddenly galvanised; the table and chairs were overset, and whites and blacks trundled, and scrambled, and bundled over and over each other, neck and crop, as if the very devil had come to invite them to dinner in *propria persona*, horns, tail, and all.

"Duppy come! Duppy come! Massa Tom Cringle ghost stand, at for we door; we all shall dead, oh—we all shall go dead, oh!" bellowed the father of gods, my old ally Jupiter.

"Guid guide us, that's an awfu' sicht?" quoth the Scotch bookkeeper.

"By the hockey, speak if you be a ghost, or I'll exercise" [exorcise] "ye with this butt of a musket," quoth the cowboy—an Irishman to be sure, whose round bullet-head was discernible in the human mass by his black, twinkling, half-drunken-looking eyes.

"Well-a-day," groaned another of them, a Welshman, I believe, with a face as long as my arm, and a drawl worthy of a Methodist parson; "and what can it be—flesh and blood it is not—can these dry bones live?"

Ill as I was, however, I could perceive that all this row had now more of a tipsy frolic in it—whatever it might have had at first—than absolute fear; for the red-faced visitor, and Mr Fyall, as if half-ashamed, speedily extricated themselves from the chaos of chairs and living creatures, righted the table, replaced the candles, and having sat down, looking as grave as judges on the bench, Aaron Bang exclaimed—"I'll bet a dozen, it is the poor fellow himself returned on our hands, half-dead from the rascally treatment he has met with at the hands of these smuggling thieves!"

"Smugglers or no," said Fyall, "you are right for once, my peony rose, I do believe."

But Aaron was a leetle staggered, notwithstanding, when I stumped towards him, as already described, and he shifted back and back as I advanced, with a most laughable cast of countenance, between jest and earnest, while Fyall kept shouting to him—"If it be his ghost, try him in Latin, Mr Bang—speak Latin to him, Aaron Bang—nothing for a ghost like Latin; it is their mother tongue."

Bang, who, it seemed, plumed himself on his erudition, forthwith began—"Quæ maribus solum tribuuntur." Aaron's conceit of exorcising a spirit with the fag-end of an old grammar rule would have tickled me under most circumstances, but I was far past laughing. I had more need, God help me, to pray. I made another step. He hitched his chair back. "Bam, Bo, Rem!" shouted the incipient planting attorney. Another hitch, which carried him clean out of the supper-room, and across the narrow piazza; but in this last movement he made a regular false step, the two back-feet of his chair dropping, over the first step of the front stairs, whereupon he lost his balance, and, toppling over, vanished in a twinkling, and rolled down half-a-dozen steps, heels over head, until he lay sprawling on the manager or mule-trough before the door, where the *beastesses* are fed under busha's own eye on all estates—for this excellent and most cogent reason, that otherwise the maize or guinea-corn, belonging of right to poor *mulo*, would generally go towards improving the condition, not of the quadruped, but of the biped quashie who had charge of him—and there he lay in a convulsion of laughter.

The two seamen, who supported me between them, were at first so completely dumfoundered by all this that they could not speak. At length, however, Timothy Tailtackle lost his patience, and found his tongue.

"This may be Jamaica frolic, good gentlemen, and all very comical in its way; but, d——n me, if it be either gentleman-like or Christian-like, to be after funning and fuddling, while a fellow-creature, and his Majesty's commissioned officer to boot, stands before you, all but dead of one of your blasted fevers."

The honest fellow's straightforward appeal, far from giving offence to the kind-hearted people to whom it was made, was not only taken in good part, but Mr Fyall himself took the lead in setting the whole household immediately to work, to have me properly cared for. The best room in the house was given up to me. I was carefully shifted and put to bed; but during all that night and the following day I was raving in a furious fever, so that I had to be forcibly held down in my bed, sometimes for half an hour at a time.

∽◦∽

I say, messmate, have you ever had the yellow fever, the *vomito prieto,* black vomit, as the Spaniards call it?—No? Have you ever had a had bilious fever, then?—No bad bilious fever either? Why, then, you are a most unfortunate creature; for you have never known what it is to be in heaven, nor eke the other place. Oh, the delight, the blessedness of the languor of recovery, when one finds himself in a large airy room, with a dreamy indistinct recollection of great past suffering endured in a small miserable vessel within the tropics, where you have been roasted one moment by the vertical rays of the sun, and the next annealed, hissing hot, by the salt sea-spray;—in a broad luxurious bed, some cool sunny morning, with the fresh sea-breeze whistling through the open windows that look into the piazza, and rustling the folds of the clean wire-gauze musquito net that serves you for bed-curtains; while beyond you look forth into the sequestered courtyard, overshadowed by one vast umbrageous kennip-tree, that makes everything look green and cool and fresh beneath, and whose branches the rushing wind is rasping cheerily on the shingles of the roof—and oh, how passing sweet is the lullaby from the humming of numberless glancing bright-hued flies, of all sorts and sizes, sparkling among the green leaves like chips of a prism, and the fitful whirring of the fairy-flitting humming-bird, now here, now there, like winged gems, or living "atoms of the rainbow," round which their tiny wings, moving too quickly to he visible, form little haloes—and the palm-tree at the house-corner is shaking its long hard leaves, making a sound for all the world like the pattering of rain; and the orange-tree top, with ripe fruit and green fruit and white blossoms, is waving to and fro flush with the windowsill, dashing the fragrant odour into your room at every *whish*; and the double jessamine is twining up the papaw (whose fruit, if rubbed on a bull's hide, immediately converts it into a tender beef-steak), and absolutely stifling you with sweet perfume; and then the sangaree—old madeira, two parts of water, no more, and nutmeg—and not a taste out of a thimble, but a rammer-full of it, my boy, that would drown your first-born at his christening, if he slipped into it. And no stinting in the use of this ocean; on the contrary, the tidy old brown nurse, or mayhap a buxom young one, at your bedside, with ever and anon a "leetle more panada," (d——n panada, I had forgotten that!) "and den some more sangaree; it will do massa good, trenthen him tomack"—and—but I am out of breath, and must lie to for a brief space.

I opened my eyes late in the morning of the second clay after landing, and saw Mr Fyall and the excellent Aaron Bang sitting one on each side of my bed. Although weak as a sucking infant, I had a strong persuasion on my mind that all danger was over, and that I was convalescent. I had no feverish symptoms whatsoever, but felt cool and comfortable, with a fine balmy moisture on my skin; as yet, however, I spoke with great difficulty.

Aaron noticed this.

"Don't exert yourself too much, Tom; take it coolly, man, and thank God that you are now fairly round the corner. Is your head painful?"

"No—why should it?

Mr Fyall smiled, and I put up my hand—it was all I could do, for my limbs appeared loaded with lead at the extremities, and when I touched any part of my frame, with my hand for instance, there was no concurring sensation conveyed by the nerves of the two parts—sometimes I felt as if touched by the hand of another; at others, as if I had touched the person of some one else. When I raised my hand to my forehead, my fingers instinctively moved to take hold of my hair, for I was in no small degree proud of some luxuriant brown curls, which the women used to praise. Alas, and alack-a-day! in place of ringlets, glossy with Macassar oil, I found a cool young tender plantain-leaf bound round my temples.

"What is all this?" said I. "A *kale-blade* where my hair used to be!"

"How came this kale-blade here,
    And how came it here?"

sang friend Bang, laughing, for he had great *powers of laughter*, and I saw he kept his quizzical face turned towards some object at the head of the bed, which I could not see.

"You may say that, Aaron—where's my wig, you rogue, eh?"

"Never mind, Tom," said Fyall, "your hair will soon grow again, won't it, miss?"

"Miss! miss!" and I screwed my neck round, and lo!—

"Ah, Mary, and are you the Delilah who have shorn my locks—you wicked young female lady, you!"

She smiled and nodded to Aaron, who was a deuced favourite with the ladies, *black*, brown, and white (I give the *pas* to the staple of the country—hope no offence), as well as with every one else who ever knew him.

"How dare you, friend Bang, shave and blister my head, you dog?" said I. "You cannibal Indian, you have scalped me; you are a regular Mohawk."

"Never mind, Tom—never mind, my boy," said he. "Ay, you may blush, Mary Palma. Cringle there will fight, but he will have '*Palmam* qui meruit ferat' for his motto yet, take my word for it."

The sight of my cousin's lovely face, and the heavenly music of her tongue, made me so forgiving that I could be angry with no one. At this moment a nice-looking elderly man slid into the room as noiselessly as a cat.

"How are you, lieutenant? Why, you are positively gay this morning! Preserve me!—why have you taken off the dressing from your head?"

"Preserve me—you may say that, doctor: why, you seem to have preserved me, and pickled me after a very remarkable fashion, certainly! Why, man, do you intend to make a mummy of me, with all your swathings? Now, what is that crackling on my chest? More plaintain-leaves, as I live!"

"Only another blister, sir."

"Only *another* blister—and my feet—Zounds! what have you been doing with my feet? The soles are as tender as if I had been bastinadoed."

"Only cataplasms, sir; mustard and bird-pepper poultices—nothing more."

"Mustard and bird-pepper poultices!—and pray, what is that long fiddle-case, supported on two chairs in the piazza?"

"What case?" said the good doctor, and his eye followed mine. "Oh, my gun-case. I am a great sportsman, you must know—but draw down that blind,—Mr Bang, if you please, the breeze is too strong."

"Gun-case! I would rather have taken it for your *game*-box, doctor. However, thanks be to heaven, you have not *bagged* me this bout."

At this moment I heard a violent scratching and jumping on the roof of the house, and presently a loud croak, and a strong rushing noise, as of a large bird taking flight—"What is that, doctor?"

"The devil," said he, laughing; "at least your evil genius, lieutenant; it is the carrion crows—the large John Crows, as they are called—flying away. They have been holding a council of war upon you since early dawn, expecting (I may tell you, now you are so well) that it might likely soon turn into a coroner's inquest."

"John Crow!—Coroner's inquest!—Cool shavers those West India chaps, after all!" muttered I; and again and again I lay back and offered up my heart-warm thanks to the Almighty for His great mercy to me a sinner.

My aunt and cousin had been on a visit in the neighbourhood, and over-night Mr Fyall had kindly sent for them to receive my last sigh, for to all appearance I was fast going. Oh, the gratitude of my heart, the tears of joy I wept in my weak blessedness, and the overflowing of heart that I experienced towards that almighty and ever-merciful Being who had spared me, and brought me out of my great sickness, to look round on dear friends, and on the idol of my heart, once more, after all my grievous sufferings! I took Mary's hand—I could not raise it for lack of strength, or I would have kissed it; but as she leant over me, Fyall came behind her and gently pressed her sweet lips to mine, while the dear girl blushed as red as Aaron Bang's face. By this my aunt herself had come into the room, and added her warm congratulations; and last, although not least, Timothy Tailtackle made his appearance in the piazza at the window, with a clean, joyful, well-shaven countenance. He grinned, turned his quid, pulled up his trousers, smoothed down his hair with his hand, and gave a sort of half-tipsy shamble, meant for a bow, as he entered the bedroom.

"You have forereached on Davy this time, sir. Heaven be praised for it! He was close aboard of you, howsomdever, sir, once or twice." Then he bowed round the room again, with a sort of swing or caper, whichever you choose to call it, as if *he* had been the party obliged.—"Kind folk these, sir," he continued, in what was meant for *sotto voce,* and for my ear alone, but it was more like the growling of a mastiff puppy than anything else—"Kind folk, sir—bad as their mountebanking looked the first night, sir. Why, Lord bless your honour, may they make a marine of me, if they han't set a Bungo to wait on us, Bill and I, that is—and we has grog more than does us good—and grub, my eye!—only think, sir,—Bill and Timothy Tailtackle waited on by a black Bungo!" and he doubled himself up, chuckling and hugging himself, with infinite glee.

"All went now merry as a marriage-bell." I was carefully conveyed to

Kingston, where I rallied under my aunt's hospitable roof, as rapidly almost as I had sickened, and within a fortnight, all bypast strangeness explained to my superiors, I at length occupied my berth in the Firebrand's gunroom as third-lieutenant of the ship.

CHAPTER XI.

MORE SCENES IN JAMAICA.

"There be land-rats and water-rats—water-thieves and
land-thieves—I mean pirates."

Merchant of Venice.

THE MALADY, from whose fangs I had just escaped, was at this time making fearful ravages amongst the troops and white inhabitants of Jamaica generally; nor was the squadron exempted from the afflicting visitation, although it suffered in a smaller degree.

I had occasion at this time to visit Up-Park camp, a military post about a mile and a half from Kingston, where two regiments of infantry and a detachment of artillery were stationed.

In the forenoon I walked out in company with an officer, a relation of my own, whom I had gone to visit—enjoying the fresh sea-breeze that whistled past us in half a gale of wind, although the sun was vertical, and shining into the bottom of a pint-pot, as the sailors have it.

The barracks were built on what appeared to me a very dry situation (although I have since heard it alleged that there was a swamp to windward of it, over which the sea-breeze blew, but this I did not see), considerably elevated above the hot sandy plain on which Kingston stands, and sloping gently towards the sea. They were splendid, large, airy, two-storey buildings, well raised off the ground on brick pillars, so that there was a perfectly free ventilation of air between the surface of the earth and the floor of the first storey, as well as through the whole of the upper rooms. A large balcony, or piazza, ran along the whole of the south front, both above and below, which shaded the brick shell of the house from the sun, and afforded a cool and convenient lounge for the men. The outhouses of all kinds were well thrown back into the rear, so that in front there was nothing to intercept the sea-breeze. The offi-

cers' quarters stood in advance of the men's barracks, and were, as might be
expected, still more comfortable; and in front of all were the field-officers'
houses, the whole of substantial brick and mortar. This superb establishment
stood in an extensive lawn, not surpassed in beauty by any nobleman's park
that I had ever seen. It was immediately after the rains when I visited it; the
grass was luxuriant and newly cut, and the trees, which grew in detached
clumps, were most magnificent. We clambered up into one of them, a large
umbrageous wild cotton-tree, which cast a shadow on the ground—the sun
being, as already mentioned, right overhead—of thirty paces in diameter; but
still it was but a dwarfish plant of its kind, for I have measured others whose
gigantic shadows, at the same hour, were upwards of one hundred and fifty feet
in diameter, and their trunks, one in particular that overhangs the Spanish
Town road, twenty feet through of *solid* timber; that is, not including the enormous spars that shoot out like buttresses, and end in strong twisted roots, that
strike deep into the earth, and form stays, as it were, to the tree in all directions.

Our object, however—publish it not in Askalon—was not so much to
admire the charms of nature as to enjoy the luxury of a real Havannah cigar in
solitary comfort; and a glorious perch we had selected. The shade was grateful
beyond measure. The fresh breeze was rushing, almost roaring, through the
leaves and groaning branches, and everything around was green, and fragrant,
and cool, and delicious—by comparison that is, for the thermometer would, I
daresay, have still vouched for eighty degrees. The branches overhead were
alive with a variety of beautiful lizards, and birds of the gayest plumage;
amongst others, a score of small chattering green paroquets were hopping
close to us, and playing at bopeep from the lower surfaces of the leaves of the
wild pine (a sort of Brobdignag parasite, that grows, like the mistletoe, in the
clefts of the larger trees), to which they clung, as green and shining as the
leaves themselves, and ever and anon popping their little heads and shoulders
over to peer at us; while the red-breasted woodpecker kept drumming on every
hollow part of the bark, for all the world like old Kelson, the carpenter of the
Torch, tapping along the top-sides for the dry rot. All around us the men were
lounging about in the shade, and sprawling on the grass in their foraging-caps
and light jackets, with an officer here and there lying reading, or sauntering
about, bearding Phœbus himself, to watch for a shot at a swallow as it skimmed
past; while goats and horses, sheep and cattle, were browsing the fresh grass,
or sheltering themselves from the heat beneath the trees. All nature seemed

alive and happy—a little drowsy from the heat or so, but that did not much signify—when two carts, each drawn by a mule, and driven by a negro, approached the tree whereon we were perched. A solitary sergeant accompanied them, and they appeared, when a bowshot distant, to be loaded with white deal boxes.

I paid little attention to them until they drove under the tree.

"I say, Snowdrop," said the noncommissioned officer, "where be them black rascals, them pioneers—where is the *fateague* party, my Lily-white, who ought to have the trench dug by this time?"

"Dere now," grumbled the negro, "dere now—easy ting to deal wid white gentleman, but debil cannot satisfy dem worsted sash." Then aloud—"Me no know, sir—me can't tell; no for me business to dig hole—I only carry what you fill him up wid;" and the vampire, looking over his shoulder, cast his eye towards his load, and grinned until his white teeth glanced from ear to ear.

"Now," said the Irish sergeant, "I could *brain* you, but it is not worth while!"—I question if he could, however, knowing, as I did, the thickness of their skulls.—"Ah, here they come!" and a dozen half-drunken, more than half-naked, bloated, villanous-looking blackamoors, with shovels and pickaxes on their shoulders, came along the road, laughing and singing most lustily. They passed beneath where we sat, and, when about a stone-cast beyond, they all jumped into a trench or pit, which I had not noticed before, about twenty feet long by eight wide. It was already nearly six feet deep, but it seemed they had instructions to sink it further, for they first plied their pickaxes, and then began to shovel out the earth. When they had completed their labour, the sergeant, who had been superintending their operations, returned to where the carts were still standing beneath the tree. One of them had *six coffins in it,* with the name of the tenant of each, and number of his company, marked in red chalk on the smallest end!

"I say, Snowdrop," said the sergeant, "how do you come to have only five bodies, when Cucumbershin there has six?"

"To be sure I hab no more as five, and weight enough too. You no see Corporal Bumblechops dere? You knows how big he was."

"Well, but where is Sergeant Heavystern?—why did you not fetch him away with the others?"

The negro answered doggedly, "Massa Sergeant, you should remember dem no die of consumption—cough you call him—nor fever and ague, nor any ting dat waste dem; for tree day gone—no more—all were mount guard—tout and fat—so, as for Sergeant Heavystern, him left in de dead-house at de hospital."

"I guessed as much, you dingy thief," said the sergeant, "but I will break your bones if you don't give me a sufficing *rason why* you left him." And he approached Snowdrop with his cane raised in act to strike.

"Top, massa," shouted the negro; "me will tell you—Dr Plaget desire dat Heavystern should be leave."

"Confound Dr Plaget!" and he smote the pioneer across the pate, whereby he broke his stick, although, as I anticipated, without much hurting his man; but the sergeant instantly saw his error, and with the piece of the baton he gave Snowdrop a tap on the shin-bone that set him pirouetting on one leg, with the other in his hand, like a teetotum.

"Why, sir, did you not bring as many as Cucumbershin, sir?"

Because," screamed Snowdrop in great wrath, now all alive and kicking from the smart—"Because Cucumbershin is loaded wid light infantry, sir, and all of mine are grenadier, Massa Sergeant—dat dem good reason surely!"

"No, it is not, sir; go back and fetch Heavystern immediately, or by the powers but I will—"

"Massa Sergeant, you must be mad—Dr Plaget—you won't yeerie—but him say, five grenadier—especially wid Corporal Bumblechop for one—is good load—ay, wery tif load—equal to seven tallion company [battalion, I presume], and more better load, great deal, den six light infantry; beside him say, Tell Sergeant Pivot to send you tack at five in de afternoon wid four more coffin, by which time he would have anoder load, and in trute de load was ready prepare in de dead-house before I come away, *only dem were not well cold just yet.*"

I was mightily shocked at all this, but my chum took it very coolly. He slightly raised one side of his mouth, and, giving a knowing wink with his eye, lighted a fresh cigar, and continued to puff away with all the composure in the world.

At length the forenoon wore away, and the bugles sounded for dinner, when we adjourned to the mess-room. It was a very large and handsome saloon, standing alone in the lawn, and quite detached from all the other buildings, but the curtailed dimensions of the table in the middle of it, and the ominous crowding together of the regimental plate, like a show-table in Rundle and Bridge's back-shop, gave startling proofs of the ravages of the "pestilence that walketh in darkness, and the destruction that wasteth at noon-day;" for although the whole regiment was in barracks, there were only *nine* covers laid, one of which was for me. The lieutenant-colonel, the major, and, I believe, fifteen other officers, had already been gathered to their fathers within four months from the day on which the regiment landed from the transports. Their warfare was o'er, and they slept well. At the first, when the insidious disease began to creep on apace, and to evince its deadly virulence, all was dismay and anxiety—downright, slavish, unmanly fear, even amongst case-hardened veterans, who had weathered the whole Peninsular war, and finished off with Waterloo. The next week passed over, the mortality increasing, but the dismay decreasing; and so it wore on, until it reached its horrible climax, at the time I speak of, by which period there was absolutely no dread at all. A reckless gaiety had succeeded—not the screwing-up of one's courage for the nonce, to mount a breach, or to lay an enemy's frigate aboard, where the substratum of fear is present, although eased over by an energetic exertion of the will; but an unnatural light-heartedness—for which account, ye philosophers, for I cannot—and this, too, amongst men who, although as steel in the field, yet whenever a common cold overtook them in quarters, or a small twinge of rheumatic pain, would, under other circumstances, have caudled and beflanneled themselves, and bored you for your sympathy, at *no allowance,* as they say.

The major elect—that is, the senior captain—was in the chair; as for the lieutenant-colonel's vacancy, that was too high an aspiration for any man in the regiment. A stranger of rank and interest and money would of course get that step, for the two deaths in the regimental staff made but one captain a major, as my neighbour on the left hand feelingly remarked. All was fun and joviality; we had a capital dinner, and no allusion whatever, direct or indirect, was made to the prevailing mortal epidemic, until the surgeon came in, about eight o'clock in the evening.

"Sit down, doctor," said the president—"take some wine; can recommend the madeira—claret but so-so—your health."

The doctor bowed, and soon became as happy and merry as the rest; so we carried on until about ten o'clock, when the lights began to waltz a little, and propagate also, and I found I had got enough, or, peradventure, a little more than enough, when the senior captain rose, and walked very composedly out of the room—but I noticed him pinch the doctor's shoulder as he passed.

The *medico* thereupon stole quietly after him; but we did not seem to miss either—a young sub had usurped the deserted throne, and there we were all once more in full career, singing and bousing, and cracking bad jokes to our heart's content. By-and-by in comes the doctor once more.

"Doctor," quoth young sub, "take some wine; can't recommend the madeira this time," mimicking his predecessor very successfully; "the claret, you know, has been condemned, but a little hot brandy-and-water, eh?"

The doctor once more bowed his pate, made his hot stuff, and volunteered a song. After he had finished, and we had all hammered on the table to his honour and glory until everything danced again, as if it had been a matter of very trivial concern, he said, "Sorry I was away so long; but old Spatterdash has got a deuced thick skin, I can tell you—could scarcely get the lancet into him: I thought I should have had to send for a spring phleme, to tip him the veterinary, you know—and he won't take physic; so I fear he will have but a poor chance."

Spatterdash was no other than mine host who had just vacated.

"What! do you really think he is in for it?" said the second oldest captain, who sat next me; and as he spoke he drew his leg from beneath the table, and turning out his dexter heel, seemed to contemplate the site of the prospective fixed spur.

"I do, indeed," quoth Dr Plaget. *He died within three days!*

But as I do not intend to write an essay on yellow fever, I will make an end, and get on shipboard as fast as I can, after stating one strong fact, authenticated to me by many unimpeachable witnesses. It is this; that this dreadful epidemic, or contagious fever—call it which you will—has never appeared, or been propagated, at or beyond an altitude of 3000 feet above the level of the sea, although people seized with it on the hot sultry plains, and removed thither, have unquestionably died. In a country like Jamaica, with a range of lofty mountains, far exceeding this height, intersecting the island through nearly its whole length, might not Government, after satisfying themselves of the truth of the fact, improve on the hint? Might not a main-guard suffice in Kingston, for instance, while the regiments were in quarters half-way up the Liguanea Mountains, within twelve miles' actual distance from the town, and within view of it, so that during the day, by a semaphore on the mountain, and another at the barrack of the outpost, a constant and instantaneous communication could be kept up, and, if need were, by lights in the night?

The admiral, for instance, had a semaphore in the stationary flag-ship at Port Royal, which communicated with another at his *Pen,* or residence, near Kingston; and this, again, rattled off the information to the mountain retreat, where he occasionally retired to careen; and it is fitting to state also, that in all the mountain districts of Jamaica which I visited there is abundance of excellent water and plenty of fuel. These matters are worth consideration, one would think; however, *allons*—it is no business of Tom Cringle's.

Speaking of telegraphing, I will relate an anecdote here, if you will wait until I mend my pen. I had landed at Greenwich wharf on duty—this was the nearest point of communication between Port Royal and the Admiral's Pen—where, finding the flag-lieutenant, he drove me up in his ketureen to lunch. While we were regaling ourselves, the old signal-man came into the piazza, and with several most remarkable obeisances gave us to know that there were flags hoisted on the signal-mast at the mountain settlement, of which he could make nothing—the uppermost was neither the interrogative, the affirmative, nor the negative, nor, in fact, anything that with the book he could make sense of.

"Odd enough," said the lieutenant; "hand me the glass," and he peered away for half a minute. "Confound me if I can make heads or tails of it either; there, Cringle, what do you think? How do you construe it?"

I took the telescope. Uppermost there was hoisted on the signal-mast a large table-cloth, not altogether immaculate, and under it a towel, as I guessed, for it was too opaque for bunting, and too white, although I could not affirm that it was fresh out of the fold either.

"I am puzzled," said I, as I spied away again. Meanwhile, there was no acknowledgment made at our semaphore. "There, down they go," I continued—"Why, it must be a mistake—Stop, here's a new batch going up above the green trees—There goes the tablecloth once more, and the towel, and—deuce take me, if I can compare the lowermost to anything but a dishclout—why, it must be a dishclout."

The flags, or substitutes for them, streamed another minute in the breeze, but as there was still no answer made from our end of the string, they were once more hauled down. We waited another minute—"Why, here goes the same signal up again, tablecloth, towel, dishclout, and all—What the *diable* have we got here? A red ball, two pennants under—What can that mean?—Ball—it is the *bonnet-rouge,* or I am a Dutchman, with two short streamers"—Another look—"A red night-cap and a pair of stockings, by all that is portentous!" exclaimed I.

"Ah, I see, I see!" said the lieutenant, laughing—"signalman, acknowledge it."

It was done, and down came all the flags in a trice. It appeared, on inquiry, that the washing-cart, which ought to have been sent up that morning, had been forgotten; and the Admiral and his secretary having ridden out, there was no one who could make the proper signal for it. So the old housekeeper took this singular method of having the cart despatched, and it was sent off accordingly.

For the first week after I entered on my new office, I was busily engaged on board, during which time my mind was quite made up, that the most rising man in his Majesty's service, beyond all compare, was Lieutenant Thomas Cringle, third of the Firebrand. During this eventful period I never addressed a note to any friend on shore, or to a brother officer, without writing in the left-hand lower corner of the envelope "Lieutenant Cringle," and clapping three dashing &c. &c. &c.'s below the party's name for whom it was intended.

"Must let 'em know that an officer of *my* rank in the service knows somewhat of the courtesies of life, eh?"

In about ten days, however, we had gotten the ship into high order and ready for sea, and now the glory and honour of command, like my *only* epaulet, that had been soaked while on duty in one or two showers, and afterwards regularly bronzed in the sun, began to tarnish, and lose the new gloss, like everything else in this weary world. It was about this time, while sitting at breakfast in the gunroom one fine morning, with the other officers of our mess, gossiping about I hardly remember what, that we heard the captain's voice on deck.

"Call the first-lieutenant."

"He is at breakfast, sir," said the man, whoever he might have been, to whom the order was addressed.

"Never mind then—Here, boatswain's mate—Pipe away the men who were captured in the boats; tell them to clean themselves, and send Mr ——— to me"—(this was the officer who had been taken prisoner along with them in the first attack)—"they are wanted in Kingston at the trial to-day—Stop—tell Mr Cringle also to get ready to go in the gig."

The pirates, to the amount of forty-five, had been transferred to Kingston jail some days previously, preparatory to their trial, which, as above mentioned, was fixed for this day.

We pulled cheerily up to Kingston, and, landing at the Wherry wharf, marched along the hot dusty streets, under a broiling sun, Captain Transom, the other lieutenant, and myself, in full puff, leading the van, followed by about fourteen seamen, in white straw-hats, with broad black ribbons, and clean white frocks and trousers, headed by a boatswain's mate, with his silver whistle hung round his neck—as respectable a tail as any Christian could desire to swing behind him; and, man for man, I would willingly have perilled my promotion upon their walloping, with no offensive weapons but their stretchers, the

Following, clay-mores and all, of any proud, disagreeable, would-be-mighty mountaineer, that ever turned up his supercilious, whisky-blossomed snout at Bailie Jarvie. On they came, square-shouldered, narrow-flanked, tall, strapping fellows, tumbling and rolling about the piazzas in knots of three and four, until, at the corner of King Street, they came bolt up upon a well-known large fat, brown lady, famous for her manufacture of spruce beer.

"Avast, avast a bit," sang out one of the topmen; "let the nobs heave ahead, will ye, and let's have a pull."

"Here, old Mother Slush," sang out another of the cutter's crew—"Hand us up a dozen bottles of spruce, do you hear?"

"Dozen battle of pruce!" groaned the old woman—"who sall pay me?"

"Why, do you think the Firebrands are thieves, you old canary, you?"

"How much, eh?" said the boatswain's mate.

"Twelve feepennies," quoth the matron.

"Oh, ah!" said one of the men—"Twelve times five is half-a-crown; there's a dollar for you, old mother Popandchokem—now give me back five shillings."

"Eigh, oh!" whined out the spruce merchant; "you dem rascal, who tell you that your dollar more wort den any one else money—eh? How can give you back five shilling and keep back twelve feepenny—eh?"

The culprit, who had stood the Cocker of the company, had by this time gained his end, which was to draw the fat damsel a step or two from the large tub half-full of water, where the bottles were packed, and to engage her attention by stirring up her bile, or *corruption*, as they call it in Scotland, while his messmates instantly seized the opportunity, and a bottle apiece also; and, as I turned round to look for them, there they all were in a circle taking the meridian altitude of the sun, or as if they had been taking aim at the pigeons on the eaves of the houses above them with Indian mouth-tubes.

They then replaced the bottles in the tub, paid the woman more than she asked; but, by way of taking out the change, they chucked her stern foremost into the water amongst her merchandise, and then shouldered the vessel, old woman and all, and away they staggered with her, the empty bottles clattering together in the water, and the old lady swearing, and bouncing, and squattering amongst them, while Jack shouted to her to hold her tongue, or they would let her go by the run bodily. Thus they stumped in the wake of their captain, until he arrived at the door of the court-house, to the great entertainment of the bystanders, cutting the strings that confined the corks of the stone bottles as they bowled along, popping the spruce into each other's faces, and the faces of the negroes, as they ran out of the stores to look at Jack in his frolic, and now and then taking a shot at the old woman's cockernony itself, as she was held, kicking and spurring, high above their heads.

At length the captain, who was no great way ahead, saw what was going on, which was the signal for doucing the whole affair, spruce-woman, tub, and bottles; and the party, gathering themselves up, mustered close aboard of us, as grave as members of the General Assembly.

The regular court-house of the city being under repair, the Admiralty Sessions were held in a large room occupied temporarily for the purpose. At one end, raised two steps above the level of the floor, was the bench, on which were seated the Judge of the Admiralty Court, supported by two post-captains in full uniform, who are ex-officio judges of this court in the colonies, one on each side. On the right, the jury, composed of merchants of the place and respectable planters of the neighbourhood, were enclosed in a sort of box, with a common white pine railing separating it from the rest of the court. There was a long table in front of the bench, at which a lot of black-robed devil's limbs of lawyers were ranged—but both amongst them, and on the bench, the want of the cauliflower wigs was sorely felt by me, as well as by the seamen, who considered it little less than murder, that men in crops—black shock-pated fellows—should sit in judgment on their fellow-creatures, where life and death were in the scales.

On the left hand of the bench, the motley public—white, black, and of every intermediate shade—were grouped; as also in front of the dock, which was large. It might have been made with a view to the possibility of fifteen unfortunates or so being arraigned at one time; but now there were no fewer than forty-three jammed and pegged together into it, like sheep in a Smithfield pen the evening before market-day. These were the *forty thieves*—the pirates. They were all, without exception, clean, well-shaven, and decently rigged in white trousers, linen or check shirts, and held their broad Panama sombreros in their hands.

Most of them wore the red silk sash round the waist. They had generally large bushy whiskers, and not a few had ear-rings of massive gold (why call wearing ear-rings puppyism?—Shakespeare wore ear-rings, or the Chandos portrait lies), and chains of the same metal round their necks, supporting, as I concluded, a crucifix, hid in the bosom of the shirt.—A Spaniard can't murder a man comfortably if he has not his crucifix about him.

They were, collectively, the most daring, intrepid, Salvator-Rosa-looking men I had ever seen. Most of them were above the middle size, and the spread of their shoulders, the grace with which their arms were hung, and finely developed muscles of the chest and neck, the latter exposed completely by the folding back of their shirt-collars, cut large and square, after the Spanish fashion, beat the finest boat's crew we could muster all to nothing. Some of them were of mixed blood, that is, the cross between the European Spaniard and the aboriginal Indian of Cuba—the latter a race long since sacrificed on the altar of Mammon, the white man's god.

Their hair, generally speaking, was long, and curled over the forehead black and glossy, or hung down to their shoulders in ringlets, that a dandy of the second Charles's time would have given his little finger for. The forehead in most was high and broad, and of a clear olive, the nose straight, springing boldly from the brow, the cheeks oval, and the mouth—every Spaniard has a beautiful mouth, until he spoils it with the beastly cigar, as far as his well-formed firm lips can be spoiled; but his teeth he generally does destroy early in life. Take the whole, however, and deduct for the teeth, I had never seen so handsome a set of men; and I am sure no woman, had she been there, would have gainsaid me. They stood up, and looked forth upon their judges and the jury like brave men, desperadoes though they were. They were, without exception, calm and collected, as if aware that they had small chance of escape, but still determined not to give that chance away. One young man especially attracted my attention, from the bold, cool self-possession of his bearing. He was in the very front of the dock, and dressed in no way different from the rest, so far as his under garments were concerned, unless it were that they were of a finer quality. He wore a short green velvet jacket, profusely studded with knobs and chains, like small chain-shot, of solid gold, similar to the shifting button lately introduced by our dandies in their waistcoats. It was not put on, but hung on one shoulder, being fastened across his breast by the two empty sleeves tied together in a knot. He also wore the red silk sash, through which a broad gold cord ran twining like the strand of a rope. He had no ear-rings, but his hair was the most beautiful I had ever seen in a male—long and black, jet-black and glossy. It was turned up and fastened in a club on the crown of his head with a large pin, I should rather say skewer, of silver; but the outlandishness of the fashion was not offensive, when I came to take into the account the beauty of the plaiting, and of the long raven lovelocks that hung down behind each of his small transparent ears, and the short Hyperion-like curls that clustered thick and richly on his high, pile, broad forehead. His eyes were large, black, and swimming, like a woman's; his nose straight and thin; and such a mouth, such an under-lip, full, and melting; and teeth regular and white, and utterly free from the pollution of tobacco; and a beautifully-moulded small chin, rounding off and merging in his round, massive, muscular neck.

I had never seen so fine a face, such perfection of features, and such a clear, dark, smooth skin. It was a finer face than Lord Byron's, whom I had seen more than once, and wanted that hellish curl of the lip; and as to figure, he could, to look at him, at any time have eaten up his lordship, stoop and roop, to his breakfast. It was the countenance, in a word, of a most beautiful youth, melancholy, indeed, and anxious—evidently anxious; for the large pearls that coursed each other down his forehead and cheek, and the slight quivering of the under-lip, every now and then evinced the powerful struggle that was going on within. His figure was, if possible, superior to his face. It was not quite filled up—*set*, as we call it—but the arch of his chest was magnificent, his shoulders square, arms well put on; but his neck—"Have you seen the Apollo, neighbour?"—"No, but the cast of it at Somerset House."—"Well, that will do—so you know the sort of neck he had." His waist was fine, hips beautifully moulded; and although his under limbs were shrouded in his wide trousers, they were evidently of a piece with what was seen and developed; and this was vouched for by the turn of his ankle and well-shaped foot, on which he wore a small Spanish grass slipper, fitted with great nicety. He was at least six feet two in height; and such as I have described him, there he stood, with his hands grasping the rail before him, and looking intently at a wigless lawyer who was opening the accusation, while he had one ear turned a little towards the sworn interpreter of the court, whose province it was, at every pause, to explain to the prisoners what the learned gentleman was stating. From time to time he said a word or two to a square-built, dark, ferocious-looking man standing next him, apparently about forty years of age, who, as well as his fellow-prisoners, appeared to pay him great respect; and I could notice the expression of their countenances change as his rose or fell.

The indictment had been read before I came in, and, as already mentioned, the lawyer was proceeding with his accusatory speech, and, as it appeared to me, the young Spaniard had some difficulty in understanding the interpreter's explanation. Whenever he saw me, he exclaimed, "Ah! aqui viene, el Señor Teniente—ahora sabremos—ahora, ahora;" and he beckoned to me to draw near. I did so.

"I beg pardon, Mr Cringle," he said in Spanish, with the ease and grace of a nobleman—"but I believe the interpreter to be incapable, and I am certain that what I say is not fittingly explained to the judges; neither do I believe he can give me a sound notion of what the advocate (avocado) is alleging against us. May I entreat you to solicit the bench for permission to take his place? I know you will expect no apology for the trouble from a man in my situation."

This unexpected address in open court took me fairly aback, and I stopped short while in the act of passing the open space in front of the dock, which was kept clear by six marines in white jackets, whose muskets, fixed bayonets, and uniform caps, seemed out of place to my mind in a criminal court. The lawyer suddenly suspended his harangue, while the judges fixed their eyes on me, and so did the audience, confound them! To be the focus of so many eyes was trying to my modesty; for, although I had mixed a little in the world, and was not altogether unacquainted with bettermost society, still, below any little manner that I had acquired, there was, and always will be, an under-stratum of bashfulness, or sheepishness, or *mauvaise honte,* call it which you will; and the torture, the breaking on the wheel, with which a man of that temperament perceives the eyes of a whole court-house, for instance, attracted to him, none but a bashful man can understand. At length I summoned courage to speak.

"May it please your honours, this poor fellow, on his own behalf, and on the part of his fellow-prisoners, complains of the incapacity of the sworn interpreter, and requests that I may be made the channel of communication in his stead."

This was a tremendous effort, and once more the whole blood of my body rushed to my cheeks and forehead, and I "sweat extremely." The judges, he of the black robe and those of the epaulet, communed together.

"Have you any objection to be sworn, Mr Cringle?"

"None in the least, provided the court considers me competent, and the accused are willing to trust to me."

"Si, si!" exclaimed the young Spaniard, as if comprehending what was going on—"Somos contentos—todos, todos!" and he looked round, like a prince, on his fellow-culprits. A low murmuring, "Si, si—contento, contento!" passed amongst the group.

"The accused, please your honours, are willing to trust to my correctness."

"Pray, Mr Cringle, don't make yourself the advocate of these men—mind that," said the lawyer *sans* wig.

"I don't intend it, sir," I said, slightly stung; "but if *you* had suffered what I have done at their hands, *peradventure* such a caution to *you* would have been unnecessary."

The sarcasm told, I was glad to see: but remembering where I was, I hauled out of action with the man of words, simply giving the last shot—"I am sure no English gentleman would willingly throw any difficulty in the way of the poor fellows being made aware of what is given in evidence against them, bad as they may be."

He was about rejoining, for a lawyer would as soon let you have the last word as a sweep or a baker the wall, when the officer of court approached and swore me in, and the trial proceeded.

The whole party were proved by fifty witnesses to have been taken in arms on board of the schooners in the cove; and further, it was proved that no commission or authority to cruise whatsoever was found on board any of them, a strong proof that they were pirates.

"Que dice, que dice?" inquired the young Spaniard already mentioned.

I said that the court seemed to infer, and were pressing it on the jury, that the absence of any commission or letter-of-marque from a superior officer, or from any of the Spanish authorities, was strong evidence that they were marauders—in fact, pirates.

"Ah!" he exclaimed; "gracias, gracias!" Then, with an agitated hand, he drew from his bosom a parchment, folded like the manifest of a merchant-ship, and at the same moment the gruff fierce-looking elderly man did the same, with another similar instrument from his own breast.

"Here, here are the commissions—here are authorities from the Captain-General of Cuba. Read them."

I looked over them; they were regular, to all appearance; at least, as there were no autographs in court of the Spanish Viceroy, or any of his officers, whose signatures, either *real* or *forged*, were affixed to the instruments, with which to compare them, there was a great chance, I conjectured, so far as I saw, that they would be acquitted: and in this case *we*, his majesty's officers, would have been converted into the transgressing party; for if it were established that the vessels taken were *bona fide guarda costas*, we should be placed in an awkward predicament, in having captured them by force of arms, not to take into account the having violated the sanctity of a friendly port.

But I could see that this unexpected production of regular papers by their officers had surprised the pirates themselves as much as it had done me—

whether it was a heinous offence of mine or not to conceal this impression from the court (there is some dispute about the matter to this hour between me and my conscience), I cannot tell; but I was determined to stick scrupulously to the temporary duties of my office, without stating what I suspected, or even translating some sudden expressions overheard by me, that would have shaken the credibility of the documents.

"Comissiones, comissiones!" for instance, was murmured by a weatherbeaten Spaniard, with a fine bald head, from which two small tufts of grey hair stood out above his ears, and with a superb Moorish face—"Comissiones es decir patentes—Si hay comissiones, el Diablo mismo las ha hecho!"

The court was apparently nonplussed—not so the wigless man of law. His pea-green visage assumed a more ghastly hue, and the expression of his eyes became absolutely blasting. He looked altogether like a cat sure of her mouse, but willing to let it play in fancied joy of escaping, as he said softly to the Jew crier, who was perched in a high chair above the heads of the people, like an ugly *corbie* in its dirty nest—"Crier, call Job Rumbletithump, mate of the Porpoise."

"Job Rumbletithump, come into court!"

"Here," quoth Job, as a stout, bluff, honest-looking sailor rolled into the witness-box.

"Now, clerk of the crown, please to swear in the mate of the Porpoise." It was done. "Now, my man, you were taken going through the Caicos Passage in the Porpoise by pirates in August last—were you not?"

"Yes, sir."

"Turn your face to the jury, and speak up, sir. Do you see any of the *honest* men who made free with you in that dock, sir? Look at them, sir."

The mate walked up to the dock, stopped, and fixed his eyes intently on the young Spaniard. I stared breathlessly at him also. He grows pale as death—his lip quivers—the large drops of sweat once more burst from his brow. I grew sick, sick.

"Yes, your honour," said the mate.

"Yes—ah!" said the devil's limb, chuckling—"we are getting on the trail at last. Can you swear to more than one?"

"Yes, your honour."

"Yes!" again responded the *sans* wig. "How many?"

The man counted them off. "Fifteen, sir. That young fellow there is the man who cut Captain Spurtel's throat, after violating his wife before his eyes."

"God forgive me, is it possible?" gasped Thomas Cringle.

"There's a monster in human form for you, gentlemen," continued the devil's limb. "Go on, Mr Rumbletithump."

"That other man next him hung me up by the heels, and seared me on the bare—." Here honest Job had just time to divert the current of his speech into a loud "whew."

"Spared you on the *whew!*" quoth the facetious lawyer, determined to have his jest, even in the face of forty-three of his fellow-creatures trembling on the brink of eternity. "Explain, sir; tell the court where you were seared, and how you were seared, and all about your being seared."

Job twisted and lolloped about, as if he was looking out for some opening to bolt through; but all egress was shut up.

"Why, please your honour," the eloquent blood mantling in his honest sun-burnt cheeks; while from my heart I pitied the poor fellow, for he was absolutely broiling in his bashfulness—"He seared me on—on—why, please your honour, he seared me on—*with* a redhot iron!"

"Why, I guessed as much, if he seared you at all; but *where* did he sear you? Come now," coaxingly, "tell the court where and how he applied the actual cautery."

Job, being thus driven to his wit's end, turned and stood at bay. "Now I will tell you, your honour, if you will but sit down for a moment, and answer me one question."

"To be sure, sir; why, Job, you brighten on us. There, I am down—now for your question."

"Now, sir," quoth Rumbletithump, imitating his tormentor's manner much more cleverly than I expected, "what part of your honour's body touches your chair?"

"How, sir!" said the man of words—"how dare you, sir, take such a liberty, sir?" while a murmuring laugh hummed through the court.

"Now, sir, since you won't answer me, sir," said Job, elevated by his victory, while his hoarse voice roughened into a loud growl, "I will answer myself. I was seared, sir, where—"

"Silence!" quoth the crier, at this instant drowning the mate's voice, so that I could not catch the words he used.

"And there you have it, sir.—Put me in jail, if you like, sir."

The murmur was bursting out into a guffaw, when the judge interfered. But there was no longer any attempt at ill-timed jesting on the part of the bar, which was but bad taste at the best on so solemn an occasion.

Job continued: "I was burnt into the very muscle, until I told where the gold was stowed away."

"Aha!" screamed the lawyer, forgetting his recent discomfiture in the gladness of his success. "And all the rest were abetting, eh?"

"The rest of the fifteen were, sir."

But the prosecutor, a glutton in his way, had thought he had bagged the whole forty-three. And so he ultimately did before the evening closed in, as most of the others were identified by other witnesses; and when they could not actually be sworn to, the piracies were brought home to them by circumstantial evidence; such, for instance, as having been captured on board of the craft we had taken, which again were identified as the very vessels which had plundered the merchantmen and murdered several of their crews, so that by six o'clock the jury had returned a verdict of Guilty—and I believe there never was a juster—against the whole of them. The finding, and sentence of death following thereupon, seemed not to create any strong effect upon the prisoners. They had all seen how the trial was going; and, long before this, the bitterness of death seemed to be past.

I could hear one of our boat's crew, who was standing behind me, say to his neighbour, "Why, Jem, surely he is in joke. Why; he don't mean to condemn them to be hanged *seriously*, without his wig, eh?"

Immediately after the judgment was pronounced, which, both as to import, and literally, I had translated to them, Captain Transom, who was sitting on the bench beside his brother officers, nodded to me, "I say, Mr Cringle, tell the coxswain to call Pearl, if you please."

I passed the word to one of the Firebrand's marines, who was on duty, who again repeated the order to a seaman who was standing at the door.

"I say, Moses, call the clergyman."

Now this Pearl was no other than the seaman who pulled the stroke-oar in the gig; a very handsome negro, and the man who afterwards forked Whiffle out of the water—tall, powerful, and muscular, and altogether one of the best men in the ship. The rest of the boat's crew, from his complexion, had fastened the *sobriquet* of the clergyman on him.

"Call the clergyman."

The superseded interpreter, who was standing near, seeing I took no notice, immediately *traduced* this literally to the unhappy men. A murmur arose amongst them.

"Que—el padre ya! Somos en Capilla, entonces—poco tiempo, poco tiempo!"

They had thought that, the clergyman having been sent for, the sentence was immediately to be executed, but I undeceived them; and in ten minutes after they were condemned, they were marched of, under a strong escort of foot, to the jail.

I must make a long story short. Two days afterwards I was ordered with the launch to Kingston, early in the morning, to receive twenty-five of the pirates who had been ordered for execution that morning at Gallows Point. It was little past four in the morning when we arrived at the Wherry Wharf, where they were already clustered, with their hands pinioned behind their backs, silent and sad, but all of them calm, and evincing no unmanly fear of death.

I don't know if other people have noticed it, but this was one of several instances where I have seen foreigners—Frenchmen, Italians, and Spaniards, for instance—meet death, *inevitable death*, with greater firmness than British soldiers or sailors. Let me explain. In the field, or grappling in mortal combat on the blood-slippery quarterdeck of an enemy's vessel, a British soldier or sailor is the bravest of the brave. No soldier or sailor of any other country, saving and excepting those damned Yankees, can stand against them—they would be utterly overpowered—their hearts would fail them; they would either be cut down, thrust through, or they would turn and flee. Yet those same men who have turned and fled will meet death—but it must be as I said, *inevitable, unavoidable death*—not only more firmly than their conquerors would do in their circumstances, but with an intrepidity—oh, do not call it indifference!—altogether astonishing. Be it their religion, or their physical conformation, or what it may, all I have to do with is the fact, which I record as undeniable. Out of five-and-twenty individuals, in the present instance, not a sigh was heard, nor a moan, nor a querulous word. They stepped lightly into the boats, and seated themselves in silence. When told by the seamen to make room, or to shift, so as not to be in the way of the oars, they did so with alacrity, and almost with an air of civility, although they knew that within half an hour their earthly career must close for ever.

The young Spaniard who had stood forward so conspicuously on the trial was in my boat; in stepping in he accidentally trode on my foot in passing forward; he turned and apologised, with much natural politeness—"he hoped he had not hurt me?"

I answered kindly, I presume; who could have done so harshly? This emboldened him apparently, for he stopped, and asked leave to sit by me. I consented, while an incomprehensible feeling crept over me; and when once I had time to recollect myself, I shrunk from him, as a blood-stained brute, with whom even in his extremity it was unfitting for me to hold any intercourse. When he noticed my repugnance to remain near him, he addressed me hastily, as if afraid that I would destroy the opportunity he seemed to desire.

"God did not always leave me the slave of my passions," he said, in a low, deep, most musical voice. "The day has been when I would have shrunk as you do—but time presses. *You have a mother?*" said he. I assented. *"And an only sister?"* As it happened, he was right here too. "And—and"—here he hesitated, and his voice shook and trembled with the most intense and heart-crushing emotion—*"y una mas cara que ambas?"*—Mary, you can tell whether in this he did not also speak truth. I acknowledged there was another being more dear to me than either. "Then," said he, "take this chain from my neck, and the crucifix, and a small miniature from my bosom; but not yet—not till I leave the boat. You will find an address affixed to the string of the latter. Your course of service may lead you to St Jago—if not, a brother officer may." His voice became inaudible; his hot scalding tears dropped fast on my hand, and the ravisher, the murderer, the *pirate*, wept as an innocent and helpless infant. "You *will* deliver it. Promise a dying man—promise a great sinner." But it was momentary—he quelled the passion with a fierce and savage energy, as he said sternly, "Promise! promise!" I did so, and I fulfilled it.

The day broke. I took the jewels and miniature from his neck, as he led the way, with the firm step of a hero, in ascending the long gibbet. The halters were adjusted, when he stepped towards the side I was on, as far as the rope would let him, *"Dexa me verla—dexa me verla, una vez mas!"* I held up the miniature. He looked—he *glared* intensely at it. "Adios, Maria, seas feliz mi querida—feliz—feliz—Maria—adios—adios—Maria—Mar—"

The rope severed thy name from his lips, sweet girl; but not until it also severed his soul from his body, and sent him to his tremendous account—young in years, but old in wickedness—to answer at that tribunal where we must all appear, to the God who made him, and whose gifts He had so fearfully abused, for thy broken heart and early death, amongst the other scarlet atrocities of his short but ill-spent life.

The signal had been given—the lumbering flap of the long drop was heard, and five-and-twenty human beings were wavering in the sea-breeze in the agonies of death! The other eighteen suffered on the same spot the week following; and for long after, this fearful and bloody example struck terror into the Cuba fishermen.

∽o∾

"Strange now, that the majority—ahem—of my beauties and favourites through life have been called *Mary*. There is my own Mary—*un peu passée*—but *deil mean* her, for half-a-dozen lit——" "Now, Tom Cringle, don't bother with your sentimentality, but get along—do." "Well, I will get along—but have patience, you Hottentot Venus. So once more we make sail."

Next Morning, soon after gun-fire, I landed at the Wherry Wharf in Port Royal. It was barely daylight, but, to my surprise, I found my friend Peregrine Whiffle seated on a Spanish chair, close to the edge of the wharf, smoking a cigar. This piece of furniture is an arm-chair, strongly framed with hard wood, over which, back and bottom, a tanned hide is stretched, which, in a hot climate, forms a most luxurious seat—the back tumbling out at an angle of 45 degrees, while the skin yields to every movement, and does not harbour a nest of biting ants, or a litter of scorpions, or any other of the customary occupants of a cushion that has been in Jamaica for a year.

He did not know me as I passed, but his small glimmering red face instantly identified the worthy little old man to me.

"Good morning, Mr Whiffle—the *top* of the morning to you, sir."

"Hillo!" responded Peregrine—"Tom, is it you?—how d'ye do, man—how d'ye do?" and he started to his feet, and almost embraced me.

Now, I had never met the said Peregrine Whiffle but twice in my life; once at Mr Fyall's, and once during the few days I remained at Kingston, before I set out on my travels; but he was a warm-hearted kindly old fellow, and, from knowing all my friends there very intimately, he, as a matter of course, became equally familiar with me.

"Why the *diable* came you not to see me, man? Have been here for change of air—to recruit, you know, after that demon, the gout, had been so perplexing me, ever since you came to anchor—the Firebrand, I mean: as for you, you have been mad one while, and philandering with those inconvenient white ladies the other. You'll cure of that, my boy—you'll come to the original comforts of the country soon, no fear!

"Perhaps I may, perhaps not."

"Oh, your cousin Mary, I forgot—fine girl, Tom—may do for you at home yonder" (all Creoles speak of England as home, although they may never have seen it), "but she can't make pepper-pot, nor give a dish of land-crabs as land-crabs should be given, nor see to the serving-up of a ringtail pigeon, nor rub a beef-steak to the rotting turn with a bruised papaw, nor compose a medicated bath, nor, nor—oh confound it, Tom, she will be, when you marry her, a cold, comfortless, motionless, Creole icicle!"

I let him have his swing. "Never mind her, then—never mind her, my dear sir; but time presses, and I must be off—I must indeed: so good morning; I wish you a good morning, sir."

He started to his feet and caught hold of me. "Sha'n't go, Tom—impossible; come along with me to my lodgings, and breakfast with me. Here, Pilfer, Pilfer," to his black valet, "give me my stick, and massu* the chair, and run home and order breakfast—cold calipiver—our Jamaica salmon, you know, Tom—tea and coffee—pickled mackerel, eggs, and cold tongue—anything that mother Dingychops can give us; so bolt, Pilfer, bolt!"

I told him that, before I came ashore, I had heard the gig's crew piped away, and that I therefore expected, as Jonathan says, that the captain would be after me immediately; so that I wished, at all events, to get away from where we were, as I had no desire to be caught gossiping about when my superior might be expected to pass.

"True, boy, true," as he shackled himself to me, and we began to crawl along towards the wharf-gate leading into the town. Captain Transom by this time had landed and came up with us.

"Ah, Transom," said Whiffle, "glad to see you. I say, why won't you allow Mr Cringle here to go over to Spanish Town with me for a couple days, eh?"

"Why, I don't remember that Mr Cringle has ever asked leave."

"Indeed, sir, I neither did ask leave, nor have I thought of doing so," said I.

"But I do for you," chimed in my friend Whiffle. "Come, captain, give him leave, just for two days—that's a prime chap. Why, Tom, you see you have got it, so off with you and come to me with your kit as soon as possible; I will bobble on and make the coffee and chocolate; and, Captain Transom, come along and breakfast with me too.—No refusal—I require society. Nearly drowned yester-day—do you know that? Off this same cursed wharf too—just here. I was looking down at the small fish playing about the piles, precisely in this position;

*Massu—lift.

one of them was as bright in the scales as a gold fish in my old grandmother's glass globe, and I had to crane over the ledge in this fashion," suiting the action to the word, "when away I went—"

And, to our unutterable surprise, splash went Peregrine Whiffle, Esquire, *for the second time,* and there he was shouting, and puffing, and splashing in the water. We were both so convulsed with laughter that I believe he would have been drowned for us; but the boat-keeper of the gig the strong athletic negro before mentioned, promptly jumped on the wharf with his boat-hook, and caught the dapper little old beau by the waistband of his breeches, swaying him up, frightened enough, with his little coat-skirts fluttering in the breeze, and no wonder, but not much the worse for it all.

"Diable porte l'amour," whispered Captain Transom.

"Swallowed a Scotch pint of salt water to a certainty.—Run, Pilfer, bring me some brandy—gout will be into my stomach, sure as fate—feel him now—run, Pilfer, run, or gout will beat you—a *dead heat* that will be!" And he *keckled* at his small joke very complacently.

We had him carried by our people to his lodgings, where, after shifting and brandying to some tune, he took his place at the breakfast table, and did the honours with his usual amenity and warmheartedness.

After breakfast, Peregrine remembered—what the sly rogue had never forgotten, I suspect—that he was engaged to dine with his friend, Mr Pepperpot Wagtail, in Kingston.

"But it don't signify; Wagtail will be delighted to see you, Tom—hospitable fellow, Wagtail; and now I recollect myself, Fyall and Aaron Bang are to be there; dang it, were it not for the gout we should have a night on't!"

After breakfast we started in a canoe for Kingston, touching at the Firebrand for my kit.

Moses Yerk, the unpoetical first-lieutenant, was standing well forward on the quarterdeck as I passed over the side to get into the canoe, with the gun-room steward following me, carrying my kit under his arm.

"I say, Tom, good for you, one lark after another."

"Don't like that fellow," quoth Whiffle; "he is quarrelsome in his drink for a thousand; I know it by the cut of his jib."

He had better have held his tongue, honest man; for as he looked up broad in Yerk's face, who was leaning over the hammocks, the scupper immediately overhead—through whose instrumentality I never knew—was suddenly cleared, and a rush of dirty water, that had been lodged there since the decks had been washed down at day-dawn, splashed slapdash over his head and shoulders and into his mouth, so as to set the dear little man a-coughing so violently that I thought he would have been throttled. Before he had recovered sufficiently to find his tongue we had pulled fifty yards from the ship, and a little farther on we overtook the captain, who had preceded us in the cutter, into which we transhipped ourselves. But Whiffle never could acquit Yerk of having been, directly or indirectly, the cause of his suffering from the impure shower.

This day was the first of the Negro Carnival, or Christmas holidays, and at the distance of two miles from Kingston the sound of the negro drums and horns, the barbarous music, and yelling of the different African tribes, and the more mellow singing of the Set Girls, came off upon the breeze loud and strong.

When we got nearer, the wharfs and different streets, as we successively opened them, were crowded with blackamoors, men, women, and children, dancing and singing and shouting, and all rigged out in their best. When we landed on the agents' wharf we were immediately surrounded by a group of these merrymakers, which happened to be the Butchers' John Canoe party, and a curious exhibition it unquestionably was. The prominent character was, as usual, the John Canoe, or Jack Pudding. He was a light, active, clean-made young Creole negro, without shoes or stockings; he wore a pair of light jean small-clothes, all too wide, but confined at the knees, below and above, by bands of red tape, after the manner that Malvolio would have called cross-gartering. He wore a splendid blue velvet waistcoat, with old-fashioned flaps coming down over his hips, and covered with tarnished embroidery. His shirt was absent on leave, I suppose, but at the wrists of his coat he had tin or white iron frills, with loose pieces attached, which tinkled as he moved, and set off the dingy paws that were stuck through these strange manacles, like black wax tapers in silver candlesticks. His coat was an old blue artillery-uniform one, with a small bell hung to the extreme points of the swallow-tailed skirts, and three tarnished epaulets—one on each shoulder; and, O ye immortal gods!—O Mars armipotent!—the biggest of the three stuck at his rump, the *point d'appui* for a sheep's tail. He had an enormous cocked-hat on, to which was appended in front a white false-face or mask, of a most methodistical expression, while, Janus-like, there was another face behind, of the most quizzical description, a sort of living Antithesis, both being garnished and overtopped with one coarse wig, made of the hair of bullocks' tails, on which the *chapeau* was strapped down with a broad band of gold lace.

He skipped up to us with a white wand in one hand and a dirty handkerchief in the other, and with sundry moppings and mowings, first wiping my shoes with his *mouchoir*, then my face (murder, what a flavour of salt fish and onions it had!), he made a smart enough pirouette, and then sprang on the back of a nondescript animal that now advanced, capering and jumping, about after the most grotesque fashion that can be imagined. This was the signal for the music to begin. The performers were two gigantic men, dressed in calf-skins entire, head, four legs, and tail. The skin of the head was made to fit like a hood, the two fore-feet hung dangling down in front, one over each shoulder, while the other two legs, or hind-feet, and the tail, trailed behind on the ground; deuce another article had they on in the shape of clothing except a handkerchief, of some flaming pattern, tied round the waist. There were also two flute-players in sheep-skins, looking still more outlandish, from the horns on the animals' heads being preserved; and three stout fellows who were dressed in the common white frock and trousers, who kept sounding on bullocks' horns. These formed the band, as it were, and might be considered John's immediate tail or following; but he was also accompanied by about fifty of the butcher negroes, all neatly dressed-blue jackets, white shirts, and Osnaburg trousers, with their steels and knife-cases by their sides, as bright as Turkish yataghans, and they all wore clean blue-and-white striped aprons. I could see and tell what *they* were; but the *Thing* John Canoe had perched himself upon I could make nothing of. At length I began to comprehend the device.

The *Magnus Apollo* of the party, the poet and chief musician—the nondescript already mentioned—was no less than the boatswain of the butcher gang, answering to the driver in an agricultural one. He was clothed in an entire bullock's hide, horns, tail, and the other particulars, the whole of the skull being retained, and the effect of the voice growling through the jaws of the beast was most startling. His legs were enveloped in the skin of the hind-legs; while the arms were eased in that of the fore, the hands protruding a little above the hoofs; and as he walked, reared upon his hind-legs, he used (in order to support the load of the John Canoe, who had perched on his shoulders like a monkey on a dancing bear) a strong stick, or sprit, with a crutch-top to it, which he leant his breast on every now and then.

After the creature—which I will call the *Device* for shortness—had capered with its extra load, as if it had been a feather, for a minute or two, it came to a standstill, and, sticking the end of the sprit into the ground, and tucking the crutch of it under its chin, it motioned to one of the attendants, who thereupon handed—of all things in the world—a *fiddle to the ox!* He then shook off the

John Canoe, who began to caper about as before, while the Device set up a deuced good pipe, and sang and played—barbarously enough, I will admit—to the tune of Guinea Corn, the following ditty :—

"Massa Buccra lob for see
Bullock caper like monkee—
Dance, and shump, and poke him toe,
Like one humane person—just so."

And hereupon the tail of the beast, some fifty strong, music men, John Canoe and all, began to rampauge about, as if they had been possessed by a devil whose name was Legion:—

"But Massa Buccra have white love,
Soft and silken like one dove.
To brown girl—him barely shivel—
To black girl—oh, Lord, de Devil!"

Then a tremendous gallopading, in the which Tailtackle was nearly capsized over the wharf. He looked quietly over the edge of it.

"Boat-keeper, hand me up that switch of a stretcher." (Friend, if thou be'st not nautical, thou knowest what a *rack-pin,* something of the stoutest, is.)

The boy did so, and Tailtackle, after moistening well his dexter claw with tobacco-juice, seized the stick with his left by the middle, and, balancing it for a second or two, he began to fasten the end of it into his right fist, as if he had been screwing a bolt into a socket. Having satisfied himself that his grip was secure, he let go the hold with his left hand, and crossed his arms on his breast, with the weapon projecting over his left shoulder, like the drone of a bagpipe.

The *Device* continued his chant, giving the seaman a wide berth, however:—

"But when him once two tree year here,
Him tink white lady wery great boder;
De coloured peoples, never fear,
Ah, him lob him de morest nor any oder."

Then another tumblification of the whole party.

"But, top—one time bad fever catch him,
Coloured peoples kindly watch him—
In sick-room, nurse voice like music—
From him hand taste sweet de physic."

Another trampoline.

"So alway come—in two tree year,
  And so wid you massa—never fear;
  Brown girl for cook—for wife—for nurse,
  Buccra lady—poo—no wort a curse."

"Get away, you scandalous scoundrel," cried I "away with you sir!"

Here the morrice-dancers began to circle round old Tailtackle, keeping him on the move, spinning round like a weathercock in a whirlwind, while they shouted, "Oh, massa, one *macaroni*,* if you please." To get quit of their importunity, Captain Transom gave them one. "Ah, good massa, tank you, sweet massa!" And away danced John Canoe and his tail, careering up the street.

In the same way all the other crafts and trades had their Gumbi-men, Horn-blowers, John Canoes, and Nondescript. The Gardeners came nearest, of anything I had seen before, to the Mayday boys in London; with this advantage, that their Jack-in-the-Green was incomparably more beautiful, from the superior bloom of the larger flowers used in composing it.

The very workhouse people, whose province it is to guard the negro culprits who may be committed to it, and to inflict punishment on them when required, had their John Canoe and Device; and their prime jest seemed to be, every now and then, to throw the fellow down who enacted the latter at the corner of a street, and to administer a sound flogging to him. The John Canoe, who was the workhouse driver, was dressed up in a lawyer's cast-off gown and bands, black silk breeches, no stockings nor shoes, but with sandals of bullock's hide strapped on his great splay feet, a small cocked-hat on his head, to which were appended a large cauliflower wig and the usual white false-face, bearing a very laughable resemblance to Chief-Justice S——, with whom I happened to be personally acquainted.

The whole party which accompanied these two worthies, musicians and tail, were dressed out so as to give a tolerable resemblance of the Bar broke loose, and they were all pretty considerably well drunk. As we passed along, the *Device* was once more laid down, and we could notice a shield of tough hide strapped over the fellow's stern-frame, so as to save the lashes of the cat, which John Canoe was administering with all his force, while the *Device* walloped about and yelled, as if he had been receiving the punishment on his naked flesh. Presently, as he had rolled over and over in the sand, bellowing to the life, I noticed the leather shield slip upwards to the small of his back, leaving

---

*A quarter dollar.

the lower storey uncovered in reality; but the driver and his tail were too drunk to observe this, and the former continued to lay on and laugh, while one of his people stood by in all the gravity of drunkenness, counting, as a first-lieutenant does, when a poor fellow is polishing at the gangway,—"Twenty—twenty-one —twenty-two"—and so on, while the patient roared you, an it were anything but a nightingale. At length he broke away from the men who held him, after receiving a most sufficient flogging, to revenge which he immediately fastened on the John Canoe, wrenched his cat from him, and employed it so scientifically on him and his followers, giving them passing taps on the shins now and then with the handle, by way of spice to the dose, that the whole crew pulled foot as if Old Nick had held them in chase.

The very children, urchins of five and six years old, had their Lilliputian John Canoes and *Devices*. But the beautiful part of the exhibition was the Set Girls. They danced along the streets, in bands of from fifteen to thirty. There were brown sets, and black sets, and sets of all the intermediate gradations of colour. Each set was dressed pin for pin alike, and carried umbrellas or parasols of the same colour and size, held over their nice, showy, well-put-on *toques*, or Madras handkerchiefs—all of the same pattern—tied round their heads, fresh out of the fold. They sang as they swam along the streets in the most luxurious attitudes. I had never seen more beautiful creatures than there were amongst the brown sets—clear olive complexions, and fine faces, elegant carriages, splendid figures—full, plump, and magnificent.

Most of the sets were as much of a size as Lord ——'s *eighteen* daughters, sailing down Regent Street, like a charity-school of a Sunday, led by a rum-looking old beadle;—others, again, had large Roman matron-looking women in the leading files—the *figurantes* in their tails becoming slighter and smaller as they tapered away, until they ended in *leetle picaniny, no bigger as my tumb*, but always preserving the uniformity of dress, and colour of the umbrella or parasol. Sometimes the breeze, on opening a corner, would strike the sternmost of a set composed in this manner of small fry, and stagger the little things, getting beneath their tiny umbrellas, and fairly blowing them out of the line, and ruffling their ribbons and finery, as if they had been tulips bending and shaking their leaves before it. But the *colours* were never blended in the same set; no blackie ever interloped with the browns, nor did the browns in any case mix with the sables, always keeping in mind, black *woman*—brown *lady*.

But—as if the whole city had been tom-fooling—a loud burst of military music was now heard, and the north end of the street we were ascending—

which leads out of the *Place d'Armes,* or parade, that occupies the centre of
the town—was filled with a cloud of dust that rose as high as the house-tops,
through which the head of a column of troops sparkled—swords and bayonets
and gay uniforms glancing in the sun. This was the Kingston regiment marching down to the court-house, in the lower part of the town, to mount the
Christmas guards, which is always carefully attended to, in case any of the John
Canoes should take a small fancy to burn or pillage the town, or to rise and cut
the throats of their masters, or any little innocent recreation of the kind, out of
compliment to Dr Lushington or Messrs Macaulay and Babington.

First came a tolerably good band, a little too drummy, but still not amiss—
well dressed, only the performers, being of all colours, from white down to
jet-black, had a curious hodgepodge or piebald appearance. Then came a dozen
mounted officers, at the very least—colonels-in-chief, and colonels, and lieu-
tenant-colonels, and majors—all very fine, and very bad horsemen. Then the
grenadier company, composed of white clerks of the place—very fine-looking
young men indeed; another white company followed, not quite so smart-look-
ing; then came a century of the children of Israel, not over-military in
appearance—the days of Joshua the son of Nun had passed away, the glory had
long departed from their house; a phalanx of light browns succeeded, then a
company of dark browns, or mulattoes—the regular half-and-half in this, as
well as in grog, is the best mixture after all; then quashie himself, or a company of free blacks, who, with the browns, seemed the best soldiers of the set,
excepting the flank companies; and after blackie the battalion again gradually
whitened away, until it ended in a very fine light company of buccras, smart
young fellows as need be; all the officers were white, and all the soldiers, whatever their cast or colour, free of course. Another battalion succeeded,
composed in the same way; and really I was agreeably surprised to find the
indigenous force of the colony so efficient. I had never seen anything more soldier-like amongst our volunteers at home. Presently a halt was called, and a
mounted officer, evidently desirous of showing off, galloped up to where we
were standing, and began to swear at the drivers of a waggon, with a long team
of sixteen bullocks, who had placed their vehicle—whether intentionally or
not I could not tell—directly across the street, where, being met by another
waggon of the same kind coming through the opposite lane, a regular jam had
taken place, as they had contrived—being redolent of new rum—to lock their
wheels, and twist their lines of bullocks together, in much-admired confusion.

"Out of the way, sir; out of the way, you black rascals—don't you see the regiment coming?"

The men spanked their long whips and shouted to the steers by name—"Back, back—Caesar—Antony—Crab, back, sir, back;" and they whistled loud and long, but Caesar and the rest only became more and more involved.

"Order arms!" roared another officer, fairly beaten by the bullocks and waggons—"Stand at ease!"

On this last signal a whole cloud of spruce-beer sellers started fiercely from under the piazzas.

"An insurrection of the slave-population, mayhap," thought I; but their object was a very peaceable one, for presently, I verily believe, every man and officer in the regiment had a tumbler of this, to me, most delicious beverage at his head; the drawing of the corks was more like street-firing than anything else—a regular *feu de joie*. In the mean time a council of war seemed to be holden by the mounted officers as to how the obstacle in front was to be overcome; but at this moment confusion became worse confounded, by the approach of what I concluded to be the white man's John Canoe party, mounted, by way of pre-eminence. First came a trumpeter, John Canoe with a *black* face, which was all in rule, as his black counterparts wore *white* ones; but his *Device*, a curious little old man, dressed in a sort of blue uniform, and mounted on the skeleton, or ghost, of a gig-horse, I could make nothing of. It carried a drawn sword in its hand, with which it made various flourishes, at each one of which I trembled for its Rosinante's ears. The *Device* was followed by about fifty other odd-looking creatures, all on horseback; but they had no more *seat* than so many pairs of tongs, which in truth they greatly resembled, and made no show and less fun. So we were wishing them out of the way, when some one whispered that the Kingston Light-Horse mustered strong this morning. I found afterwards that every man who kept a good horse, or could ride, invariably served in the foot—all free persons must join some corps or other; so that the *troop*, as it was called, was composed exclusively of those who could not ride, and who kept no saddle-horses.

The line was now formed, and after a variety of cumbrous manœuvres out of Dundas—sixteen at the least—the regiment was countermarched and filed along another street, where they gave three cheers, in honour of their having had a drink of spruce, and of having circumvented the bullocks and waggons. A little farther on we encountered four beautiful nine-pounder field-pieces, each lumbering along, drawn by half-a-dozen mules, and accompanied by three or four negroes, but with no escort whatsoever.

"I say, Quashie, where are all the bombardiers, the artillery-men?"

"Oh, massa, dem all gone to drink pruce—"

"What, more spruce!—spruce—nothing but spruce!" quoth I.

"Oh, yes, massa; after dem drink pruce done dem all go to him breakfast, massa—left we for take de gun one *feepenny,* massa"—as the price of the information, I suppose.

"Are the guns loaded?" said I.

"Me no sabe, massa—top, I shall see." And the fellow to whom I addressed myself stepped forward and began to squint into the muzzle of one of the field-pieces, slewing his head from side to side, with absurd gravity, like a magpie peeping into a marrow-bone. "Him most be load—no daylight come troo de touch-hole—take care—make me try him." And without more ado he shook out the red embers from his pipe right on the touch-hole of the gun, when the fragment of a broken tube spun up in a small jet of flame, that made me start and jump back.

"How dare you, you scoundrel!" said the captain.

"Eigh, massa, him no hax me to see if him be load—so I was try see. Indeed, I tink him is load after all yet."

He stepped forward, and entered his rammer into the cannon, after an unavailing attempt to blow with his blubber-lips through the touch-hole.

Noticing that it did not produce the ringing sound it would have done in an empty gun, but went home with a soft *thud*, I sang out, "Stand clear, sir.—By Jupiter, the gun *is* loaded."

The negro continued to *bash* at it with all his might.

Meanwhile the fellow who was driving the mules attached to the field-piece turned his head, and saw what was going on. In a trice he snatched up another rammer and, without any warning, came crack over the fellow's cranium, to whom we had been speaking, as hard as he could draw, making the instrument quiver again.

"Dem you, ye, ye Jericho! all, so you *bash* my brokefast, eh? You no see me tick him into de gun before we yoke de mule, dem, eh?—You tief you, eh?"

"No!" roared the other—"you Walkandnyam, you hab no brokefast, you liard—at least I never see him."

"Big lie dat!" replied Walkandnyam—"look in de gun."

Jericho peered into it again.

"Dere, you son of a ———" (I shan't say what)—"dere, I see de red flannin wadding over de cartridge—Your brokefast!—you be hang!" roared Jericho.

And he made at him as if he would have eaten him alive.

"You be hang youshef!" shrieked Walkandnyam—"and de red wadding be hang?" as he took a screw, and hooked out, not a cartridge, certainly, but his own nightcap, full of yams and salt-fish smashed into a paste by Jericho's rammer.

In the frenzy of his rage he dashed this into his opponent's face, and they both stripped in a second. Separating several yards, they levelled their heads like two telescopes on stands, and ran *butt* at each other like ram-goats, and quite as odoriferous, making the welkin ring again as their flint-hard skulls cracked together. Finding each other invulnerable in this direction, they closed, and began scrambling and biting and kicking, and tumbling over and over in the sand; while the skipper and I stood by cheering them on, and nearly suffocated with laughter. They never once struck with their closed fists, I noticed; so they were not much hurt. It was great cry and little wool; and at length they got tired, and hauled off by mutual consent, finishing off as usual with an appeal to us—"Beg one feepenny, massa!"

At six o'clock we drove to Mr Pepperpot Wagtail's. The party was a bachelor's one, and when we walked up the front steps, there was our host in person, standing to receive us at the door, while on each side of him there were five or six of his visitors, all sitting with their legs cocked up, their feet resting on a sort of surbase, above which the jealousies, or movable blinds of the piazza, were fixed.

I was introduced to the whole party *seriatim*—and as each of the cock-legs dropped his *trams*, he started up. caught hold of my hand, and wrung it as if I had been his dearest and oldest friend.

Were I to designate Jamaica as a community, I would call it a hand-shaking people. I have often laughed heartily upon seeing two cronies meeting in the streets of Kingston after a temporary separation; when about pistol-shot asunder, both would begin to tug and rug at the right-hand glove, but it is frequently a mighty serious affair, in that hissing hot climate, to get the gauntlet off; they approach,—one, a smart urbane little man who would not disgrace St James's Street, being more kiln-dried and less moist in his corporeals than his country friend, has contrived to extract his paw, and holds it out in act to shake.

"Ah! how do you do, Ratoon?" quoth the Kingston man.

"Quite well, Shingle," rejoins the *gloved,* a stout, red-faced, sudoriferous, yam-fed planter, dressed in blue-white jean trousers and waistcoat, with long Hessian boots drawn up to his knee over the former, and a span-new square-skirted blue coatee, with lots of clear brass buttons; a broad-brimmed black silk hat, worn white at the edge of the crown—wearing a very small neckcloth, above which shoots up an enormous shirt-collar, the peaks of which might serve for winkers to a starting horse, and carrying a large whip in his hand— "Quite well, my dear fellow," while he persists in dragging at it—the other *homo* all the while standing in the absurd position of a finger-post. At length, off comes the glove—piecemeal perhaps—a finger first, for instance,—then a thumb; at length they tackle to, and shake each other like the very devil—not a sober, pump-handle shake, but a regular jiggery jiggery, as if they were trying to dislocate each other's arm; and, confound them! even then they don't let go—they cling like sucker-fish, and talk and wallop about, and throw themselves back and laugh, and then another jiggery.

On horseback, this custom is conspicuously ridiculous. I have nearly gone into fits at beholding two men careering along the road at a hand-gallop, each on a goodish horse, with his negro boy astern of him on a mule, in clean frock and trousers and smart glazed hat with broad gold band, and massa's umbrella in a leathern case slung across his shoulders, and his portmanteau behind him on a mail pillion covered with a snow-white sheep's fleece—suddenly they pull up on recognising each other, when, tucking their whips under their arms, or crossing them in their teeth, it may be, they commence the rugging and riving operation. In this case—Shingle's bit of blood swerves, we may assume—Ratoon rides at him—Shingle fairly turns tail, and starts out at full speed, Ratoon thundering in his rear, with outstretched arm; and it does happen, I am assured, that the hot pursuit often continues for a mile before the desired clapperclaw is obtained. But when two lusty planters meet on horseback, then indeed Greek meets Greek. They begin the interview by shouting to each other while fifty yards off, pulling away at the gloves all the while—"How are you, Canetop?—glad to see you, Canetop. How do you do, I *hope*."—"How are you, Yamfu, my dear fellow?" their horses fretting and jumping all the time; and if the Jack Spaniards or gadflies be rife, they have, even when denuded for the shake, to spur at each other, more like a Knight Templar and a Saracen charging in mortal combat than two men merely struggling to be civil; and after all they have often to get their black servants alongside to hold their horses, for *shake* they must, were they to break their necks in the attempt. Why they won't shake hands with their gloves on, I am sure I can't tell. It would be much cooler and nicer—lots of *Scotchmen* in the community too.

This hand-shaking, however, was followed by an invitation to dinner from each individual in the company. I looked to Captain Transom, as much as to say, "Can they mean us to take them at their word?" He nodded.

"We are sorry that, being under orders to go to sea on Sunday morning, neither Mr Cringle nor myself can have the pleasure of accepting such kind invitations."

"Well, when you come back, you know—one day you *must* give *me*."

"And I won't be denied," quoth a second.

"Liberty Hall, you know, so to me you must come, no ceremony," said a third—and so on.

At length, no less a man drove up to the door than Judge ————. When he drew up, his servant, who was sitting behind, on a small projection of the ketureen, came round and took a parcel out of the gig, closely wrapped in a blanket—"Bring that carefully in, Leonidas," said the judge, who now stumped up stairs with a small saw in his hand. He received the parcel, and, laying it down carefully in a corner, he placed the saw on it, and then came up and shook hands with Wagtail, and made his bow very gracefully.

"What!—can't you do without your ice and sour claret yet?" said Wagtail.

"Never mind, never mind," said the judge, and here dinner being announced, we all adjourned to the dining-room, where a very splendid entertainment was set out, to which we set to, and in the end, as it will appear, did the utmost justice to it.

The wines were most exquisite. Madeira, for instance, never can be drank in perfection anywhere out of the tropics. You may have the wine as good at home, although I doubt it, but then you have not the climate to drink it in. I would say the same of most of the delicate French wines—that is, those that will stand the voyage—burgundy of course, not included; but never mind, let us get along.

All the decanters were covered with cotton bags, kept wet with saltpetre and water, so that the evaporation carried on powerfully by the stream of air that flowed across the room, through the open doors and windows, made the fluids quite as cool as was desirable to worthies sitting luxuriating with the thermometer at 80 degrees or thereby; yet, from the free current, I was in no way made aware of this degree of heat by any oppressive sensation; and I found in the West Indies, as well as in the East, although the wind in the latter is more dry and parching, that a current of heated air, if it be moderately dry even with the thermometer at 95° in the shade, is really not so enervating or oppressive as I have found it in the stagnating atmosphere on the sunny side of Pall-Mall, with the mercury barely at 75°. A cargo of ice had a little before this arrived at Kingston, and at first all the inhabitants who could afford it iced everything, wine, water, cold meats, fruits, and the Lord knows what all—tea, I believe amongst other things (by the way, I have tried this, and it *is* a luxury of its kind); but the regular old stagers, who knew what was what, and had a regard for their interiors, soon began to eschew the ice in every way, saving and excepting to cool the water they washed their thin faces and hands in; so *we* had no ice, nor did we miss it; but the judge had a plateful of chips on the table before him, one of which he every now and then popped into his long thin bell-glass of claret, diluting it, I should have thought, in rather a heathenish manner; but *n'importe,* he worked away, sawing off pieces now and then from the large lump in the blanket (to save the tear and wear attending a fracture), which was handed to him by his servant, so that by eleven o'clock at night, allowing for the water, he must have concealed his three bottles of pure claret, besides garnishing with a lot of white wines. In fine, we all carried on astonishingly, some good singing was given, a practical joke was tried on now and then by Fyall, and we continued mighty happy. As to the singing part of it, the landlord, with a bad voice and worse ear, opened the *rorytory* by volunteering a very extraordinary squeak; fortunately it was not very long, but it gave him a plea to screw a song out of his right-hand neighbour, who in turn acquired the same right of compelling the person next him to make a fool of himself; at last it came to Transom, who, by the by, sung exceedingly well, but he had got more wine than usual, and essayed the coquette a bit.

"Bring the wet nightcap!" quoth our host.

"Oh, is it that you are at?" said Transom, and he sang as required; but it was all pearls before swine, I fear.

At last we stuck fast at Fyall. Music! there was not one particle in his whole composition; so the wet nightcap already impended over him, when I sang out, "Let him tell a story, Mr Wagtail. Let him tell a story."

"Thank you, Tom," said Fyall; "I owe you a good turn for that, my boy."

"Fyall's story—Mr Fyall's story!" resounded on all hands. Fyall, glad to escape the song and wet nightcap, instantly began.

"Why, my friends, you all know Isaac Grimm, the Jew snuff-merchant and cigar-maker, in Harbour Street. Well, Isaac had a brother, Ezekiel by name, who carried on business at Curaçoa; you may have heard of him too. Ezekiel was often down here for the purpose of laying in provisions and purchasing dry goods. You all know that?"

"Certainly!" shouted both Captain Transom and myself in a breath, although we had never heard of him before.

"Hah, I knew it! Well then, Ezekiel was very rich; he came down in August last in the Pickle schooner, and, as bad luck would have it, he fell sick of the fever. 'Isaac,' quoth Ezekiel, 'I am wery sheek; I tink I shall tie.'—'Hope note, dear proder; you hab no vife, nor shildir; pity you should tie, Ezekiel. Ave you make your vill, Ezekiel?'—'Yesh; de vill is make. I leavish everyting to you, Isaac, on von condition, dat you send my pody to be bury in Curaçoa. I love dat place; twenty years since I left de Minories, all dat time I cheat dere, and tell lie dere, and lif dere happily. Oh, you most sent my pody for its puryment to Curaçoa!'—'I will do dat, mine proder.'—'Den I depart in peace, dear Isaac;' and the Israelite was as good as his word for *once*. He *did die*. Isaac, according to his promise, applied to the captains of several schooners; none of them would take the dead body. 'What shall I do?' I thought Isaac, 'de monish mosh not be loss.' So he straightway had Ezekiel (for even a Jew won't keep long in that climate) cut up and packed with pickle into two barrels, marked 'Prime mess pork, Leicester, M'Call, and Co., Cork.' He then shipped the same in the Fan Fan, taking bills of lading in accordance with the brand, deliverable to Mordecai Levi of Curaçoa, to whom he sent the requisite instructions. The vessel sailed—off St Domingo she carried away a mast—tried to fetch Carthagena under a jury-spar—fell to leeward, and finally brought up at Honduras.

"Three months after, Isaac encountered the master of the schooner in the streets of Kingston. 'Ah, mine goot captain, how is you? you lookish tin, ave you been sheek?'—'No Moses, I am well enough, thank you; poor a bit, but sound in health, thank God. You have heard of my having carried away the mainmast, and, after kicking about fifteen days on short allowance, having been obliged to bear up for Honduras?'—'I know noting of all dat,' said Isaac; 'sorry for it, captain—very sad inteed.'—'Sad! you may say that, Moses. But I am honest although poor, and here is your bill of lading for your two barrels of provisions; "Prime mess," *it* says; Damned tough, say I. Howsomdever,' pulling out his purse, 'the present value on Bogle, Jopp, and Co.'s wharf is £5, 6s. 8d. the barrel; so there are two doubloons, Moses, and now discharge the account on the back of the bill of lading, will you?'—'Vy should I take payment, captain? if de'—(pork stuck in his throat like 'amen' in Macbeth's)—'if de barrel ish lost, it can't be help—de act of God, you know.'—'I am an honest man, Isaac,' continued the captain, 'although a poor one, and I must tell the truth: we carried on with our own as long as it lasted, at length we had to break bulk, and your two barrels being nearest the hatchway, why we ate them first, that's all. Lord, what has come over you?' Isaac grew pale as a corpse. 'O mine Got—mine poor broder, dat you ever was live, to tie in Jamaic—Oh tear, oh tear!'"

"Did they eat the head and hands and—"

"Hold your tongue, Tom Cringle, don't interrupt me; *you* did not eat them; I tell it as it was told to me. So Isaac Grimm," continued Fyall, "was fairly overcome; the kindly feelings of his nature were at length stirred up, and as he turned away, he wept—blew his nose hard, like a Chaldean trumpet in the new moon—and while the large tears coursed each other down his care-worn cheeks, he exclaimed, wringing the captain's hand, in a voice tremulous and scarcely audible from extreme emotion, 'O Isaac Grimm, Isaac Grimm—tid not your heart mishgive you ven you vas commit te great plasphemy of invoish Ezekiel—flesh of your flesh, pone of your pone—as *por*—de onclean peast, I mean. If you had put invoish him ash *peef* surely te earthly tabernacle of him, as always sheet in de high places in te Sinacogue, would never have been allow to pass troo te powels of te pershicuting Nazareen. Ah, mine goot captain, mine very tear friend, vat—vat—vat av you done wid de cask, captain?'"

"Oh most lame and impotent conclusion," sang out the judge, who by this time had become deucedly prosy, and all hands arose, as if by common consent, and agreed that we had got enough.

So off we started in groups. Fyall, Captain Transom, Whiffle, Aaron Bang, and myself sallied forth in a bunch, pretty well inclined for a lark, you may guess. There are no lamps in the streets of Kingston, and as all the *decent* part of the community are in their *cavies* by half-past nine in the evening, and as it was now "the witching time o' night," there was not a soul in the streets that we saw, except a solitary town-guard now and then lurking about some dark corner under the piazzas. These same streets, which were wide and comfortable enough in the daytime, had become unaccountably narrow and intricate since six o'clock in the evening; and although the object of the party was to convoy Captain Transom and myself to our boat at the Ordnance Wharf, it struck me that we were as frequently on a totally different tack.

"I say, Cringle, my boy," stuttered out my superior, *lieutenant* and *captain* being both drowned *in* and equalised *by* the claret—"why, Tom, Tom Cringle, you dog—don't you hear your superior officer speak, sir, eh?"

My superior officer during this address was standing with both arms round a pillar of the piazza.

"I am here, sir," said I.

"Why, I know that; but—why don't you speak when I—Hilloo!—where's Aaron, and Fyall, and the rest, eh?"

They had been attracted by sounds of revelry in a splendid mansion in the next street, which we could see was lit up with great brilliancy and had at this time shot about fifty yards ahead of us, working to windward, tack and tack, like Commodore Trunnion.

"Ah, I see," said Transom; "let us heave ahead, Tom—now, do ye hear?—stand you with your white trousers against the next pillar." The ranges supporting the piazza were at distances of about twenty feet from each other. "Ah, stand there now—I see it," So he weighed from the one he had tackled to, and, making a staggering bolt of it, ran—up to the pillar against which I stood, its position being marked by my white vestment, where he again hooked on for a second or two, until I had taken up a new position.

"There, my boy, that's the way to lay out a warp—right in the wind's eye. Tom, we shall fairly beat those lubbers who are tacking in the stream—nothing like warping in the dead water near the shore-mark that down, Tom—never beat in a tide-way when you can warp up along shore in the dead water. Confound the judge's ice"—(hiccup)—"he has poisoned me with that piece he plopped in my last whitewash of madeira. He a judge! He may be a good crim—criminal judge, but no judge of wine. Why don't you laugh, Tom, eh?—and then his saw—the rasp of a saw I hate—wish it, and a whole nest more, had been in his legal stomach—full of old saws—Shakespeare—he, he! Why don't you laugh, Tom?—Poisoned by the judge, by Jupiter. Now, here we are fairly abreast of them.—Hillo!—Fyall, what are you after!"

"Hush, hush," said Fyall, with drunken gravity.

"And hush, hush," said Aaron Bang.

"Come here, Tom, come here," said Whiffle, in a whisper. We were now directly under the piazza of the fine house, in the first floor of which some gay scene was enacting. "Here, Tom, here—now stand there—hold by that pillar there. I say, Transom, give me a lift."

"Can't, Whiffle, can't, for the soul of me, Peregrine, my dear—but I see, I see."

With that the gallant captain got down on all-fours; Whiffle, a small light man, got on his back, and, with the aid of Bang and Fyall, managed to scramble up on my shoulders, where he stood, holding by the window-sill above, with a foot on each side of my head. His little red face was thus raised flush with the window-sill, so that he could see into the dark piazza on the first floor, and right through into the magnificent and sparkling drawing-room beyond.

"Now tell us what's to be seen," said Aaron.

"Stop, stop," rejoined Whiffle—"My eye, what a lot of splendid women—no men—a regular lady-party—Hush! a song." A harp was struck, and a symphony of Beethoven's played with great taste. A song, low and melancholy, from two females, followed.

"The music of the spheres!" quoth Whiffle.

We were rapt—we had been inspired before—and, drunk as we were, there we sat or stood, as best suited us, exhibiting the strange sight of a cluster of silent tipsy men. At length, at one of the finest swells, I heard a curious gurgling sound overhead, as if some one was being gagged, and I fancied Peregrine became lighter on my shoulders—Another fine die-away note—I was sure of it.

"Bang, Bang—Fyall—He is evaporating with delight—no weight at all —growing more and more ethereal—lighter and lighter, as I am a gentleman—he is off—going, going, gone—exhaled into the blue heavens, by all that is wonderful!"

Puzzled beyond measure, I stept hurriedly back, and capsized over the captain, who was still enacting the joint-stool on all-fours behind me, by which Whiffle had mounted to my cross-trees, and there we rolled in the sand, master and man.

"Murdered, Tom Cringle—murdered! you have hogged me like the old Ramilies—broke my back, Tom—spoiled my quadrilling for ever and a day: d——n the judge's ice, though, and the saw particularly."

"Where is he—where is Whiffle?" inquired all hands, in a volley.

"The devil only knows," said I; "he has flown up into the clouds, catch him who can. He has left this earth anyhow, that is clear."

"Ha, ha!" cried Fyall, in great glee, who had seen him drawn into the window by several white figures, after they had tied a silk handkerchief over his mouth; "follow me, my boys;" and we all scrambled after him to the front door of the house, to which we ascended by a handsome flight of marble steps; and when there, we began to thunder away for admittance. The door was opened by a very respectable-looking elderly gentleman, with well-powdered hair, and attended by two men-servants in handsome liveries, carrying lights. His bearing and gentlemanlike deportment had an immediate effect on me, and I believe on the others too. He knew Fyall and Whiffle, it appeared.

"Mr Fyall," he said, with much gentleness, "I know it is only meant as a frolic, but really I hope you will now end it. Amongst yourselves, gentlemen, this may be all very well, but considering my religion, and the slights we Hebrews are so often exposed to, myself and my family are more sensitive and pervious to insult than you can well understand."

"My dear fellow," quoth Fyall, "we are all very sorry: the fact is, we had some bad shaddock after dinner, which has made us very giddy and foolish somehow. Do you know, I could almost fancy I had been drinking wine."

"Cool and deliciously impudent that same—(hiccup)," quoth the skipper.

"But hand us back little Whiffle," continued Fyall, "and we shall be off."

Here Whiffle's voice was heard from the drawing-room.

"Here, Fyall!—Tom Cringle!—here, here, or I shall be murdered!"

"Ah! I see," said Mr H.; "this way, gentlemen. Come, I will deliver the culprit to you;" and we followed him into the drawing-room, a most magnificent saloon, at least forty feet by thirty, brilliantly lit up with crystal lamps and massive silver candelabra, and filled with elegant furniture, which was reflected, along with the chandeliers that hung from the centre of the coach-roof, by several large mirrors, in rich frames, as well as in the highly polished mahogany floor.

There, in the middle of the room, the other end of it being occupied by a bevy of twelve or fifteen richly-dressed females—visitors, as we conjectured—sat our friend Peregrine, pinioned into a large easy-chair, with shawls and scarfs, amidst a sea of silk cushions, by four beautiful young women, black hair and eyes, clear white skins, fine figures, and little clothing. A young Jewess is a beautiful animal, although, like the unclean—confound the metaphor—which they abhor—they don't improve by age.

When we entered, the blushing girls who had been beating Whiffle over his spindle shins with their large garden-fans, dashed through a side-door, unable to contain their laughter,—which we heard, long after they had vanished, echoing through the lofty galleries of the house. Our captive knight being restored to us, we made our bows to the other ladies, who were expiring with laughter, and took our leave, with little Whiffle on our shoulders—the worthy Hebrew, whom I afterwards knew in London, sending his servant and gig with Captain Transom and myself to the wharf. There we tumbled ourselves into the boat, and got on board the Firebrand about three in the morning. We were by this time pretty well sobered; at four a gun was fired, the topsails were let fall and sheeted home, and topgallant sails set over them, the ship having previously been hove short; at half-past, the cable being right up and down—another gun—the drums and fifes beat merrily—spin flew the capstan, tramp went the men that manned it. We were under weigh—Eastward, ho!—for Santiago de Cuba.

CHAPTER XII.

THE CRUISE OF THE FIREBRAND.

Showing, amongst other pleasant matters well worthy of being recorded, how Thomas communed with his two Consciences.

> "Oh, who can tell, save he whose heart hath tried,
> And danced in triumph o'er the waters wide,
> The exulting sense, the pulse's maddening play,
> That thrills the wanderer of that trackless way?"
>
> *The Corsair.*

WE HAD to beat up for three days before we could weather the east end of Jamaica, and tearing work we had of it. I had seen bad weather and heavy seas in several quarters of the globe—I had tumbled about, under a close-reefed main-topsail and reefed foresail, on the long seas in the Bay of Biscay—I had been kicked about in a seventy-four, off the Cape of Good Hope, as if she had been a cork—I had been hove hither and thither, by the short jumble of the North Sea, about Heligoland, and the shoals lying off the mouth of the Elbe, when everything overhead was black as thunder, and all beneath as white as snow—I had enjoyed the luxury of being torn in pieces by a northwester, which compelled us to lie-to for ten days at a stretch, under storm stay-sails, off the coast of Yankeeland, with a clear, deep, cold, blue sky above us, without a cloud, where the sun shone brightly the whole time by day, and a glorious harvest-moon by night, as if they were smiling in derision upon our riven and strained ship, as she reeled to and fro like a wounded Titan; at one time buried in the trough of the sea, at another cast upwards towards the heavens by the throes of the tormented waters, from the troubled bosom of the bounding and roaring ocean, amidst hundreds of miniature rainbows (ay, rainbows by night as well as by day), in a hissing storm of white, foaming, seething spray, torn from the curling and roaring bright green crests of the mountainous billows. And I have had more than one narrow squeak for it in the neighbourhood of the "still vexed Bermoothes," besides various other small affairs, written in this *Boke*; but the devil such another tumblification had I ever experienced—not as to danger, for there was none except to our spars and rigging, but as to discomfort—as I did in that short, cross, splashing and boiling sea off Morant Point. By noon, however, on the second day, having had a slant from the land-wind in the night previous, we got well to windward of the long sandy spit that forms the east end of the island, and were in the act of getting a small pull of the weather braces before edging away for St Jago, when the wind fell suddenly, and in half an hour it was stark calm—"una *furiosa* calma," as the Spanish sailors quaintly enough call it.

We got rolling-tackles up, and the topgallant-masts down, and studding-sails out of the tops, and lessened the lumber and weight aloft in every way we could think of, but, nevertheless, we continued to roll gunwale under, dipping the main-yardarm into the water every now and then, and setting everything adrift below and on deck that was not bolted down, or otherwise well secured.

When I went down to dinner, the scene was extremely good. Old Yerk, the first-lieutenant, was in the chair; one of the boys was jammed at his side, with his claws fastened round the foot of the table, holding a tureen of boiling pease-soup, with lumps of pork swimming in it, which the aforesaid Yerk was baling forth with great assiduity to his messmates. Hydrostatics were much in vogue—the tendency of fluids to regain their equilibrium (confound them! they have often in the shape of claret destroyed mine) was beautifully illustrated, as the contents of each carefully balanced soup-plate kept swaying about on the principle of the spirit-level. The doctor was croupier, and as it was a return-dinner to the captain, all hands were regularly figged out, the lieutenants with their epaulets and best coats, and the master, purser, and doctor, all fittingly attired. When I first entered, as I made my obeisance to the captain, I thought I saw an empty seat next him, but the matter of the soup was rather an engrossing concern, and took up my attention, so that I paid no particular regard to the circumstance; however, when we had all discussed the same, and were drinking our first glass of Teneriffe, I raised my eyes to hob and nob with the master, when—ye gods and little fishes!—who should they light on, but the merry phiz—merry, alas! no more—of Aaron Bang, Esquire, who, during the soup interlude, had slid into the vacant chair unperceived by me.

"Why, Mr Bang, where, in the name of all that is comical, *where have* you dropped from?" Alas! poor Aaron—Aaron in a rolling sea was of no kindred to

Aaron ashore. His rosy gills were no longer rosy—his round plump face seemed to be covered with parchment from an old bass-drum, cut out from the centre where most bronzed by the drum-stick—there was no speculation in his eyes that he did glare withal—and his lips, which were usually firm and open, disclosing his nice teeth in frequent grin, were held together, as if he had been in grievous pain. At length he did venture to open them—and like the ghost of Hamlet's father, "it lifted up its head and did address itself to motion, as it would speak." But they began to quiver, and he once more screwed them together, as if he feared the very exertion of *uttering* a word or two might unsettle his moniplies.

The master was an odd garrulous small man, who had a certain number of stated jokes, which, so long as they were endured, he unmercifully inflicted on his messmates. I had come in for my share, as a new-comer, as well as the rest; but even with me, although I had been but recently appointed, they had already begun to pall, and wax wearisome; and, blind as the beetle of a body was, he could not help seeing this. So poor Bang, unable to return a shot, sea-sick and crestfallen, offered a target that he could not resist taking aim at. Dinner was half over, and Bang had not eaten anything, when, unseasonable as the hour was, the little pot-valiant master, primed with two tumblers of grog, in defiance of the captain's presence, fairly fastened on him, like a remora, and pinned him down with one of his long-winded stories about Captain David Jones, in the Phantome, during a cruise off Cape Flyaway, having run foul of a whale, and thereby nearly foundered; and that at length having got the monster harpooned and speared, and the devil knows what, but it ended in getting her alongside, when they scuttled the leviathan, and then, wonderful to relate, they found a Greenlandman, with royal yards crossed, in her maw, *and the captain and mate in the cabin quarrelling about the reckoning.*

"What do you think of that, Mr Bang—as well they might be, Mr Bang—as well they might be?" Bang said nothing, but at the moment—whether the said Aaron lent wings to the bird or no, I cannot tell—a goose, swimming in apple-sauce, which he was, with a most stern countenance, endeavouring to carve, fetched way right over the gunwale of the dish, and, taking a whole boat of melted butter with it, splashed across the table during a tremendous roll, that made everything creak and groan again, right into the small master's lap, who was his *vis-à-vis*. I could hear Aaron grumble out something about—"Strange affinity—birds of a feather." But his time was up, his minutes were numbered, and like a shot he bolted from the table, sculling or rather clawing away towards the door, by the backs of the chairs, like a green parrot, until he reached the marine at the bottom of the ladder, at the door of the captain's cabin, round whose neck he immediately fetterlocked his fins.

He had only time to exclaim to his new ally, "My dear fellow, get me some brandy-and-water, for the love of mercy"—when he blew up, with an explosion like the bursting of a steam-boiler. "Oh dear, oh dear," we could hear him murmuring in the lulls of his agony—then another loud report—"there goes my yesterday's supper—hot grog and toasted cheese"—another roar, as if the spirit was leaving its earthly tabernacle—"dinner, claret, madeira—all cruel had in a second edition—cheese, teal, and ringtail pigeon—black crabs—calapi and turtle-soup"—as his fleshly indulgences of the previous day rose up in judgment against him, like a man's evil deeds on his deathbed. At length the various *strata* of his interior were entirely excavated—"Ah!—I have got to my breakfast—to the simple tea and toast at last. Brandy-and-water, my dear Transom, brandy-and-water, my darling, hot, without sugar"—and "Brandy-and-water" died in echoes in the distance as he was stowed away into his cot in the captain's cabin. It seems that it had been all arranged between him and Captain Transom, that he was to set off for St Thomas-in-the-East the morning on which we sailed, and to get a shove out in the pilot-boat schooner, from Morant Bay, to join us for the cruise; and accordingly he had come on board the night previous when I was below, and being somewhat qualmish he had wisely kept his cot; the fun of the thing depending, as it seemed, on all hands carefully keeping it from me that he was on board.

I apprehend most people indulge in the fancy that they have *Consciences*—such as they are. I myself now—even I, Thomas Cringle, Esquire—amongst sundry vain imaginings, conceive that I have a conscience—somewhat of the caoutchouc order, I will confess—stretching a little upon occasion, when the gale of my passions blows high—nevertheless a highly respectable conscience as things go—a stalwart unchancy customer, who will not be gainsaid or contradicted; but he may be disobeyed, although never with impunity. It is all true that a young, well-fledged gentlewoman, for she is furnished with a most swift pair of wings, called *Prosperity,* sometimes gets the better of Master Conscience, and smothers the *Grim Feature* for a time—under the bed of eider-down whereon you and her ladyship are reposing. But she is a sad jilt in many instances, this same Prosperity; for some fine morning, with the sun glancing in through the crevices of the window-shutters, just at the nick when, after turning yourself and rubbing your eyes, you courageously thrust forth one leg, with a determination to don your gramashes without more delay,—"Tom," says she, "Tom Cringle, I have got tired of you, Thomas; besides, I hear my next-door neighbour, Madam Adversity, tirling at the door-pin; so give me my down-bed, Tom, and I'm off." With that she bangs open the window, and, before I recover from my surprise, launches forth with a loud *whir*, mattress and all, leaving me, Pilgarlic, lying on the paillasse. Well, her nest is scarcely cold, when in comes Mistress Adversity, a wee, outspoken, sour, crab-bit, *gizzened* anatomy of an old woman—"You *ne'erdoweel*, Tam," quoth she, "is it no' enough that you consort with that scarlet limmer, who has just yescaped thorough the winday, but ye maun smoor my first-born, puir Conscience, atween ye? Whare hae ye stowed him, man—tell me that?" And the ancient damosel gives me a shrewd clip on the skull with the poker. "That's right, mother," quoth Conscience, from beneath the straw mattress,—"Give it to him—he'll no hear me—another *devel*, mother." And I found that my own weight, deserted as I was by that—ahem—Prosperity, was no longer sufficient to keep him down. So up he rose, with a loud *pech* and while the old woman keelhauled me with a poker on one side, he yerked at me on the other, until at length he gave me a regular cross-buttock, and then between them they diddled me outright. When I was fairly floored, "Now, my man," said Adversity, "I bear no spite; if you will but listen to my boy there, we shall be good friends still. He is never unreasonable. He has no objections to your consorting even with Madam Prosperity in a *decent* way; but he will not consent to your letting her get the better of you, nor to your doting on her, even to the giving her a share of your bed, when she should never be allowed to get farther than the servants' hall, for she should be kept in subjection, or she'll ruin you for ever, Thomas. Conscience is a rough lad, I grant you, and I am keen and snell also; but never mind, take his advice, and you'll be some credit to your freens yet, ye scoonrel." I did so, and the old lady's visits became shorter and shorter, and more and more distant, until at length they ceased altogether; and once more Prosperity, like a dove with its heaven-borrowed hues all glowing in the morning sun, pitched one morning on my window-sill. It was in June. "Tom, I am come back again." I glowered at her with all my bir. "Aiblins," said I, but I could go no farther. She made a step or two towards me, and the lesson of Adversity was fast evaporating into thin air, when lo! the sleeping *lion himself* awoke. "Thomas," said Conscience, in a voice that made my flesh creep, "not into your bed, neither into your bosom, Thomas. Be civil to the young woman, but remember what your best friend Adversity told you, and never let her be more than your handmaiden again; free to come, free to go, but never more to be your mistress." I screw myself about, and twist, and turn in great perplexity—Hard enough all this, and I am half-inclined to try to throttle Conscience outright.

But to make a long story short—I was resolute—"Step into the parlour, my dearest—I hope we shall never part any more; but you must not get the upper hand, you know. So step into the other room, and whenever I get my inexpressibles on, I will come to you there."

But this Conscience about which I am now *havering*, seldom acts the monitor in this way, unless against respectable crimes, such as murder, debauching your friend's wife, or stealing. But the *chield* I have to do with for the present, and who has led to this rigmarole, is a sort of *deputy Conscience*, a looker-out after small affairs—peccadilloes. The *grewsome carle, Conscience Senior,* you can grapple with, for he only steps forth on great occasions, when he says sternly—and the mischief is, that what he says we know to be true—says he, "Thomas Cringle"—he never calls me Tom, or Mister, or Lieutenant—, "Thomas Cringle," says he, "if you do that thing you shall be damned." "Lud-a-mercy," quoth I, Thomas, "I will perpend, Master Conscience"—and I set myself to eschew the evil deed with all my might. But *Conscience the Younger*—whom I will take leave to call by Quashie's appellative hereafter, *Conshy*—is a funny little fellow, and another guess sort of a chap altogether. An instance: "I say, Tom, my boy—Tom Cringle—why the *deuce* now"—he won't say "the Devil" for the world—"why the deuce, Tom, don't you confine yourself to a pint of wine at dinner, eh?" quoth Conshy. "Why will you not give up your toddy after it? You are ruining your interior, Thomas, my fine fellow—the gout is on the look-out for you—your legs are spindling, and your paunch is increasing. Read Hamlet's speech to Polonius, Tom, and if you don't find all the marks of premature old age creeping on you, then am I, Conshy, a Dutchman, that's all." Now, Conshy always lectures you in the watches of the night; I generally think his advice is good at breakfast-time, and during the forenoon, egad, I think it excellent and most reasonable, and I determine to stick by it—and if Conshy and I dine alone, I do adhere to his maxims most rigidly; but if any of my old allies should topple in to dinner, Conshy, who is a solitary mechanic, bolts instanter. Still I remember him for a time—we sit down—the dinner is good. "I say, Jack, a glass of wine—Peter, what shall we have?" and until the pint a-piece is discussed, all is right between Conshy and me. But then comes some grouse. Hook, in his double-refined nonsense, palavers about the blasphemy of white wine after *brown* game—and he is not far wrong either;—at least I never thought he was, *so long as my Hermitage lasted;* but at the time I speak of, it was still to the fore—so the moment the pint a-piece was out, "Hold hard, Tom, now," cheeps little Conshy. "Why, only one glass of Hermitage, Conshy." Conshy shakes his head. Cheese—after the manner of the ancients—Hook again—"Only one glass of port, Conshy." He shakes his head, and at length the cloth is drawn, and a confounded old steward of mine, who is now installed as butler, brings in the crystal decanters, sparkling to the wax-lights—poor as I am, I consider mutton fats damnable—and everything as it should be, down to a finger-glass. "Now, Mary, where are the children?" I am resolute. "Jack, I can't drink—out of sorts, my boy—so mind yourself, you and Peter. Now, Conshy," says I, "where are you *now*, my boy?" But just at this instant, Jack strikes out with, "Cringle, order me a tumbler—something hot—I don't care what it is."— "Ditto," quoth Peter; and down crumbles all my fine fabric of resolutions, only to be rebuilt tomorrow, before breakfast again, or at any odd moment when one's flesh is somewhat fishified.—Another instance: "I say, Tom," says Conshy, "do give over looking at that smart girl tripping it along t'other side of the street."—"Presently, my dear little man," says I. "Tight little woman that, Conshy; handsome bows; good bearings forward; tumbles home sweetly about the waist, and tumbles out well above the hips; what a beautiful run! and spars clean and tight; back-stays well set up."—"Now, Tom, you vagabond, give over. Have you not a wife of your own?"—"To be sure I have, Conshy, my darling; but *toujours per*"—"Have done now, you are going too far," says Conshy.—"Oh, you be—" "THOMAS," cries a still, stern voice, from the very inmost recesses of my heart. Wee Conshy holds up his finger, and pricks his ear. "Do you hear *him?*" says he.—"I hear," says I, *"I hear and tremble."* Now, to apply. Conshy has been nudging me for this half hour to hold my tongue regarding Aaron Bang's sea-sickness.—"It is absolutely indecent," quoth he.—"Can't help it, Conshy; no more than the extra tumbler; those who are delicate need not read it; those who are indelicate won't be the worse of it."—But," persists Conshy—"I have other hairs in your neck, Master Tommy—you are growing a bit of a buffoon on us, and sorry am I to say it, sometimes not altogether, as a man with a rank imagination may construe you, a very decent one. Now, my good boy, I would have you to remember that what you write is *condemned* in the pages of Old Christopher to an *amber immortalisation,*" (Ohon for the Provost!) "nay, don't perk and smile, I mean no compliment, for you are but the *straw* in the *amber,* Tom, and the only wonder is, *how* the deuce you got there."

"But, my dear Conshy—"

"Hold your tongue, Tom—let me say out my say, and finish my advice—and how will you answer to my father, in your old age, when youth and health and wealth may have flown, if you find anything in this your Log, calculated to bring a blush on an innocent cheek, Tom, when the time shall have for ever passed away wherein you could have remedied the injury? For *Conscience will* speak to you then; not as I do now, in friendly confidence, and impelled by a sincere regard for you, you right-hearted, but thoughtless, slapdash vagabond."

There must have been a great deal of absurd perplexity in my visage, as I sat receiving my rebuke, for I noticed Conshy smile, which gave me courage.

"I will reform, Conshy, and that immediately; but my *moral* is good, man."

"Well, well, Tom, I will take you at your word, so set about it, set about it."

"But, Conshy—a word in your starboard *lug*—why don't you go to the fountain-head—why don't you try your hand in a curtain lecture on Old Kit North himself—the hoary sinner who seduced me?"

Conshy could no longer contain himself; the very idea of old Kit having a *conscience* of any kind or description whatever, so tickled him, that he burst into a most uproarious fit of laughter, which I was in great hopes would have choked him, and thus made me well quit of him for ever. For some time I listened in great amazement, but there was something so infectious in his fun that presently I began to laugh too, which only increased his cachinnation; so there were Conshy and I roaring and shouting with the tears running down our cheeks.

"Kit, listen to me!—O Lord—"

"You are swearing, Conshy," said I, rubbing my hands at having caught *him* tripping.

"And enough to make a Quaker swear," quoth he, still laughing. "No, no, Kit never listens to me; why, he would never listen even to my father, until the gout and the Catholic Relief Bill, and, last of all, the Reform Bill, broke him down and softened his heart."

So there is an allegory for you, worthy of John Bunyan.

Next morning we got the breeze again, when we bore away for Santiago de Cuba, and arrived off the Moro Castle on the fifth evening at sunset, after leaving Port Royal harbour. The Spaniards, in their better days, were a kind of coral worms; wherever they planted their colonies, they immediately set to covering themselves in with stone and mortar—applying their own entire energies, and the whole strength of their Indian captives, first to the erection of a fort; their second object (postponed to the other only through absolute necessity) being then to build a temple to their God. Gradually vast fabrics appeared where before there was nothing but one eternal forest or a howling wilderness; and although it does come over one, when looking at the splendid moles and firm-built bastions and stupendous churches of the New World—the latter surpassing, or at the least equalling in magnificence and grandeur, those of Old Spain herself—that they are all cemented by the blood and sweat of millions of gentle Indians, of whose harmless existence in many quarters they remain the only monuments, still it is a melancholy reflection to look back and picture to one's-self what Spain was, and to compare her, in her high and palmy state, with what she is now—to compare her present condition even with what she was, when, as a young midshipman, I first visited her glorious Transatlantic colonies.

Until the Peninsula was overrun by the French, Buenos Ayres, Laguayra, Porto Cavello, Maracaibo, Santa Martha, and that stronghold of the West, the key of the Isthmus of Darien, Cartagena de las Indias, with Porto Bello, and Vera Cruz, on the Atlantic shores of South America, were all prosperous and happy—*"Llenas de plata;"* and on the western coast, Valparaiso, Lima, Panama, and San Blas, were thriving and increasing in population and wealth. England, through her colonies, was at that time driving a lucrative trade with all of them; but the demon of change was abroad, blown thither by the pestilent breath of European liberalism. What a vineyard for Abbé Sièyes to have laboured in! Every *Capitania* would have become a purchaser of one of his cut and dried constitutions; indeed he could not have turned them out of hand fast enough. The enlightened *few,* in these countries, were as a drop in the bucket to the unenlightened *many;* and although no doubt there were numbers of the former who were well-meaning men, yet they were, one and all, guilty of that prime political blunder, in common with our Whig friends at home, of expecting a set of semi-barbarians to see the beauty of, and to conform to, their newfangled codes of free institutions, for which they were as ready as I am to die at this present moment. Bolivar, in his early fever of patriotism, made the same mistake, although his shrewd mind, in his later career, saw that a despotism, *pure* or *impure*—I will not qualify it—was your only government for the *savages* he had at one time dignified with the name of fellow-patriots. But he came to this wholesome conclusion too late; he tried back, it is true, but it would not do; the fiend had been unchained, and at length hunted him, broken-hearted, into his grave.

But the men of mind tell us that those countries are now going through the *political fermentation,* which by-and-by will clear, when the sediment will be deposited, and the different ranks will each take their acknowledged and undisputed stations in society; and the United States are once and again quoted against we of the adverse faction, as if there were the most remote analogy between their population, originally composed of all the *cleverest scoundrels* of Europe, and the barbarians of Spanish America, where a few master spirits—all old Spaniards—did indeed for a season stick fiery off from the dark mass of savages amongst whom their lot was cast, like stars in a moonless night, but only to suffer a speedy eclipse from the clouds and storm which they themselves had set in motion. We shall see. The *scum* as yet is uppermost, and does not seem likely to *subside* but it may *boil over.* In Cuba, however, all was at the time quiet, and still is, I believe, prosperous, and that too without having come through this said blessed political fermentation.

During the night we stood off and on, under easy sail, and next morning, when the day broke, with a strong breeze and a fresh shower, we were about two miles off the Moro Castle, at the entrance of Santiago de Cuba.

I went aloft to look round me. The sea-breeze blew strong, until it reached within half a mile of the shore, where it stopped short, shooting in cat's-paws occasionally into the smooth belt of water beyond, where the long unbroken swell rolled like molten silver in the rising sun, without a ripple on its surface, until it dashed its gigantic undulations against the face of the precipitous cliffs on the shore, and flew up in smoke. The entrance to the harbour is very narrow, and looked from my perch like a zigzag chasm in the rock, inlaid at the bottom with polished blue steel; so clear and calm and pellucid was the still water, wherein the frowning rocks and magnificent trees on the banks and the white Moro, rising with its grinning tiers of cannon, battery above battery, were reflected *veluti in speculum,* as if it had been in a mirror.

We had shortened sail, and fired a gun, and the signal for a pilot was flying when the captain hailed me. "Does the sea-breeze blow into the harbour yet, Mr Cringle?"

"Not yet, sir; but it is creeping in fast."

"Very well. Let me know when you can run in. Mr Yerk, back the main-topsail, and heave the ship to."

Presently the pilot canoe, with the Spanish flag flying in the stern, came alongside; and the pilot, a tall brown man, a *moreno*, as the Spaniards say, came on board. He wore a glazed cocked-hat, rather an out-of-the-way finish to his figure, which was rigged in a simple Osnaburg shirt and pair of trousers. He came on the quarterdeck and made his bow to the captain with all the ease in the world, wished him a good morning, and, taking his place by the quarter-master at the conn, took charge of the ship. "Señor," quoth he to me, "is de harbour blow up yet? I mean, you see de *viento* walking into him?—de *terral*— dat is land-wind—has he cease?"

"No," I answered; "the belt of smooth water is growing narrower fast; but the sea-breeze does not blow into the channel yet. Now it has reached the entrance."

"All, den make sail, Señor Capitan; fill de main-topsail." We stood in—the scene becoming more and more magnificent—as we approached the land.

The fresh green shores of this glorious island lay before us, fringed with white surf, as the everlasting ocean in its approach to it gradually changed its dark blue colour, as the water shoaled, into a bright joyous green under the blazing sun, as if in sympathy with the genius of the fair land, before it tumbled at his feet its gently swelling billows, in shaking thunders on the reefs and rocky face of the coast, against which they were driven up in clouds, the incense of their sacrifice. The undulating hills in the vicinity were all either cleared, and covered with the greenest verdure that imagination can picture, over which strayed large herds of cattle, or with forests of gigantic trees, from amongst which, every now and then, peeped out some palm-thatched mountain settlement, with its small thread of blue smoke floating up into the calm clear morning air, while the blue hills in the distance rose higher and higher, and more and more blue and dreamy and indistinct, until their rugged summits could not be distinguished from the clouds through the glimmering hot haze of the tropics.

"By the mark seven," sang out the leadsman in the starboard chains; "Quarter less three," responded he in the larboard, showing that the inequalities of the surface at the bottom of the sea, even in the breadth of the ship, were at least as abrupt as those presented above water by the sides of the natural canal into which we were now running. By this time on our right hand we were within pistol-shot of the Moro, where the channel is not above fifty yards across; indeed, there is a chain, made fast to a rock on the opposite side, that can be hove up by a capstan until it is level with the surface of the water, so as to constitute an insurmountable obstacle to any attempt to force an entrance in time of war. As we stood in, the golden flag of Spain rose slowly on the staff at the Water Battery, and cast its large sleepy folds abroad in the breeze; but, instead of floating over mail-clad men, or Spanish soldiers in warlike array, three poor devils of half-naked mulattoes stuck their heads out of an embrasure under its shadow. "Señor Capitan," they shouted, *"una botella de Roma por el honor del pais."* We were mighty close upon leaving the bones of the old ship here, by the by; for at the very instant of entering the harbour's mouth the land-wind checked us off, and very nearly hove us broadside on upon the rocks below the castle, against which the swell was breaking in thunder.

"Let go the anchor," sang out the captain.

"All gone, sir," promptly responded the boatswain from the forecastle. And as he spoke we struck once, twice, and very heavily the third time. But the breeze coming in strong we fetched way again, and, as the cable was promptly cut, we got safely off. However, on weighing the anchor afterwards, we found the water had been so shoal under the bows, that the ship, when she stranded, had struck it, and broken the stock short off by the ring. The only laughable part of the story consisted in the old cook—an Irishman—with one leg and half an eye, scrambling out of the galley, nearly naked, in his trousers, shirt, and greasy nightcap, and sprawling on all-fours after two tubfuls of yams, which the third thump had capsized all over the decks. "Oh, you scurvy-looking tief," said he, eyeing the pilot; "if it was running us ashore you were set on, why the blazes couldn't ye wait until the yams were in the copper; bad luck to ye—and them all scraped too! I do believe, *if they even had been taties, it would have been all the same to you."* We stood on, the channel narrowing still more—the rocks rising to a height of at least five hundred feet from the water's edge, as sharply and precipitously as if they had only yesterday been split asunder; the splintered projections and pinnacles on one side having each their corresponding fissures and indentations on the other, as if the hand of a giant could have closed them together again.

Noble trees shot out in all directions wherever they could find a little earth and a crevice to hold on by, almost meeting overhead in several places, and alive with all kinds of birds and beasts incidental to the climate; parrots of all sorts, great and small, clomb and hung and fluttered amongst the branches; and pigeons of numberless varieties; and the glancing woodpecker, with his small hammer-like *tap, tap, tap;* and the West India nightingale, and humming-birds of all hues; while cranes, black, white, and grey, frightened from their fishing-stations, stalked and peeped about, as awkwardly as a warrant-officer in his long-skirted coat on a Sunday; while whole flocks of ducks flew across the mastheads and through the rigging; and the dragon-like guanas, and lizards of many kinds, disported themselves amongst the branches, not lazily or loathsomely, as we, who have only seen a lizard in our cold climate, are apt to picture, but alert, and quick as lightning—their colours changing with the changing light or the hues of the objects to which they clung—becoming, literally, in one respect, portions of the landscape.

And then the dark, transparent crystal depth of the pure waters under foot, reflecting all nature so steadily and distinctly, that in the hollows, where the overhanging foliage of the laurel-like bushes darkened the scene, you could not for your life tell where the elements met, so blended were earth and sea.

"Starboard," said I. I had now come on deck. "Starboard, or the main-topgallant-masthead *will be foul of the limb of that tree*. Foretop, there—lie out on the larboard fore-yardarm, and be ready to shove her off, if she sheers too close."

"Let go the anchor," struck in the first-lieutenant.

Splash—the cable rumbled through the hause-hole.

"Now, here are we brought up in paradise," quoth the doctor.

"Curukity coo—curukity coo," sang out a great bushy whiskered sailor from the crow's nest,—who turned out to be no other than our old friend Timothy Tailtackle, quite juvenilified by the laughing scene. "Here am I, Jack, a booby amongst the singing-birds," crowed he to one of his messmates in the maintop, as he clutched a branch of a tree in his hand, and swung himself up into it. But the ship, as Old Nick would have it, at the very instant dropped astern a few yards in swinging to her anchor, and that so suddenly, that she left him on his perch in the tree, converting his jest, poor fellow, into melancholy earnest. "O Lord, sir!" sang out Timotheus, in a great quandary. "Captain, do heave ahead a bit—Murder! I shall never get down again! Do, Mr Yerk, if you please, sir!" And there he sat twisting and craning himself about, and screwing his features into combinations evincing the most comical perplexity.

The captain, by way of a bit of fun, pretended not to hear him.

"Maintop, there," quoth be.

The midshipman in the top answered him, "Ay, ay, sir."

"Not you, Mr Reefpoint; the captain of the top I want."

"He is not in the top, sir," responded little Reefpoint, chuckling like to choke himself.

"Where the devil is he, sir?"

"*Here,* sir," squealed Timothy, his usual gruff voice spindling into a small *cheep* through his great perplexity. "*Here,* sir."

"What are you doing there, sir? Come down this moment, sir. Rig out the main-topmast-studdingsail-boom, Mr Reefpoint, and tell him to slew himself down by that long water-withe."

To hear was to obey. Poor Timothy clambered down to the fork of the tree, from which the withe depended, and immediately began to warp himself down, until he reached within three or four yards of the starboard fore-topsail-yardarm; but the corvette *still* dropped astern, so that, after a vain attempt to hook on by his feet, he swung off into mid air, hanging by his hands.

It was no longer a joke. "Here, you black fellows in the pilot canoe," shouted the captain, as he threw them a rope himself. "Pass the end of that line round the stump yonder—that one below the cliff, there; now, pull like devils—pull."

They did not understand a word he said; but, comprehending his gestures, did what he wished.

"Now, haul on the line, men—gently, that will do. Missed it again," continued the skipper, as the poor fellow once more made a fruitless attempt to swing himself on to the yard.

"Pay out the warp again," sang out Tailtackle—"quick, quick! let the ship swing from under, and leave me scope to dive, or I shall be obliged to let go, and be killed on the deck."

"God bless me, yes," said Transom; "stick out the warp, let her swing to her anchor."

In an instant all eyes were again fastened with intense anxiety on the poor fellow, whose strength was fast failing, and his grasp plainly relaxing.

"See all clear to pick me up, messmates."

Tailtackle slipped down to the extreme end of the black withe, that looked like a scorched snake, pressed his legs close together, pointing his toes downwards, and then steadying himself for a moment, with his hands right above his head, and his arms at the full stretch, he dropped, struck the water fairly, entering its dark blue depths without a splash, and instantly disappeared, leaving a white frothy mark on the surface.

"Did you ever see anything better done?" said Yerk. "Why, he clipped into the water with the speed of light, as clean and clear as if he had been a marlinspike."

"Thank Heaven!" gasped the captain; "for if he had struck the water horizontally, or fallen headlong, he would have been shattered in pieces—every bone would have been broken; he would have been as completely smashed as if he had dropped upon one of the limestone rocks on the iron-bound shore."

"Ship, ahoy!" We were all breathlessly looking over the side where he fell, expecting to see him rise again; but the hail came from the water on t'other side. "Ship, ahoy!—throw me a rope, good people—a rope, if you please. Do you mean to careen the ship, that you have all run to the starboard side, leaving me to be drowned to port here?"

"Ah, Tailtackle! well done, old boy," sang out a volley of voices, men and officers, rejoiced to see the honest fellow alive. He clambered on board, in the bight of one of twenty ropes that were hove to him.

When he came on deck, the captain slily said, "I don't think you'll go a-birdnesting in a hurry again, Tailtackle."

Tim looked with a most quizzical expression at his captain, all blue and breathless and dripping as he was; and then, sticking his tongue slightly in his cheek, he turned away without addressing him directly, but murmuring as he went, "A glass of grog now."

The captain, with whom he was a favourite, took the hint. "Go below now, and turn in till eight bells, Tailtackle. Mafame," to his steward, "send him a glass of hot brandy-grog."

"A northwester," whispered Tim aside to the functionary; "half-and-half, Tallow Chops, eh!"

About an hour after this a very melancholy accident happened to a poor boy on board, of about fifteen years of age, who had already become a great favourite of mine from his modest, quiet deportment, as well as of all the gun-room officers, although he had not been above a fortnight in the ship. He had let himself down over the bows by the cable to bathe. There were several of his comrades standing on the forecastle looking at him, and he asked one of them to go out on the spritsail-yard, and look round to see if there were any sharks in the neighbourhood; but all around was deep, clear, green water. He kept hold of the cable, however, and seemed determined not to put himself in harm's way, until a wicked little urchin, who used to wait on the warrant-officers' mess—a small meddling snipe of a creature, who got flogged in well-behaved weeks *only* once—began to taunt my little mild favourite.

"Why, you chicken-heart, I'll wager a thimbleful of grog, that such a tailor as you are in the water can't for the life of you swim out to the buoy there."

"Never you mind, Pepperbottom," said the boy, giving the imp the name he had richly earned by repeated flagellations. "Never you mind—I am not ashamed to show my naked hide, you know. But it is against orders in these seas to go overboard, unless with a sail under foot; so I shan't run the risk of being tattooed by the boatswain's mate, like some one I could tell of."

"Coward," muttered the little wasp, "you are afraid, sir;" and, the other boys abetting the mischief-maker, the lad was goaded to leave his hold of the cable and strike out for the buoy. He reached it, and then turned, and pulled towards the ship again, when he caught my eye.

"Who is that overboard? How dare you, sir, disobey the standing order of the ship? Come in, boy; come in."

My hailing the little fellow shoved him off his balance, and he lost his presence of mind for a moment or two, during which he, if anything, widened his distance from the ship.

At this instant the lad on the spritsail-yard sang out quick and suddenly, "A shark, a shark!"

And the monster, like a silver pillar, suddenly shot up perpendicularly from out the dark-green depths of the sleeping pool, with the waters sparkling and hissing around him, as if he had been a sea-demon rushing on his prey.

"Pull for the cable, Louis," shouted fifty voices at once—"pull for the cable."

The boy did so—we all ran forward. He reached the cable—grasped it with both hands, and hung on, but before he could swing himself out of the water, the fierce fish had turned. His whitish-green belly glanced in the sun—the poor little fellow gave a heart-splitting yell, which was shattered amongst the impending rocks into piercing echoes, and these again were reverberated from cavern to cavern, until they died away amongst the bellows in the distance, as if they had been the faint shrieks of the damned—yet he held fast for a second or two—the ravenous tyrant of the sea tug, tugging at him, till the stiff, taut cable shook again. At length he was torn from his hold, but did not disappear; the animal continuing on the surface crunching his prey with his teeth, and digging at him with his jaws, as if trying to gorge a morsel too large to be swallowed, and making the water flash up in foam over the boats in pursuit by the powerful strokes of his tail, but without ever letting go his hold. The poor lad only cried once more—but such a cry—oh God, I never shall forget it!—and, could it be possible, in his last shriek, his piercing expiring cry, his young voice seemed to pronounce my name—at least so I thought at the time, and others thought so too. The next moment he appeared quite dead. No less than three boats had been in the water alongside when the accident happened, and they were all on the spot by this time. And there was the bleeding and mangled boy, torn along the surface of the water by the shark, with the boats in pursuit, leaving a long stream of blood, mottled with white specks of fat and marrow in his wake. At length the man in the bow of the gig laid hold of him by the arm, another sailor caught the other arm, boat-hooks and oars were dug into and launched at the monster, who relinquished his prey at last, stripping off the flesh, however, from the upper part of the right thigh until his teeth reached the knee, where he nipped the shank clean off, and made sail with the leg in his jaws.

Poor little Louis never once moved after we took him in. I thought I heard a small still stern voice thrill along my nerves, as if an echo of the beating of my heart had become articulate. "Thomas, a fortnight ago you impressed that poor boy—who *was,* and *now is not*—out of a Bristol ship." Alas! Conscience spoke no more than the truth.

Our instructions were to lie at St Jago until three British ships, then loading, were ready for sea, and then to convey them through the Caicos, or windward passage. As our stay was, therefore, likely to be ten days or a fortnight at the shortest, the boats were hoisted out, and we made our little arrangements and preparations for taking all the recreation in our power; and our worthy skipper, taut and stiff as he was at sea, always encouraged all kinds of fun and larking, both amongst the men and the officers, on occasions like the present. Amongst his other pleasant qualities he was a great boat-racer, constantly building and altering gigs and pulling-boats at his own expense, and matching the men against each other for small prizes. He had just finished what the old carpenter considered his *chef-d'oeuvre,* and a curious affair this same masterpiece was. In the first place, it was forty-two feet long over all, and only three-and-a-half feet beam; the planking was not much above an eighth of an inch in thickness, so that, if one of the crew had slipped his foot off the stretcher, it must have gone through the bottom. There was a standing order that no man was to go into it with shoes on. She was to pull six oars, and her crew were the captains of the tops, the primest seamen in the ship, and the steersman, no less a character than the skipper himself.

Her name, for I love to be particular, was the Dragonfly; she was painted out and in of a bright red, amounting to a flame colour—oars red—the men wearing trousers and shirts of red flannel, and red net nightcaps—which common uniform the captain himself wore. I think I have said before that he was a very handsome man, but if I have not, I say so now; and when he had taken his seat, and the gigs—all fine men—were seated each with his oar held upright upon his knees ready to be dropped into the water at the same instant, the craft and her crew formed, to my eye, as pretty a plaything for grown children as ever was seen. "Give way, men;" the oars dipped as clean as so many knives, without a sparkle, the gallant fellows stretched out, and away shot the Dragonfly, like an arrow—the green water foaming into white smoke at the bows and hissing away in her wake.

She disappeared in a twinkling round the reach of the canal where we were anchored, and we, the officers—for we must needs have our boat also—were making ready to be off, to have a shot at some beautiful cranes, that, floating on their large pinions, slowly passed us with their long legs stuck straight out astern, and their longer necks gathered into their crops, when we heard a loud shouting in the direction where the captain's boat had vanished. Presently the Devil's Darning-Needle, as the Scotch part of the crew loved to call the Dragonfly, stuck her long snout round the headland, and came spinning along with a Spanish canoe manned by four negroes, and steered by an elderly gentleman, a sharp acute-looking little man, in a gingham coat, in her wake, also pulling very fast; however, the Don seemed dead beat, and the captain was in great glee. By this time both boats were alongside, and the old Spaniard, Don Ricardo Campana, addressed the captain, judging that he was one of the seamen. "Is the captain on board?" said he in Spanish. The captain, who understood the language, but did not speak it, answered him in French, which Don Ricardo seemed to speak fluently, "No, sir, the captain is not on board; but there is Mr Yerk, the first-lieutenant, at the gangway." He had come for the letter-bag, he said, and if we had any newspapers, and could spare them, it would be conferring a great favour on him.

He got his letters and newspapers handed down, and very civilly gave the captain a dollar, who touched his cap, tipped the money to the men, and, winking slightly to old Yerk and the rest of us, addressed himself to shove off. The old Don, drawing up his eyebrows a little (I *guess* he rather saw who was who, for all his make-believe innocence), bowed to the officers at the gangway, sat down, and, desiring his people to use their broad-bladed, clumsy-looking oars or paddles, began to move awkwardly away. We—that is, the gunroom officers, all except the second-lieutenant, who had the watch, and the master—now got into our own gig also, rowed by ourselves, and away we all went in a covey; the purser and doctor and three of the middies forward, Thomas Cringle, gent., pulling the stroke-oar, with old Moses Yerk as coxswain; and as the Dragonflies were all red, so we were all sea-green—boats, oars, trousers, shirts, and night-caps. We soon distanced the cumbrous-looking Don, and the strain was between the Devil's Darning-Needle and our boat, the Watersprite, which was making capital play; for although we had not the *bottom* of the *top*men, yet we had more blood, so to speak, and we had already beaten them, in their last gig, all to sticks. But Dragonfly was a new boat, and now in the water for the first time.

We were both of us so intent on our own match that we lost sight of the Spaniard altogether, and the captain and the first-lieutenant were bobbing in the stern-sheets of their respective gigs like a couple of *souple Tams,* as intent on the game as if all our lives had depended on it, when in an instant the long black dirty prow of the canoe was thrust in between us, the old Don singing out, *"Dexa mi lugar, paysanos—dexa mi lugar, mis hijos."** We kept away right and left to look at the miracle; and there lay the canoe, rumbling and splashing, with her crew walloping about, and grinning and yelling like incarnate fiends, and as naked as the day they were born, and the old Don himself, so staid and so sedate and drawley as he was a minute before, now all alive, shouting *"Tira, diablitos, tira!"†* flourishing a small paddle, with which he steered about his head like a wheel, and dancing and jumping about in his seat, as if his bottom had been a *haggis* with quicksilver in it.

"Zounds," roared the skipper,—"why, topmen—why, gentlemen, give way for the honour of the ship—Gentlemen, stretch out—Men, pull like devils; twenty pounds if you beat him."

We pulled, and they pulled, and the water roared, and the men strained their muscles and sinews to cracking; and all was splash, splash, and *whiz, whiz,* and *pech, pech,* about us; *but it would not do;* the canoe headed us like a shot, and in passing, the cool old Don again subsided into a calm as suddenly as he had been roused from it, and sitting once more, stiff as a poker, turned round and touched his *sombrero,* "I will tell that you are coming, gentlemen."

It was now the evening, near nightfall, and we had been so intent on beating our awkward-looking opponent, that we had none of us had time to look at the splendid scene that burst upon our view, on rounding a precipitous rock, from the crevices of which some magnificent trees shot up—their gnarled trunks and twisted branches overhanging, the canal where we were pulling, and antic-

---

* *"Leave me room, countrymen—leave me room, my children."*

† Equivalent to *"Pull, you devils, pull."*

ipating the fast-falling darkness that was creeping over the fair face of nature; and there we floated, in the deep shadow of the cliff and trees—Dragonflies and Water-sprites, motionless and silent, the boats floating so lightly that they scarcely seemed to touch the water, the men resting on their oars, and all of us rapt with the magnificence of the scenery around us, beneath us, and above us.

The left or western bank of the narrow entrance to the harbour, from which we were now debouching, ran out in all its precipitousness and beauty (with its dark evergreen bushes over-shadowing the deep blue waters, and its gigantic trees shooting forth high into the glowing western sky, their topmost branches gold-tipped in the flood of radiance shed by the rapidly sinking sun, while all below where we lay was grey cold shade), until it joined the northern shore, when it sloped away gradually towards the east; the higher parts of the town sparkled in the evening sun, on this dun ridge, like golden turrets on the back of an elephant, while the houses that were in the shade covered the declivity with their dark masses, until it sank down to the water's edge. On the right hand the haven opened boldly out into a basin about four miles broad by seven long, in which the placid waters spread out beyond the shadow of the western bank into one vast sheet of molten gold, with the canoe tearing along the shining surface, her side glancing in the sun, and her paddles flashing back his rays, and leaving a long train of living fire sparkling in her wake.

It was now about six o'clock in the evening; the sun had set to us, as we pulled along under the frowning brow of the cliff, where the birds were fast settling on their nightly perches with small happy twitterings, and the lizards and numberless other chirping things began to send forth their evening hymn to the great Being who made them and us, and a solitary white-sailing owl would every now and then flit spectre-like from one green tuft, across the bald face of the cliff, to another, and the small divers around us were breaking up the black surface of the waters into little sparkling circles as they fished for their suppers. All was becoming brown and indistinct near us; but the level beams of the setting sun still lingered with a golden radiance upon the lovely city, and the shipping at anchor before it, making their sails, where loosed to dry, glance like leaves of gold, and their spars and masts and rigging like wires of gold, and gilding their flags, which were waving majestically and slow from the peaks in the evening breeze; and the Moorish-looking steeples of the churches were yet sparkling in the glorious blaze, which was gradually deepening into gorgeous crimson, while the large pillars of the cathedral, then building on the highest part of the ridge, stood out like brazen monuments, softening even as we looked into a Stonehenge of amethysts. One-half of every object—shipping, houses, trees, and hills—was gloriously illuminated; but, even as we looked, the lower part of the town gradually sank into darkness, and faded from our sight; the deepening gloom cast by the high bank above us, like the dark shadow of a bad spirit, gradually crept on, and on, and extended farther and farther; the sailing water-fowl, in regular lines, no longer made the water flash up like flame; the russet mantle of eve was fast extending over the entire hemisphere; the glancing minarets, and the tallest trees, and the topgallant-yards and masts of the shipping, alone flashed back the dying effulgence of the glorious orb, which every moment grew fainter and fainter, and redder and redder, until it shaded into purple, and the loud deep bell of the convent of La Merced swung over the still waters, announcing the arrival of even-song and the departure of day.

"Had we not better pull back to supper, sir?" quoth Moses Yerk to the captain. We all started, the men dipped their oars, our dreams were dispelled, the charm was broken!—"Confound the matter-of-fact blockhead," or something very like it, grumbled the captain—"but give way, men," fast followed, and we returned towards the ship. We had not pulled fifty yards when we heard the distant rattle of the muskets of the sentries at the gangways as they discharged them at sundown, and were remarking, as we were rowing leisurely along, upon the strange effects produced by the reports, as they were frittered away amongst the overhanging cliffs in chattering reverberations, when the captain suddenly sang out, "Oars!" All hands lay on them. "Look there," he continued— "there—between the gigs—saw you ever anything like that, gentlemen?" We all leant over; and although the boats, from the *way* they had, were skimming along nearer seven than five knots—*there* lay a large shark—he must have been twelve feet long at the shortest—swimming right in the middle, and equidistant from both, and keeping way with us most accurately.

He was distinctly visible, from the strong and vivid phosphorescence excited by his rapid motion through the sleeping waters of the dark creek, which lit up his jaws, and head, and whole body; his eyes were especially luminous, while a long wake of sparkles streamed away astern of him from the lashing of his tail. As the boats lost their speed the luminousness of his appearance faded gradually as he shortened sail also, until he disappeared altogether. He was then at rest, and suspended motionless in the water; and the only thing that indicated his proximity was an occasional sparkle from the motion of a fin. We brought the boats nearer together, after pulling a stroke or two, but he seemed to sink as we closed, until at last we could merely perceive an indistinct halo far down in the clear black profound. But as we separated, and resumed our original position, he again rose near the surface, and although the ripple and dip of the oars rendered him invisible while we were pulling, yet the moment we again rested on them, there was the monster, like a persecuting fiend, once more right between us, glaring on us, and apparently watching every motion. It was a terrible spectacle, and rendered still more striking by the melancholy occurrence of the forenoon.

"That's the very identical, damnable *baste* himself, as murthered poor little Louis this morning, yeer honour; I knows him from the torn flesh of him under his larboard blinker, sir,—just where Wiggens's boathook punished him," quoth the Irish captain of the mizentop.

"A water-kelpie," murmured another of the captain's gigs—a Scotchman.

The men were evidently alarmed. "Stretch out, men; never mind the shark—he can't jump into the boat, surely," said the skipper. "What the deuce are you afraid of?"

We arrived within pistol-shot of the ship. As we approached, the sentry hailed, "Boat, ahoy!"

"Firebrand," sang out the skipper, in reply.

"Man the side—gangway lanterns there," quoth the officer on duty; and by the time we were close to there were two sidesmen over the side with the man-ropes ready stuck out to our grasp, and two boys with lanterns above them. We got on deck, the officers touching their hats, and speedily the captain dived down the ladder, saying, as he descended, "Mr Yerk, I shall be happy to see you and your boat's crew at supper, or rather to a late dinner, at eight o'clock, but come down a moment as you are. Tailtackle, bring the gigs into the cabin to get a glass of grog, will you?"

"Ay, ay, sir," responded Timothy. "Down with you, you flaming thieves, and see you don't snort and sniffle in your grog, as if you were in your own mess, like so many pigs slushing at the same trough."

"Lord love you, Tim," rejoined one of the topmen, "who made *you* master of the ceremonies, old Ironfist, eh? Where learnt you your breeding?—Among the cockatoos up yonder?"

Tim laughed, who, although he ought to have been in his bed, had taken his seat in the Dragonfly when her crew were piped over the side in the evening, and thereby subjected himself to a rap over the knuckles from the captain; but, where the offence might be said to consist in a too assiduous discharge of his duty, it was easily forgiven, unfortunate as the issue of the race had been. So down we all trundled into the cabin, masters and men. It was brilliantly lighted up—the table sparkling with crystal and wine, and glancing with silver plate; and there on a sofa lay Aaron Bang, in all his pristine beauty, and fresh from his toilet, for he had just got out of his cot after an eight-and-forty hours' sojourn therein—nice white neckcloth—white jean waistcoat and trousers, and span-new blue coat. He was reading when we entered; and the captain, in his flame-coloured costume, was close aboard of him before he raised his eyes, and rather staggered him a bit; but when seven sea-green spirits followed, he was exceedingly nonplussed, and then came the six red Dragonflies, who ranged themselves three on each side of the door, with their net-bags in their hands, smoothing down their hair, and sidling and fidgetting about at finding themselves so far out of their element as the cabin.

"Mafame," said the captain, "a glass of grog a-piece to the Dragonflies," and a tumbler of liquid amber (to borrow from my old friend Cooper) sparkled in the large bony claw of each of them. "Now, drink Mr Bang's health." They, as in duty bound, let fly at our *amigo* in a volley.

"Your health, Mr Bang."

Aaron sprang from his seat, and made his salaam, and the Dragonflies bundled out of the cabin again.

"I say, Transom, John Canoeing still—always some frolic in the wind."

We, the Watersprites, had shifted and rigged, and were all mustered aft on the poop, enjoying the little air there was, as it fanned us gently, and waiting for the announcement of supper. It was a pitch-dark night, neither moon nor stars. The murky clouds seemed to have settled down on the mastheads, shrouding every object in the thickest gloom.

"Ready with the gun forward there, Mr Catwell?" said Yerk.

"All ready, sir."

"Fire!"

Pent up as we were in a narrow channel, walled in on each side with towering precipitous rocks, the explosion, multiplied by the echoes into a whole broadside, was tremendous, and absolutely deafening.

The cold, grey, threatening rocks and the large overhanging twisted branches of the trees, and the clear black water, and the white Moro in the distance, glanced for an instant, and then all was again veiled in utter darkness, and down came a rattling shower of sand and stones from the cliffs, and of rotten branches and heavy dew from the trees, sparkling in the water like a shower of diamonds; and the birds of the air screamed, and, frightened from their nests and perches in crevices, and on the boughs of the trees, took flight with a strong rushing noise, that put one in mind of the rising of the fallen angels from the infernal council in Paradise Lost; and the cattle on the mountain-side lowed, and the fish, large and small, like darts and arrows of fire, sparkled up from the black abyss of waters, and swam in haloes of flame round the ship in every direction, as if they had been the ghosts of a shipwrecked crew, haunting the scene of their destruction; and the guanas and large lizards, which had been shaken from the trees, skimmed and struggled on the surface in glances of fire, like evil spirits watching to seize them as their prey. At length the screaming and shrieking of the birds, the clang of their wings, and the bellowing of the cattle ceased, and the startled fish subsided slowly down into the oozy caverns at the bottom of the sea, and becoming motionless, disappeared and all was again black and undistinguishable—the deathlike silence being only broken by the hoarse murmuring of the distant surf.

"Magnificent!" burst from the captain. "Messenger, send Mr Portfire here." The gunpowder functionary—he of the flannel cartridge—appeared. "Gunner, send one of your mates into the maintop, and let him burn a blue light."

The lurid glare blazed up balefully amongst the spars and rigging, lighting up the decks, and blasting the crew into the likeness of the host of Sennacherib, when the day broke on them and they were all dead corpses. Astern of us, indistinct from the distance, the white Moro Castle reappeared, and rose frowning, tier above tier, like a Tower of Babel, with its summit veiled in the clouds, and the startled sea-fowl wheeling above the higher batteries, like snow-flakes blown about in a storm; while, near at hand, the rocks on each side of us looked as if fresh splintered asunder, with the sulphureous flames which had split them still burning; the trees looked no longer green, but were sicklied o'er with a pale ashy colour, as if sheeted ghosts were holding their midnight orgies amongst their branches; cranes and water-fowl and birds of many kinds, and all the insect and reptile tribes—their gaudy noontide colours merged into one and the same fearful deathlike sameness—flitted and sailed and circled above us, and chattered and screamed and shrieked; and the unearthly-looking guanas, and numberless creeping things, ran out on the boughs to peer at us; and a large snake twined itself up a scathed stump that shot out from a shattered pinnacle of rock that overhung us, with its glossy skin, glancing like the brazen serpent set up by Moses in the camp of the Israelites; and the cattle on the beetling summit of the cliff craned over the precipitous ledge to look down upon us; and, while everything around us and above us was thus glancing in the blue and ghastly radiance, the band struck up a low moaning air; the light burnt out, and once more we were cast, by the contrast, into even more palpable darkness than before. I was entranced, and stood with folded arms, looking forth into the night, and musing intensely on the appalling scene which had just vanished like a feverish dream—"Dinner waits, sir," quoth Mafame.

"Oh! I am coming;" and, kicking all my romance to Old Nick, I descended, and we had a pleasant night of it, and some wine and some fun, and there an end; but I have often dreamed of that dark pool, and the scenes I witnessed there that day and night.

CHAPTER XIII.

THE PIRATE'S LEMAN.

"When lovely woman stoops to folly,
    And finds too late that men betray,
    What charm can soothe her melancholy,
    What art can wash her guilt away?

"The only art her guilt to cover,
    To hide her shame from every eye,
    To give repentance to her lover,
    And wring his bosom—is to die."

Vicar of Wakefield.

"Ay Dios, si sera possible que he ya hallado lugar que pueda servir de escondida sepultura a la carga pesada deste cuerpo, que tan contra mi voluntad sostengo?"

Don Quixote de la Mancha.

THE NEXT morning, after breakfast, I proceeded to Santiago, and landed at the customhouse wharf, where I found everything bustle, dust, and heat. Several of the captains of the English vessels were there, who immediately made up to me, and reported how far advanced in their lading they were, and inquired when we were to give them convoy, the latest news from Kingston, &c. At length

I saw our friend Ricardo Campana going along one of the neighbouring streets, and I immediately made sail in chase. He at once recognised me, gave me a cordial shake of the hand, and inquired how he could serve me. I produced two letters which I had brought for him, but which had been forgotten in the bustle of the preceding day; they were introductory, and, although sealed, I had some reason to conjecture that my friend, Mr Pepperpot Wagtail, had done me much more than justice. Campana, with great kindness, immediately invited me to his house. "We foreigners," said he, "don't keep your hours; I am just going home to breakfast." It was past eleven in the forenoon. I was about excusing myself on the plea of having already breakfasted, when he silenced me. "Why, I guessed as much, Mr Lieutenant, but then you have not lunched; so you can call it lunch, you know, if it will ease your conscience." There was no saying nay to all this civility, so we stumped along the burning streets, through a mile of houses, large massive buildings, but very different in externals from the gay domiciles of Kingston. Aaron Bang afterwards used to say that they looked more like prisons than dwelling-houses, and he was not in this very much out. Most of them were built of brick and plastered over, with large windows, in front of each of which, like the houses in the south of Spain, there was erected a large heavy wooden balcony, projecting far enough from the wall to allow a Spanish chair, such as I have already described, to be placed in it. The front of these verandahs was closed in with a row of heavy balustrades at the bottom, of a variety of shapes, and by clumsy carved woodwork above, which effectually prevented you from seeing into the interior. The whole had a Moorish air, and in the upper part of the town there was a Sabbath-like stillness prevailing, which was only broken now and then by the tinkle of a guitar from one of the aforesaid verandahs, or, by the rattling of a crazy *volante*—a sort of covered gig—drawn by a broken-kneed and broken-winded mule, with a kiln-dried old Spaniard or *doña* in it.

The lower part of the town had been busy enough, and the stir and hum of it rendered the quietude of the upper part of it more striking.

A shovel-hatted friar now suddenly accosted us.

"Señor Campana—ese pobre familia de Cangrejo! Lastima! Lastima! Lastima!"

"Cangrejo—Cangrejo!" muttered I; "why, it is the very name attached to the miniature."

Campana turned to the priest, and they conversed earnestly together for some moments, when he left him, and we again held on our way. I could not help asking what family that was, whose situation the *"padre"* seemed so feelingly to bemoan.

"Never mind," said he; "never mind; they were a proud family once, but that is all over now—come along."

"But," said I, "I have a very peculiar cause of interest with regard to this family. You are aware, of course, of the trial and execution of the pirates in Kingston, the most conspicuous of whom was a young man called Federico Cangrejo, from whom—"

"Mr Cringle," said he, solemnly, "at a fitting time I will hear you regarding that matter; at present I entreat you will not press it."

Good manners would not allow me to push it farther, and we trudged along together, until we arrived at Don Ricardo Campana's door. It was a large brick building, plastered over as already described, and whitewashed. There was a projecting stair in front, with a flight of steps to the right and left, with a parapet wall towards the street. There were two large windows, with the wooden verandah or lattice already described, on the first floor, and on the second a range of smaller windows of the same kind. What answered to our ground-floor was used as a warehouse and filled with dry goods, sugar, coffee, hides, and a vast variety of miscellaneous articles. We ascended the stairs and entered a lofty room, cool and dark, and paved with large diamond-shaped bricks, and every way desirable for a West India lounge, all to the furniture, which was meagre enough; three or four chairs, a wormeaten old leathern sofa, and a large clumsy hardwood table in the midst.

There were several children playing about, little sallow devils—although, I daresay, they could all of them have been furnished with certificates of white parentage—upon whom one or two negro women were hovering in attendance beyond a large folding door that fronted the entrance.

When we entered, the eldest of the children, a little girl of about eight years old, was sitting in the doorway, playing with a small blue toy that I could make nothing of, until, on a nearer inspection, I found it to be a live land-crab, which the little lady had manacled with a thread by the foot, the thread being fastened to a nail driven into a seam of the floor.

As an article of food, I was already familiar with this creature; it was in every respect like a sea-crab, only smaller, the body being at the widest not above three inches across the back. It fed without any apparent fear, and while it pattered over the tiled floor with its hard claws, it would now and then stop and seize a crumb of bread in its forceps, and feed itself like a little monkey. By the time I had exchanged a few words with the little lady, the large door that opened into the hall on the right hand moved, and mine hostess made her appearance—a small woman, dressed in a black gown, very laxly fitted. She was the very converse of our old ship, she never *missed stays*, although I did cruelly.

"This is my friend, Lieutenant Cringle," said mine host.

"*A las pies de usted, señora,*" responded your humble servant.

"I am very glad to see you," said the lady; "but breakfast is ready; welcome, sir, welcome."

The food was not amiss, the coffee decidedly good, and the chocolate, wherein, if you had planted a tea-spoon, it would have stood upright, was excellent. When we had done with substantials, *dulce*—that is, the fruit of the guava preserved, in small wooden boxes (like drums of figs), after being made into a kind of jam—was placed on the table, and mine host and his spouse had eaten a bushel of it a-piece, and drunk a gallon of that most heathenish beverage, cold clear water, before the repast was considered ended. After a hearty meal and a pint of claret I felt rather inclined to sit still, and expatiate for an hour or so, but Campana roused me, and asked whether or not I felt inclined to go and look at the town. I had no apology, and, although I would much rather have sat still, I rose to accompany him, when in walked Captain Transom and Mr Bang. They were also kindly received by Don Ricardo.

"Glad of the honour of this visit," said he in French, with a slight *lift* of the corner of his mouth; "I hope neither *you* nor your boat's crew took any harm after the *heat* of yesterday."

Transom laughed.

"Why, you did beat us very neatly, Don Ricardo. Pray, where got you that canoe? But a lady—Mrs Campana, I presume!—Have the goodness to introduce me."

The skipper was presented in due form, the lady receiving him without the least *mauvaise honte*, which, after all, I believe to be indigenous to our island. Aaron was next introduced, who, as he spoke no lingo, *as I knows of*, to borrow Timotheus Tailtackle's phraseology, but English was rather posed in the interview.

"I say, Tom, tell her I wish she may live a thousand years. Ah, so, that will do."

Madama made her *congé*, and hoped "*El señor tomaria un asiento.*"

"*Mucho, mucho,*" sang out Bang, who meant by that that he was *much* obliged.

At length Don Ricardo came to our aid. He had arranged a party into the country for next morning, and invited us all to come back to a *tertulia* in the evening, and to take beds in his house—he undertaking to provide *bestias* to carry us.

We therefore strolled out, a good deal puzzled what to make of ourselves until the evening, when we fell in with one of the captains of the English ships then loading, who told us that there was a sort of hotel a little way down the street, where we might dine at two o'clock at the *table d'hôte*. It was as yet only twelve, so we stumbled into this said hotel to reconnoitre, and a sorry affair it was. The public room was fitted with rough wooden tables, at which Spaniards, Americans, and Englishmen sat and smoked, and drank sangaree, hot punch, or cold grog, as best suited them, and committed a vast variety of miscellaneous abominations during their potations. We were about giving up all thoughts of the place, and had turned to go to the door, when in popped our friend Don Ricardo. He saw we were somewhat abroad.

"Gentlemen," said he, "if I may ask, have you any engagement to dinner?"

"No, we have none."

"Well, then, will you do me the honour of partaking of my family fare, at three o'clock? I did not venture to invite you before, because I knew you had other letters to deliver, and I wished to leave you masters of your own time." We gladly accepted his kind offer; he had made his bow, and was cruising amongst the smokers and punch-drinkers, where the blue-coated masters of the English merchantmen and American skippers were bobbing and nobbing with the gingham-coated Dons—for the whole Spanish part of the community were figged out in Glasgow and Paisley ginghams—when the priest, who had attracted our attention in the morning, came up to him and drew him aside. They talked earnestly together, the *clerigo,* every now and then, indicating, by significant nods and glances towards us, that we formed the burden of his song, whatever that might be. Campana seemed exceedingly unwilling to communicate the message, which we guessed he had been entreated to carry to us, and made one or two attempts to shove the friar *in propria persona* towards us, that he might himself tell his own story. At length they advanced together to where we stood, when he addressed me.

"You must pardon me, lieutenant; but as the proverb hath it, 'strange countries, strange manners;' my friend here, Padre Carera, brings a message from El Señor Picador Cangrejo, one of our magnates, that he will consider it an especial favour if you will call on him, either this forenoon or to-morrow."

"Why, *who is* this Cangrejo, Don Ricardo? If he be not the father of the poor fellow I mentioned, there must be some mystery about him."

"No mystery," chimed in the monk, "no mystery, God help us; but *mucha, mucha miseria, hijo mio;* much misery, sir, and more impending, and none to help save only—" He did not finish the sentence; but, taking off his shovel-hat, and showing his finely-turned bald head, he looked up to heaven and crossed himself, the tears trickling down his wrinkled checks.

"But," continued he, "you will come, Mr Cringle?"

"Certainly," said I, "to-morrow I will call, if my friend Don Ricardo will be my guide." This being fixed, we strolled about until dinner-time, friend Aaron making his remarks regarding the people and their domiciles with great *naïveté*.

"Strange now, Tom, I had expected to see little else amongst the slave-population here than misery and starvation; whereas, so far as I can observe, they are all deucedly well cared for, and fat and contented; and from the inquiries I was making amongst the captains of the merchantmen—" ("*Masters,*" interjected Captain Transom, "*Master* of a merchantman, *Captain* of a man of-war—") "Well, captains of merchantmen—masters, I mean—I find that the people whom they employ are generally free; and, further, that the slaves are not more than three to one free person, yet they export a great deal of produce, Captain Transom—must keep my eyes about me." And so he did, as will be seen by-and-by. But the dinner-hour drew near, and we repaired to Don Ricardo's, where we found a party of eight assembled, and our appearance was the signal for the repast being ordered in. It was laid out in the entrance-hall. The table was of massive mahogany, the chairs of the same material, with stuffed bottoms, covered with a dingy coloured morocco, which might have been red *once*. But devil a dish of any kind was on the snow-white tablecloth when we sat down; and our situations, or the places we were expected to fill at the board, were only indicated by a large knife and silver fork and spoon laid down for each person. The company consisted of Don Ricardo Campana, la Señora Campana, and a brother of hers, two dark young men who were Don Ricardo's clerks, and three young women, ladies, or *señoras*, as I ought to have called them, who were sitting so far back into the shade at the dark end of the room when we entered, that I could not tell what they were. Our hostess was, although a little woman, a good-looking dark Spaniard, not very polished, but very kind; and, seeing that our friend Aaron was the most helpless amongst us, she took him under her especial care, and made many a civil speech to him, although her husband did not fail to advertise her, that he understood not one word of Spanish, that is, of all she was saying to him. However, he replied to her kindnesses by never-failing exclamation of *"mucho, mucho,"* and they appeared to be getting on extremely well. "Bring dinner," quoth Don Ricardo— *"trae la comida"*—and four black female domestics entered; the first with a large dish of pillaffe, or fowls smothered in rice and onions; the second with a nondescript melange—flesh, fish, and fowl apparently—strongly flavoured with garlic; the third bore a dish of jerked beef, cut into long shreds, and swimming in *sebo*, or lard; and the fourth bore a large dish full of that indescribable thing known by those who read Don Quixote as an *olla podrida*. The sable handmaidens began to circulate round the table, and every one helped himself to the dish that he most fancied. At length they placed them on the board, and brought massive silver salvers, with snow-white bread, twisted into strands in the baking, like junks of a cable; and water-jars, and yams nicely roasted and wrapped in plantain-leaves. These were, in like manner, handed round and then deposited on the table, and the domestics vanished.

We all got on cheerily enough, and both the captain and myself were finishing off with the *olla podrida*, with which, it so happened, we were familiar, and friend Bang, taking the time from us, took heart of grace, and straightway followed our example. There was a pause—rather an irksome one from its continuance, so much so, indeed, that knocking off from my more immediate business of gorging the aforesaid *olla podrida*, I looked up, and as it so happened, by accident, towards our friend Bang—and there he was, munching and screwing up his energies to swallow a large mouthful of the mixture, against which his stomach appeared to rebel. "Smollet's feast after the manner of the ancients," whispered Transom. At length he made a vigorous effort, and straightway sang out—*"L'eau de vie,* Don Ricardibus—some brandy, *mon ami*—for the love of all the respectable saints in the calendar."

Mine host laughed, but the females were most confoundedly posed. The younger ones ran for aromatic salts, while the lady of the house fetched some very peculiar distilled waters. She, in her kindness, filled a glass and helped Bang, but the instant he perceived the flavour he thrust it away.

"Aniseed—damn aniseed—no, no—obliged—*mucho, mucho*—but brandy *plaino*, that is, simple of itself, if you please—that's it—Lord love you, my dear madam—may you live a thousand years though."

The pure brandy was administered, and once more the dark beauties reappeared, the first carrying a bottle of vin-de-grave, the second one of vinotinto, or claret, and the third one of *l'eau de vie*, for Aaron's peculiar use. These were placed before the landlord, who helped himself to half a pint of claret, which he poured into a large tumbler, and then, putting a drop or two of water into it, tasted it, and sent it to his wife. In like manner he gave a smaller quantity to each of the other señoras, when the whole female part of the family drank our healths in a volley. But all this time the devil a thing drinkable was there before we males but goblets of pure cold water. Bang's *"mucho, mucho"* even failed him, for he had only, in his modesty, got a thimbleful of brandy to qualify the *olla podrida*. However, in a twinkling a beautiful long-necked bottle of claret was planted at each of our right hands, and of course we lost no time in returning the unlooked for civility of the ladies. Until this moment I had not got a proper glimpse of the three Virgins of the Sun, who were seated at table with us. They were very pretty Moorish-looking girls, as like as peas—dark hair, black eyes, clear colourless olive complexion, and no stays; but young and elastic as their figures were, this was no disadvantage. They were all three dressed in black silk petticoats, over a sort of cambric chemise, with large frills hanging down at the bosom; but gown, properly so called, they had none, their arms being unencumbered with any clothing heavier than a shoulder strap. The eldest was a fine full young woman of about nineteen; the second was more tall and stately, but slighter; and the youngest was—oh, she was an angel of light!—such hair, such eyes, and such a mouth! then her neck and bosom—

> "Oh, my Nora's gown for me,
>   To rise and fall as nature pleases,"

when the wearer *is*, as in the present case she *was*, young and beautiful. They all wore a long plain white gauze strap, like a broad ribbon—(little Reefpoint afterwards said they wore boat-pennants at their mastheads—I don't know what Madam Maradan Carson would call it)—in their hair, which fell down from amongst the braids nearly to their heels, and then they replied in their magnificent language, when casually addressed during dinner, with so much *naïveté*. We, the males of the party, had drank little or nothing—a bottle of claret or so a-piece—and a dram of brandy, to qualify a little vin-de-grave that we had flirted with during dinner, when our landlord rose, along with his brother-in-law, wished us a good afternoon, and departed to his counting-house, saying he would be back by dark, leaving the captain and me and friend Bang to amuse the ladies the best way we could, as the clerks had taken wing along with their master. Don Ricardo's departure seemed to be the signal for all hands breaking loose, and a regular romping match took place—the girls pro-

ducing their guitars; and we were all mighty frolicsome and happy, when a couple of *padres,* from the convent of La Merced, in their white flannel gowns,
black girdles, and shaven crowns, suddenly entered the hall. We, the foreign
part of the society, calculated on being pulled up by the *clerigos,* but deuce a
bit; on the contrary, the young females clustered round them, laughing and joking, while the Señora Campana presented them with goblets of claret, in which
they drank our healths, once and again, and before long they were gamboling
about, all shaven and shorn, like a couple of three-year-olds. Bang had a large
share of their assiduity, and, to see him waltzing with a fine, active, and—what
I fancy to be a rarity—a clean-looking priest, with his ever-recurring *"mucho,
mucho,"* was rather entertaining.

The director of the post-office, and a gentleman who was called the
"Corregidor de Tabaco"—literally the "corrector of tobacco"—dropped in
about this time, and one or two ladies, relatives of Mrs Campana, and Don
Ricardo returning soon after, we had sweetmeats and liqueurs, and coffee and
chocolate, and a game at monte, and maco, and were, in fact, very happy. But
the happiest day, as well as the most miserable, must have an end, and the
merry party dropped off, one after another, until we were left all alone with our
host's family. Madama soon after took her departure, wishing us a good-night.
She had no sooner gone than Bang began to shoot out his horns a bit. "I say,
Tom, ask the Don to let us have a drop of something hot, will you, a tumbler of
hot brandy-and-water, after the waltzing, eh?—I don't see the bedroom candles yet." Nor would he, if we had sat there till doomsday. Campana seemed to
have understood Bang; the brandy was immediately forthcoming, and we drew
in to the table to enjoy ourselves—Bang waxing talkative. "Now, what odd
names; why, what a strange office it must be for his majesty of Spain to employ
at every port a *corrector of tobacco;* that his liege subjects may not be imposed
on, I suppose—what capital cigars this same *corrector* must have, eh?"

I suppose it is scarcely necessary to mention that, throughout all the
Spanish American possessions, tobacco is a royal monopoly, and that the officer above alluded to is the functionary who has the management of it. Don
Ricardo, hearing something about cigars, took the hint, and immediately produced a straw case from his pocket and handed it to Bang.

"Mucho, mucho," quoth Bang; "capital, real Havannah."

So now, since we had all gotten fairly into the clouds, there was no saying
how long we should have remained in the seventh heaven; much would have
depended upon the continuance of the supply of brandy; but two female slaves

presently made their appearance, each carrying a *quatre*. I believe I have already described this easily-rigged couch somewhere: it is a hardwood frame, like what supports the loose top of a laundry table, with canvass stretched over the top of it, but in such a manner that it can be folded up flat and laid against the wall when not in use, while a bed can be immediately constructed by simply opening it and stretching the canvass. The handmaidens accordingly set to work to arrange two beds, or *quatres*—one on each side of the table where we were sitting—while Bang sat eyeing them askance, in a kind of wonderment as to the object of their preparations, which were by no means new either to the captain or me, who, looking on them as matters of course, continued in close confabulation with Don Ricardo during the operations.

"I say, Tom," at length quoth Bang, "are you to be laid out on one of these outlandish pieces of machinery, eh?"

"Why, I suppose so; and comfortable enough beds they are, I can assure you."

"Don't fancy them much, however," said Bang; "rather flimsy the frame-work."

The servants now very unceremoniously, no leave asked, began to clear away all the glasses and tumblers on the table.

"Hillo!" said the skipper, casting an inquiring glance at Campana, who, however, did not return it, but, as a matter of course apparently, rose, and taking a chair to the other end of the room, close by the door of an apartment which opened from it, began in cold blood to unlace and disburden himself of all his apparel, even unto his shirt.

This surprised us all a good deal, but our wonderment was lost on the Don, who got up from his seat, and in his linen garment, which was deucedly lacon-ic, made his formal bow, wished us good-night, and vanished through the door. By this, the ebony ladies had cleared the table of the crystal, and had capped it with a yellow leather mattress, with pillows of the same, both embossed with large tufts of red silk; on this they placed *one* sheet, and leaving a silver appa-ratus at the head, they disappeared—*"Buenas noches, señores—las camas estan listas."*

Bang had been unable to speak from excess of astonishment; but the skip-per and I, finding there was no help for it, had followed Campana's example, and kept pace with him in our *peeling,* so that, by the time he disappeared, we were ready to topple into our *quatres,* which we accordingly did, and by this time we were both at full length, with our heads eased each in one of Don

Ricardo's silk nightcaps, contemplating Bang's appearance, as he sat in disconsolate mood in his chair at the head of the table, with the fag-end of a cigar in the corner of his cheek.

"Now, Bang," said Transom, "turn in, and let us have a snooze, will ye?"

Bang did not seem to like it much.

"Zounds, Transom, did you ever hear of a gentleman being put to bed on a table? Why, it must be a quiz. Only fancy me dished out and served up like a great calipi in the shell! However, here goes—But surely this is in sorry taste; we had our chocolate a couple of hours ago—capital it was, by the by—in vulgar Staffordshire china, and now they give us silver—"

"Be decent, Bang," cut in the skipper, who was by this time more than half asleep.—"Be decent, and go to bed—that's a good fellow."

"Ah, well;" Aaron undressed himself and lay down; and there he was laid out, with a candle on each side of his head, his red face surmounted by a redder handkerchief tied round his head, sticking out above the white sheet; and supported by Captain Transom and myself, one on each side. All was now quiet. I got up and put out the candles, and, as I fell asleep, I could hear Aaron laughing to himself—"Dished, and served up, deuced like Saint Barts. I was intended for a doctor, Tom, you must know.—I hope the Don is not a medical amateur—I trust he won't have a touch at me before morning.—Rum, *subject* I should make—he! he!" All was silent for some time.

"Hillo!—what is that?" said Aaron again, as if suddenly aroused from his slumbers—"I say, none of your fun, Transom."

A large bat was *flaffing* about, and I could hear him occasionally *whir* near our faces.

"Oh, a bat!—hate bats—how the skipper snores!—I hope there be no resurrection—men in St Jago, or I shall be stolen away to a certainty before morning.—How should I look as a skeleton in a glass—ease, eh?"

I heard no more until, it might be, about midnight, when I was awakened, and frightened out of my wits, by Bang rolling *off* the table *on* to my *quatre* which he broke in his fall, and then we both rolled over and over on the floor.

"Murder!" roared Bang.—"I am bewitched and bedevilled. Murder! a scorpion has dropped from the roof into my mouth, and stung me on the nose. —Murder! Tom—Tom Cringle—Captain—Transom, my dear fellows, awake and send for the doctor. Oh my wig!—oh dear!—oh dear!"

At this uproar I could hear Don Ricardo striking a light, and presently he appeared with a candle in his hand, more than half naked, with la señora peering through the half-opened door behind him.

"*Ave Maria purissima*—what is the matter? Where is *el Señor Bang?*"

"*Mucho, mucho,*" shouted Bang from below the table. "Send for a doctoribus, Señor Richardum. I am dead and t'other thing—help!—help!"

"*Dios guarda usted,*" again ejaculated Campana. "*What has* befallen him?" addressing the skipper, who was by this time on his head's antipodes in bed, rubbing his eyes, and in great amazement.

"Tell him, my dear Transom, that a scorpion fell from the roof, and stung me on the nose."

"What says he?" inquired the Spaniard.

Poor Transom's intellect was at this time none of the clearest, being more than half asleep, and not quite so sober as a hermit is wont to be; besides he must needs speak Spanish, of which he was by no means master, which led to a very comical blunder. *Alacran*, in Spanish, means scorpion, and *Cayman*, an alligator, not very similar in sound, certainly, but the *termination* being the same, he selected in the hurry the wrong phrase.

"He says," replied Transom in bad Spanish, "that he has swallowed an alligator, or something of that sort, sir." Then a loud yawn.

"Swallowed a what?" rejoined Campana, greatly astonished.

"No, no," snorted the captain—"I am wrong—he says he has been *stung* by alligator."

"Stung by alligator?—impossible."

"Why, then," persisted the skipper, "if he be not stung by an alligator, or if he has not *really* swallowed one, at all events, an alligator has either stung or swallowed him—so make the most of it, Don Ricardo."

"Why, this is absurd, with all submission," continued Campana; "how the deuce could he swallow an alligator, or an alligator get into my house to annoy him?"

"D——n it," said Transom, half tipsy, and very sleepy—"that's his lookout.—You are very unreasonable, Don Ricardo; all that is the affair of friend Bang and the alligator; my purpose is solely to convey his meaning *faithfully*"—a loud snore.

"Oh," said Campana, laughing, "I see, I see; I left your friend *sobre mesa*" [on the table], but now I see that he is *sub rosa.*"

"Help, good people, help!" roared Bang—"help, or my nose will reach from this to the Moro Castle—Help!"

We got him out, and were I to live a thousand years, which would be a tolerably good spell, I don't think I could forget his appearance. His nose, usually the smallest article of the kind that I ever saw, was now swollen as large as my fist, and as purple as a mulberry—the distension of the skin, from the venomous sting of the reptile—for stung he *had been* by a scorpion—made it semi-transparent, so that it looked like a large *blob* of currant jelly hung on a peg in the middle of his face, or a gigantic leech, gorged with blood, giving his visage the semblance of some grotesque old-fashioned dial, with a fantastic gnomon.

"A poultice—a poultice—a poultice, good people, or I shall presently be all nose together!"—and a poultice was promptly manufactured from mashed pumpkin, and he was put to bed, with his face covered up with it, as if an Italian artist had been taking a cast of his beauties in plaster of Paris.

In the application of this said poultice, however, we had nearly extinguished poor Aaron amongst us, by suffocating him outright; for the skipper, who was the operating surgeon in the first instance, with me for his mate, clapped a whole ladleful over his mouth and nose, which, besides being scalding hot, sealed those orifices effectually, and, indeed, about a couple of tablespoonfuls had actually been forced down his gullet, notwithstanding his struggles, and exclamations of "Pumpkin—bad—softened with castor-oil—d——n it, skipper, you'll choke me"—spurt—sputter—sputter—"choke me, man."

"Cuidado," said Don Ricardo; "let me manage"—and he got a small tube of wild cane, which he stuck into Bang's mouth, through a hole in the poultice-cloth, and set a negro servant to watch that it did not sink into his gullet as he fell asleep, and with instructions to take the poultice off whenever the pain abated; and there he lay on his back, whistling through this artificial beak, like a sick snipe.

At length, however, all hands of us seemed to have fallen asleep; but towards the dawning I was awakened by repeated bursts of suppressed laughter, and, upon looking in the direction from whence the sounds proceeded, I was surprised beyond all measure to observe Transom in a corner of the room in his trousers and shirt, squatted like a tailor on his hams, with one of the sable damsels on her knees beside him holding a candle, while his Majesty's Post-Captain was plying his needle in a style and with a dexterity that would have charmed our friend Stultze exceedingly, and every now and then bending double over his work, and swinging his body backwards and forwards, with the water welling from his eyes, laughing all the while like to choke himself. As for his bronze candlestick, I thought she would have expired on the spot, with her white teeth glancing like ivory, and the tears running down her cheeks, as she every now and then clapped a handkerchief on her mouth to smother the uncontrollable uproariousness of her mirth.

"Why, captain, what spree is this?" said I.

"Never you mind, but come here. I say, Mr Cringle, do you see him piping away there?"—and there he was, sure enough, still gurgling through the wild cane, with his black guardian, whose province it was to have removed the poultice, sound asleep, snoring in the huge chair at Bang's head, wherein he had established himself, while the candle at his patient's cheek was flickering in the socket.

My superior was evidently bent on wickedness.

"Get up and put on your trousers, man."

I did so.

"Now wait a bit till I cooper him. Here, my darling"—to the sable virgin, who was now on the *qui vive*, bustling about—"here," said the captain, sticking out a leg of Bang's trousers, "hold you there, my dear—"

She happened to be a native of Haiti, and comprehended his French,

"Now, hold *you* that, Mr Cringle."

I took hold of the other leg, and held it in a fitting position, while Transom deliberately sewed them both up.

"Now for the coat-sleeves."

We sealed them in a similar manner.

"So—now for his shirt."

We sewed up the stem, and then the stern, converting it into an outlandish-looking pillow-case, and finally both sleeves; and, last of all, we got two live land-crabs from the servants by dint of persuasion and a little *plata*, and clapped one into each stocking-foot.

We then dressed ourselves, and when all was ready we got a piece of tape for a lanyard, and made one end fast to the handle of a large earthen water-jar, full to the brim, which we placed on Bang's pillow, and passed the other end round the neck of the sleeping negro.

"Now get you to bed," said the captain to the dingy handmaiden, "and stand by to be off, Mr Cringle."

He stepped to Don Ricardo's bedroom door, and tapped loudly.

"Hillo!" quoth the Don. On this hint, like men springing a mine, the last who leave the sap, we sprang into the street, when the skipper turned, and, taking aim with a large custard-apple which he had armed himself with (I have formerly described this fruit as resembling a russet bag of cold pudding), he let fly. Spin flew the apple—bash on the blackamoor's obtuse snout. He started back, and in his terror and astonishment threw a *somersault* over the back of his chair—gush poured the water—smash fell the pipkin. "Murder!" roared Bang, dashing off the poultice-cast with such fury that it lighted in the street—and away we raced at the top of our speed.

We ran as fast as our legs could carry us for two hundred yards, and then turning, walked deliberately home again, as if we had been out taking a walk in the cool morning air.

As we approached, we heard the yells of a negro, and Bang high in oath.

"You black rascal, nothing must serve your turn but practising your John Canoe tricks upon a gentleman! Take that, you villain, as a small recompense for floating me out of my bed—or rather off the table;" and the ludicrousness of his couch seemed to come over the worthy fellow once more, and he laughed loud and long. "Poor devil, I hope I have not hurt you? Here, Quashi, there's a pistole; go buy a plaster for your broken pate."

By this time we had returned in front of the house, and as we ascended the front stairs, we again heard a loud racketing within; but blackie's voice was now wanting in the row, wherein the Spaniard and our friend appeared to be the *dramatis personæ*—and sure enough there was Don Ricardo and Bang at it, tooth and nail.

"Allow me to assist you," quoth the Don.

"Oh no—*mucho—mucho,*" quoth Bang, who was spinning round and round in his shirt on one leg, trying to thrust his foot into his trousers; but the garment was impervious; and, after emulating Noblet in a pirouette, he sat down in despair.

We appeared—"Ah, Transom, glad to see you—some evil spirit has bewitched me, I believe—overnight I was stung to death by a scorpion—half an hour ago I was deluged by an invisible spirit—and just now, when I got up, and began to pull on my stockings, Lord! a land-crab was in the toe part, and see how he has scarified me"—forking up his peg. "I then tried my trousers," he continued, in a most doleful tone—"and lo! the legs are sealed. And look at my face, saw you ever such an unfortunate? But the devil take you, Transom, I see through your tricks now, and will pay you off for this yet, take my word for it."

The truth is, that our amigo Aaron had gotten an awful fright on his first awakening after his cold bath, for he had given the poor black fellow an ugly blow upon the face before he had gathered his senses well about him, and the next moment seeing the blood streaming from his nose, and mixing with the custard-like pulp of the fruit with which his face was plastered, he took it into his noddle that he had knocked the man's brains out. However, we righted the worthy fellow the best way we could, and shortly afterwards coffee was brought, and Bang, having got himself shaven and dressed, began to forget all his botherations.

But before we left the house, madama, Don Ricardo's better-half, insisted on anointing his nose with some mixture famous for reptile bites. His natural good-breeding made him submit to the application, which was neither more nor less than an infusion of indigo and ginger, with which the worthy lady painted our friend's face and muzzle in a most ludicrous manner—it was *heads* and *tails* between him and an ancient Briton. Reefpoint at this moment appeared at the door with a letter from the merchant captains, which had been sent down to the corvette, regarding the time of sailing, and acquainting us when they would be ready. While Captain Transom was perusing it, Bang was practising Spanish at the expense of Don Ricardo, whom he had boxed into a corner; but all his Spanish seemed to be scraps of schoolboy Latin, and I noticed that Campana had the greatest difficulty in keeping his countenance. At length Don Ricardo approached us—"Gentlemen, I have laid out a little plan for the day; it is my wife's saint's day, and a holiday in the family, so we propose going to a coffee property of mine about ten miles from Santiago, and staying till morning—What say you?"

I chimed in—"I fear, sir, that I shall be unable to accompany you, even if Captain Transom should be good enough to give me leave, as I have an errand to do for that unhappy young fellow that we spoke about last evening—some trinkets which I promised to deliver; here they are"—and I produced the miniature and crucifix.

Campana winced—"Unpleasant, certainly, lieutenant," said he.

"I know it will be so myself, but I have *promised*—"

"Then far be it from me to induce you to break your promise," said the worthy man. "My son," said he, gravely, "the friar you saw yesterday is confessor to Don Picador Cangrejo's family; his reason for asking to obtain an interview with you was from its being known that you were active in capturing the unfortunate men with whom young Federico Cangrejo, his only son, was leagued. Oh that poor boy! Had you known him, gentlemen, as I knew him, poor, poor Federico!"

"He was an awful villain, however, you must allow," said the captain.

"Granted in the fullest sense, my dear sir," rejoined Campana; "but we are all frail, erring creatures, and he was hardly dealt by. He is now gone to his heavy account, and I may as well tell you the poor boy's sad story at once. Had you but seen him in his prattling infancy, in his sunny boyhood!

"He was the only son of a rich old father, an honest but worldly man, and of a most peevish, irascible temper. Poor Federico, and his sister Francisca, his only sister, were often cruelly used; and his orphan cousin, my sweet goddaughter, Maria Olivera, their playmate, was, if anything, more harshly treated; for although his mother was and is a must excellent woman, and always stood between them and the old man's ill temper, yet at the time I speak of she had returned to Spain, where a long period of ill-health detained her for upwards of three years. Federico by this time was nineteen years of age, tall, handsome, and accomplished beyond all the youth of his rank and time of life in Cuba: but you have seen him, gentlemen—in his extremity it is true; yet, fallen as he was, I mistake if you thought him a *common* man. For good or for evil, my heart told me he would be conspicuous, and I was, alas the day! too true a prophet. His attachment to his cousin, who, on the death of her mother, had become an inmate of Don Picador's house, had been evident to all but the purblind old man for a long time; and when he did discover it, he imperatively forbade all intercourse between them, as, forsooth, he had projected a richer match for him, and shut Maria up in a corner of his large mansion. Federico, haughty and proud, could not stomach this. He ceased to reside at his father's estate, which had been confided to his management, and began to frequent the billiard-table, and monte-table, and taverns, and in a thousand ways gave, from less to more, such unendurable offence, that his father at length shut his door against him, and turned him, with twenty doubloons in his pocket, into the street.

"Friends interceded, for the feud soon became public, and, amongst others, I essayed to heal it; and with the fond, although passionate father, I easily succeeded: but how true it is that 'evil communication corrupts good manners!' I found Federico by this time linked in bands of steel with a junto of desperadoes, whose calling was anything but equivocal, and implacable to a degree, that, knowing him as I had known him, I had believed impossible. But, alas! the human heart is indeed desperately wicked. I struggled long with the excellent Father Carera to bring about a reconciliation, and thought we had succeeded, as Federico was induced to return to his father's house once more, and for many days and weeks we all flattered ourselves that he had reformed; until one morning, about four months ago, he was discovered coming out of his cousin's room about the dawning by his father, who immediately charged him with seducing his ward. High words ensued. Poor Maria rushed out and threw herself at her uncle's feet. The old man, in a transport of fury, kicked her on the face as she lay prostrate; whereupon, God help me! he was felled to the earth by his own flesh and bone and blood—by his abandoned son.

> "What rein can hold licentious wickedness,
> When down the hill he holds his fierce career?"

The rest is soon told;—he joined the pirate vessels at Puerto Escondido, and, from his daring and reckless intrepidity, soon rose to command amongst them, and was proceeding in his infernal career, when the God whom he had so fearfully defied at length sent him to expiate his crimes on the scaffold."

"But the priest—" said I, much excited.

"True," continued Don Ricardo, "Padre Carera brought a joint message from his poor mother and sister, and—and, oh in darling god-child, my heart—dear Maria!—" And the kind old man wept bitterly. I was greatly moved.

"Why, Mr Cringle," said Transom, "if you *have* promised to deliver the trinkets *in propria persona*, there's an end: *take* leave—nothing doing down yonder—send Tailtackle for clothes. Mr Reefpoint, go to the boat and send up Tailtackle; so go you must to these unfortunates, and we shall then start on our cruise to the coffee estate with our worthy host."

"Why," said Campana, "the family are in the country; they live about four miles from Santiago, on the very road to my property, and we shall call on our way; but I don't much admire these interviews—there will be a *scene*, I fear—"

"Not on my part," said I; "but *call* I must, for I solemnly promised"—and presented the miniature to Don Ricardo.

Campana looked at it. It was exquisitely finished, and represented a most beautiful girl—a dark, large-eyed, sparkling, Spanish beauty. "Oh, my dear, dear child," murmured Don Ricardo, "how like this *was* to what you *were*; how changed you are *now* from what it *is*—alas! alas! But come, gentlemen, my wife is ready, and my two nieces"—the pretty girls who were of our party the previous evening—"and here are the horses."

At this moment the little midshipman, Master Reefpoint—a great favourite of mine, by the by—reappeared, with Tailtackle behind him, carrying my bundle. I was regularly caught, as the clothes, on the *chance* of a lark, had been brought from the ship, although stowed out of sight under the stern-sheets of the boat.

Here are your clothes, Mr Cringle," quoth *middy*.

"Devil confound your civility," internally murmured I.

The captain twigged, and smiled. Upon which little Reefy stole up to me—
"Lord, Mr Cringle, could you but get *me* leave to go, it would be such a—"

"Hold your tongue, boy, how can I—"

Transom struck in—"Master Reefpoint, I see what you are driving at; but
how shall the Firebrand be taken care of when *you* are away, eh? besides, *you*
have no clothes, and we shall be away a couple of days, most probably."

"Oh, yes, sir, I have clothes; I have a hair-brush and a toothbrush, and two
shirt-collars, in my waistcoat pocket."

"Very well, can we venture to lumber our kind friends with this giant, Mr
Cringle, and can we really leave the ship without him?" Little Reefy was now all
alive. "Tailtackle, go on board—say we shall be back to dinner the day after to-
morrow," said the captain.

We now made ready for the start, and certainly the cavalcade was rather a
remarkable one. First, there was an old lumbering family *volante,* a sort of gig,
with four posts or uprights supporting a canopy covered with leather, and with
a high dash-iron or splash-board in front. There were curtains depending from
this canopy, which on occasion could be let down, so as to cover in the sides and
front. The whole was of the most clumsy workmanship that can be imagined,
and hung by untanned leather straps in a square wooden frame, from the front
of which again protruded two shafts, straight as Corinthian pillars, and equally
substantial, embracing an uncommonly fine mule, one of the largest and handsomest of the species which I had seen. The harnessing partook of the same
kind of unwieldy strength and solidity, and was richly embossed with silver and
dirt. Astride on this *mulo* sat a household negro, with a huge thong of bullock's
hide in one hand and the reins in the other. In this *voiture* were ensconced La
Señora Campana, a portly concern, as already mentioned, two of her bright
black-eyed laughing nieces, and Master Reefpoint, invisible as he lay smothered amongst the ladies, all to his little glazed cocked-hat, and jabbering away
in a most unintelligible fashion, so far as the young ladies, and like the old one,
were concerned. However, they appeared all mightily tickled by little Reefy,
either mentally or physically, for off they trundled, laughing and *skirling* loud
above the noise and creaking of the *volante.* Then came three small, ambling,
stoutish, long-tailed ponies, the biggest not above fourteen hands high; these
were the barbs intended for mine host, the skipper, and myself, caparisoned

with high demipique old-fashioned Spanish saddles, mounted with silver stir-rups and clumsy bridles, with a ton of rusty iron in each poor brute's mouth for a bit, and curbs like a piece of our chain cable, all very rich, and, as before men-tioned with regard to the *volante*, far from clean. Their pace was a fast run, a compound of walk, trot, and canter, or rather of a trot and a canter, the latter broken down and frittered away through the instrumentality of a ferocious Mameluke bit, but as easy as an arm-chair; and this was—I speak it feelingly—a great convenience, as a sailor is not a Centaur—not altogether of a piece with his horse, as it were; yet both Captain Transom and myself were rather goodish horsemen for nauticals, although rather apt to go over the bows upon broaching-to suddenly. Don Ricardo's costume would have been thought a little out of the way in Leicestershire; most people put on their boots "when they do a-riding go," but he chose to mount in shoes and white cotton stockings, and white jean small-clothes, with a flowing yellow-striped gingham coat, the skirts of which fluttered in the breeze behind him, his withered face shaded by a huge Panama hat, and with enormous silver spurs on his heels, the rowels two inches in diameter.

Away lumbered the *volante,* and away we pranced after it. For the first two miles the scenery was tame enough; but after that, the gently swelling emi-nences on each side of the road rose abruptly into rugged mountains; and the dell between them, which had hitherto been verdant with waving guinea-grass, became covered with large trees, under the dark shade of which we lost sight of the sun, and the contrast made everything around us for a time almost undis-tinguishable. The forest continued to overshadow the high-road for two miles farther, only broken by a small cleared patch now and then, where the sharp-spiked limestone rocks shot up like minarets, and the fire-scathed stumps of the felled trees stood out amongst the rotten earth in the crevices, from which, however, sprang yams and cocoas, and peas of all kinds, and granadillos, and a profusion of herbs and roots, with the greatest luxuriance.

At length we came suddenly upon it cleared space—a most beautiful spot of ground—where, in the centre of a green plot of velvet grass, intersected with numberless small walks gravelled from a neighbouring rivulet, stood a large one-storey wooden edifice, built in the form of a square, with a courtyard in the centre. From the moistness of the atmosphere, the outside of the unpainted weather-boarding had a green, damp appearance, and, so far as the house itself was concerned, there was an air of great discomfort about the place. A large open balcony ran round the whole house on the outside, and fronting us there was a clumsy wooden porch, supported on pillars, with the open door yawning behind it.

The hills on both sides were cleared and planted with most luxuriant coffee-bushes and provision grounds, while the house was shaded by several splendid star-apple and kennip trees, and there was a border of rich flowering shrubs surrounding it on all sides. The hand of woman had been there!

A few half-naked negroes were lounging about, and on hearing our approach they immediately came up and stared wildly at us.

All fresh from the ship these," quoth Bang.

Can't be," said Transom—"Try and see."

I spoke some of the commonest Spanish expressions to them, but they neither understood them nor could they answer me. But Bang was more successful in Eboe and Mandingo, both of which he spoke fluently—accomplishments which I ought to have excepted, by the by, when I declared he was little skilled in any tongue but English.

Large herds of cattle were grazing on the skirts of the wood, and about one hundred mules were scrambling and picking their food in a rocky river-course which bisected the valley. The hills, tree-covered, rose around this solitary residence in all directions, as if it had been situated in the bottom of a punch-bowl; while a small waterfall, about thirty feet high, fell so near one of the corners of the building that, when the wind set that way, as I afterwards found, the spray moistened my hair through the open window in my sleeping apartment. We proceeded to the door and dismounted, following the example of our host, and proceeded to help the gentlewomen to alight from their *volante*. When we all were accounted for in the porch, Don Ricardo began to shout, *"Criados, criados, ven acá—pendejos, ven acá!"* The call was for some time unattended to; at length two tall, good-looking, decently-dressed negroes made their appearance and took charge of our bestias and carriage; but all this time there was no appearance of any living creature belonging to the family.

The dark hall, into which the porch opened, was paved with the usual diamond-shaped bricks and tiles, but was not ceiled—the rafters of the roof being exposed. There was little or no furniture in it that we could see, except a clumsy table in the centre of the room, and one or two of the leathern-backed reclining chairs, such as Whiffle used to patronise. Several doors opened from this comfortless saloon, which was innocent of paint, into other apartments, one of which was ajar.

"Estraño," murmured Don Ricardo, *"muy estraño!"*

"Coolish reception this, Tom," quoth Aaron Bang.

"Deucedly so," said the skipper.

But Campana—hooking his little fat wife under his arm, while we did the agreeable to the nieces—now addressed himself to enter, with the constant preliminary ejaculation of all well-bred Spaniards in crossing a friend's threshold, *"Ave Maria purissima,"* when we were checked by a loud tearing fit of coughing, which seemed almost to suffocate the patient, and female voices in great alarm, proceeding from the room beyond.

Presently a little anatomy of a man presented himself at the door of the apartment, wringing his hands, and apparently in great misery. Campana and his wife, with all the alacrity of kind-hearted people, immediately went up to him and said something which I did not overhear, but the poor creature to whom they spoke appeared quite bewildered. "What is it, Don Picador?" at length we could hear Campana say—"what is it?—Is it my poor dear Maria who is worse, or what?—speak man—May my wife enter?"

"Si, si—yes, yes," said the afflicted Don Picador—"yes, yes, let her go in; send—for I am unable to think or act—send one of my people back post to Santiago for the doctor—Haste, haste.—*Sangre—hecha sangre por la boca."*

"Good God, why did you not say so before?" rejoined Campana.

Here his wife called loudly to her husband, *"Ricardo, Ricardo, por amor de su alma, manda por el medico*—she has burst a bloodvessel—Maria is dying!"

"Let me mount myself; I will go myself." And the excellent man rushed for the door, when the poor heartbroken Picador clung to his knees.

"No, no, don't leave me.—Send some one else—"

"Take care, man, let me go—"

Transom and I volunteered in a breath—"No, no, I will go myself," continued Don Ricardo; "let go, man—God help me, the old creature is crazed—*el viejo no vale."*

"Here, here! help, Don Ricardo!" cried his wife.

Off started Transom for the doctor, and into the room rushed Don Picador and Campana, and from the sounds in the sick-chamber, all seemed bustle and confusion. At length the former appeared to be endeavouring to lift the poor sufferer, so as to enable her to sit up in bed; in the mean time her coughing had gradually abated into a low suffocating convulsive gasp.

"So, so, lift her up, man," we could hear Campana say; "lift her up—quick— or she will be suffocated."

At length, in a moment of great irritation, excited on the one hand by his intense interest in the poor suffering girl, and anger at the peevish, helpless Don Picador, Don Ricardo, to our unutterable surprise, rapped out, in *gude* broad Scotch, as he brushed away Señor Cangrejo from the bedside with a violence that spun him out of the door—"*God, the auld doited deevil is as fusionless as a docken.*"

My jaw dropped—I was thunderstruck; Bang's eye met mine—"Murder!" quoth Bang, so soon as his astonishment let him collect breath enough "and here I have been for two whole days practising Spanish, "to my great improvement no doubt, upon a Scotchman—how edified he must have been!"

"But the *docken*, man," said I; "*fusionless as a docken*—how classic! what an exclamation to proceed from the mouth of a solemn Don!"

"No gibes regarding the docken," promptly chimed in Bang, "it is a highly respectable vegetable, let me tell you, and useful on occasion, which is more."

The noise in the room ceased, and presently Campana joined us. "We must proceed," said he, "it will never do for you to deliver the jewels *now*, Mr Cringle; she is too much excited already, even from seeing me."

But it was more easy to determine on proceeding than to put it in execution, for a heavy cloud that had been overhanging the small valley the whole morning had by this time spread out and covered the entire face of nature like a sable pall. The birds of the air flew low, and seemed perfectly gorged with the superabundance of flies, which were thickly betaking themselves for shelter under the evergreen leaves of the bushes. All the winged creation, great and small, were fast hastening to the cover of the leaves and branches of the trees. The cattle were speeding to the hollows under the impending rocks; negroes, men, women, and children, were hurrying with their hoes on their shoulders past the windows to their huts. Several large bloodhounds had ventured into the hall, and were crouching with a low whine at our feet. The huge carrion crows were the only living things which seemed to brave the approaching *chubasco*, and were soaring high up in the heavens, appearing to touch the black agitated fringe of the lowering thunder-clouds. All other kinds of winged creatures, parrots and pigeons and cranes, had vanished by this time under the thickest trees, and into the deepest coverts, and the wild ducks were shooting past in long lines, piercing the thick air with outstretched neck and clanging wing.

Suddenly the wind fell, and the sound of the waterfall increased, and grew rough and loud, and the undefinable rushing noise that precedes a heavy fall of rain in the tropics—the voice of the wilderness—moaned through the high woods, until at length the clouds sank upon the valley in boiling mists, rolling half-way down the surrounding hills; and the water of the stream, whose scanty rill but an instant before hissed over the precipice, in a small transparent ribbon of clear grass-green, sprinkled with white foam, and then threaded its way round the large rocks in its capacious channel, like a silver eel twisting through a dry desert, now changed in a moment to a dark turgid chocolate colour; and even as we stood and looked, lo! a column of water from the mountains pitched in thunder over the face of the precipice, making the earth tremble, and driving up from the rugged face of the everlasting rocks in smoke, and forcing the air into eddies and sudden blasts, which tossed the branches of the trees that overhung it, as they were dimly seen through the clouds of drizzle, as if they had been shaken by a tempest, although there was, not a breath stirring elsewhere out of heaven; while little wavering spiral wreaths of mist rose up thick from the surface of the boiling pool at the bottom of the cataract, like miniature waterspouts, until they were dispersed by the agitation of the air above.

At length the swollen torrent rolled roaring down the narrow valley, filling the whole watercourse, about fifty yards wide, and advancing with a solid front a fathom *high*—a fathom *deep* does not convey the idea—like a stream of lava, or as one may conceive of the Red Sea, when, at the stretching forth of the hand of the prophet of the Lord, its mighty waters rolled back and stood heaped up as a wall to the host of Israel. The channel of the stream, which but a minute before I could have leaped across, was the next instant filled, and utterly impassable.

"You can't possibly move," said Don Picador; "you can neither go on nor retreat; you must stay until the river subsides." And the rain now began pattering in large drops, like scattering shots preceding an engagement, on the wooden shingles with which the house was roofed, gradually increasing to a loud rushing noise, which, as the rooms were not ceiled, prevented a word being heard.

Don Ricardo began to fret and fidget most awfully—"Beginning of the *seasons*—why, we may not get away for a week, and all the ships will be kept back in their loading."

All this time the poor sufferer's tearing cough was heard in the lulls of the rain; but it gradually became less and less severe, and the lady of the house, and Señora Campana, and Don Picador's daughter, at length slid into the room on tiptoe, leaving one of Don Ricardo's nieces in the room with the sick person.

"She is asleep—hush." The weather continued as bad as ever, and we passed a very comfortless forenoon of it, Picador, Campana, Bang, and myself, perambulating the large dark hall, while the ladies were clustered together in a corner with their work. At length the weather cleared, and I could get a glimpse of mine hostess and her fair daughter. The former was a very handsome woman, about forty; she was tall, and finely formed; her ample figure set off by the very simple, yet, to my taste, very elegant dress formerly described: it was neither more nor less than the plain black silk petticoat over a chemise, made full at the bosom, with a great quantity of lace frills: her dark glossy hair was gathered on the crown of her head in one long braid, twisted round and round, and rising up like a small turret. Over all she wore a loose shawl of yellow silk crape. But the daughter, I never shall forget her! Tall and full, and magnificently shaped—every motion was instinct with grace. Her beautiful black hair hung a yard down her back—long and glossy—in three distinct braids, while it was shaded, Madonna-like, off her high and commanding forehead. Her eyebrows—to use little Reefy's simile—looked as if cut out of a mouse's skin; and her eyes themselves, large, dark, and soft, yet brilliant and sparkling at the same time, however contradictory this may read; her nose was straight, and her cheeks firm and oval, and her mouth, her full lips, her ivory teeth, her neck and bosom, were perfect, the latter if anything giving promise of too matronly a womanhood; but at the time I saw her, nothing could have been more beautiful; and, above all, there was an *inexpressible* charm in the clear transparent darkness of her colourless skin, *into which you thought you could look;* her shoulders, and the upper part of her arms, were peculiarly beautiful. Nothing is so exquisitely lovely as the upper part of a beautiful woman's arm, and yet we have lived to see this admirable feature shrouded and lost in those abominable gigots.—I say, messmate, lend a hand and originate a crusade against those vile appendages. I will lead into action if you like,—"Woe to the women that sew pillows to all arm-holes," Ezekiel, xiii. 18. May I venture on such a quotation in such a place?—She was extremely like her brother; and her fine face was overspread with the pale cast of thought—a settled melancholy, like the shadow of a cloud in a calm day on a summer landscape, mantled over her fine features; and although she moved with the air of a princess, and was possessed of that natural politeness which far surpasses all artificial polish, yet the heaviness of her heart was apparent in every motion, as well as in all she said.

Many people labour under an unaccountable delusion, imagining, in their hallucination, that a Frenchwoman, for instance, or even an Englishwoman—nay, some have been heard to say that a Scotchwoman—has been known to *walk*. Egregious errors all! An Irishwoman of the true Milesian descent can *walk* a step or two sometimes, but all other women—fair or brown, short or tall, stout or thin—only stump, shuffle, jig, or amble—none but a Spaniard can *walk*.

Once or twice she tried to enter into conversation with me on indifferent subjects; but there was a constant tendency to approach (against her own pre-arranged determination) the one, all-absorbing one, the fate of her poor brother. "Oh, had you but known him, Mr Cringle—had you but known him in his boyhood, before bad company had corrupted him!" exclaimed she, after having asked me if he died penitent, and she turned away and wept. *"Francisca,"* said a low hoarse female voice from the other room—*"Francisca, ven acá, mi querida hermana."* The sweet girl rose, and sped across the floor with the grace of Taglioni (oh, the *legs Taglionis!*—as poor dear Bang would have ventured to have said, if the sylphide had then been known), and presently returning, whispered something to her mother, who rose and drew Don Picador aside. The waspish old man shook himself clear of his wife, as he said with indecent asperity—"No, no; she will but make a fool of herself."

His wife drew herself up, —

"She never made a fool of herself, Don Picador, but once; and God forgive those who were the cause of it!—It is not kind of you, indeed it is not."

"Well, well," rejoined the querulous old man, "do as you will, do as you will; always crossing me, always crossing."

His wife took no further notice, but stepped across the room to me,—"Our poor dying Maria knows you are here; and probably you are not aware that *he* wrote to her after his"—her voice quivered—"after his condemnation, the night before he suffered, that you were the only one who showed him kindness, and she has also read the newspapers giving an account of the trial. She wishes to see you—will you pleasure her? Señora Campana has made her acquainted that you are the bearer of some trinkets belonging to him, from which she infers you witnessed his last moments, as one of them, she was told, was her picture, poor dear girl; and she knew *that must have grown to his heart till the last.* But it will be too agitating. I will try and dissuade her from the interview until the doctor comes, at all events."

The worthy lady stepped again into Maria's apartment, and I could not avoid hearing what passed.

"My dear Maria, Mr Cringle has no objection to wait on you; but after your severe attack this morning, I don't think it will be wise. Delay it until Dr Bergara comes—at any rate, until the evening, Maria."

"Mother," she said, in a weak, plaintive voice, although husky from the phlegm which was fast coagulating in her throat—"Mother, I have already ceased to be of this world; I am dying, dearest mother, fast dying; and oh, thou all-good and all-merciful Being, against whom I have fearfully sinned, would that the last struggle were now o'er, and that my weary spirit were released, and my shame bidden in the silent tomb, and my sufferings and very name forgotten!" She paused and gasped for breath; I thought it was all over with her; but she rallied again and proceeded—"Time is rapidly ebbing from me, dearest mother—for mother I must call you, more than a mother have you been to me—and the ocean of eternity is opening to my view. If I am to see him at all, I must see him now; I shall be more agitated by the expectation of the interview than by seeing him at once. Oh! let me see him now, let me look on one who witnessed *his* last moments."

I could see Señora Cangrejo where she stood. She crossed her hands on her bosom, and looked up towards heaven, and then turned mournfully towards me, and beckoned me to approach. I entered the small room, which had been fitted up by the poor girl with some taste; the furniture was better than any I had seen in a Spanish house before, and there was a mat on the floor, and some exquisite miniatures and small landscapes on the walls. It was her boudoir, opening apparently in a bedroom beyond. It was lighted by a large open unglazed window, with a row of wooden balustrades beyond it, forming part of a small balcony. A Carmelite friar—a venerable old man, with the hot tears fast falling from his eyes over his wrinkled cheeks, whom I presently found to be the excellent Padre Carera—sat in a large chair by the bedside, with a silver cup in his hand, beside which lay a large crucifix of the same metal; he had just administered extreme unction, and the *viaticum*, he fondly hoped, would prove a passport for his dear child to another and a better world. As I entered he rose, held out his hand to me, and moved round to the bottom of the bed.

The shutters had been opened, and, with a suddenness which no one can comprehend who has not lived in these climates, the sun now shone brightly on the flowers and garden plants which grew in a range of pots on the balcony, and lighted up the pale features of a lovely girl, lovely even in the jaws of death, as she lay with her face towards the light, supported in a reclining position on cushions, on a red Morocco mattress, laid on a sort of frame or bed.

"Light was her form, and darkly delicate
That brow, whereon her native sun hath sat,
But had not marred."

She was tall, so far as I could judge, but oh, how attenuated! Her lower limbs absolutely made no impression on the mattress, to which her frame appeared to cling, giving a ghastly conspicuousness to the œdematous swelling of her feet, and to her person, for, alas! she was in a way to have become a mother—

"The offspring of his wayward youth,
When he betrayed Bianca's truth;
The maid whose folly could confide
In *him*, who made her not his bride."

Her hand, grasping her pocket-handkerchief—drenched, alas, with blood—hung over the side of the bed, thin and pale, with her long taper fingers as transparent as if they had been fresh cut alabaster with the blue veins winding through her wrists, and her bosom wasted and shrunk, and her neck no thicker than her arm, with the pulsations of the large arteries as plain and evident as if the skin had been a film; and her beautiful features—although now sharpened by the near approaching death-agony—her lovely mouth, her straight nose, her arched eyebrows, black, like pencilled jet lines, and her small ears; and oh, who can describe her rich black raven hair, lying combed out, and spread all over the bed and pillow! She was dressed in a long loose gown of white crape; it looked like a winding-sheet; but the fire of her eyes—I have purposely not ventured to describe them the unearthly brilliancy of her large, full, swimming eye!

When I entered I bowed, and remained standing near the door. She said something, but in so low a voice that I could not catch the words; and when I stepped nearer, on purpose to hear more distinctly, all at once the blood mantled in her cheeks, and forehead, and throat, like the last gleam of the setting sun; but it faded as rapidly, and once more she lay pale as her smock—

"Yet not such blush as mounts as when health would show
All the heart's hue in that delightful glow;
But 'twas a hectic tint of secret care,
That for a burning moment fevered there;
And the wild sparkle of her eve seemed caught
From high, and lightened with electric thought;

> Though its black orb these long low lashes' fringe
> Had tempered with a melancholy tinge."

Her voice was becoming more and more weak, she said, so she must be prompt. "You have some trinkets for me, Mr Cringle?" I presented them. She kissed the crucifix fervently, and then looked mournfully on her own miniature. "This was thought like *once*, Mr Cringle.—Are the newspaper accounts of his trial correct?" she next asked. I answered, that in the main facts they were. "And do you believe in the commission of all these alleged atrocities by him?" I remained silent. "Yes, they are but too true. Hush, hush," said she— "look there."

I did as she requested. There, glancing bright in the sunshine, a most beautiful butterfly fluttered in the air, in the very middle of the open window. When we first saw it, it was flitting gaily and happily amongst the plants and flowers that were blooming in the balcony, but it gradually became more and more slow on the wing, and at last poised itself so unusually steady for an insect of its class, that even had Maria not spoken, it would have attracted my attention. Below it, on the windowsill, near the wall, with head erect, and its little basilisk eyes upturned towards the lovely fly, crouched a chameleon lizard; its beautiful body, when I first looked at it, was a bright sea-green. It moved into the sunshine, a little away from the shade of the laurel bush, which grew on the side it first appeared on, and suddenly the back became transparent amber, the legs and belly continuing green. From its breast under the chin, it every now and then shot out a semicircular film of a bright scarlet colour, like a leaf of a tulip stretched vertically, or the pectoral fin of a fish.

This was evidently a decoy, and the poor fly was by degrees drawn down towards it, either under the impression of its being in reality a flower, or impelled by some impulse which it could not resist. It gradually flitted nearer and more near, the reptile remaining all the while steady as a stone, until it made a sudden spring, and in the next moment the small mealy wings were quivering on each side of the chameleon's tiny jaws. While in the act of gorging its prey, a little fork, like a wire, was projected from the opposite corner of the window; presently a small round black snout, with a pair of little fiery blasting eyes, appeared, and a thin black neck glanced in the sun. The lizard saw it. I could fancy it trembled. Its body became of a dark blue, then ashy pale, the imitation of the flower; the gaudy fin was withdrawn; it appeared to shrink back as far as it could; but it was nailed or fascinated to the window-sill, for its feet did not move. The head of the snake approached, with its long forked tongue shooting out and shortening, and with a low hissing noise. By this time about two feet of its body was visible, lying with its white belly on the wooden beam, moving forward with a small horizontal wavy motion, the head and six inches of the neck being a little raised. I shrank back from the serpent, but no one else seemed to have any dread of it; indeed, I afterwards learned, that this kind, being good mousers, and otherwise quite harmless, were, if anything, encouraged about houses in the country. I looked again; its open mouth was now within an inch of the lizard, which by this time seemed utterly paralysed and motionless; the next instant its head was drawn into the snake's mouth, and by degrees the whole body disappeared, as the reptile gorged it, and I could perceive from the lump which gradually moved down the snake's neck, that it had been sucked into its stomach. Involuntarily I raised my hand, when the whole suddenly disappeared.

I turned, I could scarcely tell why, to look at the dying girl. A transient flush had again lit up her pale wasted face. She was evidently greatly excited. "Can you read me that riddle, Mr Cringle? Does no analogy present itself to you between what you have seen, between the mysterious power possessed by these subtile reptiles, and—Look—look again."

A large and still more lovely butterfly suddenly rose from beneath where the snake had vanished, all glittering in the dazzling sunshine, and, after fluttering for a moment, floated steadily up into the air, and disappeared in the blue sky. My eye followed it as long as it was visible; and when it once more declined to where we had seen the snake, I saw a most splendid dragon-fly, about three inches long, like a golden bodkin, with its gauze-like wings moving so quickly, as it hung steadily poised in mid air, like a hawk preparing to stoop, that the body seemed to be surrounded by silver tissue, or a bright halo, while it glanced in the sunbeam.

"Can you not read it yet, Mr Cringle? can you not read my story in the fate of the first beautiful fly, and the miserable end of my Federico, in that of the lizard? And oh, may the last appearance of that ethereal thing, which but now rose, and melted into the lovely sky, be a true type of what I shall be! But that poor insect, that remains there suspended between heaven and earth—shall I say hell?—what am I to think of it?"

The dragon-fly was still there. She continued—*"En purgatorio, ah Dios, tu quedas en purgatorio,"* as if the fly had represented the unhappy young pirate's soul in limbo. Oh, let no one smile at the quaintness of the dying fancy of the poor heart-crushed girl. The weather began to lower again, the wind came past us moaningly—the sun was obscured—large drops of rain fell heavily into the room—a sudden dazzling flash of lightning took place, *and the dragon-fly was no longer there.* A long low wild cry was heard. I started, and my flesh creeped. The cry was repeated. *"Es el—el mismo, y ningun otro. Me venga, Frederico; me venga mi querido!"* shrieked poor Maria, with a supernatural energy, and with such piercing distinctness, that it was heard shrill even above the rolling thunder.

I turned to look at Maria—another flash. It glanced on the crucifix which the old priest had elevated at the foot of the bed, full in her view. It was nearer, the thunder was louder. "Is that the rain-drops which are falling heavily on the floor through the open window?" O God! O God! it is her warm heart's blood, which was bubbling from her mouth like a crimson fountain. Her pale fingers were clasped on her bosom in the attitude of prayer—a gentle quiver of her frame—and the poor brokenhearted girl, and her unborn babe, "sleeped the sleep that knows no waking."

CHAPTER XIV.

SCENES IN CUBA.

Ariel.   "Safely in harbour
Is the king's ship; in the deep nook, where once
Thou calledst me up at midnight to fetch dew
From the still-vexed Bermoothes—there she's bid."

The Tempest.

THE SPIRIT had indeed fled—the ethereal essence had departed—and the poor wasted and blood-stained husk which lay before us, could no longer be moved by our sorrows, or gratified by our sympathy. Yet I stood riveted to the spot, until I was aroused by the deep-toned voice of Padre Carera, who, lifting up his hands towards heaven, addressed the Almighty in extempore prayer, beseeching his mercy to our erring sister who had just departed. The unusualness of this startled me.—"As the tree falls, so must it lie," had been the creed of my forefathers, and was mine; but now for the first time I heard a clergyman wrestling in mental agony, and interceding with the God who hath said,

"Repent before the night cometh, in which no man can work," for a sinful creature, whose worn-out frame was now as a clod of the valley. But I had little time for consideration, as presently all the negro servants of the establishment set up a loud howl, as if they had lost their nearest and dearest. "Oh, our poor dear young mistress is dead!—She has gone to the bosom of the Virgin!—She is gone to be happy!"—"Then why the deuce make such a yelling?" quoth Bang in the other room, when this had been translated to him. Glad to leave the chamber of death, I entered the large hall, where I had left our friend.

"I say, Tom—awful work. Hear how the rain pours, and—murder—such a flash! Why, in Jamaica, we don't startle greatly at lightning, but absolutely I heard it hiss—there again." The noise of the thunder stopped farther colloquy, and the wind now burst down the valley with a loud roar.

Don Ricardo joined us. "My good friends, we are in a scrape here—what is to be done?—a melancholy affair altogether."—Bang's curiosity here fairly got the better of him.

"I say, Don Ricardibus, do—beg pardon, though—do give over this humbugging outlandish lingo of yours; speak like a Christian, in your mother tongue, and leave off your Spanish, which *now,* since I know it is all a *bam,* seems to sit as strangely on you as my grandmother's *toupée* would on Tom Cringle's Mary."

"Now do, pray, Mr Bang," said I, when Don Ricardo broke in—

"Why, Mr Bang, I am, as you now know, a Scotchman."

"How do I know any such thing—that is, for a certainty—while you keep cruising amongst so many lingoes, as Tom there says?"

"The *docken,* man," said I.—Don Ricardo smiled.

"I *am* a Scotchman, my dear sir; and the same person who, in his youth, was neither more nor less than wee Richy Cloche, in the long town of Kirkcaldy, is, in his old age, Don Ricardo Campana of St Jago de Cuba. But more of this anon; at present we are in the house of mourning, and alas the day that it should be so."

By this time the storm had increased most fearfully, and as Don Ricardo, Aaron, and myself sat in the dark corner of the large gloomy hall, we could, scarcely see each other, for the lightning had now ceased, and the darkness was so thick that, had it not been for the light from the large funeral wax tapers which had been instantly lit upon poor Maria's death in the room where she lay, that streamed through the open door, we should have been unable to see our very fingers before us.

"What is that?" said Campana; "heard you nothing, gentlemen?"

"By this the storm grew loud apace,
The water-wraith was shrieking;
And in the scowl of heaven each face
Grew dark as they were speaking."

In the lulls of the rain and the blast the same long low cry was heard which had startled me by Maria's bedside, and occasioned the sudden and fatal exertion which had been the cause of the bursting out afresh of the blood-vessel.

"Why," said I, "it *is* little more than three o'clock in the afternoon yet, dark as it is; let us sally out, Mr Bang, for I verily believe that the hollo we have heard is my captain's voice, and, if I conjecture rightly, he must have arrived at the other side of the river, probably with the doctor."

"Why, Tom," quoth Aaron, "it is only three in the afternoon as you say, although by the sky I could almost vouch for its being midnight; but I don't like that shouting—Did you ever read of a water-kelpie, "Don *Richy?*""

"Poo, poo, nonsense," said the Don; "Mr Cringle is, I fear, right enough." At this moment the wind thundered at the door and window-shutters, and howled amongst the neighbouring trees and round the roof, as if it would have blown the house down upon our devoted heads. The cry was again heard during a momentary pause.

"Zounds!" said Bang, "it *is* the skipper's voice, as sure as fate—he must be in danger—let us go and see, Tom."

"Take me with you," said Campana—the foremost always when any good deed was to be done; and, in place of clapping on his greatcoat to meet the storm, to our unutterable surprise, he began to disrobe himself, all to his trousers and large straw hat. He then called one of the servants, *"Trae me un lasso."* The *lasso,* a long thong of plaited hide, was forthwith brought; he coiled it up in his left hand. "Now, Pedro," said he to the negro servant who had fetched it—a tall, strapping fellow—"you and Gaspar, follow me.—Gentlemen, are you ready?" Gaspar appeared, properly accoutred, with a long pole in one hand and a thong similar to Don Ricardo's in the other—he, as well as his comrade, being stark naked all to their waistcloths. "Ah, well done, my sons," said Don Ricardo, as both the negroes prepared to follow him. So off we started to the door, although we heard the *tormenta* raging without with appalling fury. Bang undid the latch, and the next moment he was flat on his back, the large leaf having flown open with tremendous violence, capsizing him like an infant.

The Padre, from the inner chamber, came to our assistance, and, by our joint exertions, we at length got the door *to* again and barricaded, after which we made our exit from the lee side of the house by a window. Under other circumstances it would have been difficult to refrain from laughing at the appearance we made. We were all drenched in an instant after we left the shelter of the house, and there was old Campana, naked to the waist, with his large *sombrero* and long pigtail hanging down his back, like a mandarin of twenty buttons. Next followed his two black assistants—naked as I have described them—all three with their coils of rope in their hands, like a hangman and his deputies; then advanced friend Bang and myself, without our coats or hats, with handkerchiefs tied round our heads, and our bodies bent down so as to stem the gale as strongly as we could.

But the planting attorney—a great schemer, a kind of Will Wimble in his way—had thought fit, of all things in the world, to bring his umbrella, which the wind, as might have been expected, reversed most unceremoniously the moment he attempted to hoist it, and tore it from the staff, so that, on the impulse of the moment, he had to clutch the flying red silk and thrust his head through the centre, where the stick had stood, as if he had been some curious flower. As we turned the corner of the house the full force of the storm met us right in the teeth, when flap flew Don Ricardo's hat past us, but the two blackamoors had taken the precaution to strap each of theirs down with a strong grass lanyard. We continued to work to windward, while every now and then the hollo came past us on the gale louder and louder, until it guided us to the fording which we had crossed on our first arrival. We stopped there; the red torrent was rushing tumultuously past us, but we saw nothing save a few wet and shivering negroes on the opposite side, who had sheltered themselves under a cliff, and were busily employed in attempting to light a fire. The holloing continued.

"Why, what *can* be wrong?" at length said Don Ricardo, and he shouted to the people on the opposite side.

He might as well have spared his breath, for, although they saw his gestures and the motion of his lips, they no more heard him than we did them, as they very considerately in return made mouths at us, bellowing, no doubt, that they could not hear us.

"Don Ricardo—Don Ricardo!" at this crisis sang out Gaspar, who had clambered up the rocky to have a peep about him—*"Ave Maria—Allá son dos pobres, que peresquen pronto, si nosotros no pueden ayudarlos."*

"Whereabouts?" said Campana—"whereabouts? speak, man, speak."

"Down in the valley—about a quarter of a league, I see two men on a large rock, in the middle of the stream; the wind is in that direction, it must be them we heard."

"God be gracious to us! true enough—true enough,—let us go to them then, my children." And we again all cantered off after the excellent Don Ricardo. But before we could reach the spot we had to make a *detour,* and come down upon it from the precipitous brow of the beetling cliff above, for there was no beach nor shore to the swollen river, which was here very deep and surged, rushing under the hollow bank with comparatively little noise, which was the reason we heard the cries so distinctly.

The unfortunates who were in peril, whoever they might be, seemed to comprehend our motions, for one of them held out a white handkerchief, which I immediately answered by a similar signal, when the shouting ceased, until, guided by the negroes, we reached the verge of the cliff, and looked down from the red crumbling bank on the foaming water as it swept past beneath. It was here about thirty yards broad, divided by a rocky wedge-like islet, on which grew a profusion of dark bushes and one large tree, whose topmost branches were on a level with us where we stood. This tree was divided, about twelve feet from the root, into two limbs, in the fork of which sat, like a big monkey, no less a personage than Captain Transom himself, wet and dripping, with his clothes besmeared with mud, and shivering with cold. At the foot of the tree sat, in rueful mood, a small antique beau of an old man, in a coat which had once been blue silk, wearing breeches, the original colour of which no man could tell, and without his wig, his clear bald pate shining amidst the surrounding desolation like an ostrich's egg. Besides these worthies stood two trembling way-worn mules with drooping heads, their long ears hanging down most disconsolately. The moment we came in sight, the skipper hailed us.

"Why, I am hoarse with bawling, Don Ricardo, but here am I and El Doctor Pavo Real in as sorry a plight as any two gentlemen need be. On attempting the ford two hours ago, blockheads as we were—beg pardon, Don Pavo"—the doctor bowed, and grinned like a baboon—"we had nearly been drowned; indeed, we should have been drowned entirely, had we not brought up on this island of Barataria here.—But how is the young lady? tell me that," said the excellent-hearted fellow, even in the midst of his own danger.

"Mind *yourself,* my beautiful child," cried Bang. "How are we to get *you* on *terra firma?*"

"Poo—in the easiest way possible," rejoined he, with true seaman-like self-possession. "I see you have ropes—Tom Cringle, heave me the end of the line which Don Ricardo carries, will you?"

"No, no—I can do that myself," said Don Ricardo, and with a swing he hove the leathern noose at the skipper, and whipped it over his neck in a twinkling. The Scotch Spaniard, I saw, was pluming himself on his skill, but Transom was up to him, for in an instant he dropped out of it, while, in slipping through, he let it fall over a broken limb of the tree.

"Such an eel—such an eel!" shouted the attendant negroes, both expert hands with the *lasso* themselves.

"Now, Don Ricardo, since I am not to be had, make your end of the thong fast round that large stone there." Campana did so. "Ah, that will do." And so saying, the skipper warped himself to the top of the cliff with great agility. He was no sooner in safety himself, however, than the idea of having left the poor doctor in peril flashed on him.

"I must return—I must return! If the river rises, the *body* will be drowned out and out." And, notwithstanding our entreaties, he *did* return as he came, and, descending the tree, began apparently to argue with the little *medico,* and to endeavour to persuade him to ascend, and make his escape as he himself had done; but it would not do. Pavo Real—as brave a little man as ever was seen—made many salaams and obeisances, but move he would not. He shook his head repeatedly, in a very solemn way, as if he had said, "My very excellent friends, I am much obliged to you, but it is impossible; my dignity would be compromised by such a proceeding."

Presently Transom appeared to wax very emphatic, and pointed to a pinnacle of limestone rock, which had stood out like a small steeple above the surface of the flashing, dark red eddies, when we first arrived on the spot, but—now only stopped the water with a loud gurgle, the top rising and disappearing as the stream surged past, like a buoy *jaugling* in a tideway. The small man still shook his head, but the water now rose so rapidly that there was scarcely dry standing-room for the two poor devils of mules, while the doctor and the skipper had the greatest difficulty in finding a footing for themselves.

Time and circumstances began to press, and Transom, after another unavailing attempt to persuade the doctor, began apparently to rouse himself and muster his energies. He first drove the mules forcibly into the stream at the side opposite where we stood, which was the deepest water, and least broken by rocks and stones, and we had the pleasure to see them scramble out safe and sound; he then put his hand to his mouth, and hailed us to throw him a rope—it was done—he caught it, and then by a significant gesture to Campana, gave him to understand that now was the time. The Don comprehending him, hove his noose with great precision, right over the little doctor's head, and before he recovered from his surprise the captain slipped it under his arms and signed to haul tight, while the *medico* kicked and spurred and backed like a restive horse. At one and the same moment Transom made fast a *guy* round his waist, and we hoisted away while he hauled on the other line, so that we landed the Lilliputian Esculapius safe on the top of the bank, with the wind nearly out of his body, however, from his violent exertions and the running of the noose.

It was now the work of a moment for the captain to ascend the tree and again warp himself ashore, when he set himself to apologise with all his might and main, pleading strong necessity; and, having succeeded in pacifying the offended dignity of the doctor, we turned towards the house.

"Look out, there," sang out Campana sharply.

Time, indeed, thought I, for right ahead of us, as if an invisible gigantic ploughshare had passed over the woods, a valley or chasm was suddenly opened down the hill-side with a noise like thunder, and branches and whole limbs of trees were instantly torn away and tossed into the air like straws.

"Down on your noses, my fine fellows," cried the skipper. We were all flat in an instant, except the *medico*—the stubborn little brute—who *stood* until the tornado reached him, when in a twinkling he was cut on his back, with a violence sufficient, as I thought, to have driven his breath for ever and aye out of his body. While we lay we heard all kinds of things hurtle past us through the air, pieces of timber, branches of trees, coffee-bushes, and even stones. Presently it lulled again, and we got on end to look round us.

"How will the old house stand all this, Don Ricardo?" said the drenched, skipper. He had to shout to be heard. The Don was too busy to answer, but once more strode on towards the dwelling, as if he expected something even worse than we had experienced to be still awaiting us. By the time we reached it it was full of negroes, men, women, and children, whose huts had already been destroyed—poor, drenched, miserable devils, with scarcely any clothing; and to crown our comfort, we found the roof leaking in many places. By this time the night began to fall, and our prospects were far from flattering. The rain had entirely ceased, nor was there any lightning, but the storm was most tremendous—blowing in gusts, and veering round from east to north with the speed of thought. The force of the gale, however, gradually declined, until the wind subsided altogether, and everything became quite still. The low murmured conversation of the poor negroes who environed us was heard distinctly; the hard breathing of the sleeping children could even be distinguished. But I was by no means sure that the hurricane was over, and Don Ricardo and the rest seemed to think as I did, for there was not a word interchanged between us for some time.

"Do you hear that?" at length said Aaron Bang, as a low moaning sound rose wailing into the night air. It approached and grew louder.

"The voice of the approaching tempest amongst the higher branches of the trees," said the captain.

The rushing noise overhead increased, but still all was so calm where we sat that you could have heard a pin drop. Poo, thought I, it *has* passed over us after all—no fear now, when one reflects how completely sheltered we are. Suddenly, however, the lights in the room where the body lay were blown out, and the roof groaned and creaked as if it had been the bulkheads of a ship in a tempestuous sea.

"We shall have to cut and run from this anchorage presently, after all," said I; "the house will never hold on till morning."

The words were scarcely out of my mouth, when, as if a thunderbolt had struck it, one of the windows in the hall was driven in with a roar, as if the falls of Niagara had been pouring overhead, and the tempest having thus forced an entrance, the roof of that part of the house where we sat was blown up as if by gunpowder—ay, in the twinkling of an eye; and there we were with the bare walls, and the angry heavens overhead, and the rain descending in bucketfuls. Fortunately, two large joists or couples, being deeply imbedded in the substance of the walls, remained, when the rafters and ridgepole were torn away, or we must have been crushed in the ruins.

There was again a death-like lull, the wind fell to a small melancholy sough amongst the tree-tops, and once more, where we sat, there was not a breath stirring. So complete was the calm now, that after a light had been struck, and placed on the floor in the middle of the room, showing the surrounding group of shivering half-naked savages with fearful distinctness, the flame shot up straight as an arrow, clear and bright, although the distant roar of the storm still thundered afar off as it rushed over the mountain above us.

This unexpected stillness frightened the women even more than the fierceness of the gale, when at the loudest, had done.

"We must go forth," said Señora Campana; "the elements are only gathering themselves for a more dreadful hurricane than what we have already experienced. We must go forth to the little chapel in the wood, or the next burst may, and *will*, bury us under the walls:" and she moved towards Maria's room where, by this time, lights had again been placed. "We must move the body," we could hear her say; "we must all proceed to the chapel; in a few minutes the storm will be raging again louder than ever."

"And my wife is very right," said Don Ricardo; "so Gaspar call the other people; have some mats, and *quatres*, and mattresses carried down to the chapel, and we shall all remove, for, with half of the roof gone, it is but tempting the Almighty to remain here longer."

The word was passed and we were soon under weigh, four negroes leading the van, carrying the uncoffined body of the poor girl on a sofa; while two servants, with large splinters of a sort of resinous wood for flambeaux, walked by the side of it. Next followed the women of the family, covered up with all the cloaks and spare garments that could be collected; then came Don Picador Cangrejo, with Ricardo Campana, the skipper Aaron Bang, and myself—the procession being closed by the household negroes, with more lights, which all burned steadily and clear.

We descended through a magnificent natural avenue of lofty trees (whose brown moss-grown trunks and fantastic bough were strongly lit up by the blaze of the torches; while the fresh white splinter-marks, where the branches had been torn off by the storm, glanced bright and clear, and the rain-drops on the dark leaves sparkled like diamonds) towards the river, along whose brink the brimful red-foaming waters rushed past us close by the edge of the path, now ebbing suddenly a foot or so, and then surging up again beyond their former bounds, as if large stones or trunks of trees above were from time to time damming up the troubled waters and then giving way. After walking about four hundred yards we came to a small but massive chapel, fronting the river, the back part resting against a rocky bank, with two superb cypress-trees growing, one on each side of the door; we entered, Padre Carera leading the way. The whole area of the interior of the building did not exceed a parallelogram of twenty feet by twelve. At the eastern end, fronting the door, there was a small altar-piece of hardwood, richly ornamented with silver, and one or two bare wooden benches standing on the tiled floor—but the chief security we had that the building would withstand the storm, consisted in its having no window or aperture whatsoever, excepting two small *ports*, one on each side of the altar-piece, and the door, which was a massive frame of hardwood planking.

The body was deposited at the foot of the altar, and the ladies, having been wrapped up in cloaks and blankets, were safely lodged in *quatres*, while *we*, the gentlemen of the comfortless party, seated ourselves, disconsolately enough, on the wooden benches.

The door was made fast, after the servants had kindled a blazing wood-fire on the floor; and although the flickering light cast by the wax tapers in the six large silver candlesticks which were planted beside the bier, as it blended with the red glare of the fire, and fell strong on the pale uncovered features of the corpse, and on the anxious faces of the women, was often startling enough, yet being conscious of a certain degree of security from the thickness of the walls, we made up our minds to spend the night where we were as well as we could.

"I say, Tom Cringle," said Aaron Bang, "all the females are snug there, you see; we have a blazing fire on the hearth, and here is some comfort for *we* men slaves;" whereupon he produced two bottles of brandy. Don Ricardo Campana, with whom Bang seemed now to be absolutely *in league*, or, in vulgar phrase, as thick as pickpockets, had brought a goblet of water, and a small silver drinking cup, with him, so we passed the *creature* round, and tried all we could to while away the tedious night. But, as if a sudden thought had struck Aaron, he here tucked the brandy bottle under his arm, and asking me to carry the vessel with the water, he advanced, cup in hand, towards the ladies—

"Now, Tom, interpret carefully."

"Ahem—Madam and Signoras, this is a heavy night for all of us, but the chapel is damp—allow me to comfort you."

"Muchisimos gracias," was the gratifying answer, and Bang accordingly gave each of our fair friends a heart-warming taste of brandy-and-water. There was now a calm for a full hour, and the captain had stepped out to reconnoitre; on his return he reported that the swollen stream had very much subsided.

"Well, we shall get away, I hope, to-morrow morning, after all," whispered Bang.

He had scarcely spoken when it began to pelt and rain again, as if a water-spout had burst overhead, but there was no wind.

"Come, that is the clearing up of it," said Cloche.

At this precise moment the priest was sitting with folded arms beyond the body, on a stool or trestle, in the alcove or recess where it lay. Right overhead was one of the small round apertures in the gable of the chapel, which, opening on the bank, appeared to the eye a round black spot in the whitewashed wall.

The bright wax-lights shed a strong lustre on the worthy *clerigo*'s figure, face, and fine bald head, which shone like silver, while the deeper light of the embers on the floor was reflected in ruby tints from the larger silver crucifix that hung at his waist. The rushing of the swollen river prevented me hearing distinctly, but it occurred to me once or twice that a strange gurgling sound proceeded from the aforesaid round aperture. The *padre* seemed to hear it also, for every now and then he looked up, and once he rose and peered anxiously through it; but, apparently unable to distinguish anything, he sat down again. However, my attention had been excited, and, half asleep as I was, I kept glimmering in the direction of the *clerigo*.

The captain's deep snore had gradually lengthened out, so as to vouch for his forgetfulness, and Bang, Ricardo, Dr Pavo Real, and the ladies, had all subsided into the most perfect quietude, when I noticed, and I quaked and trembled like an aspen leaf as I did so, a long black paw thrust through, and down from the dark aperture immediately over Padre Carera's head, which, whatever it was, it appeared to scratch sharply, and then giving the *caput* a smart cuff, vanished. The priest started, put up his hand, and rubbed his head, but seeing nothing, again leant back, and was about departing to the land of *nod*, like the others, once more. However, in a few minutes the same paw again protruded, and this time a peering black snout, with two glancing eyes, was thrust through the hole after it. The paw kept swinging about like a pendulum for a few seconds, and was then suddenly thrust into the *padre*'s open mouth as he lay back asleep, and again giving him another smart crack, vanished as before.

"Hobble, gobble," gurgled the priest, nearly choked. "*Ave Maria purissima, que bocado*—what a mouthful!—What can that be?"

This was more than I knew, I must confess, and altogether I was consumedly puzzled, but, from a disinclination to alarm the women, I held my tongue. Padre Carera this time moved away to the other side from beneath the hole, but still within two feet of it; in fact, he could not get in this direction farther for the altar-piece, and being still half asleep, he lay back once more against the wall to finish his nap, taking the precaution, however, to clap on his long shovel hat, shaped like a small canoe crosswise, with the peaks standing out from each side of his head, in place of wearing it fore and aft, as usual. Well, thought I, a strange party certainly; but drowsiness was fast settling down on me also, when the same black paw was again thrust through the hole, and I distinctly heard a nuzzling, whining, short bark. I rubbed my eyes and sat up, but before I was quite awake, the head and neck of a large Newfoundland dog was shoved into the chapel through the round aperture, and making a long stretch, with the black paws thrust down and resting on the wall, supporting the creature, the animal suddenly snatched the *padre*'s hat off his head, and giving it an angry worry—as much as to say, "Confound it, I had hoped to have the head in it"—it dropped it on the floor, and with a loud yell, Sneezer, my own old dear Sneezer, leaped into the midst of us, floundering amongst the sleeping women, and kicking the firebrands about, making them hiss again with the water he shook from his shaggy coat, and frightening all hands like the—very devil.

"Sneezer, you villain, how came *you* here?" I exclaimed, in great amazement—"how came you here, sir?" The dog knew me at once, and when benches were reared against him, after the women had huddled into a corner, and everything was in sad confusion, he ran to me, and leaped on my neck, gasping and *yelping;* but finding that I was angry, and in no mood for toying, he planted himself on end so suddenly, in the middle of the floor, close by the fire, that all our hands were stayed, and no one could find in his heart to strike the poor dumb brute, he sat so quiet and motionless. "Sneezer, my boy, what have you to say—where have you come from?" He looked in the direction of the door, and then walked deliberately towards it, and tried to open it with his paws.

"Now," said the captain, "that little scamp, who would insist on riding with me to St Jago, to see, as he said, if he might not be of use in fetching the surgeon from the ship in case I could not find Dr Bergara, has come back, although I desired him to stay on board. The puppy must have returned in his cursed troublesome zeal, for in no other way could your dog be here. Certainly, however, he did not know that I had fallen in with Dr Pavo Real;" and the good-natured fellow's heart melted as he continued—"Returned! why, he may be drowned—Cringle, take care little Reefpoint be not drowned."

Sneezer lowered his black snout, and for a moment poked it into the white ashes of the fire, and then raising it and stretching his neck upward to its full length, he gave a short bark, and then a long loud howl.

"My life upon it, the poor boy is gone," said I.

"But what can we do?" said Don Ricardo; "it is as dark as pitch."

And we again set ourselves to have a small rally at the brandy-and-water, as a resolver of our doubts, whether we should sit still till daybreak, or sally forth now, and run the chance of being drowned, with but small hope of doing any good; and the old priest having left the other end of the chapel, where the ladies were once more reposing, now came to join our council of war, and to have his share of the *agua ardiente.*

The noise of the rain increased, and there was still a little puff of wind now and then, so that the *padre,* taking an *alfombra,* or small mat used to kneel on, and placing it on the step where the folding-doors opened inwards, took a cloak on his shoulders, and sat himself down with his back against the leaves, to keep them closed, as the lock or bolt was broken, and was in the act of swigging off his cupful of comfort, when a strong gust drove the door open, as if the devil himself had kicked it, capsized the *padre,* blew out the lights once more, and scattered the brands of the fire all about us. Transom and I started up, the women shrieked; but before we could get the door to again, in rode little Reefpoint on a mule, with the doctor of the Firebrand behind him, bound, or *lashed,* as we call it, to him by a strong thong. The black servants and the females took them for incarnate fiends, I fancy, for the yells and shrieks they set up were tremendous.

"Yo, ho!" sang out little Reefy; "don't be frightened, ladies—Lord love ye, I am half drowned, and the doctor here is altogether so—quite entirely drowned, I assure you. I say, *medico,* an't it true?" And the little Irish rogue slewed his head round, and gave the exhausted doctor a most comical look.

"Not quite," quoth the doctor, "but deuced near it. I say, captain, would you have known us? why, we are dyed chocolate colour, you see, in that river, flowing not with milk and honey, but with something miraculously like pea-soup—water, I cannot call it."

"But, Heaven help us, why did you try the ford, man?" said Bang.

"You may say that, sir," responded *wee* Reefy; "but our mule was knocked up, and it was so dark and tempestuous that we should have perished by the road if we had tried back for St Jago; so seeing a light here—the only indication of a living thing—and the stream looking narrow and comparatively quiet—confound it, it was all the deeper though—we shoved across."

"But, bless me, if you had been thrown in the stream lashed together as you are, you would have been drowned to a certainty," said the captain.

"Oh," said little Reefy, "the doctor was not *on* the mule in crossing—no, no, captain, I knew better—I had him in tow, sir; but after we crossed he was so faint and chill, that I had to lash myself to him to keep him from sliding over the animal's counter, and walk he could not."

"But, Master Reefpoint, why came you back? did I not desire you to remain on board of the Firebrand, sir?"

The midshipman looked nonplussed. "Why, captain, I forgot to take my clothes with me, and—and—in truth, sir, I thought our surgeon would be of more use than any outlandish *gallipot* that *you* could carry back."

The good intentions of the lad saved him further reproof, although I could not help smiling at his coming back for his clothes, when his whole wardrobe on starting was confined to the two false collars and a tooth-brush.

"But where is the young lady?" said the doctor.

"Beyond your help, my dear doctor," said the skipper; "she is dead—all that remains of her you see within that small railing there."

"Ah, indeed!" quoth the *medico*, "poor girl—poor girl—deep decline—wasted, terribly wasted," said he, as he returned from the railing of the altar-piece, where he had been to look down upon the body; and then, as if there never had been such a being as poor Maria Olivera in existence, he continued, "Pray, Mr Bang, what may you have in that bottle?"

"Brandy, to be sure, doctor," said Bang.

"A thimbleful, then, if you please."

"By all means." And the planting attorney handed the black bottle to the surgeon, who applied it to his lips without more circumlocution."

"Lord love us!—poisoned—Oh, gemini!"

"Why, doctor," said Transom, "what *has* come over you? Poisoned, captain—only taste."

The bottle contained soy. It was some time before we could get the poor man quieted; and when at length he was stretched along a bench, and the fire stirred up, and new wood added to it, the fresh air of early morning began to be scented. At this time we missed Padre Carera, and, in truth, we all fell fast asleep; but in about an hour or so afterwards I was awoke by some one stepping across me. The same cause had stirred Transom. It was Aaron Bang, who had been to look out at the door.

"I say, Cringle, look here—the *padre* and the servants are digging a grave close to the chapel—are they going to bury the poor girl so suddenly?"

I stepped to the door; the wind had entirely fallen, but it rained very fast. The small chapel door looked out on the still swollen but subsiding river, and beyond that on the mountain which rose abruptly from the opposite bank. On the side of the hill facing us was situated a negro village of about thirty huts, where lights were already twinkling, as if the inmates were preparing to go forth to their work. Far above them, on the ridge, there was a clear cold streak towards the east, against which the outline of the mountain, and the large trees which grew on it, were sharply cut out; but overhead the firmament was as yet dark and threatening. The morning star had just risen, and was sparkling bright and clear through the branches of a magnificent tree that shot out from the highest part of the hill; it seemed to have attracted the captain's attention as well as mine.

"Were I romantic now, Mr Cringle, I could expatiate on that view. How cold and clear and chaste everything looks! The elements have subsided into a perfect calm; everything is quiet and still, but there is no warmth, no comfort in the scene."

"What a soaking rain!" said Aaron Bang; "why, the drops are as small as pinpoints, and so thick!—a Scotch mist is a joke to them. Unusual all this, captain. You know *our* rain in Jamaica usually descends in bucketfuls unless it be regularly set in for a week, and then, but then only, it becomes what in England we are in the habit of calling a *soaking* rain. One good thing, however, while it descends so quietly, the earth will absorb it all, and that furious river will not continue swollen."

"Probably not," said I.

"Mr Cringle," said the skipper, "do you mark that tree on the ridge of the mountain—that large tree in such conspicuous relief against the eastern sky?"

"I do, captain. But—Heaven help us!—what necromancy is this? It seems to sink into the mountain-top—why, I only see the uppermost branches now! It has disappeared, and yet the outline of the hill is as distinct and well-defined as ever; I can even see the cattle on the ridge, although they are running about in a very incomprehensible way certainly."

"Hush!" said Don Ricardo, "hush! the *padre* is reading the funeral service in the chapel, preparatory to the body being brought out."

And so he was. But a low grumbling noise, gradually increasing, was now distinctly audible. The monk hurried on with the prescribed form—he finished it—and we were about moving the body to carry it forth, Bang and I being in the very act of stooping down to lift the bier, when the captain sang out sharp and quick—"Here, Tom!"—the urgency of the appeal abolishing the *Mister*— "Here! zounds, the whole hill-side is in motion!" And as he spoke, I beheld the negro village, that hung on the opposite bank, gradually fetch away, houses, trees, and all, with a loud, harsh, grating sound.

"God defend us!" I involuntarily exclaimed.

"Stand clear," shouted the skipper; "the whole hill-side opposite is under weigh, and we shall be bothered here presently."

He was right; the entire face of the hill over against us was by this time in motion, sliding over the substratum of rocklike a first-rate gliding along the well-greased *ways* at launching—an *earthly* avalanche. Presently the rough, rattling, and crashing sound, from the disrupture of the soil, and the breaking of the branches, and tearing up by the roots of the largest trees, gave warning of some tremendous incident. The lights in the huts still burned, but houses and all continued to slide down the declivity; and anon a loud startled exclamation was heard here and there, and then a pause, but the low mysterious hurtling wand never ceased.

At length a loud continuous yell echoed along the hill-side. The noise increased—the rushing sound came stronger and stronger—the river rose higher, and roared louder; it overleaped the lintel of the door—the fire on the floor hissed for a moment, and then expired in smouldering wreaths of white smoke—the discoloured torrent gurgled into the chapel, and reached the altar-piece; and while the cries from the hill-side were highest and bitterest and most despairing, it suddenly filled the chapel to the top of the low door-post; and although the large tapers which had been lit near the altar-piece were as yet unextinguished, like meteors sparkling on a troubled sea, all was misery and consternation.

"Have patience and be composed now," shouted Don Ricardo. "If it increases, we can escape through the apertures here, behind the altar-piece, and from thence to the high grounds beyond. The heavy rain has loosened the soil on the opposite bank, and it has slid into the river-course, negro houses and all. But be composed, my dears—nothing supernatural in all this; and rest assured, although the river has unquestionably been forced from its channel, that there is no danger, if you will only maintain your self-possession."

And there we were—an inhabitant of a cold climate cannot go along with me in the description. We were all alarmed, but we were not *chilled*—cold is a great damper of bravery. At New Orleans, the black regiments, in the heat of the forenoon, were really the most efficient corps of the army; but in the morning, when the hoar-frost was on the long wire-grass, they were but as a broken reed. "Him too *cool* for *brave* to-day," said the sergeant of the grenadier company of the West India regiment which was brigaded in the ill-omened advance when we attacked New Orleans; but here, having heat, and seeing none of the women egregiously alarmed, we all took heart of grace, and really there was no quailing amongst us.

Señora Campana and her two nieces, Señora Cangrejo and her angelic daughter, had all betaken themselves to a sort of seat, enclosing the altar in a semicircle, with the peasoup-coloured water up to their knees. Not a word— not an exclamation of fear escaped from them, although the gushing eddies from the open door showed that the soil from the opposite hill was fast settling down, and usurping the former channel of the river.

"All very fine this to read of," at last exclaimed Aaron Bang. "Zounds, we shall be drowned. Look out, Transom; Tom Cringle, look out; for my part, I shall dive through the door, and take my chance."

"No use in that," said Don Ricardo; "the two round openings there at the west end of the chapel open on a dry shelf, from which the ground slopes easily upward to the house; let us put the ladies through them, and then we males can shift for ourselves as we best may."

At this moment the water rose so high that the bier on which the corpse of poor Maria Olivera lay stark and stiff was floated off the trestles, and, turning on its edge, after glancing for a moment in the light cast by the wax tapers, it sank into the thick brown water, and was no more seen.

The old priest murmured a prayer, but the effect on us was electric. *"Sauve qui peut,"* was now the cry; and Sneezer, quite in his element, began to cruise all about, threatening the tapers with instant extinction.

"Ladies, get through the holes," shouted Don Ricardo.

"Captain, get you out first."

"Can't desert my ship," said the gallant fellow; "the last to quit where danger is, my dear sir. It is my charter; but, Mr Cringle, go you, and hand the ladies out."

"Indeed I will not," said I. "Beg pardon, sir; I simply mean to say, that I cannot usurp the *pas* from you."

"Then," quoth Don Ricardo—a more discreet personage than any of us—"I will go myself;" and forthwith he screwed himself through one of the round holes in the wall behind the altarpiece. "Give me out one of the wax tapers—there is no wind now," said Don Ricardo; "and hand out my wife, Captain Transom."

"Ave Maria!" said the matron, "I shall never get through that hole."

"Try, my dear madam," said Bang, for by this time we were all deucedly alarmed at our situation—"try, madam;" and we lifted her towards the hole —fairly entered her into it, head foremost, and all was smooth till a certain part of the excellent woman's earthly tabernacle stuck fast.

We could hear her invoking all the saints in the calendar on the outside "to make her *thin*;" but the flesh and muscle were obdurate; through she would not go, until—delicacy being now blown to the winds—Captain Transom placed his shoulder to the old lady's extremity, and with a regular "Oh, heave oh!" shot her through the aperture into her husband's arms. The young ladies we ejected much more easily, although Francesca Cangrejo did stick a little too. The priest was next passed, then Don Picador; and so we went on, until in rotation we had all made our exit, and were perched shivering on the high bank. God defend us! we had not been a minute there when the rushing of the stream increased— the rain once more fell in torrents—several large trees came down with a fearful impetus in the roaring torrent, and struck the corner of the chapel. It shook—we could see the small cross on the eastern gable tremble. Another stump surged against it—it gave way—and in a minute afterwards there was not a vestige remaining of the whole fabric.

"What a funeral for thee, Maria!" said Don Ricardo.

Not a vestige of the body was ever found.

There was nothing now for it. We all stopped, and turned, and looked— there was not a stone of the building to be seen—all was red, precipitous bank, or dark flowing river—so we turned our steps towards the house. The sun by this time had risen. We found the northern range of rooms still entire, so we made the most of it; and, by dint of the captain's and my nautical skill, before dinner-time there was rigged a canvass jury-roof over the southern part of the fabric, and we were once more seated in comparative comfort at our meal. But it was all melancholy work enough. However, at last we retired to our beds; and next morning, when I awoke, *there* was the small stream once more trickling over the face of the rock, with the slight spray wafting into my bedroom—a little discoloured, certainly, but as quietly as if no storm had taken place.

We were kept at Don Picador's for three days, as, from the shooting of the soil from the opposite hill, the river had been dammed up, and its channel altered, so that there was no venturing across. Three negroes were unfortunately drowned, when the bank *shot*, as Bang called it. But the wonder passed away; and by nine o'clock on the fourth morning, when we mounted our mules to proceed, there was little apparently on the fair face of nature to mark that such fearful scenes had been. However, when we did get under weigh, we found that the hurricane had not passed over us without leaving fearful evidences of its violence.

We had breakfasted—the women had wept—Don Ricardo had blown his nose—Aaron Bang had blundered and fidgeted about—and the *bestias* were at the door. We embraced the ladies.

"My son," said Señora Cangrejo, "we shall most likely never meet again. You have your country to go to—you have a mother. Oh, may she never suffer the pangs which have wrung my heart! But I know—I know that she never will." I bowed. "We may never—indeed, in all likelihood we shall never meet again!" continued she, in a rich, deep—toned, mellow voice; "but if your way of life should ever lead you to Cordova, you will be sure of having many visitors, and many a door will open to you, if you will but give out that you have shown kindness to Maria Olivera, or to any one connected with her." She wept, and bent over me, pressing both her hands on the crown of my head. "May that great God, who careth not for rank or station, for nation or for country, bless you, my son—bless you!"

All this was sorry work. She kissed me on the forehead, and turned away. Her daughter was standing close to her, "like Niobe, all tears." "Farewell, Mr Cringle—may you be happy." I kissed her hand—she turned to the captain. He looked inexpressible things, and, taking her hand, held it to his breast; and then, making a slight genuflection, pressed it to his lips. He appeared to be amazingly energetic, and she seemed to struggle to be released. He recovered himself, however—made a solemn bow—the ladies vanished. We shook hands with old Don Picador, mounted our mules, and bid a last adieu *to the Valley of the Hurricane.*

We ambled along for some time in silence. At length the skipper dropped astern, until he got alongside of me. "I say, Tom"—I was well aware that he never called me *Tom* unless he was *fou,* or his heart was full, honest man— "Tom, what think you of Francesca Cangrejo?"

Oh ho! sits the wind in that quarter? thought I. "Why, I don't know, captain—I have seen her to disadvantage—so much misery—fine woman though—rather large to my taste but—"

"Confound your *buts,* " quoth the captain. "But never mind—push on, push on." I may tell the gentle reader in his ear, that the worthy fellow, at the moment when I send this chapter to the press, has his flag, and that Francesca Cangrejo is no less a personage than his wife.

However, let us go along. "Doctor Pavo Real," said Don Ricardo, "now, since you have been good enough to spare us a day, let us get the heart of your secret out of you. Why, you must have been pretty well frightened on the island there."

"Never so much frightened in my life, Don Ricardo; that English captain is a most *tempestuous* man—but all has ended well; and after having seen you to the crossing, I will bid you good-bye."

"Poo—nonsense. Come along—here is the English *medico*, your brother Esculapius; so, come along, you can return in the morning."

"But the sick folk in Santiago—"

"Will be none the sicker for your absence, Dr Pavo Real," responded Don Ricardo.

The little doctor laughed, and away we all cantered—Don Ricardo leading, followed by his wife and nieces, on three stout mules, sitting, not on side-saddles, but on a kind of chair, with a foot-board on the larboard side to support the feet; then followed the two *Galens*, and little Reefpoint, while the captain and I brought up the rear. We had not proceeded five hundred yards, when we were brought to a standstill by a mighty tree, which had been thrown down by the wind fairly across the road. On the right hand there was a perpendicular rock rising up to a height of five hundred feet; and on the left an equally precipitous descent, without either ledge or parapet to prevent one from falling over. What was to be done? We could not by any exertion of strength remove the tree; and if we sent back for assistance, it would have been a work of time. So we dismounted, got the ladies to alight, and Aaron Bang, Transom, and myself, like true knights-errant, undertook to ride the *mulos* over the stump.

Aaron Bang led gallantly, and made a deuced good jump of it; Transom followed, and made not quite so clever an exhibition; I then rattled at it, and down came mule and rider. However, we were accounted for on the right side.

"But what shall become of *us!*" shouted the English doctor.

"And as for me, *I* shall return," said the Spanish *medico*.

"Lord love you, no," said little Reefpoint; "here, lash me to my beast, and no fear." The doctor made him fast, as desired, round the mule's neck with a stout thong, and then drove him at the barricade, and over they came, man and beast, although, to tell the truth, little Reefy alighted—well out on the neck, with a hand grasping each ear. However, he was a gallant little fellow, and in nowise discouraged, so he undertook to bring over the other quadrupeds; and in little more than a quarter of an hour we were all under weigh on the opposite side, in full sail towards Don Ricardo's property. But as we proceeded up the valley, the destruction caused by the storm became more and more apparent. Trees were strewn about in all directions, having been torn up by the roots— road there was literally none; and by the time we reached the coffee estate, after a ride, or scramble, more properly speaking, of three hours, we were all pretty much tired. In some places the road at the best was but a rocky shelf of limestone not exceeding twelve inches in width, where, if you had slipped, down you would have gone a thousand feet. At this time it was white and clean, as if it had been newly chiselled, all the soil and sand having been washed away by the recent heavy rains.

The situation was beautiful; the house stood on a platform scraped out of the hill-side, with a beautiful view of the whole country down to St Jago. The accommodation was good; more comforts, more English comforts, in the mansion than I had yet seen in Cuba; and as it was built with solid slabs of limestone, and roofed with strong hardwood timbers and rafters, and tiled, it had sustained comparatively little injury, having the advantage of being at the same time sheltered by the overhanging cliff. It stood in the middle of a large platform of hard sun-dried clay, plastered over, and as white as chalk, which extended about forty feet from the caves of the house, in every direction, on which the coffee was cured. This platform was surrounded on all sides by the greenest grass I had ever seen, and overshadowed, not the house alone, but the whole level space, by one vast wild fig-tree.

"I say, Tom, do you see that Scotchman hugging the Creole, eh?"

"Scotchman!" said I, looking towards Don Ricardo, who certainly did not appear to be particularly amorous; on the contrary, we had just alighted, and the worthy man was enacting groom.

"Yes," continued Bang, "the Scotchman hugging the Creole; look at that tree—do you see the trunk of it?"

I did look at it. It was a magnificent cedar, with a tall straight stem, covered over with a curious sort of fretwork, woven by the branches of some strong parasitical plant, which had warped itself round and round it by numberless snake-like convolutions, as if it had been a vegetable Laocoon. The tree itself shot up branchless to the uncommon height of fifty feet; the average girth of the trunk being four-and-twenty feet, or eight feet in diameter. The leaf of the cedar is small, not unlike the ash; but when I looked up, I noticed that the feelers of this ligneous serpent had twisted round the larger boughs, and blended their broad leaves with those of the tree, so that it looked like two trees grafted into one; but, as Aaron Bang said, in a very few years the cedar would entirely disappear, its growth being impeded, its pith extracted, and its core rotted, by the baleful embraces of the wild fig—of *"this Scotchman hugging the Creole."*

After we had fairly shaken into our places, there was every promise of a very pleasant visit. Our host had a tolerable cellar, and although there was not much of style in his establishment, still there was a fair allowance of comfort, everything considered. The evening after we arrived was most beautiful. The house—situated on its white plateau of *barbicues,* as the coffee platforms are called, where large piles of the berries in their red cherry-like husks had been blackening in the sun the whole forenoon, and on which a gang of negroes was now employed covering them up with tarpaulings for the night—stood in the centre of an amphitheatre of mountains, the front box, as it were; the stage part opening on a bird's-eye view of the distant town and harbour, with the everlasting ocean beyond it, the currents and flaws of wind making its surface look like ice, as we were too distant to discern the heaving of the swell or the motion of the billows. The fast-falling shades of evening were deepened by the sombrous shadow of the immense tree overhead, and all down in the deep valley was now becoming dark and undistinguishable, through the blue vapours that were gradually floating up towards us. To the left, on the shoulder of the Horseshoe Hill, the sunbeams still lingered, and the gigantic shadows of the trees on the right-hand prong were strongly cast across the valley on a red precipitous bank near the top of it. The sun was descending beyond the wood, flashing through the branches, as if they had been on fire. He disappeared. It was a most lovely still evening; the air—but hear the skipper—

"It is the hour when from the boughs
　The nightingale's high note is heard;
　It is the hour when lovers' vows
　Seem sweet in every whispered word;
　And gentle winds and waters near,
　Make music to the lonely ear.
　Each flower the dews have lightly wet,
　And in the sky the stars are met,
　And on the wave is deeper blue,
　And on the leaf is browner hue,
　And in the heaven that clear obscure,
　So softly dark, and darkly pure,
　Which follows the decline of day,
　When twilight melts beneath the moon away."

"Well recited, skipper," shouted Bang. "Given as the noble poet's verses should be given. I did not know the extent of your accomplishments; grown poetical ever since you saw Francesca Cangrejo, eh?"

The darkness hid the gallant captain's blushes, if blush he did.

"I say, Don Ricardo, who are those?"—half-a-dozen well-clad negroes had approached the house by this time.

"Ask them, Mr Bang; take your friend Mr Cringle for an interpreter."

"Well, I will. Tom, who are they? Ask them—do."

I put the question, "Do you belong to the property?"

The foremost, a handsome negro, answered me, "No, we don't, sir; at least, not till to-morrow."

"Not till to-morrow?"

"No, sir; *sòmos caballeros hoy*" (we are *gentlemen* to-day).

Gentlemen to-day! and, pray, what shall you be tomorrow?"

"*Esclavos otra ves*" (slaves again, sir), rejoined the poor fellow, nowise daunted.

"And you, my darling," said I to a nice well-dressed girl, who seemed to be the sister of the spokesman, "what are you to-day, may I ask?"

She laughed—"*Esclava*, a slave to-day, but to-morrow I shall be free."

"Very strange."

"Not at all, señor; there are six of us in a family, and one of us is free each day, all to father there," pointing to an old grey-headed negro, who stood by, leaning on his staff—"he is free two days in the week; and as I am going to have a child,"—a cool admission,—"I want to buy another day for myself too; but Don Ricardo will tell you all about it."

The Don by this time chimed in, talking kindly to the poor creatures; but we had to retire, as dinner was now announced, to which we sat down.

Don Ricardo had been altogether Spanish in Santiago, because be lived there amongst Spaniards, and everything was Spanish about him; so with the *tact* of his countrymen he had gradually merged into the society in which he moved, and, having married a very high-caste Spanish lady, he at length became regularly amalgamated with the community. But here, in his mountain retreat, sole master, his slaves in attendance on him, he was once more an Englishman in externals, as he always was at heart, and Richie Cloche, from the Lang Toun of Kirkcaldy, shone forth in all his glory as the kind-hearted landlord. His head household servant was an English, or rather a Jamaica negro; his equipment, so far as the dinner *set out* was concerned, was pure English; he would not even speak anything but English himself.

The entertainment was exceedingly good,—the only thing that puzzled us uninitiated subjects was a fricassee of Macaca worms, that is, the worm which breeds in the rotten trunk of the cotton-tree, a beautiful little insect, as big as a miller's thumb, with a white trunk and a black head—in one word, a gigantic caterpillar.

Bang fed thereon—he had been accustomed to it in Jamaica in some Creole families where he visited, he said—but it was beyond my compass. However, all this while we were having a great deal of fun, when Señora Campana addressed her husband—"My dear, you are now in your English mood, so I suppose we must go." We had dined at six, and it might now be about eight. Don Ricardo, with all the complacency in the world, bowed, as much as to say, "You are right, my dear, you *may* go," when his youngest niece addressed him.

"*Tio*—my uncle," said she, in a low silver-toned voice, "Juana and I have brought our guitars—"

"Not another word to be said," quoth Transom—"the guitars by all means."

The girls in an instant, without any preparatory blushing, or other botheration, rose, slipped their heads and right arms through the black ribbons that supported their instruments, and stepped into the middle of the room.

"'The Moorish Maid of Granada,'" said Señora Campana. They nodded.

"You shall take *Fernando the sailor*'s part," said Señora Candalaria, the youngest sister, to Juana, "for your voice is deeper than mine, and I shall be Anna."

"Agreed," said Juana, with a lovely smile, and an arch twinkle of her eye towards me, and then launched forth in full tide, accompanying her sweet and mellow voice on that too much neglected instrument, the guitar. It was a wild, irregular sort of ditty, with one or two startling *arabesque* bursts in it. As near as may be, the following conveys the meaning, but not the poetry:—

THE MOORISH MAID OF GRANADA.
FERNANDO.

"The setting moon hangs over the hill;
On the dark pure breast of the mountain lake
Still trembles her greenish silver *wake,*
And the blue mist floats over the rill.
And the cold streaks of dawning appear,
Giving token that sunrise is near;
And the fast-clearing east is flushing,
And the watery clouds are blushing;

And the day-star is sparkling on high,
Like the fire of my Anna's dark eye.

"The ruby-red clouds in the east
Float like islands upon the sea,
When the winds are asleep on its breast;
Ah, would that such calm were for me!

"And see, the first streamer-like ray
From the unrisen god of day,
Is piercing the ruby-red clouds,
Shooting up like golden shrouds:
And like silver gauze falls the shower,
Leaving diamonds on bank, bush, and bower,
Amidst many an unopened flower
Why walks the dark maid of Granada?"

ANNA.

"At evening when labour is done,
And cooled in the sea is the sun;
And the dew sparkles clear on the rose,
And the flowers are beginning to close,
Which at nightfall again in the calm
Their incense to God breathe in balm;
And the bat flickers up in the sky,
And the beetle hums moaningly by;
And to rest in the brake speeds the deer,
While the nightingale sings loud and clear.

"Scorched by the heat of the sun's fierce light,
The sweetest flowers are bending most
Upon their slender stems;
More faint are they than if tempest tost,
Till they drink of the sparkling gems
That fall from the eye of night.

"Hark! from lattices guitars are tinkling,
And though in heaven the stars are twinkling,
No tell-tale moon looks over the mountain,

To peer at her pale cold face in the fountain;
And serenader's mellow voice,
Wailing of war, or warbling of love,—
Of love, while the melting maid of his choice
Leans out from her bower above.

"All is soft and yielding towards night,
When blending darkness shrouds all from the sight,
But chaste, chaste, is this cold pure light,
Sang the Moorish maid of Granada."

After the song, we all applauded, and the ladies, having made their *congés*, retired. The captain and I looked towards Aaron Bang and Don Ricardo; they were tooth and nail at something which we could not understand. So we wisely held our tongues.

"Very strange all this," quoth Bang.

"Not at all," said Ricardo. "As I tell you, every slave here can have himself or herself appraised, at any time they may choose, with liberty to purchase their freedom day by day."

"But that would be compulsory manumission," quoth Bang.

"And if it be," said Ricardo, "what then? The scheme works well *here*—why should it not do so *there*—I mean with you, who have so many advantages over us?"

This is an unentertaining subject to most people, but having no bias myself, I have considered it but justice to insert in my log the following letter, which Bang, honest fellow, addressed to me, some years after the time I speak of:—

"MY DEAR CCRINGLE,—Since I last saw you in London, it is nearly, but not quite, three years ago. I considered at the time we parted, that if I lived at the rate of £3000 a-year, I was not spending one-half of my average income, and on the faith of this I did plead guilty to my house in Park Lane, and a carriage for my wife,—and, in short, I spent my £3000 a-year. Where am I now? In the old shop at Mammee Gully—my two eldest daughters, little things, in the very middle of their education, hastily ordered out—shipped, as it were, like two bales of goods—to Jamaica; my eldest nephew, whom I had adopted, obliged to exchange from the —— Light Dragoons, and to enter a foot regiment, *receiving* the difference, which but cleared him from his mess accounts. But the world says I was extravagant. Like Timon, however—no, d——n Timon—I spent money when I thought I had it, and therein I did no more than the Duke of Bedford, or Lord Grosvenor, or many another worthy peer; and now when I no longer have it, why, I cut my coat by my cloth, have made up my mind to perpetual banishment here, and I owe no man a farthing.

"But all this is wandering from the subject. We are now asked in direct terms to free our slaves. I will not even glance at the injustice of this demand, the horrible infraction of rights that it would lead to; all this I will leave untouched; but, my dear fellow, were men in your service or the army to do us justice, each in his small sphere in England, how much good might you not do us! Officers of rank are, of all others, the most influential witnesses we could adduce, if they, like you, have had opportunities of judging for themselves. But I am rambling from my object. You may remember our *escapade* into Cuba, a thousand years ago, when you were a lieutenant of the Firebrand. Well, you may also remember Don Ricardo's doctrine regarding the gradual emancipation of the negroes, and how we saw his plan in full operation—at least I did, for you knew little of these matters. Well, last year I made a note of what then passed, and sent it to an eminent West India merchant in London, who had it published in the *Courier*, but it did not seem to please either one party or the other—a signal proof, one would have thought, that there was some good in it. At a later period, I requested the same gentleman to have it published in *Blackwood*, where it would at least have had a fair trial on its own merits, but it was refused insertion. My very worthy friend ———, who acted for old Kit at that time as secretary of state for colonial affairs, did not like it, I presume; it trenched a little, it would seem, on the integrity of his great question; it approached to something like *compulsory manumission,* about which he *does* rave. Why will he not think on this subject like a Christian man? The country—I say so—*will never sanction the retaining in bondage of any slave, who is willing to pay his master his fair appraised value.*

"Our friend ——— injures *us*, and himself too, a *leetle* by his ultra notions. However, hear what I propose, and what, as I have told you formerly, was published in the *Courier* by no less a man than Lord ———:—

"'*Scheme for the gradual Abolition of Slavery.*

"'The following scheme of redemption for the slaves in our colonies is akin to a practice that prevails in some of the Spanish settlements.

"'We have now bishops (a most excellent measure), and we may presume that the inferior clergy will be much more efficient than heretofore. It is therefore proposed,—That every slave, on attaining the age of twenty-one years, should be, by Act of Parliament, competent to apply to his parish clergyman, and signify his desire to be appraised. The clergyman's business would then be to select two respectable appraisers from amongst his parishioners, who would value the slave, calling in an umpire if they disagreed.

"'As men even of good principles will often be more or less swayed by the peculiar interests of the body to which they belong, the rector should be instructed, if he saw any flagrant swerving from an honest appraisement, to notify the same to his bishop, who, by application to the governor, if need were, could thereby rectify it. When the slave was thus valued, the valuation should be registered by the rector, in a book to be kept for that purpose, an attested copy of which should be annually lodged amongst the archives of the colony.

"' We shall assume a case, where a slave is valued for £120, Jamaica currency. He soon, by working *by*-hours, selling the produce of his provision-grounds, &c., acquires £20; and how easily and frequently this is done, every one knows, who is at all acquainted with West India affairs.

"' He then *shall have a right* to pay to his owner this £20 as the price of *his Monday for ever,* and his owner shall be bound to receive it. A similar sum would purchase him his freedom on Tuesday; and other four instalments, to use a West India phrase, would *buy him free* altogether. You will notice, I consider that he is already free on the Sunday. Now, where is the insurmountable difficulty here? The planter may be put to inconvenience, certainly—great inconvenience, but *he has compensation*, and the slave *has his freedom—if he deserves it;* and as his emancipation, in nine cases out of ten, would be a work of time, he would, as he approached absolute freedom, become more civilised— that is, more fit to be free; and as he became more civilised, new wants would spring up, so that when he was finally free, he would not be content to work a day or two in the week for subsistence merely. He would work the whole six to buy many little comforts, which, *as a slave suddenly emancipated, he never would have thought of.*

"'As the slave becomes free, I would have his owner's allowance of provisions and clothing decrease gradually."

"' It may be objected—"Suppose slaves partly free to be taken in execution and sold for debt?" I answer, let them be so. Why cannot three days of a man's labour be sold by the deputy-marshal as well as six?

"'Again—"Suppose the gang is mortgaged, or liable to *judgements* against the owner of it?" I still answer, let it be so—only, in this case let the slave pay his instalments into court, in place of paying them to his owners, and let him apply to his rector for information in such a case.

"'By the register I would have kept, every one could at once see what property an owner had in his gang—that is, how many were actually slaves, and how many were in progress of becoming free. *Thus well-disposed and industrious slaves would soon become freemen. But the idle and worthless would still continue slaves, and why the devil shouldn't they?*

(Signed)   A. B.'"

There does seem to be a rough, yet vigorous sound sense in all this. But I take leave of the subject, which I do not profess to understand, only I am willing to bear witness in favour of my old friends, so far as I can conscientiously.

We returned next day to Santiago, and had then to undergo the bitterness of parting. With me it was a slight affair, but the skipper!—However, I will not dwell on it. We reached the town towards evening. The women were ready to weep, I saw; but we all turned in, and next morning at breakfast we were moved, I will admit—some more, some less. Little Reefy, poor fellow, was crying like a child; indeed he was little more, being barely fifteen.

"Oh, Mr Cringle, I wish I had never seen Miss *Candalaria de los Dolores;* indeed I do."

This was Don Ricardo's youngest niece.

"Ah, Reefy, Reefy," said I, "you must make haste, and be made post, and then—"

"What does he call her?" said Aaron.

"Señora Tomassa Candalaria de los Dolores Gonzales y Vallejo," blubbered out little Reefy.

"What a complicated piece of machinery she must be!" gravely rejoined Bang.

The meal was protracted to a very unusual length, but time and tide wait for no man. We rose. Aaron Bang advanced to make his bow to our kind hostess; he held out his hand, but she, to Aaron's great surprise apparently, pushed it on one side, and regularly closing with our friend, hugged him in right earnest. I have before mentioned that she was a very small woman; so, as the devil would have it, the golden pin in her hair was thrust into Aaron's eye, which made him jump back, wherein he lost his balance, and away he went, dragging Madama Campana down on the top of him. However, none of us could laugh *now;* we parted, jumped into our boat, and proceeded straight to the anchorage, where three British merchantmen were by this time riding, all ready for sea. We got on board. "Mr Yerk," said the captain, "fire a gun, and hoist blue Peter at the fore. Loose the foretopsail." The masters came on board for their instructions; we passed but a melancholy evening of it, and next morning I took my last look of Santiago de Cuba.

CHAPTER XV.

THE CRUISE OF THE WAVE— THE ACTION WITH THE SLAVER.

"O'er the glad waters of the dark blue sea,
    Our thoughts as boundless, and our souls as free.
    Far as the breeze can hear the billow's foam,
    Survey our empire, and behold our home,
    These are our realms, no limits to their sway—
    Our flag the sceptre all who meet obey."

The Corsair.

AT THREE o'clock next morning, about an hour and a half before day-dawn, I was roused from my cot by the gruff voice of the boatswain on deck—"All hands up anchor."

The next moment the gunroom steward entered with a lantern, which he placed on the table—"Gentlemen, all hands up anchor, if you please."

"Botheration!" grumbled one.

"Oh dear!" yawned another.

"How merrily we live that sailors be!" sang a third, in a most doleful strain, and in all the bitterness of heart consequent on being roused out of a warm nest so unceremoniously. But no help for it; so up we all got, and, opening the door of my berth, I got out, and sat me down on the bench that ran along the starboard side of the table.

For the benefit of the uninitiated, let me describe a gunroom on board of a sloop of war. Everybody knows that the captain's cabin occupies the after part

of the ship; next to it, on the same deck, is the gunroom. In a corvette, such as
the Firebrand, it is a room, as near as may be, twenty feet long by twelve wide,
and lighted by a long scuttle, or skylight, in the deck above. On each side of this
room runs a row of small chambers, seven feet long by six feet wide, boarded off
from the main saloon, or, in nautical phrase, separated from it by bulkheads,
each with a door and small window opening into the same, and, generally
speaking, with a small scuttle in the side of the ship towards the sea. These are
the officers' sleeping apartments, in which they have each a chest of drawers
and basin-stand; while overhead is suspended a cot, or hammock, kept asunder
by a wooden frame, six feet long by about two broad, slung from cleats nailed to
the beams above, by two lanyards fastened to rings, one at the head and the
other at the foot; from which radiate a number of smaller cords, which are fastened to the canvass of the cot; while a small strip of canvass runs from head to
foot on each side, so as to prevent the sleeper from rolling out. The dimensions
of the gunroom are, as will be seen, very much circumscribed by the side
berths; and when you take into account that the centre is occupied by a long
table, running the whole length of the room, flanked by a wooden bench, with a
high back to it, on each side, and a large clumsy chair at the head and another
at the foot, not forgetting the sideboard at the head of the table (full of knives,
forks, spoons, tumblers, glasses, &c. &c. &c. stuck into mahogany sockets), all
of which are made fast to the deck by strong cleats and staples, and bands of
spunyarn, so as to prevent them fetching away, or moving, when the vessel
pitches or rolls, you will understand that there is no great scope to expatiate
upon, free of the table, benches, and bulkheads of the cabins. While I sat
monopolising the dull light of the lantern, and accoutring myself as decently as
the hurry would admit of, I noticed the officers, in their nightgowns and night-
caps, as they extricated themselves from their coops; and picturesque-looking
subjects enough there were amongst them, in all conscience. At length—that
is, in about ten minutes from the time we were called—we were all at stations,
a gun was fired, and we weighed, and then stood out to sea, running along
about four knots, with the land-wind right aft. Having made an offing of three
miles or so, we outran the *terral*, and got becalmed in the belt of smooth water
between it and the sea-breeze. It was striking to see the three merchant-ships
gradually draw out from the land, until we were all clustered together in a
bunch, with half a gale of wind curling the blue waves within musket-shot,
while all was long swell and smooth water with us. At length the breeze
reached us, and we made sail with our convoy to the southward and eastward,

the lumbering merchantmen crowding every inch of canvass, while we could hardly keep astern, under close-reefed topsails, foresail, jib, and spanker.

"Pipe to breakfast," said the captain to Mr Yerk.

"A sail abeam of us to windward!"

"What is she?" sang out the skipper to the man at the masthead who had hailed.

"A small schooner, sir; she has fired a gun, and hoisted an ensign and pennant."

"How is she steering?"

"She has edged away for us, sir."

"Very well.—Mr Yerk, make the signal for the convoy to stand on. Have the men gone to breakfast?"

"No, sir, but they are just going."

"Then pipe belay with breakfast for a minute. All hands make sail, if you please. Crack on, Mr Yerk, and let us overhaul this small swaggerer."

In a trice we had all sail set, and were staggering along on the larboard tack, close upon a wind. We hauled out from the merchant-ships like smoke, and presently the schooner was seen from the deck. About this time it fell nearly calm. "Go to breakfast now." The crew disappeared, all to the officers, man at the helm, quartermaster at the conn, and signalman.

The first-lieutenant had the book open on the drum of the capstan before him. "Make our number," said the captain. It was done. "What does she answer?"

The signalmen answered from the fore-rigging, where he had perched himself with his glass—"She makes the signal to telegraph, sir—3, 9, 2, at the fore, sir"—and so on; which translated was simply this—"The Wave, with despatches from the admiral."

"Oh, ho," said Transom; "what is she sent for? Whenever the people have got their breakfast, tack, and stand towards her, Mr Yerk."

The little vessel approached. "Shorten sail, Mr Yerk, and heave the ship to," said the captain to the first-lieutenant.

"Ay, ay, sir."

"All hands, Mr Catwell."

Presently the boatswain's whistle rang sharp and clear, while his gruff voice, to which his mates bore anything but mellow burdens, echoed through the ship—"All hands shorten sail—fore and mainsails haul up—haul down the jib—in topgallant sails—now back the main-topsail."

By heaving-to, we brought the Wave on our weather bow. She was now within a cable's length of the corvette; the captain was standing on the second foremost gun, on the larboard side.

"Mafame,"—to his steward,—"hand me up my trumpet." He hailed the little vessel—"Ho, the Wave, ahoy!"

Presently the responding "hillo!" came down the wind to us from the officer in command of her, like an echo.

"Run under our stern and heave-to, to leeward."

"Ay, ay, sir."

As the Wave came to the wind, she lowered down her boat, and Mr Jigmaree, the boatswain of the dockyard in Jamaica, came on board, and, touching his hat, presented his despatches to the captain. Presently he and the skipper retired into the cabin, and all hands were inspecting the Wave in her new character of one of his Britannic Majesty's cruisers. When I had last seen her, she was a most beautiful little craft, both in hull and rigging, as ever delighted the eye of a sailor; but the dockyard riggers and carpenters had fairly bedevilled her, at least so far as appearances went. First, they had replaced the light rail on her gunwale by heavy solid bulwarks four feet high, surmounted by hammock-nettings, at least another foot, so that the symmetrical little vessel, that formerly floated on the foam light as a sea-gull, now looked like a clumsy, dish-shaped, Dutch dogger. Her long, slender wands of masts, which used to swing about as if there were neither shrouds nor stays to support them, were now as taut and stiff as church-steeples, with four heavy shrouds of a side, and stays and back-stays, and the devil knows, what all.

"Now," quoth Tailtackle, "if them *heav'emtauts* at the yard have not taken the speed out of the little beauty, I am a Dutchman." Timotheus, I may state in the bygoing, was not a Dutchman; but his opinion was sound, and soon verified to my cost. Jigmaree now approached.

"The captain wants you in the cabin, sir," said he.

I descended, and found the skipper seated at a table, with his clerk beside him, and several open letters lying before him. "Sit down, Mr Cringle." I took a chair. "There—read that," and he threw an open letter across the table to me, which ran as follows:—

"SIR,—The Vice-Admiral, commanding on the Jamaica station, desires me to say, that the bearer, the boatswain of the dockyard, Mr Luke Jigmaree, has instructions to cruise for, and if possible to fall in with you, before you weather

Cape Maize, and falling in with you, to deliver up charge of the vessel to you, as well as of the five negroes, and the pilot, Peter Mangrove, who are on board of her. The Wave having been armed and fitted with everything considered necessary, you are to man her with thirty-five of your crew, including officers, and to place her under the command of Lieutenant Thomas Cringle, who is to be furnished with a copy of this letter authenticated by your signature, and to whom you are to give instructions, that he is, first of all, to cruise in the great Cuba channel, until the 14th proximo, for the prevention of piracy, and the suppression of the slave trade carried on between the island of Cuba and the coast of Africa, and to detain and carry into Havanna, or Nassau, New Providence, all vessels having slaves on board, which he may have reason to believe have been shipped beyond the prescribed limits on the African coast, as specified on the margin; and after the 14th he is to proceed direct to New Providence, if unsuccessful, there to land Mr Jigmaree and the dockyard negroes, and await your return from the northward, after having seen the merchantmen clear of the Caicos passage. When you have rejoined the Wave at Nassau, you are to proceed with her as your tender to Crooked Island, and there to await instructions from the Vice-Admiral, which shall be transmitted by the packet to sail on the 9th proximo, to the care of the postmaster. I have the honour to be, Sir, your obedient servant,

"——— ———, Sec.

"To the Hon. Captain Transom,
"&c. &c. &c."

To say sooth, I was by no means amorous of this independent command, as an idea had, at the time I speak of, gone abroad in the navy, that lieutenants commanding small vessels seldom rose higher, unless through extraordinary interest, and I took the liberty of stating my repugnance to my captain.

He smiled, and threw over another letter to me; it was a private one from the Admiral's Secretary, and was as follows:

(*Confidential.*)

"MY DEAR TRANSOM,—The Vice-Admiral has got a hint from Sir ———, to kick that wild splice, young Cringle, about a bit. It seems he is a nephew of old Blueblazes, and as he has taken a fancy to the lad, he has promised his mother that he will do his utmost to give him opportunities of being knocked on the head, for all of which the old lady has professed herself wonderfully indebted.

As the puppy has peculiar notions, hint, directly or indirectly, that he is not to be permanently bolted down to the little Wave, and that if half-a-dozen skippers (you, my darling, among the rest) were to evaporate during the approaching hot months, he may have some small chance of t'other swab. Write me, and mind the claret and curaçoa. Put no address on either; and on coming to anchor, send notice to old Peterkin in the lodge at the Master Attendant's, and he will relieve you and the *pies de gallo,** some calm evening, of all further trouble regarding them. Don't forget the turtle from Crooked Island, and the cigars.—Always, my dear Transom, yours sincerely,

"———— ————."

"Oh, I forgot. The Admiral begs you will spare him some steady old hands to act as gunner, boatswain, &c.—elderly men, if you please, who will shorten sail before the squall strikes him. If you float him away with a crew of boys, the little scamp will get bothered, or capsized in a jiffy. All this for your worship's government. How do you live with your passenger—prime fellow, an't he? My love to him. Lady ——— is dying to see him again."

"Well, Mr Cringle, what say you?"

"Of course, I must obey, sir;—highly flattered by Mr Secretary's good opinion, anyhow." The captain laughed heartily.

"It is nearly calm, I see. We must set about manning this seventy-four for you, without delay. So, come along, Captain Cringle."

When we got on deck,—"Hail the Wave to close, Mr Yerk—I shall go in the yawl," said Transom.

"Lower away the boat, and pipe away the yawlers, boatswain's mate," quoth Yerk.

Presently the captain and I were on the Wave's deck, where I was much surprised to find no less personages than Pepperpot Wagtail and Paul Gelid, Esquires. Mr Gelid, a Conch, or native of the Bahamas, was the same yawning, drawling, long-legged Creole as ever. He had been ill with fever, and had asked a passage to Nassau, where his brother was established. At bottom, however, he was an excellent fellow, warm-hearted, honourable, and upright. As for little Wagtail—oh, he was a delight!—a small round man, with all the Jamaica Creole irritability of temper, but also all the Jamaica warmth of heart about him—straightforward, and scrupulously conscientious in his dealings, but

---

**Customhouse officers,* from the resemblance of the broad arrow, or mark of seizure, to the impression of a fowl's foot.

devoted to good cheer in every shape. He had also been ailing, and had adventured on the cruise in order to recruit. I scarcely know how to describe his figure better than by comparing his corpus to an egg, with his little feet stuck through the bottom of the shell; but he was amazingly active withal.

Both the captain and myself were rejoiced to see our old friends; and it was immediately fixed that they should go on board the corvette, and sling their cots alongside of Mr Bang, so long as the courses of the two vessels lay together. This being carried into execution, we set about our arrangements. Our precious blockheads at the dockyard had fitted a thirty-two pound carronade on the pivot, and stuck two long sixes, one on each side of the little vessel. I hate carronades. I had, before now, seen thirty-two pound shot thrown by them jump off a ship's side with a rebound like a football, when a shot from an eighteen-pounder long gun went crash, at the same range, through both sides of the ship, whipping off a leg and arm, or *aiblins* a head or two, in its transit.

"My dear sir," said I, "don't shove me adrift with that old pot there—do lend me one of your long brass eighteen-pounders."

"Why, Master Cringle, what is your antipathy to carronades?"

"I have no absolute antipathy to them, sir—they are all very well in their way. For instance, I wish you would fit me with two twelve-pound carronades instead of those two popgun long sixes. These, with thirty muskets and thirty-five men or so, would make me very complete."

"A modest request," said Captain Transom.

"Now, Tom Cringle, you have overshot your mark, my fine fellow," thought I; but it was all right, and that forenoon the cutter was hoisted out with the guns in her, and the other dismounted, and sent back in exchange; and in fine, after three days' hard work, I took the command of H.B.M. schooner Wave, with Timothy Tailtackle as gunner, the senior midshipman as master, one of the carpenter's crew as carpenter, and a boatswain's mate as boatswain, a surgeon's mate as surgeon, the captain's clerk as purser, and thirty foremast-men, besides the *blackies*, as the crew. But the sailing of the little beauty had been regularly spoiled. We could still in light winds weather on the corvette, it is true, but then she was a slow top unless it blew half a gale of wind; and as for going anything free, why a sand-barge would have beaten us.

We kept company with the Firebrand until we weathered Cape Maize. It was near five o'clock in the afternoon, the corvette was about half a mile on our lee-bow, when, while walking the deck, after an early dinner, Tailtackle came up to me.

"The commodore has hove-to, sir."

"Very like," said I; "to allow the merchant-ships to close, I presume."

"A gun," said little Reefpoint. "Ah—what signal now? It was the signal to close."

"Put the helm up and run down to him," said I. It was done—and presently the comfortable feeling of bowling along before the breeze succeeded the sharp yerking digging motion of a little vessel, tearing and pitching through a head sea close upon a wind. The water was buzzing under our bows, and we were once more close on the stern of the corvette. There was a boat alongside ready manned. The captain hailed, "I send your orders on board, Mr Cringle, to bear up on your separate cruise." At the same moment, the Firebrand's ensign and pennant were hoisted. We did the same. A gun from the commodore—ditto from the tidy little Wave—and, lo! Thomas Cringle, Esquire, launched for the first time on his own bottom.

By this time the boat was alongside, with Messieurs Aaron Bang, Pepperpot Wagtail, and Paul Gelid—the former with his cot, and half-a-dozen cases of wine, and some pigs, and some poultry, all under the charge of his black servant.

"Hillo," said I; "Mr Wagtail is at home here, you know, Mr Bang, and so is Mr Gelid; but to what lucky chance am I indebted for *your* society, my dear sir?"

"Thank your stars, Tom—*Captain* Cringle, I beg pardon—and be grateful; I am sick of rumbling tumbling in company with these heavy tools of merchantmen, so I entreated Transom to let me go and take a turn with you, promising to join the Firebrand again at Nassau."

"Why, I am delighted,"—and so I really was. "But, my dear sir, I may lead you a dance, and, peradventure, into trouble—a small vessel may catch a Tartar, you know."

"D——n the expense," rejoined my jovial ally; "why, the hot little epicurean Wagtail, and Gelid, cold and frozen as he is, have both taken a fancy to me—and no wonder, knowing my pleasant qualities as they do—ahem; so, for their sakes, I volunteer on this piece of knight-errantry as much as—"

"Poo—you be starved, Aaron dear," rapped out little Wagtail; "you came here, because you thought you should have more fun, and escape the formality of the big ship, and eke the captain's sour claret."

"Ah!" said Gelid, "my fine fellow," with his usual Creole drawl, "You did not wait for my opinion. Ah—oh—why, Captain Cringle, a thousand pardons.

Friend Bang, there, swears that he can't do without you; and all he says about me is neither more nor less than humbug—ah."

"My lovely yellowsnake," quoth Aaron, "and my amiable dumpling gentlemen both, now do hold your tongues.—Why, Tom, here we are, never you mind how, after half a quarrel with the skipper—will you take us, or will you send us back, like rejected addresses?"

"Send you back, my boys! No, no; too happy to get you." Another gun from the corvette. "Firebrands, you must shove off. My compliments, Wiggins, to the captain, and there's a trifle for you to drink my health, when you get into port." The boat shoved off—the corvette filled her maintopsail. "Put the helm up—ease off the mainsheet—stand by to run up the squaresail. How is her head, Mr Tailtackle?"

Timothy gave a most extraordinary grin at my bestowing the *Mister* on him for the first time.

"North-west, sir."

"Keep her so;" and having bore up, we rapidly widened our distance from the commodore and the fleet.

All men know, or should know, that on board of a man-of-war there is never any "yo-heave-oh-ing." That is confined to merchant vessels. But when the crew are having a strong pull of any rope, it is allowable for the man next the belaying-pin to sing out, in order to give unity to the drag, "one—two—three," the strain of the other men increasing with the figure. The tack of the mainsail had got jammed somehow, and on my desiring it to be hauled up, the men, whose province it was, were unable to start it.

"Something foul aloft," said I.

Tailtackle came up. "What are you fiddling at, men? Give me here—one—two—three."

Crack went the strands of the rope under the paws of the Titan, whereby the head of the outermost sailor pitched right into Gelid's stomach, knocked him over, and capsized him headforemost into the windsail which was let down through the skylight into the little well-cabin of the schooner. It so happened that there was a bucket fall of Spanish brown paint standing on the table in the cabin, right below the hoop of the canvass funnel, and into it popped the august pate of Paul Gelid, Esquire. Bang had, in the mean time, caught him by the heels, and with the assistance of Pearl, the handsome negro formerly noticed, who, from his steadiness, had been spared to me as quartermaster, the Conch was once more hoisted on deck, with a scalp of red paint, reaching down over his eyes.

"I say," quoth Bang, "Gelid, my darling, not quite so smooth as the real Macassar, eh? Shall I try my hand—can shave beautifully—eh?"

"Ah," drawled Gelid, "don't require it—lucky my head was shaved in that last fever, Aaron dear. Ah—let me think—you tall man—you sailor fellow—ah—do me the favour to scrape me with your knife—ah—and pray call my servant."

Timothy, to whom he had addressed himself, set to, and scraped the red paint off his poll; and having called his servant, *Chew Chew,* handed him over to the negro, who, giving his arm to him, helped him below, and with the assistance of Cologne water, contrived to scrub him decently clean.

As the evening fell, the breeze freshened; and during the night it blew strong, so that from the time we bore up, and parted company with the Firebrand, until day-dawn next morning, we had ran 130 miles or thereby to the northward and westward, and were then on the edge of the Great Bahama Bank. The breeze now failed us, and we lay roasting in the sun until mid-day, the current sweeping us to the northward, and still farther on to the bank, until the water shoaled to three fathoms. At this time the sun was blazing fiercely right overhead; and from the shallowness of the water, there was not the smallest swell or undulation of the surface. The sea, as far as the eye could reach, was a sparkling light green, from the snow-white sand at the bottom, as if a level desert had been suddenly submerged under a few feet of crystal clear water, which formed a cheery spectacle when compared with the customary leaden or dark-blue colour of the rolling fathomless ocean. It was now dead calm. "Fishing lines there—Idlers, fishing lines," said I; and in a minute there were forty of them down over the side.

In Europe, fish in their shapes partake of the sedate character of the people who inhabit the coasts of the seas or rivers in which they swim—at least I think so. The salmon, the trout, the cod, and all the other tribes of the finny people, are reputable in their shapes, and altogether respectable-looking creatures. But within the tropics, Dame Nature plays strange vagaries; and here, on the Great Bahama Bank, every new customer, as he floundered in on deck—no joke to him, poor fellow—elicited shouts of laughter from the crew. They were in no respect shaped like fish of our cold climates; some were all head—others all tail—some, so far as shape went, had their heads where, with submission, I conceived their tails should have been; and then the colours, the intense brilliancy of the scales of these *monstrous*-looking animals! We hooked up a lot of bonitos, ten pounds apiece, at the least. But Wagtail took small account of them.

"Here," said Bang, at this moment, "by all that is wonderful, look here!" And he drew up a fish about a foot long, with a crop like a pigeon of the tumbler kind, which began to make a loud snorting noise.

"Ah," drawled Gelid, "good fish, with claret sauce."

"Daresay," rejoined Aaron; "but do your Bahama fish speak, Paul, eh? Balaam's ass was a joke to this fellow."

I have already said that the water was not quite three fathoms deep, and it was so clear that I could see down to the very sand, and there were the fish cruising about in great numbers.

"Haul in, Wagtail—you have hooked him," and up came a beautiful black grouper, about four pounds weight.

"Ah, there is the regular jiggery-jiggery," sang out little Reefpoint at the same moment, as he in turn began to pull up his line. "Stand by to land him," and a red snapper, for all the world like a gigantic gold-fish, was hauled on board; and so we carried on, black snappers, red snappers, and rock fish, and a vast variety, for all of which, however, Wagtail had names pat, until at length I caught a most lovely dolphin—a beauty to look at—but dry, terribly dry to eat. I cast it on the deck, and the cameleon tints of the dying fish, about which so many lies have been said and sung, were just beginning to fade, and wax pale, and ashy, and death-like, when I felt another strong jiggery-jiggery at my line, which little Reefpoint had, in the mean time, baited afresh. "Zounds! I have caught a whale—a shark at the very least"—and I pulled him in, hand over hand.

"A most noble Jew fish," said I.

"A Jew fish!" responded Wagtail.

"A Jew fish!" said Aaron Bang.

"A Jew fish!" said Paul Gelid.

"My dear Cringle," continued Wagtail, "when do you dine?"

"At three, as usual."

"Then, Mr Reefpoint, will you have the great kindness to cast off your sink, and hook that splendid fellow by the tail—only through the gristle—don't prick him in the flesh—and let him meander about till half-past two?"

Reefy was half inclined to be angry at the idea of his Majesty's officer being converted into a cook's mate.

"Why," said I, "we shall put him in a tub of water here on deck, Mr Wagtail, if you please."

"God bless me, no!" quoth the gastronome. "Why, he is strong as an eagle, and will smash himself to mummy in half an hour in a tub. No—no; see, he weighs twelve pounds at the very lightest. Lord! Mr Cringle, I am surprised at you."

The fish was let overboard again, according to his desire, and hauled in at the very moment he indicated by his watch, when, having seen him cut up and cleaned, with his own eyes—I believe I may say with his own hand—he betook himself to his small crib to dress.

At dinner our Creole friend was very entertaining. Bang drew him out, and had him to talk on all his favourite topics, in a most amusing manner. All at once Gelid lay back on his chair.

"My God," said he, "I have broken my tooth with that confounded hard biscuit—terrible—really; ah!"—and be screwed up his face, as if he had been eating sour-crout, or had heard of the death of a dear friend.

"Poo," quoth Aaron, "any combmaker will furnish you forth as good as new; those grinders you brag of are not your own, Gelid, you know that."

"Indeed, Aaron, my dear, I know nothing of the kind; but this I know, that I have broken a most lovely white front tooth—ah!"

"Oh, you be hanged," said Aaron; "why, you have been be-chopped any time these ten years, I know."

The time wore on, and it might have been half-past seven when we went on deck.

It was a very dark night—Tailtackle had the watch. "Anything in sight, Mr Tailtackle?"

"Why, no, sir; but I have just asked your steward for your night-glass, as, once or twice—but it is so thick—Pray, sir, how far are we off the Hole in the Wall?"

"Why, sixty miles at the least."

The Hole in the Wall is a very remarkable rock in the Crooked Island Passage, greatly resembling, as the name betokens, a wall breached by the sea or by battering cannon, which rises abruptly out of the water, to a height of forty feet.

"Then," quoth Tailtackle sharply, "there must be a sail close aboard of us, to windward there."

"Where?" said I. "Quick, send for my night-glass."

"I have it here in my hand, sir."

"Let me see;" and I peered through it until my eyes ached again. I could see nothing, and resumed my walk on the quarterdeck. Tailtackle, in the mean time, continued to look through the telescope, and as I turned from aft to walk forward, a few minutes after this—"Why, sir," said he, "it clears a bit, and I see the object that has puzzled me again."

"Eh? give me the glass"—in a second I caught it. "By Jupiter, you say true, Tailtackle! beat to quarters—quick—clear away the long gun forward there!"

All was bustle for a minute. I kept my eye on the object, but I could not make out more than that it was a strange sail; I could neither judge of her size nor her rig, from the distance and the extreme darkness of the night. At length I handed the glass to Tailtackle again. We were at this time standing in towards the Cuba shore, with a fine breeze, and going along seven knots, as near as could be.

"Give the glass to Mr Jigmaree, Mr Tailtackle, and come forward here, and see all snug."

The long gun was slewed round, both carronades were run out, all three being loaded, double-shotted, and carefully primed the whole crew, with our black supernumeraries, being at quarters.

"I see her quite distinct now, sir," sang out Timotheus.

"Well, what looks she like?"

"A large brig, sir, by the wind on the same tack—you can see her now without the glass—there—with the naked eye."

I looked, and certainly fancied I saw some towering object rising high and dark to windward, like some mighty spectre walking the deep, but I could discern nothing more.

"She is a large vessel, sure enough, sir," said Timothy once more—"now she is hauling up her courses, sir—she takes in topgallant sails—why, she is bearing up across our bows, sir—mind she don't rake us."

"The deuce!" said I. I now saw the chase very distinctly bear up. "Put the helm up—keep her away a bit—steady—that will do—fire a shot across her bows, Mr Tailtackle—and, Mr Reefpoint, show the private signal." The gun was fired, and the lights shown, but our spectral friend was all darkness and silence. "Mr Scarfemwell," said I to the carpenter, "stand by the long gun. Tailtackle, I don't like that chap—open the magazine." By this time the strange sail was on our quarter—we shortened sail, while he, finding that his manœuvre of crossing our bows had been foiled by our bearing up also, got the foretack on board again, and set his topgallant sails, all very cleverly. He was not far out of pistol-shot. Tailtackle, in his shirt and trousers and felt shoes, now stuck his head up the main hatchway.

"I would recommend your getting the hatches on, sir—that fellow is not honest, sir, take my word for it."

"Never mind, Mr Tailtackle, never mind. Forward, there; Mr Jigmaree, slap a round shot into him, since he won't speak or heave-to—right between his masts, do you hear—are you ready?"

"All ready, sir."

"Fire!" The gun was fired, and simultaneously we heard a crash on board the strange sail, followed by a piercing yell, similar to what the negroes raise over a dead comrade, and then a long melancholy howl.

"A slaver, and the shot has told, sir," said Mr Handland, the master.

"Then we shall have some fun for it," thought I. I had scarcely spoken, when the brig once more shortened sail; and the instant that the foresail rose, he let fly his bow gun at us—then another, another, and another.

"Nine guns of a side, as I am a sinner," quoth Jigmaree; and three of the shot struck us, mortally wounded one poor fellow, and damaged poor little Reefy by a splinter in the side.

"Standby, men—take good aim—fire!" and we again let drive the long gun and carronade; but our friend was too quick for us, for by this time he had once more hauled his wind, and made sail as close to it as he could stagger. We crowded everything in chase, but he had the heels of us, and in an hour he was once more nearly out of sight in the dark night, right to windward.

"Keep at him, Mr Jigmaree;" and as I feared he was running us in under the land, I dived to consult the chart. There, in the cabin, I found Wagtail, Gelid, and Bang, sitting smoking on each side of the small table, with some brandy-and-water before them.

"Ah," quoth Gelid, "ah! fighting a little? Not pleasant in the evening, certainly."

"Confound you!" said Aaron; "why will you bother at this awkward moment?"

Meanwhile Wagtail was a good deal discomposed.

"My dear fellow, hand me over that devilled biscuit."

Bang handed him over the dish, slipping into it some fragments of ship biscuit, as hard as flint. All this time I was busy poring over the chart. Wagtail took up a piece and popped it into his mouth.

"Zounds, Bang!—my clear Aaron, what dentist are you in league with?—Gelid first breaks his pet fang, and now you—"

"Poo, Poo," quoth his friend, "don't bother now—hillo—what the deuce—I say, Wagtail—Gelid, my lad, look there"—as one of the seamen, with another following him, brought down on his back the poor fellow who had been wounded, and laid his bloody load on the table. To those who are unacquainted with these matters, it may be right to say that the captain's cabin, in a small vessel like the Wave, is often in an emergency used as a cockpit—and so it was in the present instance.

"Beg pardon, captain and gentlemen," said the surgeon, "but I must, I fear, perform an ugly operation on this poor fellow. I fancy you had better go on deck, gentlemen."

Now I had an opportunity to see of what sterling metal my friends were at bottom made. Mr Bang in a twinkling had his coat off.

"Doctor, I can be of use, I know it—no skill, but steady nerves,"—although he had reckoned a *leetle* without his host here. "And I can swathe a bandage too, although no surgeon," said Wagtail.

Gelid said nothing, but he was in the end the best surgeon's mate amongst them. The poor fellow, Wiggins, one of the captain's gigs, and a most excellent man in quarterdeck parlance, was now laid on the table—a fine handsome young fellow, faint and pale,—very pale, but courageous as a lion, even in his extremity. It appeared that a round shot had shattered his leg above the knee. A tourniquet had been applied on his thigh, and there was not much bleeding.

"Captain," said the poor fellow, while Bang supported him in his arms, "I shall do yet, sir; indeed I have no great pain."

All this time the surgeon was cutting off his trousers, and then, to be sure, a terrible spectacle presented itself. The foot and leg, blue and shrunk, were connected with the thigh by a band of muscle about two inches wide and an inch thick; that fined away to a bunch of white tendons or sinews at the knee, which again swelled out as they melted into the muscles of the calf of the leg; but as for the kneebone, it was smashed to pieces, leaving white spikes protruding from the shattered limb above, as well as from the shank beneath. The doctor gave the poor fellow a large dose of laudanum in a glass of brandy, and then proceeded to amputate the limb, high up on the thigh. Bang stood the knife part of it very steadily, but the instant the saw rasped against the shattered bone he shuddered.

"I am going, Cringle—can't stand that—sick as a dog;" and he was so faint that I had to relieve him in supporting the poor fellow. Wagtail had also to go on deck, but Paul Gelid remained firm as a rock. The limb was cut off, the arteries taken up very cleverly, and the surgeon was in the act of slackening the tourniquet a little, when the thread that fastened the largest or femoral artery suddenly gave way—a gush like the jet from a fire-engine took place. The poor fellow had just time to cry out, "Take that cold hand off my heart!" when his chest collapsed, his jaw fell, and in an instant his pulse stopped.

"Dead as Julius Caesar, captain," said Gelid, with his usual deliberation. Dead enough, thought I; and I was leaving the cabin to resume my post on deck, when I stumbled against something, at the ladder foot.

"Why, what is that?" grumbled I.

"It is me, sir," said a small faint voice.

"You! who are you?"

"Reefpoint, sir."

"Bless me, boy, what are you doing here? Not hurt, I hope?"

"A little, sir—a graze from a splinter, sir—the same shot that struck poor Wiggins knocked it off, sir."

"Why did you not go to the doctor, then, Mr Reefpoint?"

"I waited till he was done with Wiggins, sir; but now, since it is all over with him, I will go and be dressed."

His voice grew fainter and fainter, until I could scarcely hear him. I got him in my arms, and helped him into the cabin, where, on stripping the poor little fellow, it was found that he was much hurt on the right side, just above the hip. Bang's kind heart—for by this time a glass of water had cured him of his faintness—shone conspicuous on this occasion.

"Why, Reefy—little Reefy—you are not hurt, my man—surely you are not wounded—such a little fellow—I should have as soon thought of firing at a musquito."

"Indeed, sir, but I am; see here." Bang looked at the hurt as he supported the wounded midshipman in his arms.

"God help me?" said the excellent fellow; "you seem to me fitter for your mother's nursery, my poor dear boy, than to be knocked about in this coarse way here."

Reefy at this moment fell over into his arms in a dead faint.

"You must take my berth, with the captain's permission," said Aaron, while he and Wagtail undressed him with the greatest care, and placed him in the narrow crib.

"Thank you, my dear sir," moaned little Reefpoint; "were my mother here, sir, she would thank you too."

Stern duty now called me on deck, and I heard no more. The night was still very dark, and I could see nothing of the chase, but I made all the sail I could in the direction which I calculated she would steer, trusting that before morning we might get another glimpse of her. In a little while Bang came on deck.

"I say, Tom, now since little Reefy is asleep—what think you—big craft that—nearly caught a Tartar—not very sorry he has escaped, eh?"

"Why, my dear sir, I trust he has *not* escaped: I hope, when the day breaks, now since we have less wind, that we may have a tussle with him yet."

"No, you don't wish it, do you, really and truly?"

"Indeed I do, sir; and the only thing which bothers me is the peril that you and your friends must necessarily encounter."

"Poo, poo! don't mind us, Tom—don't mind us; but an't be too big for you, Tom?"

He said this in such a comical way, that, for the life of me, I could not help laughing.

"Why, we shall see; but attack him I must, and shall, if I can get at him. However, we shall wait till morning; so I recommend your turning in now, since they have cleared away the cockpit out of the cabin; so good-night, my dear sir—I must stay here, I fear."

"Good-night, Tom; God bless you. I shall go and comfort Wagtail and Paul."

I was at this time standing well aft on the larboard side of the deck, close abaft to the tiller-rope, so that, with no earthly disposition to be an eavesdropper, I could neither help seeing nor hearing what was going on in the cabin, as the small open skylight was close to my foot. All vestiges of the cockpit had been cleared away, and the table was laid for supper. Wagtail and Gelid were sitting on the side I stood on, so that I could not see them, although I heard every word they said. Presently Bang entered, and sat down opposite his allies. He crossed his arms, and leant down over the table, looking at them steadily.

"My dear Aaron," I could hear little Wagtail say, "speak, man, don't frighten a body so."

"Ah, Bang," drawled out Paul, "jests are good, being well timed; what can you mean by that face of yours *now*, since the fighting is all over?"

My curiosity fairly overcame my good manners, and I moved round more amidships, so as to command a view of both parties, as they sat opposite each other at the narrow table.

Bang still held his peace for another minute; at length, in a very solemn tone, he said, "Gentlemen, do you ever say your prayers?" I don't know if I mentioned it before, but Aaron had a most musical deep mellow voice, and now it absolutely thrilled to my very soul.

Wagtail and Paul looked at him, and then at each other, with a most absurd expression—between fear and jest—between crying and laughing—but gave him no answer.

"Are you, my lads, such blockheads as to be ashamed to acknowledge that you say your prayers?"

"Ah," said Gelid, "why, ah no—not—that is—"

"Oh, you Catholics are all so bigoted. I suppose we should cross ourselves, eh?" said Wagtail, hastily.

"I am a Catholic, Master Wagtail," rejoined Bang—"better that than nothing. Before sunrise, we may both have proved the truth of our creeds, if *you* have one; but if you mean it as a taunt, Wagtail, it does discredit to your judgment to select such a moment, to say nothing of your heart. However, you cannot make me angry with you, Pepperpot, you little Creole wasp, do as you will." A slight smile here curled Aaron's lip for an instant, although he immediately resumed the solemn tone in which he had previously spoken. "But I had hoped that two such old friends, as you both have been to me, would not altogether have made up their minds in cold blood, if advertised of their danger, to run the chance of dying like dogs in a ditch, without one preparatory thought towards that tremendous Being, before whom we may all stand before morning."

"Murder!" quoth Wagtail, fairly frightened; "are you *really* serious, Aaron? I did not—would not for the world hurt your feelings in earnest, my dear: why do you desire so earnestly to know whether or not I ever say my prayers?"

"Oh, don't bother, man," rejoined Bang, resuming his usual friendly tone; "you had better say boldly that you do not, without any roundaboutation."

"But why, my dear Bang—why do you ask the question?" persisted Wagtail, in a deuced quandary.

"Simply"—and here our friend's voice once more fell to the low deep serious tone in which he had opened the conference—"simply because, in my humble estimation, if you don't say your prayers tonight, it is three to one you shall never pray again."

"The deuce!" said Pepperpot, twisting himself in all directions, as if his inexpressibles had been nailed to his seat, and he was trying to escape from them. "What, in the devil's name, mean you, man?"

"I mean neither more nor less than what I say. I speak English, don't I? I say, that that pestilent young fellow, Cringle, told me half an hour ago that he was *determined*, as he words it, to stick to this Guineaman, who is three times his size, has eighteen guns, while Master Tommy has only three; and whose crew, I will venture to say, triples our number; and the snipe, from what I know of him, is the very man to keep his word—so what say you, my darling, eh?"

"Ah, very inconvenient, ah—I shall stay below," said Paul.

"So shall I," quoth Pepperpot; "won't stick my nose on deck, Aaron dear— no, not for the whole world."

"Why," said Bang, in the same steady low tone, "you shall do as you please, all"—and here he very successfully imitated our *amigo* Gelid's drawl—"and as best suits you, all; but I have consulted the gunner, an old ally of mine, who, to be plain with you—ah—says that the danger from splinter-wounds below is much greater than from their musketry on deck—ah—the risk from the round-shot being pretty equal—ah—in either situation." At this announcement you could have jumped down either Wagtail's or Gelid's throat—Wagtail's for choice—without touching their teeth. "Farther, the aforesaid Timothy, and be hanged to him! deponeth that the only place in a small vessel where we could have had a moderate chance of safety was the run—so called, I presume, from people running to it for safety; but where the deuce this sanctuary is situated I know not, nor does it signify greatly, for it is now converted into a spare powder-magazine, and of course sealed to us. So here we are, my lads, in as neat a taking as ever three unfortunate gentlemen were in, in this weary world. However, now since I have comforted you, let us go to bed-time enough to think on all this in the morning, and I am consumedly tired."

I heard no more, and resumed my solitary walk on deck, peering every now and then through the night-glass until my eyes ached again. The tedious night at length wore away, and the grey dawn found me sound asleep, leaning out at the gangway. They had scarcely begun to wash down the decks, when we discerned our friend of the preceding night, about four miles to windward, close-hauled on the same tack, apparently running in for the Cuba shore as fast as canvass would carry him. If this was his object, we had proved too quick for him, as by casting off stays and slacking shrouds, and, in every way we could think of, loosening the rigid trim of the little vessel, we had in a great measure recovered her sailing: so when he found he was cut off from the land, he resolutely bore up, took in his topgallant sails, hauled up his courses, fired a gun, and hoisted his large Spanish ensign, all in regular man-of-war fashion. By this time it was broad daylight, and Wagtail, Gelid, and Bang were all three on deck, performing their morning ablutions. As for myself, I was well forward, near the long gun. Pegtop, Mr Bang's black valet, came up to me.

"Please, Massa Captain, can you spare me any muskets?"

"Any muskets?" said I; "why, half-a-dozen if you choose."

"De wery number my massa told me to hax for. Tank you, Massa Captain." And forthwith he and the other two black servants in attendance on Wagtail and Gelid, each seized his two muskets out of the arm-chest, with the corresponding ammunition, and, like so many sable Robinson Crusoes, were stumping aft, when I again accosted the aforesaid Pegtop.

"I say, my man, now since you have got the muskets, does your master *really* intend to fight?" The negro stopped short, and faced right round, his countenance expressing very great surprise and wonderment. "Massa Bang fight! Massa Aaron Bang fight?" and he looked up in my face with the most serio-comic expression that could be imagined. "Ah, massa," continued the poor fellow, "you is joking—surely you is joking—my Massa Aaron Bang fight? Oh, massa, surely you can't know he—surely you never see *him* shoot snipe and wild-duck—oh dear! why, him kill wild-duck on de wing—ah, me often see him knock down teal wid single ball, one hundred—ah, one hundred and fifty yards—and man surely more big mark den teal?"

"Granted," I said; "but a teal has not a loaded musket in its claws, as a Spanish buccaneer may have—a small difference, Master Pegtop, in that?"

"None at all, massa," chimed in Pegtop, very energetically—"I myshef, Gabriel Pegtop, Christian man as me is, am one of de Falmouth black shot. Ah, I have been in de woods wid Massa Aaron—one time particular, when dem wery debils, Sambo Moses, Corromantee Tom, and Eboe Peter, took to de bush, at Crabyaw estate after breakfast—ten black shot—me was one—go out along wid our good massa, Massa Aaron. O Lord, we walk troo de cool wood, and over de hot cleared ground, six hour, when everybody say, 'No use dis, Massa Bang—all we tired too much—must stop here—kindle fire—cook wittal.' 'Ah, top dem who hab white liver,' said Massa Aaron; 'you, Pegtop, take you fusee and cutlass, and follow me, my shild'—Massa Aaron alway call me him *shild*, and troo enough, as parson Calaloo say, him family wery much like Joseph coat—many colour among dem, massa—though none quite so *deep* as mine eider"—and here the negro grinned at his own jest. "Well, I was follow him, or rader was go before him, opening up de pass wid me cutlass troo de wery tangle underwood. We walk four hour—see no one—all still and quiet—no breeze shake de tree—oh, I sweat too much—dem hot, massa—sun shine right down, when we could catch glimpse of him—yet no trace of de runaways. At length, on turning corner, perched on small platform of rock, overshadowed by plumes of bamboos, like ostrich feather lady wear at de ball, who shall we see but dem wery dividual d—— rascall I was mention, standing all tree, each wid one carabine pointed at us, at him shoulder, and cutlass at him side? 'Pegtop, my boy,' said Massa Aaron, 'we is *in* for it follow me, but don't fire.' So him pick off Sambo Moses—oh! cool as one cucumber. 'Now,' say he, 'man to man'—and wid dat him tro him gun on de ground, and, drawing him cutlass, we push up—in one moment him and Corromantee Tom close. Tom put up him hand to fend him head—whip—ah—massa cutlass shred de hand at de wrist, like one carrot—down Tom go—atop of him jump Massa Aaron. I master de leetle one, Eboe Peter, and we carry dem both prisoners into Falmouth. Massa Aaron fight? Ah, massa, no hax dat question again."

"Well, but will Mr Gelid fight?" said I.

"I tink him will too—great friend of Massa Bang—good duckshot too—oh yes, tink Massa Paul will fight."

"Why," said I, "your friends are all heroes, Pegtop—will Mr Wagtail fight also?" He stole close up to me, and exchanged his smart Creole gibberish for a quiet sedate accent, as he whispered—

"Not so sure of he—nice little fat man, but too fond of him belly. When I wait behind Massa Aaron chair, Pegtop sometime hear funny ting. One gentleman say—'Ah, dat month we hear Lord Wellington take Saint Sebastian—when, dat is, what time we hear dat news, Massa Wagtail?' him say, 'Eli,' say Massa Wagtail—'oh, we hear of dem news dat wery day de first of de ringtail pigeon come to market.' Den again, 'Dat big fight dem had at soch anoder place, when we hear of dat, Massa Wagtail?' say somebody else.—'Oh, oh, de wery day we hab dat beautiful grouper wid claret-sauce at Massa Whiffle's.' Oh, make me laugh to hear white gentleman mark great fight in him memory by what him eat de day de news come; so, Massa Captain Cringle, me no quite sure weder Massa Wagtail fight or no."

So saying, Pegtop, Chew Chew, and Yampea, each shouldered two muskets apiece, and betook themselves to the after-part of the schooner, where they forthwith set themselves to scour and oil and clean the same in a most skilful manner. I expected the breeze would have freshened as the day broke, but I was disappointed; it fell, towards six o'clock, nearly calm. Come, thought I, we may as well go to breakfast; and my guests and I forthwith sat down to our morning meal. Soon after, the wind died away altogether—and "out sweeps" was the word; but I soon saw we had no chance with the chase at this game, and as to attacking him with the boats, it was entirely out of the question; neither could I, in the prospect of a battle, afford to murder the people by pulling all day under a roasting sun, against one who could man his sweeps with relays of slaves, without one of his crew putting a finger to them; so I reluctantly laid them in, and there I stood looking at him the whole forenoon, as he gradually drew ahead of us. At length I piped to dinner, and the men, having finished theirs, were again on deck; but the calm still continued; and seeing no chance of it freshening, about four in the afternoon we sat down to ours in the cabin. There was little said; my friends, although brave and resolute men, were naturally happy to see the brig creeping away from us, as fighting could only bring them danger; and my own feelings were of that mixed quality, that while I determined to do all I could to bring him to action, it would not have broken my heart had he escaped. We had scarcely finished dinner, however, when the rushing of the water past the run of the little vessel, and the steadiness with which she skimmed along, showed that the light air had freshened.

Presently Tailtackle came down. "The breeze has set down, sir; the strange sail has got it strong to windward, and brings it along with him cheerily."

"Beat to quarters, then, Tailtackle; all hands stand by to shorten sail. How is she standing?"

"Right down for us, sir."

I went on deck, and there was the Guineaman, about two miles to windward, evidently cleared for action, with her decks crowded with men, bowling along steadily under her single-reefed topsails.

I saw all clear. Wagtail and Gelid had followed me on deck, and were now busy with their black servants inspecting the muskets. But Bang still remained in the cabin. I went down. He was gobbling his last plantain, and forking up along with it most respectable slices of cheese, when I entered.

I had seen before I left the deck that an action was now unavoidable, and, judging from the disparity of force, I had my own doubts as to the issue. I need scarcely say that I was greatly excited. It was my first command: my future standing in the service depended on my conduct *now*—and, God help me, I was all this while a mere lad—not more than twenty-one years old. A strange indescribable feeling had come over me, and an irresistible desire to disburden my mind to the excellent man before me. I sat down.

"Hey-day," quoth Bang, as he laid down his coffee-cup; "why, Tom, what ails you? You look deuced pale, my boy."

"Up all night and bothered all day," said I; "wearied enough, I can tell you."

I felt a strong tremor pervade my whole frame at this moment and I was impelled to speak by some unknown impulse, which I could not account for nor analyse.

"Mr Bang, you are the only friend whom I could count on in these countries; you know all about me and mine, and, I believe, would willingly do a kind action to my father's son."

"What are you at, Tom, my dear boy I come to the point, man."

"I will. I am distressed beyond measure at having led you and your excellent friends, Wagtail and Gelid, into this danger; but I could not help it, and I have satisfied my conscience on that point; so I have only to entreat that you will stay below, and not unnecessarily expose yourselves. And if I should fall—may I take this liberty, my dear sir," and I involuntarily took his hand—"if I should fall, and *I doubt if I shall ever see the sun set again,* as we are fearfully over-matched—"

Bang struck in—

"Why, if our friend be too big—why not be off then? Pull foot, man, eh?— Havannah under your lee?"

"A thousand reasons against it, my dear sir. I am a young man and a young officer; my character is to *make* in the service. No, no, it is impossible—an older and more tried hand might have bore up, but I must fight it out. If any stray shot carries me off, my dear sir, will you take"—Mary, I would have said, but I could not pronounce her name for the soul of me—"will you take charge of *her* miniature, and say I died as I have"—a choking lump rose in my throat, and I could not proceed for a second; "and will you send my writing-desk to my poor mother, there are letters in"—the lump grew bigger, the hot tears streamed from my eyes in torrents. I trembled like an aspen-leaf, and, grasping my excellent friend's hand more firmly, I sank down on my knees in a passion of tears, and wept like a woman, while I fervently prayed to that great God, in whose almighty hand I stood, that I might that day do my duty as an English seaman. Bang knelt by me. Presently the passion was quelled. I rose, and so did he.

"Before you, my dear sir, I am not ashamed to have—"

"Don't mention it, my good boy—don't mention it; neither of us, as the old general said, will fight a bit the worse."

I looked at him. "Do you then mean to fight?" said I.

"To be sure I do—why not? I have no wife"—he did not say he had no children. "Fight? To be sure I do."

"Another gun, sir," said Tailtackle through the open skylight. Now all was bustle, and we hastened on deck. Our antagonist was a large brig, three hundred tons at the least, a long low vessel, painted black out and in, and her sides round as an apple, with immensely square yards. She was apparently full of men. The sun was getting low, and she was coming down fast on us, on the verge of the dark-blue water of the sea-breeze. I could make out ten ports and nine guns of a side. I inwardly prayed they might not be long ones; but I was not a little startled to see through the glass that there were crowds of naked negroes at quarters, and on the forecastle and poop. That she was a contraband Guineaman I had already made up my mind to believe and that she had some fifty hands of a crew I also considered likely; but that her captain should have resorted to such a perilous measure—perilous to themselves as well as to us—as arming the captive slaves, was quite unexpected, and not a little alarming, as it evinced his determination to make the most desperate resistance.

Tailtackle was standing beside me at this time, with his jacket off, his cutlass girded on his thigh, and the belt drawn very tight. All the rest of the crew were armed in a similar fashion, the small-arm-men with muskets in their hands, and the rest at quarters at the guns; while the pikes were cast loose from the spars round which they had been stopped, with tubs of wadding and boxes of grape all ready ranged, and everything clear for action.

"Mr Tailtackle," said I, "you are gunner here, and should be in the magazine. Cast off that cutlass; it is not your province to lead the boarders." The poor fellow blushed, having, in the excitement of the moment, forgotten that he was anything more than captain of the Firebrand's maintop.

"Mr Timotheus," said Bang, "have you one of these bodkins to spare?"

Timothy laughed. "Certainly, sir; but *you* don't mean to head the boarders, sir, do you!"

"Who knows, now since I have learned to walk on this dancing cork of a craft?" rejoined Aaron, with a grim smile, while he pulled off his coat, braced on his cutlass, and tied a large red cotton shawl round his head. He then took off his neckerchief and fastened it round his waist as tight as he could draw.

"Strange that all men in peril—on the uneasiness, like," said he, "should always gird themselves as tightly as they can."

The slaver was now within musket-shot, when he put his helm to port, with the view of passing under our stern. To prevent being raked, we had to luff up sharp in the wind, and fire a broadside. I noticed the white splinters glance from his black wales; and once more the same sharp yell rang in our ears, followed by the long melancholy howl already described.

"We have pinned some of the poor blacks again," said Tailtackle, who still lingered on the deck; small space for remark, for the slaver again fired his broadside at us with the same cool precision as before.

"Down with the helm, and let her come round," said I; "that will do—master, run across his stern—out—sweeps forward, and keep her there—get the other carronade over to leeward—that is it—now, blaze away while he is becalmed—fire, small-arm-men, and take good aim."

We were now right across his stern, with the spanker-boom within ten yards of us; and although he worked his two stern-chasers with great determination, and poured whole showers of musketry from his rigging and poop and cabin-windows, yet, from the cleverness with which our sweeps were pulled, and the accuracy with which we were kept in our position right athwart his stern, our fire, both from the cannon and musketry, the former loaded with round and grape, was telling, I could see, with fearful effect,

Crash—"There, my lads, down goes his maintopmast—pepper him well while they are blinded and confused among the wreck. Fire away—there goes the peak, shot away cleverly, close by the throat. Don't cease firing although his flag be down—it was none of his doing. There, my lads, there he has it again; you have shot away the weather foretopsail sheet, and he cannot get from under you."

Two men at this moment lay out on his larboard fore-yardarm, apparently with the intention of splicing the sheet, and getting the dew of the foretopsail once more down to the yard; if they had succeeded in this, the vessel would again have fetched way, and drawn out from under our fire. Mr Bang and Paul Gelid had all this time been firing with murderous precision from where they had ensconced themselves under the shelter of the larboard bulwark, close to the taffrail, with their three black servants in the cabin loading the six muskets, and little Wagtail, who was no great shot, sitting on the deck, handing them up and down.

"Now, Mr Bang," cried I, "for the love of Heaven"—and may Heaven forgive me for the ill-placed exclamation—"mark these two men—down with them!"

Bang turned towards me with all the coolness in the world—"What, those chaps on the end of the long stick?"

"Yes—Yes" (I here, spoke of the larboard fore-yard-arm)—"yes, down with them."

He lifted his piece as steadily as if he had really been duckshooting.

"I say, Gelid, my lad, take you the innermost."

"Ah!" quoth Paul. They fired—and down dropped both men, and squattered for a moment in the water like wounded waterfowl, and then sank for ever, leaving two small puddles of blood on the surface.

"Now, master," shouted I, "put the helm up and lay him alongside—there—stand by with the grapplings—one round the backstay—the other through the chainplate there—so—you have it." As we ranged under his counter—"Mainchains are your chance, men—boarders, follow me!" And in the enthusiasm of the moment I jumped into the slaver's main channel, followed by twenty-eight men. We were in the act of getting over the netting when the enemy rallied, and fired a volley of small arms, which sent four out of the twenty-eight to their account, and wounded three more. We gained the quarterdeck, where the Spanish captain and about forty of his crew showed a determined front, Cutlass and Pistol in hand: we charged them—they stood their ground. Tailtackle (who, the moment he heard the boarders called, had jumped out of the magazine and followed me) at a blow clove the Spanish captain to the chine; the lieutenant, or second in command, was my bird, and I disabled him by a sabre-cut on the sword-arm, when he drew his pistol, and shot me through the left shoulder. I felt no pain, but a sharp pinch and then a cold sensation, as if water had been poured down my neck.

Jigmaree was close by me with a boarding-pike, and our fellows were fighting with all the gallantry inherent in British sailors. For a moment the battle was poised in equal scales. At length our antagonist gave way, when about fifteen of the slaves, naked barbarians, who had been ranged with muskets in their hands on the forecastle, suddenly jumped down into the waist with a yell, and came to the rescue of the Spanish part of the crew.

I thought we were lost. Our people, all but Tailtackle, poor Handlead, and Jigmaree, held back. The Spaniards rallied, and fought with renewed courage, and it was now, not for glory, but for dear life as all retreat was cut off by the parting of the grapplings and warps that had lashed the schooner alongside of the slaver, for the Wave had by this time forged ahead, and lay across the brig's bows, in place of being on our quarter, with her foremast jammed against the slaver's bowsprit, whose spritsail-yard crossed our deck between the masts. We could not therefore retreat to our own vessel if we had wished it, as the

Spaniards had possession of the waist and forecastle; all at once, however, a discharge of round and grape crashed through the bridleport of the brig, and swept off three of the black auxiliaries before mentioned, and wounded as many more, and the next moment an unexpected ally appeared on the field. When we boarded, the Wave had been left with only Peter Mangrove; the five dockyard negroes; Pearl, one of the captain's gigs, the handsome black already introduced on the scene; poor little Reefpoint, who, as already stated, was badly hurt; Aaron Bang, Paul Gelid, and Wagtail. But this Pearl without price, at the very moment of time when I thought the game was up, jumped on deck through the bowport, cutlass in hand, followed by the five black carpenters and Peter Mangrove, after whom appeared no less a personage than Aaron Bang himself and the three blackamoor valets, armed with boarding-pikes. Bang flourished his cutlass for an instant.

"Now, Pearl, my darling, shout to them in Coromantee—shout;" and forthwith the black quartermaster sang out, "Coromantee Sheik Cocoloo, kockernony populorum fiz," which, as I afterwards learned, being interpreted, is, "Behold the Sultan Cocoloo, the great ostrich, with a feather in his tail like a palm-branch; fight for him, you sons of female dogs." In an instant the black Spanish auxiliaries sided with Pearl and Bang and the negroes, and joined in charging the white Spaniards, who were speedily driven down the main hatchway, leaving onehalf of their number dead or badly wounded on the blood-slippery deck. But they still made a desperate defence by firing up the hatchway. I hailed them to surrender.

"Zounds," cried Jigmaree, "there's the clink of hammers they are knocking off the fetters of the slaves."

"If you let the blacks loose," I sang out in Spanish, "by the heaven above us, I will blow you up, although I should go with you! Hold your hands, Spaniards! Mind what you do, madmen!"

"On with the hatches, men," shouted Tailtackle.

They had been thrown overboard, or put out of the way, they could nowhere be seen. The firing from below continued.

"Cast loose that carronade there; clap in a canister of grape—so—now run it forward, and fire down the hatchway." It was done, and taking effect amongst the pent-up slaves, such a yell arose—O God! O God!—I never can forget it. Still the maniacs continued firing up the hatchway.

"Load and fire again." My people were now furious, and fought more like incarnate fiends broke loose from hell than human beings.

"Run the gun up to the hatchway once more." They ran the carronade so furiously forward that the coaming or ledge was split off, and down went the gun, carriage and all, with a crash into the hold. Presently smoke appeared rising up the fore-hatchway.

"They have set fire to the brig; overboard!—regain the schooner, or we shall all be blown into the air like peels of onions!" sang out little Jigmaree.

But where was the Wave? She had broke away, and was now a cables length ahead, apparently fast leaving us, with Paul Gelid and Wagtail, and poor little Reefpoint, who, badly wounded as he was, had left his hammock and come on deck in the emergency, making signs of their inability to cut away the halyards; and the tiller being shot away, the schooner had become utterly unmanageable.

"Up, and let fall the foresail, men—down with the foretack—cheerily now —get way on the brig and overhaul the Wave promptly, or we are lost," cried I. It was done with all the coolness of desperate men. I took the helm, and presently we were once more alongside of our own vessel. Time we were so, for about one hundred and fifty of the slaves, whose shackles had been knocked off, now scrambled up the fore-hatchway, and we had only time to jump overboard when they made a rush aft; and no doubt, exhausted as we were, they would have massacred us on the spot, frantic and furious as they had become from the murderous fire of grape that had been directed down the hatchway.

But the fire was quicker than they. The smouldering smoke, that was rising like a pillar of cloud from the fore-hatchway, was now streaked with tongues of red flame, which, licking the masts and spars, ran up and caught the sails and rigging. In an instant the fire spread to every part of the gear aloft, while the other element, the sea, was also striving for the mastery in the destruction of the doomed vessel; for our shot, or the fall of the carronade into the hold, had started some of the bottom planks, and she was fast settling down by the head. We could hear the water rushing in like a mill-stream. The fire increased—her guns went off as they became heated—she gave a sudden heel—and while five hundred human beings, pent up in her noisome hold, split the heavens with their piercing death-yells, down she went with a heavy lurch, head foremost, right in the wake of the setting sun, whose level rays made the thick dun wreaths that burst from her as she disappeared glow with the hue of the amethyst; and while the whirling clouds, gilded by his dying radiance, curled up into the blue sky in rolling masses, growing thinner and thinner until they vanished away, even like the wreck whereout they arose,—and the circling eddies, created by her sinking, no longer sparkled and flashed in the red light,—and the stilled waters where she had gone down, as if oil had been cast on them, were spread out like polished silver, shining like a mirror, while all around was dark-blue ripple,—a puff of fat black smoke, denser than any we had yet seen, suddenly emerged, with a loud gurgling noise, from out the deep bosom of the calmed sea, and rose like a balloon, rolling slowly upwards, until it reached a little way above our mastheads, where it melted and spread out into a dark pall, that overhung the scene of death, as if the incense of such a horrible and polluted sacrifice could not ascend into the pure heaven, but had been again crushed back upon our devoted heads, as a palpable manifestation of the wrath of *Him* who hath said, "Thou shalt not kill."

For a few moments all was silent as the grave, and I felt as if the air had become too thick for breathing, while I looked up like another Cain.

Presently about one hundred and fifty of the slaves, *men, women, and children,* who had been drawn down by the vortex, rose amidst numberless pieces of smoking wreck to the surface of the sea; the strongest yelling like fiends in their despair, while the weaker, the women and the helpless gasping little ones, were choking, and gurgling, and sinking all around. Yea, the small thin expiring cry of the innocent sucking infant torn from its sinking mother's breast, as she held it for a brief moment above the waters, which had already for ever closed over herself, was there.—But we could not perceive one single individual of her white crew; like desperate men, they had all gone down with the brig. We picked up about one-half of the miserable Africans, and—my pen trembles as I write it—fell necessity compelled us to fire on the remainder, as it was utterly impossible for us to take them on board. Oh that I could erase such a scene for ever from my memory! One incident I cannot help relating. We had saved a woman, a handsome, clear-skinned girl, of about sixteen years of age. She was very faint when we got her in, and was lying with her head over a portsill, when a strong athletic young negro swam to the part of the schooner where she was. She held down her hand to him; he was in the act of grasping it, when he was shot through the heart from above. She instantly jumped overboard, and, clasping him in her arms, they sank, and disappeared together. "Oh, woman, whatever may be the colour of your skin, your heart is of one only!" said Aaron.

Soon all was quiet; a wounded black here and there was shrieking in his great agony, and struggling for a moment before he sank into his watery grave for ever; a few pieces of wreck were floating and sparkling on the surface of the deep in the blood-red sunbeams, which streamed in a flood of glorious light on the bloody deck, shattered hull, and torn sails and rigging of the Wave, and on the dead bodies and mangled limbs of those who had fallen; while some heavy scattering drops of rain fell sparkling from a passing cloud, as if Nature had wept in pity over the dismal scene; or as if they had been blessed tears, shed by an angel, in his heavenward course, as he hovered for a moment, and looked down in pity on the fantastic tricks played by the worm of a day—by weak man in his little moment of power and ferocity. I said something—ill and hastily. Aaron was close beside me, sitting on a carronade slide, while the surgeon was dressing a pike-wound in his neck. He looked up solemnly in my face, and then pointed to the blessed luminary that was now sinking in the sea, and blazing up into the resplendent heavens—"Cringle, for shame—for shame—your impatience is blasphemous. Remember this morning—and thank *Him*"—here he looked up and crossed himself—"thank Him who, while He has called poor Mr Handlead and so many brave fellows to their last awful reckoning, has mercifully brought us to the end of this fearful day;—Oh, thank Him, Tom, *that you have seen the sun set once more!*"

CHAPTER XVI.

THE SECOND CRUISE OF THE WAVE.

"I longed to see the Isles that gem
Old Ocean's purple diadem;
I sought by turns, and saw them all."

Bride of Abydos.

THE PUNCTURE in Mr Bang's neck from the boarding-pike was not very deep, still it was an ugly lacerated wound; and if he had not, to use his own phrase, been somewhat bull-necked, there is no saying what the consequences might have been.

"Tom, my boy," said he, after the doctor was done with him, "I am nicely coopered now—nearly as good as new—a little stiffish or so—lucky to have such a comfortable coating of muscle, otherwise the *carotid* would have been in danger. So come here, and take your turn, and I will hold the candle."

It was a dead calm, and as I had desired the cabin to be again used as a cockpit, it was at this time full of poor fellows, waiting to have their wounds dressed whenever the surgeon could go below. The lantern was brought, and, sitting down on a wadding tub, I stripped. The ball, which I knew had lodged in the fleshy part of my left shoulder, had first of all struck me right over the collar-bone, from which it had glanced, and then buried itself in the muscle of the arm just below the skin, where it stood out as if it had been a sloe both in shape and colour. The collar-bone was much shattered, and my chest was a good deal shaken and greatly bruised but I had perceived nothing of all this at the time I was shot; the sole perceptible sensation was the feeling of cold water running down, and the pinch in the shoulder, as already described. I was much surprised (every man who has been seriously hit being entitled to expatiate) with the extreme smallness of the puncture in the skin through which the ball had entered; you could not have forced a pea through it, and there was scarcely any flow of blood.

"A very simple affair this, sir," said the surgeon, as he made a minute incision right over the ball, the instrument cutting into the cold dull lead with a *cheep*, and then pressing his fingers, one on each side of it, it jumped out nearly into Aaron's mouth.

"A pretty sugar-plum, Tom: if that collar-bone of yours had not been all the harder, you would have been embalmed in a gazette, to use your own favourite expression. But, my good boy, your bruise on the chest is serious; you must go to bed, and take care of yourself."

Alas, there was no bed for me to go to. The cabin was occupied by the wounded, where the surgeon was still at work. Out of our small crew, nine had been killed and eleven wounded, counting passengers—twenty out of forty-two—a fearful proportion.

The night had now fallen.

"Pearl, send some of the people aft, and get a spare squaresail from the sailmaker, and—"

"Will the awning not do, sir?"

"To be sure it will," said I—it did not occur to me. "Get the awning triced up to the stancheons, and tell my steward to get the beds on deck—a few flags to shut us in will make the thing complete."

It was done; and while the sharp cries of the wounded who were immediately under the knife of the doctor, and the low moans of those whose wounds had been dressed, or were waiting their turn, reached our ears distinctly through the small skylight, our beds were arranged on deck under the shelter of the awning, a curtain of flags veiling our quarters from the gaze of the crew. Paul

Gelid and Pepperpot occupied the starboard side of the little vessel, Aaron Bang and myself the larboard. By this time it was close on eight o'clock in the evening. I had merely looked in on our friends, ensconced as they were in their temporary hurricane-house; for I had more work than I could accomplish on deck in repairing damages. Most of our standing, and great part of our running rigging, had been shot away, which the tired crew were busied in splicing and knotting the best way they could. Our mainmast was very badly wounded close to the deck. It was fished as scientifically as our circumstances admitted. The foremast had fortunately escaped—it was untouched; but there were no fewer than thirteen round-shot through our hull, five of them between wind and water.

When everything had been done which ingenuity could devise, or the most determined perseverance execute, I returned to our canvass shed aft, and found Mr Wagtail sitting on the deck, arranging with the help of my steward, the supper equipment to the best of his ability. Our meal, as may easily be imagined, was frugal in the extreme—salt beef, biscuit, some roasted yams, and cold grog—some of Aaron's excellent rum. But I mark it down, that I question if any one of the four who partook of it ever made so hearty supper before or since. We worked away at the junk until we had polished the bone clean as an elephant's tusk, and the roasted yams disappeared in bushelfuls; while the old rum sank in the bottle, like mercury in the barometer indicating an approaching gale.

"I say, Tom," quoth Aaron, "how do you feel, my boy?"

"Why, not quite so buoyant as I could wish. To me it has been a day of fearful responsibility."

"And well it may," said he. "As for myself, I go to rest with the tremendous consciousness that even I, who am not a professional butcher, have this blessed day shed more than one fellow-creature's blood—a trembling consideration—and all for what, Tom? You met a big ship in the dark, and desired her to stop. She said she would not. You said, 'You shall.' She rejoined, 'I'll be d——d if I do.' And thereupon you set about compelling her; and certainly you have interrupted her course to some purpose, at the trivial cost of the lives of *only* five or six hundred human beings, whose hearts were beating cheerily in their bosoms within these last six hours, but whose bodies are now food for fishes."

I was stung. "At your hands, my dear sir, I did not expect this, and—"

"Hush," said he, "I don't blame *you*—it is all right; but why will not the Government at home arrange by treaty that this nefarious trade should be entirely put down? Surely all our victories by sea and land might warrant our stipulating for *so* much, in place of hugger-muggering with doubtful ill-defined treaties, specifying that you *John Crapeau,* and you *Jack Spaniard,* shall steal men, and deal in human flesh, in such and such a degree of latitude *only,* while if you pick up one single slave a league to the northward or southward of the prescribed line of coast, then we shall blow you out of the water wherever we meet you. Why should poor devils, who live in one degree of latitude, be allowed to be kidnapped, whilst we make it felony to steal their immediate neighbours?" Aaron waxed warm as he proceeded—"Why will not Englishmen lend a hand to put down the slave-trade amongst our opponents in sugar-growing, before they so recklessly endeavour to crush slavery in our own worn-out colonies, utterly regardless of our rights and lives? Mind, Tom, I don't defend slavery—I sincerely wish we could do without it; but am I to be the only one to pay the piper in compassing its extinction? If, however, it really *be* that Upas-tree, under whose baleful shade every kindly feeling in the human bosom, whether of master or servant, withers and dies, I ask, Who planted it? If it possess the magical, and incredible, and most pestilential quality that the English gentleman, who shall be virtuous and beneficent, and just in all his ways, *before he leaves home,* and *after he returns home,* shall, during his temporary sojourn within its influence, become a very Nero for cruelty, and have his warm heart of flesh smuggled out of his bosom by some *hocus pocus* utterly unintelligible to any unprejudiced rational being, or indurated into the flint of the *nether* mill-stone, or frozen into a lump of ice—"

"Lord!" ejaculated Wagtail, "only fancy a snowball in a man's stomach, and in Jamaica too!"

Hold your tongue, Waggy, my love," continued Aaron; "if all this were so, I would again ask, Who planted it?—Say not that *we* did it—I am a planter, but I did not plant slavery. I found it growing and flourishing, and fostered by the Government, and made my home amongst the branches like a respectable *corbie craw,* or a pelican in a wild-duck's nest, with all my pretty little tender black *branchers* hopping about me, along with numberless other unfortunates, and now find that the tree is being uprooted by the very hands that planted and nourished it, and seduced me to live in it, and all—"

I laughed aloud—"Come, come, my dear sir, you are a perfect Lord Castlereagh in the *congruity* of your figures. How the deuce can any living thing exist among the poisonous branches of the Upas-tree—or a wild-duck build—"

"Get along with your criticism, Tom, and don't laugh—hang it, don't laugh—but who told you that a corbie cannot?"

"Why *there are* no corbies in Java."

"Pah—botheration—there are pelicans then; but you know it is not an *Upas*-tree, you know it is all a chimera, and, like the air-drawn dagger of Macbeth, 'that there is no such thing.' Now, that is a good burst, Gelid, my lad, ain't it?" said Bang, as he drew a long breath, and again launched forth.

"Our Government shall quarrel about sixpence here or sixpence there of discriminative duty in a foreign port, while they have clapped a knife to our throats, and a flaming fagot to our houses, by absurd edicts and fanatical inter-meddling with our own colonies, where the slave-trade has notoriously, and to their own conviction, entirely ceased; while, I say it again, they will not put out their little finger to prevent, nay, they calmly look on and permit, a traffic utter-ly repugnant to all the best feelings of our nature, and baneful to an incalculable degree to our own West Indian possessions; provided, forsooth, the slaves be stolen within certain limits, which, as no one can prove, naturally leads to this infernal contraband, the suppression of which—Lord, what a thing to think of!—has nearly deprived the world of the invaluable services of me, Aaron Bang, Esquire, Member of Council of the Island of Jamaica, and Custos Rotulorum Populorum Jig of the Parish of—"

"Lord," said Wagtail, "why, the yam is not half done."

"But the rum *is*—ah!" drawled Gelid.

"D——n the yam and the rum too," rapped out Bang. "Why, you belly-gods, you have interrupted such a torrent of eloquence!"

I began to guess that our friends were waxing peppery. "Why, gentlemen, I don't know how *you* feel, but *I* am regularly done up—it is quite calm, and I hope we shall all sleep, so good-night."

We nestled in, and the sun had risen before I was called next morning. I hope

"I rose a sadder and a wiser man,
Upon that morrow's morn."

"On deck, there," said I, while dressing. Mr Peter Swop, one of the Firebrand's master-mates, and now, in consequence of poor Handlead's death, acting-master of the Wave, popped in his head through the opening in the flags. "How is the weather, Mr Swop?"

"Calm all night, sir; not a breath stirring, sir."

"Are the sails shifted?" said I, "and the starboard main-shrouds replaced?"

"They are not yet, sir; the sails are on deck, and the rigging is now stretching, and will be all ready to be got over the masthead by breakfast-time, sir."

"How is her head?"

"Why," rejoined Swop, "it has been boxing all round the compass, sir, for these last twelve hours; at present it is northeast."

"Have we drifted much since last night, Mr Swop?"

"No, sir—much where we were. There are several pieces of wreck and three dead bodies floating close to, sir."

By this time I was dressed, and had gone from under the awning on deck. The first thing I did was to glance my eye over the nettings, and there perceived on our quarter three dead bodies, as Mr Swop had said, floating—one a white Spaniard, and the other the corpses of two unfortunate Africans, who had perished miserably when the brig went down. The white man's remains, swollen as they were from the heat of the climate and sudden putrefaction consequent thereon, floated quietly within pistol-shot, motionless and still; but the bodies of the two negroes were nearly hidden by the clustering sea-birds which perched on them. There were at least two dozen shipped on each carcass, busy with their beaks and claws, while on the other hand, the water in the immediate neighbourhood seemed quite, alive, from the rushing and walloping of numberless fishes, who were tearing the prey piecemeal. The view was anything but pleasant, and I naturally turned my eyes forward to see what was going on in the bows of the schooner. I was startled from the number of black faces which I saw.

"Why, Mr Tailtackle, how many of these poor creatures have we on board?"

"There are fifty-nine, sir, under hatches in the forehold," said Timothy, "and thirty-five on deck; but I hope we shan't have them long, sir. It looks like a breeze to windward. We shall have it before long, sir."

At this moment Mr Bang came on deck.

"Lord, Tom, I thought it was a flea-bite last night, but, mercy! I am as stiff and sore as a gentleman need be. How do *you* feel? I see you have one of your fins in a sling—eh?"

"I am a little stiff, certainly; however, that will go off; but come forward here, my dear sir; come here, and look at this shot-hole—saw you ever anything like that?"

This was the smashing of one of our pumps from a round shot, the splinters from which were stuck into the bottom of the launch, which overhung it, forming really a figure very like the letter A.

"Don't take it to myself, Tom,—no, not at all."

At this moment the black savages on the forecastle discovered our friend, and shouts of "Sheik Cocoloo" rent the skies. Mr Bang, for a moment, appeared startled; so far as I could judge, he had forgotten that part of his exploit, and did not know what to make of it, until at last the actual meaning seemed to flash on him, when, with a shout of laughter, he bolted in through the opening of the flags to his former quarters below the awning. I descended to the cabin, breakfast having been announced, and sat down to our meal, confronted by Paul Gelid and Pepperpot Wagtail. Presently we heard Aaron sing out, the small scuttle being right overhead, "Pegtop, come here—Pegtop, I say help me on with my neckcloth—so—that will do; now I shall go on deck. Why, Pearl, my boy, what do you want?" and before Pearl could get a word in, Aaron continued, "I say, Pearl, go to the other end of the ship, and tell your Coromantee friends that it is all a humbug—that I am *not* the Sultan Cocoloo: furthermore, that I have not a feather in my tail like a palm-branch, of the truth of which I offer to give them ocular proof."

Pearl made his salaam. "Oh, sir, I fear that we must not say too much on that subject; we have not irons for one-half of them savage negirs" (the fellow was as black as a coal himself); "and were they to be undeceived, why, reduced as our crew is, they might at any time rise on and massacre the whole watch."

"The devil!" we could hear friend Aaron say; "oh, then, go forward, and assure them that I am a bigger ostrich than ever, and I shall astonish them presently, take my word for it. Pegtop, come here, you scoundrel," he continued; "I say, Pegtop, get me out my uniform coat"—our friend was a captain of Jamaica militia—"so—and my sword—that will do; and here, pull off my trousers, it will be more classical to perambulate in my shirt, in case it really be necessary to persuade them that the palm-branch was all a figure of speech. Now, my hat—there; walk before me, and fan me with the top of that herring-barrel."

This was a lid of one of the wadding-tubs, which, to come up to Jigmaree's notions of neatness, had been fitted with covers, and forth stumped Bang, preceded by Pegtop doing the honours. But the instant he appeared from beneath the flags, the same wild shout arose from the captive slaves forward, and such of them as were not fettered immediately began to bundle and tumble round our friend, rubbing their flat noses and woolly heads all over him, and taking hold of the hem of his garment, whereby his personal decency was so seriously perilled, that, after an unavailing attempt to shake them off, he fairly bolted, and ran for shelter once more under the awning, amidst the suppressed mirth of the whole crew, Aaron himself laughing louder than any of them all the while. "I say, Tom, and fellow-sufferers," quoth he, after he had run to earth under the awning, and looking down the scuttle into the cabin where we were at breakfast, "how am I to get into the cabin? if I go out on the quarterdeck but one arm's length in order to reach the companion, these barbarians will be at me again. Ah, I see!"

Whereupon, without much more ado, he stuck his legs down through the small hatch right over the breakfast table, with the intention of descending, and the first thing he accomplished was to pop his foot into a large dish of scalding hominy, or hasty-pudding, made of Indian-corn meal, with which Wagtail was in the habit of commencing his stowage at breakfast. But this proving too hot for comfort, he instantly drew it out, and, in his attempt to reascend, he stuck his bespattered toe into Paul Gelid's mouth. "Oh! oh!" exclaimed Paul, while little Wagtail lay back laughing like to die; but the next instant Bang gave another struggle, or wallop, like a *pelloch* in shoal-water, whereby Pepperpot borrowed a good kick on the side of the head, and down came the *Great Ostrich*, Aaron Bang, but without any feather in his tail, as I can avouch, slap upon the table, smashing cups and saucers and hominy, and devil knows what all, to pieces, as he floundered on the board. This was so absurd that we were all obliged to give uncontrolled course to our mirth for a minute or two, when, making the best of the wreck, we contrived to breakfast in tolerable comfort.

Soon after the meal was finished, a light air enabled us once more to lie our course, and we gradually crept to the northward until twelve o'clock in the forenoon, after which time it fell calm again. I went down to the cabin; Bang had been overhauling my small library, when a shelf gave way (the whole affair having been injured by a round shot in the action, which had torn right through the cabin), so down came several scrolls, rolled up, and covered with brown paper.

"What are all these?" I could hear our friend say.

"They are my logs," said I.

"Your what?"

"My private journals."

"Oh, I see," said Aaron, "I will have a turn at them, with your permission. But what is this so carefully bound with red tape, and sealed, and marked—let me see, 'Thomas Cringle, his Log-book.'"

He looked at me.—"Why, my dear sir, to say the truth, this is my first attempt; full of trash, believe me;—what else could you expect from so mere a lad as I was when I wrote it?"

"'The child is father to the man,' Tom, my boy; so, may I peruse it I may I read it for the edification of my learned allies, Pepperpot Wagtail and Paul Gelid, Esquires?"

"Certainly," I replied, "no objection in the world; but you will laugh at me, I know; still, do as you please—only, had you not better have your wound dressed first?"

"My wound! Poo, poo! just enough to swear by—a fleabite—never mind it; so here goes"—and he read aloud what is detailed in the "Launching of the Log," making his remarks with so much *naïveté*, that I daresay the reader will be glad to hear a few of them. His anxiety, for instance, when he read of the young aide-de-camp being shot and dragged by the *stirrup*,* to know "what became of the *empty* horse," was very entertaining; and when he had read the description of Davoust's face and person, where I describe his *nose*† "as neither fine nor dumpy—a fair enough proboscis as noses go"—he laid down the Log with the most laughable seriousness.

"Now," quoth he, "very inexplicit all this, Tom. Why, I am most curious in noses. I judge of character altogether from the nose. I never lost sight of a man's snout, albeit I never saw the tip of my own. You may rely on it that it is all a mistake to consider the regular Roman nose, with a curve like a shoemaker's paring-knife, or the straight Grecian, with a thin transparent ridge that you can see through, or the Deutsch *meerschaum*, or the Saxon pump-handle, or the Scotch *mull*, or any other nose, *that can be taken hold of,* as the standard gnomon. No, no; I never saw a man with a large nose who was not a blockhead—eh! Gelid, my love? But *allons*."—And where, having introduced the German refugees to Captain Deadeye, I go on to say that I thereupon dived into the midshipmen's berth for a morsel of comfort, and was soon "far into the secrets of a pork-pie,"§ he lay back, and exclaimed, with a long drawling emphasis, "A pork-pie!"

---

* *Page 39.*
† *Page 26.*
§ *Page 40.*

"A pork-pie!" said Paul Gelid.

"Why, do you know," said Mr Wagtail—"I—why, I never *in all my life* saw a pork-pie."

"My dear Pepperpot," chimed in Gelid, "we both forget. Don't you remember the day we dined with the Admiral at the Pen, in July last?"

"No," said Wagtail, "I totally forgot it." Bang, I saw, was all this while chuckling to himself. "I absolutely forget it altogether."

"Bless me," said Gelid, "don't you remember the beautiful calipeever we had that day?"

"Really I do not," said Pepperpot, "I have had so many good feeds there."

"Why," continued Gelid, "Lord love you, Wagtail, not remember that calipeever, so crisp in the broiling!

"No," said Wagtail "really I do not."

"Lord, man, *it had a pudding in its belly.*"

"Oh, *now* I remember," said Wagtail.

Bang laughed outright, and I could not help making a holy in my manners also, even prepared as I was for my jest by my sable crony Pegtop.—To proceed.

Aaron looked at me with one of his quizzical grins; "Cringle, my darling, do you keep these Logs still?

"I do, my dear sir, invariably."

"What," struck in little Wagtail, "the deuce!—for instance, shall I, and Paul, and Aaron there, all be embalmed or preserved" ("Say pickled," quoth the latter) "in these said Logs of yours?" This was too absurd, and I could not answer my allies for laughing. As for Gelid, he had been swaying himself backwards and forwards, half asleep, on the hind-legs of his chair all this while, puffing away at a cigar.

"Ah!" said he, half asleep, and but partly overhearing what was going on; "ah, Tom, my dear, you don't say that we shall all be handed down to our poster"—a long yawn—"to our poster"—another yawn—when Bang, watching his opportunity as he sat opposite, gently touched one of the fore-legs of the balanced chair with his toe, while he finished Gelid's sentence by interjecting "iors" as the Conch fell back and floundered over on his stern, his tormentor drawling out in wicked mimicry—

"Yes, dear Gelid, so sure as you have been landed down on your posteriors *now*—ah—you shall be handed down *to* your posterity *hereafter* by that pestilent little scamp Cringle. Ah, Tom, I know you.—Paul, Paul, it will be *paulo post futurum* with you, my lad."

Here we were interrupted by my steward's entering with his tallow face. "Dinner on the table, sir." We adjourned accordingly.

After dinner we carried on very much as usual, although the events of the previous day had their natural effect; there was little mirth, and no loud laughter. Once more we all turned in, the calm still continuing, and next morning, after breakfast, friend Aaron took to the Log again.

But the most amusing exhibition took place when he came to the description of the row in the dark stair at the agent's house, where the negroes fight for the scraps, and capsize Treenail, myself, and the brown lady, down the steps.*

"Why, I say, Tom," again quoth Aaron, "I never knew before that you were in Jamaica at the period you here write of."

"Why, my dear sir, I scarcely can say that I was there, my visit was so hurried."

"Hurried!" rejoined he, "hurried—by no means; were you not in the island for four or five hours? Ah! long enough to have authorised your writing an anti-slavery pamphlet of one hundred and fifty pages."

I smiled.

"Oh, you may laugh, my boy, but it is true: what a subject for an anti-slavery lecture!—listen, and be instructed." Here our friend shook himself as a bruiser does to ascertain that all is right before he throws up his guard, and for the first five minutes he only jerked his right shoulder this way, and his left shoulder t'other way, while his fins walloped down against his sides like empty sleeves; at length, as he warmed, he stretched forth his arms like Saint Paul in the Cartoon—and although he now and then could not help sticking his tongue in his cheek, still the exhibition was so true, and so exquisitely comical, that I never shall forget it.—"The whole white inhabitants of Kingston are luxurious monsters, living in more than Eastern splendour; and their universal practice, during their magnificent repasts, is to entertain themselves, by compelling their black servants to belabour each other across the pate with silver ladles, and to stick drumsticks of turkeys down each other's throats. Merciful heaven!—only picture the miserable slaves, each with the spaul of a turkey sticking in his gob! dwell upon that, my dearly-beloved hearers, dwell upon that—and then let those who have the atrocious hardihood to do so, speak of the kindliness of the planters' hearts. Kindliness! kindliness! to cram the leg of a turkey

---

* Page 56.

down a man's throat, while his yoke-fellow in bondage is fracturing his tender woolly skull—for all negroes, as is well known, have craniums much thinner and more fragile than an egg-shell—with so tremendous a weapon as a silver ladle! Ay, a silver ladle!!! Some people make light of a silver ladle as an instrument of punishment—it is spoken of as a very slight affair, and that the blows inflicted by it are mere child's play. If any of you, my beloved hearers, labour under this delusion, and will allow me, for your edification, to hammer you about the chops with one of the aforesaid silver soup-ladles of those yellow tyrants for one little half-hour, I pledge myself the delusion shall be dispelled once and for ever. Well, then, after this fearful scene has continued for I dare not say how long, the black butler—ay, the black butler, a slave himself—oh, my friends, even the black butlers are slaves—the very men who minister the wine in health, which maketh their hearts glad, and the castor-oil in sickness, which maketh them anything but of a cheerful countenance—this very black butler is desired, on peril of having a drumstick stuck into his own gizzard also, and his skull fractured by the aforesaid *iron* ladles—red hot, it may be—ay, and who shall say they are not full of *molten lead?* yes, molten lead: does not our reverend brother Lachrimæ Roarem say that the ladles *might* have been full of molten lead? and what evidence have we on the other side that they *were not full* of molten lead? Why, none at all, none—nothing but the oaths of all the naval and military officers who have ever served in these pestilent settlements; and of all the planters and merchants in the West Indies, the interested planters—those planters who suborn all the navy and army to a man—those planters whose molasses is but another name for human blood. (Here a large puff and blow, and a swabification of the white handkerchief, while the congregation blow a flourish of trumpets.) My friends—(another puff)—my friends—we all know, my friends, that bullocks' blood is largely used in the sugar-refineries in England; but, alas! there is no bullocks' blood used in the refineries in the West Indies. This I will prove to you on the oath of six Dissenting clergymen. No. What, then, is the inference? Oh, is it not palpable? Do you not every day, as jurors, hang men on circumstantial evidence? Are not many of yourselves hanged and transported every year, on the simple fact being proved of your being found stooping down in pity over some poor fellow with a broken head, with your hands in his breeches pockets in order to help him up? And can *you* fail to draw the proper inference in the present case? Oh no, no! my friends, *it is the blood of the negroes* that is used in these refining pandemoniums—of the poor negroes, who are worth one hundred pounds apiece to their masters, and on whose health and capacity for work these same planters absolutely and entirely depend."

Here our friend gathered all his energies, and began to roar like a perfect bull of Bashan, and to swing his arms about like the sails of a windmill, and to stamp and jump, and lollop about with his body as he went on.

"Well, this butler, this poor black butler—this poor black slave butler—this poor black Christian slave butler—for he may have been a Christian, and most likely was a Christian, and indeed must have been a Christian—is enforced, after all the cruelties already narrated, on pain of being choked with the leg of a turkey himself, and having molten lead poured down his own throat, to do what?—who would not weep?—to—to—to chuck each of his fellow-servants, poor, miserable creatures! each with a bone in his throat, and molten lead in his belly, and a fractured skull—to chuck them, neck and crop, one after another, down a dark staircase, a pitch-dark staircase, amidst a chaos of plates and dishes, and the hardest and most expensive china, and the finest-cut crystal—that the wounds inflicted may be the keener—and silver spoons, and knives, and forks—yea, my Christian brethren, carving-knives and pitchforks—right down on the top of their brown mistresses, who are thereby invariably bruised like the clown in the pantomime—at least as I am told he is, for I never go to such profane places—oh, no!—bruised as flat as pancakes, and generally murdered outright on the spot. Last of all, the landlord gets up, and kicks the miserable butler himself down after his mates, into the very heart of the living mass; and this not once and away, but every day in the week, Sundays not excepted. Oh, my dear, dear hearers, can you—can you, with your fleshy hearts thumping and bumping against your small ribs, forget the black butler, and the mulatto concubines, and the pitchforks, and the iron ladles full of molten lead? My feelings overpower me; I must conclude. Go in peace, and ponder these things in your hearts, and pay your sixpences at the doors. *Exeunt omnes*, piping their eyes, and blowing their noses."

Our shouts of laughter interrupted our friend, who never moved a muscle.

Again, where old Crowfoot asks his steward—"How does the privateer *lay?*"*

"There again, now," said Aaron, with an irritable *girn*—"why, Tom, your style is most pestilent—you *lay* here, and you *lay* there; are you sure that you are not a hen, Tom?"

One more touch at Massa Aaron, and I have done. After coming to the

* *Page 69.*

description of the horrible carnage that the fire from the transport caused on the privateer's deck before she sheered off,† I remarked, "I never recall that early and dismal scene to my recollection—the awful havoc created on the schooner's deck by our fire—the struggling and crawling, and wriggling of the dark mass of wounded men, as they endeavoured, fruitlessly, to shelter themselves from our guns, even behind the dead bodies of their slain shipmates—without conjuring up a very fearful and harrowing image."

"Were you ever at Biggleswade, my dear sir?"

"To be sure I was," said Mr Bang.

"Then did you ever see an eel-pot with the water drawn off, when the snake-like fish were twining, and twisting, and crawling, like Brobdignag maggots, in living knots, a horrible and disgusting mass of living abomination amidst the filthy slime at the bottom?"

"Ach—have done, Tom—hang your similes. Can't you cut your coat by me, man? Only observe the delicacy of mine."

"The corbie craw, for instance," said I, laughing.

"Ever at Biggleswade?" struck in Paul Gelid. "Ever at Biggleswade? Lord love you, Cringle, we have all been at Biggleswade. Don't you know" (how he conceived I should have known, I am sure I never could tell)—"don't you know that Wagtail and I once made a voyage to England, ay, in the hurricane months, too—ah—for the express purpose of eating eels there; and Lord, Tom, my dear fellow" (here he sank his voice into a most dolorous key), "let me tell you that we were caught in a hurricane in the Gulf, and very nearly lost, when, instead of eating eels, sharks would have eaten us—ah—and at length driven into Havannah—ah. And when we did get home"—(here I thought my excellent friend would have cried outright)—"Lord, sir! we found that the *fall* was not the season to eat eels in after all—ah—that is, in perfection. But we found out from Whiffle, whom we met in town, and who had learned it from the guard of the North mail, that one of the last season's pots was still on hand at Biggleswade; so down we trundled in the mail that very evening."

"And don't you remember the awful cold I caught that night, being obliged to go outside?" quoth Waggy.

"Ah, and so you did, my dear fellow," continued his ally. "But gracious—on alighting, we found that the agent of a confounded gormandising lord mayor had that very evening boned the entire contents of the only remaining pot for a cursed livery-dinner—ah. Eels, indeed! we got none but those of the new catch,

---

† *Page 71.*

full of mud, and tasting of mud and red worms. Wagtail was really very ill in consequence—ah."

Pepperpot had all this while listened with mute attention, as if the narrative had been most moving, and I question not he thought so; but Bang—oh, the rogue—looked also very grave and sympathising, but there was a laughing devil in his eye, that showed he was inwardly enjoying the beautiful rise of his friends.

We were here interrupted by a hail from the look-out man at the mast-head—"Land right ahead."

"What does it look like?" said I.

"It makes in low hummocks, sir. Now I see houses on the highest one."

"Hurrah, Nassau, New Providence, ho!"

Shortly after we made the land about Nassau, the breeze died away, and it fell nearly calm.

"I say, Thomas," quoth Aaron, "for this night at least we must still be your guests, and lumber you on board of your seventy-four. No chance, so far as I see, of getting into port to-night; at least if we do, it will be too late to go on shore."

He said truly, and we therefore made up our minds to sit down once more to our rough-and-round dinner, in the small, hot, choky cabin of the Wave. As it happened, we were all in high glee. I flattered myself that my conduct in the late affair would hoist me up a step or two on the roster for promotion, and my excellent friends were delighted at the idea of getting on shore.

After the cloth had been drawn, Mr Bang opened his fire.

"Tom, my boy, I respect your service, but I have no great ambition to belong to it. I am sure no bribe that I am aware of could ever tempt me to make 'my home upon the deep;' and I really am not sure that it is a very gentlemanly calling after all—Nay, don't look glum; what I meant was, the egregious weariness of spirit you must all undergo from consorting with the same men day after day, hearing the same jokes repeated for the hundredth time, and, whichever way you turn, seeing the same faces morning, noon, and night, and listening to the same voices. Oh! I should die in a year's time were I to become a sailor."

"But," rejoined I, "you have your land-bores in the same way that we have our sea-bores; and we have this advantage over you, that if the devil should stand at the door, *we* can always escape from them sooner or later, and can buoy up our souls with the certainty that we can so escape from them at the end of the cruise at the farthest; whereas if you happen to have taken root amidst a colony of bores on shore, why *you* never can escape, unless you sacrifice all your temporalities for that purpose; ergo, my dear sir, our life has its advantages, and *yours* has its disadvantages."

"Too true—too true," rejoined Mr Bang. "In fact, judging from my own small experience, *borism* is fast attaining a head it never reached before. Speechifying is the crying and prominent vice of the age. Why will the ganders not recollect that eloquence is the gift of heaven, Thomas? A man may improve it, unquestionably, but the Promethean fire, the electrical spark, must be from on high. No mental perseverance or education could ever have made a Demosthenes or a Cicero in the ages long past; nor an Edmund Burke—"

"Nor an Aaron Bang in times present," said I.

"Hide my roseate blushes, Thomas," quoth Aaron, as he continued. "Would that men would speak according to their gifts, study Shakespeare and Don Quixote, and learn of me; and that the real blockhead would content himself with speaking when he is spoken to, drinking when he is *drucken* to, and ganging to the kirk when the bell rings. You never can go into a party nowadays, that you don't meet with some shallow, prosing, pestilent ass of a fellow, who thinks that empty sound is conversation; and not unfrequently there is a spice of malignity in the blockhead's composition; but a creature of this calibre you can wither, for it is not worth crushing, by withholding the sunshine of your countenance from it, or by leaving it to drivel on, until the utter contempt of the whole company claps—to change the figure—a wet nightcap as an extinguisher on it, and its small, stinking flame flickers and goes out of itself. Then there is your sentimental water-fly, who *blaws* in the *lugs* of the women and clips the King's English, and your high-flying dominie body, who *whumles* them outright. I speak in a figure. But all these are as dust in the balance to the wearisome man of ponderous acquirements, the solemn blockhead who usurps the *pas*, and, if he happen to be rich, fancies himself entitled to prose and palaver away as if he were Sir Oracle, or as if the pence in his purse could ever fructify the *cauld parritch* in his pate into pregnant brain. There is a plateful of P's for you, at any rate, Tom. Beautiful exemplification of the art alliterative—ain't it?

'Oh wad some power the giftie gie us,
To see ourselves as ithers see us!'

My dear boy, speechifying has extinguished conversation. Public meetings, God knows, are rife enough, and why will the numbskulls not confine their infernal dulness to them? why not be satisfied with splitting the ears of the groundlings there? why will they not consider that convivial conversation should be lively as the sparkle of musketry, brilliant, sharp, and sprightly, and not like the thundering of heavy cannon, or heavier bombs. But no—you shall ask one of the Drawleys across the table to take wine. 'Ah,' says he—and how he makes out the concatenation, God only knows—'this puts me in mind, Mr Thingumbob, of what happened when I was chairman of the county club, on such a day. Alarming times these were, and deucedly nervous I was when I got up to return thanks. My friends, said I, this unexpected and most unlooked-for honour—this—' Here, blowing all your breeding to the winds, you fire a question across his bows, into the fat pleasant fellow, who speaks for society, beyond him, and expect to find that the dull sailor has hauled his wind, or dropped astern—(do you twig how nautical I have become in my lingo, under Tailtackle's tuition, Tom?)—but, alas! no sooner has the sparkle of our fat friend's wit lit up the whole worshipful society, than at the first lull, down comes Drawley again upon you, like a heavy-sterned Dutch dogger, right before the wind—'As I was saying—this unexpected and most unlooked-for honour'—and there you are pinned to the stake, and compelled to stand the fire of all his blunt bird-bolts for half an hour on end. At length his mud has all dribbled from him, and you hug yourself—'Ah, come, here *is* a talking man opening his fire, so we shall have some conversation at last.' But alas and alack-a-day! *Prosey* the second chimes in, and works away, and hems and haws, and hawks up some old scraps of schoolboy Latin and Greek, which are all Hebrew to you, honest man, until at length he finishes off by some solemn twaddle about fossil turnips and vitrified brickbats; and thus concludes *Fozy* No. 2. Oh, shade of Edie Ochiltree! that we should stand in the taunt of such unmerciful spendthrifts of our time on earth. Besides, the devil of it is, that whatever may be said of the flippant *palaverers,* the heavy bores are generally most excellent and amiable men, so that one can't abuse the *sumphs* with anything like a quiet conscience."

"Come," said I, "my dear sir, you are growing satirical."

"Quarter less three," sang out the leadsman in the chains.

We were now running in past the end of Hog Island to the port of Nassau, where the lights were sparkling brightly. We anchored, but it was too late to go on shore that evening, so, after a parting glass of swizzle, we all turned in for the night.

To be near the wharf, for the convenience of refitting, I had run the schooner close in, being aware of the complete security of the harbour, so that in the night I could feel the little vessel gently take the ground. This awoke me and several of the crew; for, accustomed as sailors are to the smooth bounding motion of a buoyant vessel rising and falling on the heaving bosom of the ocean, the least touch on the solid ground, or against any hard floating substance, thrills to their hearts with electrical quickness. Through the thin bulkhead I could hear the officers speaking to each other.

"We are touching the ground," said one.

"And if we be, there is no sea here—all smooth—land-locked entirely," quoth another.

So all hands of us, except the watch on deck, snoozed away once more into the land of deep forgetfulness. We had all for some days previously been over-worked, and over-fatigued; indeed, ever since the action had caused the duty of the little vessel to devolve on one-half of her original crew, those who had escaped had been subjected to great privations, and were nearly worn out.

It might have been four bells in the middle watch when I was awakened by the *discontinuance* of Mr Swop's heavy step overhead; but judging that the poor fellow might have toppled over into a slight temporary snooze, I thought little of it, persuaded as I was that the vessel was lying in the most perfect safety. In this belief I was falling over once more, when I heard a short startled grunt from one of the men in the steerage—then a sudden sharp exclamation from another-a louder ejaculation of surprise from a third—and presently Mr Wagtail, who was sleeping on a mattress spread on the locker below me, gave a spluttering cough. A heavy splash followed, and, simultaneously, several of the men forward shouted out, "Ship full of water—water up to our hammocks;" while Waggy, who had rolled off his narrow couch, sang out at the top of his pipe, "I am drowned, Bang. Tom Cringle, my dear—Gelid, I am drowned—we are all drowned—the ship is at the bottom of the sea, and we shall have eels enough here, if we had none at Biggleswade. Oh! murder! murder!"

"Sound the well," I could hear Tailtackle, who had run on deck, sing out.

"No use in that," I called out, as I splashed out of my warm cot up to my knees in water. "Bring a light, Mr Tailtackle; a bottom plank must have started, or a butt, or a hidden-end. The schooner is full of water beyond doubt, and as the tide is still making, stand by to hoist out the boats, and get the wounded into them. But don't be alarmed, men; the schooner is on the ground, and it is near high-water. So be cool and quiet. Don't bother now—don't—"

By the time I had finished my extempore speech I was on deck, where I soon found that, in very truth, there was no use in sounding the well, or manning the pumps either, as some wounded plank had been crushed out bodily by the pressure of the vessel when she took the ground; and there she lay—

the tidy little Wave—regularly bilged, with the tide flowing into her.

Every one of the crew was now on the alert. Bedding and bags and some provisions were placed in the boats of the schooner, and several craft from the shore, hearing the alarm, were now alongside; so danger there was none, except that of catching cold, and I therefore bethought me of looking in on my guests in the cabin. I descended and waded into our late dormitory with a candle in my hand, and the water nearly up to my waist. I there found my steward, also with a light, splashing about in the water, catching a stray hat here, and fishing up a spare coat there, and anchoring a chair, with a piece of spunyarn, to the pillar of the small side-berth on the starboard side, while our friend Massa Aaron was coolly lying in his cot on the larboard, the bottom of which was by this time within an inch of the surface of the water, and bestirring himself in an attempt to get his trousers on, which by some lucky chance he had stowed away under his pillow overnight; and there he was, sticking up first one peg and then another, until, by sidling and shifting in his narrow lair, he contrived to rig himself in his nether garments. "But, steward, my good man," he was saying when I entered, "where is my coat, eh?" The man groped for a moment down in the water, which his nose dipped into, with his shirt-sleeves tucked up to his armpits, and then held up some dark object, that, to me at least, looked like a piece of black cloth hooked out of a dyer's vat. Alas! this was Massa Aaron's coat; and while the hats were bobbing at each other in the other corner like seventy-fours, with a squadron of shoes in their wakes, and Wagtail was sitting in the side-berth, with his wet night-gown drawn about him, his muscular development in high relief through the clinging drapery, and bemoaning his fate in the most pathetic manner that can be conceived, our ally Aaron exclaimed, "I say, Tom, how do you like the cut of my Sunday coat, eh?" while our friend Paul Gelid, who, it seems, had slept through the whole row, was at length startled out of his sleep, and, sticking one of his long shanks over the side of his cot in act to descend, immersed it in the cold salt brine.

"Lord, Wagtail!" he exclaimed, "my dear fellow, the cabin is full of water—we are sinking—ah! Deucedly annoying to be drowned in this hole, amidst dirty water, like a tubful of ill-washed potatoes—ah."

"Tom—Tom Cringle," shouted Mr Bang at this juncture, while he looked over the edge of his cot on the *stramash* below, "saw ever any man the like of that? Why, see there—there, just under your candle, Tom—a bird's nest floating about with a *mavis* in it, as I am a gentleman."

"D——n your bird's nest and *mavis* too, whatever that may be," roared little Mr Pepperpot. "By Jupiter, it is my wig with a live rat in it!"

"Confound your wig!—ah," quoth Paul, as the steward fished up what I took at first for a pair of brimful water-stoups. "Zounds! look at my boots."

"And *confound* both the wig and boots, say I," sang out Mr Bang. "Look at my Sunday coat. Why, who set the ship on *fire*, Tom?"

Here his eye caught mine, and a few words sufficed to explain how we were situated, and then the only bother was how to get ashore, and where we were to sojourn, so as to have our clothes dried, as nothing could now be done until daylight. I therefore got our friends safely into a Nassau boat alongside, with their wet trunks and portmanteaus in charge of their black servants, and left them to fish their way to their lodging-house as they best could. BY this our negro captives had been landed, and delivered over to the proper authorities, and the wounded and the sound part of the crew had been placed on board of two merchant brigs that lay close to us: the masters of them proving accommodating men, I got them alongside, as the tide flowed, one on the starboard, the other on the larboard side, right over the Wave; and next forenoon, when they took the ground, we rigged two spare topmasts from one vessel to another, and making the main and fore-rigging of the schooner fast to them as the tide once more made, we weighed her, and floated her alongside of the sheer-hulk, against which we were enabled to heave her out, so as to get at the leak, and then by rigging bilge-pumps we contrived to free her and keep her dry. The damaged plank was soon removed; and, being in a fair way to surmount all my difficulties, about half-past five in the evening I equipped myself in dry clothes, and proceeded on shore to call on our friends at their new domicile. When I entered I was shown into the dining-hall by my ally, Pegtop.

"Massa will be here presently, sir."

"Oh—tell him he need not hurry himself. But how are Mr Bang and his friends?"

"Oh, dem all wery so-so, only Massa Wagtail hab take soch a terrible cold, dat him tink he is going to dead; him wery sorry for himshef, for true, massa."

"But where are the gentlemen, Pegtop?"

"All, every one on dem, is in him bed. Wet clothes have been drying all day."

"And when do they mean to dine?"

Here Pegtop doubled himself up, and laughed like to split himself.

"Dem is all dining in bed, massa. Shall I show you to dem?"

"I shall he obliged; but don't let me intrude. Give my compliments, and say I have looked in simply to inquire after their health."

Here Mr Wagtail shouted from the inner apartment.

"Hillo! Tom, my boy!—Tom Cringle!—here, my lad here!"

I was shown into the room from whence the voice proceeded, which happened to be Massa Aaron's bedroom; and there were my three friends stretched on sofas, in their night-clothes with a blanket, sheet, and counterpane over each forming three sides of a square round a long table, on which a most capital dinner was smoking, with wines of several kinds, and a perfect galaxy of wax candles, and their sable valets, in nice clean attire and smart livery-coats, waiting on them.

"Ah, Tom," quoth Massa Paul, "delighted to see you;—come, you seem to have dry clothes on, so take the head of the table."

I did so, and broke ground forthwith with great zeal.

"Tom, a glass of wine, my dear," said Aaron. "Don't you admire us—classical, after the manner of the ancients, eh? Wagtail's head-dress and Paul's nightcap—oh, the comforts of a woollen one! Ah, Tom, Tom, the Greeks had no Kilmarnock—none."

We all carried on cheerily, and Bang began to sparkle.

"Well, now since you have *weighed* the schooner and *found not much wanting*, I feel my spirits rising again.—A glass of champagne, Tom—your health, boy.—The dip the old hooker has got must have surprised the rats and cockroaches. Do you know, Tom, I really have an idea of writing a history of the cruise; only I am deterred from the melancholy consciousness that every blockhead nowadays fancies he can write."

"Why, my dear sir, are you not coquetting for a compliment? Don't we all know that many of the crack articles in Ebony's Mag—"

"Bah," clapping his hand on my mouth; "hold your tongue; all wrong in that—"

"Well, if it be not you then, I scarcely know to whom to attribute them.—Until lately, I only knew you as the warmhearted West Indian gentleman; but now I am certain I am to—"

"Tom, hold your tongue, my beautiful little man. For although I must plead guilty to having mixed a little in literary society in my younger days—

"Alas! my heart, those days are *gane*."

Ah, Mr Swop," continued Mr Bang, as the master was ushered into the room. "Plate and glasses for Mr Swop."

The sailor bowed, perched himself on the very edge of his chair, scarcely within long arm's-length of the table, and sitting bolt upright as if he had swallowed a spare studding-sail-boom, drank our healths and smoothed down his hair on his brow.

"Captain, I come to report the schooner ready to—"Poo," rattled out Mr Bang; "time for your tale by-and-by;—help yourself to some of that capital beef, Peter,—so—Yes, my love," continued our friend, resuming his *yarn*, "I once coped even with John Wilson himself. Yea, in the fulness of my powers, I feared not even the Professor."

"Indeed!" said I.

"True, as I am a gentleman. Why, I once, in a public trial of skill, beat him, even *him*, by eighteen measured inches, from toe to heel."

I stared.

"I was the slighter man of the two, certainly. Still, in a flying leap, I always had the best of it, until he astonished the world with the 'Isle of Palms.' From that day forth my springiness and elasticity left me. 'Fallen was my muscles' brawny vaunt.' I quailed. My genius stood rebuked before him. Nevertheless at *hop-step-and-jump* I was his match still. When out came the 'City of the Plague!' From that hour the Great Ostrich could not hold the candle to the Flying Philosopher. And now, Heaven help me! I can scarcely cover nineteen feet, with every advantage of ground for the run. It is true, the Professor was always in condition, and never required training; now, unless I had time for my hard food, I was seldom in wind."

Mr Peter Swop, emboldened and brightened by the wine he had so industriously swilled, and willing to contribute his quota of conversation, having previously jumbled in his noddle what Mr Bang had said about an ostrich and hard food, asked across the table

"Do you believe ostriches eat iron, Mr Bang?"

Mr Bane, slowly put down his glass, and, looking with the most imperturbable seriousness the innocent master right in the face, exclaimed—

"Ostriches eat iron!—Do I believe ostriches eat iron, did you say, Mr Swop? Will you have the great kindness to tell me if this glass of madeira be poison, Mr Swop? Why, when Captain Cringle there was in the Bight of Benin, from which

'One comes out
Where a hundred go in,'

on board of the—what d'ye call her? I forget her name—they had a tame ostrich, which was the wonder of the whole squadron. At the first go-off it had plenty of food, but at length they had to put it on short allowance of a Winchester bushel of tenpenny nails and a pumpbolt a day; but their supplies failing, they had even to reduce this quantity, whereby the poor bird, after unavailing endeavours to get at the iron ballast, was driven to pick out the iron bolts of the ship in the clear moonlight nights, when no one was thinking of it; so that the craft would soon have been a perfect wreck. And as the commodore would not hear of the creature being killed, Tom here undertook to keep it on copper bolts and sheathing until they reached Cape Coast. But it would not do; the copper soured on its stomach and it died. Believe an ostrich eats iron, quotha! But to return to the training for the jump—I used to stick to beefsteaks and a thimbleful of Burton ale; and again I tried the dried knuckle parts of legs of five-year-old blackfaced muttons; but, latterly, I trained best on birsled peas and whisky—"

"On what?" shouted I, in great astonishment; "on what?"

"Yes, my boys; parched peas and whisky. Charge properly with birsled peas, and if you take a caulker just as you begin your run, there is the linstock to the gun for you, and away you fly through the air on the principle of the Congreve rocket. Well might that amiable, and venerable, and most learned Theban, Cockibus Bungo, who always held the stakes on these great occasions, exclaim, in his astonishment, to Cheesey, the Janitor of many days—as

'Like fire from flint I glanced away,'

disdaining the laws of gravitation—

Ερασμίη πέλεια,
Πόθεν, πόθεν πέτασαι.

By Mercury, I swear—yea, by his winged heel, I shall have at the Professor yet, if I live, and whisky and birsled peas fail me not."

Here Paul and I laughed outright; but Mr Wagtail appeared out of sorts somehow; and Swop looked first at one and then at another, with a look of the most ludicrous uncertainty as to whether Mr Bang was quizzing him, or telling a verity.

"Why, Wagtail," said Gelid, "what ails you, my boy?"

I looked towards our little amiable fat friend. His face was much flushed, although I learned that he had been unusually abstemious, and he appeared heated and restless, and had evidently feverish symptoms about him.

"Who's there?" said Wagtail, looking towards the door with a *raised* look.

It was Tailtackle, with two of the boys carrying a litter, followed by Peter Mangrove, as if he had been chief mourner at a funeral. Out of the litter a black paw, with *fishes* or splints whipped round it by a band of spunyarn, protruded, and kept swaying about like a pendulum.

"What have you got there, Mr Tailtackle?"

The gunner turned round.

"Oh, it is a vagary of Peter Mangrove's, sir. Not contented with getting the doctor to set Sneezer's starboard fore-leg, he insists on bringing him away from amongst the people at the capstan-house."

"True, massa—Massa Tailtackle say true; de poor dumb dog never shall cure him leg, none at all, 'mong de men dere; dey all love him so mosh, and make of him so mosh, and stuff him wid salt wittal so mosh, till him blood inflammation like a hell; and den him so good temper, and so gratify wid dere attention, dat I believe him will eat till him kickeriboo of sorefut [surfeit, I presumed]; and, beside, I know de dog healt will instantly mend if him see you. Oh, Massa Aaron [our friend was smiling], it not like you to make fun of poor black fellow, when him is take de part of soch old friend as poor Sneezer. De captain dere cannot laugh, dat is if him will only tink on dat fearful cove at Puerto Escondido, and what Sneezer did for bote of we dere."

Well, well, Mangrove, my man," said Mr Bang, "I will ask leave of my friends here to have the dog bestowed in a corner of the piazza; so let the boys lay him down there, and here is a glass of grog for you—so. Now go back again,"—as the poor fellow had drunk our healths.

Here Sneezer, who had been still as a mouse all this while, put his black snout out of his hammock, and began to cheep and whine in his gladness at seeing his master, and the large tears ran down his coal-black muzzle as he licked my hand, while every now and then he gave a short fondling bark, as if he had said, "Ah, master, I thought you had forgotten me altogether, ever since the action where I got my leg broke by a grape-shot, but I find I am mistaken."

"Now, Tailtackle, what say you?"

"We may ease off the tackles to-morrow afternoon," said the gunner, "and right the schooner, sir, we have put in a dozen cashaw knees, as tough as leather, and bolted the planks tight and fast. You saw these heavy quarters did us no good, sir; I hope you will beautify her again, now since the Spaniard's shot has pretty well demolished them already. I hope you won't replace them, sir. I hope Captain Transom may see her as she should be—as she was when your honour had your first pleasure cruise in her." Here—but I may have dreamed it—I thought the quid in the honest fellow's cheek stuck out in higher relief than usual for a short space.

"We shall see—we shall see," said I.

"I say, Don Timotheus," quoth Bang, "you don't mean to be off without drinking our healths?" as he tipped him a tumbler of brandy-grog of very dangerous strength.

The warrant-officer drank it and vanished; and presently Mr Gelid's brother, who had just returned from one of the *out* islands, made his appearance, and, after the greeting between them was over, the stranger advanced, and with much grace invited us *en masse* to his house. But by this time Mr Wagtail was so ill that we could not move that night, our chief concern now being to see him properly bestowed; and very soon I was convinced that his disease was a violent bilious fever.

The old brown landlady, like all her caste, was a most excellent nurse; and after the most approved and skilful surgeon of the town had seen him, and prescribed what was thought right, we all turned in. Next morning, before any of us were up, a whole plateful of cards were handed to us, and during the forenoon these were followed by as many invitations to dinner. We had difficulty in making our election, but that day I remember we dined at the beautiful Mrs C——'s, and in the evening adjourned to a ball—a very gay affair; and I do freely avow that I never saw so many pretty women in a community of the same size before. Oh! it was a little paradise, and not without its Eve. But such an Eve! I scarcely think the old Serpent himself could have found it in his heart to have beguiled her.

"I say, Tom, my dear boy," said Mr Bang, "do you see that darling? Oh, who can picture to himself, without a tear, that such a creature of light, such an ethereal-looking thing, whose step 'would ne'er wear out the everlasting flint,' that floating gossamer on the thin air, shall one day become an anxious-looking, sharp-featured, pale-faced, loud-tongued, thin-bosomed, broad-hipped wife!"

The next day, or rather in the same night, his Majesty's ship Rabo arrived, and the first tidings we had of it in the morning were communicated by Captain Qeuedechat himself, an honest, uproarious sailor, who chose to begin, as many a worthy ends, by driving up to the door of the lodging in a cart.

"Is the captain of the small schooner that was swamped here?" he asked of Massa Pegtop.

"Free and easy this," thought I.

"Yes, sir, Captain Cringle is here, but him no get up yet."

"Oh, never mind; tell him not to hurry himself. But where is the table laid for breakfast?"

"Here, sir," said Pegtop, as he showed him into the piazza.

"Ah, that will do—so, give me the newspaper—tol de rol!" and he began reading and singing, in all the buoyancy of mind consequent on escaping from shipboard after a three months' cruise.

I dressed and came to him as soon as I could; and the gallant captain, whom I had figured to myself a fine light gossamer lad of twenty-two, stared me in the face as a fat elderly cock of forty at the least; and as to bulk, I would not have guaranteed that eighteen stone could have made him kick the beam. However, he was an excellent fellow, and that day he and his crew were of most essential service in assisting me in refitting the Wave, for which I shall always be grateful. I had spent the greater part of the forenoon in my professional duty, but about two o'clock I had knocked off in order to make a few calls on the families to whom I had introductions, and who were afterwards so signally kind to me. I then returned to our lodgings in order to dress for dinner, before I sallied forth to worthy old Mr N——'s, where we were all to dine, when I met Aaron.

"No chance of our removing to Peter Gelid's this evening."

"Why?" I asked.

"Oh, poor Pepperpot Wagtail is become alarmingly ill; inflammatory symptoms have appeared, and—" Here the colloquy was cut short by the entrance of Mrs Peter Gelid—a pretty woman enough. She had come to learn herself from our landlady how Mr Wagtail was, and with the kindliness of the country she volunteered to visit poor little Waggy in his sickbed. I did not go into the room with her but when she returned, she startled us all a good deal by stating her opinion that the worthy man was really very ill, in which she was corroborated by the doctor, who now arrived. So soon as the *medico* saw him, he bled him, and after prescribing a lot of effervescing draughts and various febrifuge mixtures, he left a large blister with the old brown landlady, to be applied over his stomach if the wavering and flightiness did not leave him before morning. We returned early after dinner from Mr N——'s to our lodgings, and as I knew Gelid was expected at his brother's in the evening, to meet a large assemblage of kindred, and as the night was rainy and tempestuous, I persuaded him to trust the watch to me; and as our brown landlady had been up nearly the whole of the previous night, I sent for Tailtackle to spell me, while the black valets acted with great assiduity in their capacity of surgeon's mates. About two in the morning Mr Wagtail became delirious, and it was all that I could do, aided by my sable assistants and an old black nurse, to hold him down in his bed. Now was the time to clap on the blister, but he repeatedly tore it off, so that at length we had to give it up for an impracticable job; and Tailtackle, whom I had called from his pallet, where he had gone to lie down for an hour, placed the *caustico*, as the Spaniards call it, at the side of the bed.

"No use in trying this any more at present," said I we must wait until he gets quieter, Mr Tailtackle; so go to your bed, and I shall lie down on this sofa here, where Marie Paparoche" (this was our old landlady) "has spread sheets, I see, and made all comfortable. And send Mr Bang's servant, will you?" (friend Aaron had ridden into the country after dinner to visit a friend and the storm, as I conjectured, had kept him there); "he is fresh, and will call me in case I be wanted, or Mr Wagtail gets worse."

I lay down, and soon fell fast asleep, and I remembered nothing until I awoke about eleven o'clock next morning, and heard Mr Bang speaking to Wagtail, at whose bedside he was standing.

"Pepperpot, my dear, be thankful—you are quite cool—a fine moisture on your skin this morning—be thankful, my little man—how did your blister rise?"

"My good friend," quoth Wagtail, in a thin weak voice, "I can't tell—I don't know; but this I perceive, that I am unable to rise, whether it has risen or no."

"Ah—weak," quoth Gelid, who had now entered the room.

"Nay," said Pepperpot, "not so weak as deucedly sore, and on a very unromantic spot, my dears."

"Why," said Aaron, "the pit of the stomach is not a very genteel department, nor the abdomen neither."

"Why," said Wagtail, "I have no blister on either of those places, but if it were possible to dream of such a thing, I would say it had been clapped on—"

Here his innate propriety tongue-tied him.

"Eh?" said Aaron; "what! has the *caustico* that was intended for the *frontiers* of *Belgium*, been clapped by mistake on the broad *Pays Bas!*"

And so in very truth it turned out; for while we slept the patient had risen, and sat down on the blister that lay, as already mentioned, on a chair at his bedside, and, again toppling into bed, had fallen into a sound sleep, from which he had but a few moments before the time I write of awoke.

"Why, now," continued Aaron to the doctor of the Wave, who had just entered—"why, here *is* a discovery, my dear doctor. You clap a *hot* blister on a poor fellow's head to cool it, but Doctor Cringle there has cooled Master Wagtail's brain by blistering his stern—eh? Make notes, and mind you report this to the College of Surgeons." *

I cleared myself of these imputations. Wagtail recovered: our refitting was completed; our wood and water and provisions replenished; and after spending one of the happiest fortnights of my life, in one continued round of gaiety, I prepared to leave—with tears in my eyes, I will confess—the clear waters, bright blue skies, glorious climate, and warm-hearted community of Nassau, New Providence. Well might that old villain Blackbeard have made this sweet spot his favourite *rendezvous*. By the way, this same John Teach, or Blackbeard, had fourteen wives in the lovely island; and I am not sure but I could have picked

---

* *In the manuscript Log forwarded by Mr Bang, who kindly undertakes to correct the proofs during his friend Cringle's absence in the North Sea, there is a leaf wafered in here, with the following in Mr Aaron's own handwriting:—*

"Master Tommy has allowed his fancy some small poetical licences in this his Log. First of all, in Chapter II of this volume, he lays me out on the table, and makes the scorpion sting me in the night, at Don Ricardo Campana's, whereas the villain himself was the hero of the story, and the man on whom Transom played off his tricks. But not content with this, he makes a bad pun, when speaking of Francesca Cangrejo, which he puts into my mouth, forsooth, as if I had not sins enough of my own to answer for. And, secondly, in the present chapter, why, he was himself in very truth the real King of the Netherlands, the integrity of whose low countries was violated, and not poor Wagtail—as thus: Squire Pepperpot, in his delirium, irritated by the part that Cringle had good-naturedly taken in endeavouring to clap the blister on his stomach, watched his opportunity, and when all hands had fallen into a sound sleep, he got up and approached the sofa, where the *nautical* was snoozing. Tom, honest fellow! dreaming no harm, was luxuriating in the genial climate, and sleeping very much as we are given to believe little pigs do, as described in the old song, so that Pepperpot had no difficulty in applying the argument *a posteriori;* and having covered up the sleeping man-of-war, with the *caustico* adhering to his latter end like bird-lime, he retired noiseless as a cat to his own quarters. Time ran on, and when the blister should have *risen* next morning on Wagtail's stomach, Captain Cringle could not *rise*, and the jest went round; but Thomas nevertheless went about as usual, and was the gayest of the gay, dancing and singing; but whenever he dined out, he always carried a *brechum* with him. This I vouch for. —A. B."

out something approximating to the aforesaid number myself, with time and opportunity, from among such a galaxy of loveliness as then shone and sparkled in this dear little town. Speaking of the pirate Blackbeard, I ought to have related that one morning when I was at breakfast at Mrs C——'s, the amiable and beautiful and innocent girl-matron—ay, you supercilious son of a sea-cook, you may turn tip your nose at the expression, but if you could have seen the burden of my song * as I saw her, and felt the elegancies of her manner and conversation as I felt them—but let us stick to Blackbeard, if you please. We were all comfortably seated at breakfast; I had finished my sixth egg, had concealed a beautiful dried snapper, before which even a *rizzard* haddock sank into insignificance, and was bethinking me of finishing off with a slice of Scotch mutton-ham, when in slid Mr Bang. He was received with all possible cordiality, and commenced operations very vigorously.

He was an amazing favourite of our hostess (as where was he not a favourite?), so that it was some time before he even looked my way. We were in the midst of a discussion regarding the beauty of New Providence, and the West India islands in general; and I was remarking that nature had been liberal, that the scenery was unquestionably magnificent in the larger islands, and beautiful in the smaller; but there were none of those heart-stirring reminiscences, none of those thrilling electrical associations, which vibrate to the heart at visiting scenes in Europe famous in antiquity—famous as the spot in which recent victories had been achieved—famous even for the very freebooters, who once held unlawful sway in the neighbourhood. "Why, there never has flourished hereabouts, for instance, even one thoroughly melodramatic thief." Massa Aaron let me go on, until he had nearly finished his breakfast. At length he fired a shot at me.

"I say, Tom, you are expatiating, I see. Nothing heart-stirring, say you? In *new* countries it would bother you to have *old* associations certainly; and you have had your Rob Roy, I grant you, and the old country has had her Robin Hood. But has not Jamaica had her Three-fingered Jack? Ay, a more gentleman-like scoundrel than either of the former. When did Jack refuse a piece of yam, and a cordial from his horn, to the wayworn man, white or black? When did he injure a woman? When did Jack refuse food and a draught of cold water—the greatest boon, in our ardent climate, that he could offer—to a wearied child? Oh, there was much poetry in the poor fellow! And here, had they not that most

---

* *"Burden.*—Tom was right here; she was within a week of her confinement.—A. B."

melodramatic (as you choose to word it) of thieves, *Black*beard, before whom *Blue*beard must for ever hide his diminished head? Why Bluebeard had only one wife at a time, although he murdered five of them, whereas Blackbeard had seldom fewer than a dozen, and he was never known to murder above three. But I have fallen in with such a treasure! Oh, such a discovery! I have been communing with Noah himself—with an old negro who remembers this very Blackbeard—the pirate Blackbeard."

"The deuce!" said I; "impossible!"

"But it is true. Why, it is only ninety-four years ago since the scoundrel flourished, and this old cock is one hundred and ten. I have jotted it down—worth a hundred pounds. Read, my adorable Mrs C——, read."

"But, my dear Mr Bang," said she, "had you not better read it yourself?"

"You, if you please," quoth Aaron, who forthwith set himself to make the best use of his time.

MEMOIR OF JOHN TEACH, ESQUIRE, VULGARLY CALLED BLACKBEARD, BY AARON BANG, ESQUIRE, F.R.S.

> "He was the mildest-mannered man
> That ever scuttled ship, or cut a throat;
> With such true breeding of a gentleman,
> You never could discern his real thought.
> Pity he loved adventurous life's variety,
> He was so great a loss to good society."

John Teach, or Blackbeard, was a very eminent man—a very handsome man, and a very devil amongst the ladies.

He was a Welshman, and introduced the leek into Nassau about the year 1718, and was a very remarkable personage, although, from some singular imperfection in his moral constitution, he never could distinguish clearly between *meum* and *tuum*.

He found his patrimony was not sufficient to support him, and, as he disliked agricultural pursuits as much as mercantile, he got together forty or fifty fine young men one day, and *borrowed* a vessel from some merchants that was lying at the Nore, and set sail for the Bahamas. On his way he fell in with several West Indiamen, and, sending a boat on board of each, he asked them for the *loan* of provisions and wine, and all their gold and silver and clothes, which request was, in every instance but one, civilly acceded to; whereupon, drinking their good healths, he returned to his ship. In the instance where he had been uncivilly treated, to show his forbearance he saluted them with twenty-one guns; but by some accident the shot had not been withdrawn, so that, unfortunately, the contumacious ill-bred craft sank, and, as Blackbeard's own vessel was very crowded, he was unable to save any of the crew. He was a great admirer of fine air, and accordingly established himself on the island of New Providence, and invited a number of elegant young men, who were fond of pleasure cruises, to visit him, so that presently he found it necessary to launch forth, in order to *borrow* more provisions.

At this period he was a great dandy; and, amongst other vagaries, he allowed his beard to grow a foot long at the shortest, and then plaited it into three strands, indicating that he was a bashaw of no common dimensions. He wore red breeches, but no stockings, and sandals of bullock's hide. He was a perfect Egyptian in his curiousness in fine linen, and his shirt was always white as the driven snow *when* it was clean, which was the first Sunday of every month. In waistcoats he was especially select; but the cut of them very much depended on the fashion in favour with the last gentleman he had *borrowed* from. He never wore anything but a full-dress purple velvet coat, under which bristled three brace of pistols, and two naked stilettoes, only eighteen inches long, and he had generally a lighted match, *fizzing* in the bow of his cocked scraper, whereat he lighted his pipe, or fired of a cannon, as pleased him.

One of his favourite amusements, when he got half slewed, was to adjourn to the hold with his compotators, and, kindling some brimstone matches, to dance and roar as if he had been the devil himself, until his allies were nearly suffocated. At another time he would blow out the candles in the cabin, and blaze away with his loaded pistols at random, right and left, whereby he severely wounded the feelings of some of his intimates by the poignancy of his wit, all of which he considered a most excellent joke. But he was kind to his fourteen wives so long as he was sober, as it is known that he never murdered above three of them. His *borrowing,* however, gave offence to our government, no one can tell how; and at length two of our frigates, the Lime and Pearl, then cruising off the American coast, after driving him from his stronghold, hunted him down in an inlet in North Carolina, where, in an eight-gun schooner, with thirty desperate fellows, he made a defence worthy of his honourable life, and fought so furiously that he killed and wounded more men of the attacking party than his own crew consisted of; and, following up his success, he boarded, sword in hand, the headmost of the two armed sloops, which had been detached by the frigates, with ninety men on board, to capture him; and being followed by twelve men and his trusty lieutenant, he would have carried her out and out, maugre the disparity of force, had he not fainted from loss of blood, when, falling on his back, he died where he fell, like a hero—

"His face to the sky, and his feet to the foe"—

leaving eleven forlorn widows, being the fourteen wives, minus the three that he had throttled.

ᑐᵒᑐ

"No chivalrous associations indeed! Match me such a character as this."

We all applauded to the echo. But I must end my song, for I should never tire in dwelling on the happy days we spent in this most enchanting little island. The lovely blithe girls, and the hospitable kind-hearted men, and the children! I never saw such *cherubs*—with all the sprightliness of the little pale-faced creoles of the West Indies, while the healthy bloom of Old England blossomed on their cheeks.

"I say, Tom," said Massa Aaron, on one occasion when I was rather tedious on the subject, "all those little cherubs, as you call them, at least the most of them, are the offspring of the cotton bales captured in the American war."

"The what?" said I.

"The children of the American war—and I will prove it thus—taking the time from no less an authority than Hamlet, when he chose to follow the great Dictator, Julius Caesar himself, through all the corruption of our physical nature, until he found him stopping a beer barrel—(only imagine the froth of one of our *disinterested* friend Buxton's beer barrels, savouring of quassia, not hop, fizzing through the clay of Julias Caesar the Roman!)—*as* thus: If there had been no Yankee war, there would have been no prize cargoes of cotton sent into Nassau; if there had been no prize cargoes sent into Nassau, there would have been little money made; if there had been little money made, there would have been fewer marriages; if there had been fewer marriages, there would have been fewer cherubs. There is logic for you, my darling."

"Your last is a *non sequitur,* my dear sir," said I, laughing. "But, in the main, Parson Malthus is right—out of Ireland, that is—after all."

That evening I got into a small scrape, by impressing three apprentices out of a Scotch brig, and if Mr Bang had not stood my friend, I might have got into serious trouble. Thanks to him, the affair was soldered.

When on the eve of sailing—having received a letter ordering me to join the

Firebrand at Crooked Island—my excellent friends, Messrs Bang, Gelid, and Wagtail, determined, in consequence of letters which they had received from Jamaica, to return home in a beautiful armed brig that was to sail in a few days, laden with flour. I cannot well describe how much this moved me. Young and enthusiastic as I was, I had grappled myself with hooks of steel to Mr Bang; and now, when he unexpectedly communicated his intention of leaving me, I felt more forlorn and deserted than I was willing to plead to.

"My dear boy," said he, "make my peace with Transom. If urgent business had not pressed me, I would not have broken my promise to rejoin him; but I am imperiously called for in Jamaica, where I hope soon to see you." He continued, with a slight tremor in his voice, which thrilled to my heart, as it vouched for the strength of big regard—"If ever I am where you may come, Tom, and you don't make *my* house *your* home, provided you have not a better of your own, I will never forgive you." He paused. "You young fellows sometimes spend faster than you should do, and quarterly bills are long of coming round. I have drawn for more money than I want. I wish you would let me be your banker for a hundred pounds, Tom."

I squeezed his hand. "No, no—many, many thanks, my dear sir—but I never outrun the constable. Good-by, God bless you. Farewell, Mr Wagtail—Mr Gelid, adieu." I tumbled into the boat and pulled on board. The first thing I did was to send the wine and sea stock, a most exuberant assortment unquestionably, belonging to my Jamaica friends, ashore; but, to my surprise, the boat was sent back, with Mr Bang's card, on which was written in pencil, "Don't affront us, *Captain* Cringle." Thereupon I got the schooner under weigh, and no event worth narrating turned up until we anchored close to the post-office at Crooked Island, two days after.

We found the Firebrand there, and the post-office mail-boat, with her red flag and white horse in it, and I went on board the corvette to deliver my official letter detailing the incidents of the cruise, and was most graciously received by my captain.

There was a sail in sight when we anchored, which at first we took for the Jamaica packet; but it turned out to be the Tinker, friend Bang's flour-loaded brig; and by five in the evening our allies were all three once more restored to us, but, alas! so far as regarded two of them, only for a moment. Messrs Gelid and Wagtail had, on second thoughts, it seems, hauled their wind to lay in a stock of turtle at Crooked Island, and I went ashore with them, and assisted in the selection from the turtle-crawls filled with beautiful clear water and lots of fine lively fresh-caught fish, the postmaster being the turtle-merchant.

"I say, Paul, happier in the fish way here than you were at Biggleswade, eh?" said Aaron.

After we had completed our purchases, our friends went on board the corvette, and I was invited to meet them at dinner, where the aforesaid post-master, a stout conch, with a square-cut coatee and red cape and cuffs, was also a guest.

He must have had but a dull time of it, as there were no other white inhabitants, that I saw, on the island besides himself; his wife having gone to Nassau, which he looked on as a prime city of the world, to be confined, as he told us. Bang said that she must rather have gone to be *delivered* from *confinement;* and, in truth, Crooked Island was a most desolate domicile for a lady; our friend the postmaster's family, and a few negroes employed in catching turtle, and making salt, and dressing some scrubby cotton-trees, composing the whole population. In the evening the packet did arrive, however, and Captain Transom received his orders.

"Captain Transom, my boy," quoth Bang, towards nightfall, the best of friends must part—we must move—good-night—we shall be off presently—good-by," and he held out his hand.

"Devil a bit," said Transom; "Bang, you shall not go, neither you nor your friends. You promised, in fact shipped with me for the cruise, and Lady ——— has my word and honour that you shall be restored to her longing eye sound and safe; so you must all remain, and send down the flour brig to say you are coming."

To make a long story short, Massa Aaron was boned, but his friends were obdurate, so we all weighed that night, the Tinker bearing up for Jamaica, while we kept by the wind, steering for Gonaives in St Domingo.

The third day we were off Cape St Nicholas, and, getting a slant of wind from the westward, we ran up the Bight of Leogane all that night, but towards morning it fell calm: we were close in under the high land, about two miles from the shore, and the night was the darkest I ever was out in anywhere. There were neither moon nor stars to be seen, and the dark clouds settled down until they appeared to rest upon our mastheads, compressing, as it were, the hot steamy air upon us until it became too dense for breathing. In the early part of the night it had rained in heavy showers now and then, and there were one or two faint flashes of lightning, and some heavy peals of thunder, which rolled amongst the distant hills in loud shaking reverberations, which gradually became fainter and fainter, until they grumbled away in the distance in hoarse murmurs, like the low notes of an organ in one of our old cathedrals; but now there was neither rain nor wind—all nature seemed fearfully hushed; for where we lay, in the smooth bight, there was no swell, not even a ripple, on the glass-like sea; the sound of the shifting of a handspike, or the tread of the men as they ran to haul on a rope, or the creaking of the rudder, sounded loud and distinct. The sea in our neighbourhood was strongly phosphorescent, so that the smallest chip thrown overboard struck fire from the water, as if it had been a piece of iron cast on flint; and when you looked over the quarter, as I delight to do, and tried to penetrate into the dark clear profound beneath, you every now and then saw a burst of pale light, like a halo, far down in the depths of the green sea, caused by the motion of some fish, or of what Jack, no great natural philosopher, usually calls *blubbers;* and when the dolphin, or skipjack, leapt into the air, they sparkled out from the still bosom of the deep dark water like rockets, until they fell again into their element in a flash of fire. This evening the corvette had showed no lights, and although I conjectured she was not far from us, still I could not with any certainty indicate her whereabouts. It might now have been about three o'clock, and I was standing on the aftermost gun on the starboard side, peering into the impervious darkness over the taffrail, with my dear old dog Sneezer by my side, nuzzling and fondling after his affectionate fashion, while the pilot, Peter Mangrove, stood within handspike length of me. The dog had been growling, but all in fun, and snapping at me, when in a moment he hauled off, planted his paws on the rail, looked forth into the night, and gave a short anxious bark, like the solitary pop of the sentry's musket to alarm the main-guard in outpost work.

Peter Mangrove advanced, and put his arm round the dog's neck. "What you see, my shild?" said the black pilot.

Sneezer uplifted his voice, and gave a long continuous growl.

"Ah!" said Mangrove, sharply, "Massa Captain, someting near we—never doubt dat—de dog yeerie someting we can't yeerie, and see someting we can't see."

I had lived long enough never to despise any caution, from whatever quarter it proceeded. So I listened, still as a stone. Presently I thought I heard the distant splash of oars. I placed my hand behind my ear, and waited with breathless attention. Immediately I saw the sparkling dip of them in the calm black water, as if a boat, and a large one, was pulling very fast towards us. "Look-out, hail that boat," said I.

"Boat ahoy!" sang out the man to whom I had spoken. No answer. "Coming here?" reiterated the seaman. No better success. The boat or canoe, or whatever it might be, was by this time close aboard of us, within pistol-shot at the farthest—no time to be lost; so I hailed myself, and this time the challenge did produce an answer.

"Sore boat—fruit and wegitab."

"Shore boat, with fruit and vegetables, at this time of night—I don't like it," said I. "Boatswain's mate—all hands—pipe away the boarders. Cutlasses, men—quick—a piratical rowboat is close to." And verily we had little time to lose, when a large canoe or row-boat, pulling twelve oars at the fewest, and carrying twenty-five men or thereabouts, swept up on our larboard quarter, hooked on, and the next moment upwards of twenty unlooked-for visitors scrambled up our shallow side, and jumped on board. All this took place so suddenly that there were not ten of my people ready to receive them, but those ten were the prime men of the ship.

"Surrender! you scoundrels—surrender! You have boarded a man-of-war. Down with your arms, or we shall kill you to a man."

But they either did not understand me, or did not believe me, for the answer was a blow from a cutlass, which, if I had not parried with my night-glass, which it broke in pieces, might have effectually stopped my promotion.

"Cut them down, boarders! down with them—they are pirates!" shouted I; "heave cold shot into their boat alongside—all hands, Mr Rouse-em-out" (to the boatswain), "call all hands."

We closed. The assailants had no firearms, but they were armed with swords and long knives, and as they fought with desperation, several of our people were cruelly haggled; and after the first charge, the combatants on both sides became so blended that it was impossible to strike a blow without running the risk of cutting down a friend. By this time all hands were on deck; the boat alongside had been swamped by the cold shot that had been hove crashing through her bottom, when down came a shower from the surcharged clouds, or waterspout—call it which you will—that absolutely deluged the decks, the scuppers being utterly unable to carry off the water. So long as the pirates fought in a body, I had no fears, as, dark as it was, our men, who held together, knew where to strike and thrust; but when the torrent of rain descended in bucketfuls, the former broke away, and were pursued singly into various corners about the deck, all escape being cut off from the swamping of their boat. Still they were not vanquished, and I ran aft to the binnacle, where a blue-light was stowed away—one of several that we had got on deck to burn that night, in order to point out our whereabouts to the Firebrand. I fired it, and, rushing forward cutlass in hand, we set on the gang of black desperadoes with such fury, that, after killing two of them outright, and wounding and taking prisoners seven, we drove the rest overboard into the sea, where the small-armed men, who by this time had tackled to their muskets, made short work of them, guided as they were by the sparkling of the dark water as they struck out and swam for their lives. The blue-light was immediately answered by another from the corvette, which lay about a mile off; but before her boats, two of which were immediately armed and manned, could reach us, we had defeated our antagonists, and the rain had increased to such a degree, that the heavy drops, as they fell with a strong rushing noise into the sea, flashed it up into one entire sheet of fire.

We secured our prisoners, all blacks and mulattoes, the most villanous-looking scoundrels I had ever seen, and shortly after it came on to thunder and lighten, as if heaven and earth had been falling together. A most vivid flash—it almost blinded me. Presently, the Firebrand burnt another blue-light, whereby we saw that her maintopmast was gone close by the cap, with the topsail and upper spars and yards and gear all hanging down in a lumbering mass of confused wreck; she had been struck by the levin brand, which had killed four men and stunned several more.

By this time the cold grey streaks of morning appeared in the eastern horizon—soon after the day broke; and by two o'clock in the afternoon both corvette and schooner were at anchor at Gonaives. The village, for town it could not be called, stands on a low hot plain, as if the washings of the mountains on the left-hand side as we stood in had been carried out into the sea and formed into a white plateau of sand; all was hot and stunted and scrubby. We brought up, inside of the corvette, in three fathoms water. My superior officer had made the private signal to come on board and dine. I dressed, and the boat was lowered down, and we pulled for the corvette, but our course lay under the stern of two English ships that were lying there loading cargoes of coffee.

"Pray, sir," said a decent-looking man, who leant on the taffrail of one of them—"Pray, sir, are you going on board of the commodore?"

"I am," I answered.

"I am invited there too, sir; will you have the kindness to say I will be there presently?"

"Certainly—give way, men."

Presently we were alongside the corvette, and the next moment we stood on her deck, holystoned white and clean, with my stanch friend Captain Transom and his officers, all in full fig, walking to and fro under the awning, a most magnificent naval lounge, being thirty-two feet wide at the gangway, and extending fifty feet or more aft, until it narrowed to twenty at the taffrail. We were all—the two masters of the merchantmen, decent respectable men in their way, included—graciously received, and sat down to an excellent dinner, Mr Bang taking the lead as usual in all the fun; and we were just on the verge of cigars and cold grog when the first-lieutenant came down and said that the captain of the port had come off, and was then on board.

"Show him in," said Captain Transom, and a tall vulgar-looking blackamoor, dressed apparently in the cast-off coat of a French grenadier officer, entered the cabin with his chapeau in his hand, and a Madras handkerchief tied round his woolly skull. He made his bow, and remained standing near the door.

"You are the captain of the port?" said Captain Transom. The man answered in French, that he was. "Why, then, take a chair, sir, if you please."

He begged to be excused, and after tipping off his bumper of claret, and receiving the captain's report, he made his bow and departed.

I returned to the Wave, and next morning I breakfasted on board of the commodore, and afterwards we all proceeded on shore to Monsieur B——'s, to whom Massa Aaron was known. The town, if I may call it so, had certainly a very desolate appearance. There was nothing stirring; and although a group of idlers, amounting to about twenty or thirty, did collect about us on the end of the wharf—which, by the by, was terribly out of repair—yet they all appeared ill-clad, and in no way so well furnished as the blackies in Jamaica; and when we marched up through a hot, sandy, unpaved street into the town, the low, one storey, shabby-looking houses were fallen into decay, and the streets more resembled river-courses than thoroughfares, while the large carrion-crows were picking garbage on the very crown of the causeway, without apparently entertaining the least fear of us, or of the negro children who were playing close to them—so near, in fact, that every now and then one of the urchins would aim a blow at one of the obscene birds, when it would give a loud discordant croak, and jump a pace or two with outspread wings, but without taking flight. Still, many of the women, who were sitting under the small piazzas or projecting eaves of the houses, with their little stalls filled with pullicate handkerchiefs, and pieces of muslin, and ginghams for sale, were healthy-looking, and appeared comfortable and happy. As we advanced into the town, almost every male we met was a soldier, all rigged, and well dressed too, in the French uniform; in fact, the remarkable man, King Henry, or Christophe, took care to have his troops well fed and clothed in every case. On our way we had to pass by the Commandant, Baron B——'s house, when it occurred to Captain Transom that we ought to stop and pay our respects; but Mr Bang, being bound by no such etiquette, bore up for his friend, Monsieur B——'s. As we approached the house—a long, low, one-storey building, with a narrow piazza, and a range of unglazed windows, staring open, with their wooden shutters, like ports in a ship's side, towards the street—we found a sentry at the door, who, when we announced ourselves, carried arms, all in regular style. Presently a very good-looking negro, in a handsome aide-de-camp's uniform, appeared, and, hat in hand, with all the grace in the world, ushered us into the presence of the Baron, who was lounging in a Spanish chair half asleep; but on hearing us announced, he rose, and received us with great amenity. He was a fat elderly negro, so far as I could judge, about sixty years of age, and was dressed in very wide jean trousers, over which a pair of well-polished Hessian boots were drawn, which, by adhering close to his legs, gave him, in contrast with the wide puffing of his garments above, the appearance of being underlimbed, which he by no means was, being a stout old Turk.

After a profusion of congees and fine speeches, and superabundant assurances of the esteem in which *his* master King Henry held *our* master King George, we made our bows, and repaired to Monsieur B——'s, where I was engaged to dine. As for Captain Transom, he went on board that evening to superintend the repairs of the ship.

There was no one to meet us but Monsieur B—and his daughter, a tall and very elegant brown girl, who had been educated in France, and did the honours incomparably well. We sat down, Massa Aaron whispering in my *lug*, that in Jamaica it was not quite the thing to introduce brown ladies at dinner; but, as he said, "Why not? Neither you nor I are high-caste creoles—so *en avant.*"

Dinner was nearly over, when Baron B——'s aide-de-camp slid into the room. Monsieur B—— rose. "Captain Latour, you are welcome—be seated. I hope you have not dined?"

"Why, no," said the negro officer, as he drew a chair, while he exchanged glances with the beautiful Eugenie, and sat himself down close to *el Señor* Bang.

"Hillo, Quashie! Whereaway, my lad? a little above the salt, ain't you?" ejaculated our *amigo;* while Pegtop, who had just come on shore, and was standing behind his master, stared and gaped in the greatest wonderment. But Mr Bang's natural good-breeding and knowledge of the world instantly recalled him to time and circumstances; and when the young officer looked at him, regarding him with some surprise, he bowed, and invited him, in the best French he could muster, to drink wine. The aide-de-camp was, as I have said, jet-black as the ace of spades; but he was, notwithstanding, so far as figure went, a very handsome man—tall and well made, especially about the shoulders, which were beautifully formed, and, in the estimation of a statuary, would probably have balanced the cucumber curve of the shin; his face, however, was regular negro—flat nose, heavy lips, fine eyes, and beautiful teeth; and he wore two immense gold ear-rings. His woolly head was bound round with a pullicate handkerchief, which we had not noticed until he took off his laced cocked-hat. His coat was the exact pattern of the French staff uniform at the time—plain blue, without lace, except at the cape and cuffs, which were of scarlet cloth covered with rich embroidery. He wore a very handsome straight sword, with steel scabbard, and white trousers and long Hessian boots already described as part of the costume of his general.

Mr Bang, as I have said, had rallied by this time, and, with the tact of a gentleman, appeared to have forgotten whether his new ally was black, blue, or green, while the claret, stimulating him into self-possession, was evaporating in broken French. But his man, Pegtop, had been pushed off his balance altogether; *his* equanimity was utterly gone. When the young officer brushed passed him, at the first go off, while he was rinsing some glasses in the passage, his sword banged against Pegtop's *derrière* as he stooped down over his work. He started and looked round, and merely exclaimed—"*Eigh*, Massa Niger, wurra dat!" But now, when standing behind his master's chair, he saw the aide-de-camp consorting with *him*, whom he looked upon as the greatest man in existence, on terms of equality, all his faculties were paralysed.

"Pegtop," said, "I hand me some yam, if you please."

He looked at me all agape, as if he had been half strangled.

"Pegtop, you scoundrel!" quoth Massa Aaron, "don't you hear what Captain Cringle says, sir?"

"Oh yes, massa;" and thereupon the sable valet brought me a bottle of fish-sauce, which he endeavoured to pour into my wineglass. All this while Eugenie and the aide-de-camp were playing the agreeable—and in very good taste, too, let me tell you.

I had just drunk wine with mine host, when I cast my eye along the passage

that led out of the room, and there was Pegtop dancing and jumping and smiting his thigh, in an ecstasy of laughter, as he doubled himself up, with the tears
welling over his cheeks.

"O Lord! Oh!—Massa Bang bow, and make face, and drink wine, and do
everyting shivil, to one dam black rascall nigger!—Oh, blackee more worser
dan me, Gabriel Pegtop—O Lard!—ha! ha! ha!"—Thereupon he threw himself
down in the piazza, amongst plates and dishes, and shouted and laughed in a
perfect frenzy, until Mr Bang got up, and thrust the poor fellow out of doors, in
a pelting shower, which soon so far quelled the hysterical passion, that he came
in again, grave as a judge, and took his place behind his master's chair once
more, and everything went on smoothly. The aide-de-camp, who appeared quite
unconscious that he was the cause of the poor fellow's mirth, renewed his
attentions to Eugenie; and Mr Bang, M. B——, and myself, were again engaged
in conversation, and our friend Pegtop was in the act of handing a slice of
melon to the black officer, when a file of soldiers with fixed bayonets, stepped
into the piazza, and ordered arms, one taking up his station on each side of the
door. Presently another aide-de-camp, booted and spurred, dashed after them
and, as soon as he crossed the threshold, sang out, *"Place pour Monsieur le
Baron."*

The electrical nerve was again touched—"Oh!—oh!—oh! Garamighty! here
comes anoder on dem," roared Pegtop, sticking the slice of melon, which was
intended for *Mademoiselle Eugenie,* into his own mouth, to quell the paroxysm, if possible (while he fractured the plate on the black aide's skull), and
immediately blew it out again, with an explosion, and a scattering of the fragments, as if it had been the blasting of a stone quarry.

"Zounds, this is too much!" exclaimed Bang, as he rose and kicked the poor
fellow out again with such vehemence, that his skull, encountering the paunch
of our friend the baron, who was entering from the street at that instant, capsized him outright, and away rolled his Excellency the Général de Division,
Commandant de l'Arrondissement, &c. &c., digging his spurs into poor Pegtop's
transom, and *sacréing* furiously, while the black servant roared as if he had
been harpooned by the very devil. The aides started to their feet—and one of
them looked at Mr Bang and touched the hilt of his sword, grinding the word
"satisfaction" between his teeth, while the other ordered the sentries to run
the poor fellow, whose mirth had been so uproarious, through. However, he got
off with one or two *progues* in a very safe place; and when Monsieur B——

explained how matters stood, and that the *"pauvre diable,"* as the black baron coolly called him, was a mere servant, and an uncultivated creature, and that no insult was meant, we had all a hearty laugh, and everything rolled right again. At length the baron and his black tail rose to wish us a good-evening, and we were thinking of finishing off with a cigar and a glass of cold grog, when Monsieur B——'s daughter returned into the piazza very pale, and evidently much frightened. *"Mon père,"* said she—while her voice quavered from excessive agitation—"My father—why do the soldiers remain?"

We all peered into the dark passage, and there, true enough, were the black sentries at their posts beside the doorway, still and motionless as statues. Monsieur B——, poor fellow, fell back in his chair at the sight, as if he had been shot through the heart.

"My fate is sealed—I am lost—O Eugenie!" were the only words he could utter.

"No, no," exclaimed the weeping girl, "God forbid—the baron is a kindhearted man, King Henry cannot—no, no—he knows you are not disaffected, he will not injure you."

Here one of the black aides-de-camp suddenly returned. It was the poor fellow who had been making love to Eugenie during the entertainment. He looked absolutely blue with dismay; his voice shook, and his knees knocked together as he approached our host.

He tried to speak, but could not. *"O Pierre, Pierre,"* moaned, or rather gasped Eugenie, "what have you come to communicate? what dreadful news are you the bearer of?" He held out an open letter to poor B——, who, unable to read it from excessive agitation, handed it to me. It ran thus:

> MONSIEUR LE BARON,—Monsieur —— has been arrested here this morning: he is a white Frenchman, and there are strong suspicions against him. Place his partner M. B—— under the surveillance of the police instantly. You are made answerable for his safe custody.
>
> "Witness his Majesty's hand and seal, at Sans Souci, this . . .
>
> "THE COUNT ——."

"Then I am doomed," groaned poor M. B——. His daughter fainted, the black officer wept, and, having laid his senseless mistress on a sofa, he approached and wrung B——'s hand. "Alas, my dear sir—how my heart bleeds! But cheer up—King Henry is just—all may be right—all may still be right; and so far as my duty to him will allow, you may count on nothing being done here that is not absolutely necessary for holding ourselves blameless with the Government."

Enough and to spare of this. We slept on shore that night, and a very neat catastrophe was likely to have ensued thereupon. Intending to go on board ship at daybreak, I had got up and dressed myself, and opened the door into the street to let myself out, when I stumbled unwittingly against the black sentry, who must have been half asleep, for he immediately stepped several paces back, and, presenting his musket, the clear barrel glancing in the moonlight, snapped it at me. Fortunately it missed fire, which gave me time to explain that it was not M. B—— attempting to escape; but that day week he was marched to the prison of La Force, near Cape Henry, where his partner had been previously lodged; and *from that hour to this, neither of them were ever heard of.* Next evening I again went ashore, but I was denied admittance to him; and, as my orders were imperative not to interfere in any way, I had to return on board with a heavy heart.

The day following Captain Transom and myself paid a formal visit to the black baron, in order to leave no stone unturned to obtain poor B——'s release if we could. Mr Bang accompanied us. We found the sable dignitary lounging in a grass hammock (slung from corner to corner of a very comfortless room, for the floor was tiled, the windows were unglazed, and there was no furniture whatever but an old-fashioned mahogany sideboard and three wicker chairs) apparently half asleep, or *ruminating* after his breakfast. On our being announced by a half-naked negro servant, who aroused him, he got up and received us very kindly—I beg his lordship's pardon, I should write graciously—and made us take wine and biscuit, and talked and rattled; but I saw he carefully avoided the subject which he evidently knew was the object of our visit. At length, finding it would be impossible for him to parry it much longer single-handed, with tact worthy of a man of fashion, he called out, "Marie! Marie!" Our eyes followed his, and we saw a young and very handsome brown *lady* rise, whom we had perceived seated at her work when we first entered, in a small, dark, back porch, and advance, after curtsying to us *seriatim*, with great elegance, as the old fat *nigger* introduced her to us as Madame la Baronne."

"His *wife?*" whispered Aaron; "the old rank goat!"

Her brown ladyship did the honours of the wine-ewer with the perfect quietude and ease of a well-bred woman. She was a most lovely, clear-skinned, quadroon girl. She could not have been twenty; tall, and beautifully shaped. Her long coal-black tresses were dressed high on her head, which was bound round with the everlasting Madras handkerchief, in which pale blue was the prevailing colour; but it was elegantly adjusted, and did not come down far enough to shade the fine development of her majestic forehead—Pasta's in *Semiramide* was not more commanding. Her eyebrows were delicately arched and sharply defined, and her eyes of jet were large and swimming; her nose had not utterly abjured its African origin, neither had her lips, but, notwithstanding, her countenance shone with all the beauty of expression so conspicuous in the Egyptian sphinx—Abyssinian, but most sweet; while her teeth were as the finest ivory, and her chin, and threat, and bosom, as if her bust had been an antique statue of the rarest workmanship. The only ornaments she wore were two large virgin gold ear-rings, massive yellow hoops without any carving, but so heavy, that they seemed to weigh down the small thin transparent ears which they perforated; and a broad black velvet band round her neck, to which was appended a large massive crucifix of the same metal. She also wore two broad bracelets of black velvet clasped with gold. Her beautifully moulded form was scarcely veiled by a cambric *chemise*, with exceedingly short sleeves, over which she wore a rose-coloured silk petticoat, short enough to display a finely-formed foot and ankle, with a well-selected pearl-white silk stocking, and a neat low-cut French black kid shoe. As for gown, she had none. She wore a large sparkling diamond ring on her marriage finger, and we were all bowing before the deity when our attention was arrested by a cloud of dust at the top of the street, and presently a solitary black dragoon sparked out from it, his accoutrements and headpiece blazing in the sun, then three more abreast, and immediately a troop of five-and-twenty cavaliers, or thereabouts, came thundering down the street. They formed opposite the Baron's house, and I will say I never saw a better appointed troop of horse anywhere. Presently an aide-de-camp scampered up; and having arrived opposite the door, dismounted, and entering, exclaimed, *"Les Comtes de Lemonade et Marmalade."*—"The who?" said Mr Pang; but presently two very handsome young men of colour, in splendid uniforms, rode up, followed by a glittering staff, of at least twenty mounted officers. They alighted, and entering, made their bow to Baron B——. The youngest, the Count Lemonade, spoke very decent English; and what between Mr Bang's and my bad, and Captain Transom's very good, French, we all made ourselves agreeable. I may state here that *Lemonade* and *Marmalade* are two districts of the island of St Domingo, which had been pitched on by

Christophe to give titles to two of his fire-new nobility. The grandees had come on a survey of the district; and although we did not fail to press the matter of poor B——'s release, yet they either had no authority to interfere in the matter, or they would not acknowledge that they had, so we reluctantly took leave and went on shipboard.

"Tom, you villain," said Mr Bang, as we stepped into the boat, "if my eye had caught yours when these *noblemen* made their *entrée*, I should have exploded with laughter, and most likely have had my throat cut for my pains. Pray, did his Highness of *Lemonade* carry a punch-ladle in his hand? I am sure I expected he of *Marmalade* to have carried a jelly-can! Oh, Tom, at the moment I heard them announced, my old dear mother flitted before my mind's eye, with the bright, well-scoured, large brass pans in the background, as she superintended her handmaidens in their annual *preservations*."

After the fruitless interview, we weighed, and sailed for Port-au-Prince, where we arrived the following evening.

I had heard much of the magnificence of the scenery in the Bight of Leogane, but the reality far surpassed what I had pictured to myself. The breeze, towards noon of the following day, had come up in a gentle air from the westward, and we were gliding along before it like a spread eagle, with all our light sails abroad to catch the sweet zephyr, which was not even strong enough to ruffle the silver surface of the land-locked sea that glowed beneath the blazing mid-day sun, with a dolphin here and there cleaving the shining surface with an arrowy ripple, and a brown-skinned shark glaring on us, far down in the deep, clear, green profound, like a water fiend, and a slow-sailing pelican overhead, after a long sweep on poised wing, dropping into the sea like lead, and flashing up the water like the bursting of a shell, as we sailed up into a glorious amphitheatre of stupendous mountains, covered with one eternal forest, that rose gradually from the hot sandy plains that skirted the shore; while what had once been smiling fields and rich sugar-plantations, in the long misty level districts at their bases, were now covered with brushwood, fast rising up into one impervious thicket; and, as the island of Gonave closed in the view behind us to seaward, the sun sank beyond it, amidst rolling masses of golden and blood-red clouds, giving token of a goodly day tomorrow, and gilding the outline of the rocky islet (as if to a certain depth it had been transparent) with a golden halo, gradually deepening into imperial purple. Beyond the shadow of the tree-covered islet, on the left hand, rose the town of Port-au-Prince, with its long streets rising like terraces on the gently swelling shore, while the mountains behind it, still gold-tipped in the declining sunbeams, seemed to impend frowningly over it —and the shipping in the roadstead at anchor off the town were just beginning to fade from our sight in the gradually increasing darkness—and a solitary light began to sparkle in a cabin window and then disappear, and to twinkle for a moment in the piazzas of the houses on shore like a will-of-the-wisp—and the chirping buzz of myriads of insects and reptiles was coming off from the island astern of us, borne on the wings of the light wind, which, charged with rich odours from the closing flowers, fanned us "like the sweet south, soft breathing o'er a bed of violets"—when a sudden flash and a jet of white smoke puffed out from the hill-fort above the town, the report thundering amongst the everlasting hills, and gradually rumbling itself away into the distant ravines and valleys, like a lion growling itself to sleep, and the shades of night fell on the dead face of nature like a pall, and all was undistinguishable. When I had written thus far—it was at Port-au-Prince, at Mr S——'s—Mr Bang entered—"Ah! I Tom—at the Log, polishing—using the *plane*—shaping out something for Ebony—let me see."

Here our friend read the preceding paragraphs. They did not please him. "Don't like it, Tom."

"No? Pray, why, my dear sir?—I have tried to—"

"Hold your tongue, my good boy.

> 'Cease, rude Boreas, blustering railer,
>> List, old ladies, o'er your tea,
> At description Tom's a tailor,
>> When he is compared to me.
>>> Tooral looral loo.'

Attend—brevity is the soul of wit—ahem. Listen how I shall crush all your lengthy yarn into an eggshell. 'The Bight of Leogane is a horseshoe—Cape St Nicholas is the caulker on the northern heel—Cape Tiberoon, the ditto on the south—Port-au-Prince is the tip at the toe towards the east—Gonaives, Leogane, Petit Trouve, &c. &c. &c., are the nails, and the island of Gonave is the frog.' Now every human being who knows that a horse has four legs and a tail—of course this includes all the human race, excepting tailors and sailors—must understand this at once; it is palpable and plain, although no man could have put it so perspicuously, excepting my friend William Cobbett, or myself. By the way, speaking of horses, that blood thing of the old baron's nearly gave you your *quietus* t'other day, Tom. Why will you always pass the flank of a horse in place of going ahead of him, to use your own phrase? Never ride near a led horse on passing when you can help it; give him a wide berth, or clap the groom's *corpus* between you and his heels; and never, never go near the croup of any quadruped bigger than a cat, for even a cow's is inconvenient, when you can by any possibility help it."

I laughed—"Well, well, my dear sir,—but you undervalue my equestrian capability somewhat too, for I do pretend to know that a horse has four legs and a tail."

There was no pleasing Aaron this morning, I saw.

"Then, *Tummas*, my man, you know a deuced deal more than I do. As for the tail, conceditur—but devilish few horses have *four* legs nowadays, take my word for it. However, here comes Transom; I am off to have a lounge with him, and I will finish the veterinary lecture at some more convenient season. Tol lol de rol."—*Exit* singing.

The morning after this I went ashore at daylight, and, guided by the sound of military music, proceeded to the Place Republican, or square before President Petion's palace, where I found eight regiments of foot under arms, with their bands playing, and in the act of defiling before General Boyer, who commanded the *arrondissement*. This was the garrison of Port-au-Prince; but neither the personal appearance of the troops, nor their appointments, were at all equal to those of King Henry's well-dressed and well-drilled cohorts that we saw at Gonaives. The president's guards were certainly fine men, and a squadron of dismounted cavalry, in splendid blue uniforms, with scarlet trousers richly laced, might have vied with the *élite* of Nap's own, barring the black faces. But the *materiel* of the other regiments was not *superfine,** as M. Boyer, before whom they were defiling, might have said.

I went to breakfast with Mr S——, one of the English merchants of the place, a kind and most hospitable man; and under his guidance, the captain, Mr Bang, and I, proceeded afterwards to call on Petion. Christophe, or King Henry, had some time before retired from the siege of Port-au-Prince, and we found the town in a very miserable state. Many of the houses were injured from shot; the president's palace, for instance, was perforated in several places, which had not been repaired. In the antechamber you could see the blue heavens through the shot-holes in the roof. "Next time I come to court, Tom," said Mr Bang, "I will bring an umbrella." Turning out of the parade, we passed

---

* *The present excellent President of the Haytian Republic had at one time been a tailor, I believe.*

through a rickety, unpainted open gate, in a wall about six feet high; the space beyond was an open green or grass-plot, parched and burned up by the sun, with a common fowl here and there fluttering and *hotching* in the hole she had scratched in the arid soil; but there was neither sentry nor servant to be seen, nor any of the usual pomp and circumstance about a great man's dwelling. Presently we were in front of a long, low, one-storey building, with a flight of steps leading up into an entrance-hall, furnished with several gaudy sofas and half-a-dozen chairs—with a plain wooden floor, on which a slight approach to the usual West India polish had been attempted, but mightily behind the elegant domiciles of my Kingston friends in this respect. In the centre of this room stood three young officers, fair mulattoes, with their plumed cocked-hats in their hands, and dressed very handsomely in French uniforms; and it always struck me as curious, that men who hated the very name of Frenchman, as the devil hates holy water, should copy all the customs and manners of the detested people so closely. I may mention here, once for all, that Petion's officers, who, generally speaking, were all men of colour, and not negroes, were as much superior in education, and, I fear I must say, in intellect, as they certainly were in personal appearance, to the black officers of King Henry, as *his* soldiery were superior to those of the neighbouring black republic.

"*Ah, Monsieur S——, comment vous portez-vous? Je suis bien aise de vous voir,*" said one of the young officers; "how are you, how have you been?"

"*Vous devenez tout à fait rare,*" quoth a second. "*Le president* will be delighted to see you. Why, he says he thought you must have been dead, and *les messieurs là—*"

"Who?—Introduce us."

It was done in due form—the Honourable Captain Transom, Captain Cringle of his Britannic Majesty's schooner Wave, and Aaron Bang, Esquire. And presently we were all as thick as pickpockets.

"But come, the president will be delighted to see you." We followed the officer who spoke, as he marshalled us along; and in an inner chamber, wherein there were also several large holes in the ceiling through which the sun shone, we found President Petion, the black Washington, sitting on a very old ragged sofa, amidst a confused mass of papers, dressed in a blue military undress frock, white trousers, and the everlasting Madras handkerchief bound round his brows. He was much darker than I expected to have seen him, darker than one usually sees a mulatto, or the direct cross between the negro and the white, yet his features were in no way akin to those of an African. His nose was as high, sharp, and well defined as that of any Hindoo I ever saw in the Hoogly, and his hair was fine and silky. In fact, dark as he was, he was at least three removes from the African; and when I mention that he had been long in Europe—he was even for a short space acting adjutant-general of the army of Italy with Napoleon—his general manner, which was extremely good, kind, and affable, was not matter of so much surprise.

He rose to receive us with much grace, and entered into conversation with all the ease and polish of a gentleman—"*Je me porte assez bien aujourd'hui;* but I have been very unwell, M. S——, so tell me the news." Early as it was, he immediately ordered in coffee; it was brought by two black servants, followed by a most sylph-like girl, about twelve years of age, the president's natural daughter; she was fairer than her father, and acquitted herself very gracefully. She was rigged, pin for pin, like a little woman, with a perfect turret of artificial flowers twined amongst the braids of her beautiful hair; and although her neck was rather overloaded with ornaments, and her poor little ears were stretching under the weight of the heavy gold and emerald ear-rings, while her bracelets were like manacles, yet I had never seen a more lovely little girl. She wore a frock of green Chinese crape, beneath which appeared the prettiest little feet in the world.

We were invited to attend a ball in the evening, given in honour of the president's birthday, and after a sumptuous dinner at our friend Mr S——'s, we all adjourned to the gay scene. There was a company of grenadiers of the president's guard, with their band, on duty in front of the palace, as a guard of honour; they carried arms as we passed, all in good style; and at the door we met two aides-de-camp in full dress, one of whom ushered us into an anteroom, where a crowd of brown, with a sprinkling of black ladies, and a whole host of brown and black officers, with a white foreign merchant here and there, were drinking coffee, and taking refreshments of one kind or another. The ladies were dressed in the very height of the newest Parisian fashion of the day—hats and feathers, and jewellery, real or fictitious, short sleeves, and shorter petticoats—fine silks, and broad blonde trimmings and flounces, and low-cut *corsages*—some of them even venturing on rouge, which gave them the appearance of purple dahlias; but as to manner, all lady-like and proper; while the men, most of them *militaires,* were as fine as gold and silver lace, and gay uniforms, and dress-swords could make them—and all was blaze, and sparkle, and jingle; but the black officers, in general, covered their woolly pates with Madras handkerchiefs, as if ashamed to show them, the brown officers alone venturing to show their own hair. Presently a military band struck up with a sudden crash in the inner-room, and the large folding door being thrown open, the ball-room lay before us, in the centre of which stood the president, surrounded by his very splendid staff, with his daughter on his arm. He was dressed in a plain blue uniform with gold epaulets, and acquitted himself extremely well; conversing freely on European politics, and giving his remarks with great shrewdness, and a very peculiar *naïveté*. As for his daughter, however much she might appear to have been overdressed in the morning, she was now simple in her attire as a little shepherdess—a plain white muslin frock, white sash, white shoes, white gloves, pearl ear-rings and necklace, and a simple, but most beautiful, camilla japonica in her hair. Dancing now commenced, and all that I shall say is, that before I had been an hour in the room, I had forgotten whether the faces around me were black, brown, or white; everything was conducted with such decorum. However, I could see that the fine jet was not altogether the approved style of beauty, and that many a very handsome woolly-headed *belle* was destined to ornament the walls, until a few of the young white merchants made a dash amongst them, more for the fun of the thing, as it struck me, than anything else, which piqued some of the brown officers, and for the rest of the evening *blackee,* had it hollow. And there was friend Aaron waltzing with a very splendid woman, elegantly dressed, but black as a coal, with long kid gloves, between which and the sleeve of her gown a space of two inches of the black skin, like an ebony armlet, was visible; while her white dress, and rich white satin hat, and a lofty plume of feathers, with a pearl necklace and diamond ear-rings, set off her loveliness most conspicuously. At every wheel round Mr Bang slewed his head a little on one side and peeped in at one of her bright eyes, and then tossing his cranium on t'other side, took a squint in at the other, and then cast his eyes towards the roof, and muttered with his lips as if he had been shot all of a heap by the blind boy's butt-shaft; but every now and then as we passed, the rogue would stick his tongue in his cheek, yet so slightly as to be perceptible to no one but myself. After this heat, Massa Aaron and myself were perambulating the ball-room, quite satisfied with our own prowess, and I was *churming* to myself *"Voulez-vous danser, mademoiselle"*—*"De tout mon cœur,"* said a buxom brown dame, about eighteen stone by the coffee-mill in St James's Street. The devil Aaron gave me a look that I swore I would pay him for, the villain, as the extensive mademoiselle, suiting the action to the word, started up, and hooked on, and as a cotillon had been called, there I was, figuring away most emphatically, to Bang and Transom's great entertainment. At length the dance was at an end, and a waltz was once more called, and having done my duty, I thought I might slip out between the acts; so I offered to hand my solid armful to her seat—*"Certainement vous pouvez bien rester encore un moment."* The devil confound you and Aaron Bang, thought I; but waltz I must, and away we whirled until the room span round faster than we did, and when I was at length emancipated, my dark fair and fat one whispered, in a regular die-away, *"J'espère vous revoir bientôt."* All this while there was a heavy firing of champagne and other corks, and the fun grew so fast and furious, that I remembered very little more of the matter, until the morning breeze whistled through my muslin curtains, or mosquito net, about noon on the following day.

I arose, and found mine host setting out to bathe at Madame Le Clerc's bath, at Marquesan. I rode with him; and after a cool dip we breakfasted with President Petion at his country-house there, and met with great kindness. About the house itself there was nothing particularly to distinguish it from many others in the neighbourhood; but the little statues, and fragments of marble steps, and detached portions of old-fashioned wrought-iron railing, which had been grouped together so as to form an ornamental terrace below it, facing the sea, showed that it had been a compilation from the ruins of the houses of the rich French planters, which were now blackening in the sun on the plain of Leogane. A couple of Buenos Ayrean privateers were riding at anchor in the bight just below the windows, manned, as I afterwards found, by Americans. The president, in his quiet way, after contemplating them through his glass, said, *"Ces pavillons sont bien neuf."*

The next morning, as we were pulling in my gig, no less a man than Massa Aaron steering, to board the Arethusa, one of the merchantmen lying at anchor off the town, we were nearly run down by getting athwart the bows of an American schooner standing in for the port. As it was, her cutwater gave us so smart a crack that I thought we were done for; but our Palinurus, finding he could not clear her, with his inherent self-possession put his helm to port, and kept away on the same course as the schooner, so that we got off with the loss of our two larboard oars, which were snapped off like parsnips, and a good heavy bump that nearly drove us into staves.

"Never mind, my dear sir, never mind," said I; "but hereafter listen to the old song—

'Steer clear of the stem of a sailing ship.'"

Massa Aaron was down on me like lightning—

"Or the stern of a kicking horse, Tom"

While I continued—

"'Or you a wet jacket may catch, and a dip—'"

He again cleverly clipped the word out of my mouth—

"Or a kick on the croup, which is worse, Tom."

"Why, my dear sir, you are an *improvisatore* of the first quality."

We rowed ashore, and nothing particular happened that day until we sat down to dinner at Mr S——'s. We had a very agreeable party. Captain Transom and Mr Bang were, as usual, the life of the company; and it was verging towards eight o'clock in the evening, when an English sailor, apparently belonging to the merchant service, came into the piazza, and planted himself opposite to the window where I sat.

He made various nautical salaams until he had attracted my attention. "Excuse me," I said to Mr S——,"there is some one in the piazza wanting me." I rose.

"Are you Captain Transom?" said the man.

"No, I am not. There is the captain; do you want him?"

"If you please, sir," said the man.

I called my superior officer into the dark narrow piazza.

"Well, my man," said Transom, "what want you with me?"

"I am sent, sir, to you from the captain of the Haytian ship, the E——, to request a visit from you, and to ask for a prayerbook."

"A what?" said Transom.

"A prayerbook, sir. I suppose you know that he and the captain of that other Haytian ship, the P——, are condemned to be shot to-morrow morning."

"I know nothing of all this," said Transom. "Do you, Cringle?"

"No, sir," said I.

"Then let us adjourn to the dining-room again; or, stop, ask Mr S—— and Mr Bang to step here for a moment."

They appeared; and when Transom explained the affair, so far as consisted with his knowledge, Mr S—— told us that the two unfortunates in question were, one of them a Guernsey man, and the other a man of colour, a native of St Vincent's, whom the president had promoted to the command of two Haytian ships that had been employed in carrying coffee to England; but on their last return voyage, they had introduced a quantity of base Birmingham coin into the republic; which fact having been proved on their trial, they had been convicted of treason against the state, condemned, and were now under sentence of death; and, the government being purely military, they were to be shot tomorrow morning. A boat was immediately sent on board, the messenger returned with a prayerbook; and we prepared to visit the miserable men.

Mr Bang insisted on joining us—ever first where misery was to be relieved—and we proceeded towards the prison. Following the sailor, who was the mate of one of the ships, presently we arrived before the door of the place where the unfortunate men were confined. We were speedily admitted; but the building had none of the common appurtenances of a prison. There were neither long galleries nor strong iron-bound and clamped doors to pass through, nor jailers with rusty keys jingling, nor fetters clanking; for we had not made two steps past the black grenadiers who guarded the door, when a sergeant showed us into a long ill-lighted room, about thirty feet by twelve—in truth, it was more like a gallery than a room—with the windows into the street open, and no precautions taken, apparently at least, to prevent the escape of the condemned. In truth, if they had broken forth, I imagine the kind-hearted president would not have made any very serious inquiry as to the *how.*

There was a small rickety old card-table, covered with tattered green cloth, standing in the middle of the floor, which was composed of dirty unpolished pitch pine planks, and on this table glimmered two brown wax candles, in old-fashioned brass candlesticks. Between us and the table, forming a sort of line across the floor, stood four black soldiers, with their muskets at their shoulders, while beyond them sat, in old-fashioned armchairs, three figures, whose appearance I never can forget.

The man fronting us rose on our entrance. He was an uncommonly handsome elderly personage; his age I should guess to have been about fifty. He was dressed in white trousers and shirt, and wore no coat; his head was very bald, but he had large and very dark whiskers and eyebrows, above which towered a most splendid forehead, white, massive, and spreading. His eyes were deep-set and sparkling, but he was pale, very pale, and his fine features were sharp and pinched. He sat with his hands clasped together, and resting on the table, his fingers twitching to and fro convulsively, while his under jaw had dropped a little, and, from the constant motion of his head and the heaving of his chest, it was clear that he was breathing quick and painfully.

The figure on his right hand was altogether a more vulgar-looking personage. He was a man of colour; his caste being indicated by his short curly black hair, and his African descent vouched for by his obtuse features; but he was composed and steady in his bearing. He was dressed in white trousers and waistcoat, and a blue surtout; and on our entrance he rose, and remained standing. But the person on the elder prisoner's left hand riveted my attention more than either of the other two. She was a respectable-looking, little, thin woman, but dressed with great neatness, in a plain black silk gown. Her sharp features were high and well formed; her eyes and mouth were not particularly noticeable, but her hair was most beautiful—her long shining auburn hair—although she must have been forty years of age, and her skin was like the driven snow. When we entered, she was seated on the left hand of the eldest prisoner, and was lying back on her chair, with her arms crossed on her bosom, her eyes wide open, and staring upwards towards the roof, with the tears coursing each other down over her cheeks, while her lower jaw had fallen down, as if she had been dead—her breathing was scarcely perceptible—her bosom remaining still as a frozen sea for the space of a minute, when she would draw a long breath with a low moaning noise, to which succeeded a convulsive crowing gasp, like a child in the hooping-cough, and all would be still again.

At length Captain Transom addressed the elder prisoner.

"You have sent for us, Mr ——; what can we do for you—in accordance with our duty as English officers?"

The poor man looked at us with a vacant stare, but his fellow-sufferer instantly spoke. "Gentlemen, this is kind—very kind. I sent my mate to borrow a prayerbook from you, for our consolation now must flow from above; man cannot comfort us."

The female, who was the elder prisoner's wife, suddenly leant forward in her chair, and peered intently into Mr Bang's face. "Prayerbook," said she; "prayerbook—why, I have a prayerbook. I will go for my prayerbook," and she rose quickly from her seat.

"*Restez,*" quoth the black sergeant. The word seemed to rouse her; she laid her head on her hands, on the table, and sobbed out as if her heart were bursting—"O God! O God!" is it come to this—is it come to this?" the frail table trembling beneath her, with her heart-crushing emotion. His wife's misery now seemed to recall the elder prisoner to himself. He made a strong effort, and in a great degree recovered his composure.

"Captain Transom" said he, "I believe you know our story. That we have been justly condemned, I admit, but it is a fearful thing to die, captain, in a strange country, and by the hands of these barbarians, and to leave my own dear—" Here his voice altogether failed him; presently he resumed. "The government have sealed up my papers and packages, and I have neither Bible nor prayer-book—will you spare us the use of one, or both, for this night, sir?"

The captain said he had brought a prayerbook, and did all he could to comfort the poor fellows. But, alas! their grief "knew not consolation's name."

Captain Transom read prayers, which were listened to by both of the miserable men with the greatest devotion, but all the while the poor woman never moved a muscle, every faculty appearing to be once more frozen up by grief and misery. At length, the elder prisoner again spoke, "I know I have no claim on you, gentlemen; but I am an Englishman—at least I hope I may call myself an Englishman—and my wife there is an Englishwoman: when I am gone—oh, gentlemen, what is to become of her? If I were but sure that she would be cared for and enabled to return to her friends, the bitterness of death would be past." Here the poor woman threw herself round her husband's neck, and gave a shrill sharp cry, and, relaxing her hold, fell down across his knees, with her head hanging back, and her face towards the roof, in a dead faint. For a minute or two, the husband's sole concern seemed to be the condition of his wife.

"I will undertake that she shall be sent safe to England, my good man," said Mr Bang.

The felon looked at him—drew one hand across his eyes, which were misty with tears, held down his head, and again looked up; at length he found his tongue. "That God who rewardeth good deeds here, that God whom I have offended, before whom I must answer for my sins by daybreak to-morrow, will *reward* you; I can only thank you." He seized Mr Bang's hand and kissed it.

With heavy hearts we left the miserable group; and I may mention here, that Mr Bang was as good as his word, and paid the poor woman's passage home, and, so far as I know, she is now restored to her family.

We slept that night at Mr S——'s, and as the morning dawned we mounted our horses, which our worthy host had kindly desired to be ready, in order to enable us to take our exercise in the cool of the morning. As we rode past the *Place d'Armes,* or open space in front of the president's palace, we heard sounds of military music, and asked the first chance passenger what was going on. *"Execution militaire;* or rather," said the man, "the two sea-captains, who introduced the base money, are to be shot this morning—there, against the rampart." Of the fact we were aware, but we did not dream that we had ridden so near the whereabouts.

"Ay, indeed!" said Mr Bang. He looked towards the captain. "My dear Transom, I have no wish to witness so horrible a sight, but still—what say you—shall we pull up, or ride on?"

The truth was, that Captain Transom and myself were both of us desirous of seeing the execution—from what impelling motive, let learned blockheads, who have never gloated over a hanging, determine; and quickly it was determined that we should wait and witness it.

First advanced a whole regiment of the president's guards, then a battalion of infantry of the line, close to which followed a whole bevy of priests clad in white, which contrasted conspicuously with their brown and black faces. After them marched two firing parties of twelve men each, drafted indiscriminately, as it would appear, from the whole garrison; for the grenadier cap was there intermingled with the glazed shako, of the battalion company and the light morion of the dismounted dragoon. Then came the prisoners; the elder culprit respectably clothed in a white shirt, waistcoat, and trousers, and blue coat, with an Indian silk yellow handkerchief bound round his head. His lips were compressed together with an unnatural firmness, and his features were sharpened like those of a corpse. His complexion was ashy blue. His eyes were half shut, but every now and then he opened them wide, and gave a startling rapid glance about him, and occasionally he staggered a little in his gait. As he approached the place of execution, his eyelids fell, his under-jaw dropped, his arms hung dangling by his side like empty sleeves; still he walked on, mechanically keeping time, like an automaton, to the measured tread of the soldiery. His fellow-sufferer followed him. His eye was bright, his complexion healthy, his step firm, and he immediately recognised us in the throng, made a bow to Captain Transom, and held out his hand to Mr Bang, who was nearest to him, and shook it cordially. The procession moved on. The troops formed into three sides of a square, the remaining one being the earthen mound that constituted the rampart of the place. A halt was called. The two firing parties advanced to the sound of muffled drums, and having arrived at the crest of the glacis, right over the counterscarp, they halted on what, in a more regular fortification, would have been termed the covered-way. The prisoners, perfectly unfettered, advanced between them, stepped down with a firm step into the ditch, led each by a grenadier. In the centre of it they turned and kneeled, neither of their eyes being bound. A priest advanced, and seemed to pray with the brown man fervently; another offered spiritual consolation to the Englishman, who seemed now to have rallied his torpid faculties; but he waved him away impatiently, and, taking a book from his bosom, seemed to repeat a prayer from it with great fervour. At this very instant of time Mr Bang caught his eye. He dropped the book on the ground, placed one hand on his heart, while he pointed upwards towards heaven with the other, calling out in a loud clear voice, "Remember!" Aaron bowed. A mounted officer now rode quickly up to the brink of the ditch, and called out *"Dépêchez."*

The priests left the miserable men, and all was still as death for a minute. A low solitary tap of the drum—the firing parties came to the recover, and presently, taking the time from the sword of the staff-officer who had spoken, came down to the present, and fired a rattling, straggling volley. The brown man sprang up into the air three or four feet, and fell dead; he had been shot through the heart; but the white man was only wounded, and had fallen, writhing and struggling and shrieking, to the ground. I heard him distinctly call out, as the reserve of six men stepped into the ditch, *"Dans la tête, dans la tête."* One of the grenadiers advanced, and, putting his musket close to his face, fired. The ball splashed into his skull through the left eye, setting fire to his hair and clothes and the handkerchief bound round his head, and making the brains and blood flash up all over his face and the person of the soldier who had given him the *coup de grace*.

A strong murmuring noise, like the rushing of many waters, growled amongst the ranks and the surrounding spectators, while a short sharp exclamation of horror every now and then gushed out shrill and clear, and fearfully distinct, above the appalling monotony.

The miserable man stretched out his legs and arms straight and rigidly, a strong shiver pervaded his whole frame, his jaw fell, his muscles relaxed, and he and his brother in calamity became a portion of the bloody clay on which they were stretched.

CHAPTER XVII.

THE THIRD CRUISE OF THE WAVE.

"Roll on, thou deep and dark blue ocean—roll!
Ten thousand fleets sweep over thee in vain:
Man marks the earth with ruin—his control
Stops with the shore,—upon the watery plain
The wrecks are all thy deed, nor doth remain
A shadow of man's ravage, save his own,
When for a moment, like a drop of rain,
He sinks into thy depths with bubbling groan,
Without a grave, unknelled, uncoffined, and unknown."

Childe Harold.

I HAD been invited to breakfast on board the corvette, on the morning after this; and Captain Transom, Mr Bang, and myself, were comfortably seated at our meal on the quarterdeck, under the awning, screened off by flags from the view of the men. The ship was riding to a small westerly breeze that was rippling up the bight. The ports on each quarter, as well as the two in the stern, were open, through which we had an extensive view of Port-au-Prince and the surrounding country.

"Now, Transom," said our *amigo,* Massa Aaron, "I am quite persuaded that the town astern of us there must always have been, and is now, exceedingly unhealthy. Only reflect on its situation: it fronts the west, with the hot sickening afternoon's sun blazing on it every evening, along the glowing mirror of the calm bight, under whose influence the fat black mud that composes the beach must send up most pestilent effluvia; while in the forenoon it is shut out from the influence of the regular easterly sea-breeze, or trade-wind, by the high land behind. However, as I don't mean to stay here longer than I can help, it is not my affair; and as Mr S—— will be waiting for us, pray order your carriage, my dear fellow, and let us go on shore."

The carriage our friend spoke of was the captain's gig, by this time alongside, ready manned each of the six seamen who composed her crew with his oar resting between his knees, the blade pointed upwards towards the sky. We all got in. "Shove off"—dip fell the oars into the water. "Give way, men"—the good ash staves groaned, and cheeped, and the water buzzed, and away we shot towards the wharf. We landed, and having proceeded to Mr S——'s, we found horses ready for us, to take our promised ride into the beautiful plain of the *Cul de Sac,* lying to the northward and eastward of the town; the cavalcade being led by Massa Aaron and myself, while Mr S—— rode beside Captain Transom.

Aforetime, from the estates situated on this most magnificent plain (which extends about fifteen miles into the interior, while its width varies from ten to five miles, being surrounded by hills on three sides) there used to be produced no less than thirty thousand hogsheads of sugar. This was during the *ancien régime;* whereas now, I believe, the only articles it yields beyond plantains, yams, and pot herbs for the supply of the town, are a few gallons of syrup, and a few puncheons of *tafia,* a very inferior kind of rum. The whole extend of the sea-like plain, for there is throughout scarcely any inequality higher than my staff, was once covered with well-cultivated fields and happy homes; but now, alas! with brushwood from six to ten feet high—in truth, by one sea of jungle, through which you have to thread your difficult way along narrow, hot, sandy bridle-paths (with the sand-flies and mosquitoes flaying you alive), which every now and then lead you to some old ruinous courtyard, with the ground strewed with broken boilers and mill-rollers, and decaying hardwood timbers, and crumbling bricks; while, a little farther on, you shall find the blackened roofless walls of what was most probably an unfortunate planter's once happy home, where the midnight brigand came, and found peace and comfort and all the elegancies of life, and left—blood and ashes; with the wildflowers growing on the window-sills, and the prickly pear on the tops of the walls, while marble steps, and old shutters, and window-hinges, and pieces of china, are strewn all about; the only tenant now being most likely an old miserable negro who has sheltered himself in a coarsely-thatched hut, in a corner of what had once been a gay and well-furnished saloon.

After having extended our ride, under a hot broiling sun, until two o'clock in the afternoon, we hove about and returned towards the town. We had not ridden on our homeward journey above three miles, when we overtook a tall good-looking negro dressed in white Osnaburg trousers rolled up to his knees, and a check shirt. He wore neither shoes nor stockings, but his head was bound round with the usual handkerchief, over which he wore a large glazed cocked-hat, with a most conspicuous Haytian blue-and-red cockade. He was goading on a jackass before him, loaded with a goodly burden apparently; but what it was we could not tell, as the whole was covered by a large sheepskin, with the wool outermost. I was pricking past the man, when Mr S—— sang out to me to shorten sail, and the next moment he startled me by addressing the pedestrian as Colonel Gabaroche. The colonel returned the salute, and seemed in no way put out from being detected in this rather unmilitary predicament. He was going up to Port-au-Prince to take his turn of duty with his regiment. Presently up came another half-naked black fellow, with the same kind of glazed hat and handkerchief under it; but he was mounted, and his nag, was not a bad one by any means. It was Colonel Gabaroche's captain of grenadiers, Papotiere by name. He was introduced to us, and we all moved jabbering along. At the time I write of, the military force of the Haytian Republic was composed of one-third of the whole male population capable of bearing arms, which third was obliged to be on permanent duty for four months every year; but the individuals of the quota were allowed to follow their callings as merchants, planters, or agriculturists, during the remaining eight months; they were, I believe, fed by government during their four months of permanent duty. The weather, by the time we had ridden a couple of miles farther, began to lower, and presently large heavy drops of rain fell, and, preserving their globular shape, rolled like peas, or rather like bullets, amidst the small finely pulverised dust of the sandy path. "Umbrella" was the word; but this was a luxury unknown to our military friends. However, the colonel immediately unfurled a blanket from beneath the sheepskin, and sticking his head through a hole in the centre of it, there he stalked like a herald in his tabard, with the blanket hanging down before and behind him. As for the captain, he dismounted, disencumbered himself of his trousers, which he crammed under the mat that served him for a saddle, and, taking off his shirt, he stowed it away in the capacious crown of his cocked-hat, while he once more bestrid his Bucephalus *in puris naturalibus,* but conversing with all the ease in the world and the most perfect *sang froid,* while the thunder-shower came down in bucketfuls. In about half an hour we arrived at the skirt of the brushwood or jungle, and found on our left hand some rice-fields, which from appearance we could not have distinguished from young wheat; but on a nearer approach, we perceived that the soil, if soil it could be called on which there was no walking, was a soft mud, the only passages through the fields and along the ridges being by planks, on which several of the labourers were standing as we passed, one of whom, turning to look at us, slipped off, and instantly sank amidst the rotten slime up to his waist. The neighbourhood of these rice-swamps is generally extremely unhealthy. At length we got on board the Firebrand, drenched to the skin, to a late dinner, after which it was determined by Captain Transom—of which intention, by the by, with all his familiarity, I had not the smallest previous notice—that I should cross the island to Jacmel, in order to communicate with the merchant-ships loading there; and by the time I returned, it was supposed the Firebrand would be ready for sea, when I was to be detached in the Wave, to whip in the craft at the different outports, after which we were all to sail in a fleet to Port Royal.

"I say, skipper," quoth Mr Bang, "I have a great mind to ride with Tom; what say you?"

"Why, Aaron, you are using me ill; that shaver is seducing you altogether; but come, you won't be a week away, and if you want to go, I see no objection."

It was fixed accordingly, and on the morrow Mr Bang and I completed our arrangements, hired horses and a guide, and all being in order, clothes packed, and everything else made ready for the cruise, we rode out along with Mr S——— (we were to dine and sleep at his house) to view the fortifications on the hill above the town, the site of Christophe's operations when he besieged the place; and pretty hot work they must have had of it, for in two different places the trenches of the besiegers had been pushed on to the very crest of the glacis, and in one the counterscarp had been fairly blown into the ditch, disclosing the gallery of the mine behind, as if it had been a cavern, the crest of the glacis having remained entire. We walked into it, and Mr S——— pointed out where the president's troops, in Fort Républicain, had countermined, and absolutely entered the other chamber from beneath, after the explosion, and, sword in hand, cut off the storming party (which had by this time descended into the ditch), and drove them up through the breach into the fort, where they were made prisoners.

The *assault* had been given three times in one night, and he trembled for the town; however, Petion's courage and indomitable resolution saved them all. For by making a sally from the south gate at grey dawn, even when the firing on the hill was hottest, and turning the enemy's flank, he poured into the trenches, routed the covering party, stormed the batteries, spiked the guns, and that evening's sun glanced on the bayonets of King Henry's troops as they raised the siege, and fell back in great confusion on their lines, leaving the whole of their battering train and a great quantity of ammunition behind them.

Next morning we were called at daylight, and having accoutred ourselves for the journey, we descended, and found two stout ponies, the biggest not fourteen hands high, ready saddled, with old-fashioned demipiques, and large holsters at each of the saddlebows. A very stout mule was furnished for Monsieur Pegtop; and our black guide, who had contracted for our transit across the island, was also in attendance, mounted on a very active, well-actioned horse. We had coffee, and started. By the time we reached Leogane, the sun was high and fierce. Here we breakfasted in a low one-storey building, our host being no smaller man than Major L—— of the Fourth Regiment of the line. We got our chocolate, and eggs, and fricasseed fowl, and roasted yam, and in fact made, even according to friend Aaron's conception of matters, an exceedingly comfortable breakfast.

Mr Bang here insisted on being paymaster, and tendered a sum that the black major thought so extravagantly great, considering the entertainment we had received, that he declined taking more than one-half. However, Mr Bang, after several unavailing attempts to press the money on the man—who, by the by, was simply a good-looking blackamoor, dressed in a check shirt, coarse but clean white trousers, with the omnipresent handkerchief bound round his head—and finding that he could not persist without giving offence, was about pocketing the same, when Pegtop audibly whispered him, "Massa, you ever shee black niger refuse money before? but don't take it to heart, massa; me, Pegtop, will pocket him, if dat foolis black person won't."

"Thank you for nothing, Master Pegtop," said Aaron.

We proceeded, and rode across the beautiful plain, gradually sloping up from the mangrove-covered beach, until it swelled into the first range of hills that formed the pedestal of the high precipitous ridge that intersected the southern prong of the island, winding our way through the ruins of sugar-plantations, with fragments of the machinery and implements employed in the manufacture scattered about, and half sunk into the soil of the fields, which were fast becoming impervious jungle, and interrupting our progress along the narrow bridle-paths. At length we began to ascend, and the comparative coolness of the climate soon evinced that we were rapidly leaving the hot plains as the air became purer and thinner at every turn. After a long, hot, hot ride, we reached the top of the ridge, and, turning back, had a most magnificent view of the whole Bight of Leogane, and of the Horseshoe, and Aaron's Frog; even the tops of the mountains above the Mole, which could not have been nearer than seventy miles, were visible, floating like islands or blue clouds in the misty distance. Aaron took off his hat, reined up, and, turning the head of his Bucephalus towards the placid waters we had left, stretched forth his hand—

> "'Ethereal air, and ye swift-winged winds,
> Ye rivers springing from fresh founts, ye waves
> That o'er th' interminable ocean wreath
> Your crispèd smiles, thou all-producing Earth,
> And thee, bright Sun, I call, whose flaming orb
> Views the wide world beneath—See!'—

Nearly got a stroke of the sun, Tom—what Whiffle would call a *cul de sac*—by taking off my chapeau in my poetical frenzy; so shove on."

We continued our journey through most magnificent defiles, and under long avenues of the most superb trees, until, deeply embosomed in the very heart of the eternal forest, we came to a shady clump of bamboos, overhanging, with their ostrich-feather-like plumes, a round pool of water, mantled or creamed over with a bright green coating, as if it had been vegetable velvet, but nothing akin to the noisome scum that ferments on a stagnant pool in England. It was about the time we had promised ourselves dinner, and in fact our black guide and Pegtop had dismounted to make their preparations.

"Why, we surely cannot dine here? You don't mean to drink of that stagnant pool, my dear sir?"

"*Siste paulisper,* my boy," said Mr Bang, as he stooped down and skimmed off the green covering with his hand, disclosing the water below, pure and limpid as a crystal-clear fountain. We dined on the brink, and discussed a bottle of vin-de-grave apiece, and then had a small pull at brandy-and-water; but we ate very little, although I was very hungry—but Mr Bang would not let me feed largely.

"Now, Tom, you really do not understand things. When one rides a goodish journey on end—say seventy miles or so—on the same horse, one never feeds the trusty creature with half a bushel of oats; at least, if any wooden spoon does, the chances are he knocks him up. No, no; you give him a *mouthful* of corn, but *plenty* to drink—a little meal-and-water here, and a bottle of porter in water there, and he brings you in handsomely. Zounds! how would you yourself, Tom, like to dine on turtle soup and venison in the middle of a hissing hot ride of sixty miles, thirty of them to be covered after the feed? Lord! what between the rich food and the punch, you would have fermented like a brewer's vat before you reached the end of the journey; and if you had not a boll imperial measure of carbonate of soda with you, the chances are you would explode like a catamaran—your head flying through some old woman's window, and capsizing her teapot on the one hand, while on the other your four quarters are scattered north, south, east, and west. But *gaudeamus*—sweet is pleasure after pain, Tom, and all you sailors and tailors—I love to class you together—are tender—not *hearted*—creatures. Strange now that there should be three classes of his Majesty's subjects who never can be taught to ride—to whom riding is, in fact, a physical impossibility; and these three are the aforesaid sailors, and tailors, and dragoon officers. However, hand me the brandy-bottle; and Pegtop, spare me that black jack that you are rinsing—so. Useful commodity a cup of this kind"—here our friend dashed in a large qualifier of cognac—"it not only conceals the quality of the water, for you can sometimes perceive the animalculæ hereabouts without a microscope, but also the strength of the libation. So—a piece of biscuit now, and the smallest morsel of that cold tongue—your health, Thomas"—a long pull—"speedy promotion to you, Thomas." Here our friend rested the jug on his knee. "Were you ever at a *gaudeamus* of Presbyterian clergymen on the Monday after the Sacrament Sunday, Tom—that is, at the dinner at the manse?"

"No, my dear sir; you know I am an Episcopalian."

"And I am a Roman Catholic. What then? I have been at a *gaudeamus*, and why might not you have been at one too? Oh, the fun of such a meeting! the feast of reason and the flow of Ferintosh, and the rich stories, ay, fatter than even I would venture on, and the cricket-like chirps of laughter of the probationer, and the loud independent guffaw of the placed minister, and the sly innuendos, when our *freens* get half *foo*. Oh, how I honour a *gaudeamus!* And why," he continued," should the excellent men not rejoice, Tom? Are they not the very men who should be happy? Is a minister to be for ever boxed up in his pulpit—for ever to be wagging his pow, bald, black, or grizzled, as it may be, beneath his sounding-board, like a bullfrog below a toadstool? And, like the aforesaid respectable quadruped or biped (it has always puzzled me which to call it), is he never to drink anything stronger than water? Hath not a minister eyes? hath not a minister hands, organs, dimensions, senses, affections, passions? Fed with the same food, hurt with the same weapons, subject to the same diseases, healed by the same means, warmed and cooled by the same winter and summer, that another man is? If you prick them, do they not bleed? If you tickle them, do they not laugh? And shall we grudge them a *gaudeamus* now and then? Shall *opera peracta ludemus* be in the mouths of all mankind, from the dirty little greasy-faced schoolboy who wears a red gown, and learns the Humanities and Whiggery in the Nineveh of the West, as the Bailie glories to call it, to the King upon his throne, and a dead letter, as well as a dead language, to them, and them only? Forbid it, the Honourable the Lord Provost; forbid it, the Honourable the Lord Provost and all the Bailies; forbid it, the Honourable the Lord Provost and all the Bailies, and those who sit in Council with them! Forbid it, the whole august aggregate of terror to evil-doers and praise of them who do well! Forbid it, the devil and Dr Faustus!"

By this time I had smuggled the jug out of our *amigo*'s claw and had done honour to his pledge. "Do you know, my dear Mr Bang, I have always been surprised that a man of your strong intellect, and clear views of most matters, should continue, in profession at least, a Roman Catholic?"

Aaron looked at me with a seriousness, an unaffected seriousness, in his manner, that possessed me with the notion that I had taken an unwarrantable liberty. "Profession," at length said he, slowly and deliberately, apparently weighing every word carefully as it fell from him, as one is apt to do when approaching an interesting subject on which you desire not to be misunderstood—"Profession!—what right have you to assume this of me or any man, that my mode of faith is but profession?" and then the kind-hearted fellow, perceiving that his rebuke had mortified me, altering his tone, continued, but still with a strong tinge of melancholy in his manner, "Alas! Tom, how often will weak man, in his great arrogance, assume the prerogative of his Maker, and attempt to judge—honestly, we will even allow, according to his conception—of the heart and secret things of another, but too often, in reality, by the evil scale of his own! Shall the potsherd say to his frail fellow, 'Thou art weak, but I am strong?' Shall the *moudiewort* say to his brother mole (I say, Quashie, mind that mule of yours don't snort in the water, will ye?)—'Blind art thou, but lo, I see?' All, Tom, I am a Roman Catholic! but is it thou who shalt venture down into the depths of my heart, and then say, whether I be so in profession only, or in stern, unswerving sincerity?"

I found I had unwittingly touched a string that vibrated to his heart.

"I am a Roman Catholic, but, I humbly trust, not a bigoted one; for were it not against the canons of both our churches, I fear I should incline to the doctrine of Pope—

'He can't be wrong whose life is in the right.'

My fathers, Tom, were all Catholics before me; they may have been wrong; but I am only my father's son—not a better, and, I fear, I fear, not so wise a man. Pray, Tom, did you ever hear of even a *good* Jew, who, being converted, did not become a *bad* Christian? Have you not all your life had a repugnance to consort with a sinner converted from the faith of his fathers, whether they were Jews or Gentiles, Hindoos or Mohammedans, dwellers in Mesopotamia, or beyond Jordan? You *have* such a repugnance, Tom, I know; and *I* have it too."

"Well," I proceeded, on the strength of the brandy grog, "in the case of an unenlightened, or ignorant, or half-educated man, I *might*, indeed, suspect duplicity, or even hypocrisy, at the bottom of the abjuration of his fathers' creed; but in a gentleman of your acquirements and knowledge—"

"There again now, Cringle, you are wrong. The clodhopper might be conscientious in a change of creed; but as to the advantage I have over him from superior knowledge!—Knowledge, Tom! what do I know—what does the greatest and the best of us know—to venture on a saying somewhat of the tritest—but that he knows nothing? Oh, my dear boy, you and I have hitherto consorted together on the *deck* of life, so to speak, with the bright joyous sun sparkling, and the blue heavens laughing overhead, and the clear green sea dancing under foot, and the merry breeze buzzing past us right cheerily. We have seen but the fair-weather side of each other, Thomas, without considering that all men have their deep feelings, that lie far, far down in the *hold* of their hearts, were they but stirred up. Ay, you smile at my figures, but I repeat it—in the deep *hold* of their hearts; and may I not follow out the image with verity and modesty, and say that those feelings, often too deep for tears, are the *ballast* that keeps the whole ship in trim, and without which we should be every hour of our existence liable to be driven out of our heavenward course, yea, to broach to, and founder, and sink for ever, under one of the many squalls in this world of storms? And here, in this most beautiful spot, with the deep, dark, crystal-clear pool at our feet, fringed with that velvet grass, and the green quivering leaf above flickering between us and the bright blue cloudless sky—and the everlasting rocks, with those diamond-like tears trickling down their rugged cheeks impending over us—and those gigantic gnarled trees, with their tracery of black withes fantastically tangled, whose naked roots twist and twine amongst the fissures, like serpents trying to shelter themselves from the scorching rays of the vertical sun—and those feather-like bamboos high arching overhead, and screening us under their noble canopy—and the cool plantains, their broad ragged leaves bending under the weight of dew-spangles, and the half-opened wild-flowers—yea, even here, the ardent noontide sleeping on the hill, when even the quick-eyed lizard lies still, and no longer rustles through the dry grass, and there is not a breath of air strong enough out of heaven to stir the gossamer that floats before us, or to wave that wild-flower on its hair-like stem, or to ruffle the fairy plumage of the humming-bird, which, against the custom of its kind, is now quietly perched thereon; and while the bills of the chattering paroquets, that are peering at us from the branches above, are closed, and the woodpecker interrupts his tapping to look down upon us, and the only sound we hear is the moaning of the wood-pigeon, and the lulling buzz of myriads of happy insects booming on the ear, loud as the rushing of a distant waterfall—(Confound these mosquitoes, though!) Even here, on this

> 'So sweet a spot of earth, you might, I ween,
> Have guessed some congregation of the elves,
> To sport by summer moons, had shaped it for themselves.'

Even in such a place could I look forward without a shudder to set up my everlasting rest, to lay my weary bones in the earth, and to mingle my clay with that whereout it was moulded. No fear of being *houcked* here, Thomas, and preserved in a glass case, like a stuffed woodcock, in Surgeon's Hall. I am a barbarian, Tom, in these respects; I am a barbarian, and nothing of a philosopher. *Quiero Paz* is to be my epitaph. *Quiero Paz*—'Cursed be he who stirs these bones.' Did not even Shakespeare write it? What poetry in this spot, Thomas! Oh,

> 'There is a pleasure in the pathless woods,
> There is a rapture on the lonely shore,
> There is society, where none intrudes,
> By the deep sea, and music in its roar:
> I love not man the less, but nature more,
> From these our interviews, in which I steal
> From all I may be, or have been before,
> To mingle with the universe, and feel
> What I can ne'er express, yet cannot all conceal.'

Yes, even here, where nature is all beautiful and *everything,* and man abject and *nothing*—even here, Tom, amidst the loneliness of earth, rugged and half-mad as you must sometimes have thought me, a fellow wholly made up of quips and jests,—even *I* at this moment could, like an aboriginal Charib of the land, 'lift up my voice to the Great Spirit,' and kneel, and weep, and pray."

I was much moved.

"You have spoken of knowledge, Tom. Knowledge! what do I know? Of myself I know as little as I do of any other grub that crawls on the surface of this world of sin and suffering; and what I do know, adds little to my self-esteem, Tom, and affords small encouragement to inquire farther. Knowledge, say you? How is that particle of sand here? I cannot tell. How grew that blade of grass? I do not know. Even when I look into that jug of brandy grog (I'll trouble you for it, Thomas), all that I know is, that if I drink it, it will make me drunk, and a more desperately wicked creature, if that were possible, than I am already. And when I look forth on the higher and more noble objects of the visible creation, abroad on this beautiful earth, above on the glorious universe studded with shining orbs, without number numberless, what can I make of *them?* Nothing—absolutely nothing; yet they are all creatures like myself. But if I try—audaciously try—to strain my *finite* faculties in the futile attempt to take in what is infinite—if I aspiringly, but hopelessly, grapple with the idea of the immensity of space, for instance, which my reason yet tells me must of necessity be boundless—do I not fall fluttering to the earth again, like an owl flying against the noontide sun? Again, when I venture to think of eternity—ay, when, reptile as I feel myself to be, I even look up towards heaven, and bend my erring thoughts towards the Most High, the Maker of all things, who was, and is, and is to come; whose flaming minister, even while I speak, is pouring down a flood of intolerable day on one-half of the dry earth, and all that therein is; and when I reflect on what this tremendous, this inscrutable Being has done for me and my sinful race, so beautifully shown forth in both our creeds, *what I do I know?* but that I am a poor miserable worm, crushed before the moth, whose only song should be the *miserere,* whose only prayer 'God be merciful to me a sinner!'"

There was a long pause, and I began to fear that my friend was shaken in his mind, for he continued to look steadfastly into the clear black water, where he had skimmed off the green velvet coating with his stick.

"Ay, and is it even so? and is it Tom Cringle who thinks and says that I am a man likely to profess to believe what he knows in his heart to be a lie? *A Roman Catholic!* Had I lived before the Roman Conquest I would have been a *Druid,* for it is not under the echoing domes of our magnificent cathedrals, with all the grandeur of our ritual, the flaming tapers, and bands of choristers, and the pealing organ, and smoking censers, and silver-toned bells, and white-robed priests, that the depths of my heart are stirred up. It is *here,* and not in a temple made with hands however gorgeous—*here,* in the secret places of the everlasting forest; it is in such a place as this that I feel the immortal spark within me kindling into a flame, and wavering up heavenward. I am superstitious, Thomas, I am superstitious, when left alone in such a scene as this. I can walk through a country churchyard at midnight, and stumble amongst the rank grass that covers the graves of those I have lived with and loved, even if the be 'green in death, and festering in their shrouds,' with the wind moaning amongst the stunted yew-trees, and the rain splashing and scattering on the moss-covered tombstones, and the blinding blue lightning flashing, while the headstones glance like an array of sheeted ghosts, and the thunder is grumbling overhead, without a qualm; direness of this kind cannot once daunt me. It is *here* and *now*, when all nature sleeps in the ardent noontide, that I become superstitious, and would not willingly be left alone. Thoughts too deep for tears!—ay, indeed, and there be such thoughts, that, long after time has allowed them to subside, and when, to the cold eye of the world, all is clear and smooth above, will, when stirred up, like the sediment of this fountain of the wood, discolour and embitter the whole stream of life once more, even after the lapse of long long years. When my heart-crushing loss was recent—when the wound was green, I could not walk abroad at this to me witching time of day, without a stock or a stone, a distant mark on the hill-side, or the outline of the grey cliff above, taking the very fashion of *her* face, or figure, on which I would gaze, and gaze, as if spell-bound, until I knew not whether to call it a grouping of the imagination, or a reality from without—of *her* with whom I fondly hoped to have travelled the weary road of life. Friends approved—fortune smiled— one little month, and we should have been one; but it pleased *Him,* to whom in my present frame of mind I dare not look up, to blight my beautiful flower, to canker my rose-bud, to change the fair countenance of my Elizabeth, and send her away. She drooped and died, even like that pale flower under the scorching sun; and I was driven forth to worship Mammon in these sweltering climes; but the sting remains, the barbed arrow sticks fast."

Here the clear surface of the water, into which he was steadfastly looking, was gradually contracted to a small round spot about an foot in diameter, by the settling back of the green floating matter that he had skimmed aside. His countenance became very pale; he appeared even more excited than he had hitherto been.

"By heavens! look in that water, if the green covering of it has not arranged itself round the clear spot into the shape of a medallion—into *her* features! I had dreamed of such things before, but now it is a palpable reality—it is her face—her straight nose—her Grecian upper lip—her beautiful forehead, and her very bust!—even,

> 'As when years apace
> Had bound her lovely waist with woman's zone.'

Oh, Elizabeth—Elizabeth!"

Here his whole frame shook with the most intense emotion, but at length tears, unwonted tears, *did* come to his relief, and he hid his face in his hands and wept bitterly. I was now convinced he was mad, but I durst not interrupt him. At length he slowly removed his hands, by which time, however, a beautiful small black diver, the most minute species of duck that I ever saw—it was not so big as my fist—but which is common in woodland ponds in the West Indies, had risen in the centre of the eye of the fountain, while all was so still that it floated quietly like a leaf on the water, apparently without the least fear of us.

"The devil appeared in paradise under the shape of a cormorant," said Mr Bang, half angrily, as he gazed sternly at the unlooked-for visitor; "what imp art thou?"

Tip—the little fellow dived; presently it rose again in the same place, and, lifting up its little foot scratched the side of its tiny yellow bill and little red-spotted head, shook its small wings, bright and changeable as shot silk, with a snow-white pen-feather in each, and then tipped up its little purple tail, and once more disappeared.

Aaron's features were gradually relaxing; a change was coming over the spirit of his dream. The bird appeared for the third time, looked him in the face, first turning up one little sparkling eye, and then another, with its neck changing its hues like a pigeon's. Aaron began to smile; he gently raised his stick—"Do you cock your *fud* at me, you tiny thief, you?"—and thereupon he struck at it with his stick. *Tip*—the duck dived, and did not rise again; and all that he got was a sprinkling shower in the face, from the water flashing up at his blow, and once more the green covering settled back again, and the bust of his dead love, or what he fancied to be so, disappeared. Aaron laughed outright, arose, and began to shout to the black guide, who, along with Pegtop, had taken the beasts into the wood in search of provender. *"Ayez le bonté de donner moi mon cheval. Bringibus the horsos, Massa Bungo—venga los quadrupedos—* make haste, *vite, mucho, mucho."*

Come, there *is my* Massa Aaron once more, at all events, thought I; but oh, how unlike the Aaron of five minutes ago!

"So now let us mount, my boy," said he, and we shoved along until the evening fell, and the sun bid us good-by very abruptly. "Cheep, cheep," sang the lizard—"chirp, chirp," sang the crickets—"snore, snore," moaned the tree-toad—and it was night.

"Dame Nature shifts the scene without much warning here, Thomas," said Massa Aaron; "we must get along. *Dépêchez, mon cher—dépêchez; diggez votre* spurs into the *flankibus of votre cheval, mon ami,*" shouted Aaron to our guide.

"*Oui, monsieur,*" replied the man, "*mais—*"

I did not like this ominous "*but,*" nevertheless we rode on. No more did Massa Aaron. The guide repeated his *mais* again. "*Mais, mon filo,*" said Bang, "*mais—que meanez-vous* by baaing *comme un* sheep, eh? *Que vizzy-vous,* eh?*"

We were at this time riding in a bridle-road, to which the worst sheep-paths in Westmoreland would have been a railway, with our horses every now and then stumbling and coming down on their noses on the deep red earth, while we as often stood a chance of being pitched bodily against some tree on the pathside. But we were by this time all alive again, the dulness of repletion having evaporated; and Mr Bang, I fancied, began to peer anxiously about him, and to fidget a good deal, and to murmur and grumble something in his gizzard about "arms—no arms," as, feeling in his starboard holster, he detected a regular long cork of claret, where he had hoped to clutch a pistol, while in the larboard, by the praiseworthy forethought of our guide, a good roasted capon was ensconced. "I say Tom—*tohoo*—mind I don't shoot you," presenting the bottle of claret. "If it had been soda-water, and the wire not all the stronger, I might have had a chance in this climate; but we are somewhat caught here, my dear—we have no arms."

"Poo," said I, "never mind; no danger at hand, take my word for it."

"Maybe not, maybe not—but, Pegtop, you scoundrel, why did you not fetch my pistols?"

"*Eigh,* you go fight, massa?

"Fight! no, you booby; but could not your own numskull—the fellow's a fool—so come—ride on, ride on."

Presently we came to an open space, free of trees, where the moon shone brightly; it was a round precipitous hollow, that had been excavated apparently by the action of a small clear stream or spout of water, that sparkled in the moonbeams like a web of silver tissue, as it leaped in a crystal arch over our heads from the top of a rock about twenty feet high, that rose on our right hand, the summit clearly and sharply defined against the blue firmament, while, on the left, there was a small hollow or ravine, down which the rivulet gurgled and vanished; while ahead the same impervious forest prevailed, beneath which we had been travelling for so many hours.

The road led right through this rugged hollow, crossing it about the middle, or, if anything, nearer the base of the cliff; and the whole clear space between the rock and the branches of the opposite trees might have measured twenty yards. In front of us, the path took a turn to the left, as if again entering below the dark shadow of the wood; but towards the right, with the moon shining brightly on it, there was a most beautiful bank, clear of underwood, and covered with the finest short velvet grass that could be dreamed of as a fitting sward to be in the centre of the open space.

"See how the moonlight sleeps on yonder bank!" said I.

"I don't know what sleeps there, Tom," said Aaron; "but does that figure sleep, think you?" pointing to the dark crest of the precipitous eminence on the right hand, from which the moonlight rill was gushing, as if it had been smitten by the rod of the prophet.

I started, and looked—a dark half-naked figure, with an enormous cap of the shaggy skin of some wild creature, was kneeling on one knee, on the very pinnacle, with a carabine resting across his thigh. I noticed our guide tremble from head to foot, but he did not speak.

"Vous avez des arms?" said Bang, as he continued, with great fluency, but little grammar; *"ayez le bonté de cockez votre pistolettes?"*

The man gave no answer. We heard the click of the carabine lock.

"Zounds!" said Aaron, with his usual energy when excited, "if you won't use them, give them to me;" and forthwith he snatched both pistols from our guide's holsters. "Now, Tom, get on. Shove t'other blackie ahead of you, Pegtop, will you? Confound you for forgetting my Mantons, you villain! I will bring up the rear."

"Well, I will get on," said I; "but here, give me a pistol."

"Ridez-vous en avant, blackimoribus ambos—en avant, you black rascals—*laissez le capitan* and me *pour fightez,"* shouted Bang, as the black guide, guessing his meaning, spurred his horse against the moonlight bank.

"Ah-ah!" exclaimed the man, as he wheeled about, after he had ridden a pace or two under the shadow of the trees—*"Voila ces autres brigands là."*

"Where?" said I.

"There," said the man, in an ecstasy of fear—"there" and, peering up into the forest, where the checkering dancing moonlight was flickering on the dun, herbless soil, as the gentle night-breeze made the leaves of the trees twinkle to and fro, I saw three dark figures advancing upon us.

"Here's a catastrophe, Tom, my boy," quoth Aaron, who, now that he had satisfied himself that the pistols were properly loaded and primed, had resumed all his wonted coolness in danger. "Ask that fellow who is enacting the statue on the top of the rock what he wants. I am a tolerable shot, you know; and if he means evil, I shall nick him before he can carry his carabine to his shoulder, take my word for it."

"Who is there, and what do you want?" No answer; the man above us continued as still as if he had actually been a statue of bronze. Presently one of the three men in the wood sounded a short snorting note on a bullock's born.

It would seem that until this moment their comrade above us had not been aware of their vicinity, for he immediately called out in the *patois* of St Domingo, "Advance, and seize the travellers;" and thereupon was in the act of raising his piece to his shoulder, when—crack—Bang fired his pistol. The man uttered a loud *hah,* but did not fall.

"Missed him, by all that is wonderful!" said my companion. "Now, Tom, it is your turn."

I levelled, and was in the very act of pulling the trigger, when the dark figure fell over slowly and stiffly on his back, and then began to struggle violently, and to cough loudly as if he were suffocating. At length he rolled over and down the face of the rock, where he was caught by a strong clump of brushwood, and there he hung, while the coughing and crowing increased, and I felt a warm shower, as of heated water, sputter over my face. It was hot hot, and salt—God of my fathers! *it was blood.* But there was no time for consideration; the three figures by this time had been reinforced by six more, and they now, with a most fiendish yell, jumped down into the hollow basin and surrounded us.

"Lay down your arms," one of them shouted.

"No," I exclaimed; "we are British officers, and armed, and determined to sell our lives dearly; and if you do succeed in murdering us, you may rest assured you shall be hunted down by bloodhounds."

I thought the game was up, and little dreamed that the name of Britain would, amongst the fastnesses of Hayti, have proved a talisman; but it did so. "We have no wish to injure you, but you must follow us and see our general," said the man who appeared to take the lead amongst them. Here two of the men scrambled up the face of the rock, and brought their wounded comrade down from where he hung, and laid him on the bank; he had been shot through the lungs, and could not speak. After a minute's conversation, they lifted him on their shoulders; and as our guide and Monsieur Pegtop had been instantly bound, we were only two to nine armed men, and accordingly had nothing for it but to follow the bearers of the wounded man, with our horses tumbling and scrambling up the river-course, into which, by their order, we had now turned.

We proceeded in this way for about half a mile, when it was evident that the jaded beasts could not travel farther amongst the twisted trunks of trees and fragments of rock with which the river-course was now strewed. We therefore dismounted, and were compelled to leave them in charge of two of the brigands, and immediately began to scramble up the hill-side through a narrow foot-path, in one of the otherwise most impervious thickets that I had ever seen. Presently a black savage, half-naked like his companions, hailed, and told us to stand. Some password that we could not understand was given by our captors, and we proceeded, still ascending, until, turning sharp off to the left, we came suddenly round a pinnacle of rock, and looked down into a deep dell, with a winding path leading to the brink of it. It was a round cockpit of a place, surrounded with precipitous limestone rocks on all sides, from the fissures of which large trees and bushes sprang, while the bottom was a level piece of ground, covered with long hay-like grass, evidently much trodden down. Close to the high bank, right opposite, and about thirty yards from us, a wood fire was sparkling cheerily against the grey rock; while, on the side next us, the roofs of several huts were visible, but there was no one moving about that we could see. The moment, however, that the man with the horn sounded a rough and most unmelodious blast, there was a buzz and a stir below, and many a short grunt arose out of the pit, and long yawns, and *eigh, eighs!* while a dozen splinters of resinous wood were instantly lit, and held aloft, by whose light I saw fifty or sixty half-naked but well-armed blacks, gazing up at us from beneath, their white eyes and whiter teeth glancing. Most of them had muskets and long knives, and several wore the military *shako,* while others had their heads bound round with the never-failing handkerchief. At length a fierce-looking fellow, dressed in short drawers, a round blue jacket, a pair of epaulets, and a most enormous cocked hat, placed a sort of rough ladder, a plank with notches cut in it with a hatchet, against the bank next us, and in a loud voice desired us to descend. I did so with fear and trembling, but Mr Bang never lost his presence of mind for a moment; and, in answer to the black chief's questions, I again rested our plea on our being British officers, despatched on service from a squadron (and as I used the word, the poor little Wave and solitary corvette rose up before me) across the island to Jacmel, to communicate with another British force lying there. The man heard me with great patience; but when I looked round the circle of tatterdemalions, for there was ne'er a shirt in the whole company—Falstaff's men were a joke to them—with their bright arms sparkling to the red glare of the torches, that flared like tongues of flame overhead, while they grinned with their ivory teeth, and glared fiercely with their white eyeballs on us I felt that our lives were not worth an hour's purchase.

At length the leader spoke—"I am General Sanchez, driven to dispute President Petion's sway by his injustice to me—but I trust our quarrel is not hopeless; will you, gentlemen, on your return to Port-au-Prince, use your influence with him to withdraw his decree against me?"

This was so much out of the way—the idea of our being deputed to mediate between such great personages as President Petion and one of his rebel generals was altogether so absurd, that, under other circumstances, I would have laughed in the black fellow's face. However, a jest here might have cost us our lives; so we looked serious, and promised.

"Upon your honours!" said the poor fellow.

"Upon our words of honour," we rejoined.

"Then embrace me"—and the savage thereupon, stinking of tobacco and cocoa-nut oil, hugged me, and kissed me on both cheeks, and then did the agreeable in a similar way to Mr Bang. Here the coughing and moaning of the wounded man broke in upon the conference.

"What is that?" said Sanchez. One of his people told him. "Ah!" said he, with a good deal of savageness in his tone"—"Aha! Blood?"

We promptly explained how it happened; for a few moments, I did not know how he might take it.

"But I forgive you," at length, said he; "however, my men may revenge their comrade. You must drink and eat with them."

This was said aside to us, as it were. He ordered some roasted plantains to be brought, and mixed some cruel bad tafia with water in an enormous gourd. He ate, and then took a pull himself—we followed; and he then walked round the circle, and carefully observed that every one had tasted also. Being satisfied on this head, he abruptly ordered us to ascend the ladder and to pass on our way.

The poor fellow was mad, I believe. However, some time afterwards, the president hunted him down, and got hold of him, but I believe he never punished him. As for the wounded man

"Whether he did live or die,
Tom Cringle does not know."

We were reconducted by our former escort to where we left our horses, remounted, and, without further let or hindrance, arrived by day-dawn at the straggling town of Jacmel. The situation is very beautiful; the town being built on the hill-side, looking out seaward on a very safe roadstead, the anchorage being defended to the southward by bright blue shoals, and white breakers, that curl and roar over the coral-reefs and ledges. As we rode up to Mr S——'s, the principal merchant in the place, and a Frenchman, we were again struck with the dilapidated condition of the houses, and the generally ruinous state of the town. The brown and black population appeared to be lounging about in the most absolute idleness; and here, as at Port-au-Prince, every second man you met was a soldier. The women sitting in their little shops, nicely set out with a variety of gay printed goods, and the crews of the English vessels loading coffee, were the only individuals who seemed to be capable of any exertion.

"I say, Tom," quoth Massa Aaron, "do you see that old fellow there?"

"What! that old grey-headed negro sitting in the arbour there?"

"Yes; the patriarch is sitting under the shadow of his own *Lima bean*."

And so in very truth he was. The stem was three inches in diameter, and the branches had been trained along and over a sparred arch, and were loaded with pods.

"I shall believe in the story of Jack and the Beanstalk henceforth and for ever," said I.

We were most kindly entertained by Mr S——, and spent two or three days very happily. The evening of the day on which we arrived, we had strolled out about nine o'clock to take the air—our host and his clerks being busy in the counting-house—and were on our way home, when we looked in on them at their desks before ascending to the apartments above. There were five clerks and Mr S——, all working away on the top of their tall mahogany tripods, by the light of their brown homemade wax candles, while three masters of merchantmen were sitting in a corner, comparing bills of lading, making up manifests, and I do not know what beside.

"It is now about time to close," said Mr S——; "have you any objection to a little music, gentlemen? or are you too much fatigued?"

"Music—music," said Mr Bang; "I delight in good music, but—" He was cut short by the whole bunch, the clerks and their master, closing their ledgers and journals and day-books and cash-books with a bang, while one hooked up a fiddle, another a clarionet, another a flute, &c., while Mr S—— offered, with a smile, his own clarionet to Massa Aaron, and holding out at the same time, with the true good-breeding of a Frenchman, a span-new reed. To my unutterable surprise he took it—sucked in his lips—wet the reed in his mouth; then passing his hand across his muzzle, coolly asked Mr S—— what the piece was to be? *"Adeste fideles,* if you please," said S——, rather taken aback. Mr Bang nodded, sounded a bar or two, gave another very scientific flourish, and then calmly awaited the opening. He then tendered a fiddle to me—altogether beyond my compass—but I offered to officiate on the kettledrum, the drummer being competent to something else. At a signal from our host away they all launched, in full *crash,* and very melodious it was too, let me tell you, Aaron's instrument telling most famously.

The next day we went to visit a tafia property in the neighbourhood. On our way we passed a dozen miserable-looking blacks, cleaning canes, followed by an ugly Turk of a brown man, almost naked, with the omnipresent glazed cocked-hat, and a drawn cutlass in his hand. He was abusing the poor devils most lustily as we rode along, and stood so pertinaciously in the path that I could not for the life of me pass without jostling him. *"Je vous demande pardon,"* said I, with a most abject salaam to my saddle-bow. He knit his brows and shut his teeth hard, as he ground out between the glancing ivory, *"Sacré! voila ces foutres blancs là,"* clutching the hilt of his couteau firmly all the while. I thought he would have struck me. But Mr S——, coming up, mollified the savage, and we rode on.

The tafia estate was a sore affair. It had once been a prosperous sugar-plantation, as the broken panes and ruined houses, blackened by fire, were melancholy vouchers for; but now the whole cultivation was reduced to about a couple of acres of wiry sugar-canes, and the boiling and distilling were carried on in a small unroofed nook of the original works.

Two days after this we returned to Port-au-Prince, and I could not help admiring the justness of Aaron's former description; for noisome exhalations were rising thick, as the evening sun shone hot and sickly on the long bank of fat black mud that covers the beach beneath the town. We found Captain Transom at Mr S——'s. I made my report of the state of the merchantmen loading on the south side of the island, and retired to rest, deucedly tired and stiff with my ride. Next morning Bang entered my room.

"Hillo, Tom! the skipper has been shouting for you this half-hour; get up, man—get up."

"My dear sir, I am awfully tired."

"Oh!" sang Bang—

"'I have a silent sorrow here'—

eh?"

It was true enough; no sailor rides seventy miles on end with impunity. That same evening we bade adieu to our excellent host Mr S——, and the rising moon shone on us under weigh for Kingston, where two days after we safely anchored with the homeward-bound trade.

"The roaring seas
Is not a place of ease,"

says a *Point* ditty. No more is the command of a small schooner in the West Indies. We had scarcely anchored when the boarding-officer from the flag-ship brought me a message to repair thither immediately. I did so. As I stepped on deck, the lieutenant was leaning on the drum-head of the capstan, with the signal-book open before him, while the signal-man was telling off the semaphore, which was rattling away at the Admiral's pen, situated about five miles off.

"Ah! Cringle," said he, without turning his head, "how are you? glad to see you—wish you joy, my lad. Here lend me a hand, will you? it concerns you." I took the book, and as the man reported, I pieced the following comfortable sentence together.

"Desire—Wave—fit—wood—water—instantly—to take convoy—to Spanish Main—to-morrow morning—Mr Cringle—remain on board—orders will be sent—evening."

"Heigh ho, says *Rowley*,"

sang I Thomas, in great wrath and bitterness of spirit, "D——d hard; am I a duck, to live in the water altogether, entirely?"

"Tom, my boy," sang out a voice from the water. It was Aaron Bang's, who, along with Transom, had seen me go on board the receiving ship. "Come along, man—come along; Transom is going to make interest to get you a furlough on shore; so come along, and dine with us in Kingston."

"I am ordered to sea to-morrow morning, my dear sir," said I, like to cry.

"No!" "Too true, too true." So no help for it, I took a sad farewell of my friends, received my orders, laid in my provisions and water, hauled out into the fairway, and sailed for Santa Martha next morning at daybreak, with three merchant schooners under convoy—one for Santa Martha, another for Carthagena, and the third for Porto-Bello.

We sailed on the 24th of such a month, and, after a pleasant passage, anchored at Santa Martha at 8 A.M. on the 31st. When we came to anchor we saluted, which seemed to have been a somewhat unexpected honour, as the return was fired from the fort after a most primitive fashion. A black fellow appeared with a shovel of live embers, one of which another *sans culotte* caught up in his hand, chucking it from palm to palm until he ran to the breech of the first gun, where, clapping it on the touch-hole, he fired it off, and so on *seriatim* through the whole battery, until the required number of guns were given, several of which, by the by, were shotted, as we could hear the balls whiz overhead. The town lies on a small plain, at the foot of very high mountains, or rather on a sand-bank, formed from the washings from these mountains. The summit of the highest of them, we could see from the deck, was covered with snow, which at sunrise, in the clear light of the cool grey dawn, shone, when struck by the first rays of the sun, like one entire amethyst. Oh, how often I longed for the wings of the eagle, to waft me from the hot deck of the little vessel, where the thermometer in the shade stood at 95°, far up amongst the shining glaciers, to be comforted with cold!

One striking natural phenomenon is exhibited here, arising out of the vicinity of this stupendous prong of the Cordilleras. The sea-breeze blows into the harbour all day, but in the night, or rather towards morning, the cold air from the high regions rushes down, and blows with such violence off the land, that my convoy and myself were nearly blown out to sea the first night after we arrived; and it was only by following the practice of the native craft, and anchoring close under the lee of the beach—in fact, by having an anchor high and dry on the shore itself—the *playa*, as the Spaniards call it—that we could count on riding through the night with security or comfort.

There are several small islands at the entrance of the harbour, on the highest of which is a fort that might easily be rendered impregnable; it commands both the town and harbour. The place itself deserves little notice: the houses are mean, and interspersed with negro huts, but there is one fine church with several tolerable paintings in it. One struck me as especially grotesque, although I had often seen queer things in Roman Catholic churches in Europe.

It was a representation of Hell, with Old Nicholas, under the guise of a dragon, entertaining himself with the soul of an unfortunate heretic in his claws, who certainly appeared far from comfortable, while a lot of his angels were washing the sins off a set of fine young men, as you would the dirt off *scabbit* potatoes, in a sea of liquid fire. But their saints!—I often rejoiced that Aaron Bang was not with me; we should unquestionably have quarreled; for as to the manner in which they were dressed and decorated, the most fantastic *mode* a girl ever *did* up her doll in was a joke to it. Still these wooden deities are treated with such veneration, that I do believe their ornaments, which are of massive gold and silver, are never, or very rarely, stolen.

On the evening of the 2d of the following month, we sailed again, but having been baffled by calms and light winds, it was the 4th before we anchored off the St Domingo gate at Carthagena, and next morning we dropped down to Boca Chica, and saw our charge, a fine dashing schooner of 150 tons, safe into the harbour. About 9 A.M. we weighed, but we had scarcely got the anchor catted, when it came on to blow great guns from the north-west—a most unusual thing hereabouts—so it was down anchor again; and as I had made up my mind not to attempt it again before morning, I got the gig in the water with all convenient speed; and that same forenoon I reached the town, and immediately called on the Viceroy, but under very different circumstances from the time Mr Splinter and I had entered it along with the conquering army.

We dined with the magnate, and found a very large party assembled. Amongst others, I especially recollect that the *Inquisidor-General* was conspicuous; but every one, with the exception of the Captain-General and his immediate staff, was arrayed in gingham jackets; so there was not much style in the affair.

I had before dinner an opportunity to inspect the works of Carthagena at my leisure. It is unquestionably a very strong place, the walls, which are built of solid masonry, being armed with at least three hundred pieces of brass cannon, while the continual ebb and flow of the tide in the ditch creates a current so strong, that it would be next to impossible to fill it up, as fascines would be carried away by the current; so that, were the walls even breached, it would be impracticable to storm them. The appearance of Carthagena from the sea— that is, from a vessel anchored off the St Domingo gate—is singularly beautiful and picturesque. It is situated on a sandy island, or rather a group of islands; and the beach here shoals so gradually, that boats of even a very small draught of water cannot approach within musket-shot. The walls and numerous batteries have a very commanding appearance. The spires and towers on the churches are numerous, and many of them were decorated with flags when we were there; and the green trees, shooting up amidst the red-tiled houses, afforded a beautiful relief to the prospect. A little behind the town, on a gentle acclivity, is the citadel, or Fort San Felipe, whose appearance conveys an idea of impregnable strength (but all this sort of thing, is it not written in *Roderick Random*?), and on the ship-like hill beyond it, the only other eminence in the neighbourhood, stands the convent of the Popa, like a poop lantern on the high stern of a ship, from which, indeed, it takes its name. This convent had been strongly fortified; and, commanding San Felipe, was of great use to Morillo, who carried it by assault during the siege, and held it until the insurgents shelled him out from the citadel. The effect, when I first saw it, was increased by the whole scene—city, and batteries, and Popa—being reflected in the calm smooth sea as distinctly as if it had been glass; so clear, in fact, was the reflection, that you could scarcely distinguish the shadow from the reality. We weighed next morning—that is, on the 6th of the month, and arrived safe at Porto-Bello on the 11th, after a tedious passage, during which we had continual rains, accompanied with vivid lightning and tremendous thunder. I had expected to have fallen in with one of our frigates here; but I afterwards learned that, although I had slid down cheerily along shore, the weather current that prevailed farther out at sea had swept her away to the eastward; so I ran in and anchored, and immediately waited on the Governor, who received me in what might once have been a barn, although it did not now deserve the name.—

Porto-Bello was originally called Nombre de Dios, having received the former name from the English when we took it. It is a miserable, dirty, damp hole, surrounded by high, forest-clad hills, round which everlasting mists curl and obscure the sun, whose rays, at any chance moment when they do reach the steamy swamp on which it is built, or the waters of the lead-coloured land-locked cove that constitutes the harbour, immediately exhale a thick sickly moisture, in clouds of sluggish white vapours, smelling diabolically of decayed vegetables and slime and mud. I will venture a remark that will be found, I am persuaded, pretty near the truth, that there were twenty carrion crows to be seen in the streets for every inhabitant. The people seem every way worthy of such an abode—saffron, dingy, miserable, emaciated-looking devils. As for the place itself, it appeared to my eyes one large hospital, inhabited by patients in the yellow fever. During the whole of the following day there was still no appearance of the frigate, and I had in consequence now to execute the ulterior part of my orders, which were, that if I did not find her at anchor when I arrived, or if she did not make her appearance within forty-eight hours thereafter, I was myself to leave the Wave in Porto-Bello, and to proceed overland across the isthmus to Panama, and to deliver, on board of H. M. S. Bandera, into the captain's own hands, a large packet with despatches from the Government at home, as I understood, of great importance, touching the conduct of our squadron, with reference to the vagaries of some of the mushroom American Republics on the Pacific. But if I fell in with the frigate, then I was to deliver the said packet to the captain, and return immediately in the Wave to Port Royal.

Having, therefore, obtained letters from the Governor of Porto-Bello to the Commandant at Chagres, I chartered a canoe, with four stout canoemen and a steersman, or *patron*, as he is called, to convey me to Cruzes; and having laid in a good stock of eatables and drinkables, and selected the black pilot, Peter Mangrove, to go as my servant, accompanied by his never-failing companion, Sneezer, and taking my hammock and double-barrelled gun, and a brace of pistols with me, we shoved off at 6 A.M. on the morning, of the 14th.

It was a rum sort of conveyance this said canoe of mine. In the first place, it was near forty feet long, and only five wide at the broadest, being hollowed out of one single wild cotton-tree; how this was to be pulled through the sea on the coast, by four men, I could not divine. However, I was assured by the old thief who chartered it to me, that it would be all right; whereas, had my innocence not been imposed on, I might, in a *caiuco*, or smaller canoe, have made the passage in one half the time it took me.

About ten feet of the afterpart was thatched with palm leaves, over a framework of broad ash hoops; which awning, called the *toldo*, was open both towards the steersman that guided us with a long broad-bladed paddle in the stern, and in the direction of the men forward, who, on starting, stripped themselves stark naked, and, giving a loud yell every now and then, began to pull their oars, or long paddles, after a most extraordinary fashion. First, when they lay back to the strain, they jumped backwards and upwards on the thwart with their feet, and then, as they once more feathered their paddles again, they came crack down on their bottoms with a loud *skelp* on the seats, upon which they again mounted at the next stroke, and so on.

When we cleared the harbour it was fine and serene, but about noon it came onto blow violently from the north-east. All this while we were coasting it along about pistol-shot from the white coral beach, with the clear light green swell on our right hand, and beyond it the dark and stormy waters of the blue rolling ocean; and the snow-white roaring surf on our left. By the time I speak of, the swell had been lashed up into breaking waves, and, after shipping more salt water than I had bargained for, we were obliged, about 4 P.M., to shove into a cove within the reef, called Naranja.

Along this part of the coast there is a chain of salt-water lagoons, divided from the sea by the coral beach, the crest of which is covered here and there with clumps of stunted mangroves.

This beach, strangely enough, is higher than the land immediately behind it, as if it had been a dyke, or natural breakwater thrown up by the sea. Every here and there there were gaps in this natural dyke, and it was through one of these we shoved, and soon swung to our grapnel in perfect security, but in a most outlandish situation certainly.

As we rode to the easterly breeze, there was the beach as described, almost level with the water, on our left hand, the land or lee side of it covered with most beautiful white sand and shells, with whole warrens of land-crabs running out and in their holes like little rabbits, their tiny green bodies seeming to roll up and down, for I was not near enough to see their feet, or the mode of their locomotion, like bushels of grapeshot trundling all about on the shining white shore. Beyond, the roaring surf was flashing up over the clumps of green bushes and thundering on the seaward face. On the right hand, ahead of us and astern of us, the prospect was shut in by impervious thickets of mangroves, while in the distance the blue hills rose glimmering and indistinct as seen through the steamy atmosphere. We were anchored in a stripe of clear water, about three hundred yards long by fifty broad. There was a clear space abeam of us, landward, of about half an acre in extent, on which was built a solitary Indian hut close to the water's edge, with a small canoe drawn up close to the door. We had not been long at anchor when the canoe was launched, and a monkey-looking naked old man paddled off, and brought us a most beautiful chicken-turtle, some yams, and a few oranges. I asked him his price. He rejoined, *"por amor de Dios;"* that it was his mint's day, and he meant it as a gift. However, he did not refuse a dollar when tendered to him before he paddled away.

That night, when we were all at supper, master and men, I heard and felt a sharp crack against the side of the canoe. "Hillo, Peter, what is that?" said I.

"Nothing, sir," quoth Peter, who was enjoying his scraps abaft with the headman, *patron*, or whatever you may call him, of my crew. There was a blazing fire kindled on a bed of white sand, forward in the bow of the canoe, round which the four *bogas*, or canoemen, were seated, with three sticks stuck up triangularly over the fire, from which depended an earthen pot, in which they were cooking their suppers.

I had rigged my hammock between the foremost and aftermost hoops of the *toldo*, and as I was fatigued and sleepy, and it was now getting late, I desired to betake myself to rest; so I was just flirting with a piece of ham, preparatory to the cold grog, when I again felt a similar thump and rattle against the side of the canoe. There was a small aperture in the palm thatch, right opposite to where I was sitting, on the outside of which I now heard a rustling noise, and presently a long snout was thrust through, and into the canoe, which kept opening and shutting with a sharp rattling noise. It was more like two long splinters of mud-covered and half-decayed timber, than anything I can compare it to; but as the lower jaw was opened, like a pair of Brobdignag scissors, a formidable row of teeth was unmasked, the snout from the tip to the eyes being nearly three feet long. The scene at this moment was exceedingly good, as seen by the light of a small, bright, silver lamp, fed with spirits of wine, that I always travelled with, which hung from one of the hoops of the *toldo*. First, there was our friend Peter Mangrove, cowering in a corner under the afterpart of the awning, covered up with a blanket and shaking, as if with an ague-fit, with the *patron* peering over his shoulder, no less alarmed. Sneezer, the dog, was sitting on end, with his black nose resting on the table, waiting patiently for his crumbs; and the black boatmen were forward in the bow of the canoe, jabbering, and laughing, and munching, as they clustered round a sparkling fire. When I first saw the apparition of the diabolical-looking snout, I was in a manner fascinated, and could neither speak nor move. Mangrove and the *patron* were also paralysed with fear, and the others did not see it; so Sneezer was the only creature amongst us, aware of the danger, who seemed to have his wits about him, for the instant he noticed it, he calmly lifted his nose off the table, and gave a short startled bark, and then crouched and drew himself back as if in act to spring, glancing his eyes from the monstrous jaws to my face, and nuzzling and whining with a laughing expression, and giving a small yelp now and then, and again riveting his eyes with intense earnestness on the alligator, telling me as plainly as if he had spoken it—"If you choose, master, I will attack *it* as in duty bound, but really such a customer is not at all in my way." And not only did he say this, but he showed his intellect was clear, and no way warped through fear, for he now stood on his hind legs, and, holding on the hammock with his forepaws, he thrust his snout below the pillow, and pulled out one of my pistols, which always garnished the head of my bed on such expeditions as the present.

My presence of mind returned at witnessing the courage and sagacity of my noble dog. I seized the loaded pistol, and as by this time the eyes of the alligator were inside of the *toldo,* I clapped the muzzle to the larboard one and fired. The creature jerked back so suddenly and convulsively, that part of the *toldo* was torn away: and as the dead monster fell off, the canoe rolled as if in a seaway. My crew shouted *"Que es esto?"* Peter Mangrove cheered; Sneezer barked and yelled at a glorious rate, and could scarcely be held in the canoe; and looking overboard, we saw the monster, twelve feet long at least, upturn his white belly to the rising moon, struggle for a moment with his short paws, and after a solitary heavy lash of his scaly tail, he floated away astern of us, dead and still. To proceed: poor Peter Mangrove, whose nerves were consumedly shaken by this interlude, was seized during the night with a roasting fever, brought on in a great measure, I believe, by fear, at finding himself so far out of his latitude; and that he had grievous doubts as to the issue of our voyage, and as to where we were bound for, was abundantly evident. I dosed him most copiously with salt water, a very cooling medicine, and no lack of it at hand.

We weighed at grey dawn, on the morning of the 15th, and at 11 o'clock A.M. arrived at Chagres, a more miserable place, were that credible, even than Porto-Bello. The eastern side of the harbour is formed by a small promontory that runs out into the sea about five hundred yards, with a bright little bay to windward; while a long muddy mangrove-covered pit forms the right-hand bank as you enter the mouth or estuary of the river Chagres on the west. The easternmost bluff is a narrow saddle, with a fort erected on the extreme point facing the sea, which, so far as situation is concerned, is, or ought to be, impregnable; the rock being precipitous on three faces, while it is cut off to landward by a deep dry ditch, about thirty feet wide, across which a movable drawbridge is let down, and this compartment of the defences is all very regular, with scarp and counterscarp, covered-way, and glacis. The brass guns mounted on the castle were numerous and beautiful, but everything was in miserable disrepair; several of the guns, for instance, had settled down bodily on the platform, having fallen through the crushed rotten carriages. I found an efficient garrison in this stronghold of three old negroes, who had not even a musket of any kind, but the commandant was not in the castle when I paid my visit; however, one of the invincibles undertook to pilot me to El Señor Torre's house, where his honour was dining. The best house in the place this was, by the by, although only a thatched hut; and here I found his Excellency the Commandant, a little shrivelled insignificant-looking creature. He was about sitting down to his dinner, of which he invited me to partake, alongside of El Señor Torre, who was neither more nor less than a reputable negro; and as I was very hungry, I contrived to do justice to the first dish, but my stomach was grievously offended at the second, which seemed to me to be a compound of garlic, brick-dust, and train-oil, so that I was glad to hurry on board of my canoe, to settle all with a little good madeira.

At 4 P.M. I proceeded up the river, which is here about a hundred yards across, and very deep; it rolls sluggishly along through a low swampy country, covered to the water's edge with thick sedges and underwood, below which the water stagnates, and generates myriads of mosquitoes and other troublesome insects, and sends up whole clouds of noxious vapours, redolent of yellow fever and ague and cramps, and all manner of comfortable things.

At 10 P.M. we anchored by a grapnel in the stream, and I set Peter Mangrove forthwith to officiate in his new capacity of cook, and really he made a deuced good one. I then slung my hammock under the *toldo,* and, lighting a slow match at the end of it forwards to smoke away the mosquitoes—having previously covered the aftermost end with a mat—I wrapped myself in my cloak and turned in to take my snooze. We weighed again about two in the morning. As the day dawned the dull grey steamy clouds settled down on us once more, while the rain fell in a regular waterspout. It was anything but a cheering prospect to look along the dreary vistas of the dull brimful Lethe-like stream, with nothing to be seen but the heavy lowering sky above, the red swollen water beneath, and the gigantic trees high towering overhead, and growing close to the water's edge, laced together with black snake-like withes, while the jungle was thick and impervious, and actually grew down into the water, for beach, or shore, or cleared bank, there was none—all water and underwood, except where a soft slimy steaming black bank of mud hove its shining back from out the dead waters near the shore, with one or more monstrous alligators sleeping on it, like dirty rotten logs of wood, scarcely deigning to lift their abominable long snouts to look at us as we passed, or to raise their scaly tails, with the black mud sticking to the scales in great lumps—oh! horrible—most horrible! But the creatures, although no beauties certainly, are harmless after all. For instance, I never heard a well-authenticated case of their attacking a human being hereabouts; pigs and fowls they do tithe, however, like any parson. I don't mean to say that they would not make free with a little fat dumpling of a *piccaniny*, if he were thrown to them, but they seem to have no ferocious propensities. I shot one of them; he was about twelve feet long; the bullet entered in the joints of the mail, below the shoulder of the forepaw, where the hide was tender; but if you fire at them *with* the scale—that is, with the monster looking at you—a musket-ball will glance. I have often in this my Log spoken of the Brobdignag lizards, the guanas. I brought down one this day, about three feet long, and found it, notwithstanding its dragon-like appearance, very good eating. At 11 A.M., on the 18th, we arrived at the village of Cruzes, the point where the river ceases to be navigable for canoes, and from whence you take horse, or rather mule, for Panama. For about fifteen or twenty miles below Cruzes the river becomes rapid, and full of shoals, when the oars are laid aside, and the canoes are propelled by long poles.

The Town, as it is called, is a poor miserable place, composed chiefly of negro huts; however, a Spanish trader of the name of Villaverde, who had come over in the Wave as a passenger, and had preceded me in a lighter canoe, and to whom I had shown some kindness, now repaid it as far as lay in his power.

He lodged me for the night, and hired mules for me to proceed to Panama in the morning; so I slung my hammock in an old Spanish soldier's house, who keeps a kind of *posada*, and was called by my friend Villaverde at daydawn, whose object was, not to tell me to get ready for my journey, but to ask me if I would go and bathe before starting. Rather a rum sort of request, it struck me; nevertheless, a purification, after the many disagreeables I had endured, could not come amiss; and slipping on my trousers, and casting my cloak on my shoulders, away we trudged to a very beautiful spot, about a mile above Cruzes, where, to my surprise, I found a score of *Crusaños*, all *ploutering* in the water, puffing and blowing and shouting. "Now an alligator might pick and choose," thought I; however, no one seemed in the least afraid, so I dashed amongst them. Presently, about pistol-shot from us, a group of females appeared. "Come," thought I, "rather too much for a modest young man this too," and deuce take me, as I am a gentleman, if the whole bevy did not disrobe in cold blood, and squatter, naked as their mother Eve was in the garden of Eden, before she took to the herbage, right into the middle of the stream, skirling and laughing, as if not even a male mosquito had been within twenty miles. However, my neighbour took no notice of them; it seemed all a matter of course. But let that pass. About 8 o'clock A.M. I got under weigh, with Peter Mangrove, on two good stout mules, and a black guide running before me with a long stick, with which he sprang over the sloughs and stones in the road with great agility; I would have backed him against many a passable hunter, to do four miles over a close country in a steeple-chase.

Panama is distant from Cruzes about seven leagues. The road is somewhat like what the Highland ones must have been before General Wade took them in hand, and only passable for mules; indeed, in many places where it has been hewn out of the rock in zigzags on the face of the hill, it is scarcely passable for two persons meeting. But the scenery on each side is very beautiful, as it winds, for the most part, amongst steep rocks, overshadowed by magnificent trees, amongst which birds of all sizes, and of the most beautiful plumage, are perpetually glancing; while a monkey, every here and there, would sit grimacing and chattering and scratching himself in the cleft of a tree.

I should think, judging from my barometer—but I may have made an inaccurate calculation, and I have not Humboldt by me—that the ridge of the highest is fifteen hundred feet above the level of the ocean, so that it would be next to impossible to join the two seas at this point by a canal *with water in it*. However, I expect to see a Joint Stock Company set agoing some fine day yet, for the purpose of cutting it—that is, when the national capital next accumulates (and Lord knows when that will be) to a plethora, and people's purses become so distended that they require bleeding.

After travelling about twenty miles, the scene gradually opens, and one begins to dream about Vasco Nuñez and the enthusiastic first explorers of the Isthmus; but my first view of the Pacific was through a drenching shower of rain, that wet me to the skin, and rather kept my imagination under; for this said imagination of mine is like a barn-door chuckey, brisk and *crouse* enough when the sun shines, and the sky is blue, and plenty of grub at hand; but I can't write poetry when I am *cauld* and hungry and *drooked*. Still, when I caught my first glimpse of the distant Pacific, I felt that, even through a miserable drizzle, it was a noble prospect.

As you proceed, you occasionally pass through small open savannahs, which become larger, and the clear spaces wider, until the forest you have been travelling under gradually breaks into beautiful clumps of trees, like those in a gentleman's park, and every here and there a placid clear piece of water spreads out, full of pond turtle, which I believe to be one and the same with the tortoise and eels—the latter of which, by the by, are very sociable creatures—for in the clear moonlight nights, with the bright sparkling dew on the short moist grass, they frequently travel from one pond to another, wriggling along the grass like snakes. I have myself found them fifty yards from the water; but whether the errand was love or war, or merely to drink tea with some of the slippery young females in the next pool, and then return again, the deponent sayeth not.

As you approach the town the open spaces, before mentioned, become more frequent, until at length you gain a rising-ground about three miles from Panama, where, as the sun again shone out, the view became truly enchanting.

There lay the town of Panama, built on a small tongue of land jutting into the Pacific, surrounded by walls, which might have been a formidable defence once; but I wish my promotion depended on my rattling the old bricks and stones about their ears, with one single frigate, if I could only get near enough; but in the impossibility of this lies the strength of the place, as the water shoals so gradually that the tide retires nearly a mile and a half from the walls, rising, I consider, near eighteen feet at the springs; while, on the opposite side of the isthmus, at Chagres for instance, there is scarcely any at all, the Gulf stream neutralising it almost entirely.

On the right hand a hill overhangs the town, rising precipitously to the height of a thousand feet or thereabouts, on the extreme pinnacle of which is erected a signal station, called the *Vigia,* which, at the instant I saw it, was telegraphing to some craft out at sea. As for the city, to assume our friend Mr Bang's mode of description, it was shaped like a tadpole, the body representing the city, and the suburb the tail; or a stewpan, the city and its fortifications being the pan, while the handle, tending obliquely towards us, was the *Raval* or long street, extending savannahward, without the walls. At the distance from which we viewed it, the red-tiled houses, cathedral with its towers, and the numerous monasteries and nunneries, seemed girt in with a white ribbon; while a series of black spots here and there denoted the cannon on the batteries. To the left of the town there was a whole flotilla of small craft, brigs, schooners, and vegetable boats; while farther out at sea, beyond the fortifications, three large ships rode at anchor; and beyond them again, the beautiful group of islands lying about five miles off the town, appeared to float on and were reflected in, the calm glass-like expanse of the Pacific, like emeralds chased in silver, while the ocean itself, towards the horizon, seemed to rise up like a scene in a theatre, or a burnished bright silver wall, growing more and more blue and hazy and indistinct as it ascended, until it melted into the cloudless heaven, so that no one could tell where water and sky met.

"Thou glorious mirror,

  .   .   .   .   .   . in all time,

Calm or convulsed—in breeze, or gale, or storm,

Icing the pole, or in the torrid clime

Dark heaving—boundless, endless, and sublime.

The image of Eternity—the throne

Of the Invisible."

While a sperm-whale every now and then rose between us and the islands, and spouted up a high double jet into the air, like a blast of steam, and then, with a heavy flounder of his broad tail, slowly sank again; and a boat here and there glided athwart the scene, and a sleepy sail arose, with a slow motion and a fitful rattle and a greasy cheep, on the mast of some vessel getting all ready to weigh; while small floating trails of blue smoke were streaming away astern from the tiny cabooses of the craft at anchor, and a mournful distant "Yo, heave oh!" came booming past us on the light air; and the everlasting tinkle of the convent bells sounded cheerily, and the lowing of the kine around us called up old associations in my bosom, as I looked forth on the glorious spectacle from beneath a magnificent bower of orange-trees and shaddocks, while all manner of wild-flowers blossomed and bloomed around us.

We arrived at Panama about 3 P.M., covered to the eyes with mud, and after some little difficulty I found out Señor Hombrecillo Justo's house, who received me very kindly. Next morning I waited on the Governor, made my bow, and told him my errand. He was abundantly civil, professing himself ready to serve me in any way, and promising to give me the earliest intelligence of the arrival of the Bandera. I then returned to mine host's, to whom I had strong letters of introduction from some Kingston friends.

I soon found that I had landed amongst a family of originals. Mine host was a little thin withered body, with a face that might have vied with the monkey whom the council of Aberdeen took for a sugar-planter. He wore his own grey hair in a long greasy queue, and his costume, when I first saw him, was white cotton stockings, white jane small-clothes and waistcoat, and a little light-blue silk coat; he wore large solid gold buckles in his shoes, and knee-buckles of the same. His voice was small and squeaking and when heated in argument, or crossed by any member of his family—and he was very touchy—it became so shrill and indistinct that it pierced the ear without being in the least intelligible. In those paroxysms he did not walk, but sprung from place to place like a grasshopper with unlooked-for agility, avoiding the chairs and tables and other movables with great dexterity. I often thought he would have broken whatever came in his way; but although his erratic orbit was small, he performed his evolutions with great precision and security. His general temper, however, was very kind, humane, and good-humoured, and he seldom remained long under the influence of passion. His character, both as a man and a merchant, was, unimpeachable, and indeed proverbial in the place. His better half appeared to be some years older, and also a good deal of an original. She was a little short thick woman; but stout as she was when I had the honour of an embrace, she must have been once much stouter, for her skin appeared, from the colour and texture, to have come to her at secondhand, and to have originally belonged to a much larger person, for it bagged and hung in flaps about her jowls and bosom like an ill-cut maintopsail which sits clumsily about the clews. I think I could have reefed her with advantage below the chin.

Her usual dress was a shift, with a whole sail-room of frills about the sleeves and bosom, and a heavy pink taffeta petticoat (gowns being only worn by those fair ones as you put on a greatcoat—that is, when they go abroad), and a small round apron like a flap of black silk. Over these she wore a Spanish aroba, or 25 lb. weight of gold chains, saints, and crucifixes, and a large black velvet patch, of the size of a wafer, on each temple, which I found, by the by, to be an ornament very much in fashion amongst the fair of Panama. Her hair, or rather the scanty remnant thereof, was plaited into two grizzled braids, with a black bow of ribbon at the end of each, and hung straight down her back. Like many excellent wives, she loved to circulate her spouse's blood by a little well-timed opposition now and then; but she never tried her strength too far, and she always softened down in proportion as he waxed energetic and began to accelerate his motions, so that by the time he had given one or two hops, she had either fairly given in, or moved out. They had no children, but had in a manner adopted a little black creature about four years old, which, being a female, the lady had christened by the familiar diminutive of *Diablita*.

Another curiosity was the maternal aunt of Don Hombrecillo, a little superannuated woman about four feet high if she could have stood erect, but old age had long since bent her nearly double; she was on the verge of eighty-five years of age, and had outlived all her faculties. This poor old creature, in place of being respectably lodged and taken care of, was allowed to go about the house, tame, without any fixed abode, so far as I could learn; nor did she always meet with that attention, I am sorry to say it, from the family, or even from the servants, that she was entitled to from her extreme helplessness. She had a droll custom of eating all her meals walking, and it was her practice to move round the dinner-table in this her dotage, and to commit pranks that, against my will, made me laugh, and even in despite of the feelings of pity and self-humiliation that arose in my bosom at the sight of such miserable imbecility in a fellow-creature. Thus keeping on the wing as I have described, it was her practice to cruise about behind the chairs, occasionally snatching pieces of food from before the guests, so slyly, that the first intimation of her intentions was the appearance of her yellow shrivelled bird-like claw in your plate.

The brother of our host was a little stout man, but still very like Señor Justo himself. For instance, I always gloried in likening the latter to a dried prune; then, to conceive of his plump brother, imagine him boiled, and so swell out the creases in his skin, and there you have him.

This little dumpling was very asthmatic, and used to blow like a porpoise by the time he reached the top of the stairs. The only time he had ever been out of Panama was whilst he made a short visit to Lima, the wonders of which he used to chant unceasingly. But the continual cause of my annoyance—I fear I must write disgust—was the stepmother of mine host, a large fat dirty old woman. She had a pouch under her chin like a pelican, while her complexion, from the quantity of oil and foul feeding in which she delighted, was a greasy mahogany. She despised the unnatural luxuries of knives and forks, constantly devouring her meat with her fingers, whatever its consistency might be; if flesh, she tore it with both hands; if soup, she—bah! and, as the devil would have it, the venerable beauty chose to take a fancy to me. Oh, she was a baloon! I have often expected to see her rise to the roof.

These polished personages may be called Señor Justo's family, but it was occasionally increased by various others; none of whom, however, can I heave-to to describe at present.

The day after my arrival, the operation of covering dollar-boxes with wet hides had been going on in the dinner saloon the whole forenoon, which drove me forth to look about me; but I returned about half-past two, this being the hour of dinner, and found all the family, excepting mine hostess, assembled, and my appearance was the signal for dinner being ordered in. I may mention here that this worthy family were all firmly impressed with the idea that an Englishman was an ostrich, possessing a stomach capable of holding and digesting four times as much as any other person; and under this belief they were so outrageously kind that I was often literally stuffed to suffocation when

I first came amongst them; and when at length I resolutely refused to be immo-
lated after this fashion, they swore I was sick, or did not like my food, which
was next door to insulting them. El Señor Justo's fat dumpling of a brother
thought medical advice ought to be taken, for when he was in Lima several seamen belonging to an English whaler had died, and he had remarked, the
twaddling body, that they had invariably lost their appetites previous to their
dissolution.

But to return. Dinner, being ordered, was promptly placed on the table, and
mine host insisted on planting me at the foot thereof, while he sat on my left
hand; so the party sat down; but the chair opposite, that ought to have been
filled by *Madama* herself, was still vacant.

"Adonde esta su ama," quoth Don Hombrecillo to one of the black waiting-
wenches. The girl said she did not know, but she would go and see. It is
necessary to mention here that the worthy Señor's counting-house was in a
back building, separated from the house that fronted the street by a narrow
court; and in a small closet off this counting-house my *quatre* had been rigged
the previous night, and there had my luggage been deposited. Amongst other
articles in my commissariat there was a basket with half-a-dozen of champagne, and some hock, and a bottle of brandy, that I had placed under Peter
Mangrove's care, to comfort us in the wilderness. We all lay back in our chairs
to wait for the lady of the house, but neither did she nor Tomassa, the name of
the handmaiden who had been despatched in search of her, seem inclined to
make their appearance. Don Hombrecillo became impatient.

"Josefa"—to another of the servants—"run and *desire* your mistress to
come here immediately." Away she flew, but neither did this second pigeon
return. Mine host now lost his temper entirely, and spluttered out, as loud as he
could roar, *"Somos comiendo, Panchita, somos comiendo;"* and forthwith, as if
in spite, he began to fork up his food, until he had nearly choked himself.
Presently a short startled scream was heard from the counting-house, then a
low suppressed laugh, then a loud shout, a long uproarious peal of laughter, and
the two black servants came thundering across the wooden gangway or drawbridge that connected the room where we sat with the outhouse, driven
onwards by their mistress herself. They flew across the end of the dining-room
into the small balcony fronting the lane, and began without ceremony to shout
across the narrow street to a Carmelite priest, who was in a gallery of the opposite monastery, "that their mistress was *possessed*."

Presently in danced our landlady, *in propriâ personâ,* jumping and screaming and laughing, and snapping her fingers, and spinning round like a Turkish dervish,—*"Mira el fandango, mira el fandango—dexa me baylar, dexa me baylar*—See my fandango, see my fandango!—let me dance—let me dance—ha, ha, ha!"

"Panchita!" screamed Justo, in extreme wrath, *"tu es loco,* you are mad—sit down, *por amor de Dios—seas decente—*be decent."

She continued gamboling about, *"Joven soy y virgin—*I am young and a virgin—*y tu Viejo diablo que queres tu—*and you, old devil, what do you want, eh?—*Una virgin por Dios soy—*I am young," and, seizing a boiled fowl from the dish, she let fly at her husband's head, but missed him fortunately; whereupon she made a regular grab at him with her paw, but he slid under the table in all haste, roaring out,—*"Ave Maria, que es esso—manda por el padre—*Send for the priest, *y trae una puerca, on donde echar el demonio manda, manda*—send for a priest, and a pig, into which the demon may be cast,—send—" *"Dexa me, dexa me baylar,"* continued the old dame—*"tu no vale, bobo viejo,*—you are of no use, you old blockhead—you are a forked radish and not a man—let me catch you, let me catch you!" and here she made a second attempt, and got hold of his queue, by which she forcibly dragged him from beneath the table, until, fortunately, the ribbon that tied it slid off in her hand, and the little Señor instantly ran back to his burrow, with the speed of a rabbit, while his wife sang out, *"Tu gastas calzones, eh? para que, damelos damelos, yo los quitare?"* and if she had caught the worthy man, I believe she would really have shaken him out of his garments, peeled him on the spot, and appropriated them to herself, as her threat ran. "I am a cat, a dog, and a devil—hoo—hoo—hoo!—let me catch you, you miserable wretch, you forked radish, and if I don't peel off your breeches—I shall wear them, I shall wear them—*Ave Maria.*" Here she threw herself into a chair, being completely blown; but after a gasp or two she started to her legs again, dancing and singing and snapping her fingers as if she had held castanets between them, *"Venga—Venga—dexa me baylar—Dankee, Dankee la—Dankee, Dankee la—mi guitarra—mi guitarra—Dankee, Dankee la—ha, ha, ha!"*—and away she trundled down-stairs again, where she met the priest, who had been sent for, in the lower hall, who happened to be a very handsome young man. Seeing the state she was in, and utterly unable to account for it, he bobbed as she threw herself on him, eluded her embraces, and then bolted up-stairs, followed by Mrs Potiphar at full speed.—*"Padre,* father!" cried she, "stop till I peel that forked radish there, and I will give you his breeches—*Dankee, Dankee la.*" All this while Don Hombrecillo was squeaking out from his lair, at the top of his pipe—"*Padre, padre, trae la puerca, venga la puerca—echar el demonio— echar el demonio*—bring the pig, the pig, and cast out the devil."—"*Mi guitarra, canta, canta y bayle, viejo diablito, canta o yo te matarras*—Bring my guitar, dance, dance and sing, you little old devil you, or I'll murder you!— *Dankee, Dankee la.*"

In fine, I was at length obliged to lend a hand, and she was bodily laid hold of and put to bed, where she soon fell into a profound sleep, and next morning awoke in her sound senses, totally unconscious of all that had passed, except- ing that she remembered having taken a glass of the Englishman's *small-beer.*

Now the secret was out. The worthy woman, like most South American Spaniards, was distractedly fond of *cervesa blanca*, or small-beer, and seeing the champagne-bottles with their wired corks (beer requiring to be so secured in hot climates) in my basket, she could not resist making free with a bottle, and, as I charitably concluded, small-beer being a rarity in those countries, she did not find out the difference until it was made evident by the issue; however, I have it from authority that she never afterwards ventured on anything weaker than brandy, and from that hour utterly eschewed that most dangerous liquor, *cervesa blanca.*

CHAPTER XVIII.

TROPICAL HIGH-JINKS.

"Now, Massa, pipe belay
    Wid your weary, weary Log, O!
Peter sick of him, me say,
    Ah! sick more as one dog O!"
                    The humble Petition of Peter Mangrove, Branch Pilot.

LIKE ALL Portuguese towns, and most Spanish, Panama does not realise the idea which a stranger forms of it from the first view, as he descends from the savannah. The houses are generally built of wood, and three storeys high: in the first or ground floor are the shops, in the second the merchants have their warehouses, and in the third they usually live with their families. Those three different regions, sorry am I to say it, are all very dirty; indeed, they may be said to be the positive, comparative, and superlative degrees of uncleanness. There are no glazed sashes in the windows, so that when it rains, and the shutters are closed, you are involved in utter darkness. The furniture is miserably scanty— some old-fashioned, high-backed, hardwood chairs, with a profusion of tarnished gilding; a table or two in the same style, with a long grass hammock slung from corner to corner, intersecting the room diagonally, which, as they hang very low, about six inches only from the floor, it was not *once* only, that entering a house during the *siesta,* when the windows were darkened, I have tumbled headlong over a Don or Doña taking his or her forenoon nap. But if *movables* were scarce, there was no paucity of silver dishes; basins, spitboxes, censers, and utensils of all shapes, descriptions, and sizes, of this precious metal, were scattered about without any order or regularity, while some name-less articles, also of silver, were thrust far out of their latitude, and shone conspicuously in the very centre of the rooms. The floors were usually either of hardwood plank, ill kept, or terraced, or tiled; some indeed were flagged with marble, but this was rare; and as for the luxury of a carpet, it was utterly unknown the nearest approach to it being a grass mat, plaited prettily enough, called an *estera*. Round the walls of the house are usually hung a lot of dingy-faced, worm-eaten pictures of saints, and several crucifixes, which appear to be held in great veneration. The streets are paved, but exceedingly indifferently; and the frequent rains or rather waterspouts (and from the position of the place, between the two vast oceans of the Atlantic and Pacific, they have con-siderably more than their own share of moisture), washing away the soil and sand from between the stones, render the footing for *bestias* of all kinds extremely insecure. There are five monasteries of different orders, and a con-vent of nuns, within the walls, most of which, I believe, are but poorly endowed. All these have handsome churches attached to them; that of La Merced is very splendid. The cathedral is also a fine building, with some good pictures, and several lay relics of Pizarro, Almagro, and Vasco Nuñez, that riveted my atten-tion; while their fragments of the *Vera Cruz*, and arrow-points that had quivered in the muscles of St Sebastian, were passed by as weak inventions of the enemy.

The week after my arrival was a fast, the men eating only once in the twen-ty-four hours (as for the women, who the deuce can tell how often a woman eats?), and during this period all the houses were stripped of their pictures, lamps, and ornaments, to dress out the churches, which were beautifully illu-minated in the evenings, while a succession of friars performed service in them continually. High mass is, even to the eye of a heretic, a very splendid ceremony; and the music in this outlandish corner was unexpectedly good, everything considered; in the church of La Merced especially, they had a very fine organ, and the congregation joined in the *Jubilate* with very good taste. By the way, in this same church, on the right of the high altar, there was a deep and lofty recess, covered with a thick black veil, in which stood concealed a figure of our Saviour, as large as life, hanging on a great cross, with the blood flowing from his wounds, and all kinds of horrible accompaniments. At a certain stage of the service, a drum was beaten by one of the brethren, upon which the veil was withdrawn, when the whole congregation prostrated themselves before the image, with every appearance of the greatest devotion. Even the passengers in the streets within ear-shot of the drum stopped and uncovered themselves, and muttered a prayer; while the inmates of the houses knelt and crossed themselves with all the externals of deep humility; although, very probably, they were at the moment calculating in their minds the profits on the last adventure from Kingston. One custom particularly struck me as being very beautiful. As the night shuts in, after a noisy prelude on all the old pots in the different steeples throughout the city, there is a dead pause; presently the great bell of the cathedral tolls slowly, once or twice, at which every person stops from his employment, whatever *that* may be, or wherever *he* may be, uncovers himself, and says a short prayer—all hands remaining still and silent for a minute or more, when the great bell tolls again, and once more everything rolls on as usual.

On the fourth evening of my residence in Panama I had retired early to rest. My trusty knave, Peter Mangrove, and trustier still, my dog Sneezer, had both fallen asleep on the floor, at the foot of my bed—if the piece of machinery on which I lay deserved that name—when in the dead of night I was awakened by a slight noise at the door. I shook myself and listened. Presently it opened, and the old woman that I have already described as part and portion of Don Hombrecillo Justo's family, entered the room in her usual very scanty dress, with a lighted candle in her hand, led by a little naked negro child. I was curious to see what she would do, but I was not certain how the dog might relish the intrusion; so I put my hand over my *quatre*, and, snapping my finger and thumb, Sneezer immediately rose and came to my bedside. I immediately judged, from the comical expression of his face, as seen by the taper of the intruder, that he thought it was some piece of fun, for he walked quietly up, and, confronting the old lady, deliberately took the candlestick out of her hand. The little black urchin thereupon began shouting, *"Perro Demonio—Perro Demonio"*—and in their struggle to escape, she and the old lady tumbled headlong over the sleeping pilot, whereby the candle was extinguished, and we were left in utter darkness. I had therefore nothing for it but to get out of bed, and go down to the cobbler, who lived in the *entresol*, to get a light. He had not gone to sleep, and I gave him no small alarm—indeed, he was near absconding at my unseasonable intrusion; but at length I obtained the object of my visit, and returned to my room, when, on opening the door, I saw poor Mangrove lying on his back in the middle of the floor, with his legs and arms extended as if he had been on the rack, his eyes set, his mouth open, and every faculty benumbed by fear. At his feet sat the negro child, almost as much terrified as he was, and crying most lamentably; while at a little distance sat the spectre of the old woman, scratching its head with the greatest composure, and exclaiming in Spanish, "A little brandy for love of the Holy Virgin." But the most curious part of it was the conduct of our old friend Sneezer. There he was, sitting on end upon the table, grinning and showing his ivory teeth, his eyes of jet sparkling like diamonds with fun and frolic, and evidently laughing after his fashion, like to split himself, as he every now and then gave a large sweeping whisk of his tail, like a cat watching a mouse. A length I got the cobbler and his sable rib to take charge of the wanderers, and once more fell asleep.

On my first arrival I was somewhat surprised at my Spanish acquaintances always putting up their umbrellas when abroad after nightfall in the streets; the city had its evil customs, it seemed, as well as others of more note, with this disadvantage, that no one had the discretion to sing out *gardyloo*.

There was another solemn fast about this time, in honour of a saint having had a tooth drawn, or some equally important event, and Don Hombrecillo and I had been at the evening service in the church of the convent of La Merced, situated, as I have already mentioned, directly opposite his house, on the other side of the lane; and this being over, we were on the eve of returning home, when the flannel-robed superior came up and invited us into the refectory, whereunto, after some palaver, we agreed to adjourn, and had a *good* supper, and some *bad* Malaga wine, which, however, seemed to suit the palates of the *Frailes*, if taking a very decent quantity thereof were any proof of the same. Presently two of the lay brothers produced their fiddles, and as I was determined not to be outdone, I volunteered a song, and, as a keystone to my politeness, sent to Don Hombrecillo's for the residue of my brandy, which, coming after the bad wine, acted most cordially opening the hearts of all hands like an oyster-knife, the Superior's especially, who in turn drew on his private treasure also, when out came a large green vitrified earthen pipkin, one of those round-bottomed jars that won't stand on end, but must perforce be on their sides, as if it had been a type of the predicament in which some of us were to be placed ere long through its agency. The large cork, buried an inch deep in green wax, was withdrawn from the long neck, and out gurgled most capital old *Xeres*. So we worked away until we were all pretty well *fou*, and anon we began to dance; and there were half-a-dozen friars, and old Justo and myself, in great glee, jumping and gamboling about, and making fools of ourselves after a very fantastic fashion—the witches in Macbeth as an illustration.

At length, after being two months in Panama, and still no appearance of the Bandera, I received a letter from the Admiral desiring me to rejoin the Wave immediately, as it was then known that the line-of-battle ship had returned to the River Plate. Like most young men who have hearts of flesh in their bosoms, I had in this short space begun to have my likings—may I not call them friendships?—in this, at the time I write of, most primitive community; and the idea of bidding farewell to it, most likely for ever, sank deep. However, I was His Majesty's officer, and my services and obedience were his, although my feelings were my own; and accordingly, stifling the latter, I prepared for my departure.

On the very day whereon I was recalled, a sister of mine host's—a most reverend mechanic, who had been fourteen years married without chick or child—was brought to bed, to the unutterable surprise of her spouse, and of all the little world in Panama, of a male infant. It had rained the whole day, notwithstanding which, and its being the only authenticated production ever published by the venerable young lady, the *piccaniny* was carried to the Franciscan church, a distance of half a mile, at nine o'clock at night, through a perfect storm, to be christened, and the evil star of poor Mangrove rose high in the ascendant on the occasion.

After the ceremony, I was returning home chilled with standing uncovered for an hour in a cold damp church, and walking very fast in order to bring myself into heat, when on turning a corner, I heard a sound of flutes and fiddles in the street, and from the number of lanterns and torches that accompanied it, I conjectured rightly that it was a *Function* of no small importance—no less, in fact, than a procession in honour of the Virgin. Poor Mangrove at this time was pattering close to my heels, and I could hear him chuckling and laughing to himself.

"What dis can be—I say, Sneezer?"—to his never-failing companion—

"what you tink? *John Canoe,* after Spanish fashion, it mosh be, eh?"

The dog began to jump and gambol about.

"Ah," continued the black pilot, "no doubt it must be *John Canoe*—I may dance—why not—eh?—oh, yes—I shall dance."

And as the music struck into rather a quicker tune at the moment, our ebony friend began to caper and jump about as if he had been in Jamaica at Christmas-time, whereupon one of the choristers, or music-boys, as they were called, a beautiful youth about forty years of age, six feet high, and proportionably strong, without the least warning, incontinently smote our *amigo* across the pate with a brazen saint that he carried, and felled him to the earth; indeed, if el Señor Justo had not been on the spot to interfere, we should have had a scene of it in all likelihood, as the instant the man delivered his blow, Sneezer's jaws were at his throat, and had he not fortunately obeyed me, and let go at the sound of my voice, we might have had a *double* of *Macaire* and the dog of Montargis. As it was, the noble animal, before he let go, brought the culprit to the ground like a shot. I immediately stood forward and got the feud soldered as well as I could, in which the worthy Justo cordially lent me a hand.

Next morning I rode out on my mule, to take my last clip in the Quebrada of the Loseria, a rapid in a beautiful little rivulet distant from Panama about three miles; and a most exquisite bath it was. Let me describe it. After riding a couple of miles, and leaving the open savannah, you struck off sharp to the left through a narrow bridle-path into the wood, with an impervious forest on either hand, and proceeding a mile farther, you came suddenly upon a small, rushing, roaring, miniature cascade, where the pent-up waters leaped through a narrow gap in the limestone rock, that you could have stepped across, down a tiny fall about a fathom high, into a round foaming buzzing basin, twenty feet in diameter, where the clear cool water bubbled and eddied round and round like a boiling caldron, until it rushed away once more over the lower ledge, and again disappeared, murmuring beneath the thick foliage of the rustling branches. The pool was about ten feet deep, and never was anything more luxurious in a hot climate.

After having performed my morning ablutions, and looking with a heavy heart at the sweet stream, and at every stock and stone, and shrub and tree, as objects I was never to see again, I trotted on, followed by Peter Mangrove, my man-at-arms, who bestrode his mule gallantly, to Don Hombrecillo's pen, as the little man delighted to call his country-house, situated about five miles from Panama, and which I was previously informed had been given up to the use of his two maiden sisters. I got there about half-past ten in the forenoon, and found that el Señor Justo had arrived before me. The situation was most beautiful; the house was embosomed in high wood, the lowest spurs put forth by the gigantic trees being far above the ridgepole of the wooden fabric. It was a low one-storey building of unpainted timber, which, from the action of the weather, had been bleached on the outside into a whitish-grey appearance, streaked by numerous green weather-stains, and raised about five feet on wooden posts, so that there was room for a flock of goats to shelter themselves below it. Access was had to the interior by a rickety rattletrap of a wooden ladder or stair of half-a-dozen steps, at the top of which you landed in an unceiled hall, with the rafters of the roof exposed, and the bare green vitrified tiles for a canopy, while a small sleeping apartment opened off each end. In the centre room there was no furniture except two grass hammocks slung across the room, and three or four old-fashioned leather or rather *hide* covered chairs, and an old rickety table; while overhead the tiles were displaced in one or two places, where the droppings from the leaves of the trees, and the *sough* of their rustling in the wind, came through. There were no inmates visible when we entered but a little negro girl, of whom el Señor Hombrecillo asked "where the Señoras were?"—"*En cavilla,*" said the urchin. Whereupon we turned back and proceeded to a little tiny stone chapel, little bigger than a dog-house, the smallest affair in the shape of a church I had ever seen, about a pistol-shot distant in the wood, where we found the two old ladies and Señor Justo's natural son engaged at their devotions. On being aware of our presence they made haste with the service, and, having finished it, arose and embraced their brother, while the son approached and kissed his hand.

One of the ancient *demoiselles* appeared in bad health; nevertheless, they both gave us a very hearty reception, and prepared breakfast for us; fricasseed fowls, a little too much of the lard, but still ———, fish from the neighbouring stream, &c.; and I was doing the agreeable to the best of my poor ability, when el Señor Justo asked me abruptly if I would go and bathe. A curious country, thought I, and a strange way people have of doing things. After a hearty meal, instead of giving you time to ruminate, and to allow the gastric juices to operate, away they lug you to be plumped over head and ears into a pool of ice-cold water. I rose, confoundedly against my inclination, I will confess, and we proceeded to a small rocky waterfall, where a man might *wash* himself, certainly, but as to swimming, which is to me the grand *desideratum,* it was impossible; so I prowled away down the stream, to look out for a pool, and at last I was successful. On returning, as I only took a dip to swear by, the situation of my venerable Spanish ally was entertaining enough. There he was, the most forlorn little mandrake eye ever rested on, cowering like a large frog under the tiny cascade, stark naked, with his knees drawn up to his chin, and his grey queue gathered carefully under a green gourd or calabash that he wore on his head, while his natural son was dashing water in his face, as if the shower-bath overhead had not been sufficient.

"*Soy bañando—soy bañando, capitan—fresco—fresquito!*" squealed Hombrecillo; while, splash between every exclamation, his dutiful son let fly a gourdful of *agua* at his head.

That same evening we returned to Panama; and next morning, being the 22d of such a month, I left my kind friends, and, with Peter Mangrove, proceeded on our journey to Cruzes, mounted on two stout mules. I got there late in the evening, the road, from the heavy rains, being in sad condition; but next morning the *recua*, or convoy of silver, which was to follow me for shipment on merchants' account to Kingston, had not arrived. Presently I received a letter from Don Justo, sent express, to intimate that the muleteers had proceeded immediately after we had started for about a mile beyond the suburbs, where they were stopped by the officer of a kind of military post or barrier, under pretence of the passport being irregular; and this difficulty was no sooner cleared up than the accounts of a bull-fight, that was unexpectedly to take place that forenoon, reached them, when the whole bunch, half drunk as they were, started off to Panama again, leaving the money with the soldiers; nor would they return, or be prevailed on to proceed, until the following morning. However, on the 24th, at noon, the money did arrive, which was immediately embarked on board of a large canoe that I had provided; and having shipped a beautiful little mule also, of which I had made a purchase at Panama, we proceeded down the river to the village of Gorgona, where we slept. My apartment was rather a primitive concern. It was simply a roof or shed, thatched with palm-tree leaves, about twelve feet long by eight broad, and supported on four upright posts at the corners, the eaves being about six feet high. Under this I slung my grass hammock transversely from corner to corner, tricing it well up to the rafters, so that it hung about five feet from the ground; while beneath Mangrove lit a fire, for the twofold purpose, as it struck me, of driving off the mosquitoes, and converting his Majesty's officer into ham or hung beef; so after having made *mulo* fast to one of the posts, with a bundle of *malojo*, or the green stems of Indian corn or maize, under his nose, he borrowed a plank from a neighbouring hut and laid himself down on it at full length, covered up with a blanket, as if he had been a corpse, and soon fell fast asleep. As for Sneezer, he lay with his black muzzle resting on his fore-paws, which were thrust out straight before him, until they almost stirred up the white embers of the fire, with his eyes shut, and apparently asleep; but from the constant nervous twitchings and pricking up of his ears, and his haunches being gathered up well under him, and a small quick switch of his tail now and then, it was evident he was broad awake, and considered himself on duty. All continued quiet and silent in our bivouac until midnight, however, except the rushing of the river hard by, when I was awakened by the shaking of the shed from the violent struggles of *mulo* to break loose, his strong tremblings thrilling along the taut cord that held him, down the lanyard of my hammock to my neck, as he drew himself in the intervals of his struggles as far back as he could, proving that the poor brute suffered under a paroxysm of fear. "What noise is that?" I roused myself. It was repeated. It was a wild cry, or rather a loud shrill *mew*, gradually sinking into a deep growl. "What the deuce is that, Sneezer?" said I. The dog made no answer, but merely wagged his tail once, as if he had said, "Wait a bit now, master; you shall see how well I shall acquit myself, for *this is* in my way." Ten yards from the shed under which I slept there was a pig-sty, surrounded by a sort of tiny stockade a fathom high, made of split cane, wove into wicker-work between upright rails sunk into the ground; and by the clear moonlight I could, as I lay in my hammock, see an animal larger than an English bull-dog, but with the stealthy pace of the cat, crawl on in a crouching attitude until within ten feet of the sty, when it stopped, looked round, and then drew itself back, and made a scrambling jump against the cane defence, hooking on to the top of it by its fore-paws, the claws of its hind-feet scratching and rasping against the dry cane splits, until it had gathered its legs into a bunch, like the aforesaid puss, on the top of the enclosure; from which elevation the creature seemed to be reconnoitring the unclean beasts within. I grasped my pistols. Mangrove was still sound asleep. The struggles of *mulo* increased; I could hear the sweat raining off him; but Sneezer, to my great surprise, remained motionless as before. We now heard the alarmed grunts, and occasionally a sharp squeak, from the piggery, as if the beauties had only now become aware of the vicinity of their dangerous neighbour, who, having apparently made his selection, suddenly dropped down amongst them; when *mulo* burst from his fastenings with a yell, enough to frighten the devil, tearing away the upright to which the lanyard of my hammock was made fast, whereby I was pitched like a shot right down on

Mangrove's corpus, while a volley of grunting and squeaking split the sky, such as I never heard before; in the very nick, Sneezer, starting from his lair with a loud bark, sprang at a bound into the enclosure, which he topped like a first-rate hunter; and Peter Mangrove, awakening all of a heap from my falling on him, jumped upon his feet as noisy as the rest.

"Garamighty in a tap—wurra all dis—my tomach bruise home to my back-bone like one pancake;" and while the short fierce bark of the noble dog was blended with the agonised cry of the *gatto del monte,* the shrill treble of the poor porkers rose high above both, and *mulo* was galloping through the village with the post after him, like a dog with a pan at his tail, making the most unearthly noises; for it was neither bray nor neigh. The villagers ran out of their huts headed by the *padre cura,* and all was commotion and uproar. Lights were procured. The noise in the sty continued, and Mangrove, the warm-hearted creature, unsheathing his knife, clambered over the fence to the rescue of his four-footed ally, and disappeared, shouting, "Sneezer often fight for Peter, so Peter now will fight for he;" and soon began to blend his shouts with the cries of the enraged beasts within. At length the mania spread to me upon hearing the poor follow shout, "Tiger here, captain—tiger here—tiger too many for we—Lud-a-mercy—tiger too many for we, sir—if you no help we, we shall be torn in piece." Then a violent struggle, and a renewal of the uproar, and of the barking and yelling and squeaking. It was now no joke; the life of a fellow-creature was at stake. So I scrambled up after the pilot to the top of the fence with a loaded pistol in my hand, a young active Spaniard following with a large brown wax candle, that burned like a torch; and, looking down on the *mêlée* below, there Sneezer lay with the throat of the leopard in his jaws, evidently much exhausted, but still giving the creature a cruel shake now and then, while Mangrove was endeavouring to throttle the brute with his bare hands. As for the poor pigs, they were all huddled together, squeaking and grunting most melodiously in the corner. I held down the light. "Now, Peter, cut his throat, man—cut his throat."

Mangrove, the moment he saw where he was, drew his knife across the leopard's *weasand,* and killed him on the spot. The glorious dog, the very instant he felt he had a dead antagonist in his fangs, let go his hold, and, making a jump with all his remaining strength, for he was bleeding much, and terribly torn, I caught him by the nape of the neck, and, in my attempt to lift him over and place him on the outside, down I went, dog and all, amongst the pigs, upon the bloody carcass; out of which mess I was gathered by the *cura* and the standers-by in a very beautiful condition; for, what between the filth of the sty and blood of the leopard, and so forth, I was not altogether a fit subject for a side-box at the opera.

This same tiger or leopard had committed great depredations in the neighbourhood for months before, but he had always escaped, although he had been repeatedly wounded; so Peter and I became as great men for the two hours longer that we sojourned in Gorgona, as if we had killed the dragon of Wantley. Our quarry was indeed a noble animal, nearly seven feet from the nose to the tip of the tail. At day-dawn, having purchased his skin for three dollars, I shoved off; and on the 25th, at five in the evening, having had a strong current with us the whole way down, we arrived at Chagres once more. I found a boat from the Wave waiting for me, and, to prevent unnecessary delay, I resolved to proceed with the canoe along the coast to Porto-Bello, as there was a strong weather-current running, and little wind; and, accordingly, we proceeded next morning, with the canoe in tow, but towards the afternoon it came on to blow, which forced us into a small cove, where we remained for the night in a very uncomfortable situation, as the awning proved an indifferent shelter from the rain that descended in torrents.

We had made ourselves as snug as it was possible to be in such weather, under an awning of boat-sails, and had kindled a fire in a tub at the bottom of the boat, at which we had made ready some slices of beef, and roasted some yams, and were—all hands, master and men—making ourselves comfortable with a glass of grog, when the warp by which we rode suddenly parted, from a puff of wind that eddied down on us over the little cape, and before we could get the oars out we were tailing on the beach at the opposite side of the small bay. However, we soon regained our original position, by which time all was calm again where we lay; and this time we sent the end of the line ashore, making it fast round a tree, and once more rode in safety. But I could not sleep, and the rain having ceased, the clouds broke away, and the moon once more shone out cold, bright, and clear. I had stepped forward from under the temporary awning, and was standing on the thwart, looking out to windward, endeavouring to judge of the weather at sea, and debating in my own mind whether it would be prudent to weigh before daylight or remain where we were. But all in the offing, beyond the small headland, under the lee of which we lay, was dark and stormy water, and white-crested howling waves, although our snug little bay continued placid and clear, with the moonbeams dancing on the twinkling ripple, that was lap, lapping, and sparkling like silver on the snow-white beach of sand and broken shells; while the hills on shore, that rose high and abrupt close to, were covered with thick jungle, from which here and there a pinnacle of naked grey rock would shoot up like a gigantic spectre, or a tall tree would cast its long black shadow over the waving sea of green leaves that undulated in the breeze beneath.

As the wind was veering about rather capriciously, I had cast my eye anxiously along the warp, to see how it bore the strain, when, to my surprise, it appeared to thicken at the end next the tree, and presently something like a screw, about a foot long, that occasionally shone like glass in the moonlight, began to move along the taut line, with a spiral motion. All this time one of the boys was fast asleep, resting on his folded arms on the gunwale, his head having dropped down on the stem of the boat; but one of the Spanish *bogas* in the canoe, which was anchored close to us, seeing me gazing at something, now looked in the same direction; the instant he caught the object he thumped with his palms on the side of the canoe, exclaiming, in a loud, alarmed tone— *"Culebra—culebra!*—a snake, a snake!"—on which the reptile made a sudden and rapid slide down the line towards the bow of the boat where the poor lad was sleeping, and immediately afterwards dropped into the sea.

The sailor rose and walked aft, as if nothing had happened, amongst his messmates, who had been alarmed by the cries of the Spanish canoeman, and I was thinking little of the matter when I heard some anxious whispering amongst them.

"Fred," said one of the men, "what is wrong, that you breathe so hard?"

"Why, boy, what ails you?" said another.

"Something has stung me," at length said the poor little fellow, speaking thick, as if he had laboured under sore throat. The truth flashed on me, a candle was lit, and, on looking at him, he appeared stunned, complained of cold, and suddenly assumed a wild startled look.

He evinced great anxiety and restlessness, accompanied by a sudden and severe prostration of strength—still continuing to complain of great and increasing cold and chilliness, but he did not shiver. As yet no part of his body was swollen, except very slightly about the wound; however, there was a rapidly increasing rigidity of the muscles of the neck and throat, and within half an hour after he was bit he was utterly unable to swallow even liquids. The small whip-snake—the most deadly asp in the whole list of noxious reptiles peculiar to South America—was not above fourteen inches long; it had made four small punctures with its fangs, right over the left jugular vein, about an inch below the chin. There was no blood oozing from them, but a circle, about the size of a crown-piece, of dark red surrounded them, gradually melting into blue at the outer rim, which again became fainter and fainter, until it disappeared in the natural colour of the skin. By the advice of the Spanish boatmen, we applied an embrocation of the leaves of the *palma Christi,* or castor-oil nut, as hot as the lad could bear it, but we had neither oil nor hot milk to give internally, both of which, they informed us, often proved specifics. Rather than be at anchor until morning under these melancholy circumstances, I shoved out into the rough water, but we made little of it, and when the day broke I saw that the poor fellow's fate was sealed. His voice had become inarticulate, the coldness had increased, all motion in the extremities had ceased, the legs and arms became quite stiff, the respiration slow and difficult, as if the blood had coagulated, and could no longer circulate through the heart, or as if, from some unaccountable effect of the poison on the nerves, the action of it had been impeded; still the poor little fellow was perfectly sensible, and his eye bright and restless. His breathing became still more interrupted—he could no longer be said to breathe, but gasped—and in another half hour, like a steam engine when the fire is withdrawn, the strokes, or contractions and expansions of his heart, became slower and slower until they ceased altogether.

From the very moment of his death the body began rapidly to swell and become discoloured; the face and neck especially were nearly as black as ink within half an hour of it, when blood began to flow from the mouth, and other symptoms of rapid decomposition succeeded each other so fast that, by nine in the morning, we had to sew him up in a boatsail, with a large stone, and launch the body into the sea.

We continued to struggle against the breeze until eleven o'clock in the forenoon of the 27th, when the wind again increased to such a pitch that we had to cast off our tow and leave her on the coast under the charge of little Reefpoint, with instructions to remain in the creek where he was until the schooner picked him up; we then pushed once more through the surf for Porto-Bello, where we arrived in safety at 5 P.M. Next morning at daylight we got under weigh, and stood down for the canoe; and having received the money on board, and the Spaniards who accompanied it, and poor *mulo,* we made sail for Kingston, Jamaica, and on the 4th of the following month were off Carthagena once more, having been delayed by calms and light winds. The captain of the port shoved out to us, and I immediately recognised him as the officer to whom poor old Deadeye once gave a deuced fright, when we were off the town, in the old Torch, during the siege, shortly before she foundered in the hurricane; but in the present instance he was all civility. On his departure we made sail, and arrived at Kingston, safe and sound, in the unusually short passage of sixty hours from the time we left Carthagena.

Here the first thing I did was to call on some of my old friends, with one of whom I found a letter lying for me from Mr Bang, requesting a visit at his domicile in St-Thomas-in-the-Vale so soon as I arrived; and through the extreme kindness of my Kingston allies, I had, on my intention of accepting it being known, at least half-a-dozen gigs offered to me, with servants and horses, and I don't know what all. I made my selection, and had arranged to start at day-dawn next morning, when a cousin of mine, young Palma, came in where I was dining, and said that his mother and the family had arrived in town that very day, and were bound on a pic-nic party next morning to visit the Falls in St David's. I agreed to go, and to postpone my visit to friend Aaron for the present; and very splendid scenery did we see; but as I had seen the Falls of Niagara, of course I was not *astonished.* There was a favourite haunt and cave of Three-fingered Jack shown to us in the neighbourhood, very picturesque and romantic, and all that sort of thing; but I was escorting my Mary, and the fine scenery and roaring waters were at this time thrown away on me. However, there was one incident amusing enough. Mary and I had wandered away from the rest of the party, about a mile above the cascade, where the river was quiet and still, and divided into several tiny streams or pools, by huge stones that had rolled from the precipitous banks down into its channel, when, on turning an angle of the rock, we came unexpectedly on my old ally Whiffle, with a cigar in his mouth, seated on a cane-bottomed chair, close to the brink of the water, with a little low table at his right hand, on which stood a plate of cold meat, over which his black servant held a green branch, with which he was brushing the flies away, while a large rummer of cold brandy grog was immersed in the pool at his feet, covered up with a cool plantain leaf. He held a long fishing-rod in his hands, eighteen feet at the shortest, fit to catch salmon with, which he had to keep nearly upright, in order to let his hook drop into the pool, which was not above five feet wide; why he did not heave it by hand I am sure I cannot tell; indeed, I would as soon have thought of angling for goldfish in my aunt's glass globe—and there he sat fishing with great complacency. However, he seemed a little put out when we came up. "Ah, Tom how do you do?—Miss, your most obsequious—No rain—mullet deucedly shy, Tom—ah! what a glorious nibble —there—there again—I have him;" and sure enough, he had hooked a fine mountain mullet, weighing about a pound and a half, and in the ecstasy of the moment, and his hurry to land him handsomely, he regularly capsized in his chair, upset the rummer of brandy grog, and table and all the rest of it. We had a good laugh, and then rejoined our party, and that evening we all sojourned at Lucky Valley, a splendid coffee estate, with a most excellent man and an exceedingly obliging fellow for a landlord.

Next day we took a long ride, to visit a German gentleman, who had succeeded in a wonderful manner in taming fish. He received us very hospitably, and after lunch we all proceeded to his garden, through which ran a beautiful stream of the clearest water. It was about four feet broad and a foot deep, where it entered the garden, but gradually widened in consequence of a dam with stakes at the top having been erected at the lower part of it, until it became a pool twelve feet broad, and four feet deep, of the most beautiful crystal-clear water that can be imagined, while the margin on both sides was fringed with the fairest flowers that Europe or the tropics could afford. We all peered into the stream, but could see nothing except an occasional glance of a white scale or fin now and then.—"Liverpool!" shouted the old German who was doing the honours,—"Liverpool, come bring de food for de fis." Liverpool, a respectable-looking negro, approached, and stooping down at the water-edge, held a piece of roasted plantain close to the surface of it. In an instant, upwards of a hundred mullet, large fine fish, some of them above a foot long, rushed from out the dark clear depths of the quiet pool, and jumped, and walloped, and struggled for the food, although the whole party were standing close by. Several of the ladies afterwards tried their hand, and the fish, although not apparently quite so confident, after a tack here and a tack there, always in the end came close to and made a grab at what was held to them.

That evening I returned to Kingston, where I found an order lying for me to repair as second-lieutenant on board the Firebrand once more, and to resign the command of the Wave to no less a man than Moses Yerk, Esquire; and a happy man was Moses, and a gallant fellow be proved himself in her, and earned laurels and good freights of specie, and is now comfortably domiciled amongst his friends.

The only two *Waves* that I successfully made interest at their own request to get back with me were Tailtackle and little Reefpoint.

Time wore on—days and weeks and months passed away, during which we were almost constantly at sea; but incidents worth relating had grown scarce, as we were now in piping times of peace, when even a stray pirate had become a rarity, and a luxury denied to all but the small craft people. On one of our cruises, however, we had been working up all morning to the southward of the Pedro shoals, with the wind strong at east, a hard fiery sea-breeze. We had hove about, some three hours before, and were standing in towards the land, on the starboard tack, when the look-out at the masthead hailed.

"The water shoals on the weather-bow, sir;" and presently, "Breakers right ahead."

"Very well," I replied—"all right!"

"We are nearing the reefs, sir," said I, walking aft, and addressing Captain Transom; "shall we stand by to go about, sir?"

"Certainly—heave in stays as soon as you like, Mr Cringle." At this moment the man aloft again sang out—"There is a wreck on the weathermost point of the long reef, sir."

"Ay! what does she look like?"

"I see the stumps of two lower masts, but the bowsprit is gone, sir—I think she must be a schooner or a brig, sir."

The captain was standing by, and looked up to me, as I stood on the long eighteen at the weather-gangway.

"Is the breeze not too strong, Mr Cringle?"

I glanced my eye over the side—"Why, no, sir—a boat will live well enough—there is not so much sea in shore here."

"Very well—haul the courses up, and heave to."

It was done.

"Pipe away the yawlers, boatswain's mate."

The boat over the lee-quarter was lowered, and I was sent to reconnoitre the object that had attracted our attention. As we approached we passed the floating swollen carcasses of several bullocks, and some pieces of wreck; and getting into smooth water, under the lee of the reef, we pulled up under the stern of the shattered hull which lay across it, and scrambled on deck by the boat-tackles that hung from the davits, as if the jolly-boat had recently been lowered. The vessel was a large Spanish schooner, apparently about one hundred and eighty tons burden, nearly new; everything strong and well fitted about her, with a beautiful spacious flush deck, surrounded by high solid bulwarks. All the boats had disappeared; they might either have been carried away by the crew, or washed overboard by the sea. Both masts were gone about ten feet above the deck, which, with the whole of their spars and canvass, and the wreck of the bowsprit, were lumbering and rattling against the lee-side of the vessel, and splashing about in the broken water, being still attached to the hull by the standing rigging, no part of which had been cut away. The mainsail, gaff-topsail, foresail, fore-topsail, fore-staysail, and jib were all set, so she must most likely have gone on the reef, either under a press of canvass in the night, in ignorance of its vicinity, or by missing stays.

She lay on her beam-ends across the coral rock, on which there was about three feet water where shallowest, and had fallen over to leeward, presenting her starboard broadside to the sea, which surged along it in a slanting direction, while the lee gunwale was under water. The boiling white breakers were dashing right against her bows, lifting them up with every send, and thundering them down again against the flint-hard coral spikes, with a loud gritting rumble; while every now and then the sea made a fair breach over them, flashing up over the whole deck aft to the taffrail in a snowstorm of frothy flakes. Forward in the bows there lay, in one horrible fermenting and putrifying mass, the carcasses of about twenty bullocks, part of her deck-load of cattle, rotted into one hideous lump, with the individual bodies of the poor brutes almost obliterated and undistinguishable, while streams of decomposed animal matter were ever and anon flowing down to leeward, although as often washed away by the hissing waters. But how shall I describe the scene of horror that presented itself in the after-part of the vessel, under the lee of the weather-bulwarks!

There, lashed to the ring-bolts, and sheltered from the sun and sea by a piece of canvass, stretched across a broken oar, lay, more than half naked, the dead bodies of an elderly female, and three young women; one of the latter with two lifeless children fastened by handkerchiefs to her waist, while each of the other two had the corpse of an infant firmly clasped in her arms.

It was the dry season, and as they lay right in the wake of the windward ports, exposed to a thorough draft of air, and were defended from the sun and the spray, no putrefaction had taken place; the bodies looked like mummies, the shrunken muscles and wasted features being covered with a dry horny skin, like parchment; even the eyes remained full and round, as if they had been covered over with a hard dim scale.

On looking down into the steerage we saw another corpse, that of a tall young slip of a Spanish girl, surging about in the water, which reached nearly to the deck, with her long black hair floating and spread out all over her neck and bosom, but it was so offensive and decayed, that we were glad to look another way. There was no male corpse to be seen, which, coupled with the absence of the boats, evinced but too clearly that the crew had left the females, with their helpless infants, on the wreck to perish. There was a small round-house on the afterpart of the deck, in which we found three other women alive, but wasted to skeletons. We took them into the boat, but one died in getting her over the side; the other two we got on board, and I am glad to say that they both recovered. For two days neither could speak; there seemed to be some rigidity about the throat and mouth that prevented them; but at length the youngest—(the other was her servant)—a very handsome woman, became strong enough to tell us, "that it was the schooner Caridad that we had boarded, bound from Rio de la Hache to Savana la Mar, where she was to have discharged her deck-load of cattle, and afterwards to have proceeded to Batabano, in Cuba. She had struck, as I surmised, in the night, about a fortnight before we fell in with her; and next morning, the crew and male passengers took to the boats, which with difficulty contained them, leaving the women under a promise to come back that evening, with assistance from the shore, but they never appeared, nor were they ever after heard of." And here the poor thing cried as if her heart would break. "Even my own Juan, my husband, left me and my child to perish on the wreck. O God! O God! I could not have left *him*—I could not have left *him*."

There had been three families on board, with their servants, who were emigrating to Cuba, all of whom had been abandoned by the males, who, as already related, must in all human probability have perished after their unmanly desertion. As the whole of the provisions were under water, and could not be got at, the survivors had subsisted on raw flesh so long as they had strength to cut it, or power to swallow it; what made the poor creature tell it, I cannot imagine, if it were not to give the most vivid picture possible, in her conception, of their loneliness and desolation, but she said, "no sea-bird even ever came near us."

It were harrowing to repeat the heart-rending description given by her, of the sickening of the heart when the first night fell, and still no tidings of the boats; the second sun set—still the horizon was speckless; the next dreary day wore to an end, and three innocent helpless children were dead corpses; on the fourth, madness seized on their mothers, and—but I will not dwell on such horrors.

During these manifold goings and comings I naturally enlarged the circle of my acquaintance in the island, especially in Kingston, the mercantile capital; and often does my heart glow within me when the scenes I have witnessed in that land of fun and fever rise up before me after the lapse of many years under the influence of a good fire and a glass of old madeira. Take the following example of Jamaica High-Jinks as one of many: On a certain occasion I had gone to dine with Mr Isaac Shingle, an extensive American merchant, and a most estimable man, who considerately sent his gig down to the wherry-wharf for me. At six o'clock I arrived at my friend's mansion, situated in the upper part of the town, a spacious one-storey house, overshadowed by two fine old trees, and situated back from the street about ten yards—the intervening space being laid out in a beautiful little garden, raised considerably above the level of the adjoining thoroughfare, from which it was divided by a low parapet wall, surmounted by a green painted wooden railing. There was a flight of six brick steps from the street to the garden, and you ascended from the latter to the house itself, which was raised on brick pillars a fathom high by another stair of eight broad marble slabs. The usual verandah, or piazza, ran along the whole front, beyond which you entered a large and lofty, but very darksome hall, answering to our European drawing-room, into which the bedrooms opened on each side. It did strike me at first as odd, that the principal room in the house should be a dark dungeon of a place, with nothing but borrowed lights, until I again recollected that darkness and coolness were convertible terms within the tropics. Advancing through this room you entered, by a pair of folding doors, on a very handsome dining-room, situated in what I believe is called a back-jamb, a sort of outrigger to the house, fitted all round with movable blinds, or *jealousies*, and open like a lantern to all the winds of heaven except the west, in which direction the main body of the house warded off the sickening beams of the setting sun. And how sickening they are, let the weary sentries under the pillars of the Jamaica viceroy's house in Spanish Town tell, reflected as they were there from the hot brick walls of the palace.

This room again communicated with the back-yard, in which the negro houses, kitchen, and other offices were situated, by a wooden stair of the same elevation as that in front. Here the table was laid for dinner, covered with the finest diaper, and snow-white napkins, and silver wine-coolers, and silver forks, and fine steel, and cut-glass, and cool green finger-glasses with lime-leaves floating within, and tall wax-lights shaded from the breeze in thin glass barrels, and an epergne filled with flowers, with a fragrant fresh-gathered lime in each of the small leaf-like branches, and salt-cellars with red peppers in them, &c. &c., all of which made the *tout ensemble* the most captivating imaginable to a hungry man.

I found a large party assembled in the piazza and the dark hall, to whom I was introduced in due form. In Jamaica, of all countries I ever was in, it is a most difficult matter for a stranger to ascertain the real names of the guests at a bachelor dinner like the present, where all the parties were intimate—there were so many *sobriquets* amongst them; for instance, a highly respectable merchant of the place, with some fine young women for daughters, by the way, from the peculiarity of a prominent front tooth, was generally known as the Grand Duke of Tuscany; while an equally respectable elderly man, with a slight touch of paralysis in his head, was christened Old Steady in the West, *because* he never kept his head still; so, whether some of the names of the present party were real or fictitious I really cannot tell.

First, there was Mr Seco, a very neat gentleman-like little man, perfectly well-bred, and full of French phrases. Then came Mr Eschylus Stave, a tall, raw-boned, well-informed personage; a bit of a quiz on occasion, but withal a pleasant fellow. Mr Isaac Shingle, mine host, a sallow, sharp, hatchet-faced, small *homo,* but warm-hearted and kind, as I often experienced during my sojourn in the West, only sometimes a little peppery and argumentative. Then came Mr Jacob Bumble, a sleek fat-pated Scotchman. Next I was introduced to Mr Alonzo Smoothpate, a very handsome fellow, with an uncommon share of natural good-breeding and politeness. Again I clapper-clawed, according to the fashion of the country, a violent shake of the paw being the Jamaica infeftment to acquaintanceship, with Mr Percales, whom I took for a foreign Jew somehow or other at first, from his uncommon name, until I heard him speak, and perceived he was an Englishman; indeed, his fresh complexion, very neat person, and gentleman-like deportment, when I had time to reflect, would of themselves have disconnected him from all kindred with the sons of Levi. Then came a long, dark-complexioned, curly-pated slip of a lad with white teeth and high strongly marked features, considerably pitted with smallpox. He seemed the great promoter of fun and wickedness in the party, and was familiarly addressed as the Don, although I believe his real name was Mr Lucifer Longtram. Then there was Mr Aspen Tremble, a fresh-looking, pleasant, well-informed man, but withal a little nervous, his cheeks quivering when he spoke like shapes of calf's-foot jelly; after him came an exceedingly polite old gentleman, wearing hair-powder and a queue, ycleped Nicodemus; and a very devil of a little chap of the name of Rubiochico, a great ally in wickedness with Master Longtram; the last in this eventful history being a staid, sedate-looking, elderly-young man, of the name of Onyx Steady, an extensive foreign merchant, with a species of dry caustic readiness about him that was dangerous enough.—We sat down, Isaac Shingle doing the honours, confronted by Eschylus Stave, and all was right and smooth and pleasant, and in no way different from a party of well-bred men in England.

When the second course appeared I noticed that the blackie, who brought in two nice tender little ducklings, with the concomitant green peas, both just come in season, was chuckling and grinning, and showing his white teeth most vehemently, as he placed both dishes, right under Jacob Bumble's nose. Shingle and Longtram exchanged looks. I saw there was some mischief toward, and presently, as if by some preconcerted signal, everybody asked for duck, duck, duck. Bumble, with whom the dish was a prime favourite, carved away with a most stern countenance, until he had got half through the second bird, when some unpleasant recollection seemed to come over him, and his countenance fell; and lying back on his chair, he gave a deep sigh. But, "Mr Bumble, that breast, if you please—thank you." "Mr Bumble, that back, if you please,"—succeeded each other rapidly, until all that remained of the last of the ducklings was a beautiful little leg, which, under cover of the following story, Jacob cannily smuggled on to his own plate.

"Why, gentlemen, a most remarkable circumstance happened to me while dressing for dinner. You all know I am next-door neighbour to our friend Shingle—our premises being only divided by a brick wall, about eight feet high. Well, my dressing-room window looks out on this wall, between which and the house, I have my duck-pen—"

"Your what?" said I.

"My poultry-yard—as I like to see the creatures fed myself—and I was particularly admiring two beautiful ducklings which I had been carefully fattening for a whole week" (here our friend's voice shook, and a tear glistened in his eye)—"when first one and then another jumped out of the little pond, and successively made a grab at something which I could not see, and immediately began to shake their wings, and struggle with their feet, as if they were dancing, until, as with one accord—deuce take me!" (here he almost blubbered aloud)—"if they did not walk up the brick wall with all the deliberation in the world, merely helping themselves over the top by a small flaff of their wings; and where they have gone, none of Shingle's people know."

"I'll trouble you for that leg, Julius," said Longtram, at this juncture, to a servant, who whipped away the plate from under Bumble's arm, before he could prevent him, who looked after it as if it had been a pound of his own flesh. It seemed that Longtram, who had arrived rather early, had found a fishing-tackle in the piazza, and knowing the localities of Bumble's premises, as well as his peculiarities, he, by way of adding his quota to the entertainment, baited two hooks with pieces of raw potatoes, and throwing them over the wall, had, in conjunction with Julius the black, hooked up the two ducklings out of the pen, to the amazement of Squire Bumble.

By-and-by, as the evening wore on, I saw the Longtram lad making demonstrations to bring on a general drink, in which he was nobly seconded by Rubiochico; and, I grieve to say it, I was noways loth, nor indeed were any of the company. There had been a great deal of mirth and frolic during dinner—all within proper bounds however—but as the night made upon us, we set more sail—more, as it turned out, than some of us had ballast for—when lo! towards ten of the clock, up started Mr Eschylus to give us a speech. His seat was at the bottom of the table, with the back of his chair close to the door that opened into the yard; and after he had got his breath out, on I forget what topic, he sat down, and lay back on his balanced chair, stretching out his long legs with great complacency. However, they did not prove a sufficient counterpoise to his very square shoulders, which, obeying the laws of gravitation, destroyed his equilibrium, and threw him a somersault, when exit Eschylus Stave, Esquire, head foremost, with a formidable rumble-tumble and hurry-scurry, down the back steps, his long shanks disappearing last, and clipping between us and the bright moon like a pair of flails. However, there was no damage done; and, after a good laugh, Stave's own being loudest of all the Don and Rubiochico righted him, and helped him once more into his chair.

Jacob Bumble now favoured us with a song that sounded as if he had been barrelled up in a puncheon, and was *cantando* through the bunghole; then Rubiochico sang, and the Don sang and we all sang and bumpered away; and Mr Seco got on the table and gave us the newest quadrille step; and, in fine, we were all becoming dangerously drunk. Longtram, especially, had become uproarious beyond all bounds, and getting up from his chair, he took a short run of a step or two, and sprang right over the table, whereby he smashed the epergne, full of fruit and flowers, scattering the contents all about like hail, and driving a volley of preserved limes like grapeshot, in all their syrup and stickiness, slap into my face—a stray one spinning with a sloppy *whit* into Jacob Bumble's open mouth as he sang, like a musket-ball into a winter turnip; while a fine preserved pine-apple flew bash on Isaac Shingle's sharp snout, like the bursting of a shrapnel shell.

"D——n it," hiccuped Shingle, "I won't stand this any longer, by Ju-Ju-

Jupiter! Give over your practicals, Lucifer. Confound it, Don, give over—do, now, you mad long-legged son of a gun!" Here the Don caught Shingle round the waist, and whipping him bodily out of his chair, carried him, kicking and spurring, into the hall, now well lit up, and laid him on a sofa, and then returning, coolly installed himself in his seat.

In a little we heard the squeaking of a pig in the street, and our friend Shingle's voice high in oath. I sallied forth to see the cause of the uproar, and found our host engaged in single combat with a drawn sword-stick that sparkled blue and bright in the moonbeam, his antagonist being a strong porker that he had taken for a town-guard, and had hemmed into a corner formed by the stair and the garden wall, which, on being pressed, made a dash between his spindle-shanks, and fairly capsized him into my arms. I carried him back to his couch again; and, thinking it was high time to be off, as I saw that Smoothpate and Steady and Nicodemus, and the more composed part of the company, had already absconded, I seized my hat, and made sail in the direction of the former's house, where I was to sleep, when that devil Longtram made up to me.

"Hillo, my little man of war—heave-to a bit, and take me with you. Why, what *is* that? what the deuce *is* that?" We were at this time staggering along under the dark piazza of a long line of low wooden houses, every now and then thundering against the thin boards, or bulkheads, that constituted the side next the street, making, as we could distinctly hear, the inmates start and snort in the inside, as they turned themselves in their beds. In the darkest part of the piazza there was the figure of a man in the attitude of a telescope levelled on its stand, with its head, as it were, countersunk or mortised into the wooden partition. Tipsy as we both were we stopped in great surprise.

"D——n it, Cringle," said the Don, his philosophy utterly at fault, "the trunk of a man without a head!—How is this?"

"Why, Mr Longtram," I replied, "this is our friend Mr Smoothpate, or I mistake greatly."

"Let me see," said Longtram; "if it be him, he used to have a head somewhere, I know.—Let me see.—Oh, it is him; you are right, my boy; and here *is* his head after all, and a devil of a size it has grown to since dinner-time, to be sure. But I know his features—bald pate—high forehead and cheekbones."

Nota Bene.—We were still in the piazza, where Smoothpate was unquestionably present in the body, but the head was within the house, and altogether, as I can avouch, beyond the Don's ken.

"Where?" said I, groping about—"very odd, for deuce take me if I can see his head. Why, he has none—a phenomenon—four legs and a tail, but no head, as I am a gentleman—lively enough, too, he is—don't seem to miss it much." Here poor Smoothpate made a violent walloping in a vain attempt to disentangle himself.

We could now hear shouts of laughter within, and a voice that I was sure belonged to Mr Smoothpate, begging to be released from the pillory he had placed himself in, by removing a board in the wooden partition, and sliding it up, and then thrusting his caput from without into the interior of the house, to the no small amazement of the brown fiddler and his daughter who inhabited the same, and who had immediately secured their prize by slipping the displaced board down again, wedging it firmly on the back of his neck, as if he had been fitted for the guillotine, thus nailing him fast, unless he had bolted, and left his head in pawn.

We now entered, and perceived it was really Don Alonzo's flushed but very handsome countenance that was grinning at us from where it was fixed, like a large peony rose stuck against the wall. After a hearty laugh we relieved him, and being now joined by Percales, who came up in his gig, with Mr Smoothpate's following in his wake, we embarked for an airing at half-past one in the morning—Smoothpate and Percales, Longtram and Tom Cringle. Amongst other exploits we broke into a proscribed conventicle of drunken negroes—but I am rather ashamed of this part of the transaction, and intended to have held my tongue, had Aaron managed his, although it was notorious as the haunt of all the thieves and slight ladies of the place; here we found Parson Charley, a celebrated black preacher, *three parts drunk, extorting*, as Mawworm says, a number of devotees, male and female, all very tipsy, in a most blasphemous fashion, the table being covered with rummers of punch and fragments of pies and cold meat; but this did not render our conduct more excusable, I will acknowledge. Finally, as a trophy, Percales, who was a wickeder little chap than I took him for, with Longtram's help, unshipped the bell of the conventicle from the little belfry, and fastening it below Smoothpate's gig, we dashed back to Mr Shingle's with it clanging at every jolt. In our progress the hone took fright, and ran away, and no wonder.

"Zounds, Don, the weather-rein has parted—what shall we do?" said I.

"Do I?" rejoined Lucifer, with drunken gravity,—"haul on the other, to be sure—there is one left, ain't there?—so hard a-port, and run him up against that gun at the street corner, will ye?—That will stop him, or the devil is in it."

Crash—it was done—and over the horse's ears we both flew like skyrockets; but, strange to tell, although we had wedged the wheel of the ketureen fast as a wreck on a reef, with the cannon that was stuck into the ground postwise between it and the body, there was no damage done beyond the springing of the starboard shaft; so, with the assistance of the negro servant, who had been thrown from his perch behind, by a shock that frightened him out of his wits, we hove the *voiture* off again, and arrived in safety at friend Shingle's once more. Here we found the table set out with devilled turkey, and a variety of high-spiced dishes; and, to make a long story short, we had another set-to, during which, as an interlude, Longtram capsized Shingle out of the sofa he had again lain down on, in an attempt to jump over it, and broke his arm; and, being the soberest man of the company, I started off, guided by a negro servant, for Doctor Greyfriars. On our return, the first thing that met our eyes was the redoubted Don himself, lying on his back where he had fallen at his leap, with his head over the step at the door of the piazza. I thought his neck was broken; and the doctor, considering that he was the culprit to be carved, forthwith had him carried in, his coat taken off, and was about striking a phleme into him, when Isaac's voice sounded from the inner apartment, where he had lain all the while below the sofa like a crushed frog; the party in the background, who were *boosing* away, being totally unconscious of his mishap, as they sat at table in the room beyond, enjoying themselves, impressed apparently with the belief that the whole affair was a lark.

"Doctor, doctor," shouted he in great pain,—"here, here—it is me that is murdered—that chap is only *dead* drunk, but I am really *dead,* or will be, if you don't help."

At length the arm was set, and Shingle put to bed, and the whole crew dispersed themselves, each moving off as well as he could towards his own home.

But the cream of the jest was richest next day. Parson Charley, who, drunk as he had been overnight, still retained a confused recollection of the parties who had made the irruption, in the morning applied to Mr Smoothpate to have his bell restored, when the latter told him, with the utmost gravity, that Mr Onyx Steady was the culprit, who, by the by, had disappeared from Shingle's before the bell interlude, and, in fact, was wholly ignorant of the transaction. "Certainly," quod Smoothpate, with the greatest seriousness, "a most unlikely person, I will confess, Charley, as he is a grave, respectable man; still, you know, the most demure cats sometimes steal cream, Charley; so, parson, my good man, Mr Onyx Steady has your bell, and no one else."

Whereupon, away trudged Charley to Mr Steady's warehouse, and, pulling off his hat with a formal salaam, "Good Massa Onyx—sweet Massa Teady—pray give me de bell." Here the sable *clerigo* gathered himself up, and leant composedly on his long staff, hat still in hand, and ear turned towards Mr Steady, awaiting his answer.

"Bell?" ejaculated Steady, in great amazement—"bell! what bell?"

"Oh, good, sweet Massa Onyx, dear Massa Onyx Teady, everybody know you good person—quiet, wise somebody you is—all person sabe dat," whined Charley; then slipping near our friend, he whispered to him—"But de best of we lob bit of fun now and den—de best of we lef to himshef sometime."

"Confound the fellow!" quoth Onyx, rather pushed off his balance by such an unlooked-for attack before his clerks; "get out of my house, sir; what the mischief do I know of you or your infernal bell?—l wish the tongue of it was in your stomach—get out, sir, away with you."

Charley could stand this no longer, and losing patience, "D——n me eye, you *is* de tief, sir—so give me de bell, Massa Teady, or I sall pull you go before de Mayor, Massa Teady, and you sall be shame, Massa Teady; and, it may be, you sall be export to de Bay of Honduras, Massa Teady. Aha, how you will like dat, Massa Teady? you shall be export, maybe, for break into chapel during sarvice, and teal bell—aha, teal bell—whoever yeerie one crime equal to dat?"

"My good man," quoth Onyx, who now felt the absurdity of the affair, "I know nothing of all this—believe me, there is a mistake.—Who sent you here?"

"Massa Smoothpate," roared Charley—"Massa Smoothpate he who neber tell lie to nobody. Massa Smoothpate sent me, sir; so de debil if you no give up de bell, I sall—"

"Mr Smoothpate—oh ho!" sang out Steady, "I see, I see—." Finally, the affair was cleared up; a little hush-money made all snug, and Charley, having got back his instrument, bore no malice; so he and Steady resumed their former friendly footing—the *"statu quo ante bellum."*

Another story, and I have done—

About a week after this several of the same party again met at dinner, when my excellent friend Mr Nicodemus amused us exceedingly by the following story, which, for want of a better title, I shall relate under the head of

A SLIPPERY YOUTH.

"We all know," quoth old Nic, "that house robberies have been very rife of late, and on peril even of having the laugh against me, I will tell you how I

TOM CRINGLE'S LOG

suffered, no longer than three nights ago; so, Tom Cringle, will you and Bang have the charity to hold your tongues, and be instructed?

"Old Gelid, Longtram, Steady, and myself, had been eating *ratoons*, at the former's domicile, and it was about nine in the evening when I got home. We had taken next to no wine, a pint of madeira a-piece during dinner, and six bottles of claret between us afterwards, so I went to bed as cool as a cucumber, and slept soundly for several hours, until awakened by my old gander—now, do be quiet, Cringle—by my old watchman of a gander, cackling like a hero. I struck my repeater—half-past one—so I turned myself, and was once more falling over into the arms of Morpheus, when I thought I saw some dark object flit silently across the open window that looks into the piazza, between me and the deep blue and as yet moonless sky. This somewhat startled me, but it might have been one of the servants. Still I got up and looked out, but I could see nothing. It did certainly strike me once or twice that there was some dark object cowering in the deep gloom caused by the shade of the orange-tree at the end of the piazza, but I persuaded myself it was fancy, and once more slipped into my nest. However, the circumstance had put sleep to flight. Half an hour might have passed, and the deep dark purity of the eastern sky was rapidly quickening into a greenish azure, the forerunner of the rising moon"—("Oh, confound your poetry," said Rubiochico)—"which was fast swamping the sparkling stars, like a bright river flowing over diamonds, when the old gander again set up his gabblement and trumpeted more loudly than before. 'If you were not so tough, my noisy old cock,' thought I, 'next Michaelmas should be your last.' So I now resolutely shut my eyes and tried to sleep perforce, in which usually fruitless attempt I was actually beginning to succeed, do you know, when a strong odour of palm oil came through the window, and, on opening my eyes, I saw by the increasing light a naked negro standing at it, with his head and shoulders in sharp relief against the pale broad disc of the moon, at that moment just peering over the dark summit of the Long Mountain.

"I rubbed my eyes and looked again; the dark figure was still there; but, as if aware that some one was on the watch, it gradually sank down, until nothing but the round bullet head appeared above the window-sill. This was trying enough, but I made an effort and lay still. The stratagem succeeded: the figure, deceived by my feigned snoring and quietude, slowly rose, and once more stood erect. Presently it slipped one foot into the room, and then another, but so noiselessly that, when I saw the black figure standing before me on the floor, I had some misgivings as to whether or not it was really a being of this world.

However, I had small space for speculation, when it slid past the foot of the bed towards my open bureau; I seized the opportunity—started up—turned the key of the door, and planted myself right between the thief and the open window. 'Now, you scoundrel, surrender, or I will murder you on the spot.' I had scarcely spoken the words when, with the speed of light, the fellow threw himself on me—we closed—I fell—when, clip, he slipped through my fingers like an eel—bolted through the window, cleared the balcony at a bound, and disappeared. The thief had stripped himself as naked as he was born, and soaped his woolly skull, and smeared his whole corpus with palm oil, so that in the struggle I was charmingly lubricated."

Nicodemus here lay back on his chair, evidently desirous of our considering this the *whole* of the story, but he was not to be let off so easily, for presently Longtram, with a wicked twinkle of his eye, chimed in—

"Ay, and what happened next, old Nic—did nothing follow, eh?"

Nic's countenance assumed an irresolute expression; he saw he was jammed up in the wind, so at a venture he determined to sham deafness—

"Take wine, Lucifer—a glass of hermitage?"

"With great pleasure," said his Satanic majesty. The propitiatory libation, however, did not work, for no sooner had his glass touched the mahogany again than he returned to the charge.

"Now, Mr Nicodemus, since you won't, I will tell the company the reason of so nice an old gentleman wearing Baltimore flour in his hair instead of perfumed Mareschale powder, and none of the freshest either, let me tell you; why, I have seen three weavels take flight from your august pate since we sat down to dinner."

Old Nic, seeing he was caught, met the attack with the greatest good-humour—

"Why, I will tell the whole truth, Lucifer, if you don't bother."—("The devil thank you," said Longtram.)—"So you must know," continued Nicodemus, "that I immediately roused the servants, searched the premises in every direction without success—nothing could be seen; but, at the suggestion of my valet, I lit a small spirit-lamp, and placed it on the table at my bedside, on which it pleased him to place my brace of Mantons, loaded with slug, and my naked small sword, so that, thought I, if the thief ventures back, he shall not slip through my fingers again so easily. I do confess that these imposing preparations did appear to me somewhat preposterous, even at the time, as it was not, to say the least of it, very probable that my slippery gentleman would return the same night. However, my servant in his zeal was not to be denied, and I was not so fit to judge as usual, from having missed my customary quantity of wine after dinner the previous day; so, seeing all right, I turned in, thus bristling like a porcupine, and slept soundly until daylight, when I bethought me of getting up. I then rose, slipped on my nightgown, and,"—here Nicodemus laughed more loudly than ever,—"as I am a gentleman, my spirit-lamp, naked sword, loaded pistols, my diamond breast-pin, and all my clothes, even unto my unmentionables, had disappeared; but what was the cruelest cut of all, my box of Mareschale powder, my patent puff, and all my pomade divine, had also vanished; and, true enough, as Lucifer says, it so happened that, from the delay in the arrival of the running ships, there was not an ounce of either powder or pomatum to be had in the whole town, so I have been driven in my extremity— oh most horrible declension!—to keep my tail on hog's lard and Baltimore flour ever since."

"Well, but," persisted Lucifer, "who the deuce was the man in the moon? Come, tell us. And what has become of the queue you so tenderly nourished, for you sport a crop, Master Nic, now, I perceive?"

Here Nicodemus was neither to hold nor to bind; he was absolutely suffocating with laughter, as he shrieked out, with long intervals between—

"Why the robber was my own favourite body-servant, Crabclaw, after all, and be d——d to him—the identical man who advised the warlike demonstrations; and as for the pigtail, why, on the very second night of the flour and grease, it was so cruelly damaged by a rat while I slept, that I had to amputate the whole affair, stoop and roop, this very morning." And, so saying, the excellent creature fell back in his chair, like to choke from the uproariousness of his mirth, while the tears streamed down his cheeks, and washed channels in the flour, as if he had been a tatooed Mandingo.

CHAPTER XIX.

THE LAST OF THE LOG— TOM CRINGLE'S FAREWELL.

"And whether we shall meet again, I know not."
Brutus to Cassius, in Julius Caesar.

ONE FINE morning about this time we had just anchored on our return from a cruise, when I received, as I was dressing, a letter from the secretary, desiring me instantly to wait on the Admiral, as I was promoted to the rank of commander (how I did dance and sing, my eye!), and appointed to the Lotus-Leaf, of eighteen guns, then refitting at the dockyard, and under orders for England.

I accordingly, after calling and making my bow, proceeded to the dockyard to enter on my new command, and I was happy in being able to get Tailtackle and Reefpoint once more removed along with me.

The gunner of Lotus-Leaf having died, Timotheus got an acting warrant, which I rejoice to say was ultimately confirmed, and little Reefy, now a commander in the service, weathered it many a day with me afterwards, both as midshipman and lieutenant.

After seeing everything in a fair train on board, I applied for a fortnight's leave, which I got, as the trade which I was to convoy had not yet congregated, nor were they likely to do so before the expiry of this period.

Having paid my respects at the Admiral's pen, I returned to Kingston. Most of the houses in the lower part of the town are surmounted by a small *look-out*, as it is called, like a little belfry fitted with green blinds, and usually furnished with one or more good telescopes. It is the habit of the Kingstonians to resort in great numbers to those *gardemange*-looking boxes whenever a strange sail appears in the offing, or any circumstance takes place at sea worth reconnoitring. It was about nine o'clock on a fine morning, and I had taken my stand in one of them, peering out towards the east, but no white speck on the verge of the horizon indicated an approaching sail; so I slewed round the glass to the westward, to have a squint at the goings-on amongst the squadron, lying at anchor at Port Royal, about six miles off, then mustering no fewer than eighteen pennants; viz., one line-of-battle ship, one fifty, five frigates, two corvettes, one ship-sloop, four eighteen-gun brigs, three schooners, and a cutter. All was quiet, not even one solitary signal making amongst them; so I again scoured the horizon towards the east, when I noticed a very dashing schooner, which had sailed that morning, as she crept along the Palisadoes. She was lying up the inner channel, taking advantage of the land-wind, in place of staggering away to the southward through the ship-channel, already within the influence of the sea-breeze, but which was as yet neutralised close in-shore where she was by the terral. The speed of the craft—the rapidity with which she slid along the land with the light air—riveted my attention. On inquiry I found she was the Carthaginian schooner Josefa. At this moment the splash of oars was heard right below where we stood, and a very roguish-looking craft, also schooner-rigged, about a hundred tons burden apparently, passed rapidly beneath us, tearing up the shining surface of the sleeping harbour with no fewer than fourteen sweeps. She was very heavily rigged, with her mainmast raking over the taffrail, and full of men. I noticed she had a long gun on a pivot, and several carronades mounted. Presently there was a good deal of whispering amongst the group of half-a-dozen gentlemen who were with me in the look-out, who, from their conversation, I soon found were underwriters on the schooner outside.

"Heyday," said one, "the Antonio is off somewhat suddenly this morning."

"Where may that schooner that is sweeping so handsomely down harbour belong to?" said I to the gentleman who had spoken.

"To Havanna," was the answer; "but I fear he intends to overhaul the Josefa there, and she would be a good prize to him, now since Carthagena has thrown off allegiance to Spain."

"But he will never venture to infract the neutrality of the waters, surely," rejoined I, "within sight of the squadron too?"

The gentleman I spoke to smiled incredulously; and as I had nothing particular to do for a couple of hours, I resolved to remain and see the issue. In a few minutes the sea-breeze came thundering down, in half a gale of wind, singing through the rigging of the ships alongside of the wharfs, and making the wooden blinds rattle again. The Antonio laid in her sweeps, spread her canvass in an instant, and was lying-to, off the fort at Port Royal, to land her pass, in little in more than half an hour from the time she passed us, a distance of no less than seven miles, as she had to sail it. In a minute the jibsheet was again hauled over to leeward, and away she was like an arrow, crowding all sail. I had seldom seen a vessel so weatherly before. In an hour more she was abreast of the town and abeam of the Josefa, who, from being cooped up in the narrow inner channel, had, ever since the sea-breeze set down, been bothering with short tacks, about and about, every minute. Presently the Antonio dashed in through a streak of blue water in the reef, so narrow, that, to look at it, I did not think a boat could have passed, and got between the Josefa and Port Royal, when he took in his gaff-topsail and hauled down his flying-jib, but made no hostile demonstration, beyond keeping dead to leeward, tack for tack with the Josefa; and once, when the latter seemed about to bear up and run past him, I noticed the foot of his foresail lift, and his sails shiver as he came to the wind, as much as to say, "Luff again, my lady, or I'll fire at you." It was now clear Josefa did not like her playmate, for she cracked on all the canvass she could carry; and having tried every other manœuvre to escape without effect, she at length, with reckless desperation, edged away a point, and flew like smoke through another gap, even smaller and shallower than the one the Antonio had entered by. We all held our breath until she got into blue water again, expecting every moment to see her stick fast, and her masts tumble over the side; but she scraped clear very cleverly, and the next moment was tearing and plunging through the tumbling waves outside of the reefs. Antonio, as I expected, followed her, but all very quietly, still keeping well to leeward, however. Thus they continued for half an hour, running to the southward and eastward, when I noticed the Havanero, who had gradually crept up under the Josefa's lee-quarter, hoist his colours and pennant, and fire a gun at her. She immediately tacked in great confusion, and made all sail to get back through the canal into the inner channel, with the other schooner close at her heels, blazing away from his long gun as fast as he could load. A Spaniard, who was one of the principal owners of the Josefa's cargo, happened to be standing beside me in the lookout; at every shot, he would, with a face of the most intense anxiety, while the perspiration hailed off his brow, slap his hands on his thighs, and shrink down on his hams, cowering his head at the same time, as if the shot had, been aimed at him and he was trying to shun it, apostrophising himself, with an agitated voice, as follows:

"Valga me Dios, que demonio, que demonio! Ah, Pancho Roque, tu es ruinado, mi amigo." Another shot. "Tu es ruinado, chicatico, tan çierto como navos no son coles." A third flash. "Oh, rabo de lechon de Sail Antonio, que es eso, que es eso!"*

Neck and neck, however, in came the Josefa, staggering right through the narrow channel once more, persecuted by the Antonio, with the white breakers

---

*Thus freely:—"Heaven defend me, what a devil! Ah, Pancho Roque, you are ruined, my fine fellow—you are ruined, my little man, so sure as turnips am not cauliflowers. Oh, tail of St Anthony's pig, that it should come to this!"

foaming and flashing close to on each side of her; but by this time there was a third party in the game. I had noticed a lot of signals made in the flag-ship. Presently one of the sloops of war fired a gun, and before the smoke blew off she was under weigh, with her topsails, foresail, spanker, and foretopmast-staysail set. This was his Majesty's sloop-of-war Seaflower, which had slipped from her moorings, and was now crowding all sail in chase of the arrogant Don, who had dared to fire a shot in anger in the sanctuary of British waters. All this while the Antonio had been so intent on hooking the Carthaginian, that the sloop was nearly up to him before he hove about and gave up the chase; and now the tables were beautifully turned on him, for the Seaflower's shot was flying over and over him in whole broadsides, and he must have been taken, when, crack! away went the sloop's foretop-gallant-mast, which gave the rogue a start. In an hour he was away to windward as far as you could see, and his pursuer and the Josefa were once more at anchor in Port Royal.

That evening I returned to the dockyard, where I found everything going on with Lotus-Leaf as I could wish. So I returned, after a three days' sojourn on board, to Kingston, and next afternoon mounted my horse, or rather a horse that a friend was fool enough to lend me, at the agent's wharf, with the thermometer at ninety-five in the shade, and, cantering off, landed at my aunt Mrs Palma's mountain residence, where the mercury stood at sixty-two at nightfall, just in time to dress for dinner. I need not say that we had a pleasant party, as Mary was there; so, having rigged very killingly, as I thought, I made my appearance at dinner, a mighty man, indeed, *with my two epaulets;* but, to my great disappointment, when I walked into the piazza, not a soul seemed to acknowledge my promotion. "How blind people are!" thought I. Even my cousins, little creole urchins, dressed in small transparent cambric shifts tied into a knot over their tails, and with devil the thing else on, seemed to perceive no difference, as they pulled me about, with a volley of "Cousin Taam, what you bring we?"

At length dinner was announced, and we adjourned from the dark balcony to the dining-room. "Come, there is light enough here; my rank will be noticed now, surely; but no—so patience." The only males of the party were the doctor of the district, two Kingston gentlemen, young Palma, and Colonel B—— of the Guards; the ladies at dinner being my aunt, Mary, and her younger sister. We sat down all in high glee; I was sitting opposite my dearie. "Deuced strange—neither does *she* take any notice of my two epaulets;" and I glanced my eye, to be sure that they were both really there. I then, with some small misgivings, stole a look towards the Colonel—a very handsome fellow—with all the ease and polish of a soldier and a gentleman about him. "The devil, it cannot be, surely!" for the black-eyed and black-haired pale face seemed annoyingly attentive to the *militaire*. At length this said officer addressed me, "Captain Cringle, do me the honour to take wine." Mary started at the *Captain*—

> "She gazed, she reddened like a rose,
> Syne pale as ony lily."

"Aha," thought I, "all right still." She trembled extremely, and her mother at length noticed it, I saw; but all this while B—— was balancing a land-crab on his silver fork, while, with a wine-glass in his other claw, he was ogling me in some wonderment. I saw the awkwardness of the affair, and seizing a bottle of catchup for one of sercial, I filled my glass with such vehemence that I spilt a great part of it; but even the colour and flavour did not recover me; so, with a face like a north-west moon, I swilled off the potion, and instantly fell back in my chair—"Poisoned I by all that is nonsensical—poisoned—catchup—O Lord!" and off I started to my bedroom, where, by dint of an ocean of hot water, I got quit of the sauce, and, clinching the whole with a caulker of brandy, I returned to the dinner-table a good deal abashed, I will confess, but endeavouring most emphatically all the while to laugh it off as a good jest. But my Mary was flown; she had been ailing for some days, her mother alleged, and she required rest. Presently my aunt rose, and we were left to our bottle, and, sorry am I to say it, I bumpered away from some strong unaccountable impulse until I got three parts drunk, to the great surprise of the rest of the party, for guzzling wine was not certainly a failing of mine, unless on the strong provocation of good fellowship.

Mary did not appear that evening, and I may as well tell the whole truth, that she was pledged to marry me whenever I got my step; and next morning all this sort of thing was duly communicated to mamma, &c. &c. &c., and I was the happiest, and so forth—all of which, as it concerns no one but myself, if you please, we shall say no more about it.

The beautiful cottage where we were sojourning was situated about three thousand feet above the level of the sea, and halfway up the great prong of the Blue Mountains, known by the name of the Liguanea range, which rises behind, and overhangs the city of Kingston. The road to it, after you have ridden about five miles over the hot plain of Liguanea, brings you to Hope estate, where an

anatomy of an old watchman greeted me with the negro's constant solicitation—"Massa, me beg you for one feepenny." This youth was, as authentic
records show, one hundred and forty years old *only*—The Hope is situated in
the very gorge of the pass, wherein you have to travel nine miles further,
through most magnificent scenery; at one time struggling among the hot stones
of the all but dry river-course, at others winding along the breezy cliffs, on
mule-paths not twelve inches wide, with a perpendicular wall of rock rising five
hundred feet above you on one side, while a dark gulf, a thousand feet deep,
yawned on the other, from the bottom of which arose the hoarse murmur of the
foliage-screened brook. Noble trees spread their boughs overhead, and the
most beautiful shrubs and bushes grew and blossomed close at hand, and all
was moist and cool and fresh until you turned the bare pinnacle of some lime-
stone-rock, naked as the summit of the Andes where the hot sun, even through
the thin attenuated air of that altitude, would suddenly blaze on you so fiercely
that your eyes were blinded and your face blistered, as if you had been suddenly transported within the influence of a sirocco. Well, now since you know the
road, let us take a walk after breakfast. It shall be a beautiful clear day—not a
speck or cloud in the heavens. Mary is with me.

"Well, Tom," says she, "you were very sentimental last evening."

"Sentimental! I was deucedly sick, let me tell you; a wine-glassful of cold
catchup is rather trying even to a lover's stomach, Mary. Murder! I never was so
sick, even in my first cruise in the old Breeze. Bah! Do you know I did not think
of you for an hour afterwards?—not until that bumper of brandy stayed my
calamity. But come, when shall we be married, Maria? Oh! have done with your
blushing and botheration—to-morrow or next day? It would not be quite the
thing this evening, would it?"

"Tom, you are crazy.—Time enough, surely, when we all meet in England."

"And when may that be?" said I, drawing her arm closer through mine. "No,
no—to-morrow I will call on the Admiral; and as you are all going to England in
the fleet at any rate, I will ask his leave to give you a passage, and—and—
and—"

All of which, as I said before, being parish news, we shall drop a veil over
it—so a small touch at the scenery again.

Immediately under foot rose several lower ranges of mountains—those
nearest us, covered with the laurel-looking coffee-bushes, interspersed with
negro villages hanging amongst the fruit-trees like clusters of birds' nests on
the hill-side, with a bright green patch of plantain-suckers here and there, and

a white painted overseer's house peeping from out the wood, and herds of cattle in the Guinea-grass pieces. Beyond these stretched out the lovely plain of Liguanea, covered with luxuriant cane-pieces, and groups of negro-houses, and Guinea-grass pastures of even a deeper green than that of the canes; and small towns of sugar-works rose every here and there, with their threads of white smoke floating up into the clear sky, while, as the plain receded, the cultivation disappeared, and it gradually became sterile, hot, and sandy, until the Long Mountain hove its back like a whale from out the sea-like level of the plain, while to the right of it appeared the city of Kingston, like a model, with its parade, or *place d'armes* in the centre, from which its long lines of hot sandy streets stretched out at right angles, with the military post of Up-park Camp, situated about a mile and a half to the northward and eastward of the town. Through a tolerably good glass, the church-spire looked like a needle, the trees about the houses like bushes, the tall cocoa-nut trees like harebells; a slow crawling black speck here and there denoted a carriage moving along; while waggons, with their teams of eighteen or twenty oxen, looked like so many centipedes. At the camp, the two regiments drawn out on parade, with two nine-pounders on each flank, and their attendant gunners, looked like a red sparkling line, with two black spots at each end, surrounded by small black dots. Presently the red line wavered, and finally broke up as the regiments wheeled into open column, when the whole fifteen hundred men crawled past three little scarlet spots, denoting the general and his staff. When they began to manœuvre, each company looked like a single piece in a game at chess, and, as they fired by companies, the little tiny puffs of smoke floated up like wreaths of wool, suddenly surmounting and overlaying the red lines; while the light companies, breaking away into skirmishers, seemed for all the world like two red bricks suddenly cast down, and shattered on the ground, whereby the fragments were scattered all over the green fields, and under the noble trees, the biggest of which looked like *small* cabbages. At length the line was again formed, and the inspection being over, it broke up once more, and the minute red fragments presently vanished altogether like a nest of ants—the guns looking like so many barley-corns, under the long lines of barracks, that seemed no bigger than houses in a child's toy. As for the other *arm*, we of the navy had no reason to glorify ourselves; for while the review proceeded on shore, a strange man-of-war hove in sight in the offing, looming like a mussel-shell, although she was a forty-four gun frigate, and ran down before the wind close to the Palisadoes, or natural tongue of land, which juts out like a bow from Rock Fort, to the eastward of Kingston, and hoops in the harbour, and then lengthens out, trending about five miles due west, where it widens out into a sandy flat, on which the town and forts of Port Royal are situated. She was saluting the Admiral when I first saw her. A red spark and a small puff on the starboard side—a puff, but no spark on the larboard, which was the side farthest from us, but no report from either reached our ears; and presently down came the little red flag, and up went the St George's ensign, white, with a red cross, while the sails of the gallant craft seemed about the size of those of a little schoolboy's plaything. After a short interval the flag-ship, a seventy-four, lying at Port Royal, returned the salute. She, again, appeared somewhat loftier; she might have been an *oyster*-shell; while the squadron of four frigates, two sloops of war, and several brigs and schooners, looked like ants in the wake of a beetle. As for the dear little Wave, I can compare her to nothing but a mosquito, and the large 500-ton West Indiamen lying off Kingston, five miles nearer, were but as small cock-boats to the eye. In the offing the sea appeared like ice, for the waves were not seen at all, and the swell could only be marked by the difference, in the reflection of the sun's rays as it rose and fell, while a hot haze hung over the whole, making everything indistinct, so that the water blended into sky without the line of demarcation being visible. But, even as we looked forth on this most glorious scene, a small black cloud rose to windward. At this time we were both sitting on the grass on a most beautiful bank, beneath an orange-tree. The ominous appearance increased in size, the sea-breeze was suddenly stifled, the swelling sails of the frigate that had first saluted, fell, and, as she rolled, flattened in against the masts—the rustling of the green leaves over-head ceased.

The cloud rolled onward from the east, and spread out, and out, as it sailed in from seaward, and on, and on, until it gradually covered the whole scene from our view (shipping and harbour and town and camp and sugar estates), boiling and rolling in black eddies under our feet. Anon the thunder began to grumble, and the zigzag lightning to fork out from one dark mass into another, while all where we sat was bright and smiling under the unclouded noonday sun. This continued for half an hour, when at length the sombre appearance of the clouds below us brightened into a sea of white fleecy vapour like wool, which gradually broke away into detached masses, discovering another layer of still thinner vapour underneath, which again parted, disclosing through the interstices a fresh gauzelike veil of transparent mist, through which the lower ranges of hills and the sugar estates and the town and shipping were once more dimly visible; but this in turn vanished, and the clouds, attracted by the hills, floated away, and hung around them in festoons, and gradually rose and rose until presently we were enveloped in mist, and Mary spoke—"Tom, there will be thunder here—what shall we do?"

"Pooh, never mind, Mary; you have a conductor on the house."

"True," said she; "but the servants, when the post that supported it was blown down t'other day, very judiciously unlinked the rods, and now, since I remember me, they are, to use your phrase, *'stowed away'* below the house;" and so they were, sure enough. However, we had no more thunder, and soon the only indications of the spent storm were the increased distinctness of objects at a distance, the coolness and purity of the air, the brighter green of the cane-fields, and the red discoloured appearance of the margin of the harbour, from the rush of muddy water off the land, and the chocolate colour of the previously snow-white sandy roads, that now twisted through the plain like black snakes, and a fleecy dolphin-shaped cloud here and there stretching out, and floating horizontally in the blue sky, as if it had been hooked to the precipitous mountain-tops above us.

Next day it was agreed that we should all return to Kingston and the day after that, we proceeded to Mr Bang's Pen, on the Spanish Town road, as a sort of half-way house or stepping-stone to his beautiful residence in St-Thomas-in-the-Vale, where we were all invited to spend a fortnight. Our friend himself was on the other side of the island, but he was to join us in the valley, and we found our comforts carefully attended to; and as the day after we had set up our tent at the Pen was to be one of rest to my aunt, I took the opportunity of paying my respects to the Admiral, who was then careening at his mountain retreat in the vicinity with his family. Accordingly, I took horse, and rode along the margin of the great lagoon, on the Spanish Town road, through tremendous defiles; and after being driven into a watchman's hut by the rain, I reached the house, and was most graciously received by Sir Samuel Semaphore and his lady and their lovely daughters.—Oh, the most splendid women that ever were built! The youngest is now, I believe, the prime ornament of the Scottish Peerage; and I never can forget the pleasure I so frequently experienced in those days in the society of this delightful family. The same evening I returned to the Pen. On my way I fell in with three officers in white jackets and broad-brimmed straw hats, wading up to the waist amongst the reeds of the lagoon, with guns held high above their heads. They were shooting ducks, it seemed; and their negro servants were heard ploutering and shouting amidst the thickets of the crackling reeds, while their dogs were swimming all about them.

"Hillo!" shouted the nearest—"Cringle, my lad—whither bound? how is Sir Samuel and Lady Semaphore, eh? Capital sport, ten brace of teal—there;" and the spokesman threw two beautiful birds ashore to me. This wise man of the bulrushes was no less a personage than Sir Jeremy Mayo, the commander of the forces, one of the bravest fellows in the army, and respected and beloved by all who ever knew him, but a regular dare-devil of an Irishman, who, not satisfied with his chance of yellow fever on shore, had thus chosen to hunt for it with his staff in the *Caymanas Lagoon.*

Next morning we set out in earnest on our travels for St Thomas-in-the-Vale, in two of our friend Bang's gigs, and my aunt's ketureen, laden with her black maiden and a lot of bandboxes, while two mounted servants brought up the rear, and my old friend Jupiter, who had descended—not from the clouds, but from the excellent Mr Fyall, who was by this time gathered to his fathers—to Massa Aaron, rode a musket-shot ahead of the convoy to clear away or give notice of any impediments of waggons or carts, or droves of cattle, that might be meeting us.

After driving five miles or so we reached the seat of government, Spanish Town. Here we stopped at the Speaker's house—by the way, one of the handsomest and most agreeable men I ever saw—intending to proceed in the afternoon to our destination. But the rain in the forenoon fell so heavily that we had to delay our journey until next morning; and that afternoon I spent in attending the debates in the House of Assembly, where everything was conducted with much greater decorum than I ever saw maintained in the House of Commons, and no great daring in the assertion either. The Hall itself, fitted with polished mahogany benches, was handsome and well aired, and between it and the grand court, as it is called, occupying the other end of the building, which was then sitting, there is a large cool saloon, generally in term time well filled with wigless lawyers and their clients. The House of Assembly (this saloon and the court-house forming one side of the square) is situated over against the Government House; while another side is occupied by a very handsome temple, covering in a statue erected to Lord Rodney, the saver of the island, as he is always called, from having crushed the fleet of Count de Grasse.

At length, at grey dawn the next day, as the report of the morning gun came booming along the level plain from Port Royal, we weighed, and finally started on our cruise. As we drove up towards St-Thomas-in-the-Vale from Spanish Town, along the hot sandy road, the plain gradually roughened into small rocky eminences, covered with patches of bushes here and there, with luxuriant Guinea-grass growing in the clefts; the road then sank between abrupt little hills, the Guinea-corn fields began to disappear, the grass became greener, the trees rose higher, the air felt fresher and cooler, and, proceeding still farther, the hills on either side swelled into mountains and became rocky and precipitous, and drew together, as it were, until they appeared to impend over us. We had now arrived at the gorge of the pass leading into the valley, through which flowed a most beautiful limpid clear blue stream, along the margin of which the road wound, while the tree-clothed precipices rose five hundred feet perpendicularly on each brink. Presently we crossed a wooden bridge, supported by a stone pier in the centre, when Jupiter pricked ahead to give notice of the approach of waggons, that our cavalcade might haul up, out of danger, into some nook in the rock, to allow the lumbersome teams to pass.

"What is that?"—I was driving my dearie in the leading gig—"is that a pistol-shot?" It was the crack of the long whip carried by the negro waggoner, reverberated from hill to hill, and from cliff to cliff; and presently the father of gods came thundering down the steep acclivity we were ascending.

"Massa, draw up into dat corner; draw up."

I did as I was desired, and presently the shrill whistle of the negro waggoners, and the increasing sharpness of the reports of their whips, the handles of which were as long as fishing-rods, and their wild exclamations to their cattle, to whom they addressed themselves by name, as if they had been reasonable creatures, gave notice of the near approach of a train of no fewer than seven waggons, each with three drivers, eighteen oxen, three hogsheads of sugar, and two puncheons of rum.

"Come," thought I; "if the negroes are overworked, it is more than the bullocks are, at all events." They passed us with abundance of yelling and cracking, and as soon as the coast was clear we again pursued our way up the ravine, than which nothing could be more beautiful or magnificent. On our right hand now rose, almost perpendicularly, the everlasting rocks, to a height of a thousand feet, covered with the richest foliage that imagination can picture; while here and there a sharp steeple-like pinnacle of grey stone, overgrown with lichens, shot up and out from the face of them into the blue sky, mixing with the tall forest trees that overhung the road, festooned with ivy and withes of different kinds like the rigging of a ship, round which the tendrils of many a beautiful wild-flower crept twining up, while all was fresh with the sparkling dew that showered down on us, with every breath of wind, like rain. On our left foamed the roaring river, and on the other brink the opposite bank rose equally precipitously, clothed also with superb trees, that spread their blending boughs over the chasm, until they wove themselves together with those that grew on the side we were on, qualifying the noonday fierceness of a Jamaica sun into a green cool twilight, while the long misty reaches of the blue river, with white foaming rapids here and there, and the cattle wading in them, lengthened out beneath in the distance. Oh! the very look of it refreshed one unspeakably.

Presently a group of half-a-dozen country *buccras*—overseers, or coffee-planters, most likely, or possibly larger fish than either—hove in sight, all in their blue-white jane trousers, and long Hessian boots pulled up over them, and new blue, square-cut, bright-buttoned coatees, and threadbare, silk, broad-brimmed hats. They dashed past us on goodish nags, followed at a distance of three hundred yards by a covey of negro servants, mounted on mules, in white Osnaburg trousers, with a shirt or frock over them, no stockings, each with one spur, and the stirrup-iron held firmly between the great and second toes, while a snow-white sheep's fleece covered their massas' portmanteaus, strapped on to the mail pillion behind. We drove on for about seven miles, after entering the pass—the whole scenery of which was by far the finest thing I had ever seen—the precipices on each side becoming more and more rugged and abrupt as we advanced, until all at once we emerged from the chasm on the parish of St-Thomas-in-the-Vale, which opened on us like a magical illusion, in all its green luxuriance and freshness. But by this time we were deucedly tired, and Massa Aaron's mansion, situated on its little airy hill above a sea of canes, which rose and fell before the passing breeze like the waves of the ocean, was the most consolatory object in the view; and thither we drove as fast as our wearied horses could carry us, and found everything most carefully prepared for our reception. Having dressed, we had a glorious dinner and lots of good wine; and, the happiest of the happy, I tumbled into bed, dreaming of leading a division of line-of-battle ships into action, and of Mary, and of our eldest son being my first-lieutenant, and

"Massa," quoth Jupiter—"you take cup of coffee dis marning, massa?"

"Thank you; certainly."

It was by this time grey dawn. My window had been left open the evening before, when it was hot and sultry enough; but it was now cold and clamp, and a wetting mist boiled in through the open sash, like rolling wreaths of white smoke.

"What is that—where are we—in the North Sea, or on the top of Mont Blanc? Why, clouds may be all in your way, Massa Jupiter, but—"

"Cloud!" rejoined the deity—"him no more den marning fag, massa; always hab him over de Vale in de marning, until de sun melt him. And where is you?—why, you is in Massa Aaron house, here in St-Thomas-in-de-Vale—and Miss—"

"—Miss!" said I—"what Miss?"

"Oh, for you Miss," rejoined Jupiter, with a grin. "Miss Mary up and dress already, and de horses are at de door; him wait for you to ride wid him before breakfast, massa, and to see de clearing of de fag."

"Ride before breakfast!—see the clearing of the fog!" grumbled I. "Romantic it may be, but consumedly inconvenient." However, my knighthood was at stake; so up I got, drank my coffee, dressed, and adjourned to the piazza, where my adorable was already rigged with riding-habit and whip. Straightway we mounted, she into her side-saddle, with her riding-habit and who knows how many petticoats beneath her, while I, Pilgarlic, embarked in thin jane trousers upon a cold, damp, indeed wet saddle, that made me shiver again. But I was understood to be in love, *ergo*, I was expected to be agreeable. However, a damp saddle and a thin pair of trousers allay one's ardour a good deal too. But if any one had seen the impervious fog in which we sat—why, you could not see a tree three yards from you—a cabbage looked like a laurel-bush, Sneezer became a dromedary, and the negroes passing the little gate to their work were absolute Titans.—*Boom*—a long reverberating noise thundered in the distance and amongst the hills, gradually dying away in a hollow rumble. "The Admiral tumbling down the hatchway, Tom—the morning gun fired at Port Royal," said Mary; and so it was.

The fire-flies were still glancing amongst the leaves of the beautiful orange-trees in front of the house; but we could see no farther, the whole view being shrouded under the thick watery veil which rolled and boiled about us, sometimes thick, and sometimes thinner, hovering between a mist and small rain, and wetting one's hair and face and clothes most completely. We descended from the eminence on which the house stood, rode along the level at the foot of it, and, after a canter of a couple of miles we began to ascend a bridle-path, through the Guinea-grass pastures, which rose rank and wet, as high as one's saddlebow, drenching me to the skin in the few patches where I was not wet before. All this while the fog continued as ever; at length we suddenly rose above it—rode out of it, as it were.

St-Thomas-in-the-Vale is, as the name denotes, a deep valley, about ten miles long by six broad, into which there is but one inlet comfortably passable for carriages—the road along which we had to come. The hills, by which it is surrounded on all sides, are, for the most part, covered with Guinea-grass pastures—on the lower ranges, and with coffee plantations and provision grounds higher up. When we had ridden clear of the mist the sun was shining brightly overhead, and everything was fresh and sparkling with dewdrops near us; but the vale was still concealed under the wool-like sea of white mist, only pierced here and there by a tall cocoa-nut tree rising above it, like the mast of a foundered vessel. But anon the higher ridges of the grass pieces appeared, as the fog undulated in fleecy waves in the passing breeze, which, as it rose and sank like the swell of the ocean, disclosed every now and then the works on some high-lying sugar estate, and again rolled over them like the tide covering the shallows of the sea, while shouts of laughter and the whooping of the negroes in the fields, rose from out the obscurity, blended with the signal-cries of the sugar boilers to the stokeholemen of "Fire, fire—grand copper, grand copper," and the *ca-ca'ing*, like so many rooks, of the children driving the mules and oxen in the mills, and the everlasting splashing and panting of the waterwheel of the estate immediately below us, and the crashing and smashing of the canes, as they were crushed between the mill rollers; and the cracking of the wain and waggonmen's long whips, and the rumbling, and creaking and squealing of the machinery of the mills, and of the carriage-wheels; while the smoke from the unseen chimney-stalks of the sugar-works rose whirling darkly up through the watery veil, like spinning waterspouts, from out the bosom of the great deep. Anon the veil rose, and we were once more gradually enveloped in vapour. Presently the thickest of the mist floated up, and rose above us like a gauze-like canopy of fleecy clouds overhanging the whole level plain through which the red quenched sun, which a moment before was flaming with intolerable brightness overhead, suddenly assumed the appearance of a round red globe in an apothecary's window, surrounded by a broad yellow sickly halo, which dimly lit up, as if the sun had been in eclipse, the cane fields, then *in arrow*, as it is called (a lavender-coloured flower, about three feet long, that shoots out from the top of the cane, denoting that it is mature, and fit to be ground), and the Guinea-grass plats, and the nice-looking houses of the bushas, and the busy mill-yards, and the noisy gangs of negroes in the field, which were all disclosed, as if by the change of a scene.

At length, in love as we were, we remembered our breakfast; and, beginning to descend, we encountered in the path a gang of about three dozen little glossy black piccaninies going to their work, the oldest not above twelve years of age, under the care of an old negress. They had all their little *packies*, or calabashes, on their heads, full of provisions; while an old cook, with a bundle of fagots on her head, and a *fire*-stick in her hand, brought up the rear—her province being to cook the food which the tiny little workpeople carried. Presently several bookkeepers, or deputy white superintendents on the plantation, also passed—strong healthy-looking young fellows—in stuff jackets and white trousers, and all with good cudgels in their hands. The mist, which had continued to rise up and up, growing thinner and thinner as it ascended, now rent overhead about the middle of the vale, and the masses, like scattered clouds, drew towards the ledge of hills that surrounded it, like floating chips of wood in a tub of water, sailing in long shreds towards the most precipitous peaks, to which, as they ascended, they attached themselves and remained at rest. And now the fierce sun, reasserting his supremacy, shone once more in all his tropical fierceness right down on the steamy earth, and all was glare and heat and bustle.

Next morning I rode out at daylight along with Mr Bang, who had arrived on the previous evening. We stopped to breakfast at a property of his about four miles distant, and certainly we had no reason to complain of our fare; fresh fish from the gully, nicely-roasted yams, a capital junk of salt beef, a dish I always glory in on shore, although a hint of it at sea makes me quake; and, after our repast, I once more took the road to see the estate in company of my learned friend. There was a long narrow saddle, or ridge of limestone, about five hundred feet high, that separated the southern quarter of the parish from the northern. The cane-pieces, and cultivated part of the estate, lay in a dead level of deep black mould, to the southward of this ridge, from out there, the latter rose abruptly. The lower part of the ridge was clothed with the most luxuriant orange, shaddock, lime, star-apple, bread-fruit, and custard-apple trees, besides numberless others that I cannot particularise, while the summit was shaded by tall forest timber. Proceeding along a rough bridle-path for the space of two miles, we attained the highest part of the saddle, and turned sharp off to the right to follow a small footpath that had been *billed in the bush,* being the lines recently *run* by the land-surveyor between Mr Bang's property and the neighbouring estate, the course of which mine host was desirous of personally inspecting. We therefore left our horses in charge of our servants, who had followed us, running behind, holding on by their tails, and began to brush through the narrow path cut in the hot underwood. After walking a hundred yards or so, we arrived at the point where the path ended abruptly, abutting against a large tree that had been felled, about three feet high, and at least five in diameter. Mr Bang immediately perched himself on it to look about him, to see the *lay* of the land over the sea of brushwood. I remained below, complaining loudly of the heat and confined air of my situation, and swabbing all the while most energetically, when I saw my friend start.

"Zounds, Tom, look behind you!" We had nothing but our riding-switches in our hands. A large snake, about ten feet long, had closed up the path in our rear, sliding slowly from one branch to another, and hissing and striking out its forked tongue as it twisted itself, at the height of my head from the ground, amongst the trees and bushes, round and round about, occasionally twining its neck round a tree as thick as my body, on one side of the path, and its tail round another, larger in girth than my leg, on the other; when it would, with prodigious strength but the greatest ease and the most oily smoothness, bend the smaller tree like a hoop, until the trunks nearly touched, although growing full six feet asunder, as if a tacklefall or other strong purchase, had been applied; but continuing all the while it was putting forth its power to glide soapily along, quite unconcernedly, and to all appearance as pliant as a leather thong, shooting out its glancing neck, and *glowering* about with its little blasting fiery eyes, and sliding the forepart of the body onwards without pausing, as if there had been no strain on the tail whatsoever, until the stems of the two trees were at length brought together, when it let the smaller go with a loud spank, that shook the dew of the neighbouring branches, and the perspiration from Tom Cringle's forehead—whose nerves were not more steady than the tree—like rain, and frightened all the birds in the neighbourhood; while it, the only unstartled thing, continued steadily and silently on its course, turning and looking at us and poking its head within arm's length, and raising it with a loud hiss, and a threatening attitude, on our smallest motion.

"A modern group of the Laocoon; lord, what a neckcloth we shall both have presently!" thought I.

Meanwhile, the serpent seemed to be emboldened from our quietude, and came so near that I thought I perceived the hot glow of its breath, with its scales glancing like gold and silver, and its diamond-like eyes sparkling; but all so still and smooth that, unless it were an occasional hiss, its motions were noiseless as those of an apparition.

At length the devil came fairly between us, and I could stand it no longer. We had both up to this period been really and truly *fascinated;* but the very instant that the coast was clear in my *wake,* by the snake heading me, and gliding between me and Mr Bang, my manhood forsook me all of a heap, and, turning tail, I gave a loud shout and started off down the path at speed, never once looking behind, and leaving Bang to his fate, perched on his pedestal, like the laughing satyr; however, the next moment I heard him thundering in my rear. My panic had been contagious, for the instant my sudden motion had frightened the snake out of its way, Bang started forth after me at speed, and away we both raced, until a stump caught my foot, and both of us, after flying through the air a couple of fathoms or so, trundled head over heels, over and over, shouting and laughing. Pegtop now came up to us in no small surprise, but the adventure was at an end, and we returned to Mr Bang's to dinner.

Here we had an agreeable addition to our party in Sir Jeremy Mayo, and the family of the Admiral, Sir Samuel Semaphore, his lady, his two most amiable daughters, and the husband of the eldest.

Next morning we rode out to breakfast with a very worthy man, Mr Stornaway, the overseer of Mount Olive estate, in the neighbourhood of which there were several natural curiosities to be seen. Although the extent of our party startled him a good deal, he received us most hospitably. He ushered us into the piazza, where breakfast was laid, when up rose ten thousand flies from the breakfast-table, that was covered with marmalade, and guava jelly, and nicely-roasted yams, and fair white bread, and the fragrant bread-fruit roasted in the ashes and wrapped in plantain-leaves; while the chocolate and coffee pots—the latter equal in cubic contents to one of the Wave's water-butts—emulated each other in the fragrance of the odours which they sent forth; and avocado pears, and potted calipiver, and cold pork hams, and—really, I cannot repeat the numberless luxuries that flanked the main body of the entertainment on a side-table—all strong provocatives to fall to.

"You, Quacco—Peter—Monkey," shouted Stornaway, "where are you, with your brushes? don't you see the flies covering the table?" The three sable pages forthwith appeared, each with a large green branch in his hand, which they waved over the viands, and we sat down and had a most splendid breakfast. Lady Semaphore and I—for I have always had a touch of the old woman in me—were exceedingly tickled with the way in which the *piccaniny mummas,* that is, the mothers of the negro children, received our friend Bang. After breakfast, a regular muster took place under the piazza of all the children on the property under eight years of age, accompanied by their mothers.

"Ah, Massa Bang," shouted one, "why you no come see we oftener? you forget your poor piccaniny hereabout."

"You grow foolish old man now," quoth another.

"You no wort—you go live in town, an' no care about we who make massa money here; you no see we all tarving here;" and the nice cleanly-looking fat matron, who made the remark, laughed loudly.

He entered into the spirit of the affair with great kindliness, and verily, before he got clear, his pockets were as empty as a half-pay lieutenant's. His *fee-pennies* were flying about in all directions.

After breakfast we went to view the natural bridge—a band of rock that connects two hills together—and beneath which a roaring stream rushes, hid entirely by the bushes and trees that grow on each side of the ravine. We descended by a circuitous footpath into the river-course, and walked under the natural arch, and certainly never was anything finer; a regular *Der Freyschutz* dell. The arch overhead was nearly fifty feet high, and the echo was superb, as we found, when the sweet voices of the ladies, blending in softest harmony— (lord, how fine you become, Tom!)—in one of Moore's melodies, were reflected back on us at the close with the most thrilling distinctness; while a stone, pitched against any of the ivy-like creepers with which the face of the rock was covered, was sure to dislodge a whole cloud of birds, and not unfrequently a slow-sailing white-winged owl. Shortly after the Riomagno Gully, as it is called, passes this most interesting spot, it sinks, and runs for three miles underground, and again reappears on the surface, and go over the stones, as if nothing had happened. By the by, this is a common vagary of nature in Jamaica. For instance, the Rio Cobre, I think it is, which, after a subterranean course of three miles, suddenly gushes out of the solid rock at Bybrook estate, in a solid cube of clear cold water, three feet in diameter; and I remember, in a cruise that I had at another period of my life, in the leeward part of the island, we came to an estate where the supply of water for the machinery rose up within the bounds of the mill-dam itself, into which there was no flow, with such force, that above the spring, if I might so call it, the bubbling water was projected into a blunt cone like the bottom of a caldron, the apex of which was a foot higher than the level of the pond, although the latter was eighteen feet deep.

After an exceedingly pleasant day we returned home, and next morning, when I got out of bed, I complained of a violent itching and pain, a sort of non-descript sensation, a mixture of pain and pleasure, in my starboard great toe, and on reconnoitring, I discovered it to be a good deal inflamed on the ball, round a blue spot about the size of a pin-head. Pegtop had come into the room, and while he was placing my clothes in order, I asked him "What this could be—gout, think you, Massa Pegtop—gout?"

"Gote, massa—gote—no, no; him chiger, massa—chiger—little something like one flea, poke him head under de kin, dere lay egg; ah, great luxury to creole gentleman and lady dat chiger; sweet pain, creole miss say—nice for cratch him, him say."

"Why, it may be a creole luxury, Pegtop, but I wish you would relieve me of it."

"Surely, massa, surely, if you wish it" said Pegtop, in some surprise at my want of taste. "Lend me your penknife den, massa;" and he gabbled as he extracted from my flesh the chiger bag—like a blue pill in size and colour.

"O, massa, top till you marry creole wife, she will tell you me say true; ah, daresay Miss Mary himself love chiger to tickle him—to be sure him love to be tickle—him love to be tickle— ay, all creole miss love to be tickle—he, he, he!"

By agreement, Mr Bang and I met Mr Stornaway this morning, in order to visit some other estates together and during our ride I was particularly gratified by his company. He was a man of solid and very extensive acquirements, and far above what his situation in life at that time led one to expect. When I revisited the island, some years afterwards, I was rejoiced to find that his intrinsic worth and ability had floated him up into a very extensive business, and I believe he is now a man of property. I rather think he is engaged in some statistical work connected with Jamaica, which, I am certain, will do him credit whenever it appears. Odd enough, the very first time I saw him I said I was sure he would succeed in the world; and I am glad to find I was a true prophet. To return: Our chief object at present was to visit a neighbouring estate, the overseer of which was, we were led to believe, from a message sent to Mr Bang, very ill with fever. He was a most respectable young man, Mr Stornaway told me, a Swede by birth, who had come over to England with his parents at the early age of eight years, where both he and his cousin Agatha had continued, until he embarked for the West Indies. This was an orphan girl whom his father had adopted, and both of them, as he had often told Mr Stornaway, had utterly forgotten their Swedish; in fact, they understood no language but English at the time he embarked. I have been thus particular, from a very extraordinary phenomenon that occurred immediately preceding his dissolution, of which I was a witness.

We rode up in front of the door, close to the fixed manger, where the horses and mules belonging to the busha are usually fed, and encountered a negro servant on a mule, with an umbrella-case slung across his back, and a portmanteau behind him, covered with the usual sheep's fleece, and holding a saddle-horse.

"Where is your master?" said Mr Bang.

"De dactor is in de hose," replied Quashie. "Busha dere upon dying."

We ascended the rocky unhewn steps, and entered the cool dark hall, smelling strong of camphor, and slid over the polished floors towards an open door, that led into the back piazza, where we were received by the head bookkeeper and carpenter. They told us that the overseer had been seized three days before with fever, and was now desperately ill; and presently the doctor came forth out of the sick-room.

"Poor Wedderfelt is fast going, sir; cold at the extremities already—very bad fever—the bilious remittent of the country, of the worst type."

All this while the servants, male and female, were whispering to each other, while a poor little black fellow sat at the door of the room, crying bitterly—this was the overseer's servant. We entered the room, which was darkened from the *jealousies* being all shut, except one of the uppermost, which happening to be broken, there was a strong *pensil* of light cast across the head of the bed where the sick man lay, while the rest of the apartment was involved in gloom.

The sufferer seemed in the last stage of yellow fever; his skin was a bright yellow, his nose sharp, and his general features very much pinched. His head had been shaven, and there was a handkerchief bound round it over a plantain-leaf, the mark of the blister coming low down on his forehead, where the skin was shrivelled like dry parchment; apparently it had not risen. There was also a blister on his chest. He was very restless, clutching the bedclothes, and tossing his limbs about; his mouth was ulcerated, and blood oozed from the corners; his eyes were a deep yellow, with the pupil much dilated, and very lustrous; he was breathing with a heavy moaning noise when we entered, and looked wildly round, mistaking Mr Bang and me for some other persons. Presently he began to speak very quickly, and to lift one of his hands repeatedly close to his face, as if there was something in it he wished to look at. I presently saw that it held a miniature of a fair-haired, blue-eyed, Scandinavian girl; but apparently he could not see it, from the increasing dimness of his eyes, which seemed to distress him greatly. After a still minute, during which no sound was heard but his own heavy breathing, he again began to speak very rapidly, but no one in the room could make out what he said. I listened attentively; it struck me as being like—I was certain of it—*it was Swedish*, which in health he had entirely forgotten but now in his dying moments vividly remembered. Alas! it was a melancholy and a moving sight, to perceive all the hitherto engrossing thoughts and incidents of his youth and manhood, all save the love of one dear object, suddenly vanished from the tablet of his memory, ground away and abrased, as it were, by his great agony; or like worthless rubbish, removed from above some beautiful ancient inscription, which for ages it had hid, disclosing in all their primeval freshness, sharp cut into his dying heart, the long-smothered but never-to-be-obliterated impressions of his early childhood. I could plainly distinguish the name Agatha, whenever he peered with fast glazing eyes on the miniature. All this while a nice little brown child was lying playing with his watch and seals on the bed beside him, while a handsome coloured girl, a slight young creature, apparently its mother, sat on the other side of the dying man, supporting his head on her lap, and wetting his mouth every now and then with a cloth dipped in brandy.

As he raised the miniature to his face, she would gently endeavour to turn away his hand, that he might not look at one whom she, poor thing, no doubt considered was usurping the place in his fluttering heart that she long fancied had been filled by herself solely; and at other times she would vainly try to coax it out of his cold hand, but the dying grasp was now one of iron, and her attempts evidently discomposed the departing sinner; but all was done kindly and quietly, and a flood of tears would every now and then stream down her cheeks, as she failed in her endeavours, or as the murmured, gasped name, *Agatha,* reached her ear.

"Ah!" said she, "him heart not wid me now—it far away in him own country—him never will make me yeerie what him say again no more."

Oh, woman, woman! who can fathom that heart of thine! By this time the hiccup grew stronger, and all at once he sat up strong in his bed without assistance, "light as if he felt no wound;" but immediately thereafter gave a strong shudder, ejecting from his mouth a jet of dark matter like the grounds of chocolate, and fell back dead—whereupon the negroes began to howl and shriek in such a horrible fashion that we were glad to leave the scene.

Next day, when we returned to attend the poor fellow's funeral, we found a complete *bivouac* of horses and black servants under the trees in front of the house, which was full of neighbouring planters and overseers, all walking about, and talking, and laughing, as if it had been a public meeting on parish business. Some of them occasionally went into the room to look at the body as it lay in the open coffin, the lid of which was at length screwed down, and the corpse carried on four negroes' shoulders to its long home, followed by the brown girl and all the servants, the latter weeping and howling; but she, poor thing, said not a word, although her heart seemed, from the convulsive heaving of her bosom, like to burst. He was buried under a neighbouring orange-tree, the service being read by the Irish carpenter of the estate, who got half a page into the marriage service by mistake before either he or any one else noticed he was wrong.

Three clays after this the Admiral extended my leave for a fortnight, which I spent in a tour round this most glorious island with friend Aaron, whose *smiling* face, like the sun (more like the nor'west moon in a fog, by the by), seemed to diffuse warmth and comfort and happiness wherever he went, while Sir Samuel and his charming family, and the general, and my dearie and her aunt, returned home; and after a three weeks' philandering I was married, and all that sort of thing, and a week afterwards embarked with my treasure—for I had half a million of dollars on freight, as well as my own particular jewel; and don't grin at the former, for they gave me a handsome sum, and helped to rig us when we got to *Ould* England, where Lotus-Leaf was paid off, and I settled for a time on shore, the happiest, &c. &c. &c., until some years afterwards, when the *wee* Cringles began to tumble home so deucedly fast that I had to cut and run, and once more betake myself to the salt sea. My aunt and her family returned at the same time to England, in a merchant-ship under my convoy, and became our neighbours. Bang also got married soon after to Miss Lucretia Wagtail, by whom he got the Slap estate. But old Gelid and my other allies remain, I believe, in single blessedness until this hour.

〜o〜

My tale is told—my yarn is ended; and were I to spin it longer I fear it would be only bending it "end for end;" yet still I linger, "like the sough of an auld sang" on the ear, loth to pronounce that stern heart-crushing word, that yet "has been and must be," and which, during my boisterous and unsettled morning, has been, alas! a too familiar one with me. I hope I shall always bless Heaven for my fair blinks, although, as the day has wore on, I have had my own share of lee-currents, hard gales, and foul weather; and many an old and dear friend has lately swamped alongside of me, while few new ones have shoved out to replace them. But suffering, that scathes the heart, does not always make it callous; and I feel much of the woman hanging about mine still—even now, when the tide is on the turn with me, and the iron voice of the inexorable First-Lieutenant, Time, has sung out, "Strike the bell eight,"—every chime smiting on my soul as if an angel spoke, to warn me that my stormy forenoon watch is at length over; that the sun, now passing the meridian, must soon decline towards the western horizon, and who shall assure himself of a cloudless setting?

I have, in very truth, now reached the summit of the bald spray-washed promontory, and stand on the slippery ledge of the cliff that trembles to the thundering of the surge beneath; but the plunge must be made—so at once, Farewell, all hands, and God bless ye! If, while chucking the cap about at a venture—but I hope and trust there has been no such thing—it has alighted on the head of some ancient ally, and pinched in any the remotest degree, I hereby express my most sincere and heartfelt regret; and to such a one I would say as he said who wrote for all time,

> "I have shot
> Mine arrow o'er the house, and hurt my brother."

Thus I cut my stick while the play is good, and before the public gets wearied of me; and as for the Log, it is now launched, swim or founder: if those things be good, it will float from its own buoyancy; if they be naught, let it sink at once and for ever—all that Tom Cringle expects at the hands of his countrymen, is—A CLEAR STAGE, AND NO FAVOUR.

THE END.